Jonathon Karagiannis lives in Melbourne, Victoria, and has a Bachelor of Arts majoring in Archaeology & Ancient History with a minor in philosophy and literary studies. He is currently doing a second Bachelor in Theology majoring in Biblical Studies, whilst also conducting research on ancient Southwest Asia, focusing on the late Bronze Age Hittites.

Combining his fascination of ancient cultures, religion, literature and philosophy, Jonathon's debut novel *Omega Plan* is the first novel in a seven-part mythopoetic sci fi fantasy epic called *The Era of the End*. A saga that explores the apocalypse from a unique angle, focusing on the problem of evil, conspiracy and ultimately, faith and hope.

THE ERA OF THE END

OMEGA PLAN

VOLUME ONE

JONATHON KARAGIANNIS

Escarpment Publishing

Jonathon Karagiannis
The Era of the End: Omega Plan, Volume 1
Jonathon Karagiannis
Copyright © 2025
Published by Escarpment Publishing, an Imprint of Alkira Publishing, Australia
ABN: 32736122056
http://www.alkirapublishing.com

ISBN: 978-1-922329-77-6

In memory of Rob Skiba II (1969 - 2021)

A charismatic and passionate

Brother and storyteller.

Sower of the seeds of inspiration.

All for God - the Creative Creator.

PROLOGUE
INUMA ILU AWILUM

7975 BCE

"And I will put enmity
between you (the snake) and the woman,
between your seed and her seed;
it will strike your head,
and you will strike its heel."
—From the Scroll of Genesis, c. 6th century – c. 5th century BCE. Tim Mackie's
Literal-Literary Translation. Protoevangelium of the redemption of humankind of a
Chosen Seed that will defeat the Snake.

Scents of blood and smoke blew far, from a scourged Garden among flames. A hope of return, taken away.

In times when gods were human and humans were gods, the Sage watched the sun sink like a pink head on a dune, all its heat tardy. His vision blurred – he may as well watch through closed eyes, not willing to accept that the divine gift of the Garden had fallen into chaos. His bones felt numb from the persistent battle, his skin blighted by burns and from the east wind.

Yared ben Mahalal'el – the Chosen Seed – opened his eyes. He sat crouched in a cleft of rock, overlooking nothingness. He wore white and blue – a colour of purity, a colour of promise.

But the nightmares remained. Body upon body, covered in dust, grey black streaks of char and ash, Yared saw them, dead. The biggest beasts lay with slender elongated bodies, segmented legs, carapace, claws, wings and stingers. Those that were human-like had protruding bumps from their marbled flesh, brown and red in the setting sun, that one could've mistaken them for desert hills.

The spiritual flesh was still. Just seeing them there, their bodies double the height of a man, sent shivers down Yared's spine, hearing again the tormented sounds and their ability to destroy so much. Yet thousands of the Eternal Ones lay massacred, sure in death.

The gods that destroyed humanity could fall just like humanity.

Once this great void that devoured mountains had used to be, only a day ago, a lust verdant jungle – with rushing rivers, hooting with monkeys, swathed in gentle dew. Billowing smoke replaced soaring utiles. The fourfold rivers were now fourfold rivers of lava. The Tree of Life, which once lit up the land of Eden in the east like a second sun, had crumbled, the light of its leaves vanished. To the east, parties of raiders – both friend and foe – scattered into the wild and waste, as many as the sand of the sea.

Yared leaned his forehead on his blade, his only support. The cold evening wind struck him and his stomach seethed, unsettled. He'd survived immense doom.

Only to live on… On with darkness.

Caws of great anzuds echoed. He saw a pair of gigantic bat storks, wings thundering like great hearts and huge lance beaks jutting out of their heads, carrying a handful of survivors on their backs.

Who won this battle? Was violence and killing necessary to save lives?

Hefting his completely crystal Vanquishblade, Yared inhaled. A jet of bright amber wind rushed down from on high, infusing him with a dazzling radiance, glowing smoke billowing off his body. The Holy Wind – gushed through every corner of his tent, awakening him from his banality like a splash of cold water. The invisible Wind that guided reality; whatever it impacted, it rendered neutral and useful.

Yared coursed gracefully off the chalky spire, the Wind carrying him towards the anzud birds. He did not need wings. He merged away ahead of the stork bats, hovering in the air, to a lofty mountain, overlooking Eden. Cloudy smoke of white and black hugged the mountain, giving it the illusion that it floated above the land.

He landed before the rock shelter, on a platform large enough to accommodate six anzuds.

Yared trudged lightly on his sore feet into the cave entrance. The shade was cool, sheltering him from the sun's heat. He dragged his great sword like a burden towards the flat rock table inside the shelter. It lay in front of the ancestral resting place of Red Life – the representatives of El: Adapa and Khavva. In it, was a tomb for their children: the shepherd Hebel – the victim of foul fratricide – and his brother that he never knew – Sheth. Sheth had made the calling to return to the Garden, to cleanse the blood guilt, and since then, humans had sworn to be loyal to El – the one true creator God. Yet now . . .

Yared slowed to a stop in the gloom, before the flat rock. The rock shelter was sad and estranging. The brisk moaning mountain air oddly perturbed, blew with no genesis and no destination. With insipid eyes he studied the rock table inscribed with symmetrical seven sided shapes. There, already on the table, were three magnificent swords, pure crystal, deposited before the crypt.

He recognised each sword and their owners – the Sages, the Watchers, of every power. *Oh tragic. If one doesn't start, then who will? When one falls, so shall the rest follow? This is the tear of a unified family. I shall be a curse in the land.*

Outside the rock shelter, Yared heard Uan leap off the anzud's back. More footfalls crunched behind, approaching Yared. More Sages. More Watchers.

"Uan. Paradise is lost," Yared remarked flatly.

Uan appeared as the dirge of the anzud sounded behind him, and Enmebulugga and the acolyte Ninmada followed. They were ageless despite their wise eyes that had seen much, witnessed much. Every single one of them had grey hair. Because eventually, they would die. All because of the great lie of the Evil One, Shaitan, denying Khavva and humanity eternal life.

Uan carried a body in his arms – a dead woman. Hair as fair as the gleanings of wheat and barley in the time of harvest – none had so gold of hair than Baraka. Yared's wife.

What was the point of living? What was the point of a good life, if life itself was enslaved to vain oblivion? Why did he not perform an elegiac over such despair? Here, before his eyes, was a woman . . . a glorious stoic ally had died. The potential for life, his wife . . . He could not come to saying it. His only ensconcing attempts of sorrow were a hovering grimy hand over his wife's face and the stroking of her buttery hair. *Your blood cries out to El Baraka. You are in the land, my garden.*

The Garden… gone.

Not meeting anyone's eyes, Yared managed to let out a melancholy whisper. "Where are the others?"

"Driven out," Uan exhaled deeply, laying Baraka's body to rest in a small alcove in the crypt.

"They saw the truth then. El destroyed everything we hoped for. I knew this would happen." Yared swallowed, throat throbbing with frustration. He could've said simply, that he and the Sages self-deceived themselves.

Uan placed his sword on the flat rock in the gap reverently between the other blades. It was a sword for a Preserver – those Sages who could grow and regrow – and the blade with its slender, elegant look, edged on both sides, twisted in vine patterns at pommel and cross-guard. A Preserver's blade. All Vanquishblades were forged by Tubal-Qayin with the aid of the Fallen Gods – the Anunna.

"Leave your sword," Yared demanded to his brother Enmebulugga.

"What?" he blurted. "Brother? The Calling of Sheth—"

"It's all gone! We will never return to the Garden of Rest!" Yared trembled. When did he become so weak? "Leave your sword and turn away!"

"I cannot," Enmebulugga said, dazed, eying his blade longingly. "I . . . don't want to."

Ninmada wordlessly placed her elegant crystal blade next to Uan's, ambling away. Enmebulugga's distressed eyes trailed her.

"Ah, but we are to reckon the Anunna, Yared," Enmebulugga said.

"We cannot reckon the gods!" Yared snapped. Surprising how he felt anger now of all things. He'd been disciplined as a Sage otherwise. "I am *not* the Chosen Seed." Enmebulugga gasped. "I desire giving up being a Sage and a Watcher. Where is the sinless man? Where are the saviours? I do not know who the saviour for our failures will be. For all we know, there could be no one of the seed of Khavva in our lifetime, that will crush the head of the Snake Shaitan. Humanity is utterly hopeless. How can we enter into Eternal Rest? What can we do if the Abzu and Tiham of Formlessness threatens us?" Tiham were the salt waters of chaos. Abzu were the abyss of the ocean, the waters of the universe.

He looked into his brother's eyes, darkened with fatigue, colourless and lethargic. In this man, there was anguish – a man hanging off a cliff, grasping desperately onto trust in El. *El,* Yared said within his heart. *He's broken! Everyone is broken! Why have you done this to us!? You promised justice! What has madness done to us, killing and killing? Like Qayin?*

"They see us semi-divine," Enmebulugga spoke, glowering. "Without us, humankind will be bad."

"Never has a sinless child been born of its mother. A sinless youth has not existed from old. Humans don't need Sages." Those words – vexed hisses

– were cathartic, after years of meditation. "They need trust," Yared said.

"What about your son?" Enmebulugga said. "Do you trust him?"

"My son is improper for the Watcher's task," Yared whispered coldly. "He's not so bellicose."

Enmebulugga twitched, emitting a shaking breath. Then with a dead voice, he moaned, "Then I'm a lie . . . We're *all* a lie!"

Devastated, Enmebulugga half dropped, and half threw his weapon onto the table, but he stumbled as if suffering a fit. The amazing weapon flipped off the lip of the table, crashing to the floor with a tumultuous cacophony. Arms trembling with strain, Enmebulugga stooped to pick it up, hand only opening and closing aimlessly over the hilt.

"What do we say to the refugees in Havilah?" Enmebulugga fretted.

"We will tell them we finally won. The fallen Anunna bound in the Underworld. A half-truth – at least. One day, perhaps, it will become the truth." Shivering, Yared hugged his own blade, closing his eyes, trying to keep himself small and warm from the bitter mountain wind.

He could not. For the first time in a long time, Yared felt what it was like to be utterly alone.

Yared's gaze remained fixed on the table as Enmebulugga slogged back outside into the dark, sword still discarded on the ground.

Yared laid his own sword down. Grunting, he picked Enmebulugga's sword up next to his and closed his eyes.

He slumped, cowering as a great darkness enveloped him. The skies were no longer his. The Presence of God's Holy Wind had abandoned him.

And then finally, he let go. The Vanquishblade fell on the table.

Good to perish now, than live to look upon evil.

He turned. He followed his brother with a cadaverous stride.

And yet, Yared couldn't help glancing back at the table and at the single space. The seventh blade unaccounted, given to his one-of-a-kind son.

Hanok.

———

"Now that they have been given great responsibility to rule, they have defiled their promise of loyal love. Now that they have turned from face-to-face, they sought their own desires, good to their eyes, to make them wise. Now that they have fallen to this abominable sin, they took might and pain. The holy Garden of Eden descending into the Grave, until bitterness and torment remains. Where shall humans dwell then?

"Now that they shed blood, the land shall be flooded with blood. Now shall the number of humanity's days be shortened. The independence of the human heart is so easily corrupted. Falling short to recognising their depravity, from sorrow to violence…When will they see this and, desiring to return, take life?"

But there was no one to hearken to his laments in the skies. From the barrier of the heavens, the mountains rose to sheer, dark, dreadful heights. Only the circular motions of swirling clouds hung densely in cool dark space, shrouding the dark precipices with crowns of white ice. A foreboding scent lingered, a scent that would plunge the world into further decay.

Floating out of a funnel of mist, Mikael, the Merciful and Long-Suffering, dismissed his helmet visor.

Before him a volcanic peak rose, domed, covered with ice and fire, smoke and ash gushing out of its crater like a burning city. At first it seemed like the orange glow of the lava danced sway over the tremendous volcano, but the way they shifted, protesting against the mountains, resembled toilsome bramble.

There were no clouds here. The volcano of the south pole ruled even the clouds, that no bird of the air could fly over the peak.

The confirmation before Mikael's eyes filmed them with tears. Within the crater, stuck inside the boiling pinnacle of magma and gouts of lava were the wretched bodies of the Fallen. The sight brought shivers down Mikael's spine, even despite being kept from hearing the bawls of the spirits.

Great spirit beings died behind the veil, in the heart of the volcano. It was their just punishment for causing so much suffering to millions.

Why did this happen? Because the humans and spirits failed to love the Khesed Bond – fulfilling service to El not out of duty, but out of love, loyalty and mercy, not expecting reciprocity in return. *How can humans be trusted anymore to be El's image!*

Mikael saw those haunted, pale ichor spirits in the great lake of magma within the volcano, longing to die like flesh beings. Some twisted, mangled on top of each other, pressing against an unseen transparent veil, trying doggedly to escape from the burns. The ash.

Yet, Mikael could do nothing but watch.

Spirit beings… traitors. Humans… seditious. Could Mikael himself face even *this* enemy? Unfaithfulness?

It all seemed too difficult. Why would El allow humans and spirits to come together in his name to establish the Khesed Bond, if it was bound for failure?

He turned his pauldroned shoulder, blessed that the Spiritual Realm was sealed off from the Physical Realm so he would not have to listen to those cries, and break . . .

No, Mikael the Great Prince *will never break*. Never will he break Khesed!

We have come to this! The unmade will come on men. On men . . . *and women. And their offspring. It will come. Soon.*

But I shall have mercy on the merciless.

Those spirits there – the Anunna – had made their *graves* in their sin to bond with humans. Now they died like humans, defining good and evil for themselves.

Justice had been satisfied.

Namely, Mikael the Long-Suffering would bear the agonies in the Bottomless Pit. Even in the Underworld, he shall stand in the gap. It was his function, to keep wicked and destructive spirits like these from returning to the land and the skies.

Mikael the Merciful skimmed away, leaving behind this recreance.

PART I

REVEAL, OUR TYRANNICAL PSYOP

1

FORSWORN

"Behold I will make the last as the first."
—From the Epistle of Barnabas, c. 100 CE. Author likely pseudepigraphal.

Michael Oppenheim strode meticulously through the jungle of stony corners and hanging alcoves. He wore white on red – knife hidden, ready to kill a guru.

The summer night around him was balmy, whispering songs of anticipatory caution, embracing him with impulses of revenge and justice.

Question everything. Be acute. Be aware. The words Ludwig, his dead father, had once said to him. It had become Michael's mantra. *Question everything, Socrates said. Be acute. Be aware.*

Do not trust everything the elites say.

The Third Reich had begun long ago, when the love of his life could not make it to the art history expedition. He looked forward to that night, as rainy and dreary as it was. When he returned home from the Neues Museum, he walked into his room and found her with a gash at her throat and his baby boy kidnapped.

Michael's stomach had heaved; he could not remember if he vomited, screamed or both. The men with red arm bands, puppets of the Agarthan guru, had singled him out by murdering his loved ones.

Even in death, Valentina looked gorgeous to draw, but he couldn't draw her. He didn't want to ruin the image of her that he had in his mind.

There was a massive search for Michael's lost child, and, five days later, he found his frozen corpse in the Black Forest.

That was when Michael met his master and friend, Alfred Bonner, on the investigation for the kidnappers and killers. Neither Michael, nor the Social Democrats, enemies of the Reich – the *Bundischen* – could ever understand why his loved ones died. Was it because his wife had Russian heritage? No matter, Michael was Forsworn to Hitler and to the Nazi's Aryanism.

Ahead of Michael was a tour group of German archaeologists – followers of the occultist Heinrich Himmler. They laughed with their girlfriends all blasé, and at their head, was the guru Michael would kill. The Brahmin of the Cult of Agartha. As pollen drew in bees, the Nazis followed the gimpy elderly man, withered by ages of scheming. He had wrinkled skin stretched tightly over his skull-like face, a white wiry beard and red-orange robes, stark bright in the moonlight.

Michael kept an adequate distance behind the last German guard, remaining hidden as a shadow. Watching.

He gawked at the surreal incisions within the stone. Stone. Ellora was an entire *mountain* hewed into elaborate stupas of monasteries, courtyards, circular daises and caves, pillars adorned with ornamental knops delicately framed with reliefs of posing, dancing, multi-armed gods and legendary figures within petrified façades, ghastly in the moon shadows.

This was it. With his own eyes. In his schooling days, Michael had always wanted to become a sculptor, an artist, yet his father, being a renowned Sanskritologist whom, in his works on the Orient combined his acquaintance with the mystic painter Nicholas Roerich, had given Michael a wealth of knowledge of the East. Now, with trained eyes, especially now, when he had cracked the code – the mystery behind the dreadnaught of the Swastika became clear.

Thule Society. Nazis and Patala or Agartha in a guild working a filthy alliance.

Michael focused on the Brahmin leading the group into his little cave. *Tonight*, Michael thought. *Tonight, I am not here as an artist, a scholar, nor as a performer. I am . . . death.*

Footfalls grinding gravel, Michael followed into a deep colonnade hall, proceeding into the bowels of the mountain.

A mission like this would undermine the entire Germanic race, according to the National Socialists. Germans *were not* Aryans. Hitler used it ethnically, to refer to light-skinned, fair-haired, tall Caucasians. The Celtic Blue Bloods.

An erroneous misconception. For Aryan in Sanskrit was a social term meaning "civilised", "noble", or "free". Could not Michael be that? Noble and free? His father told him these things once, as if he foreknew the venal Nationalist Socialist Party would rise, vilifying this word. His father, a guardian of the East, was a nobler Aryan than Adolf Hitler.

Tonight, master Bonner's command included wearing a dhoti kurta – Indian eastern wear. Effeminate in appearance, with fancy embroidery and zari work, it was no longer exclusive to women. Michael's filmy long-sleeved white top, with a short button placket, was sliced open at his right hip, exposing his scarlet draping garment.

White to not blend into the night. Red under white. Blood leaching under skin. It was not the clothing for a killer, but that was what made it so menacing. It didn't blend with anything but was humble in appearance. Bonner and the *Bund* told him that this was a symbol for the victims to see before they died. A sudden revelation.

These white sepulchres who killed his heart, were *not* noble Aryans. They were stained red; the knife ready to gouge out the truth of bloody guilt underneath.

My boy was almost ready to walk!

Michael turned right, vengeance imbuing, following these power-hungry pilgrims, their voices echoing off the cavern walls. These walls were crudely cut and undecorated unlike above, but down below, there was light coming from the other side. Michael followed with anticipation.

Spanning before him was a subterranean temple. Just like above – so there was a temple below. In the shape of a gigantic horseshoe, it had a large oval with alcoves and walls arranged in ascending circles, with an architecture that immediately struck Michael as unusual.

There were no planes or angles. Everything had sinuous curves with metal inlay. There were round windows and intricate slices of infinitesimal confections set over pinecone stupas and archways. It was simply beautiful. The teal and ultra-violet light emanated from flameless crystal lamps lining the stairs and passageways. Yes, those were powered by what Michael understood from his studies, as Vril – a rare type of energy produced entirely from sound, tuned into a frequency that emitted light.

I am seeing Agarthan culture close up, Michael thought excitedly, struggling not to show it.

"This civilisation of Shambala lies just beneath our feet, brethren," one of the female servants of the guru said to the German anthropologists with a thick accent, her German just passable. "Until now, it has never been seen by the eyes of Westerners. So, I imagine, you feel very special at this point."

The agreeing group issued out past a mushroom grove towards the inner vault. Michael joined the woman who had just spoken. Luckily, these people didn't pay much attention to Michael because nobody was supposed to. But Michael did eye them. Were those revolver holsters hidden within their garments? *These ladies are not going to depart from the guru's side, are they?* Michael thought. *I'm going to have to distract them to get to the guru. Cause a ruckus . . . Somehow.*

At the small opening of the horseshoe was a second cavern hewed out of the rock, a raised superstructure with a single stone runway cutting through the centre, leading into an obscured corridor. He pursed his lips, observing its curved lintel marked by a large ancient swastika with four dots in the middle of each right-angled arms. The Antediluvian Proto-Indo-European symbol of wellbeing, life and good luck. Flanking this detestable door were two horned serpent statues of a style similar to the Naga . . .

Stop. Focus. This mission I cannot fail.

The scenery. It was a spell having captivated him. Alluring all his senses, past and present to ecstasy.

I am death.

Finally, Michael passed through the dark, the Vril lights fading behind into the gloom. The hall was squared, bare and narrow, with space for only one person at a time.

I am death.

As the party descended, the air became soft, perfumed with an aromatic essence. His feet made no sound on the polished floor.

I love you so much, Valentina. The child . . . I love you too.

They were going in a straight line. When Michael thought he was going mad, the group finally entered a Vril lit cellar with a bench and a massive door. The Ksitigarbha Vault that had been sealed shut, required nine numbers to turn the mandala dial. The door had nine knobs and locks coloured by the gemstones representing the planets.

The guru did the honours as some of the Germans rested on the benches. Michael mingled with servants surrounding the guru in a semicircle for protection. Now was not the ideal time to strike – he was so close; he felt a thrill within him.

But he needed to kill when the guru was alone.

The guru rubbed the knobs imbedded into the metal door with his bare hands. He seemed to loom his head over them, mumbling and exhaling like a child trying to fog up a window with his warm breath. As he did so, the gems began to *glow* with a turbid white colour. *What is this that he's doing? Some occult magic?*

Michael could not help eavesdropping in one of the young woman's conversations nearby, because she was fluent in German. She was definitely the youngest, possibly twenty-five, diminutive with long brown hair and elegant chocolate skin.

"I've been inside a Ksitigarbha – the Earth Matrix – only once, and they contain the greatest earth store in the world," she whispered. "They've never seen the light of day, but you will not believe how much treasure there is here."

Treasure?

"They're worthless, Aditi," an older woman replied. "They come to no practical use and collect dust."

"But Ksitigarbha is sacred," Aditi intoned. "And what about the new minerals that they harvested? It has something profound trapped within it. Something ancient."

Voidstone . . . Bonner mentioned the treasure he wanted down here.

Once all nine knobs had been vigorously rubbed by the guru, the Ksitigarbha door finally opened with a resounding thump. The guru gestured and everyone got up, ready to enter.

Standing by the open door stood two guards. Not human guards, but two males with bizarre grey and red marbled skin and huge feline green eyes. Their facial features resemble a frog, and they stood slimly, eight feet in height.

Michael took a good look at the two giants in wonder – at their wonderful otherworldly, leathery uniforms and their strange crossbow guns, resembling a beaked cone.

The guru spoke something to the frog-like humanoids in another language.

The guards nodded, stepping back, lowering their weapons. Once they were all in, Michael heard a thumping sound and, looking behind, saw the marbled-skinned guards closing the door behind him, locking it in place.

No, I need time to find another escape route. How was Bonner going to get in? He'd better have a way out.

They walked down another dark hallway, this one was filled with metal racks of dun gems – said to be the batteries that powered travel and commerce in Patala. These gemstones were stored in display boxes, catalogued by a plate of metal glued to its bottom on the racks. To Michael, the numbers inscribed on them were meaningless, but he had a feeling that the richness of Agartha relied much on this merchandise.

Then they approached a grand atrium containing multiple locked vaults. The entire place was dark, so the Germans were requested to turn on their torches again to help aid the guru unlock the door. Yet as the door opened, and the Germans cast the lights within, a thick darkness *blocked* the light.

The guru and his followers exchanged wary glances, proceeding into the dark. Michael followed with tense unease.

Here it was. The sacred treasure that beguiled Nazi avarice.

The dark orb sat in a bronze cage – a large ruby the size of a man's head. Cordate, the caged gem was infused with a dark purple-and-red light, which in essence, brought on a deeper darkness within the entire chamber. Even when the Germans shined their light on the core, the darkness seemed to be *consuming* the light into a formless void. So, they turned them off, muttering perplexed to their friends, some giggling like all of this was some circus horror house.

Michael could tell this because the only thing he could see in the blackness was the dense dark red glow of the heart of darkness, which swirled inside with dancing wisps. These seemed vaguely human, with ever-shifting figures, forms and shapes made of congealed red shadows.

A voidstone. A crystal infused by wispy spirits like smoky ectoplasm. They had to be demons in there; he could feel their scratching on the wall of his psyche like rats, making him feel nauseous. They were trapped inside the crystal; however, they danced in the quartz with beautiful ruddy motions.

Michael... A still small voice.

The guru stepped towards the voidstone, lacing his hands slyly under his orange robes. Michael broke his eyes from the stone's captivating allure and noticed that everyone in the room had gone silent. Someone coughed as the guru stood frozen like a dark statue of the goddess Kali – the dank colour making his appearance next to the voidstone salient. As he spoke, a male translator stood unseen for the benefit of Michael and the Germans.

"Sorry for the darkness," the guru said. "But I wanted eagerly to show you the Thule Society's most valuable artefact."

"Yes. It's what Himmler and the Führer desires, guru," one of the German secretaries commented passionately. "It matches the description."

The guru nodded. "For thousands of years, the voidstone has remained as it is. This heart is effused with the spirit of an ancient god." The Germans stirred with a frenzied enthusiasm. Michael heart thudded harder in his chest. *A god?* "A crystal's lattice alone would store Pneuma without severe leakage," the guru went on, "but when they are properly housed in metal cages, you can manage the leakage's duration. See how the light consumes all external light? My friends, this ancient god *is* Dark Matter." The guru, by example, grabbed one of the torches, flashed it at the gemstone, but nothing happened, only invisible dimness. "Dark Matter is discerned from its gravitational attraction rather than its luminosity. It's a fact; most of the universe is composed of darkness." As the guru lectured, Michael listened to his enthralling smooth voice, noting the remarkable semblance between the sciences and the so-called superstition of arts and spirituality.

Spirituality that could be a weapon of mass destruction.

Is this darkness the return of the Nephilim? The foes of humanity? Michael wished someone could answer these questions, but his assassination task to avenge his family was paramount. There wasn't anything nobler that he could do. He would worry about the spiritual threat of the Nephilim and dark gods later. His honour demanded it.

The German anthropologists hummed gleefully among themselves.

A throbbing wave of anger stirred up within Michael, as easily as a fire over a dry land. What more did he need to justify the assassination, but to commit *theft* as well? To steal a demonic device that had the potential to turn humans into dark gods of terror. This wasn't just being *obedient* to his master, or a personal vendetta. This was saving the *human race* from extinction! *The mystics that my father had known spoke about the voidstone's potential! The spirits of the Nephilim!*

Michael rooted himself in place, shrouded and veiled in black – a mere shadow on the wall – as he observed the guru and the tour group leave the chamber. One by one, they were escorted out.

"We'll get the word out," one of the Germans mumbled blandly as the party departed.

Portentous silence followed. Michael's eyes became heavy as he froze meditatively within the light-quenched room. He became banal - the feeling of self no longer existing - experiencing a loss of affinity towards the slight inklings of evil in the ineffable he could not understand.

Banality. His destiny . . . An unscrupulous fate.

The entire chamber plummeted to a biting cold, and Michael felt very unwell suddenly, his stomach aching with nausea. The dark red heart of the void digested all life. As he stayed in its presence long enough, it made him sick. It beckoned for Michael to breathe it in – the demonic Pneuma. It was pensive.

Unleash me, Michael. You know who I am. I am death, the destroyer of -

No! Michael countered the temptation. *Remember the plan. Go. Trust in Bonner.*

For Valentina. Destroy those villains for Valentina.

What voices flooding into his head! Was this the symptom of extreme stress and trauma? He hoped so. The trance had almost devoured Michael.

"Focus on the task at hand," Michael whispered to himself, nodding. "I am death." Bonner did say specifically that the guru must be killed when he was alone, distracted from the Ksitigarbha – the Earth Matrix or Womb – of the voidstone. Bonner *promised* he would do the rest later. He had not given him any more information.

So, Michael slipped out of the sicking chamber and proceeded into a faintly lit hallway which tricked his eye into appearing almost opalescent. Adrenaline washing over him, eyes adjusting to the ultraviolet Vril lighting, Michael picked his way through the maze of corridors. Getting into a soft run, he slipped behind a round pillar, surreptitiously watching giant guards patrolling alongside the party. Here, Michael watched them enter a main atrium room, distinctly shaped as a lotus flower where flights of stairs led upwards towards galleries and accommodations.

In this place, everything was a twisting labyrinth of tunnels, architecturally made to make the peregrine feel unwelcomed.

This was why he had brought his father's map. The lotus atrium led upwards and back around where he had come from, stretching along a series of balustrades, ramps and bridges made of pure white stone and complex ornate patterns.

There, if the timing were right, he could create a ruse nearby so the women and the Germans would be too enmeshed in their discourse to react.

Perfect.

Michael slipped back the way he came, weaving through the corridors. He emerged out of the doorway and back through the hall, slowing down to a walk. He eyed the second-level railing above, picking up the mutterings and the footfalls of the party. His time was short.

He spied a pair of the giant troglodyte soldiers guarding one of the Ksitigarbhas in the shadows. They saw him approach, and one held up his right hand warningly. So, Michael with his two hands, grabbed it and twisted, shattering the guard's wrist. He smashed an elbow into the creature's groin, sending him backing against the wall, grunting. His body flickered and flashed when Michael attacked him, as if encased inside an invisible blue bubble.

"The hell?!" Michael cursed, clutching the troglodyte's gun as the stunned companion opened his mouth to yell. But Michael shot them both, the gun emitting a low-sounding thrum.

And both of their bodies flashed and blurred, the blue body energy making a thick crackling sound. The projectiles *deflected* off the alien creatures' bubbles, hitting the stone walls. The blue body bubbles faded.

Michael held the gun, stunned. Then, seeing the giants were still stirring, he ran back the way he came. He gazed up at the balcony, spying the guru and the Nazis.

While on the run, Michael shot directly at the party. The shock wave of the bullets sheared off the railing, just missing the guru's head. The way every single person in the train staggered, covering their heads at the same time, looked rather amusing. He deliberately missed again, projectiles ripping through the railing, casting mortar over the Germans diving for cover. The Hindu women shrieked and just as Michael wanted, the guards scattered.

"It came from down the hall!" the German officers barked, cocking their guns. "Hurry! Back that way!"

"Protect the guru!" the company of women shouted, pulling out their revolvers. They raced away towards the sounds of the gunshots, leaving behind a sole straggler alone with the guru. He saw the guru retreat into the farthest accommodation room just before the section of the hallway, where the open railing ended.

Michael dashed back down the corridors towards the lotus atrium room. Slipping behind a pillar, Michael, just managing to stay hidden, let the Germans and Hindu women charge past, down the passage. Once clear, Michael raced up the stairs two steps at a time.

He darted around the loop, as swift as shadows in the wind. He skidded to a halt and saw the long straight hallway with the open-balustrade balcony extending before him. He burst into a sprint. It felt *so good* to feel the wind rush through his hair and against his body.

He reached the final door, kicking it open. Within the Mughal-styled room, well lit with bookcases, spacious with long elegant rugs and an indoor fountain, there, the guru sat writing furiously at his desk. He shot up to his feet with a recoiling jolt. Terror manipulated his wrinkled face.

Michael strode forward, aiming the alien gun.

A lady leapt out from the left, whipping out her revolver.

Shooting her first, Michael dodged her fire, as the woman crashed into him, knocking the gun out of his hand.

Michael scrambled to his feet. He leapt, sliding onto the long table.

Frozen in shock, the guru hardly staggered away. Knocking over plates and books in his path, Michael used the friction to stand up, ramming into the guru, grappling him. They rolled over on the ground, tumbling at the fountain's base. Michael pried the guru's neck, his knees on the old man's chest to debilitate him.

The guru gagged, thrashing about, but Michael squeezed tightly with both hands, constricting the life out of the guru. The old man contorted his face, his curly beard prickling Michael's hands.

All Michael had to do, was strangle.

The guru in his arms went stiff. He ceased to resist.

Wetting his lips, Michael got up slowly, leaving guru's carcass sprawled on the floor, eyes wide open with terror.

"Valentina," Michael said softly. Painfully. "My boy. I did it."

A bloodied hand slammed on the table, gripping for a firm purchase. Michael got into fighting stance.

The Hindi woman was Aditi, hair dishevelled, and right hand clutching her gory side, stood up swaying, leaning on the table.

The lady was defenceless. Wounded. And Michael had the upper hand. Was it honourable to kill this wounded person – let alone a woman – all to keep dangerous information of a demonic capsule from getting in the hands of the Führer? Michael couldn't philosophise deeply on that at the moment. He sprung.

He tackled the yelping woman. She spun, falling to her knees as he dragged her around, putting her in a firm headlock. With his right hand, he pulled out his knife, pointing it at Aditi's throat.

He held her there, her breathing ragged and savage in his ears. The woman was about to wail.

"Stop! Or I'll plunge this through your eye!"

Luckily, she understood, her hicks and yelps easing down. "Who? What is this?" she gasped in German on the verge of tears. "Who are you?"

"I'm . . . sorry. I can't. The . . ." Michael swallowed, trembling. *Who* had he become?

"Forsworn of the Führer."

Another voice. A sound of stone rolling on stone.

Aditi hissed. Michael held the knife at her eye. He cut her slightly on the side of her head, causing a single drop of her blood to smear down her cheek like a crimson tear.

Master Alfred Bonner emerged from the open door. He affixed Michael with a calculated stare, portentous and measured. The man was menacing and broad. Six foot six, he wore a polished grey *schutzstaffel* uniform with black boots – a deceitful disguise – and such grey made him appear an iron hill, with strong shoulders. Alfred Bonner was Bavarian – shockingly handsome, squared to the point. His eyebrows – perfect arches – made his blue eyes so diminutively sunken that they looked like lanterns in caves. He had stark blond hair, gelled back, buzz cut, spiky and short, bright as a bundle of hay and sharp as icicles. He was perfection in every way. This man who was said to have discovered the secret of immortality via age reversal technology developed here in Patala. It explained his youthful look, despite being in his mid-thirties.

However, the only blemish to this man's immaculate body was a long depression streaking across his left cheek from his nose to his jaw. A battle scar of tightened skin – a slash from a rapier – though healed, it remained, never going away. To Michael, the scar told a story that this man had endured a tumultuous existence, hardship to stand for the good against fascism. The hardened look, *durchalten* (holding out) that stood against the machinery of the Third Reich, against the odds, in no-man's-land.

In the crook of his arm was the infused voidstone, dimming all the candle-shaped lamps and chandeliers into its deeper darkness. How could Bonner hold such an… abomination and not feel anything? As Michael thought about that, biliousness struck his senses. He strained, almost throwing up.

Bonner lowered his gaze towards the voidstone. Michael witnessed the face of a man who had been betrayed by his family, friends and nation – he'd become hard, there were few men he could trust. Hardened, to singlemindedness. Convinced in his heart that his purposes were good.

"Bilge Cabal. Your bilge caprice, dehumanising humanity," Bonner grumbled with a cold voice. He strode into the room. "How could it have come to this? Down here? Harnessing demonic power of the Nephilim?"

Aditi growled attempting a word of protest, but Michael beat her left breast to silence her.

The Nephilim. The creatures of chaos that caused the Flood. If Himmler was trying to manifest them…

"My lord, what are we to do if Himmler is retrieving the voidstone?" Michael begged, showing his master that this artefact had genuinely horrified him. "Are the Nephilim returning? We must do something to stop this!"

Bonner smirked. "Michael. This began as an investigation to find the murderers of your wife and child. We are superfluous criminal youths, but before us is a path of glory. Your family's killers have been avenged, and I and the *Bund* will go and bring just innovation to the new world. This war is not over."

"The Cabal . . . killed her . . ." Michael's mouth went dry.

"Michael. I'm sorry. Your family was doomed ever since Patala entered into your father's mind. See how bad this world has become? This is clearly *not* the Aryan Germany originally envisioned."

He raised the unclean stone, the Dark Matter within the caged heart pulsing, eager to suck in all hope – all things good – instantaneously. Luckily, the caged metal restrained it. Bonner's eyes glinted with curiosity. "The voidstone has many secrets. The Nephilim *are not* returning. They are *already here*. This calls for a new idea. We need to become the Alliance. To ally together as one humanity to destroy tyranny. You are the only one that can help me in this, Michael." He craned his neck, staring at Michael. The man was perfectly chiselled, like Greek classical marble. "You understand the Cabal. You have proven you can kill them. This is your new purpose, if you want. Join the Alliance, or… you could go home."

"I do not want to go back," Michael called passionately, his sickness still present. "I have no home. I have nothing. I want to join you. Your vision is my vision."

Bonner's lower lip protruded. "Hmm. Indeed. The Alliance is making promises, against the Cabal's Nazi Empire. The Alliance shall bring back the Ascended Masters. And they shall defeat the Nephilim. The Cabal's dominion is up."

"You speak lies!" Aditi hissed, her hair a mangled veil over her face. "You do not know what Adolf has done for us all. He gave my people an identity to be proud of. To be free. Free from Britain. And you—"

"Ah, woman! It is *never* good to favour one race over the other," Bonner snarled with a sly, Bavarian accent. He slowly glanced to the left, towards an arched doorway leading to a staircase descending below. And Michael instantly knew, *an escape route.*

Outside, the confusing barks of the Germans could be heard. Michael felt a heave of panic in his loins. But Bonner remained standing, calm as ever.

"What is this that you mentioned?" Michael asked. "The Alliance?"

"Humanity against tyranny. The Ascended Masters shall return. Lacking imperfect thoughts, surrendered to God."

The voices intensified.

"Uh, lord . . . I will foresee the way," Michael said, feeling convicted, adrenaline pushing through his sickness. "I will see the Ascended Masters return! If that means justice!"

Aditi yowled to get the pursuers' attention.

End it.

Michael jerked the knife in a quick, efficient slice, opening Aditi's throat and spilling her spurting life blood all over her cream kurta.

Aditi fell to the ground, thrashing and convulsing weakly with wide eyes before Alfred Bonner's feet.

Indifferent, Michael heaved a sigh, staring at the woman's trembling body. A reinforcing atonement. For his family.

Finally, Bonner strode swiftly towards the escape route. Michael yelped pathetically at his own clothes, drenched in Aditi's blood. For now, the pursuers would find two dead bodies and a missing voidstone, and garner a potential death sentence from their lords.

"The world will see and know in time that they need the Ascended Masters to defeat the Nephilim," Bonner said, marching down the stairs. "It will take time to liberate, time for the truth, time for the masses to awake."

"Yes. Master, when the Cabal come for us, I want you to train me," Michael said with anticipation. For Valentina, and for his father, he could redeem himself of the guilt this way. He could become something more, something greater than a mere art historian and sculptor. "How can we be ready? How can I become an Ascended Master?"

"Ambitious," Bonner extolled. "The process to start the Alliance would be effective."

They approached a stone door with a glowing, teal swastika emblazoned on it. Bonner pressed his free hand on the symbol and the stone door rolled open, silently rising. It revealed a dark passageway leading to – well, anywhere. The cave systems under India were as complex as the highways and subways of Berlin.

Bonner rubbed Michael's shoulder as he sighed. "The Tibetan monks will teach you all you need to know."

Michael swallowed, setting his jaw staring into the dark ever-expanding maze. The monks. The devotees of Gautama Siddhartha. This was it; Michael saw the old, the sick, and the dead. He saw Samsara - the wheel of time, life, death . . .

The wheel of rebirth.

So, the master and student stepped forth – down the lonely enclosure of winding tunnels, progressing into the foreboding darkness.

2

APOCALYPSE

SAN ANTONIO, TEXAS, AUGUST 2002.

*My name is James Casbolt. I was trained under Michael Oppenheim, Son of Danu —
the ancestral mother of my people the Tuatha Dé Danann. I am a white boy, raised by an
elite paedophile and a drug addict. I am neither a good nor a bad, but I've experienced both.*

*When I was a teenager, Matrika Semjase, the Great Mother in Antarctica, called
for our blood, and I became a super soldier. The Redlion. A real genetic mutant. You may
have never heard of me, but what you will take from this is knowing the true man behind
these words: a man who self-loathes himself over his sins.*

*Of course, the advancements in Antarctica did not stop with genetic enhancement.
My people could astral travel into different realms, use our powers to forge new technologies,
adapt to the storms, create AI. We had to touch the other universes beyond the ice, to feel
the possibilities and take them.*

God said no.

*Heteronomy of ourselves hindered us. I have let my handlers use me as a tool: to remote
view, a living computer and a drug runner. I let them rape me, molest me and indoctrinate
me with their ideals, all for the sake of the sisterhood of the Nindingir — whose great
intellectual capabilities use genetic experimentation and training, to hone incredible skills
of influence, to guide humanity subtly through diplomacy, to make way for the Übermensch.*

*I was to be groomed by the Nindingir, with my brother Maximilian Bates Spiers, to
lead armies of super soldiers to fight against the Galactic Tyranny.*

*I know. At this point, you may consider me a madman who has gone too deep into
the rabbit hole. I'm certain some will feel threatened by this record. I'm exposing secrets and*

conspiracies not known to the public. Some few may feel liberated by this. Most will simply feel that it should not exist. I needed to write it anyway.

Imagine you were sexually abused, knowing that you should be like the normal people out there, but you are molested and shamed all the time. This was my grim childhood.

I wish I could go back in time and change everything. Now I have to live with the Bleakness.

These secret societies that used me – the Light Alliance and the Dark Cabal – follow elements from the Theosophical Society, and Thelema occult magic. Their claim to legitimacy was to utilise people like me – the Aes Sidhe. The Indigo Children.

I was part of the Alliance corporation. It was founded by the Bavarian polymath Alfred Bonner. Despite the Alliance's problematic training, unlike the Cabal, among their soldiers, I made friends. The Alliance is a dampened Socialism – the lesser of two evils.

But after the Cold War, the Iraq-Iran War and the beginning of the 1991 Gulf War, an arms race in the Middle East began for each of these secret societies; the Alliance and the Cabal. There had been much talk with the Aes Sidhe in Antarctica about the Alliance's role in American geo-politics and the Cabal's operations behind the scenes, aiming to intervene in the Middle East, in order to save the present from the apocalypse of the Galactic Tyranny.

Is the Galactic Tyrant an evil god that became immortal? (Gods in non-literate Celtic culture were not Creators or Devils, mind you. They were people, ancestors with natural virtues and vices. Julius Caesar observed and commented on this, but Christianity turned our gods into fairies). Is the Galactic Tyrant a force behind climate change? A consequence of human avarice that would come back to burn the whole world to ashes? Is it an alien invader? I, James Casbolt and the Aes Sidhe destined to face the Tyrant, don't even know what it actually is. No one told us. I did not dare question anything. Just blindly obeyed the system.

What does this all mean? That is why I wrote this book. I'm still trying to put the pieces all together so to speak. I have done much harm to many people, so I ask not that you forgive me, nor that you find this amusing. I hope this work can be an apocalypse (a revelation) for you. This shall be the last time the Redlion tries to do some good before I descend into madness. I ask only that you read or listen to these words. In this record, I hold nothing back. I will try not to shy away from difficult topics or paint myself in a dishonest heroic light. You must know what has been done to me, and what my actions or lack of action has cost me. I have no doubt that you are smarter than I am. I am not a scholar, a scientist, a poet, or a philosopher. I am a witness: of my murders, of my terrible actions, of my humanity.

—James Casbolt, Agaid Tara Chief of the McMurdo Dry Valleys of the Iceni Aes Sidhe.

James Casbolt finished typing on his computer and saved the document that contained the brief account of his life. The life that he remembered at least. He had been as honest as possible, except for the instance when Perseus Euergetes compared elite Mr Whitmore to a male Adelie penguin ejaculating over the bodies of dead chicks and females.

James Casbolt laughed to himself, guffawing in long croaks. "Delightful!" he said aloud. "Delightful!"

Those *disgusting* paedophiles who took him from his flat and from school to do experiments on him as a boy in Wiltshire, Glastonbury and Anglesey, were going have a hard time trying to cover up their acts when this book was published. Why would he lie about the paedophiles in his life? They were *bastards*. All the time, his stepfather Neil would return from "work" with Krispy Kreme donuts, swearing and saying vulgar things about women, like his mother Kate. To Casbolt, even at a young age, he knew it seemed perverted, not understanding why he hated Neil with all his heart.

Justice could be done in a unique way then – by publishing the sincere account of his life. Kate could be vindicated, as well as the many unnamed people who had suffered the same abuse.

Casbolt's light eyes slowly focused to his large, calloused hand which lay on the desk, over a therapist certificate. An official diagnosis for DID – dissociative identity disorder. There were many symptoms to this mental illness, some of which included crippling depression, confusion and anxiety.

James Casbolt did not laugh then. He slumped, reminded of his failure of his Iceni, the Aes Sidhe and Max Spiers. He felt *so weak* and wanted *so* desperately to get better. But now that he had been exiled for breaking the UN Antarctic Treaty, never before had he been so self-conscious. Violence and war were prohibited in the South Pole, but the Alliance's Aes Sidhe super soldier program of Antarctica often found loopholes to transgress these restrictions. But ultimately, his self-ostracism had been for self-preservation and reflection on what he had done.

People wanted revenge against James Casbolt. The law condemned him. The UN wanted to put him on trial.

For an entire year, in hiding, alone in America, his memories of his heinous past returned. He had to tell his story, to write down his apocalypse. He had to spread the word, to bring awareness to the conspiracies of the secret societies and child sex trafficking.

Casbolt heaved himself from his chair, feeling weary, staring ahead at the bars of light banded from the slits of his blinds from the windows of his apartment in San Antonio, Texas. Exiled in an unfamiliar land was for the purpose of evading agents from the deep state – the Cabal – who could so easily locate him, arrest him, take him back to Antarctica to shame him or worse, assassinate him. He hardly got out much for that reason, isolated in his little prison of a rented shack.

During his time in hiding, Casbolt's Aes Sidhe friends would be training and researching and living in Antarctic bases during the six months of winter. Antarctica had become the Tuatha Dé Danann's Inisfail – the Island of Destiny. During winter, a convenient time for the Alliance, offered the opportunity for them to pursue their secret science in peace while most of the secular scientists and tourists were gone. During his childhood, Casbolt used to think Antarctica and its ways, and its weather as the only world where he felt alive.

The only world that felt *real*. Tangible.

Max Spiers. Heather Baglio. Kenneth Marrow. All friends from school. Friends that wept and struggled with him. Friends that inflicted pain on Casbolt from not seeing them again.

"It's not a good to feel like this, now that the book is done," James Casbolt said to himself. He had gotten into the habit of talking to himself over the last year. It wasn't as if he had anyone else to talk to besides the therapist occasionally, and the personalities in his head, which created a space for him to comprehend his day-to-day ruminations. Good thing that he could have someone listening to him. In his mind. "I could finally do something."

"That's good," Michael Prince said. Every time the Michael Prince personality spoke up, Casbolt relaxed, sharing his mind openly with this another side of himself. He developed Michael Prince as a personality when James Casbolt was readopted by his mother Kate Casbolt, after Michael Oppenheim saved him. He became a Casbolt, given a new identity and name under Kate's authority. But Michael Prince, the embryonic core to who Casbolt was, always remained alive; an active and comforting personal friend of his childhood and teenage life. "I'm proud of you, Casbolt. See what we can accomplish together? See? Giving up is never an option because look what you have done so far! *Agent Buried Alive is finished!* Now the world can know about the secret societies, and awareness can be raised to help the victims of child sex trafficking. Perhaps something could be done about it."

"Yeah, finally," Casbolt grumbled. "Now we have another challenge to face." He peered through the blinds longingly, prying them with his fingers and looking outside at the park and the trees. The light and verdant colour astounded him. The leaves and the clouds, and the birds singing – simply sublime. Antarctica had none of that. "I'm just nervous at what people would think of me, Michael."

"You're worrying again, man," Michael Prince replied. "*Don't worry* about what people think. Take a deep breath. You're a strong man, and you've come through the other side and solved problems where many would have given up trying."

"I have come this far," Casbolt whispered, scowling. "There is no turning back now."

No turning back . . . He always considered it a selfish futile exercise to feel respite from pain by assuming any normal person that underwent his sufferings would fail and go through worse than he did. The mindset of an Aes Sidhe was the most *selfish* survival of the fittest. *Others out there going through worse than I . . .*

"I need to tell my story so other victims of abuse can speak out," Casbolt said. "I'm a voice in the wilderness. I have no predecessor. I have no one that cares for me."

"You *do* have people that care about you, Casbolt," Michael reassured. "I was created just to protect you, Spartan."

Casbolt smiled. Spartan. It had been a compliment that Michael Oppenheim, Son of Danu had used, after Casbolt accomplished something he thought was not a big deal. The only time Casbolt experienced love was from Michael Oppenheim, Kate and his auntie – Max Spiers' mother – those memories were sensations of warmth and loss. All of them converged into this one personality of Michael Prince. *Good on ya, Spartan. Good on ya.*

The therapist said that the best way to heal – not resolve – his dissociative identity disorder was to create bonds and relationship with the alter egos. If they were active. Many more, naturally, would remain dormant.

Two alters (personalities) had surfaced so far, Casbolt could not know precisely how many were to be identified, but two were prominent. Michael Prince was the truth worthy, talkative one. He had been the one that had a lot of the earlier memories of his childhood up to his teenage life and early twenties. The other, Redlion, had been precisely created by his own mind so Casbolt could endure the brutality of the sexual and ritual abuse, to numb the fear of dying. The therapist said these personalities were ways his human body, his psyche, created resilient coping mechanisms to kept him functioning.

He told Casbolt to embrace his condition and make use of it.

Casbolt felt like the only person in the world going through the torment of reliving.

His dreadful apocalypse – his reprograming from the indoctrination of the Alliance – begun on the slopes of Fenriskjeften, where Casbolt had remembered enjoying killing – killing more than he had ever killed before. He'd broken *every* Antarctic Treaty article created by the United Nations – entailing serious reprimands for the Aes Sidhe program and the Alliance. Casbolt felt unbearable shame for Max, he knew leaving him to Antarctica alone would make people think Casbolt a coward, unwilling to face the consequences of his reckless actions. *No, they were wrong!*

"What was that?"

Suddenly, Casbolt's hairs rose, and he turned, staring at the computer. The hyper Parvus Perception of his sensitive receptors could tell him if someone were watching via radio waves or via radar keenly, and he sensed a frequency now.

"Oh, so you think you can watch me and monitor me, eh?" he said, stomping towards the web cam on top of his computer, tapping it. He should have covered it long ago. "If you think you can stop me, know that I am not what I am. I've changed!"

The computer did not respond. Luckily. Casbolt chuckled to himself again, rubbing his temples, feeling a strange emptiness engulf him. He *was* mad, and *not* normal, alienated from all the world around him.

His therapist once said that "there are state of affairs that are intrinsically more valuable than others. Being unhappy on contemplating the undeserved suffering of others you caused is a better state of affairs than someone's being happy and not feeling guilt for causing the undeserved suffering of others. The truth is entirely incompatible with someone's being happy or sad."

Writing his autobiography *Agent Buried Alive* had, on one hand, been extremely traumatic, toilsome and frustrating to work on. Two times he had saved the work, and even after the computer shut off, the file had lost all the revisions he'd made. Two times! One instance, he'd lost everything and had to try all over again. A hole in the wall remained a testament of what that loss had done to him.

The second time, he'd lost only a week's worth of work, to reconstruct it made him feel sick. "Losing something and remaking it," Casbolt muttered. "Hmmm. I don't know if I loathe this record more now, because knowing it was not what it once was? Or do I cherish it more now that I have it back? For sure, the hackers are tracking my computer down. They don't want this story out."

On the other hand, writing had been therapeutic, to release all his amounting worries in one place, to record them, letting experience flow freely on a page.

Memories were responsibility and choices, a reckoning.

If there had been no meaning to publishing *Agent Buried Alive*, then Casbolt was sure he could not live with himself anymore.

"It is what it is," Casbolt said. "I did all I could. I can help other people feel comfortable to step out and talk about their pain and traumas." He pulled out a cigarette and walked over towards the porch to get some fresh brisk winter air. The day was so blue, reminding him of Antarctic summers. The way he liked it. "I'm publishing the truth and only the truth." He took a drag and exhaled a puff.

—

Three months later, after publishing *Agent Buried Alive* on the online Bases Forum website, in November 2002, James Casbolt got a call from a US marine living in San Juan Puerto Rico named Julian. He was a friend of the Actionman. The world-famous actor.

But Julian was more than a random person. He was also, a victim of trauma.

Casbolt requested that he come to help Julian with his strange hallucinations of nocturnal erotic behaviour with a woman, surges of anger, night terrors and above all, the strange, adoptee girls. Surprisingly, Julian was even kind enough to offer Casbolt a chance to redeem himself. Suspending disbelief to Casbolt's personal narrative, Julian wanted him – a struggling super soldier. He was keen to enlist Casbolt into the US marine force to fight Islamic terrorists in Afghanistan at the end of the year. *Killing two birds with one stone!*

Putting down the phone, Casbolt pulled out his Green Card – representing his permanent resident alien status, and he grinned. At last, he can bring awareness to child trafficking and the secret societies.

"At last! I can do something! Hey, Michael! I've finally done it! I'm finally going to help someone! Finally, I have a chance to show the world that James Casbolt is a free man!"

At least, fighting terrorists after 9/11 would make him a vigilante.

3

THE JAWS OF THE WOLF

"Max Spiers is not my biological brother. His father is from Latvia and his mother from Poland, but he is still the closest I can call family. Despite his childhood being full of dares and reckless behaviour, now he's a person of scientific discoveries and honour.

Since only the Celtic Blue Bloods can worthily run for chieftain, Max and I didn't 'rise to power' as rising up the ranks, but only in proving ourselves that we could maintain our inevitable destiny mentally and physically. It is not about merit either for Aes Sidhe – beforehand, you recall in our private lives, Max and I used to run amuck with gangs at schools and rob stores together, smoke and chase girls at nightclubs in England. Not so chief-like.

Aes Sidhe society is based off honour and shame. Ideally, the notion of geas – a idiosyncratic taboo, whether of obligation or prohibition on one hand, a cursed fate on another. If one incurred geas, it was important to fulfil it."

—From *Agent Buried Alive*, James Casbolt's Autobiography, 2001.

The low sun had not yet disappeared beyond the horizon, and eternal twilight had not yet come, impending upon the wind-flayed white desert at the bottom of the world. Dry minus zero air on the horizon shimmered with a jubilant glory, celebrating the coming warmth of the sun's rays embracing the hard ice that mimicked its golden glow. It reflected upwards the heat from the wind lashed sastrugi – a perpetual glare of whiteness that would make one snow blind. The visors of James Casbolt's helm had been built just for that – a

22

thick clear polarised vision against the sun's strong reflected glare off the snow. There, through the lens of rosy pigmentation, he saw the promontories of Mundlauga Crags thrusting vertically out of the barren snow surface.

Casbolt danced on one foot into the snow, stepping out of the skidoo carrier, feeling the new power, the strength and energy in each step. Goibniuium Armour – a suit of heat-insulating plate developed by cybernetic engineers from the remains of metal armour from fallen meteorites – or gods according to the Nindingir. He could not *believe* he had won his own set in a duel! Now the world had changed, and the stakes had changed, no longer could he contain the excitement at the back of his mind anymore. Now all he needed was to earn a Curruid Spear – weapons of lore, weapons of magic.

Until then, he would be a true Celtic hero.

"Calm down, James," Temarunda of the Aquarian super soldiers said from behind. She didn't have the armour but wore circular snow goggles and a beany cap resembling a retro biplane pilot of the early twentieth century, clad in red and black thick padded coats with a fur hood and a black neck warmer that muffled her voice partly. Occasionally, she would pluck it outwards to let out a squall of warm fog breath. The woman was beautiful, yet fiercely stout with fair skin and a Norwegian accent. Behind her was a small land contingent of twenty Aquarians – loyal to the chiefs. "Patience, James. Crevasses. I shouldn't be saying this to a chief of the Iceni and Taradan!" She sounded irked.

Casbolt smiled within his helm. He wanted to fight. He wanted to prove to these other Aquarians here in the Mundlauga Crags, that there were consequences for violating *geas*. The Aquarians had held his Iceni friends hostage. He promised those friends years ago during the Agoge that he would protect them from predators.

Now, the predator Aquarian chief found them, and Casbolt gained his armour.

Death was inevitable, and Casbolt didn't care. *Geas.* He promised. He hoped Temarunda and her soldiers could understand why.

"Man, easy man. It would not do any good if you wrongly step." Max Spiers of the Berserkirs, clad in white and purple aqua armour, was here too. His feet worked with faint hydraulics, enhancing of speed and agility, as he hiked the incline of rubble strewn with snow. He looked glorious, powerful and majestic.

"Admit it," Casbolt gloated. "Max, you were excited when you won your armour too. Who on earth wouldn't be?!"

"We need some brains than brawn ultimately," Temarunda sniffed with a nasal voice.

Casbolt shifted, feeling the morning cold frigid wind from the seams of his armour, blundering his ears. The cold was very good the druids said; it heightened the acute awareness accuracy. He could confirm that, from his training with fresh starts jogging in the morning, but the freedom Goibniuium Armour brought . . .

Behind him, an army of disciplined clan members of the Berserkirs of the Ronne Ice Shelf Aes Sidhe and Aquarians of the Orvin Mountains marched patiently, their footsteps plodding through the snow. Most of them were tall and fit with brown and fair hair, and all light eyes.

With this suit of interlocking armour, Casbolt felt that he did not need these super soldiers. Including his blaster canons and shield in his red gauntlets, he had a thick hammer called Icebreaker slung onto his jet pack. To Casbolt, it felt as light as a feather. The unlimited power he now had in his hands was incredible.

"You forgotten my advice, Casbolt?" Temarunda said tartly, almost annoyed by his enthralment. "You're actively seeking retribution on my clan because of failure of communication with your society. If you had been eager to speak to Tulugaak first about the Iceni's skidoo survey for meltwater glaciers in Queen Maud Land, then everything would have been different. The 'capture' of Heather Baglio's skidoo that crashed around here doesn't *appear* to be a kidnapping. Could it just be a voluntary action?

"Blake and Heather may have been seeking shelter in the nearest base for a while to pass the last blizzard, and maybe decided to stay a little longer because of the hospitality?" The woman sighed. "But you Iceni *love* your contests. You never seem to wait a single moment, and you're actively seeking out another challenge after challenge. We need to be *wise* – this does not have to be a bloodbath between us like you did with the Carnutes."

"I'm thinking about it," Casbolt intoned. No . . . He tried to ignore her. Great *geas* had been committed towards Casbolt's best friends, demanding great retribution. *On the battlefield, one has no time to think. The Carnutes' war was an exception because they swore allegiance to the Cabal by trying to begin illegal mining operations for fossil fuels at the Filchner Ice Shelf.*

The Aquarians have done the same. They wanted to exploit resources and human labour.

Max summoned his barbed dark-gold Curruid Spear, Gáe Buidhe, from the Otherworld. He splayed his right hand out, and twisting lines of mist gathered in the air, coalescing in his hand. A massive Spear appeared, shimmering gold, barbed and sinuous with a rippled eel-like point and crusted crystal ridges along the hand guard on the shaft. It dripped with condensation which gleamed in the sunlight.

According to legend, the notorious Curruid Spears were first carried by the Tuatha Dé Danann when they arrived from the Atlantic and the English Channel to settle Ireland to trade during the Middle Bronze Age. James Casbolt's Celtic ancestors worshipped the alloy that formed these weapons, believed to be meteorites that fell from the sky at night. The souls of broken gods, those rocks had been called. A master forger by the wisdom of the gods could change their shape.

The Curruid Spear was made to fight only one foe: Fomorians. The Nindingir wanted to make sure the Fomorians – forces of the Galactic Tyranny – did not return past the barrier of the South Pole. Also known as Ophidians or Nephilim, these demonic creatures from the air and sea represented the destructive powers of nature, personifications of chaos, darkness and death. They could take beautiful human forms, were reptilian in nature, and were the Aes Sidhe's ancient enemy.

Were the Carnutes and the Aquarians Fomorians in disguise? Perhaps. When your foes were supernatural warriors, bronze was useless. Something supernal was required.

"You know you could have married Temarunda, Cas, and we wouldn't have to do this," Max Spiers said.

Casbolt shrugged.

"Marriage is for winning new political alliances, Casbolt," Temarunda spoke. "Only four of the thirteen Aes Sidhe clans have recognised Max Spiers by the title Eurypontid Tara Chief. You should have arranged a marriage with Fiacha. Or Fiacha to Blake Gates. But yes." She gazed at Casbolt. "You should have arranged a marriage with me, Redlion."

"You bloody still on that?" Casbolt said. "It's too late now. Blake was kidnapped and we're here to save him. Let's fight already. These Aquarians have incurred serious *geas* upon us. Enough of politics!"

"You cannot escape forever, Casbolt," Max uttered. "As chief, you are married to everything. The money, base infrastructure, ice-penetrating radars, wildlife and green sustainability. It's all *politics*."

"Says who? How is it like to go against your own people?" Casbolt asked the Aquarian, ignoring Spiers.

Temarunda shrugged, but her face in the folds of her neckwarmer, flushed. "The societies made a grave mistake to anger the Iceni. History has proven that."

The misty morning fog began to disperse, and the crags appeared rising out of the snow down the valley. They were a string of partly covered rocky aretes isolated in a white ocean, glowing a metallic brown gold in the orange sun. Like rows of canine teeth, the peaks were split in V formations caused by wind erosion. Others were needle-like towers petrified and hallowed with a round crescent bases, packed up with two hundred and fifty metres of snow upon their slopes. The largest of the mountains, the base difficult to spot in this direction, was named Fenriskjeften, also known as the Jaws of the Wolf: the Aquarian base.

"Tulugaak has Heather and the Iceni captured in there," Casbolt said. "He's a human trafficker with a Spear."

"A demigod from Canada," Spiers cut in. "His mother was a Cabal clairvoyant, and rumours say his father was the god Loki. You cannot get any more suspicious than this." Spiers' helm and visor morphed, clicking into place, forming a pointed mask with an intimidating triangular pointed helmet. A white-and-purple plume, arched from one side of his helmet to the other. Around his neck, just like Casbolt's own armour, was an exquisitely decorated torc – a divine mark of warrior rank.

"He's mine. Time to test this baby," Casbolt whispered. Grinning, he took off running and Max joined him, boots grinding against ice. This armour – besides its innovative technology, had magical elements. It gave one extreme mobility, speed and agility, as well as strength.

Casbolt leapt over a lightning-shaped crevice beginning to appear, momentum unaltered. As everything should be, James Casbolt and Max Spiers together. Other responsibilities did not matter. All life was about the thrill. A good fight, a day on the ice or in the underground arenas, and the sauna, and a good vintage of wine or ale in the tavern. *This is Antarctica!*

Cracks of webbed ice were already forming the closer Casbolt got to the edge of the glacier. Once he reached the cliff, he leapt with a mighty jump.

His jet pack activated with a roar, surging his body upwards at incredible speed. Another bonus: the suit reduced Gs, not ceasing it entirely.

Thrusting upwards then curving back around, Casbolt gained a tentative equilibrium on an updraft, sighing with relief. He had learnt how to fly in the skydiving machines in the bases, but not really flying with armour on.

"Jesus Christ!" Casbolt laughed.

"Woah! Man, you all good?" Max sounded he was having the time of his life. "You almost rocketed into the stratosphere!"

Casbolt looked down and realised, Max Spiers was below him, flying, many meters down above the ground in the air. Casbolt carefully, pulled back, sinking back down to join his brother's attitude. Flying in Goibniuium Armour felt like swimming, in some sense. One had to use their arms, legs, and body to stir and turn and change speed while soaring.

"Do you think so, man? This is unreal!" Casbolt shouted, genuinely surprised by his childlike excitement.

"Carry on!"

"Wait! I got a hold of it now!"

"Alright. Alright, man. If you say so."

Casbolt drifted behind Max soaring downwards steadily towards the fang-toothed arete looming above.

Promptly, he surged towards the snowy slope, landed, scaling up the crenels of rock. Out of the clefts of ice caves, tanned men, veiled with neck warmers and fury-maned hoods in padded armour, disgorged from caves with hammers, harpoons and guns. Their eyes were filled with provocation and their body language, hesitation. They did not want to fight.

Detaching the hammer from off his jet pack, Casbolt flung it down, crushing the enemy. He threw a back fist at three men, hurtling them broken and mewling. At that instant, the Aquarians broke out of their shock – knowing the decay of international law – they attacked.

What a joke! This was bloody easy! Seizing the hammer, he brought it around in a wide arc, swung it, sweeping men off their feet, dashing them against the wall like autumn leaves. Before they died, he saw the terror and numb fierceness in their eyes realising they had met their doom. Above on the vertical ridge, Max swooped, leaving behind a wormlike trail of smoke. Up here, well defended within the natural fortifications of the eroded arete, Aquarian Aes Sidhe held their base.

Ripping through them, Casbolt killed more men than he had in his entire life. A maelstrom of incredible destruction, compacted foes dying from a mere swing of his hammer breaking bones, sending them sliding down, flaccid. An Aes Sidhe could fight an Aes Sidhe fairly, but with an Aes Sidhe in magical armour . . . Casbolt laughed. At that he felt less remorse, but more pride. One could place a worthless helot inside this armour and if they even had their wits about them, they would annihilate. Combat in the Agoge did not matter for Goibniuium Armour. Casbolt was sure, the Nindingir martial art teacher Scáthach would be shaking her head in appalling asperity at him for fighting like this, or even box him for it; she'd been conservatively against technology made to kill without the art of form stances.

Gritting his teeth, he dug deep within the thrill of battle, the Redlion waiting.

He embraced the beast.

In less than a moment, he was tumbling out roars of pleasure; blow after blow, destruction streaking blood through the snow, wreaking ruin upon these men. He was a conqueror. He was glorious blizzard of death. He was a *god*.

Suddenly the snowy slope rumbled and roared, the ground sliding away. Casbolt activated his jet pack, thrusters lurching him into the air. He watched the Aes Sidhe below scream, floundering and drowning under the avalanche, thundering down the crag.

Now, Casbolt – the Redlion – had nature on his side.

Landing on solid ground, rocks crunched like skulls beneath his sabatons, as he charged across the rusty battlefield, scourged by wind and snow. His elite reinforcements pounded below, up the other side of the peak. His handpicked force of Iceni of the McMurdo Dry Valleys Aes Sidhe swarmed in the bowl of the bronze crag, beating their spears or guns on their bucklers, neck warmers and hoods veiling their faces. Guns crackled and spears thrashed as battle unleashed at the bowels of the closed slope end of the fanged peak.

More Aquarians appeared from out of clefts, and Casbolt attacked them, hammer raised. The rhythm of the war sung within him as he swung – before him a tower of stone and snow, and behind him, a trail of corpses.

Then something hard banged against his back, with enough impact that it sent him stumbling. Scanning, in the distance, he spied sniper rifles from up on the tower fang of rock. Easy target. Marking them, Casbolt pulled into the stance Iceberg Breaks off the Glacier, stomping on bodies, aiming his right arm and transforming it into a tubular blaster, glowing blue, white from the seams, and fired. It did not need a direct aim, the projectile arched a trail of smoke, struck the rock nearby, and the explosion did the rest of the job.

More gunfire railed him. Growling, he fired again, killing more Aes Sidhe, sending them spinning in the air. He spun, slaying, Max flying alongside with him looking . . . uncertain.

"To the peak!" Casbolt roared. "To the peak!"

Below, his men and women imbuing vengeance for the incurred *geas* roared in response, surging forward, pressing the Aquarians. It was a vitality better than youth, better than any pleasure he could know of. His power. A skilful passion better than a lifetime of bleak drudgery and torture. Aquarian after Aquarian fell before his hammer. The sheer momentum of attacks often sent them stumbling backwards and falling off the cliff from the viciousness of his swings. Right then, he saw the enemy Aes Sidhe breaking, fleeing from Casbolt. He grinned. Aes Sidhe *never* gave up a fight.

"Always running into things without thinking, Cas! At ease," Max snapped from the other side of the ridge. What? Why did he sound mad?

Down the V-shaped cliffs forming the arete was a silk-like pocket of ice lodged between twin peaks, forming a wedged bridge. A perfect lookout for James Casbolt and Max Spiers while a perfect defence to hide not just from a blizzard, but from Fomorian Ophidian spirits. And also, it was a great place to hold hostage prisoners like Heather Baglio and the lost Iceni.

"Our chance to win!" Casbolt said. Breathing deeply, he raised his hammer above his head posing, reflecting sunlight. His armour glowing, below his Aes Sidhe roared and cheered, calls that rose above the Aquarian cries.

This was it!

Amidst the sounds, cries erupted, soaring into the air. "Redlion! Redlion! Redlion!"

"Hang on," Max said frantically, removing his visor up from his eyes. "Hang on! Stop! Stop what you're doing! Something is wrong! Something . . ."

Idiot! He *ruined* his moment! Wanting to crush Max's skull, Casbolt rasped a growl. "Why do you have to . . ."

Max stalked up to him, pulling his arm. "Come and look at this!"

Together, they went towards the cliff, watching the glacier walls in the distance from where the assault had begun. A series of ropes hung off the glacier, where the soldiers had abseiled down. Where were Casbolt's Aquarian reinforcements? The scouts should be—

Casbolt removed his visor, his bare sweaty skin freezing. Wind gushed, blundering his ears, powerful enough to make him lose balance. Shaking, Casbolt scrambled to one of the jutting square-shaped overhangs to get a better view of the valley. Here, he knew the tactics of a battle as a chef knew cooking: Max was right, something smelled off.

Two hundred metres below in the shadow of the tower compacted in between two of the Mundlauga Crags, the Aquarians did not fare well as the fight continued, but the retreating soldiers clogged both passes, trapping the Iceni and Berserkirs simultaneously, potentially if Tulugaak had reinforcements – he had to be smarter than that to do it if he had been expecting a siege – the tables would turn. The cries of battle echoed, but unless Casbolt could gather more reinforcements . . .

Max pointed northward towards the circling glacier where the skidoos were. Northward, beyond the ice wall, towards Temarunda. Casbolt squinted at the burning white down below.

"Oh no," he rasped.

Temarunda was retreating – she hadn't even scaled down the glacier – back across the white desert, abandoning the staging camp.

Temarunda had given up on the chief's troops, leaving them in enemy territory. Abandoning them.

"Tulugaak's doing!" Casbolt roared, stalking back down the rocky slope towards the wedge of hardened ice. He stood on the edge, his boot thumping the ice, his hammer ready to pound it. "I told you, Max! I *told you* I didn't want to marry her! She's a snake!"

"We walked right into this!" Max shouted, following behind. "We were domed. We shouldn't have brought our troops. They were eager to fight. The *geas* was too much, and now Temarunda has brought double!" Then the man stiffened.

A crack of ice appeared under Casbolt's feet faster than he could blink.

"Go!" Casbolt just managed as the entire floe shattered underneath. He caught a glimpse of his brother, scrabbling on all fours on the dry rocks, looking back in horror as Casbolt toppled into the rift, backwards, face towards the tranquil unpolluted sky.

Everything spun round him in pale blue-black, chunks of ice hanging still around him.

A moment later, he found himself crashing into a dark building with an awful *crunch*! Something hard hit his arm, the impact so powerful he felt his gauntlet crumple, hurting his arm, breaking his fingers.

But the structure had failed to stop him. A metal juggernaut, he tore right through the floor, and continued to fall, helmet grinding, hitting a concrete surface with a loud crash, finally stopping. Residue, fallen ice, and debris rained upon him. The sounds were so deafening, it drowned out his groans.

A sharp pain raced up his numb left hand. He shook his head, finding himself facing the damp cold ground, gingerly prying himself up, realising it was not a ground but an concrete bridge that spanned a massive cave. He shook his head, staring upwards at what had to have been a fifty-foot drop, shattering a section of the sealed subterranean base. Large lights illuminated the hallows, casting an eerie fluorescent glow across the chamber.

He was inside the frigid Jaws of the Wolf! A fitting trap with a fitting name.

Casbolt shifted, feeling the pain in his left hand, making him wince. His red vambrace down his left lower arm had been sheered, crumpled and broken, and his pinkie and index looked swollen, the other fingers still encased in dinted crimson metal. Bits of the gauntlet had been destroyed, its interlocking bits were sparkling with detached wires. Growling, Casbolt found his hammer, with its handle completely bent under him. How could regular steel do that!?

Perhaps the Goibniuium alloy was a stronger metal, perhaps similar metal forged from meteorites as the Curruid Spear. In order to not catch himself by surprise anymore – he could never afford that – he would wear the armour day and night, heck he might even *sleep in it* if that what it took to get used to it.

Then, Casbolt backed into a woman in a researcher uniform with a family of young people, screaming, pulling back against the wall. Apparently, Tulugaak hadn't warned that his trap would affect the people without a proper evacuation. Indeed, the Treaty forbade sieges, so the people in the base were not used to battle.

The Treaty would crumble sooner than later. The Galactic Tyranny.

Ignoring the cowering people, he shoved through the door with his enhanced strength, and walked out onto a wooden landing frosted hard with ice.

Streams of bullets hailed upon him. He turned his right shoulder, growling gutturally in anger, shielding himself – he was without the function of his left vambrace that could summon the shield. The best he could do in the flurry, was inspect the attack and move.

Up in the caves, around fifteen gunmen with scoped semi-automatics fired from a good sniper's distance. Idiots with their guns breaking the law! On the other side of the bridge, Aes Sidhe carrying harpoons and more guns, stormed towards him. They all wore bands around their foreheads with the symbol of Aquarius – two wavy lines on top of each other.

In that troop on the top of a large rock wall was a tall man, who Casbolt supposed to be Tulugaak himself. He had the look of a grizzly bear in his layered coat, and furry hood like a lion, bearing a large red lance in his hand. A lethal impressive weapon, it rose high above the troops like a war banner, its crimson surface burnished, a work of art, its tip barbed with a spiked starburst, a sinuous point at the top. The Spear felt ancient somehow, *alien*, crafted in another age when gods walked the earth. It made harpoons and guns seem pitiful.

By the time this was over, Casbolt would have that Curruid Spear.

Revelling in the thrill of the Redlion that drove all pain and anxiety away, Casbolt charged in, facing the Aes Sidhe, ignoring the bullets.

Right hand becoming a blaster, he fired back, aiming hazardously, certain to hit a target with the enemy packed so tightly. Defending men and women dropped left right and centre, making the other troops stagger and recoil. Shouts bellowing, bullets clanging loudly on armour, Casbolt alone faced the guard.

Firing his blaster at some of the gunner men on the sides, Casbolt watched the Aquarians barking commands. Pairs went out on the sides of the bridge, using saws to cleave the support beams and the railings on the crag's interior. Some sections were made of frosted metal, and they would surely give way if the weight of Goibniuium could weaken it.

The walkway shook under Casbolt's feet, snow pouring down the cracks.

A single stream of bullets racked through the ranks of leading Aes Sidhe, mowing them down to a thrashing death. That same stream killed the men sawing the railing and beams.

It was none other than Blake Gates. That warrior of the Iceni had such accuracy with the gun. He had made it inside, to free Heather. The woman looked like she could eat rock and ice all at once with that glower, but she was a graceful fighter.

"Blake! You miracle!" Casbolt called, but his mind was on a better prize. "Hey, Heather!"

"You've come with a show!" the woman called out.

Casbolt chuckled. Reaching for a discarded harpoon from a fallen Aes Sidhe, he charged up the frosty ramp to where he saw Tulugaak.

He met the man on a wide wooden and metal-bolted platform, arched by a large cave made of rock and limpid ice. Slinking around the Indigo Child were five bodyguards, all wearing the Aquarian bands of blue, white and red wavy lines on their foreheads. Puffing inside his helmet, Casbolt took a step forward.

Ordering his men to lower their guns, Tulugaak with his Spear in both hands, strode towards Casbolt.

But everyone was fixed on the blood-red Curruid Spear. No one knew how many Spears were out there. The Tuatha Dé Danann when they arrived in Ireland, thousands of years ago, fighting in the glorious *Cath Maige Tuired* against the Fir Bolg and Fomorians, made many Spiritual weapons. Over time, as the Aes Sidhe retreated into the Otherworld, into earthen mounds and ring barrows (sidhe), the Spears were passed down by nobles, chiefs of tribes during the Roman empire. In Arthur's day facing the English Anglo-Saxons, the weapons were relics of power. By the Christian Middle Ages up until the original settlers on John Davis' whaling ship – the first landing on Antarctica – the weapons were heirlooms. On that ship, one man had a fascination for Celticism. In finding Antarctica, never explored by man, he was said to have found more Spears here. Weapons like this went back further to the days of the Celtic gods of Europe, because the Curruid Spears did not belong to endemic peoples already living here. Antarctica was *terra nullius* and yet, endemic of spirit beings. These were *their* Spears as they were gods. Antarctica was the gods' land and wherever the gods went, their magical items inevitably followed.

Thrill thrummed inside Casbolt thinking about how he could win the weapon – just a single solid hit and the bout would be over. He picked up a harpoon, which felt like a toy in comparison to the Curruid Spear.

"You should not have come here, James," Tulugaak said with his distinctive native north-Canadian accent.

"You kidnapped my family. Why? Now the Chief has come to rescue them. It could have made things a lot easier if you'd just gave them back." His dinted armour clicked as he began to circle the Indigo Child while trying to keep a shrewd eye on his gun men.

"What!?" the Aquarian leader exclaimed in derision. "This is *ridiculous!* This is a free unpolluted land, protected by all nations! You're breaking the laws of the Treaty!"

"Says you with bodyguards and a private army! Semjase chooses only the best to protect this land!"

Roaring, Tulugaak twirled the barbed Spear savagely, and Casbolt lunged back. The half hit his pauldron, but on the drawback, one of the blades on the barb jammed into his left pauldron. It jerked his body towards Tulugaak, but Casbolt resisted, getting into Starfish Caught in a Brinicle – a firm deep-rooted stance with slightly bent knees and a thrusted pelvis.

Tugging and grunting, Tulugaak pushed forward, dislodging the Spear, evading backwards with three steps. Casbolt had to be careful, to wait for the right moment. But the Redlion was a self-exalting spur.

Ideally, Casbolt would rely on the armour's vigour to prolong the fight. Unfortunately, the armour was badly dinted, and his left vambrace and part of his gauntlet completely ruined, and he had more men to deal with. So he played along with what Tulugaak expected; dodging into the stances he learnt in the Agoge – Orca on the Wave, Seal Slides the Floe and Squall Dips the Permafrost.

Attacking, Tulugaak swung directly downward. The Spear was long and lethal, slicing the air sharply with the force of a crashing wave. Casbolt blocked with his vambrace, perfunctorily striking with his harpoon.

Tulugaak, manoeuvring, thrust. Casbolt brushed against icicles with a zigzagging Iceberg Breaks off the Glacier. The Redlion called to him. It numbed the dislocated fingers on his left hand.

Stall him. Distract him as long as you can . . .

Tulugaak thrust at Casbolt's stomach, sparks streaking the air, spinning the weapon around to trip him. Casbolt stepped into him, moving faster, slamming his shoulder into his padded chest.

Winded, Tulugaak gasped, crashing to the ground. The platform shook as Casbolt, from the force of his shoulder strike, fell on top of his opponent, dropping the harpoon.

At last, Casbolt rolled, positioning himself on top of Tulugaak, where the weight of Goibniuium would keep him pinned. Just as Casbolt expected, at that moment, the Aquarians cocked their guns and attacked. From all sides.

But they were not ready to see how fast Casbolt could respond. Scooping up his harpoon, getting on his feet, he bore the barrage of incoming fire. He managed to deflect shrapnel into a man's face. Dropping the harpoon into his left hand, he punched with his right into a man, blasting him backwards with his canon. When he swung the harpoon, he had *power*.

Dropping gunmen with the flurry of his strikes, he crashed into them, cleaving pockets out of their ranks.

"You speak of protection?" Tulugaak said hoarsely, his hand clutching his chest, having trouble breathing. "If you were for the land, why are you killing like a savage!?"

The cries were numbed by the thrill of the Redlion.

"Uncivilised machine! You monster, look at you! Look at you!"

"Aes Sidhe are breed for battle," Casbolt shouted. Gripping a floundering man in his hands, Casbolt stalked nonchalantly, raising him up, slowly crushing the man's throat. Pure anguish marred his victim's expression. He had red hair and bulging blue eyes and freckles – an Aes Sidhe. It could have been any one of Casbolt's family.

Casbolt ended his misery by imbedding the harpoon deep into his chest. Then he discarded the body, tossing it like a rag doll with a roar.

The remaining Aes Sidhe trembled, looking upon him. "When there is power, there will always be suffering!" Casbolt said. "Face it, man! Bloodshed is inevitable!"

"You don't have to crush random people! I and they will go to Valhalla's Halls rewarded! While you remain on Earth, with orphans as your servants and your loved ones burning up in the fire of your guilt! Who's the real winner then? Who's the loser!?

"Until the Heralds of the end come,

you shall fear your own glory,

and fall with wrath,

drunken by strength, your anguish.

The Judge's end.

Red runs the Spear of Abaddon's Champion.

Blue Blood."

Such strange words for an Indigo Child.

Tulugaak coughed, blood brimming his lips. "For the sake of the gods," he rasped in wounded agony. "I will do one last service." He raised the Spear.

The last of the gunners opened fire.

Casbolt roared as waves of rapid-fire bullets crashed into him, sending him sliding backwards from the impact; sparks flashed everywhere in his vision, his armour rattling terribly. Then, throwing himself onto the ground, Casbolt punched the platform. It dislodged around him and the gunners, and Tulugaak slipped on the ice, tumbling off he platform and smashing into the rocks. He heard the men scream in pain.

He felt his helmet had been greatly damaged, so Casbolt ripped it off to breathe. His right arm hurt too. Grimacing, he faced the Aquarians with guns charging towards him.

Shooting to his feet, dazed, Casbolt realised then that the Aes Sidhe were not coming for him. They huddled around Tulugaak's body where it had fallen from the platform, dashed against the stones. They hauled him and the Spear, fleeing.

Casbolt roared, stumbling in pursuit. No, not now after all this time, his prize, that Spear, would be taken from him! Not now after so much effort, after so much thrill from killing. The pain in his arms made him mad with rage, but the Redlion drove him forward.

Casbolt ran up the ramp along the side of the cavern, his legs screaming with pain, chasing after the men carrying their leader away. Right gauntlet turning into a blaster he fired, but just missed, sheering a block of ice. Growling, he stumbled to a stop, aimed for a moment and fired. But just when the men entered into a hidden door, he killed one of the carriers. Dragging the body, the surviving Aquarian carriers pulled inside with Casbolt in hot pursuit.

Though helmless, Casbolt saw red in a tunnel of white. He fired, and fired and fired.

Casbolt kicked open a door, his sabaton smashing it into pieces, his blaster aimed and whirling with power. The tunnel inside the bunker had sterile light glowing with a blanched colour, and to his bare face, it felt warmer inside, much warmer than a fridge. Following the trail of blood, he found another room, with one guard on post. He gave a start. This person did not believe a charging warrior could kill him in Antarctica. The Treaty of peace was this fool's only shield.

Casbolt finished him with a single blast.

The next room had a bronze serpent coiled around a tall pole hanging on the wall, and Tulugaak laying on the ground. His eyes were closed, blood smearing his body. Next to him, was a beautiful distraught woman, rocketing up from her feet. Tulugaak's wife. She raised a jug, screaming so loudly it could have made the ice break.

She threw the jug. Casbolt dodged and punched her in the stomach. He heard ribs and bones crunch. The woman flew, crashing into the wall, roaring for breath, wheezing and coughing up gouts of blood violently, her body wringing madly. The gauntlet, forming into his blaster, he aimed at her. The woman in an excruciating fit, drummed her legs weaky to ward him off, struggling to survive, her eyes wide in her pale face.

There was another sound in the room that made Casbolt hesitate. An abject moaning cry. The only other person in room was the young boy, six or seven. Tears streaking down his face, he struggled to lift Tulugaak's Curruid Spear in both hands.

Casbolt froze, muscles taut. Those eyes . . . What did this heroic boy see above him? A monster in impervious armour? The thrill of battle started to dwindle, but Redlion hardened his heart.

"You cannot have my daddy," the boy sobbed. "You cannot have my mommy. Please."

Redlion shot the groaning agonised woman. The boy squealed, taking a step forward. "No! Mommy!"

With his wounded left hand, Redlion grabbed the haft of the Spear, yanking the boy off his feet. Sobbing, the boy fell on his knees.

Only a child . . . A child of a perverted father that abducted his friends. Redlion will cease this generational curse. Son of Loki. Cabal spawn.

If Casbolt could take away what Tulugaak held dear, then the gods have come to punish *him* for his terrible *geas*.

You uncivilised machine.

But Redlion *needed* the Spear. He needed to protect his family from potential enemies. There was a greater force out there to fight. The Fomorians. The Galactic Tyranny.

The child's wet face glowed under the barrel of Redlion's blaster above.

—

A few hours later, Casbolt sat on the edge of Fenriskjeften, the Drygalski nunataks strewn across the snow – gnarled black teeth on a plain of white desert. The sky hung with ghostly mundane clouds, roiling with a few white whisps that rasped the course of the slanting crags forming smearing shadows across the land. The wind was frigid, making his face prickle, burning his nose.

In Casbolt's lap, laying parallel to the ground, was his new Curruid Spear. His armour had been removed, carried away to be repaired by the engineers. He was now dressed in his regular puffy jacket, his left hand bandaged. Below, the Iceni and the Berserkirs regrouped, packing up on snowmobiles and carrier aircraft.

In his snow jacket and out of his suit, Max Spiers gingerly hiked up the incline, flanked by two Aes Sidhe women – Heather Baglio who still looked sullen and despondent from her experience as a hostage – and red-haired Caitlin McLeod. Both women were mature adults now, youthful and lean. At the wave of the chief's hand, the two women kept a good distance behind, and Casbolt knew, looking into Heather's eyes, not a little bit of gratitude resided in there. Afterall, she did not need Casbolt and Max's help; Blake Gates, Casbolt's school friend, was the true hero of the battle. He'd gotten himself free.

Despite his fatigue, Max looked thoughtful. Growing up, Max had been excellent in schooling both in mundane life and in the Agoge, with the exception for Casbolt who thought the man to always be right with everything, even if he disagreed with him.

"What have we done?" Max sighed wearily, rubbing his gloved hands together for warmth. "This battle made no sense. No sense. No sense whatsoever." Grinding his jaw, he looked at the wind-scourged crags rising out of the barren snow desert. "This will cost us."

"What do we do with them, Max?" Casbolt said. "The UN?"

"We cannot be enemies to the people we ought to save," Max said bleakly. "Danu gave birth to us to be scions of peace in this Inisfail. We need to give the Aquarians back their livelihoods and their families. They did not come to stay in Antarctica to die. Antarctica is no place you would want to die."

The boy's wide shimmering eyes smeared across Casbolt's consciousness. "James?"

"Why do they train us? What are we fighting for? Is it for honour? *Geas*? The universe? Or for ourselves?" As an obligation that can be imposed on anyone, *geas* was a duty to create peace and honour or a curse, namely if one was reckoning it or incurring it. Casbolt felt its weight upon his shoulders as a cold curse.

Max slanted his head in thought. "We need to stop squabbling and remember why Danu gave birth to us – the Aes Sidhe program was to prevent the Galactic Tyranny. That's all. Have we been so blind?"

Casbolt closed his eyes, shame slipping from his fatigue, filling him with reproach. "What even is the Galactic Tyranny?!" he hissed. "We were never told what it is!"

"That's not the point! You're a crazy, bloodthirsty, voracious animal," Max said, anger riddling his voice. He pointed at Casbolt, looming over him. "You're a *disgrace!*"

Casbolt smirked but forced it away. That would be inappropriate. "Ahh. The programming . . . I'm . . . am I not strong? The druids told us to be strong."

"No, no! We can't afford another civil war! We need to be strong to unite the world against the Tyrant, not kill each other!" Max paused. "The Galactic Tyrant is an alien invasion. An evil god, bent to burn us all in his wrath. War is coming between the forces of the gods and the Fomorians. Until then, there will be no more fighting as chief… I'm married now, James. I will be having a family now – fighting will have to stop."

For the first time in his life, Casbolt felt the idea of a chiefdom headed by the Aes Sidhe horrifying. He had to unite societies that had different intrigues. Remind them of their goal – the destiny to thwart the Galactic Tyranny and the Fomorians. A responsibility, and it made Casbolt feel impossibly weak.

"This is the last time," Max said half-heartedly, standing up, responding to some calls from the women for him. "Enjoy Gáe Bulg."

"Gáe Bulg?" Casbolt almost said Gale Bulge.

"The Curruid Spear," Max said curtly. "It used to belong to Diarmuid Ua Duibhne the *Fianna*. One day, one time long ago. It's yours now. Use it wisely."

Casbolt shifted the Spear in his lap, letting it play in the dull sunlight along its crimson edge.

Max Spiers hiked away with his escort. And then Casbolt was alone. Alone to think. Alone for a *long* time.

He rammed the barb of the Spear into the stone, and leaned back, burying his face in his gloved hands. They were cold, but the assault of ice came from more than just the below zero temperature. As if wounded by arrows and sword gashes, Casbolt gasped and gritted his teeth in agony from some strange desolation. How? And again, pain stung, clamping around his chest like Goibniuium armour fitting too tightly. He trembled violently from it. Loneliness ruined his soul.

The sound of the brave boy crying . . .

"No . . . It wasn't me! It wasn't me!" he rasped. "What . . .? I'm supposed to be a hero! I'm a . . . I'm a bloodthirsty animal." He refrained from speaking for a *long* time. He let the bout of silent sobs and tears pass. He felt too exhausted, and cold, to even move his lips. *Why do I feel so . . . alone?*

Guilt had won in the end. He had won a great victory, but inside, he felt life – a crystalline structure – shatter into bright sharp shards that left him bleeding. A great moulin. No way of going back to the bases like this. Now, convulsing, Casbolt *loathed* everything. He had to leave Antarctica. Now!

I and they will go to Valhalla's Halls rewarded! While you remain on Earth, with orphans as your servants and your loved ones burning up in the fire of your guilt! Who's the real winner then? Who's the loser!?

You're a disgrace!

Casbolt, on the fang-like slopes of Fenris Wolf on a desolate white continent – the driest place on the Earth – was afflicted by a death he could not understand.

Slowly, truly, the memories of his past unspooled, descending unto him as vividly as the present clouds consumed the landscape.

4

THE MAN IN BLACK

"The Nindingir are all-women conciliators, scientists, occultists, astronomers, philosophers and theologians who use genetic experimentation to further control every muscle, abstaining from wrongdoing and sexual intercourse. They would control the fibres of the body to train super soldiers in the Agoge school, furthering their own agenda of ascending the human race with the advent of their chosen one – the Übermensch. Most of them are Welsh and Highland Scottish minorities – but they are really open to Eastern forms of spirituality such as Theosophy developed in the nineteenth century. Along with their male counterparts, the druids, Nindingir have a profound tribal authority and are able to unify groups cohesively. They have counterparts, sex trafficker beauty queens that work for the Cabal as well. The Cabal have their own Aes Sidhe – the apostate Carnutes society – that I so shamefully took part in purging. In this way, the Indigo Children can be used by both Alliance and Cabal secret societies."

—From *Agent Buried Alive*, James Casbolt's Autobiography, 2001.

Julian beamed, chuckling as he poured two large jars of beer for himself and his friend, from the tap at the nozzle of a rose metallic barrel. Around him, glasses clinked, feet clomped on floorboards and peopled murmured indistinctly. Spanish music played along in the background in the Barachina restaurant.

The cuisine lived up to its name; it was professional and posh, while casual at the same time, lavishly decorated, infused with the manifold of scents: of fillets, of seafood, garlic and vegetables, of mofongo and of la parrilla steak. Scents of a cornucopia.

As Julian wove through the torrid heat of the bustling people in the bar –

the restaurant was packed today – he passed a black-aproned waitress, tapping in a docket on the machine at the counter. She met his eyes – a brown-haired, slim, pale-cheeked beauty. Her voluptuous hips went pleasantly well with her tight shorts. All the waitresses here were pretty. The walls of the building were washed with hot-pink arches and corridors, pots of large tropical jungle plants and small palms decorated the verdant courtyard. Over the bar was a canopy of roses and green flowers attached in brocaded streams. Paintings hung on the walls, framed elegantly, depicting stylised relaxing scenes in smooth tones. Mirthful families and friends drank, ate and laughed.

Just the sort of place Julian preferred; it fairly oozed comfort and an air of money. A couple minutes down the road from his apartment, Barachina was the ideal meeting place for a get-together, when confronted with a lack of which restaurants to go to – in which there were so many in the old city San Juan, it felt as if one could not choose – Barachina was that default choice. If one wasted considerable time to find a booking, why not do Barachina?

Carrying the drinks back to his seat, Julian found his good friend Benjamin DePaula, who sat alone indulging in a medium bowl of sweet potato fries. Of course, he wasn't alone all the time. Just a few minutes ago, a young girl and her brother asked for Ben to sign his autograph on their caps and take a photo with them. The Actionman always had a texter in handy.

What would it be like to be a famous Hollywood star to have your life constantly at the attention of others? Julian thought. *How disturbing. I would hate to be Ben. He's very lucky that he can interact with women, but I would not relax with people chasing me, stalking me, asking me to take a photo for them. And then you have to deal with the creepy ones that try to seduce you . . . Ridiculous!*

Rescinding that envy, Julian nevertheless leered, placing the drinks on the table. Benjamin DePaula – the Actionman – the man, the myth, the legend, did not disappoint when you pictured a professional model and stuntman made special forces marine. It made logical sense why most young girls randomly around the world would want to take a selfie with him. The man was quirky and hilarious. Broad and slender as he was tall, his body was sculpted with tanned muscles. He wore a nicely fitting pink shirt with dark biker pants, bald as an egg, with a clean-shaven beard. He had the determined look which inclined people to mistake Ben for a hairless Sylvester Stallone. He *did* look like Rocky, Julian had to admit.

"Looking too sexy, Ben," Julian commented jauntily. "You took some more photos?"

Ben raised his squared head, his temple muscles moving as he chewed.

"Too many that I forgot to count, man."

"So, what do you rate them?" Julian said, as he sat down handing Ben his drink. It had become a tradition that every time Ben went to a new restaurant, and if they made sweet potatoes, he would taste them and rate their quality. He had to order sweet potatoes *before* even meeting with James Casbolt.

Often, Ben complained how soggy, burnt and salty the sweet potatoes normally were, but here, by the looks of it, Ben was going to rate Barachina in San Juan quite highly. He took another bite, shaking his head, munching.

"You know, these little guys I have to say are exquisite," Ben said with a slight southern Arizonian accent, picking at one of the lean and golden orange fries in one hand. "Well seasoned. The way they *masterfully* blend sweetness with a slight crisp is excellent." He kissed his fingers. "*Meravigliosa.*"

Julian grinned, itching his brown sideburns. They were just sweet potatoes and Ben really did make a show of his effort to learn Spanish. "You know, you'd be surprised how it is that everything traditional here is top notch."

Clutching his beer, Ben spoke as a cocky comedian. "I know, bro, but as you can see, I *suck* when it comes to learning new languages. Bro, frown at me all you want because, when I said a word wrong *pierdas*, it's none of yah business. But I'm an Italian man, not Spanish, give me a break! Mamamia! I'm trying to *learn* Spanish. So, I only know *holla* and *gracias* and *amigo* and get lost, that's pretty much it. So alas, you have to be my speaker." Ben chugged down a nice gulp of beer, smacking his lips. "Rule of thumb. As long as I add an 'o' to every word I say then, I can wing it!"

Julian laughed, hitting the table. "No! No! Where did you get that?"

"A goof told me. Hehe." That goof, had to be no one but himself. They both took a swig. "So, Julz. Can you speak more about this new amigo of yours enlisting in the Marine Corps?"

"Yeah, for sure. James Casbolt is – well – he's literally *the* man. He'll be a great addition to the Rangers."

Ben looked offended. He sarcastically stiffed his back and eyed Julian with a raised eyebrow. "But *I'm* da man!"

"Yes!"

"Oh, I know what you're doing." Grinning impishly, Ben shook his finger in a mocking fashion. "You're making a rival for me. Are you making a rival for me?"

"No. You're just a cool stuntman. But James Casbolt is Captain America. I can tell you that for sure. But the problem is, the guy's lonely and needs some attention. Like you get."

Ben's eyebrow crept up his face. "I imagined he was a scholar! I thought you said he wrote a book!"

"No one reads it, Ben! Only those that are already conspiracy theorists do. It's nothing professional or anything."

Ben sniffed, his sun-kissed complexion grimacing. "Strange. You'd think people would dig a super soldier hero – a real-life Captain America." Ben nodded with a half grin, one Julian knew masked incredulity. "This must be *some* amigo."

"Oh, he's more than *just an amigo,* Ben." Julian leaned his head on his hand. "They call him a chief of the Iceni Aes Sidhe. Claiming patrilineage from the magical elves of Celtic folklore. Trained from birth by a super assassin to fight terrorists and suspected alien bounty hunters worldwide."

"Bounty hunters? *Aliens?*" Ben chuckled with amusement. Yeah, Ben was *not* going to be taking *anything* to do with James Casbolt seriously, or at the least any of the claims about him at face value. Fair enough. "Eh. Brother, take me to the movies. If any man has a reputation like that, I mean . . . *Man,* I don't know if I should be mad jealous or grateful. James' book sounds like a Hollywood script!"

"Ben, you will like him. Casbolt's life *is* a movie but in *real life*. Doesn't that sound the least bit interesting? Aliens?"

"Hmm. It's *alien*ating. I'm interested about myself because I also play superheroes killing aliens you know?" He took a haughty sip.

Well, apparently, flash news: you are not the only top dog in town, Actionman! Why did he *always* bolster that point as a famous world-class stuntman in the movie industry? Truth be told, there was a saying that truth was stranger than fiction. "Where abouts are you getting your information about him?" Ben said.

"Dude, come on. Keep up. His autobiography – *Agent Buried Alive*. It's a best seller for the alternative fringe community."

Ben beamed. "That's a flop."

"It is. It's because its content is the first and most detailed account of ritual abuse in the top-secret government programs in America and England. Casbolt is the pioneer for survivors to be brave, step out and share their testimonies worldwide. Thousands upon thousands of people with dissociative identity disorder are coming out of the closest with stories of sexual abuse, after Casbolt foreran with his unprecedented book. It made history."

"And when was this?" Ben said quizzically.

"Only a few months ago."

"Jesus." Ben whistled.

"And he's bringing awareness," Julian replied.

"Fascinating and crazy," Ben said flatly, obviously because he thought conspiracy theories were an embarrassment to humanity and academia – mere science fiction. He mouthed another sweet potato, chomping on it vigorously at the side of his mouth.

"I think so too," Julian said, picking his left sideburn. "I'm not saying I believe in this fool – he is a fool – but, hey, Casbolt is an *honourable* man for his honesty. It doesn't hurt to respect him. He's crazy but he cares about my daughters. He's a soldier that wants to change his ways, to help do some good and fight against Saddam Hussein and bin Laden."

Julian reached for a sweet potato which on reflex, caused Ben to slap Julian's hand away. The two froze, eyeing each other, yet Ben beamed, a smile that could light up Vegas. "No hard feelings, bro. Have one."

Julian clicked his tongue, picking a nice crispy wedge. He took a bite. *Ah. These* are *addictive.*

"Anyways, what am I saying?"

"To be honest the things around Casbolt and super soldiers sounds like a centre for bad ideas," Ben remarked. "I've had my fair share of interesting people with bizarre beliefs. Not saying they're bad, yah know, just, *hard to understand.* I think they are bored and make sweeping generalisations about problems in the world in order to give themselves a sense of comfort. It often scapegoats people, even if they have to pull stuff out of their asses to prove their points. Hehe, respect to that." Julian noticed Ben slumping his head, drawing his lips to a tight line as he uttered those prejudices. *Ah, he's had a bad experience with one of these conspiracy theorists, did he?* "It is one thing to listen to gossip," Ben continued, "but it is another to start building your life around association fallacies – flimsy information, self-deceiving yourself and calling it fact."

"Where did you learn those words?" Julian said quizzically. "Association fallacy. What is that?"

Ben shrugged. "It's something like . . . boy, you've got me working! It's when something is inherently like something else, but their qualities are completely irrelevant. Heard it somewhere. Hm, it's like saying . . . Mark Zuckerberg is a reptilian hybrid because he says he *loves* Emperor Augustus, that supposedly said he was a chameleon, so therefore, Zuckerberg's a reptilian from outer space! Yeah, that's a *crap* example, but you see the point. Association fallacies. I'm *not* a fan of conspiracy theorists. They commit them *all the time.*"

Julian nodded. One would not contend with the Actionman when he was sure and firmly convicted with his beliefs.

"I do hope Casbolt is a good man," Ben proceeded. "I don't like men who try to force me to bend to their views – it's a sign that their arguments are sloppy." Ben fidgeting with his napkin, had a tone sounding more sombre than conceited and condescending, though Julian was convinced it was both. He took a sip from his beer as Ben stared off into the distance at nothing. "So, we were saying," Ben continued, regaining his joyful expression. "Casbolt's here because you think your adopted stepdaughters are super soldiers?"

Julian blinked and hesitated. "What? What do you mean?"

"But you've had sex with your wife, right? They're your daughters or your stepdaughters?" Ben asked, taking a sip from his mug of beer, a mischievous wink flashing from his left eye.

"Bah." Julian felt his face burn. "It's complicated, man. I don't know if they're super soldiers, but Casbolt thinks they very well could be. You know I'm not married, but I've met someone who had adopted them. Guanina. I told you about her."

"You did." Ben nodded.

"You know how I am like around women. After dating that last one . . . You cannot understand them, so why marry them."

Ben laughed. "Yes. Yes. I understand how that feels! I've had my share of women! You were saying that you 'did it' *before* getting married?"

"Whatever. It was my amigo Canimao. He said that his sister Guanina had become the owner of two orphaned girls. She doesn't think they're super soldiers, and since Canimao is a fighter pilot for our air force, I just so happened to meet Guanina one day after Desert Storm. She brought the girls and we had a great time together. She's young, single and we're amigos now. Thus, we started dating and I opted to move in with her to help raise her girls." At that moment Ben's face narrowed, not at all helping Julian to retain his bearings. "Long story short, they're adopted girls with unknown parents."

That was the tricky part Julian hoped Casbolt could answer. Intuitively, Julian knew his stepdaughters had nothing to do with his previously promiscuous behaviour around young women. Casbolt could sense things beyond any normal human, supposedly, he knew there was something fishy going on in Julian's situation. *Why me? This wasn't a dream like those nightmares with that woman in my room after I started going through the hippy phase collecting tarot cards and crystals. Had that all been real?* "Yeah . . . That's the point. Canimao and Guanina should be able to know."

At that moment, a large man with a thick head and a stern jaw loomed at the restaurant entrance. Wearing a checker green-blue-and-white shirt, he looked – surprisingly – slightly younger than Julian, maybe twenty-eight? But he contained an air of discipline and authority. He stood posed and alert, head scanning the restaurant with an officer by his side, an imperious bodyguard. They had intense eyes – eyes that didn't trust anybody.

—

Casbolt was brought face to face with a scarlet macaw, perching on a strip of bark inside a small lattice of sticks resembling an aviary. A *bird* in the middle of a restaurant?

Casbolt eyed his bodyguard Carl, passing through the small pink courtyard. Once he spotted the man in question: Julian, Casbolt trudged up to him awkwardly.

"Ah well uhm. I'm here." *You snow chick! Introduce yourself!* Casbolt held out a sweaty hand to Julian. "Nice to meet you, Julian. How are you? I am – James Casbolt. Well. You knew that."

"Well amigo, it was kind of obvious once I saw you," Julian replied. "I'm doing well. Is that a bodyguard you have there?"

"Yeah. His name is Carl."

Casbolt very much hated his heavy British accent – it made him sound timid, and a goddamn mumbler. Julian beamed, gripping Casbolt's hand with a taut grip. "No words can explain my appreciation right now. Sit."

Casbolt grimaced. Parvus Perception ingrained within him, read Julian's eyes and he could tell he too was uneasy. "So . . . This place is rather nice."

Right there and then, he lost control of the conversation, for Julian left walking up to talk with his friend. And Casbolt stood there, procrastinating.

Whipping around like a fool, he turned, nearly running into a Spanish lady pushing a pram with a young child inside. Apologising perfunctorily, he collapsed into a chair sighing and holding his head.

"God help me, Carl. I'll kill myself with embarrassment one of these days."

Carl was a robot of a man – he never spoke. Casbolt heaved out another sigh. What's the point travelling on a plane and coming here, not speaking to anyone?

If I'm going to speak out, I need to build confidence. Despite his insurgence of wanting to share his story, seeking recognition from other people appeared prohibitable. *You want to be alone? No, I'm already here. So, let's try. Just be honest.*

Once Casbolt and Carl had ordered their late lunch, he played the thing he was most talented at: watching. Doing nothing.

He would do this commonly when Max was at his conference meetings and Casbolt wasted his time in the background, twiddling his thumbs.

Casbolt was close, but distant enough to not interfere with Julian's marine acquaintance, clinking glasses and laughing. Casbolt knew he should join in, but he couldn't bother. Fear of ridicule rescinded him.

Casbolt now had to await his food. Even something as simple as waiting could be a mission for espionage. Since the Alliance's enemies monitored the entire world, he knew that the Cabal had a rough idea where he was by now. That meant he must be very vigilant. Being the man he was, he could not afford to sit down and relax like everyone else in this building especially American marines who were getting ready for the great campaign of great irony – the War on Terror – war on the Middle East. Absolutely he knew, you make one mistake, make one impulsive decision that couldn't be undone, you have the power to not just destroy many lives, but destroy your own if you didn't have a hard heart.

At a grimace from Carl, Casbolt stopped gouging his fork along his napkin, sheering holes into it. This place was *far* too warm, sweat prickled in his armpits and forehead. Stupid low-budget air fans. *I'm already missing the snow and ice.*

As the waitress brought them some water, Casbolt scanned the maroon restaurant. Then Casbolt's Parvus Perception went on high alert. A spike in his stomach, a jolt of sheer awryness brought to his cognition with the monitoring minutiae of the five senses – the Parvus Perception – a Nindingir druid ability that could detect concealed emotions, motivations, agendas, or even physical things such as concealed weapons and a false accent. He heard a dark voice undulating like a dry leaves rustled by wind, amidst the din of voices, the zipping of vehicles, Spanish music buzzing. A report. A call. A positive remark for reinforcements.

Intelligence were here.

Then Casbolt saw a man in a black suit and a fedora hat with sunglasses leaning on a wall, trench coat covering him well to his boot tops – not suitable for the heat of the day. The man in black stood far off in the distance that he could not have noticed Casbolt without Parvus sensitivity. Casbolt scanned. *Who is this?* Cadaverous white in complexion biting on a tube of tobacco, the man chewed on the death stick as if half asleep, fingers in a V shape, glazing over its length. He pulled it out, sending a small braid of pungent smoke into the air, a ghostly veil that wrapped around him. That man did look like Carl his bodyguard, but the resemblance ended with the poise. . . The man's skin was deathly pallid. His cloak hung motionless, not a rustle, nor a stir from the breeze outside rippled it.

Queasiness settled in Casbolt's stomach. The shadowy energy from the mysterious newcomer had a fierce sharpness, an energy that hated everything that lived.

"Hey," Casbolt leaned in to whisper to Carl, trying not draw attention. "Just keep an eye on that man, will yah?"

Marking the man, Carl nodded, biting his lip pensively. *Another one of those Cabal spies,* Casbolt thought.

Once the food arrived, Casbolt barely enjoyed his fillet. He observed tirelessly at the man in black, dipping his gaze every once in a while, to look at the food, to drink and glimpse Julian's table, who laughed as if danger did not exist. They had no sense, no priori senses for the paranormal.

But swiftly, the man in black got up, craned his neck this way and that, then slipped out the restaurant on the footpath with serpent grace down the narrow street, and was gone. Vanished. The man in black was certainly a master stealth agent. The man vanished within a shadow on the street, there was not much of a hiding place to see where he had disappeared, yet he was nowhere to be seen.

Trance like, Casbolt turned to his indifferent bodyguard. "Carl, I think we need to get moving." Promptly Casbolt got up to use this chance to inform Julian's famous Desert Storm Major: Benjamin DePaula.

"Hullo, Actionman," Casbolt said, grinning and gaining Ben's attention. "I'm James Casbolt. It's a pleasure to meet you."

"Ah! It's Captain America!" Ben perkily slapped Casbolt on the back, rather informally, shaking his hand, squeezing it tightly. "Nice to meet you too! Your friend here has spoken very highly of you, sir," Ben said with a grin, gesturing to Julian as he stood up. "So, what's the hurry?"

Casbolt swallowed, unable to stop glancing outside the windows. "I want to warn you, Julian. Ben. I have had constant death threats, and even intelligence people die in very suspicious circumstances, hours before arranged meetings with them." He clicked open the handle of his suitcase with a stiff grip.

Let's just hope that seeing one agent of the Cabal was a one off, Michael Prince said uneasily in Casbolt's head.

——

"My story is a long story, so I think we need to start with a brief history lesson."

Casbolt was very pleased with himself that he had successfully scared Ben and Julian out of Barachina from potential enemy eyes. He'd offered them a request to walk around the old San Juan and they complied freely. Julian, to Casbolt's convenience, was delighted to show him around the area, to mill about in the balmy afternoon along the snaking crumbling ruins of the old fort Castillo San Felipe del Morro – dark bare balustrades of brick and stone morphed into crude slate jetties running along the contours of the rocky promontory with a beach churning with swirling white waves below. A single solitary castle tower stood in the distance, before a large green oval of tended grass where families sat on picnic blankets, walking their dogs and flying kites. It was not just an occasion for Casbolt to stretch his legs and smell the salty air, it was to have a sense of life without worries.

"Will the man in black know where my stepdaughters are?" Julian asked, concerned.

"If they were at the restaurant, then not yet," Casbolt spoke firmly. "Even if they did, wouldn't the stepmother notice?"

Julian patted his pocket. "Oh yeah. Good point. I remember one time a bad man tried to break down our door when she ran down the hall shrieking and roaring so loudly the man flinched and scrambled away." Julian grinned and Ben laughed at the story. "Yeah, I would have *absolutely* gotten a call – and a screaming voice message if one of those spies tried to break into my house."

Casbolt laughed. "I would suspect it would be very unpleasant."

"Phantom espionage, eh?" Ben sighed, running his hand along the stone wall of the sixteenth century conquistador fort. He spoke with an edge of cynicism. "So, tell me? Who do they work for, Casbolt? What's the story?"

"Competing mafias – each one behind the façade of a national empire, itching to see the other go down. All that for one goal: world domination to avert calamity. I was part of the Left Alliance. The men in black might be part of the Right Cabal but I'm not too sure. They're a mystery, the men in black. It's very complex, but basically, the ideology is mainly eastern mysticism. The Alliance rule for peace. Make everyone think you are tolerant and wise; accept everyone and men in power are held in everyone's trust and allegiance, despite apparent inconsistences in their behaviour." Casbolt lectured, technically reiterating details in his book instead of making something up on the spot.

He could just do that, actually. He doubted someone like Ben had the time to bother reading three hundred pages. "You can become influential by doing good and ridding the world of corruption."

"You believe these men needs girls?" Ben retorted his forehead creased eye squinting in the glare. "Why do they want girls?"

"The elites are paedophiles and child traffickers."

"Foolish," Ben muttered awkwardly. "Baloney."

Quelling an impulse of wounded anger, Casbolt passed by little vibrant plump houses nestled together in rows down the narrow streets, exotic and full of taverns and shops – some hugged by vines of budding flowers and banana trees. Casbolt and the others trekked the well-travelled cobblestone streets, as they heard him lecture on about his family and parents. Indeed, the walking did help Casbolt alleviate most of his anxiety, reinforcing his resolve.

The men in black smelled of hair gel, they were coming discreetly in their numbers now, human ravens, intelligent beyond belief and well hidden, not giving Casbolt, Ben, Julian and Carl any more mind than they gave anyone else in the steady throng of the laneway streets. Their cold suspicious stare beneath dunce sunglasses and the shade of fedora hats like urban ghosts of the undead, they walked invisible among humans, tucking away vengeful hands within the folds of their inert trench cloaks. The relief was palpable, when those dead eyes, unfeeling eyes, swept past. Casbolt with his enhanced Parvus Perception – besides the sweet chemical smell of the rare encounters and sightings of vampiric men hiding, in trees, alleys, vendors and multitudes – sensed the refuse, food, leather, swearing and other pungent scents and sounds from stores and the occasional exhausts. Clusters of people in shorts, t-shirts, singlets and flip flops walked around, languid amigos lounging on chairs at vendors, some leaning on the crumbling remnants of an old rampart there, inhaling away at an ignited withering grey stick without care for tomorrow. Children played and ran giddily. Tourists weaved in and out in clumps of colour and multicultural complexions, bursting the seams of grimy narrow crisscrossing streets. Even a busker sat on a small pink step of an apartment, singing a Spanish folk song with his guitar pouring liveliness into the old city, while awaiting change in his upturned hat. The bustling life brought a sense of relief and peace to Casbolt, he'd never been so sure how much he had missed out on during the last year in self-imposed curfew, and how much he missed communicating to real people. Soon, the men in black ceased to exist, no longer seen.

Julian watched Casbolt, thoroughly rubbing his chin. "So now, in your book you claimed to have been born right in the middle of a conspiracy am I right?"

"Yes. Yes. You see, in 1976, when my first memories come to light, forty-two children and I were taken to Project Vortigern – a Cabal program that invited the Alliance, by exchanging their children to develop stronger super soldiers to expel the . . . well for better training facilities in Antarctica. But the Cabal deceived the Alliance, took the children and never returned them." In reality, and what Casbolt did not disclose to these men, was Project Vortigern, consequently, would help strengthen Aes Sidhe ranks against Fomorian and the Galactic Tyrant's attacks.

Casbolt leaned on a stone embrasure looking out beyond at the bay. "My past is extremely slow moving, bleak and foul so I'll try to stick to the important parts," he uttered, eyes affixed to a passing yacht cruising along in the placid wind, the people on the vessels looking so calm, and above all ignorant – better to be ignorant and virtuous than all in the know and guilty about not changing the state of affairs with one's power. "I don't know for sure, but I think my father Neil, after I was born in Wimbledon, he sent me on a plane to Canada."

Suddenly, the darkness of Michael Prince's past shrouded Casbolt like a shawl of melancholy. Smell of the pine trees from the cold winter nights in the mountains drifted on the winds.

"So, in your book," Julian said, "you explained that Alfred Bonner and Michael Oppenheim's secret government called the Alliance saved you from these Carnutes?"

"Yes. Because I am a test tube-baby; I was not a result of God's hands – or nature – depending on what you believe. I was designed to have the required genes to become a chief of the Aes Sidhe."

"Do you get a chance to live a normal life?" Ben said with an interesting smirk pasted on his face which Casbolt was increasingly finding annoying, as if he was deceptively masking a grudge too hard. However, that smile according to his Parvus Perception said, 'Did you even live a normal life so I can discriminate against you?'

"As you can imagine soldiers, many of the children at the Cabal's Project Vortigern did not make it. If we did . . . Yeah, we end up just living amongst, um, normal society. Serial killers and school shooters could get jobs, live a social life and still, all of sudden, commit heinous crimes. That's what I could have become with Carnute handlers." *I'm easily giving all these people who I barely know my life story, so they could just as easily weaponise it against me.*

"Interesting. So, you're saying," Julian interjected, "my two daughters are some of these super soldiers?"

"There will always be one parent that is not present at home when I hear the reports of super soldier childhoods." Casbolt glanced at Julian. "There is an abduction case by a mother of an Indigo Child, who had many occasions spoke and bonded with an alien being while she was sleeping. One instance, her alien showed her a picture of their son and asked what the difference between them was? She said, 'Everyone looks the same.' 'Isn't that wonderful?' the alien replied passionately. 'Isn't that beautiful? Pretty soon in the future, we will all be together. Pretty soon, you will not be able to tell the difference between us and you. It will be wonderful.'"

Perspiration manifested on Julian's forehead. Fear sweat.

I'm sorry, Julian. But sometimes the truth can hurt. You wanted me to give answers, well, here's one the Parvus has detected.

"Julian, I am not saying the girl's mother was an alien just… I don't know. I'm putting a possibility out there."

"You're kidding me?! You're kidding me, right!?" Julian blurted out franticly. "Aliens… That's insane."

Casbolt chuckled at that. "I guess it is. I want to talk about the part where I was as a little baby in the Carnutes' Project Vortigern and my befriending of a she wolf. The best part!"

"A *wolf?*" Both Julian and Ben said at once.

"Ahhh yes," Casbolt chuckled. Reminiscing those hazy days, wonderful how far back the human mind could be cast, like a drag net widening into the endless ocean of consciousness. "We were crafted into the perfect super soldiers. The Cabal left us out to sleep, doors and windows open to let the harsh cold mountain elements blow inside. If we were concerned about the next crisis, and we had anxiety about that, we wouldn't be able to carry out orders. But in our mindset, if we believed we were designed for endless warfare, we were just able to accept that."

"That's why they named you the Redlion," Julian spoke, surprised. "People would describe you as a mindless, ruthless machine. You're like a real-life superhero in their eyes!"

God. The Redlion . . . slaughtered the Carnutes' and the Aquarians' families, Casbolt thought, troubled.

"I— Ugh. Yes . . . To some, yes. He was a hero." Casbolt swallowed, bitterness racking his throat. "I ugh. I get really twitchy talking about this." Flashing the briefest of grins, Casbolt rubbed his head. "It's tough to live through it. Another to do it again. Happens less every time. Don't worry about me." Ben and Julian asked him to sit down or to have a cup of coffee, but he refused and went on to tell his story.

The one that he remembered.

5

OPERATION PUER LIBERTATEM

NELSON, CANADA - 1979

"These Indigos can have precognitive paranormal/psychic abilities, but the Nindingir's Übermensch is the ultimate Indigo Child with the abilities of prescience, bilocation, and extreme energy medicine. All 'normal' super soldiers like me contain expanded life, extra endurance, Parvus Perception and have Rh-Negative blood. This is a very rare blood type and makes up about five percent of the human population. I believe Rh-Negative means oxygen is processed in the blood differently to people with Rh-Positive blood. The amount of oxygen processed by the body makes all the difference as an Aes Sidhe.

There is a theological issue with Rh-Negative connected to the so-called ancient Nephilim of the Bible. This text I think tells us why the Tribe of Danu are kidnapping children, but I'd rather not say explicitly. I might not live long enough to complete this work if I do."

—From *Agent Buried Alive*, James Casbolt's Autobiography, 2001.

Michael Oppenheim, Just Son of Danu, Forsworn of the Führer, sat inside a blaring UH-60 Black Hawk, chasing down elite child traffickers.

He tucked an AK-47 rifle under the crook of his arm, as the helicopter made a tight left turn. Below was the vast continuum of the mountains of British Colombia, flanked by flaky bare pines veiled by the snow.

The men inside stared at the silvery-blue, woad dye paint streaking over his large eyes. Four of them – two over each eye – swirling like the storm winds. The tattoos, when applied to the flesh, were said to provide magic providence when worn in battle.

And these soldiers had no idea at what he could do as an Aes Sidhe Disciple of the Second Initiation now.

"Target's in site. Suit up, men!" The call of the pilot went through a crackling filtered speaker, popping as he breathed.

So, at last, Alfred Bonner setting up the Light Alliance as a stronghold in the New World, in the name of Danu, sent three Black Hawks to save the forty-two children hostages of Project Vortigern that – bizarrely – actually made the job to train a new generation of Aes Sidhe easier. The man had said at the Alliance cabinet meeting in Vancouver, that there was a ring of Cabal sex trafficking operations from Canada, Bangkok, Mexico, Ecuador and Moscow. The Alliance had to save these kids, or else the paedophiles would launch their global campaign to advertise their new sex hotel, with twenty-four-seven, full access to teenage 'chickens'.

Do not hesitate. Just begin Operation Puer Libertatem.

The Cabal took the children of Danu and let them pass the long nights in the cold. According to satellite footage – they were treated like exposed invalids on Taygetus. Now they were stored within convoys sent towards a new Cabal base.

Michael never even thought of raising or having children. It probably wasn't interesting enough to have to go that route in life as his calling to attain nirvana, and justice in a tumultuous world, was purely paramount for him. Why have children in a world full of suffering and pain? It would be cruel to bring more children into this world of gratuitous suffering. But, if Michael saved a child, he was going to have to brace for the possibility of becoming attached to him or her.

It was integral on Michael's part however, to restore light and truth to an evil world. As part of his mastery over the physical body to his soul, he now harnessed the opposite to Dark Matter. Michael used Pneuma – human spirits – within voidstones.

And by wielding Pneuma, Michael was a warrior wielding a thousand arms. A god with a thousand arms.

Reckoning.

Justice.

Fidgeting with his belt, it contained piles of small voidstones, hidden inside camo coating. Michael opened the velcro of one of the pouches along his belt and beheld the even blue glow of the infused stones.

So much control. The primordial energy. Pneuma. Human spirits.

In his long years to become the Disciple of the Second Initiation, he had to pass the First. The First was the awakening into the Spiritual World. It was the attainment of the True Self, making one worthy to inhale the Pneuma and store it within one's body. By being born into the new life of the Spirit, and the expanding of consciousness, Michael could be powered by human spirits. In doing this, the ego and the lower self can reach upwards into the buddhic plane, the plane of unity, to cast off delusions of the self. In this way, one can pass to the Second Initiation, which was one of the most difficult and painful. The candidate had to control all emotions and take action to get rid of negative desire. A candite of the Second could infuse oneself with Pneuma when one had broken off the three fetters: selfishness, doubt and superstition (belief in lies).

Once free, the candidate could be enhanced by having complete mastery over the physical and emotional bodies, empowered by the flowing energy of Pneuma.

What had blocked Michael to gain the Third Initiation, was his insufficient thirst for not judging anyone or anything. He had self-control, he accepted all beings. But for Michael, being a Just Agent of Danu, was it even possible to never judge the Cabal? Michael judged what was good and bad. Was discernment a defilement? A paradox?

No matter. Michael had all the time in the world to overcome this great block. Aes Sidhe life expectancy exceeded twice the human lifespan.

Michael's insides stirred with adrenaline as the soldiers around him loaded their guns, standing up to prepare for the drop off. They were given orders by Sergeant Murry McHolden that as soon as they got out of the gunner door, they would immediately raid the road and blockade it. First waiting to let the officers surrender the hostages, and if that failed, to hijack the convoy by deadly force, with as few hostage casualties as possible.

The Black Hawk's blades roared with quickening intensity as they went skyward. Vertigo seized Michael as they dipped back down again. Outside, he saw the winding highway and the convoy of military SUVs, most of them pulling large grey rectangular trailers, bumper to bumper, clogging up the road. They had officially startled the Carnutes' convoy, and they hadn't even started the breadth of their journey.

Enthralled and ready, the soldiers clutched their guns, waiting frenzied for the side to open. The helicopter spun around to land in the woods, a fair distance away from the objective.

Michael rolled his shoulders, bounced on his feet, his heart racing.

The side doors opened with a roar. Light and wind gushed through his vision. Everyone charged.

"Go, go, go!" voices blared. The helicopter's blades beat the air above, bending the grass, making a whirlwind out of snow. Michael and his squad charged across the clearing, weaving between the trees. Above, the two other helicopters hovered through the dense foliage of trees nearby, disgorging their own attack squads.

Michael inhaled a smidgin of Pneuma. It was just enough to keep him alert, enough to level his mind, but not enough for the men to see the strands of blue smoke in daylight. In the enhanced *sati*, he suddenly became aware of faint wails of children, like spectres of some ghostly stadium cheering him on in the background.

He picked up speed, getting ahead of his men breathing heavily, leaping over snow-caked logs and ducking under overreaching trees hanging limp with icicles like melted wax. Sticks and leaves snapped and crunched under his feet.

Up an incline and past the corridor, the road clogged up with SUVs lay before him. As he weaved through the lines of trees, he could see hulking dark figures – humanoid – appearing around the trucks. Black guns in hand, the soldiers clomped, all wearing respiratory masks. Michael began to slow down, hunching over. He raised a hand signal.

"Hold!"

As the incentive repeated down the line, hunkering down under branches hiding behind thickets, all of Michael's soldiers quietly got into defence positions, guns aiming.

Now, from a clear vantage point, Michael could see who they were fighting. They were certainly neo-nazi Carnutes – an Aes Sidhe society of the Horned Ones. They all had a thin crimson band around their left forearms. Completely black, these were heavy armed Carnutes guards wearing onyx-plated armour over a laced suit. Their boots were studded with razor-sharp points like shark teeth, carrying semi-automatics and masked in dark stormtrooper helmets – respiratory like – some with thin red slits for eye holes and others with circular gas mask goggles. Each of the Cabal Carnutes wore tri-crested metal war hats. The horns of the Carnutes.

Intimidating, yes, but Michael had learnt in his time facing enemy militia organisations that no matter how scary the opponent may be, if they can't maintain effective strategy, it was all a front.

The question remained. Who was the Carnutes' new leader? Or leaders?

"This is Com-12 Naval Intelligence of the Alliance!" Michael declared, yelling loud enough so all could hear. His voice echoed down the hills, through the mountain passes. "Drop your weapons now, release the hostages, and you can be on your way!"

A grinding sound, like a roller door being slammed open broke the silence. Michael whipped his head around and, there, he saw what looked like to be the commander Waffen, draped in a dark cape, a white swastika on his lapel, strapped with an assortment of bullet magazines chained around himself.

But it was inside the trailer this Waffen had opened that made Michael gasp aloud. Children. Crying and whimpering children inside the van, huddling in blankets.

Presently, a pair of Carnutes marched up towards the open trailer, cocking their guns.

The shootout happened faster than Michael could forecast. The Carnutes demonstrated no mercy, opening fire at Com-12, pelleting them with deadly bullets. Michael inhaled more Pneuma as he twisted around the tree trunk. His men yelled, seizing cover, bullets zipping and whistling, chipping off splinters of bark and crushing branches. One of his men – Randolph – was shot in the neck howling in shock.

If only Pneuma could heal wounds, Michael thought desperately.

Sergeant Murry McHolden, crouching behind the fork of a trunk, snapped his hand forward.

"GO!"

Michael turned, punching the trigger. They could stay here and endure the Carnutes within the trees, being snuffed out one by one. Or Com-12 could adamantly risk it.

Michael took off, Pneuma humming within empowering him as he pumped his legs. A poor soldier by his side was bombarded rapidly with bullets, dead in a blink, unable to yell.

Following Michael's lead, the soldiers broke forth in a frantic charge, howling guns crackling. While men struggled to run across the corridor, up the incline towards the road, Michael had an advantage – Pneuma endowed one with perfect awareness and agility. He moved aside from bullets as if he was the wind itself, shoved to the side, unable to be touched like two opposite poles of a magnet. Everything appeared to move slightly slower running infused with Pneuma. Though bullets darted past, Michael could sense the air being disturbed before they came.

Around him, his men hunkered low in the ditch within the clearing, covering their commander's back.

Michael hunkered down under a discarded log, backing against it, heart thumping, his breath visible and azure in hue before him. He was closer to the jeeps, just out of sight from the Carnutes. Bullets skipped and ricocheted off doors and trailers above Michael, popping in flashes, ringing his ears. Gruff calls – garbled German – clattered in the cacophony.

Then there also was the ever-present whines and blays of the children – like thorns in Michael's psyche.

Come on!

A Carnute near Michael unwisely attempted to scramble around the nose of the truck, reaching out to attack Michael. He didn't even get on two feet as Michael's bullet erupted in his face, the force knocking him down on the frosty asphalt.

"Forward!" Michael howled over his shoulder, flipping on stomach in a military crawl, elbows digging in the grass, gun lined with his spine at his chest.

"Let's go, let's go!" His men closed in.

Something arced in the air. Something dark and egg shaped.

Michael gasped, unconsciously taking in more Pneuma, coursing within him, pressured like pins and needles. By Carnute hand, something flew not too far away, towards the tree line where his men were emerging.

"WATCH OUT!"

About five of his men were caught in the explosion. Garret, JP, Aaron, Luke and Nigel. Their truncated bodies flew apart monstrously, other men tripping, rolling and hollering. He saw someone fly backwards, legs drumming, slamming back into tree trunks with a horrible crack. Bark and smoke drifted everywhere; the unlucky Com-12 men thrashed in death throes.

Michael blared his teeth. He was nearly there! Just one more run!

The cry of the children penetrated him, bawling and calling.

"Danu!" Michael sailed over the log, sprinting furiously up the incline.

The leading vehicle screeched, taking off at the periphery of his vision. He noted that, if any Carnutes got away, the attack helicopter should be able to track them down effortlessly. These *cowards* thought they could get away with it!

Squatting down behind the tyre of an abandoned jeep, Michael pressed the side of his face and body against the truck. Inside, he could hear the children. One kid was screeching at the top of his lungs throwing a tantrum, at a voice-breaking pitch, banging the sides of the trailer.

Damn it, pup! Easy!

Before him, Michael saw his men pushing on to the road, the battle making progress for the Alliance, the Cabal's formations beginning to buckle.

Suddenly, the door behind Michael opened, and a man leapt on top of him. Winded, Michael rammed into the side of the jeep, crushing the attacker. He met his gaze. The driver of the jeep agitatedly clawed at Michael, arms reaching out. He hammered at him with sporadic hits, but Michael landed a vicious elbow into the man's right shoulder, jamming a gun into the man's ribs. Michael fired and ended the Carnute's life, blood spraying over the trailer.

Michael sniffed at the filthy work, hefting his gun, taking long stealthy steps to circumvent the trailer. Expecting to find an enemy, he turned pointing his gun, finding that the first jeep was clear. He promptly opened the trailer roller door, startling the children within. They all rubbernecked, eyes wide with bewilderment. Five children crawled inside, shivering from the cold – two young girls and three boys – one of which was large with bright red flaming hair; he was standing up, beating the side of the jeep. He looked at Michael with a fearful azure-eyed gaze.

"Don't worry, I'm here to save you," Michael said attempting to calm them down. "I'm not going to hurt you. The bad guys are going to go now." Michael turned to his right. "Liam, I need your help! Children!"

Liam – one of the lieutenants – rushed over to Michael. "Take the children back into the chopper. Check for wounds and signs of distress. Get them warm and reassure them that they're going to be taken home."

"Yes, sir, Commander," Liam nodded, hopping into the trailer.

"Leave none of them behind," Michael called. "None! You hear me!? Quickly, Liam!"

Picking his way towards the next jeep in line, Michael nearly staggered with a numbing wave of shock. From the second cargo came the screeching of squirming young girls and children in distress. Rapid firing of bullets ricocheted *within* the carriage.

No!

Michael blundered around the truck.

"NO!"

He performed a Pneuma-enhanced flying side kick into the Waffen, causing him to buckle, misfiring, shattering the windscreen ahead. He grunted, fumbling with his gun and crashing into the side of the trailer, spinning to the ground in a heap.

Teeth gritted with indignation, Michael growled, getting on top of the Waffen and jabbing with his gun. He pressed the trigger and—

His gun *jammed!* He pressed it again.

The Waffen roared, flipping back up on his feet. Michael, too stunned to react, suffered a hook, right in the face. He blindly bashed into the trailer, tripping over. With one hand Michael braced himself, dropping his gun, dazed. His jaw throbbed, feeling bruised.

The Waffen took a step, breathing heavily, ripping out a Swiss army knife.

Michael picked up a glimmer of light from the corner of his eye, like a mirage. Within the carriage, he saw a young dark-red-haired boy around six years old, hugging two little boys protecting one with brown hair covering his forehead. The six-year-old protecting the two boys had three bloody bullet wounds in his back. Michael felt pain compact his chest as he saw three more children laying lifeless in heaps of blood within the trailer.

I couldn't save them. They had to save themselves.

Michael growled, seeing his foe holding his knife downwards. So, he flipped his feet around behind him, inhaling vast swaths of Pneuma. The selfless power of distressed spirits spurred him on, a storm that could not be stopped. His muscles burned with energy, the desire to move. The tempest spread within, pushing at his skin, causing his blood to pump in a powerful rhythm. His expert martial arts training flashed in his mind clearly.

The Waffen stabbed downwards, but Michael twisted out of the way, parrying the blow with a right block. Michael landed a Pneuma-infused palm heel, but the Waffen evaded, hissing, slashing at Michael who dodged.

He swung again with a wide strike, but Michael twisted his body, ramming into the Waffen, backing up against him. He caught the attacking arm with a body block, grabbed it with both hands, and performed a reverse figure four, bending the elbow, twisting the arm downwards, away from himself. The Waffen resisted dangerously.

Michael spun, controlling the Waffen, yanking his knife hand. One foot behind the Waffen's front leg, he tossed his body with his hips as a lever. It made the Waffen trip, but Michael, still grasping the knife hand, sent the wretch dangling on the ground. Wisely, the Waffen braced his fall, slapping his left arm rigidly on the road.

The Waffen's masked face was pitiful. Only cowards wore masks because they couldn't bear to face their opponent eye to eye. The Cabal were as shameful as a serpent, their intimidation 'tactics' proving no purpose.

Yelling in anger, the Waffen kicked up, getting Michael in the ribs, making him drop the knife hand. The Waffen rolled on the ground gaining distance to evade Michael's advances, backing up against the road rail.

Michael anticipated his moment, getting into *sanchin* stance – left foot in front of the right, shoulder width apart – the left toe orientated slightly inwards on an angle. He loosened his knees and locked his pelvis outwards, rooting himself deeply.

The *sanchin* was the struggle of three. Its diaphragmatic breathing enhanced *pranayama* (breathing exercises) and *bandhas* (muscular contractions), loosening his being for better breathing action to infuse Pneuma – the flow of the winds.

As he inhaled sharply, flaring his nostrils, a grandiose gush of Pneuma inundated him, blue smoke rising from his skin all over his body, burning radiantly. His chest inflated, frigid from the thrumming raging storm winds within his lungs and veins, infusing his spirit.

Michael's whole being felt so free and rigid at the same time. His mouth pulled tightly into a shape of a crude smile as he clenched hands to fists, drawing them back, right fist billowing with Pneuma, frothing with vengeance. Then he inhaled briskly, puffing smoke from his mouth.

His fist *flew*.

His dazzling hand morphed into a palm, slamming right into the Waffen's chest. The Carnute folded, sailing from the attack. For a split second, Michael saw that he had caused an accordion effect – the Waffen's body trailed behind a dark black aura. Streaking farther from his body behind a translucent blue afterimage – vague and indistinct of any features.

All this happened in a second. The apparitions zoomed back into the Waffen's body, flipping over the railing, and tumbled off the cliff, down into the abyss below, howling shockingly.

"Road's secure, Commander," a voice said from behind. Victor.

Michael spun around, catching a few soldiers off guard, staggering. They saw him glowing with the smoke, but Michael snapped out of his stupor, marching towards the carriage and getting inside.

"Good. Come on," Michael said. "Secure the kids. Round them up and abide by the pilot's orders. I want all the children that are alive – even the ones in the rogue bogey down road." Michael pointed to the jeeps before him down the road where Com-12 soldiers started to unload them. "Get these ones here ready before the escort comes back! Move!" Pneuma faded in wisps around Michael as he spoke, but it still puffed like fog from his mouth. Gratefully, all the soldiers in his unit got to work, calling to one another opening the doors in the jeeps. Certainly, the word would spread about the blue smoke coming out of Michael, but it was inevitable, his men were prone to think Michael as a special leader in their eyes.

Michael met the two young timid boys in the corner of the trailer – the only two survivors. They glanced up at him, fascinated. Michael looked upon one of the boys who looked only four years old, with light eyes and flat soft-brown hair. The kid looked scrawny, despite his intense eyes. Next to that boy was another, who looked more docile than the first, shying away from Michael's intense glance.

His heart fluttered with warmth to see the two children all calm. Outside he heard wailing and crying from anxious children being led away – their souls of pure darkness and sadness for haven't experienced the embodiment of love and kindness.

I did what I can. If that's not enough . . .

"What are your names?" Michael asked softly. But the children were nervous, losing his gaze, looking around desultory at the dead bleeding bodies of their companions. Michael grinned kindly. "Don't worry, the bad guys are all dead now. Here, let's get to safety. It's quite cold up here, don't you think?" Michael held out a hand for the brown-haired kid, the youngest. The child stared at Michael's strange cobalt war paint, looking intimidated. Nevertheless, he reluctantly hovered a hand towards Michael who nodded, keeping a straight smile.

They linked hands.

A distant boom echoed, trembling the entire mountain. The child's grip slipped from Michael's.

"Shhhh. It's okay. That's us. The last baddy is gone," Michael said. Indeed, that was clearly the sound of a missile strike from the helicopter in the distance, hopefully to trap the Cabal's fleeing vehicle – the leader? – by destroying the road ahead in the distance. "Come on. Let's go."

Soon, Michael was gently leading the frightened children off the carriage, huddling in their blankets, towards the grassy corridor in between the road and the tree line. The soldiers rounded all the children up in tight bundles, setting up tents while waiting for their escort, staying close to them as snow began to fall gently from the grey sky.

———

Michael had changed into a black woollen fleece, pushing aside the flap of the tent containing the children he had saved in the first two jeeps. Most slept cosily and soundly in thick bundles of blankets, provided by the soldiers.

Some stayed up, languid, not talking, nervous and too stunned to consider taking a nap.

The children were beautiful; no wonder the secret societies wanted the bloodline of Danu to be their real life Übermensch. But the sight wasn't exactly pleasing either – the children were all cold, trembling, hardened by the Cabal's traumatic experiments, their life devoid from their husks. These children would not have a childhood like his own. They didn't even look to greet Michael to reward his selfless act. They just sat there, broken. Waiting for someone to give them orders.

Delusion arises from the duality of attraction and aversion, the Vishnu avatar Krishna said in the Gita. *Every creature is deluded by these from birth.*

What did Michael attract? What did he averse?

Sitting down at the mouth of the tent, letting out an enervated sigh, he got into a bandha – a firm, rooted meditation pose the yoga teachers taught him. They were very proud of the Marxist Alliance's adoption of Dravidian Nationalism, incorporating many forms of yoga – literally to be yoked to the gods – for their Aes Sidhe Initiates. India, according to his mentor philosopher Jiddu Krishnamurti, was a second Promised Land because they were the only country that attained a sense of compassionate authenticity during World War II. India did not kill the Jews. Michael did not know how that could be related to anything, but his mentors believed it. After all, years ago, he had assassinated a powerful Brahmic cult leader who had given upstream information and Patalan technology to Hitler and the Cabal. Hitler had his own Tantric guru from India that was behind the genocide of many people. India a Promised Land?

Focus . . . A mind that can focus was better than one distracted.

Then he heard the voices, for the first time. The Pneuma spoke within the *sunyata* – the Emptiness. The Void when the kundalini energy could be tapped into within his mental, physical and emotional body. By displacing his three vessels, his enlightenment came as a result of slowly becoming a less material and more indifferent state of consciousness. That helped him focus, emptying his mind of all thought.

Death. SCREAMS.

The Void withered. The cries of the dammed souls that he had killed in the last decade or so vibrated evanescently and whispered again – on and off like the faraway waves of the sea.

Michael's eyes fluttered open. His block to the Third Initiation involved the ultimate comprehending and overcoming what was most natural to the human condition – judgment.

God judged people, making him unworthy to be worshipped. A lower being.

Beings of higher states of consciousness accepted everything, no matter what they were. But how could one accept paedophiles and Nazis? Despite Michael's virtue ethics, he did not understand *why* an Ascended Master of the Sixth Initiation could never ever have no imperfect or judgmental thoughts towards anyone.

Michael had judged and killed. He'd only killed a handful of people deemed corrupted as part of his mission, mostly those that merited it, like slaying Adam Glauer, elites from the Soviet Union and poisoning Jack Parsons. But then there were souls that were not complicit. Souls that he'd killed close up and personal. Of simple soldiers and servants like Aditi and now the jeep driver.

These ignorant people were only following orders – they were defiled and could never attain nirvana. Michael only quickened their passing into the next life. A better life, hopefully.

Rustling.

Michael opened his eyes. The little boy whom he saved had curiosity in his blue eyes. Gingerly, the boy bravely sat down next to Michael.

"What's your name?" Michael asked tenderly, an affable smirk growing on his lips. "Did you think I wouldn't ask? You didn't ask me in the jeep, boyo."

The boy just stared at him in the bandha pose, mute and insipid, his mouth hanging open slightly.

"You don't know?"

The kid shook his head very carefully.

"Well. My name is Michael Oppenheim," he intoned affectionately.

"Mic . . . hael . . ." The boy attempted to say his name, mouth trying to grin but failing. So tragic. The kid had no name but found his own name fond.

"You like that name? Do you?" Michael said, feeling touched by the boy's attempt of kindness.

He watched the nameless little boy rummage for something in his pocket and handed to Michael a crumpled-up sticker in his hand. Michael studied it and eyeing the boy sympathetically, he took the worn sticker, opening it up. On it, it said one word in dark marker: Prince.

"Prince?" Michael uttered, surprised, trying to not wake up the children still asleep. "That's your name?"

The young boy waited for a long while and nodded. A nod that was full of insecurity – a worry that the abashment of answering wrong would have him punished. But he just nodded in order to show respect and to get along. *Good boy*, Michael thought. He saw no agreement in Prince's eyes. Prince didn't know *what* to agree with. Only with love.

"Michael – Prince . . ."

A pensive cohesion gripped Michael as he uttered those words to the beautiful child – a cohesion cold as tragedy and as profound as the joy of celebration. He contemplated Prince, his eyes orbs of awe. An enlightenment – a great epiphany. Here, Michael saw someone with much frailty, pure as a callow. He was in need of a new identity. Michael Prince needed a carer.

And at that very moment of revelation, Michael bowed his head with a hurtful moan, more concerned for the boy's self than his own.

6

SURVIVOR'S GUILT

"The Antarctic Treaty was signed in Washington on December 1st 1959. It entered into international force in 1961 and has since been acceded to by many other nations. The Antarctic Treaty has weathered sixty years since its first signing, transforming from a baseline of scientific freedoms and territorial coexistence to encompass broad swathes of environmental protection and ever-changing delineations in the world's atlas of political relationships. It's interesting that the countries who participated in the treaty have put aside their political animosities for the sake of peace, science, environment and tourism.

Many Middle Eastern countries did not participate.

What do these treaties mean now — for Antarctica itself, for the Aes Sidhe and for global ideas of governance — as geopolitical alliances and desires shift and change, as the race for new resources heats up, and as the results of a changing climate and exceeded tipping points come into play? Should the overarching issue of the Galactic Tyranny be the concern to bring us together? Or peace with the world? Or both?"

—From *Agent Buried Alive*, James Casbolt's Autobiography, 2001.

Casbolt strolled down Plaza Darsena, feeling uplifted. He knew sharing his testimony would help sedate himself from the guilt of his alienating memories, though he pretended to feel that such times would not be as transitory as they often were. However, this moment was something different. He had lifted most of the burden off his shoulders in the retelling.

The evening was balmy as Julian, Ben, Carl and Casbolt milled about at the La Casita – its pools gargling softly with light blue undulating water from four fountains therapeutic to the ears and sight.

"I want you to meet the girls, Casbolt," Julian said, hands in pockets.

Ben DePaula paced around casually; eyes uncontrollably active when people came near; a look as if they would ambush him off guard. "Yeah, we should meet the girls. How are they?"

"Not too bad," Julian shrugged.

"I will be more than happy to meet your daughters," Casbolt offered.

"Sounds like a good plan," Julian said standing up, stretching.

Your job is to wake up the sheep, Michael said in his mind. *They're in a dream world, they will think your trauma and experience mean nothing. Illusions of happiness. Hedonistic in prosperity. They know no better. Only those who are awake would be humble.*

Casbolt narrowed his eyes as he watched Ben. A spike of annoyance and envy pricked him, and for a moment he embraced it, thinking it to be right. It felt natural – right in his own eyes.

Rowdy eater, the Redlion growled, crouching in the gloom.

Chills engulfed Casbolt as he considered those thoughts seemingly not his own, all the while standing up to follow Julian into the crowd. Casbolt tried hard to pull his gaze from the tall, happy and well-built Benjamin DePaula.

Hollywood. The den of serpents. The den of sex offenders wearing fancy celebrity clothing with annoying voices and vulgar quirks with their runway porn stars – mind-controlled slaves. Getting away with trafficking and praised by the world as a pantheon of idols! And Ben had a place among them!

Yes, meet blood with blood. All of them, the Redlion of thrill said. *Kill him! Kill him! Kill him now!*

Shut up! No! I am James Casbolt. The Redlion croaked, retreating in the back, feeling convicted for even thinking such vulgar thoughts. But he couldn't blame himself. The Redlion had developed as a mechanism to cope with trauma, making sure his body never encountered abuse again. Casbolt was sweating as he walked faster, trying not to trot.

We share truth for mercy. That's all we need, Michael Prince interjected as Casbolt took control of his alters.

Enough. I am James Casbolt. I'm peaceful. I'm a normal man. He twitched, glad all faces were turned away. *I am . . . James Casbolt.*

The group hiked up the blue cobblestone footpath of Julian's Calle San Jose Street. Crumbling pastel houses nestled narrowly above the street, where banana trees were planted around sparsely across the footpaths. Julian led the way as a skinny white-and-orange cat – a stray by its patches of hair and its malnutrition – suddenly scuttled from out of nowhere. It ran across the road, under an old rusty red car that looked like it hadn't seen the road in years.

When Casbolt saw the girls, he saw them all giddy, chasing the cat. The youngest lay on her stomach reaching for it under the car. She looked to be four or five years old, wearing purple bather shorts and a dark purple polo shirt, her long black hair was tied up in a single braid draping over her shoulders. Bare foot, skin tanned to a light brown, she chirped, gasping juvenilely, jiggling her legs.

"Hullo! Little wid! Eeee! Look at them!"

The older sister stood quietly by a brick fence patting a large white cat resting on top. Sharing resemblances to her sister, she had the height and elegance, an exquisite beauty as Blue Bloods always were. Her longer straight black hair was left loose and fuzzy over her shoulder, partially covering her face. She looked around ten to thirteen years old.

These were the supposed Indigo Children and they seemed closer to normal than expected. Supervising them was a Spanish woman in her early thirties, with brown hair tied up in a bun, tall and willowy. The adoptive mother, Guanina.

Guanina was nice as she greeted Ben, Julian and Casbolt, exchanging remarks: "We were just leaving to meet you. Perfect timing." "Well, what do you know? Hi, everyone!"

While he expressed his greetings with Guanina, Casbolt approached the eldest daughter. She aimlessly stroked the neck of the purring white cat, lost in thought.

"Hullo," Casbolt said timorously. Surprisingly, he got her attention, light eyes monitoring his every move attentively. She was a pretty and young girl – Casbolt felt uneasy remembering the things he and his stepfather Neil did, telling him that he will never be able to stop lusting for women. That made Casbolt sweat even more.

No! No! I'm a better man!

"My name is James Casbolt and I'm just like you." He found himself patting the white cat, the Parvus Perception transmitting a reception of information from the girl's body language.

Her face morphed into an unreadable expression – transient.

"Boofs! There are so many boof cats! Say hi-yah! Yieep!"

Casbolt turned to the sibling who was kneeling back down under the car again, where three cats and a kitten, curled up together looking appallingly horrified with their disc eyes gazing at their overtly kind visitor who loomed above.

Casbolt brought his lips to a taut line as he saw Julian yanking his daughter impetuously by the shirt. "Lluvia!" he barked sharply. "What are you doing? People are here! *¡Vamos! ¡Modales!*"

"*Aperd . . .*" Lluvia sighed, stamping one foot in annoyance.

"Lluvia, say hi to James Casbolt."

Gazing into the mahogany eyes of the little girl, Casbolt placed a friendly hand on her arm.

And it was only then the memories returned all at once.

Purple clothes. Purple light. Purple ribbon – *Purple girl!*

The wolf!

Casbolt tensed, eyes gazing at his hand, slipping away from any form of sane soundness as he beheld . . . Danu. An emblem of his guilt, an emblem of his failures and an emblem of his sexual perversion. He sweated profoundly.

Casbolt wasn't worthy to help smuggle children. He let children be abducted and he'd been the one who indulged in the fantasy of sexually abusing them.

Hypocrite.

Pure pain pounded his soul. A lauding, wicked, sonorous voice swept through the deep recesses of his mind, pulling up the purple ribbon for a . . . A Celtic human sacrifice of placation.

Pretence. Children.

Danu... It was her fault.

Casbolt! Don't give in! Michael Prince screamed.

Hypocrite!

Where? Am . . .?

Strangers in the driveway, calling him.

"They're coming!" Seizing the startled Lluvia tightly to protect her, Casbolt squeezed for his life. She yelped in shock in Casbolt's arms, his eyes twitching madly as he fell back into the crevasse of his mind.

———

Wiltshire, October 31st, 1981

Michael Prince – now James Casbolt – sat insipidly in the back of the Alfa Romeo. Snatched from the cares of his mother. This had been her doing, it *had* to be. Nothing bad about these lot.

Yet he still cried and sobbed?

"Have more of this, Michael," said a laid-back thick Welsh voice. Casbolt had no concept of time, gazing deliriously up at the orbs of orange lights rising and falling in the damp darkness of the night.

"Hullo hullo! Earth to Michael?" said the same voice. A headache wrenched Casbolt awake, eyes dreary with daze and fatigue. He glimpsed a blurry outline of someone reaching back from the passenger seat of the car towards him. He was offering him something. It looked like a glass.

"It's water, son. Water," the Welsh man confirmed blandly.

Okay. Water. Throat parched, and thinking it kind, Casbolt took the cup but as he did, the man placed something small, hard and round in his other hand.

"Oi! Here, okay take this too, boyo."

Whatever the thing was, it was the size of a pea, a vitamin his mother would give him when he caught colds. Nice little things. Studying it, Casbolt confirmed in his feeble mind, for sure, that this was a vitamin in his palm. For sure.

"Now, put the pill on your tongue, Michael," the strange man instructed.

"I'm tired," Casbolt mumbled.

"This will make you awake," the man said. "Put it in your mouth. Keep it on your tongue but do not bite it or chew when you swallow because it will taste horrible if you do. So go on?"

Don't bite on it? "I don't—"

"Quick, man!" he snapped. "Just put it in your mouth and do not eat it! Capisce?"

"Hey, take it easy over there, Hywel!" The driver was Scottish.

"But he's giving me a hard time, man!"

"Oh, what do you expect, Hywel? Hm? It's almost twelve thirty, and the kid has no idea what we're about to do to him. He's probably thinking we're out to take him trick or treating or something!" The driver laughed. "The time when the veil is thinnest and when Danu returns to her children every year. Halloween night is when her children go to Antarctica."

"Nah. Don't worry Michael. This is not for you."

"The kid's spooked out as it is, man. Take it easy."

"Bah! Hodge! You just as easily get spooked out by the Morrigan and the customs! I mean, you hear the things they do in the program eh!? I don't see yah doing anything! Wonder why Whitmore gave us the lousy job doing bus runs! Bah! And I'm stuck with you too, always complaining!" The man named Hywel, turning focus to Casbolt, remained obscured in shadows. "Now, boyo. Grab the water and drink it. Make sure the pill washes down your throat as you do. On with it. Go on."

"When will I go home?"

"Oh cutie. Take the pill and you will. Your parents are completely aware of what we are doing."

Trusting him, Casbolt gingerly placed the pill in his little mouth and then tried to swallow it by taking a drink from the cup. Did it work? Hywel's darkened expression seemed to deny that.

"Well? Did you swallow it?!"

Casbolt sat there with a mouth full of water, worried that if he swallowed this strange vitamin whole, it could make him choke.

The man got frustrated. "Now swallow the damn thing! Quickly, man! It will help you later!"

Panicking, Casbolt lifted his chin, screwing his eyes shut tight and swallowed as hard as he could. He felt the capsule squeeze down his gullet, bruising it. Another tear slithered down his face.

"*Good.* There yah go, cutie." The man sighed coaxingly.

A lapse of time occurred; the dark car seemed to instantly become a large tunnel with clamorous sounds of feral beasts, and the Gaelic man's voice the roars of blabbering men.

"Wakey wakey cuties!" Banging. "Wakey wakey!"

Casbolt's ears popped, nausea taking hold, opening his eyes wide, taking in his surroundings. He saw a large room of infrared and sapphire dark-blue lighting illuminating the skin of operators to the far left. It reminded Casbolt of the school discos. But there was no music. It smelled of wee and poo. A zoo disco?

A long aisle stretched out before him, glowing blue on each end, marking out the passage in the dark. And along the aisle, rendered ghastly by the infrared, were large cells containing all kinds of wild animals, mostly dogs and wolves.

To his left, he saw a cluster of women in dark cowls; like witches, they held strange wands, walking in a tranquil file towards . . . something ahead. The smell of incense was strong.

"It is time to act as one mind now! To see who the gods of the barrows and hill forts – our ancestors – will prove worthy to begin the departure to Inisfail! Druid Whitmore! Sisters of the Nindingir, we shall begin training my children!"

"Mother Danu has spoken, and we will do!" the witches chanted in unison.

Mother Danu. He remembered her from the audition photoshoots for dancing and modelling. She came into full view before Casbolt and the small group of children next to him. He saw little Heather Baglio, pretty and petite with light-brown hair at her shoulders greasy, eyes frozen in a stupor staring at nothing – that girl that was from his school. Kenneth Marrow – a large red head also from his school – was on his other side, drooling and softly mumbling for his brothers to keep quiet.

Every one of his friends from Danu's photo and modelling audition looked tired and bored. Casbolt blinked in fatigue. He wanted a bed.

"Stand up in front of the cages! Everyone!" yelled an injunction. Druid Whitmore escorted the children, rounding them up towards the cages, the banging, the barking and the screeching unbearably loud.

The Nindingir slid into their positions besides the wooden chair at the far end of the room. On the chair sat Danu – a grave, tall, slender woman, leaning her hands on the S shaped crossguard of a completely crystal sword, bright, short, thin and double-edged.

Her fair face glowed a sunset hue. No sign of age was upon her, unless it were hidden within the depths of her keen eyes; cool as lances in moonlight and profoundly rich in memory of epochs long gone. Sublime as her complexion was, her face had a tone of freckles over the bridge of her nose, eyebrows upturned wings, and light-amber tresses reaching her waist, bound by a diadem of golden knots and a horse across her forehead. One leg over the other, she appeared naked from the cuts of her princess dress of green and warm colours, draping languidly. Her firm aqua-green brocaded bodice under her draping cloak created a considerable cleavage, where a silver necklace sat above her breasts; the triangular triple spiral. Danu smelled faintly of oak wood and pollen. As she spoke, her voice ran like many waters, musical and frisky.

"My little cuties," Danu smiled. She stood, descending the throne. She leaned her crystal sword on the throne, leaving it there. "We are going to play a game!" Her eyes swept over Casbolt and the other children – her children – as waves over a sea. "Isn't that exciting!?"

His skin crawled. His gut seethed. Casbolt felt a pressure on his chest for some reason he couldn't understand. He let out a brisk sigh fearing that even *that* could possibly get him sentenced for a misdemeanour.

Danu folded her arms behind her back, confronting a wild dog behind the cage, bashing the cell. It repeatably barked with vicious vigour, so deep Casbolt could *feel* the sound.

He cuddled up with all the kids with their blankets for protection as they gawked at the monster behind bars. A gigantic wild Alsatian dog aggressively clawed the cage on its hind legs. It got down back on its feet, snarling, dripping torrents of saliva from its frothing maw.

Danu scrutinised the dog and then the children with an increasing intensity, as if she were trying to decipher an obscure text. "Mac Tíre – son of the country – has agreed to choose the chosen to depart to Inisfail. Mac Tíre knows that you, the Tomorrow Children, have my blessing as the defenders of the Earth against the evil Galactic Tyrant and the evil Fomorians. Mac Tíre shall give you a great privilege, to go to the frontier of human endeavour of the South Pole, to face the wall that divides worlds."

Danu studied the cage again with a peculiar gaze, fluttering her luscious eyebrows and said with a loud voice, "DOWN!"

Casbolt shivered from the force of that single cracked word – it *struck* his awareness violently. At the command, the wild dog paced, gradually ceasing its startled movements, barks reduced to rumbles. The spiky fur on its back flattened.

Shocked, Casbolt gawked at Danu's swaying elegant cloak, ripping with the texture of moss. She clasped her hands together with a dominating air, turning to the men who brought her a board, pinned with fifteen ribbons, each of different colours, and rested it on a small table, leaning against a pillar. Casbolt eyed the rainbow vivacious glow on that board.

"Pick one please," Danu said with a stately dulcet. But something did not feel right to Casbolt; the animals and the air dulled as if obstructed.

One by one, Whitmore led each child to pick their ribbons. Before him, Casbolt's friend Heather Baglio went for her turn. Casbolt watched her intensely, occasionally eyeing the rabid dog prowling and licking its chops.

Heather approached the board, her hand about to pick the brilliant purple ribbon but she froze. Casbolt focused and noticed that her hand was shivering with tension.

It was then when Casbolt's heart began to thump; thumping like a drum in his little rib cage, that he'd thought Danu would surely hear it and punish him for it.

Heather Baglio, at the last second, twitched, plucking the yellow ribbon, returning to her place, relieved from the oppression of the stares of men.

"Your turn," Whitmore grumbled and Casbolt glanced up at another girl placing her choice. A game? The game made Casbolt's body quiver like water in a bowl just waiting . . .

Then came his turn. Once before the board, he procrastinated for a long time, the vibrant superb colours spellbinding him. But why did it feel so wrong to select a colour? He had no precognitive idea of where this game of Danu's was going, but he never thought selecting would become *so hard*. The foreboding warm stenches of urine struck him, the noises of the animals ebbing and flowing, masking the wafts of Danu's pleasant smell of a grove. He found pleasant to the eyes, a deep ocean blue ribbon for his taking.

He plucked it as if a fruit from a branch.

As Casbolt returned, Kenneth Marrow proceeded to select emerald green. Next, Casbolt's best friend in the world – Max Spiers – picked a blushing red. Casbolt's head throbbed, hoping he would not die.

And then last but not least, it was a girl's turn Casbolt barely knew. The girl in purple. Casbolt could predict what colour she would choose by her violet-clad clothes.

She had curly red hair and a smooth round head, no younger than five years old. She stepped forward peering with excited eyes at the magical colours. Danu loomed in the shadows, imperious eyes watching her.

The girl picked magenta purple.

The wolf separated by only a cage, emitted a piercing growl of hunger. Danu frowned, as if *grieved*. Before Casbolt could comprehend why, the goddess gradually plucked a dark purple ribbon from the fold of her pleats.

Casbolt's heart leapt. For a dreadful second, he thought that he chose that same pink-purple ribbon. He looked down and found that his ribbon was in fact a similar-hued deep blue. He relaxed greatly.

"Who has magenta?" Danu intoned lugubriously.

That friendly wide-eyed purple girl put her hand up. "Me. Me."

The dog let out an ear-splitting cackle.

A grin crept on Danu's face and voice cooler than a winter bog said, "Come here."

Casbolt and all the other children rubbernecked to watch the red-haired girl in purple stride forward, all attention suddenly imposed forcefully unto her. Her wide eyes were glazed with fright. She held Danu's slim hand, as the wild dog unable to restrain itself pounced with loud metallic snarls. Casbolt thought he heard the girl whimper; he saw her bare legs tremble.

Oh no.

Casbolt's bowels cramped. He knew something bad, *very* bad was about to happen. But why was Danu *so sweet* and *nice* about it? It made no sense!

The girl held up the ribbon for Danu to take back. But the goddess did not even offer out a hand.

"Please bring back my mummy. You are the mean one," the girl bravely scowled at Danu. But the conniving woman beamed with a deadly smile. She was acting as the type of person not willing to cradle a crying child, the woman who would let it cry itself to sleep. The entire room held its breath, suspended, ready to plummet down a cliff. Casbolt could almost smell it in the air. Someone had pooed their pants.

"I will give you back your mummy, darling," Danu whispered with a smooth rounded voice, her eyes locked on the girl. She stroked her chin delicately. "In the Otherworld."

Suddenly, Druid Whitmore, snatched the girl's orange hair cruelly. He bound a cord around her body, garrotting her slowly. She screamed in shocking agony, crying until she gushed blood, coughing. She thrashed in his arms, limbs tied tight within the cords and Whitmore, lifting her garrotted body over his shoulder, opened the cage.

The wild dog sat by Danu's power.

Casbolt dropped his blue ribbon. That could have been him! He could have spared that girl's life, instead of – instead of . . .

Living with guilt and pain.

He covered his eyes, tears breaching forth. All he heard was the maelstrom of wild noises: rasping girl, a barking monster, and a sliding of the cage door. He only suffered to the sounds of her being mauled to death. Cracking bones. Intense blares gargling into hollering whimpers, fading.

It was all to dehumanise the innocent. Desensitise the ones who were.

A sacrifice to save the world.

7

SCREAMS OF ARMAGEDDON

"And one of the elders said to me, 'Do not weep! Behold, the lion of the tribe of Judah, the root of David, has conquered, so that he can open the scroll and its seven seals. And I saw in the midst of the throne. . . a Lamb standing as though slaughtered, having seven horns and seven eyes."

—From the Scroll of Revelation, John the Apostle, 95 - 96 CE.

What's happening to him?!" Ben spanned his hand out on the ground, to pin Casbolt convulsing madly as Julian's daughters eased away, huddling around their father and stepmother, utterly bewildered.

"He just had a seizure!" Ben barked with a severity Julian knew so well in Operation Desert Storm when crisis gripped them. "Carl, call 911."

"Casbolt!" Julian shouted. "Hey, Casbolt's awake!"

Casbolt rubbed his face, disorientated, Ben and Guanina gathering around him. "Cas, are you alright?" Ben said. "Were you hurt? We were about to call the ambulance—"

"No!" Casbolt protested with fierce slurred words, hand to his forehead. "No, don't call. Don't worry. You'll call the men in black . . ." His face flushed red. "Ah . . . Don't worry. It's fine. It's fine. This happens. I'm okay."

"You sure?"

"Yes! This happens!"

Ben was utterly stunned. "*All the time*? No. Dude, I'm calling."

"No," Casbolt insisted again. He sighed and holding his head. "Please. They will have no explanation for my condition. They'll end up locking me up in a mental asylum and . . ." Casbolt let out a broken sigh. "And we can't have that. We can't. It's deprogramming from the Nindingir. It's normal for people like me."

"*This* happens?" Julian asked aghast. "Seizures?"

"Unless I am triggered, which is not common," Casbolt said in a matter-of-fact way, though he got a very distant gaze in his eyes. Guanina, hurrying from inside the house, knelt at Casbolt's side, carrying a glass in her hand. "Thank you. I don't want a drink either."

"Are you sure?" the woman said.

"This is good thanks. This is a good thing . . . I remember more." Casbolt placed a hand on his suitcase nearby, stroking it with an uncanny fondness. "Julian?"

"Yes?"

"Can I steal you for moment please? In private?," Casbolt said.

Julian led Casbolt into his room. He was granted the permission to speak to *a chief* who ruled over an occult society of super soldiers in Antarctica.

He knows something is up about my contact with the mediums, Julian reasoned in himself.

Julian grabbed a cloth in his room by the bed stand, covering a display of crystals just as the super soldier locked the door behind him.

"So, Casbolt, what happened to you back there?" Julian said out of sheer inquisitiveness, to divert the man's attention away from the crystals which he knew had a link with the dreams of the nocturnal woman. "Was that one of your trigger moments, when memories awoke?"

Casbolt began his inspection of Julian's room. *Good, he's not looking at those crystals there,* Julian contemplated, his eyes widening. Casbolt peered at the family heirloom housed in glass on the wall near the door – the gold rapier of Pirate Roberto Cofresi – an inheritance of swashbuckling buccaneers and conquerors. He nodded at the sword. "I had a flashback, Julian. I'm sorry."

"You do not have to apologise, amigo," Julian said, crossing his arms hoping he did not look suspect, though he could feel heat on his skin perspiring.

"I had a flashback of the time I was taken away from my family, trafficked off to Antarctica to train vigorously and tediously. But before that, I went near Stonehenge on Halloween night for a sacrifice to the gods to ensure good luck. To ensure good passage."

Julian's face went slack. "And what happened?"

"Danu is a monster," Casbolt whispered, a rictus forming on his mouth. "The gods are monsters, they don't have human's best interests in mind. Danu sacrificed a beautiful Gaelic girl to the Celtic gods. A sacrifice to save the world."

Julian went taut. "How do you know if this is true? You never wrote about girls being kidnapped to be sacrificed at Stonehenge!"

"Julian, what I wrote in the book were the memories that I could remember. But it seems as I'm triggered, more come to light." Julian frowned. "You have to realise something. Memory is dynamic. It's alive, it takes you where you need to go, constructs who you are. Where there are gaps in memory, it fills up with experiences that I cannot discern if they were mine, or if they even happened at all. Invention, forgery or both, memory takes you on nevertheless. And in the end, it's inextricably yours. What I remember, is mine and mine alone. The ancient gods are moral monsters. They're *tyrants*."

"Who was there with you when you met Danu?" Julian said. "The goddess of the Aes Sidhe?" The very air in the room, Julian perceived, became static at the pronunciation of her name. His eyes darted to the crystal set on his table unconsciously.

"Max Spiers," Casbolt said. "And Heather Baglio from school . . ."

"So, what was the purpose to get Antarctica?"

"The Galactic Tyranny, man. The war in the Middle East. Climate change. Resources. Everything. It's all leading up to a culmination – the Last Battle – on such a massive scale, that the world will burn. But unless all nations can come together and put aside their differences, we can face a common enemy and thwart the threat of humankind. The evil god, this alien invasion, is the only hope for our world. Ironically. It's probably what inflates his ego. By being an enemy, he has power over the world."

Julian swayed on one foot, greatly dissatisfied with how Casbolt concluded the matter. "So, my daughters are in danger of being trafficked because of the Galactic Tyrant?" He said this containing his boiling frustration. "The aliens?"

"I'm sorry, but I think you're right. There is no other reason to explain why the secret societies would take children away. I'm here to stop this from happening. Children *are not* for sale. They don't have to be snatched from their parents for this enterprise. We have more than enough super soldiers via genetic modification to fight the Tyrant and defend Earth."

Why me? Why did it have to be me to get stuck into this end game? "Yes of course. But… How can this be? Secret societies. Conspiracies. It will make me go mad. You can't trust anything, criticising what's accepted, making it sound as if people were deliberately deceiving you. Have you ever wondered if you were doing that sometimes, Casbolt!?"

Casbolt, a chief of the Aes Sidhe, actually appeared vulnerable. His face turned a dark crimson. "I . . . Look, I was just as hesitant meeting you, as you are meeting me," he said, splaying his fingers on Julian's table. "I don't have all the answers but I have to trust my memories as they arise to reconstruct my past. Ultimately, I want to help other victims face their past and heal. This is my mission."

It was there that Julian snapped. Nourishing the consternation of his life, and the great grievance in his mind all day – ever since he made the request for Casbolt to come. "Then why didn't you tell me this before!? If you just told me all this, then I wouldn't have put my daughters in danger by calling you over!"

"Julian!" Casbolt said, shocked. "Without proper education, the girls will not be able to survive."

"But that man in black at Barachina!" Julian hissed. "You bring *so much* attention. Everything was going perfectly fine without you."

"Well congratulations! You finally decided to *change your mind*. You want me to join your Marines or not!? Okay! I guess my job here is done then."

"But—"

Casbolt moved past Julian, reaching for the exit. "I expected this to happen. Not surprised. Not surprised."

"Wait, Casbolt. I . . . Wait! I'm sorry! Sorry!"

Turning his back Casbolt stood by the door and froze.

"Hey, are you guys done in there?" Ben's voice from right behind the door. "Guanina and I want to head back down the street."

"Just – hang on a minute." Casbolt turned back to Julian getting into his face, expression poisonous. "I have to deal with *this*."

A chill racked Julian's spine at that objectification. "What do you want?" Julian whispered swiftly.

"I . . ." Casbolt hesitated. "I was a violent machine once. Born to lead armies at Armageddon against the Galactic Tyrant. The gods are getting desperate. There is a sense of agency in the air. The powers, the occult, is seething with dread at the Galactic Tyrant's coming. As we speak, a line is being drawn in the sand." He met Julian's eyes – *like the ice cold of a predator!* "And I don't want you on the wrong side.

"This is why I *must* enlist in Marines while I am in exile. Because I hope serving in Operation Enduring Freedom will revoke my ban from Antarctica so I can return home to help my friends prepare for Armageddon. It's for God's sake, that we protect our planet from the forces of Satan. This is why I *need* to enlist in the Marines so I can return home and wake up the Aes Sidhe enslaved to the super soldier program to the truth. It's the *only way* I can improve myself. The *only way*. I'm enlisting because I need to prove myself that I am *not* a wretch, but that I am hero. I need to prove to the United Nations and to the Nindingir that *I am not* an unstable psychopath. Fighting in Iraq can do that. I *pray* it can do that. I want to know what it is like to serve the greater good in freedom for a change." Casbolt relaxed, cracking his wrists. "Was that all clear?"

"Clear as crystal." Julian cringed. "I… I will help you enlist. Just…"

"Good. Good to hear. I trust you Julian," Casbolt said. "A loyal reader of my book." The chief smiled, inclining his head. "Thank you. You're good at opening your mind."

8

KLEOS

"When he (the living creature) opened the fifth seal, I saw under the altar the souls of those who had been slain because of the word of God and because of the testimony which they had. They cried out in a loud voice, 'How long, Sovereign Lord, holy and true, until you judge the inhabitants of the earth and avenge our blood?' Then each of them was given a white robe, and they were told to wait a little longer, until the full number of their fellow servants, their brothers and sisters, were killed just as they had been."
—From the Scroll of Revelation, John the Apostle, 95 - 96 CE.

Once Ben helped Julian finish organising the Marine enlisting for deployment into Afghanistan, feeling surprised that Casbolt actually *passed* his in-processing and medical evaluation due to his history with DID – the departure to the airport could not have been any better. Ben was *baffled* at how James Casbolt could pass to be enlisted – he was a resident alien with a Green Card and not well in the head. *Probably because he's being favoured as a super soldier. Ridiculous.*

But now it was too late – James Casbolt had proven himself just eligible enough to be enlisted. Unbelievable. How could being a super soldier guarantee one's enlistment into the Marines?

I have a madman in my ranks now, Ben thought morbidly.

To put all that aside, he was now back in active duty. A part of him was enraptured, but another part of him, depressed. Again, another half a year without seeing his daughter Veronica. Another half a year without seeing his wife and spending time with family.

Ben really had to set his priorities straight. He needed to at least call his wife. He needed to check on Veronica.

They'd both miss him dearly.

One time, on the trip to the airport, James Casbolt asked what movies Ben took part in. As a part-time stuntman he'd been in action blockbusters like *The Matrix*, *Die Hard* and *The Rock*. He even mentioned, though quite reluctantly, he did some Power Ranger stunts as well for the kids. Casbolt laughed, congratulating Ben, but he could not seem to understand why Casbolt's eyes quivered and twitched as he probed him. All these things Casbolt spoke often about had no empirical evidence and were very likely association fallacies. He needed to prove himself a soldier if he were to get on Ben's good books.

Concurring with his departure, Julian had left the girls in the hands of his maid back at San Juan, under guard by one of James Casbolt's bodyguards with Guanina and her brother Canimao who were also connected to military intelligence, for extra safe security. It sounded alright, though Ben thought it was overkill, but he was willing to be nice enough to go along with the idea the girls were peculiar. Canimao was an honourable man and a Taino to be trusted – but Casbolt had yet to earn Ben's trust.

While waiting in the terminal hanging out in the lounge with the other marines of the area, enrolling for George Bush's goal to begin the crusade into the Middle East, Ben called his wife Brianna.

Excusing his men, Ben retreated towards a quiet secluded corner of the lounge room, facing the window looking out onto the tarmac and the boarding bridges for passenger aircraft.

"Hey," he said nonchalantly.

"Hey, Ben, hey how you are doing?"

"Everything is going absolutely wonderful," Ben lauded, happily looking around. "We are about to be deployed now. I'm at the airport, honey."

"Alright." She sounded bummed. Who wouldn't with a husband gone for most of the year.

"How's Veronica going?" Ben asked.

His young daughter Veronica DePaula was born to a different mother. The mother, Cleo, had not been polite at all with Brianna and her family – so Ben knew when he married Brianna, after divorcing Cleo, challenges would inevitably rise. Cleo, the fashion designer and model married Ben DePaula the world-famous actor. It made sense. But there was no deep love.

Ben had thought, haunted many times over the years, of sending Veronica to Cleo, but who knew what a mess that woman had gotten herself into now with her affairs. She might send Veronica off to sex traffickers for all he knew!

Veronica's mother had the mansions, the pools, the servants and the nice Bugatti and was friends with the wrong crowd. But then the whole reason for their initial separation had come as a result of her addiction to gambling and drugs.

The snares of Hollywood. Ben wouldn't have divorced Cleo, if she hadn't been the promiscuous piece of work that she'd been.

Family. It wasn't so easy. The Actionman could wriggle out and improvise in impossible situations on a movie set or in war, but in family life, even after the last decade, it exhausted Ben. All a true father wanted was for his children to flourish and prosper, more than himself, because the strenuous effort he'd put into raising Veronica, had to pay off.

But life . . . Ben remembered a joke from a pastor that Ben's father Joseph knew. He'd claimed there were three intertwined rings of family: the ring of dating, the ring of marriage and last but not least, the suffe*ring*. Well, Amen! Many times, in Ben's chaotic neckbreak speed life, wondered if family suffering was worth it.

"Veronica? She's perfectly fine," Brianna said sounding soft spoken and exhausted.

The DePaulas are tough oxen. "That's good to hear. How are you? Is Veronica home?"

"Unfortunately, no, she's busy at school."

The DePaulas are always busy, Ben thought, amused.

"Nice I'm here just waiting for the plane."

"Well, I wish I was there. I'm just in a middle of an investigation." Brianna sighed, sounding truly drained. As an FBI agent, she could face the most gnarliest of situations and endure them impressively. If this woman was tired, she'd been in some case. Hardy, determined and persistent, Ben never recalled Brianna ever sleeping in, she'd always be up early before sunrise, to continue her work. "Manslaughter and a series of uncontrolled child abductions. These cases are all happening back-to-back. It's bogged down. People lose sight of the victims, and in this case, these Muslim migrant women related to the victims are very vulnerable. I told them to make use of a sympathetic ear once they got it."

Ben shifted on his feet, turning around from the terminal window to leer at his marines across the lounge room, laughing, acting as youths. All his men were youths at heart, and they never grew up. A blessing. "Well, I hope those women are doing well in your care. And that those children are found.

That's rough."

Islam and Muslims . . . What an international crisis. Ben thought about the implications of the war against the Taliban, Saddam Hussein, Osama bin Laden's al-Qaeda and how any ordinary person could brand all Arabs as villains, just because of prominent terrorism. Arabs were Arabs. America was going *to save* the Arabs. That's what Judd Pounders and the officers had told him their mission objective was anyway. America – most of the world – was a friend of the Middle East – a whole other universe, a whole other culture, and a whole other society, so far away and maybe even backwards compared to the States. Perhaps the latter may be biased, but Ben wondered, reluctantly, if his father Joseph, as a historian, knew why and when and how that backwardness happened in history. Why did Ben have to live in the West? What would have happened if the Europeans had never discovered the Americans but the Muslims? Would he be living in New Doha?

"They're well but . . ." She paused. "Ben don't worry for me. It's just the Islamophobia. No one likes them. For good reasons. You do your duty; I wish you luck. I love you and . . ." She trailed off, her voice sounding ambivalent.

"Well, I just wanted to wish you a merry Christmas and a happy new year," Ben said, filling in for the unaccounted-for moment of silence. "Say to Veronica, I love her and that I hope she has a merry Christmas."

"I promise I will. Thank you. Please, Ben, don't get reckless. We need to catch up."

"Agreed," Ben said. "Duty calls. See yah."

Another Christmas comes where I don't get to see my daughter Veronica, Ben thought in dismay, stalking back to his lean and mean marines, ruffling each other up, each with multiple perspectives in problem-solving, bringing diversity to how situations could be dealt with. Competition was highly encouraged among the marines, bettering the vitality of a mobile strike force to be sent during an emergency within six hours. The phrase, "Send the Marines", had been uttered at least once by every US President in the last century. *If only I could have sent Veronica a letter that Daddy will come back, victorious. A glamorous hero.*

The whole issue began when Operation Enduring Freedom was declared on October 7th 2001, when B-2 and B-52 bombers attacked many Taliban bases in Afghanistan and ten days later, four-star army general Tommy Franks, commander of the US central command, launched a revolution to stir up support with US and native intelligence to combat against Islamic terrorism – who all believed they were part of the historical struggle against the crusaders. Tommy Franks had called the shots first after 9/11 – George W Bush had warned that he would make no distinction between the terrorist who committed the attacks, and those who harboured them. Ben remembered the craze, coming back from his part-time stunt for a fight scene in *The Last Samurai* with Tom Cruise, when Colonel Judd Pounders gave him the call. The World Trade Centre Towers had fallen. Stunt work would have to wait.

Of course, it had come from the national security organisation of CENTCOM, stationed in spangled regions from the Horn of Africa across the Near East, into the Hindu Kush – attaining full control and power over the heart of the globe. To root out al-Qaeda and Taliban, asymmetric warfare was needed in addition of marine intervention, General Tommy Franks and his ad hoc superiors organised to train indigenous and American soldiers. It was done once the marines got a word of respect, demonstrating credibility in combat expertise from the civilian population in the region; thus, peacekeeping and stability operations could remain under wraps until the crisis cooled down. Under wraps. The *worst* part of being a marine.

Ben had always wished that he had a son, because then, at least, he could convince himself as he consoled that little Simba of his self-confidence, his competence and courage.

But at the moment, for now, he would be more than happy to fight the hyenas for Veronica.

—

When James Casbolt went through the final enlisting process, approving his deployment with Colonel Judd Pounders, he had never been so nervous and so enthralled. When the Colonel responded to Casbolt's question about what General Harrel's counterterrorism meant, he said, "I can't tell you. It's focal point."

Focal to 99.99 per cent of people who knew the entire point of the war! It was above top secret. Likely many of the President Bush's Alliance or Cabal lackies had full discretion.

"Count me in," Casbolt replied, considering the weight of his decision. The uncertainty of how Harrel's counterterrorism would look like in action disturbed him. But, the western world relied on the vital coherence of the marines on the frontier of the zone of crisis – the Middle East. Without them, regardless of how they conducted the operation, there would be chaos. It was flimsy to build civilisation off the expenditure of others, but he knew this idea was historical and subtly drilled into the heads of all these officers and soldiers in the Marine Corps. But for Casbolt, it would redeem his reputation in the eyes of the Aes Sidhe. Weather the counterterrorism was problematic ethically or not.

The trip to Afghanistan on the matte-grey C-130 Hercules cargo plane, had a one stop at Adana, Turkey, before landing in Kandahar airport. The cabins inside looked like the anatomy of a whale – ribcage and all. The seats were fold ins with red sinews of crimson netting dangling, confining apparatus behind the rows of seats. The seats were next to one another, side by side, cramped in rows along the tubular walls. When one sat down, they were facing the other row of seats directly, meaning Casbolt could not hide from the eyes of the marines, he had no excuse to not speak to them. The seats were built inside a stressful dark cage, in order to build bonds between the all-male soldiers. It seemed not too dissimilar to what Casbolt learnt in Antarctic training with the Aes Sidhe.

Casbolt did try to familiarise himself with the soldiers and the crew onboard, realising how hard and strenuous it was to make new friends. To commit to his mission – to spread awareness of abuse and conspiracy, to serve in war and to fight for a noble cause – would go far if he could learn to make friends. He'd been ostracised from Antarctica for breaking international law, and he'll been a criminal in the eyes of the people who actually knew who he was by reading his book – and most people have not and would not. Despite this, he felt like a pretender among lighthearted, honest middle-class American men who had normal lives and families to protect. They had a lot to lose and Casbolt had none. If he was caught by people of the law, it would have nothing to do with his service in the marines.

Because becoming a marine meant he could gain favour once more with the Aes Sidhe and the Nindingir, and, hopefully, he could mitigate his crimes.

Military service might – and he hoped it would – appeal his breech of the United Nations Treaty. For there was nothing else Casbolt could do, without descending into oblivion.

———

Casbolt hated airports.

They had a sickly, grimy feel to them, an artery for dull ennui. It agitated Michael Prince in his head, who knew very well that the journey to the Antarctic began at an airport, with Mr Whitmore after Danu's sacrifice of the purple girl to the gods at Wiltshire. It brought back the vileness that seemed to seep from its sterile walls.

When the Hercules landed after a fifteen-hour flight to Adana airport, docking by the military sector to reload on fuel, Casbolt, after relieving himself in the toilets, heard some of the marines talking.

Peeking around the corner of the lounge, Ben – tall, graceful and cocky – blabbered to Julian and his friends.

"Casbolt is utterly blasé and disingenuous," Ben said tersely. "He's so soft spoken and yet, he speaks about some of the *most ridiculous* stuff ever." The marines holding cups of beer, coffee and other refreshing beverages, laughed. "I don't buy him one bit. But as a guy, he's cool. I like a super soldier on my team, no doubt!" Ben was sarcastic; he grinned as the marines guffawed raucously. "I do not like people getting brainwashed on my team. I've seen it done before; you know. And it's bad. Trust me. It's not my fault people do crap things because of me. Every human being in their own right shall own their responsibility."

"Come on, Ben," Julian chided. "What's up with you? You're bullying."

"Well, look, bro. Casbolt is what he is. Just suggesting that he hasn't proven to us anything he said in his book. Why should I believe anything he says. I don't want him to cry out wolf."

"Yeah, true dat," a marine remarked.

"Ben?" Derek Fish, one of the marines said, chortling. "Ben, why would someone make up stories of them being sexually abused?"

Ben raised an eyebrow. "You believe him? I mean, cool that you do. I'm jealous of you because I wish I could believe. But I can't you know. I wish super soldiers were real. Heck I want to slap Captain America's ass for real, you know?!" A wave of snickering and knee slapping went on as Ben spoke. "You believe him on that basis because it is cool?!"

"Casbolt *does not* have America's greatest ass!" shouted a blond-haired five-foot ten man with slender limbs, underweight, like someone who'd played more video games than the gym, let alone fight a battle. Despite that, the man had determined hazel eyes, enlarged by his large spectacles that gave him a Mr Smart Guy look. "He's English! He has England's greatest ass."

"Hey!' Derek snapped. "Stop bullying Casbolt, Jason Laycock!"

"I'm not!" whined the blond nerdy marine. "If it's a *compliment* for Steve Rogers, why not for James Casbolt?"

"You ever seen his ass, Ben?" chuckled a young marine wrapping an arm around a marine with a bandana.

"No, Brody! Breaking news: I'm not gay!" Ben exclaimed.

"Logical," said a marine with a bandana around his head. "Right, Brody?" Brody blushed at his friend's look.

"Dan! Okay, Dan! But conspiracies are a *terrible* basis for belief," Jason Laycock said.

The Parvus Perception told Casbolt that Ben hated him. Jason Laycock as well as Dan. Why? It appeared the answer could not so easily be discerned. All Casbolt had done was tell the truth as it came to him from his memories, trying to be objective about it . . . No Casbolt *deserved* to be disliked. He expected this feedback. Casbolt pressed his back on the wall, standing still – it was hard not to – and listened.

"It makes more sense that Casbolt just made it all up to just get a book out," Ben said. "Anyone can write a book if they wanted to."

At that moment, Casbolt doubted himself, detesting Ben. His very bones were repelled by him, that *abstemious* man was foul and dull minded.

Show them, Michael Prince asserted. *Show the selfish terrible world that discriminates those who are different that you are James Casbolt – a new man.*

Casbolt appeared in the open, and all eyes turned to him. The marines went dead silent.

"Goodnight men," Casbolt said with a dishonest grin. "Nice to see you are ready to fight with me. Nice to see." He bit his lip.

The marines groaned, some gazing up at their idol Ben, expressions unreadable.

"James," Ben said sternly, clearing his throat. "You know . . . You know we were only joking, right?"

Casbolt felt fury wash his body with sweat. *Liar,* Redlion whispered. *He must be destroyed!*

Wait! Casbolt trembled. His nose flared.

I will break your neck!

I'm James Casbolt!

"Ben, you don't joke about the family member who wounded you, am I correct?" Casbolt watched Ben's eyes widen, recoiling in shock. Once again, his Parvus Perception had ostensibly given Casbolt a hint about this, the body language of Ben indicated he'd been affected once in the past by a man with "bad ideas", thinking outside the box. "You're making fun of me because I'm different? Come on. You have an African American man in your crew, and you treat him well?" He gestured to Derek Fish. "Listen to me. Isn't the number one rule in the Marine Corps comradeship? No matter our differences?"

Casbolt felt slighted. Who was he – James Casbolt the American marine – talking *back* to Ben, a major in the marines? In this setting, Casbolt was not a chief anymore.

"I don't mean to bring anything up to aggravate you, man," Casbolt uttered, walking slowly towards Ben. "But you're wrong about me. *Very wrong.*"

Ben, lowering his glance, tightened his fists. "You know Joseph?" Casbolt nodded. Joseph was Ben's father, a public speaker of fringe Christianity. Ben's voice sounded husky. "He used to be family, but things happened. I don't even see him anymore. He doesn't celebrate Christmas or Easter. Or anything." Emotion riddled Ben's raspy voice.

Why now was Ben compromising and opening up his chest? "I do. What about him? You dehumanise your father too? Calling him a stupid tinfoil asshole?"

Ben groaned, his cheeks turning considerably red. "No I—"

Casbolt took a step forward. "Listen, Ben. You should learn respect. Let these marines know that the Actionman is a bully."

That had gone too far, yet Ben had incurred an offence – a *geas* in which an obligation must be made. Casbolt could restore his own honour, the ancient Aes Sidhe way. To build his self-esteem from a lowly state, after the damages of reprograming, and after the Bleakness. If Casbolt was a new man, he had incurred *geas to* Ben.

Fool! Fool! Fool! Michael Prince hissed in Casbolt's head. *Don't become a hypocrite!*

Ben's face contorted. "You really are mad. What they say about you."

"Snots like you could believe whatever you like about people," Casbolt said, the Redlion enjoying the aggressive discourse. *Only conflict is interesting. Only evil is intellectually stimulating*, Great Semjase used to say. "But it is not right to speak behind my back." Casbolt cupped his ear for good measure. "I'm a super soldier, aren't I?"

Ben's nostrils flared, then looking as if he were about to scream at his face in wrath, he turned away, sighing. "This is very stupid, James. Sorry. I am *sorry* about what I said. I take it back. You're right. I should not be bullying you because you are crazy and amazing all at once." Chuckling, Ben placed a hand on Casbolt's shoulder. "Bros again?"

Not genuine, Casbolt thought as he looked into the light-brown eyes of the handsome bold man, a man any woman could love . . . At first sight of course. So full of *conceit.* So *abstemious.*

Casbolt paused at that comment as a torrent of memories flashed before his eyes, memories where he had forced respect and his way to be done to normal children at school, bullying them through violence and abuse. He was such a *hypocrite*. Such a *fool.* What right did he have to demand Ben how to live his ordered life when Casbolt lived his so poorly? A loner, stuck in rabbit holes and talking to himself all the time?

"James? James!"

Casbolt started, realised that he had almost succumbed to his knees. Ben grasped his shoulder so tight that it hurt like an iron clamp. "Bro. You're sweating like a pig, and you almost hit your head!"

Casbolt felt the marines' gazes, all the shock and humiliation.

It's happening again, Michael Prince confirmed. *The Bleakness. The Triggers. They know you're not right in the head.*

Suddenly, Casbolt felt a chill drip down his spine. Would going out to fight the Taliban in the mountains of Kandahar be the best idea after all?

But he *had* to fight for a better cause! He had to prove to the UN he was noble. He had to help liberate the Middle East for his own sake, for Max Spier's sake, for the Iceni's sake.

"You need some rest, bro."

"Yes," Casbolt said dryly.

No, I don't want your kindness, a part of Casbolt said.

"You look tired."

"We're all tired."

"And there's a big day tomorrow." Ben bit his lower lip, turning to his men. "Alright, boys, time to retire." The marines, grunting incoherently to each other, roused from their chairs. Ben turned to Casbolt, smiling reassuringly. "Bro, it's okay. Pounders will not like us hitting heads. It's not very pragmatic when you think about it. So, I've got to get going." Ben looked at his watch, putting on a mock snarl. "It's getting pretty late. Before sunrise at five fifteen we're packing and flying to Kandahar at six forty on the dot. Days of sleeping in are over. Night, James." Ben hesitated, not completely mollified. "Again, I'm sorry about what I said. I take it back. Really." And with that, Ben turned and left to the lounge at the end of the room where the marines set up their supplies sleeping on the couches.

Giving him the benefit of the doubt then . . . Relaxing his shoulders, Casbolt recognised that Ben had only attempted simple honesty – he'd been too honest about his father Joseph — and Casbolt too, had been honest, albeit he had spoken the truth from knowledge. Ben spoke it through resentment.

"Sorry, Ben," Casbolt whispered alone. "I shouldn't have said anything about your father."

Did Ben even *know* his father? Did he *love* his father, or did he feel sorry that they'd separated and blamed himself for it? The father set an example, for Casbolt, he had been unlucky, to have Neil as a father who was aggressive and hopelessly arrogant.

Only conflict is interesting. Only evil is intellectually stimulating.

———

After staying the night at Adana airport, and once the Hercules had its fuel tanks filled, Casbolt walked down the aisle, strapping himself to a fold-up seat, into the cargo netting, his duffel bag a heap at his feet.

There was a fair number of marines on duty today, many of whom he only got to learn about recently. He nodded good morning to Konstantinos – Demos – the Greek man from New York – a prosecutor, restaurant waiter, and a history buff. He was reading Homer's *Iliad* that had seen its days, a crinkled book, all annotated and patched with sticky notes. A nerd in ancient things was so rare in a capitalist world – perhaps Casbolt was not alone after all. He found the man to be a delight very quickly and their chemistry flourished.

They couldn't cease taking. They spoke about the ancient Greek virtues and the Delphic latinity, revealing that the druids seemed to have adopted similar ideas due to a common Proto-Indo-European tradition thousands and thousands of years before the Greek and the Celts. As Casbolt spoke about his Nindingir virtues and traditions, Demos spoke about the Homeric Greek philosophical virtues and found striking similarities with his Aes Sidhe culture: *arete* (excellence of any kind), *metis* (wit) and *themis* (what's right). Demos smiled with pride and slapped Casbolt's hand with a high five.

"Yeah man! We're the warriors of a lifetime!"

"Time for attaining *kleos*!" Casbolt said jubilantly. The glorious death of *kleos* – it perfectly aligned with the epic poetry strung by the bard Taliesin of Urien, king of the ancient Welsh territory of Rheged during the Saxon invasion of Britain and Scotland – the era of King Arthur. Demos laughed. Such silly romance this all was.

Casbolt would use glorious virtue as his standard. He would die a hero to show everyone that he was no longer a bastard Aes Sidhe.

I will rest when I die.

Casbolt resonated with what Demos told him. It gave him the vigour to discuss his own culture of his people – the Celts. What he knew about the epic cycles *Leabhar Gabhala* (The Book of Invasions), which was found in the *Leadhar Laignech* in medieval times, was that it recounted the mythical invasion of the Everlasting Ones, the children of Danu, coming to Ireland. There was also the *Togial Bruidne Da Derga,* and the accounts the Ulster Cycle of the king Conchobar mac Nessa of Emain Macha, of the demigod hero Cú Chulainn, son of Lugh, and their contentions with the nefarious Connachta queen, Medb.

From now on, Demos' comradery helped Casbolt forge a path that he must go on with full marching velocity, as his graceful warrior ancestors did in the epic past – Lugh Lamhfada the Long Arm and Achilles the Runner, all had the same core Indo-European notion – legendary champions, attaining glory in battle. *Kleos* made one a hero.

The noise of the engines changed pitch and the entire plane trembled, beginning to drop for landing. Landing in Kandahar.

Demos said it was a city that bore the name Alexandria Arachoton. It was named after Alexander the Great, a heroic man of Macedonian royalty that conquered the Persians and the known world. He came to Afghanistan with his companion troops inspired by the Iliad – the Indo-European warrior tradition.

But now I, Casbolt thought, *an Aes Sidhe chief of the McMurdo Dry Valleys Iceni Aes Sidhe, with America's marines, for the first time I shall step foot in the Middle East – the heart of the earth.* A sense of awe overtook Casbolt at his once in a lifetime opportunity to travel. He was going to the Middle East!

The landing experience was in no way a comforting one, such as the "prepare for landing" ease on commercial flights. Instead the plane shifted from the left and to the right, undergoing extreme turbulence that made Casbolt grip his seat tightly, his stomach lurching with every move. A noise like an elevator cable cut loose whirled back and forth as the plane banked and boomed for landing. Most of the marines were quiet now, yet some still persistently joked with one another – Julian, Dan, Brody and Laycock.

The aircraft thundered on the runway, the engines roaring to slow the plane down, the cabin shuddering and quaking along. Then, a few loadmasters appeared once the plane had reached a taxied speed and signalled everyone to get packed. One of these officers and loadmasters, Marcus Theis, gathered his belongings and stood up tall. The thirty-year-old man – his general appearance reminded Casbolt of the movie actor Jason Statham that had a DePaulan look to him – a bald head, meticulously shaved short beard and tough build.

"Alright let's go meet the babysitters," Marcus Theis slurred with languid bravura, striding past them down the aisle towards the ramp under the tail of the plane. Casbolt followed suit and collected his baggage, unbuckling himself.

Once the hydraulics activated, blighting light beamed within the plane, the blaring hissing noises of engines roaring and gushing over everyone's voices. A squall of hot air, carrying spicy scents, scorched rubber, and fuel, burst within the confines of the cold plane hitting Casbolt hard. He had to squint from the unbelievable heat and brightness. He watched Derek Fish coolly pulling out a pair of soldier-model sunglasses over his eyes.

Casbolt took a deep breath as he found himself marching down the tail ramp into the heat of the Afghani sun, which drifted towards the western horizon indicating late afternoon. The sky was devoid of clouds. The valley was surrounded by a mountain range appearing prehistoric, many of which still had their icy summits shimmering white. The skin on Casbolt's arms burst with sweat then evaporated, the tarmac burning through his boots. The distance shimmered, burning in a liquid mirage. The bases where air conditioning would be held, flickered like holograms.

Casbolt stood in a line with a group of twenty or so soldiers, Ben DePaula and Marcus Theis as commanding officers for their crews, stoically meeting the so-called "babysitters".

"Major Theis and DePaula," the first officer said, shaking firm hands with both of them. "You've come just in time. We have a situation."

That was it. Their welcome. Not unfriendly, nor over friendly, it wasn't surprising either. Looking at the officers and the soldiers in this small airport base, they looked like a rag-tag bunch, some having gone native like the officers with their short beards and headcloths wrapped around their heads. Casbolt could see most of the people gathered at Kandahar base were battle hardened, the youngest was maybe in their mid-twenties, and each the best of what he or she had to offer to the table.

Casbolt studied the second officer scanning the newly arrived crew in silence. His skin was wrinkly with hard-slated scowling lines and the hair peeking out from underneath his patched red-and-white head covering looked grey. "Let's talk inside," he said in a gravelly voice.

The general lay out of the American base was rather bizarre – a remnant of the ugly poured-concrete structure of Soviet infrastructure. The navigation, very poor and unwelcoming, facilitated a base that housed nine large arched roofed buildings in a circle around the operation centre where small planes, sheds for fighter jets, and helicopters where parked, and small luggage cars which sped around on errands. It looked vacant and fairly uneventful. But once Casbolt and the marines strode in through the middle, past the Afghani security guards, passing through a series of doors inside, they waited for the first one to close until opening the next, to maintain light and noise discipline.

Casbolt saw why as he passed. A dozen guys sat in dim cool rooms in front of video and computer screens wearing headsets, monitoring satellite feeds streaming from different bases all over the mountainous country. Another dozen men in khaki and camo shirts, discussed strategy, plotting and tracking recent enemy activity, in front of laminated maps. None of these men ever looked up.

At the rear of the base, Casbolt and the marines congregated around in a semicircle before a table where two large maps were laid out with a map of Afghanistan's terrain in intricate detail.

"Earlier today," the scowling officer uttered, holding his hands together behind his back, "at three thirty we sent out a routine patrol of infantrymen into the remote mountains, looking for high-value targets and to report back to the Northern Alliance who are currently undergoing a ground campaign."

Jason Laycock adjusted his glasses. "Taliban targets you say, sir?"

"Yes," grumbled the tall man. "After their leader Mohammed Omar was giving the ultimatum from President Bush to close down all al-Qaeda training camps, he ordered the slaughter of two thousand innocent people. The Northern Alliance was dispatched for tracking any of these remaining terrorists to further uproot the Taliban. One patrol had been dropped off by helicopter into a secluded mountainous location to the north."

The officer picked up a large, laminated satellite photograph of the mountains that looked like the rough festered sores on an elephant seal bull – the uninhabitable, unforgiving hide of Kandahar. How Alexander and his companion cavalry navigated through such treacherous terrain in the fourth century BCE was beyond Casbolt. The Macedonian boy was ruthlessly tenacious and disciplined.

Ben DePaula nodded. "Do we have the precise coordinates of the last reported rally point?"

"We do," the first officer replied. He showed everyone a piece of paper where the coordinates had been written down. It read: *32.3907615, 66.5857229.* "They were dropped off a few clicks south from here," the first officer continued.

"May I?" Marcus Theis, receiving a copy of the coordinates, pinpointed the last made checkpoint on their inevitable mission in the middle of the rugged mountain range on the map.

"While on their reconnaissance mission, our marines failed to report in, missing two of their check-in times," the second officer began. "All units in the field have a radio operator, and there are appointed times when the patrol is required to check in with a situation report, but this failure of meeting this basic requirement has been extremely frustrating." He stretched his fingers and leaned them on the table, sighing stressfully, occasionally glancing up at the other officer.

He knows this situation is not a normal one, Casbolt thought. *Not Taliban. But something else is out there... But what?*

"There is . . ." the officer stammered, sweat appearing on his forehead. "A great level of uncertainty for the safety of the unit. They simply vanished. This failure to communicate may suggest – they're in danger or dead."

"They couldn't just *die* out there," Laycock commented vehemently. "They've got to be somewhere. Surely."

"Do you think they were hostages?" Casbolt postulated. "Did they get mowed down on sight and left out to die? Or were they captured by al-Qaeda as interrogation hostages and all communications were cut off so their locations cannot be uncovered?"

The old stern officer shook his head, giving him an eye that saw right past him. This man had no idea who he was. "I was thinking around the same lines." The officer scratched his head. "It could be a stalling or taunting tactic . . . Well. We simply have no idea why and where they vanished."

Casbolt frowned.

"That's not normal," Julian said. "You'd call for air support, something, but you saying that there was *nothing*? You think it might have been a landslide? Wiped out by some natural hazard? Maybe heat stroke got to them and they fainted? I don't know. They ran out of water?"

"All those things are our best guesses, Lieutenant," the officer said, nodding to the side. "That may be the only explanation we have now. However, our soldiers are diligent and well trained. Heat stroke and lack of water is unlikely. They are well aware of natural hazards too. The weather was partly sunny when they were deployed. Surely at daytime, we would have traces of them."

God, this is ridiculous, Casbolt thought. *I've just gotten here, haven't even unpacked and the universe had set this up for me. I'm seriously dealing with a strange disappearance now?* Casbolt would prepare for the paranormal in whatever form it would take.

The first officer dabbed his forehead with a handkerchief. "We are starting to conduct search investigations, and if we do not get any more information by tonight, we will be sending you as a fresh unit in the morning to retrace our lost patrol team's steps from the rally point given."

"So," Derek Fish said, crossing his huge arms. "Off the grid we go. Those mountains are extremely treacherous, sir. You're confident we will find them?"

The officer replied, "If you stay to the path they took, maybe. Not to mention that you are required to examine the surrounding area for signs of hostilities."

"Of course, sir," came Marcus' firm positive rejoinder.

"How long ago did they fail to report in?" Ben asked.

"5.00 pm, around. Only an hour ago."

"Okay. Sir, we will up turn the mountains to find our brothers if we have to, sir."

"Good, DePaula."

"Sir, you can count on us. We need at least tonight to get ready, sir," Marcus said confidently. "Five wake-up time. Five thirty dispatch. When it is still cool. We do not want to be out in the heat for long. We need all eyes on the road, any sign of clothing, footprints or traces, we will report back to you, sir."

"Done." The officer slapped the table, rolling up the map into a scroll and the team dispersed.

—

Casbolt followed the marines to settle in the thatched roofed barracks into the cool afternoon light outside. The twenty-eight-degree air was fresh and the marines were still rowdy, even after a whole day flying.

"The mysteries. Ohhhh," Dan teased wiggling his fingers into Derek's face. "A UFO beamed them up and took them to another planet!"

"Bullocks!" Laycock laughed.

Or a gateway, Casbolt thought. *A portal into the Underworld is not entirely out of possibility.*

"Oh, give me a break, Danny boy." Laycock nudged him, grinning. "You want to go up to another planet yourself?"

"Nah, I dunno," Dan said, kicking some dirt as the marines trudged towards the barracks and the outdoor showers. Casbolt could see the arms of hairy men raising a pan the size of a baking dish and a bottle of water above their heads, splashing water upon themselves. Such "bathing" in a facility that had scarce water supply, that could not waste drinking water after cleaning sweaty dirty men, was pragmatic. Casbolt smiled watching the showers and thought it new. Survival was fun when it removed the necessities of life. Like some of the Antarctic bases.

"Man, why would an animal want to mess with a bunch of special forces? It doesn't make any sense to me," Brody Nathan said, the youngest boy in the incongruous base and best friend of Dan Markowitz.

"Well, you never know, bud," Dan said falling behind to meet his mate. "I have a feeling something is very fishy about this."

Dan leered at Derek Fish who turned around startled. "What? Don't look at me."

"Merry Christmas, Fish!" Dan said, adjusting his bandana. It seemed the boy wore it just because he was in the Middle East and wanted to suit for the occasion.

"What are you talking about, Danny boy! You're the one who loves the creepy stuff! You watch too many movies!"

"But whatever happened certainly is interesting. We will have to wait to find out tomorrow," Julian remarked, striding in the group carrying his duffel bag over his shoulder, walking backwards and grinning all the while. "Besides, *qué es —*"

"*Spanish*! You son of a—" Derek leapt in the air like a basketball player, knocking Julian with his body. The collision sent Julian stumbling into a patchy concrete wall, dropping his bag. A lone basketball ring stood nearby and already some of the marines were getting ideas, flinging their bags down to go hunt for a ball.

"Hey! Hey man," Randall called out.

Throwing back his head, Derek let out a curt hysterical laugh ramming and thumping Julian back against the wall, groaning and grunting, leaping with his rear and side, smothering him as if he was shooting for the ring for a lay-ups. Harmlessly of course, a big sweaty man playing roughly with a slim Spanish boy could end heinously. It all managed to paste a wry smile on Casbolt's face, as the marines burst out laughing.

"Wooh! Oh! Yeah! Ugh! Beat that!"

"Stop!" Julian resisted. "Wait! Watch it! You'll – ohff! Ah, you gonna – Agh! My bone!"

"Huh!" Derek disengaged, only to get Julian in a headlock. "Boi! Kiss the dirt!"

"Take it easy, Fish. You aren't Drill Sergeant around here." Ben DePaula broke up the mock fight, towering, his bald head gleaming in the setting sun, holding his luggage to expose his body-building biceps. "We've got another early night tonight, boys! Come on! No more games!"

"It's a ritual now," Derek said, letting Julian go to rub his bruises. He staggered, relieved to have air to breathe. "You start rambling in Spanish again, I'll give you wake-up call, you hear me? Haha."

"If you can't understand, then *why* didn't you take Spanish in college?" Julian replied contentiously. "Like, bro, chill!"

"Hehe, I didn't," Derek said. "Because I couldn't be bothered. I just wanted to practise to see if my skills are still smooooth!" He pointed at Julian and then to the ring. "You fed me up? You're schooled!"

"Yo, buds." Dan patted Derek on the back. "Wanna play basketball?"

"Shirts vs skins!" Derek took off his shirt, clapping. "You're on, yo!"

Dan bit his lip with a crazed expression as Ben turned, rolling his eyes and grinning like a goof. "Alright," he said, sighing. "For half an hour until we have dinner. But remember to get all your stuff inside like mommy back at home."

"Love you, homie," Derek replied, blow kissing. "Love you, Actionman!"

"Love you too, Fisherman!"

"Hey!?"

Some of the younger marines – not newbies, but those who had some experience – started to break up into teams. After they rushed inside to put their bags in their cabins, they raided the square near the concrete wall like desultory bandits. Soon, they were playing an intense match, cheering and having fun.

Casbolt wondered about why he was here – he was here to prove himself, to regain his reputation amongst the Aes Sidhe and world. He hoped his efforts could revoke his ban from returning to Antarctica with his friends, his people the Iceni. But he was here now, in Afghanistan – the forefront of the great beast of war that was brewing within Iraq – the cradle of civilisation. The next step Casbolt could make was simple enough – save lives. Not to worry at all about the hours organising and leading troops, he only had to follow the major.

A part of him hated this, a part of him loathed this.

I am a chief.

Casbolt knew such a deduction of himself was good for him, despite how it exceeded Nindingir social mores. He chose to be public about many things in his past and about the secret societies, he knew it would get him in trouble. But if the Galactic Tyrant was coming, wouldn't the whole world know about the secret societies anyway? Above all, Casbolt *had* to set the example for any Aes Sidhe that suffered the Bleakness of deprograming and sexual abuse. If the Alliance was about peace and healing, they *needed* the chief to change, to be responsible. Perhaps Max Spiers could follow his example in this.

I am not *a disgrace!*

And perhaps it was by taking a break from being chief for once, that it would be the way to outweigh the avaricious choices Casbolt had been responsible for committing. Maybe it was just that. Become an ordinary guy.

A guy who could play a simple game of basketball and laugh about life.

And then, maybe then, he would become more capable to do good.

"What better way," Casbolt muttered to himself, "to defeat the darkness, than the one responsible for it?"

9

ATTACK FROM BELOW

DECEMBER 21ST, 2002

"Iraq – the birthplace of culture, writing, law, science and literature. The place of great riches. But that was four to three thousand years ago. History tells us that over the centuries, the Silk Roads were fought over by power-hungry European nations. The Spanish, Dutch, Portuguese and British dextrously pursued the East's imperial riches.

Iraq is dying. A new feudalism took root when Britain wringed its hands tightly over its oil supplies, partitioning fragments of the Ottoman Empire, curtailing social inequality, religious frustration and fanning dissatisfaction in rural communities. Not only that, Iraq is also backwards because everything about its British-given geography sucks. Landlocked between a desert to the east and Zagros mountains to the west, with a wedged coast stuffed between Kuwait and Iran; it can easily be blockaded from supplies. Its oil is distributed unevenly between ethnoreligious groups, generating instability. And you wonder why Iraq lashes out? And on top of that, the Mosel Dam by miracle, almost flooded the Tigris, and as a result of the desperate construction of dams by Turkey and Syria upriver, could very well shut down all the water supply at will, thus drying up the Euphrates River. Dry up. I don't know about you Bible nerds, but those things make you say, hmmmmm?"

—Lecture on *The Omega Plan*, Joseph DePaula, at Global Kairos for Justice, Portland, Oregon, 11 September 2002.

The smouldering incoming heat was partially blanketed by bleak grey clouds, as the marines traversed the ridges, expecting danger at every turn. The sun was just peaking over the horizon, stretching long rippling shadows across angled plains of mountain valleys and peaks, sun baking them dark black with crevasses. And yet, this land was so deceptively beautiful and sublime. Dawn's warmth was already giving way to the heat of the day. The air would swelter once the sun reached its summit, and Ben was already beginning to sweat.

He watched the helicopter's slicing blades that had dropped them off, fading to a distant incorporeal *crack*. Since the floors of the Hindu Kush Mountain ranges were at fifteen hundred feet, the conditions would make helicopter operations through the mountains a fruitless payload.

Ben's superiors had offered his men to wear Afghan headcloths in order to not be picked off so easily by enemy mountain snipers. Down treacherous slopes, weaving between boulders, so high up in the sky on edge, the odds were risky.

Then again, Ben thought, if they were without helicopter aid at a certain altitude, it would save a lot of their equipment, while at the cost of having men suffer from frostbite and exposure. A balance needed to be reached then, to not waste a sand load of lives establishing a military presence. But weighing out riding on horseback, getting saddle sore and paranoid like the 2001 Army Special Forces did, or walking on his own two feet and receiving the patty hose from getting all dirty and dusty, Ben preferred the latter. His experience riding horses in movies was bad enough for his balls.

Carrying his M4 gun in his hands, he surveyed the breathtaking rugged mountains; perhaps there might have been a landside and no enemy at all. *Well, at least I'll get some exercise.*

Ben hiked beside Marcus in silence, the goat trails virgins to the boots of men were rugged, dusty and unkept, with loose rocks clanking on each footfall. Only a mild mountain breeze kept the mission bearable despite its uncertain swings. Mountains, from one direction to the other, expanded before Ben – many very similar but each individually distinct with different hues and shadows and shapes, some purple, brown, snow-capped, others hazy. Mountains that were closer apeared to be a part of the distant ranges, but Ben knew, being in such a vast open space, perspective was an illusion.

And this was why he loved being a marine. Seeing sights he'd never thought existed. Seeing sights he wished Veronica could see too, sights he could take her too when she got old enough to travel with him.

Going on missions wasn't like travelling as a celebrity stuntman, following around a director and movie crew to some landscape set. He'd been there and done that a thousand times over and got the t-shirts. The Marine Corps sent

Ben to *real* places. The remote, the unhabitable, the magnificent.

To Ben's right a soldier, his name escaping him, placed one foot on a raised rock, getting out his communication device and GPS. He brought his left hand out as he raised the satellite phone to his mouth. "Kandahar Base. This Patrol Ranger 75 squad. We've met the recon point: four clicks from the original drop off of the routine patrol. Status: negative. No signs of the Taliban nor the lost patrol. Over."

Ben glanced towards the craggy passes before him, beams of the orange morning sunlight slanting through the clouds in bands and sheets, casting a crispy glare over the shrubby patches along the wild mountain side. A very cold northerly breeze made his damp skin frigid, and he shivered.

Taliban. Animals. Fallen rocks. Anything. Stay alert. Ben spurred on ahead faster to keep his body warm, his boots clanking rocks of the goat path which sloped downwards into a rising incline of a land bridge, spanning a chasm of two dramatic peak faces plummeting below. An alienated squall of wind buffeted the marines, moaning through the shattered hills and valleys with cries that lamented a change in the world.

Another uneven goat trail caused Ben and the soldiers to walk in single file, passing underneath an eroded domed archway of prehistoric earth towards a massive plateau. Approximately thirty-five to forty feet wide, on the left, was a massive cliff cascading down into sheer oblivion about five hundred feet or more. Up to the right, a small mound rose which levelled out again leading up to the mouth of a very large cave imbedded within a gigantic metamorphic cairn.

Ben raised up a stiff hand signal for his men to halt. An adequate, interesting place to stop and scout. It had a cave. The Taliban loved their cave warfare.

As the soldiers responded, the air did so too. As if they had approached an altitude where the air was thinner and very cold, Ben could hear nothing, not even a distant whistle, only his own rushing blood.

However, there was movement. Up in the sky.

Ben jolted his head up, squinting at a circling ring of sinuous shadows. The first signs of life . . . Vultures that lived off the detritus.

"There's death," whispered Ben.

Perceiving the ghoulish birds, his marines loitered gingerly onto the plateau. They prowled as Ben saw Jason Laycock crane his head over the cliff, detaching himself from the unit to observe the outer perimeter of the plateau and the cliff.

"Keep tight," Ben said, clutching his gun, wacthing Marcus and another dude – his name also leaving Ben. The vultures' caws echoed eerily, dismal and fomented, possibly vexed by the signs of movement that troubled their tranquillity of dining with the dead.

Something died here, Ben thought. *And not too long ago.*

The guy who Ben called "Moron One" came from behind carrying his .308 sniper rifle. He began to take it upon himself to examine the multitude of rocks like a geologist for any signs of clues. Ben did not see how that could be useful, but he looked back up at the vultures screeching above trying to gauge the situation. Brianna taught him a thing or two about inference in detective work. With his sniper, he pointed it, staring at the cave and narrowing his eyes.

Something dead. Let's make sure it's a goat and not our men.

But Ben caught something with his eye that drew his attention. A rippled strand of rock and dirt, laying on the ground just by Moron One's boot. The soldier, stooping down, *peeled* it to the side with his hand. Then, scrupulously, he picked up a cloth – like that from a garment – dangling in his hands.

Ben scowled. *Oh, well done!* It turned out he had begun revealing a piece of camo combat uniform still partially attached to a long grey slate of rock. No. Moron One, did not find a rock at all – he'd picked up a femur bone!

Some suspenseful jolt in his body made Ben shudder, and it was beyond the cold. His heart began to pulse. The vultures never lied.

"Found something, sir," Moron One exclaimed, turning around. "I found something!"

Ben got up and continued to investigate. He bit his peeled lips as Marcus Theis signalled everyone to go into overwatch, defensive positions covering the entire plateau space.

"Disperse," Ben commanded to Moron One, Casbolt, Julian and Dan, pointing to Derek Fish with his Barrett .50 BMG. "See if this one is ours."

Derek nodded curtly as Ben took a deep composing breath. Derek grunted in disgust picking up what appeared to be a boot half buried in the sand and, within it, something white snapped in half. He reported in that on the torn boot was the American Army insignia. The distinctive coat of arms of his country. The American eagle could not be mistaken.

"Jesus Christ. I think we just found our patrol squad," Ben whispered. They had been rendered to dust, indistinguishable from the rock-strewn earth overnight. Clicking his tongue, gingerly taking a few steps, he heard his boot crunch something, break something. Lifting his boot, he saw a broken communication device, as flattened and as crushed as the pounded stones themselves. Dread instantly gripped him.

No one in their right mind, left com kits out like this in enemy territory!

"It's them," Derek said from behind and Ben stood up, making the associations. Someone or *something* had ambushed the crew, leaving their remains for the vultures.

"Strange. I see no evidence of explosives," the soldier who discovered the uniform and femur bone said cautiously from the far side of the plateau. "If it was a raid, I cannot see artillery marks. They would've been smart to have taken the communication devices, but they were just... left there."

True observation.

James Casbolt stormed up to Ben, resolute with intense glints in his blue watery eyes. He was crying? Shocked, Ben asked what was wrong, but Casbolt, smearing his eyes, said, "Just feeling lightheaded, Ben. We need to be *very careful*. I have a bad feeling about this place. The com kit... Be careful. I sense *something*." The super soldier, stout, half mad, yet keen and passionate, blanched in the face. "If the kill is down here, then *why* are those birds still flying? I sense they are wary of something," he said through gritted teeth, lowering his glance. "Animals have a sixth sense, Ben, you know?"

Ben licked his lips, assessing Dan warily stepping over ahead at the small rise towards the cavity of the cave, gun at his chest. *Sixth sense... This plateau would make a perfect goddamn outpost,* Ben supposed. *It looks abandoned though, unless... That's what they* want *us to believe.*

"Maybe an animal?" Laycock theorised, sounding more at ease, but Casbolt did not look any better about it. He looked sick, mouth hanging open, not even aware he was picking at his rifle in his hands.

Marcus Theis scowled, looking inside at the boot and femur that Derek had found. "Nah, there's no tracks. But whatever it was, it put up a hell of a fight." He tossed the boot away, grimacing without an inch of respect. Well, if the unfortunate marine had been this unmade, the human remains were more than disrespected.

"It would make a good ambush," Julian said nervously.

"Osama bin Laden," someone intoned.

"Makes no sense, actually," Laycock uttered, concerned. "There is no strategic value to this location whatsoever. Not even for that troglodyte."

"No signs of a landslide either," Ben mused in consternation. The exposed com kit device bothered him overwhelmingly.

Near the cave, Dan gasped, prompting all the marines into red-alert mode.

"What!?" Ben demanded. "Dan, what is it?"

"It's a *bloodbath*," Dan exclaimed in terror. "Blood . . . Oh, holy crap! Guys!"

Heart thundering, jogging up the incline towards the cave, Ben's eyes widened. Dan stood in the middle of what first looked like streaks of orange soil of rusty pigment, the sort of rust staining rocks, but once that he put it that way – a bloodbath – Ben could never unsee the macabre of shredded flesh, the deposited piled remains of tattered clothing, rib cages and larger segments of human bones and broken skulls, sprawled all over the ground.

Goosebumps raced up Ben's arms. If bin Laden could do this . . .?
No, he couldn't.

Adrenaline surged through Ben – he felt it in his bones. The sensation of a persisting terror, binding his feet into the ground.

Something *lurked* in the cave's mouth, in the shade. Stupefied, Dan stepped back, gun raised. Ben took a few steps back, because he thought he heard a croaking belch echo along the rocky confines, gushing out of the cave in a putrid stale wind.

It was *not* Osama bin Laden. And Ben wished it was.

Stomping out of the dark hole in the mountain, a *gigantic* mass hurled out of the cave, hair catching the light, igniting with red fiery intensity. Its skin was hairless, the colour of basalt. A caveman! A naked beast in nothing but a tattered loin cloth, wielding in one hand a long pike and a worn-out shield in the other. It bellowed loudly, emitting a sound Ben had never heard before. A gargle rising with such a provoked upsurge that Ben's eyes watered – it made his rib cage tremble as the soundwave *molested* him internally, cudgelling into the marines, clouding their awareness – a stunning of the prey.

In his stupor, Ben saw Dan breaking out, instinctively opening fire.

Faster than he could blink, Dan was skewered upwards through the chest with the pike. The giant snarling a rictus at his victim, Ben watched supine Dan sliding deeper into the shaft with a wet crack, blood dripping down its length, gun dangling lifelessly in his arms.

Combat muscle memory kicked it. "DAN!"

Ben fired and fired, until his arms quivered from recoil.

Bullets skimming across its shield, the giant roared, and even his gunfire could not drown out its long abominable bellow.

Ben fell back, Julian and all the soldiers bracketing him, forming a perimeter around the giant.

He did not need to tell them to unleash deadly force.

Through the buzz of bullets, the giant, gritting its teeth, resisted the assault from all sides. Soon that shield would give way, but it would be suicidal wasting bullets on it. Ben lurched backwards purely out of reflex as the giant leapt. It pushed Ben and the marines back, towards the cliff and the cliff pushed them towards the monster – they'd either be stomped or plumet.

Nevertheless, the marines, standing their ground, shouted in unison panic.
"Shoot in the face!"
"Shoot him in the face!"
"Shoot him in the face!"
The creature manoeuvred with such spryness unsuited for its size, it made Ben yelp in horror. Dodging, his men scrambled, maintaining as much distance as they could.

He saw Casbolt's commando roll in a ball of dust, firing at the behemoth's feet, causing the giant to lower its guard. The creature let out a grievous gasp, spitting saliva over Casbolt. It walked backwards, retreating, shield lowered. Its eyes . . . They were huge, oversized and babylike.

Only then did the bullets find their places. Splattering blood with dull thuds rapidly wounding thick polychrome skin felt *so* empowering. Retrieving the upper hand, Ben, his panic vanishing, pushed *forward*. The archaic shield and spear fell, bullets shredding the beast. It expressed pure agony it its large eyes. A hand rose to shield his face.

Ben grinded his teeth. Blood gushed from the giant's face, swaying backwards. Ben would waste all his ammunition on this thing – he did not care – he fired, fired and fired and fired.

Come on! Come on! There you go! There!
The giant ceased, overwhelmed, its head flinging back red tresses. On its fall, Dan rolled with the spear, as the giant crumpled to the earth with an echoing crash. Guns still fired a few seconds afterward, pelting its husk until the rush of battle ended and the monster was dead.

Muscles the size of an oak trunk, thick and lithe, it had to be twelve feet tall. The skin had the look of polished marble – rippling veined colours of silvery shades, dark and light. Its back bore scabs and welts, scars that had a foamy texture like blubber, but Ben was not yet ready to lay a hand on the abomination. Other parts of its mangled body were also unusual: its elbows and knees had a sort of lighter tone from the rest of the body, ridges of rougher calloused skin that too closely resembled a carapace growing from within the tissue.

A monster.
Oh my God . . .

Ben forgot how to swallow. He could feel his hands shaking from more than just the recoil of his gun burning in his hands. His hazy awareness made him dimly aware of his crew, who stood tense, breathing heavily, all eyes fastened on the beast and the younger boy, Dan, pale faced from shock, eyes half closed, twitching, the spear pierced through his body. A gargling sound. A croak from his crimson-filled mouth.

Dan. He was *still alive* and in *excruciating* pain.

10

HEAVY CARGO

"From the invasion of Kuwait and 9/11, the new Omega Plan kicked into play. The United States' hold of the British mantle in the Middle East is no small irony; political and military objectives were central to a free democratic world from the days of the Cold War to now. But for the Plan to run on ground, it needed to be built by a series of strong men, with very unsavoury and very undemocratic ways of staying in power. Irangate proved our childishness and, therefore, our troops were discharged to Afghanistan and Iraq under the banner Operation Enduring Freedom. Now we know this Freedom failed, why the hell try do it again?

Because it's an enduring illusion to save a ruined Middle East. The Luciferin Left and the Satanic Right are just looking for the most believable excuse to sell us out. The great American pursuits of a megalomaniacal goal as the British and the European powers did centuries before, is being repeated. 9/11 triggered a supernatural tsunami. It is a phantasmagoric endgame and we're that generation fortunate to live through it."

—Lecture on *The Omega Plan*, Joseph DePaula, at Global Kairos for Justice, Portland, Oregon, 11 September 2002.

Dazed, Casbolt sat rubbing dust out of his eyes, staring at the ground while the beleaguered American marines moped in the sun, which now beamed with full force out from the clouds. No one could cease staring at the monster that had been barraged to death in a bright spray of blood around its bulk; and, streaming off it, an odoriferous smell of rotten corpses.

Casbolt scowled, getting to his feet, his skull blistered by the headache. Upon hiking up to this spot, Casbolt had gradually begun to feel a heaviness in his chest. That heaviness only increased as time progressed, to a sensation of panic – of a powerful intuition to turn back and leave immediately. His eyeballs began to throb, becoming disorientated. He did all he could to combat it with an outburst of Nindingir bodily discipline. By then, it was already too late.

Casbolt did not realise he stumbled until Julian held his arm.

"It's okay, I got you."

"I felt something powerful hit me." His headache still made his head throb from the infrasound. *Infrasound, it had been from the giant.*

"Cas," Julian whispered aghast. "We had just killed . . . a . . . a . . ."

"A giant."

Like the Fomorians of old it should have astounded him too, though he was more concerned of his troubles than the creature right now. A giant suspect – the incredible pretext to why the druids and Nindingir had created the Aes Sidhe program in Antarctica.

Casbolt, swallowing his pride, found himself struck by gratefulness offered by Julian's kindness. Julian was the only one who had taken the time to read and believe his book *Agent Buried Alive.*

Recovered and feeling slightly better about himself, Casbolt beheld their perished suspect. It produced an unpleasant odour of a skunk, making the soldiers gag and one of the young marines to empty his stomach.

He always knew that there were Nephilim genetics still out there in the modern world. They were rare, but this one resembled none of the Fomorians that had been encountered. This one had no body hair but thick grey-marbled skin, its red hair twisted in dishevelled knots over the ogre's sweaty bloodied face, an unrecognisable ruin of red and black. One eyeball, half intact, stared up at the sky all gelatinous, slimy and cloudy. Cloudy as if it were blind. *Blind unless it was a troglodyte kind of Fomorian, not used to sunlight.* Casbolt could see that its upper jawbone had been blasted away, exposing two rows of heinous yellow teeth on the lower jaw.

He swallowed, trying not to double over from the putrid stench. The giant wouldn't exactly be fortunate enough to have access to the proper bathing facilities if it lived as a troglodyte . . .

How were these marines to report back to base *about this*?

"I can't believe it." Ben's voice was husky, muffled as he raised his arm to cover his nose and mouth. "No . . . This is impossible . . ."

"Weeeellll," Derek groaned. "This was *not* what I was expecting. What is it? What the hell? You gotta to be joking? Somebody punch me. Tell me, am I dreaming?"

"You're not, man," Julian grumbled. "We are all dreaming."

Suddenly, a long-afflicted groan came from Brody drawing everyone's attention. He knelt feebly at Dan Markowitz's side. He looked elegiac. "No. Daniel." He shook his head, hand to his mouth. "No. No. Hey, Daniel, hey man. Daniel, listen to me."

Casbolt scurried to comfort the boy. Inconsolable seeing the gore of his friend covering his hands, he broke down, turning away from Casbolt.

No, do something. Help Dan. Do something good!

"We need a medic!" Casbolt shouted. "Get a medic now! Don't just stand there like penguins, do something! A medic! That's an order! Go!" He really shouldn't be ordering the major of the unit around too, but Dan was dying. "Medivac now!" Casbolt and Brody together, pulled out a medical blanket from the first-aid pack unfolding it, swathing Dan.

Casbolt met the young man in the eyes, staring intently at them. Within his eyes, a spark refused to die.

Dan's lips quivered, croaking, "Marching through the earth, he . . . He casts his lightnings. The great harvest has come, the land melts. He wields a rod of iron, smashing . . ."

He heaved blood. And then falling still, his eyes stared upwards, gore trickling down his chin.

Casbolt sat back, stunned. He felt so tired, so hopeless, that he could do nothing. It had not been his role in Antarctica to bind wounds.

"He's gone," Brody groaned.

"CENTCOM, this is Ranger 75, we need an urgent nine-line immediately," Mark Randall said into his communication with a stern voice, restraining all his shock.

"Ranger 75 this is CENTCOM prepared to copy," said a dry, tranquil male voice.

"Six clicks from the recon point of lost routine patrol Nautilus."

Casbolt went to aid the majors tending Dan's body as Randall proceeded with the nine-line call. At the conclusion of it, Casbolt overheard him add, "We've found the Nautilus patrol who are no more. And our suspect disabled. Eh . . . And It's – heavy hardware. Over."

"Affirmative, standby," the dry voice through the intercom said, cutting off, drawing out a sigh of relief from Randall.

Once Ben and Marcus were able to slide poor Dan off the pike, albeit with much grumbling and contorting expressions, Casbolt saw Dan's guts issue forth from the gaping wound, squirming like crimson streams in rivulets down a rocky cataract on the ground. The marines hastily bound up the hole in his torso with bandages, laying him on a stretcher while his grievous wounds were cleaned by the soldiers' own water bottles, water, now when they needed it most to stay hydrated. They had to wait patiently with the dead colossal corpse for about fifteen minutes for the air lift to arrive from base.

During this wait, Brody Nathan lost it. As Casbolt helped lay Dan on the stretcher, the boy cursed the medivac for taking too long. He started throwing rocks off the cliff to vent his anger and loss. Eventually, though at first an umbrage, everyone ultimately sympathised with Brody's petulance. Nevertheless, waiting around with him sulking, assaulted by the acrid stink, was extremely unpleasant.

Casbolt glanced towards the cave's entrance, seeking for a way to evade the stink. *If it lived in a cave . . . The Hallow Earth.*

It clicked then. Could it be that this giant was a denizen of the Hallow Earth? The civilisation of Patala as it was known in Sanskrit? Curiously, obstinate to answer his speculation, he got up, sauntering over towards the hanging rock, M16 in both hands.

Littered all over the cave's entrance were scattered pieces of flesh, clothes, rib cages and even skulls all clean of flesh. Both animal and human alike.

It made him shudder, realising that these bones were fresh: bones belonging to unlucky young men who had no idea they would end up lost and killed by a maneater. Those who perished had families and friends awaiting their return, never to be reunited again. To the giant, it may have been its lucky day to have a five-course meal with many leftovers to spare. In a corner, Casbolt saw a large pile of guns from the first assault team all organised and neatly stacked on a flat stone surface. The cave giant had some dignity it seemed, even though that tangy smell of wet vomit permeated the very air, the order was astoundingly un-barbaric. The creature was a wretched being, and Casbolt wondered why? If it came from the Hallow Earth – Patala, a place of legend and virtue – why did wild humans roam from its caverns?

"Where do you come from?" Casbolt muttered nasally.

The cave's interior, characterised by greasy smooth stones – platforms, he realised – were eroded over as if they had been touched and walked upon for years upon years. Casbolt ran his hand along the wall. "We interrupted its dinner. Was there a family of Nephilim? A whole tribe? Are there more of these things perhaps out there?" So many mysteries unanswered. The possibilities fascinated Casbolt beyond understanding. "I think this might be it," Casbolt said to himself. "Patala." The place underneath the feet. "Yes. Michael, remind me to tell Max to organise an expedition into the Hallow Earth. I think there could be so much under our feet we are yet to uncover. *So much* still yet to be discovered."

The sound of a rapid thudding heart, the beats of the large helicopters could be heard outside. One day, he could explore the Hallow Earth. But alas, he'd rather not go missing, exacerbating the terrible day that had transpired already. Next time, he try and find Patala. Michael Oppenheim had been close.

Emerging from the darkness, Casbolt adjusted to the sunlight. The marines enthusiastically got up on their toes, eager for the escort; he could perceive that respite in their body language clearly. They wanted to end this day, and the heat was not aiding to sooth Casbolt's throbbing headache. As the thudding sounds got louder and louder, worsening his headache, Casbolt found himself approaching the husk of the giant to examine it for himself.

"Not native. That skin is not suited for outside. We need to do DNA tests to substantiate something," Casbolt muttered. "And . . . Hold on." Leaning closer, Casbolt counted the caveman's fingers, finding that it had *six*, not five. The nails were gnarly green, cracked and pointed, six digits on all hands and feet. Casbolt scowled. "What was the condition called again? Rhymed with pterodactyl . . ."

Sonorous thudding of the massive CH47 helicopter rose grandly, whipping up winds of dust, hovering closely above in the air providing a lift for the soldiers from the hatch.

"That's impossible. Impossible," Ben kept on saying, his voice strained and trembling. "Julian, what are we going to do?" he said in dismay.

Marcus Theis got out his communication device, eyeing the CH47 tersely. "We're ready to move the heavy cargo! We're going to need some crates! Over!"

Soon, from the side of the CH47, a series of thick rigging and cargo nets dangled to the ground, lowering a large durable flat crate. Seeing the marines' reluctance, Casbolt took the initiative first to lead, mostly to encourage the others' distraught nature to move the heinous Fomorian. He braved the revolting smell which tried to make him heave out his stomach many times.

"Come on! Its dead, you snow chicks. Give me a hand, will yah," Casbolt managed. Promptly, Marcus and Ben were at Casbolt's aid, their support tipping the giant's right arm over and rolling him on his belly as they groaned and sighed. But they still needed to roll the hulk one more time, so they slid it across, to properly secure it on the crate and into the surrounding cargo net. Soon Laycock, Randall, Bill Sargent and Derek were seeing to him, helping to push the thing over again. Yet that smell destroyed them all, eye watering and so penetrating it got into Casbolt's mouth, making him unable to continue. Many times, he tried to hold his mouth closed, feeling for sure he would vomit. The unbearable stomach pain slowly dwindled, eventually, as the gushing air from the helicopter helped revive him.

"Yeah, it's too big. You think you're strong enough to move it, Derek?" Laycock remarked unenthusiastically, looking unwilling.

"Gowwffh! It smells worse than a skunk!" Bill complained.

Finally, they all rolled the beast onto its back on the crate.

"Wow wee!" Derek said, holding his nose. "That *was nasty!*"

"Yeah," Laycock remarked, coughing. Julian looked so pale, and he sat down off in the distance, heaving.

"No way I'm doing that again!" Randall wheezed. "No way!"

Hands on his hips, Marcus gave a thumbs up to the pilots in the CH47. The wind buffeted Casbolt's hair madly as the helicopter blades spun faster, slowly lifting the dead giant, up into the thundering air. Casbolt watched the creature glide over the cliff towards the base, as the medivac helicopter appeared. Everyone was keen to get inside and buckle in, even dignified Marcus Theis. Already half the day had passed, but it felt like a full day. A few marines loaded Dan's body onboard and Brody, sitting in the back compartment, stayed with Dan resting in his lap, not moving, silent and staring at nothing.

"Gosh, Ben, you need a shower," Derek teased. "I can still smell that mother on you in here."

"We all need shower, bro." Ben looked away, gazing out the window with a sombre look. A shower . . . Casbolt frowned. A shower with just a pan and a bottle of water.

—

Once everyone was back resting in their quarters in the barracks, Casbolt pissed blood.

His urine in the toilet was not yellow, but light red. And it stank, cramping his bowels.

His conclusion: the infrasound from the mountain preceding the giant ambush, did this to him. During his research for his autobiography, Casbolt heard eyewitness accounts of violent encounters with Bigfoot (Fomorians), symptoms included reported memory loss, headaches and such extreme fear that, in a few hours, they returned home very sick, suffering strange bodily emissions. *Is this same thing happening to me too?*

As he sat stuck on the toilet for a good hour, Casbolt groaned, feeling as wretched and as unworthy as a snow chick in a winter storm. If the infrasound had long-term damage to him, he worried that he could never make his case to appeal his transgression of the Antarctic Treaty to the UN. Never would he be able to spread the truth and make right to the Aes Sidhe. Never would he serve in the military.

I will.

When he finally flushed, lumbering with aching pains down the hall to his room – with a thatched roof that offered not enough privacy – he entered into his empty barrack, collapsing in his bed, sighing and groaning.

That shock wave, said Michael Prince in his head. *It did something to you.*

Prince was right. It only made sense that he was hit by the infrasound – he remembered.

A low-frequency sound wave undetectable to human ears – it was not fundamentally exclusive to Fomorians. Animals used such frequencies for stunning prey and communication – species such as tigers and whales. It had been proven by departments of health and human services that a fluctuation of infrasound resonance amplitude of 3Hz to 20Hz had an array of adverse effects on the human body.

Casbolt felt numb, thinking that he had to keep his illness secret so he wouldn't have to be taken back home. He had chosen to serve and had chosen to face his crimes against the Antarctic Treaty. The Aes Sidhe needed to see that he cared and that he was still strong to live a good life. He couldn't afford to be sick!

But letting one's reach exceed his grasp, would only have his arm cut off in places like this. He lived among stone-cold professionals in the US military and Casbolt realised the dreadful possibility that he could fail in his mission and everything he set out to do to build himself back up could be in vain.

Gasping, Casbolt buried his face in his hands. He was so tired, and his stomach still roiled.

Don't be surprised, you fool, remarked a firm chastising voice from within. *Casbolt is used to letting people die. Casbolt is used to having to put up with browbeating. Casbolt expects to be mistreated. Yes, Casbolt doesn't care. Casbolt is a worm!* He stared at the ceiling, face to face with a haunted-eyed man that had been molested, that had given up on caring and trying.

"I have changed," Michael Prince whispered, recomposing himself. "I am not a murderer. I am not a wretch. I can rebuild myself. I can appeal my crimes. I can show the UN and the Aes Sidhe that I haven't perished. I will change!"

He begged, looking towards the dark ceiling of his empty room on the bunk, hoping that if there was a God or gods up there, they would give him an answer. He could be yelling at the bleak wretch up there too. But God, he *needed* an answer. "Protecting this world from evil, from the Fomorians and the Cabal, is more important than my wretchedness. I want the people around me to live and not go through what I have endured. At the very least, that is all I want. Please. Please, God? Help me save them. Please." His voice sounded raspy to his ears as he bowed his head in loathing, pouring his soul from the deep recesses of his heart. "Save me from myself."

That was it. He was trapped in a mind filled with conflicting personas that clashed in his head like icebergs at sea during a storm.

The super soldier's burden, Michael thought.

When the darkness finds us, we will face it – alone . . . Casbolt thought.

11

NEPHILIM

"As Dr Karla Turner states in her book Into the Fringe; these spiritual beings have always wanted to probe us. In fact, forget Independence Day, these parasites need us as hosts to survive! Every time a person is abducted there is an invasion. There are many sophisticated ways to invade than to just use weapons of mass destruction. If the principalities and powers behind government systems that neglect the oppressed can control the way we think, the things we see, the things we learn and how we emotionally respond to the news, then Satan has already won the world."

—*Lecture on The Omega Plan*, Joseph DePaula, at Global Kairos for Justice, Portland, Oregon, 11 September 2002.

Arhat Alfred Bonner of the Alliance arrived at Kandahar yesterday, following James Casbolt to keep intelligence security over him. He *could not* afford the Redlion to become a lose canon, especially after the disaster in Antarctica, but also, he could not let him know that he was here. The Bennu bird had led Alfred to this place for something else. The Bennu had sung the Dynamics to him verse by verse – the document he wrote that would save the world from the Galactic Tyrant.

Rostau. The key to the clamorous geopolitical, social human mess. That tomb had to be somewhere in Warka. He hoped the archaeologists were not aware of it, and he especially hoped the marines would begin their invasion into Iraq soon so that operations could be underway smoothly to attain the tomb.

But today, Alfred left that agenda aside and manoeuvred out towards the roaring loading bay docking a grey Boeing C-17. The report came in this morning; James Casbolt's rescue patrol unit had found a suspect, sent an emergency medical vac *and* a large cargo, to import back something . . . significantly giant.

Today, Alfred thought, *the gods are returning.*

There, laying before the colossal plane, was a large crate covered by a huge blue tarp. If anything like this was lying out in the open, news would spread, and pandemonium would burn with it.

The pilot of the Globemaster approached Alfred with his headphones and mic on his head. Alfred, clasping both hands around his back, towered over this unenlightened gentleman, the sonorous noises of the engine blaring loudly, inhibiting easy speech. Scattering all the maintenance workers, they went to work, making sure the plane was ready and refilled for the next flight.

"Sir," he said to Alfred, making himself heard. Alfred glanced towards the two babysitters of the cargo – three-star air force generals – who approached the newly arrived batch of American troops for announcements.

One of them caught Alfred's eye, a younger slender marine, carrying a digital camera who looked like someone who wanted to take photo of everything and send them back to his parents to cherish his journeys. Alfred Bonner, long, long ago had been like that to an extent. Eager to show everyone what he knew, in order to not be neglected.

"Hey, no cameras," a babysitter said strictly to the boy and, frowning ruefully, he lowered the camera. "Nobody is taking pictures here. We are moving some high-value hardware. Top secret, boys."

The pilot gawked at the general, looking curious, clearing his throat. "Eh, will I be moving *this* hardware sir? Is this why you came?" He pointed to the massive pallet.

"Yes," the elderly general replied. "Director Alfred Bonner has authorised that we do not have the facilities to leave this laying around here, do we?"

"You are correct, sir," Alfred remarked over the surging engines. "I'll take it from here."

A forklift vehicle whirled from within the holding compartments, ready to escort the cargo. The pilot noted that, nodding in affirmative. "So you are Director Bonner? Alright. I will just – Oh!" The pilot held his nose. "What is *that?*"

Alfred gazed at the tarp. And that smell billowing out of it was indeed filthy and needed to be put away immediately. "Another one," Alfred intoned turgidly. He covered his nose, sauntering towards the pallet, and lifted a portion of the tarp.

Exposed was a pale marbled knee, dangling off the edge of the crate, connected by extraordinary lean sinews. Asura skin – coarse yet smooth bumpy tissue. Afghanistan's native people here did not closely resemble the Nephilim's pale complexion. Definitely a rogue Ullikummi from Patala. Aggregations of flies and maggots buzzed around within the tarp over the giant's rotting corpse. Peering at the feet, and just as Alfred expected, just as the Hebrew Bible said, he saw the feet had an extra, incongruous digit.

Polydactyl.

The six nails were pointed and cracked like rows of shark teeth growing fungus. A common trait of the Nephilim – offspring of the gods and the daughters of men. Creatures of nightmares. Bringers of chaos.

"It was transloaded out of the mountains by a CH47, Director, after a firefight," said the general to the pilot.

"Get the next flight to America to export the specimen," Alfred said. "Take it to Wright Patterson Air Force Base for further examination."

"Yes, Director." The general turned to the pilot. "Excuse me."

Alfred turned back to the pilot. "Pilot, do everything I say."

"Yes, Director!"

The pilot began to examine the creature, utterly marvelled. He took his foot and placed it next to the giant foot for comparison – twice as large as his own. He slumped, looking up at Alfred in astounded disbelief.

"No way," the lugubrious man intoned. "No . . ."

"Fascinating, isn't it?" Alfred lingered behind the pilot. "And disturbing. Yes, just wait until the world sees this."

The pilot blanched and Alfred smiled. "But he's . . . Has to be *half a ton*! I'm taking this?"

"Yes. You take it." And Alfred expected that these people knew *exactly* what they were doing – it was not his business – they would perfunctorily take the Nephilim away, and he would continue his whole purpose here – keeping James Casbolt from ruining Alliance plans to secure Warka – the ultimate aim of the American war effort. And these officers followed orders from people of the higher echelons of society ignorantly, blindly and without question. Sometimes it did not hurt to tell a lie that had no intrinsic weight to it. They would never see it in their apathy. "We need to keep the public safe from fear. Experiments need to be done as soon as possible. We are not alone."

Alfred stared down at the bewildered pilot. If everyone knew about the existence of ancient giants roaming the wilderness, mountains and forests, then they would go extinct. It was simply public safety requirements and common sense, which needed no epiphanies from the Bennu to know. Cover up needed no dark conspiracy at all, only public safety and wildlife preservation, so that no one would panic and pillage.

So that *no one* would waste their lives trying to hunt these beings; there were already too many fools out there trying to catch them on tape – the world needed fewer.

The hunters would never discover the cryptid – a trivial unknown creature – until the creatures *wanted* to be discovered. Alfred knew, the Dynamics foretold, and because he had spoken to the Gla-kees (Hairy Ones in Navajo) of the American woods themselves, he knew. Known locally as Sasquatch, they were all over the Earth: Wendigo, Almas, Mapinguari, Yeti, Yeren, Yowie. Reclusive to humans, the woods were their homes, the leaves their beds and fruit their food. Extreme measures to incorporate these giants back into the fold of society were both a logical and pragmatic.

By taming the forces of chaos, the Nephilim could be defeated.

Alfred said, "This is the official report: we do not have any record about a special forces member killed by a giant in Kandahar. It is a tall tale from bored marines trying to kill time." He turned to the crewmen. "Get us fuelled up ready to go. Set course for Ohio."

12

TO TAILOR DEATH AND DECEIT

"But all this said, remember Romans 13. Let every person be subject to the governing authorities. For there is no authority except from God, whoever resists the authorities resists God. So, I encourage you, pray for the peace of Babylon. Pray for America and Israel, folks, for goodness' sake. Do not fight against Israeli occupation. Protest for peace, yes, but do not fight. God placed us in this time, where wicked rulers rule over us, because we are wicked people. Pray for the peace of Babylon...

Bush and the United States government are not just looking for oil in the Middle East, I can bank on it. It's more complex than this. These white European secret societies that have ruled our nation since the founding fathers, need avatars of persuasion. Avatars of spirituality. Avatars of sorcery.

They need the Beast, from the cradle of civilization."

—*Lecture on* The Omega Plan, Joseph DePaula, at Global Kairos for Justice, Portland, Oregon, 11 September 2002.

Chain of command insists that you *all* rewrite your after-action reports, to negate and keep under wraps any reference to the *unusual* in your mission. Let's keep this quick. Without any hassle."

Lieutenant Colonel Judd Pounders was a tanned, bald and stout man, with a short neatly kept beard, and a large forehead. Grey hairs streaked the corners of his face, though still retaining a lean body, he possessed a disfigured nose that had been broken many times while in battle. He wore an immaculate formal dark green general uniform patrolling through the room as though he were a disappointed principal, his voice hardened but measured. He was in his fifties.

However, Ben *did* feel like he was at some after school detention, as if his men had violated the wildlife. He soberly sat attentive, and reluctant, before a computer screen with hands hovering over the keyboard. Why should he be disciplined anyway for following protocols and remaining honest with his superiors? What did he, and any of his men, *do* wrong? If any enemy provoked attack, one did all that it takes . . . Right?

Bastard protocols and regulations, Ben grumbled bitterly to himself. He glanced at the soldiers around him, all tense and wincing.

"I have a question, Lieutenant Colonel," Derek Fish said gingerly.

Pounders stopped pacing, turning daggers back at Derek. He maintained his poise, looking pathetically frustrated to have been interrupted.

"What about the death of Lieutenant Daniel?" Derek asked. Were these Afghanistan authorities going to be that cruel and bury him in secret without a funeral because "a giant that doesn't exist" killed him? The Marine Corps couldn't go that far lying how their man had died without an honourable procession march. It went against their purpose. Self-sacrifice would always be privileged over superstition, even one that Ben knew he could never deny. And yet, he had a feeling deep down that the biased world did not operate as simply as that. That Galileo Effect indeed!

Pounders paused for a long time; the silence buzzing in Ben's ears. "I understand the frustration. But if you want to continue in the Marine Corps, then all information regarding the creature cannot be spoken of. It will draw too much attention. America is just about to mobilise into Iraq, and we cannot be associated with fairytales of trolls. It is common sense." Pounders grimaced sourly with an abhorrence to this negligence to Dan. "I am just as prohibited to be outspoken about it to anyone. As you know, Derek Fish, that means Dan died in a routine training exercise . . . *Unfortunately.*"

Ben rubbed his face in frustration. An overwhelming sense of disapprobation emitted from the soldiers. Ben frowned, wrath coalescing within his chest as he saw the newbie Brody Nathan flaring his nostrils disparagingly. Ben jolted out of his seat then sank back down again abashed by such fury. He wanted to punch something. He glared at Pounders and oh, how he wanted to pound that Pounders good!

The Colonel sighed. "Look. I understand the concerns, and the CIA have this under control. They have concluded that this debriefing must be in respect to the native Afghani villagers. By the broadcasting of a legendary race of giants to the world, it will allow for cults and ambitious entrepreneurs to flock into the country and the Afghani don't need that. We are at war here. We are protecting the people from the Taliban. That means at times, compromise must be made if we are going to strive for the greater good. In the meantime, then, the mandatory requirement and task for you, is to sign a confidential." He placed cold hands on Ben and Casbolt's shoulders, leaning his head in between them. "And that is final," he concluded softly.

—

"When you're wounded and left on Afghanistan's plains," Demos recited as he folded the ironed pants of a dead man. "And the women come up to cut up what remains, jest roll to your rifle and blow out your brains, an' go to your Gawd like a soldier."

"What was that?" Casbolt asked dryly. "The way you said it, it sounded British." The motes of death clung to every part of Dan's possessions as he ironed the Class A blazer.

"Kipling," Demos replied, seemingly trifled.

Quite inappropriate, Casbolt contemplated, *but Demos has his fascinating artistic quirks.*

Yet again, it would have been nice in a heavy-hearted way to remember Dan, however, he knew this tedium would be all for nothing. To make a lie out of Dan's death.

Blast out my brains this is morbid. May Dan's soul dwell in the Otherworld in peace. Forgetting this world where he's been dishonoured and his heroic death against a Fomorian slighted. May he always forget this world in the Otherworld. May he.

While ironing Dan's blazer, Casbolt dazed about the futility of life and the futility of the deaths at his hand.

"Disclosure agreement . . ." Ben scoffed, with stammering lips. With a steady stagnant wipe of his hand, he polished Dan's M4 carbine and his other weapons with a cloth. "I know. I know. This sucks. Freakin' hate my life. I want to die like Dan."

"Dan deserves more," Demos said. "He needs Hector's burial."

"What?"

Demos chuckled.

"Look man, I do not know what is more embarrassing," Laycock said while pulling out Dan's boots. "Telling everyone Dan was skewered by a naked caveman or his obit saying he died during a *training course. A training course! Crap!* How humiliating!"

"Right. Or you could always say the Taliban snipers got him," Brody Nathan said, bumping into Casbolt nonchalantly, carrying Dan's casual wear to the table nearby to fold them. "Ha. Lie upon lie, upon lie, upon lie. Just lie and be cool with it!" Suddenly, Brody slammed his fist on the table. "*Far out!* Can't even tell his *family!*"

"I know. I know," Casbolt said. While neatly laying out Dan's service ribbons, he sighed. Service ribbons of honour and an honourable young man who had died in a training exercise. A sheer paradox – a shameful humiliation to Dan's family, incurring great *geas.*

After cleaning out the locker, Randall came down to Casbolt and Ben as he carefully folded and placed Dan's beret in Ben's stack to clean and dust. Both men were still tense in body language, and Casbolt noticed an unconscious stigma coordinating him and Ben while Randall ironed. His face looked so hard he could chew on that burning iron and not even care he'd been marred.

"Well, we know the truth and that is all the really matters . . ." Casbolt said. He wanted to say something more to lighten the mood but lost the words. "It's in our hearts."

"In our hearts," Demos parroted sourly.

"So, you're saying those in power have a vestige to keep this story covered up? And you are just going to let them do it? Let them get away with it?" Ben placed the gun down, a blood vessel in his neck protruding from stress. "And we have to all *shut up?*" Ben roughly shoved one of the guns onto Casbolt's operation desk to clean. But that was not his job. "I'm going to the toilet."

"Best not to talk about it right now," Julian said, taking initiative to continue cleaning the guns that Ben had left behind. "It's been a rough day."

"Agreed," Laycock said.

Casbolt proceeded ironing the arm of Dan's Class A jacket, which would soon be worn on the corpse in the coffin to decay. What was the point of that then? Who was he grooming for? The worms? Or perhaps the gods? Even though he contemplated the purpose of ironing the uniform, it just felt *honourable* and just to do so, despite how futile it logically seemed to honour the individual transient lives each human lived. All this effort to tailor death in a morgue of decay.

A memory rose to the surface, of Druid Dwyvan – a man of erudition. When he first met Casbolt, learning he had family in London, he called it "that wild place" and Casbolt, a "wild one". A joke Casbolt himself never understood to this day. *Death is never the conqueror,* Dwyvan had said. *Death is a door of reincarnation into the Otherworld – the ideal paradise. A birth of a child meant death from the Otherworld. This was why Greeks and Latins were confused when they saw Celtic peoples greeting birth with mourning and death with feasting and celebration. Transmutation is not a Hindu-yoga thing. It is a cultural Indo-European, Yamnaya thing that adapted and changed in different regions. We, the West, lost this reckoning due to Christianity. But to Xenophnes' bafflement, even Zalmoxis of Thrace and the great Pythagoras, knew the druids.*

Dan, therefore, was comforted in Paradise.

Bill Sargent finished polishing Dan's boots. "You know, I think Ben's right. People have the right to know what is going on. I believe what I saw. I am not mad."

Just then, a door in the delta common room burst open, with Derek Fish tumbling inside, gripping a blank piece of paper in his hand. "Yo, where's Ben?" he asked, looking around the room. "I have been looking for him. He has a eulogy to write."

Laycock pointed out the door. "He's at the toilet, Derek."

"Okay. Thanks." As Derek left, closing the door, everyone turned their eyes to Casbolt.

"Casbolt, come with me," Demos said and together they both began to gather the cleaned polished uniform, preparing to dress Dan's corpse. They entered into another room to await the funeral supervisors who were coming with the washed and embalmed body.

Casbolt shivered. When an Aes Sidhe died, they were not cleaned or tailored. Their state was left as they were – once they entered into the ice pit, they would freeze solid and remain as they were in the state of perpetual honour – at the point of *kleos* as they had died – a warrior, to enter into the halls of Valhalla. The ultimate *nostos* – homecoming – into the bosom of the gods. For Casbolt, tailoring death reminded him of a type of materialistic unsavoury Egyptian's obsession with death that spent too many resources on the transient.

"Soon, Casbolt, soon, we Achaeans are going to have to meet Priam and give back the body of Hector, so his spirit can be at rest and Troy too, at least."

Demos' literary analogy made perfect sense. He hoped the injustice around Dan's death could be dealt with. "For now." Casbolt nodded, holding Dan's clothes in both hands as the coffin rolled inside pushed by the funeral attendants. Made up and covered in a cloth was Dan's perfect ageless face. Crusts of dried mucus sealed his mouth, eyelids. In the end, Casbolt had a vague idea how the story of Troy finished.

A tragedy via deceit, in a world of collapse, fires, sacking, slaughtering, and dislocated peoples.

—

Rushing down the hallway, weaving in and out of bystanders, Ben hunted and finally found Pounders. He could not explain it or understand why he wanted to fuss over the killing of a giant, but something about today's events made a part of him want to break free. To do something about it when it did not seem right.

"Colonel, sir," Ben said abruptly grabbing Pounders' shoulder. As he turned around looking indignant, Ben took a deep breath. "It is not right. We have no right to discredit Daniel's death without his family's permission. I'm sorry, sir. I need to find an alternative or I cannot live with myself and the men."

Pounders responded with a single-sided grin. "You got any other ideas, soldier?" He chuckled. "And stop being so dramatic."

"Sir, with all due respect," Ben remarked, "to be recognised for one's participation in war is to be valued. Not to be pushed aside for some insidious agenda to hold back information."

"Ben." Pounders sighed, rubbing his temples, his eyes searching Ben's face. "It is not about an *insidious agenda* to hold back information. I agree with everything you said, but I can't guarantee people are ready for the truth. I am *extremely* sorry for Daniel's passing. I really am. Nothing can be done about it." He looked behind his shoulder and whispered, "Unless you swear to tell the truth to those that are closest to him of what happened, but on this condition. Tell them they are to keep it to themselves."

"But *why?*" Ben said, lowering his voice so only Pounders could hear. "Why not tell everyone that a giant killed him? What will it achieve but more . . ."

"We are bound by professional ethics to keep institutions safe," Pounders remarked dryly, an ingenious spark in his eyes. "*This is why*. If we tell the truth, everyone will think we *are* lying and the consequences? The President and his cabinet officials have the right to annul us from serving in the war for disapprobation and ineffectiveness. And then? Iraq and Afghanistan will never be saved. Terrorism will take over the Middle East. It's for the sake of our country and the people of Iraq. My agenda, Ben, is *honour*."

"Yeah but . . ." Ben stammered, truly stumped. He lowered his glance, not willing show weakness to the man he had looked up to for a good while in his life. Irked, Ben trembled. What would people think of him being humbled and castigated? Ben scowled so hard he heard Pounders sigh. "I . . . just don't want to be part of a *conspiracy*."

"Ben." Pounders sniffed with amusement, sounding friendly. "Ben. Sometimes you need to slow down and realise you do not always have full control of everything in your life. A man cannot be a man if he is so arrogant to hold on to everything and refuse to respect the circumstances around him. We need to know what to do with the time that is given to us. It's no use to complain. After all these years I have come to know you very well. You have a wonderful family, a wife and a daughter. Everyone is inspired by you. They imitate you and look up to you. Even I cannot help myself sometimes to go – wow, this man never lets anything bring him down. I *know* I can rely on you, and you have *never* failed me. There is nothing more profound than a man's trust in honour – the ones he cares for. You *are* that ideal man, DePaula." Pounders then smiled. Ben stared at him, shocked. "I know. *I know*. Sometimes, in life, you need to make difficult choices that your instincts may not always agree with."

Those words rang within Ben like a bell fusing into his being. He felt some pride dashed out, stress dithering, relaxing. Yes, feeling more confident *always* helped. Confidence was what made a man and if a man lost confidence, he need not be afraid to ask for help from a man that did. Responsibility, Ben knew, made heroes out of men who learnt from the heroes that came before them. Then they *acted*. A man of action. He shall be the inspiration of strength, self-esteem and courage to the young men around the world that lacked that. Such confidence kept Ben alive.

And on top of that, *true honour, dignity, involved a great sacrifice. And in this situation . . .*

God. *Now* Ben understood the full picture. He shook his head in abashment. "I'm so sorry, Colonel. I am wasting your time, aren't I? Sorry."

"No," Pounders said, remaining dead serious but intimate at the same time. "Not at all. You are a good man, Ben, and I thank you for being there for everyone. People will listen if you're passionate."

Passion . . . I could use passion to portray myself better.

"Major! There you are!" Derek Fish was running down the hallway desperately.

"What's the rush, Derek Fish?"

"Colonel, sir," Derek said, saluting, out of breath. "Here, Ben, it's for the funeral. You're speaking for our boy."

Ben took the paper and thanked Derek because he knew in this speech, he could be the best passionate inspiration for everybody.

13

THE SHINAR MISSION

"Imperial history often concentrates on military rule, but it's more often than not revealed by interventionism of alliances, protectorates and trade concessions to secure imperial interests. Britain displayed its preference in the Middle East. When British occupying forces in Baghdad or Jerusalem partitioned the fragments of the slain Ottoman Empire after its six hundred years of rule, they proclaimed that they came as liberators, seen when T E Lawrence and his Arab Bureau enthusiasts promised Sharif Hussein of Mecca and his son Faisal an Arab state. These promises were not cynical ploys aimed at tittivating annexation; they were part of a strategy of influence and hegemony that was always central to British imperialism."

—From *Omega Plan: The Epicenter of Light and Darkness*, Joseph DePaula.

Ben held his head feeling trapped, sitting against his will in the briefing room surrounded by the marines, most of whom he never knew. Here, he found it increasingly frustrating to see the three Colonels standing still in front of each of the locked doors behind them, reducing any snooping.

But what haunted him above all, what chilled him to the bones, was the giant of Kandahar and the consequences and the implications. The fear he felt was unlike anything he'd experienced in his life. He still couldn't wrap his head around why the secrecy over Dan's death at the hands of the creature if the Marine Corps truly cared about Dan. If they did…

Ben sighed, too tired and too dumb to figure out and resolve this ethical conundrum himself. Let alone Pounders. It seemed a cop out and unethical to flippantly diminish the giant's importance and lie about Dan's death. Lying was a vice, but was it *always*? Was honesty unhelpful in *some* circumstances? If only Ben could have done something different about this, if only he could change, to take matters into his own hands... But there was no use now.

Once everyone was dismissed, Ben followed his team in silence when he felt a hand on his shoulder. "Benjamin, can you come with me, please?" He turned around and found Judd Pounders awaiting him.

"Colonel, sir," Ben blurted out.

"You're not in trouble," he said, voice low. "Just want to have a few words with you." He smiled. *What is he at here?* Ben must have looked befuddled as Pounders patted him on the back, escorting him away from the group and leading him to his office past the operator station.

Once inside, Ben, after being told to close the door and to sit down in front of Pounders' desk, the Colonel went to consult a stack of files on his shelf. "You are probably already aware of why you are here," he said as he slid one particular file out, placing it before Ben on the desk. On its cover it said, stamped in ink-black characters: SECRET.

Procrastinating, Ben bit his lips as Pounders offered him a seat, but he refused to sit down. "Colonel. And what exactly will we be looking for then?"

"You will be fighting the war you signed up for. You will be facing off Saddam's regime, but you will be stationed in places that have peculiarities." He performed a swirling motion in his chair with diplomatic hands in a diamond shape under his chin. "It has been confirmed to offer you a new assignment. The Shinar Mission."

"Yes, sir," Ben said, nodding, a bitter taste forming in his mouth. *Shinar . . .* "And this came about after the killing of the Kandahar giant?" Even just saying that sounded jarring to Ben.

"Yes. And it pays for a re-action and a solution. This will be a great experience for you as well as the other men. I detect potential for astounding change. Ever since 1947, countless documents and data has been assembled over the decades to confirm that there is indeed a legitimate threat out there."

1947? What threat? Ben shifted on his feet uncomfortably, his hand beginning to fiddle with the document. He curled his lip. "In what way will this mission help us depose of this threat?"

Pounders leaned back on his chair, interlacing his fingers together. "That is a good question to ponder, Benjamin," he said. "To not overwhelm you, in essence, there have been sites hidden in Iraq for centuries that might be helpful in our situation."

Oh great. What did I expect? The next expedition of a lifetime, the next page in history will be Ben and his marines, finding that giants truly do exist. Why not just kill some terrorists and go back and play stuntman for another blockbuster?

Ben raised an eyebrow. "Are you serious?"

"The Pentagon and the Alliance has authorised that three units of seven men for field ops to lead scouting teams outside Baghdad, Warka and Samawah," Pounders said in a matter-of-fact manner, not breaking Ben's gaze. "We will have other checkpoints along the way too. So, I decided to put you in position as Captain of the Eidolons – a unit within the broader 75th Ranger Regiment led by Colonel Mulholland."

Ben started. "*Captain*, sir?"

"The chain of command must be established," Pounders replied, his voice sharply potent. "That said, you will still retain a great amount of your autonomy. Not only because of your father's service during the Vietnam War, but your proficiency overall and diligence and passion, makes me believe you are suitable for this job."

Ben, feeling torn, shifted weight from one foot to the other, watching Pounders reach down, acquiring a sheet of paper titled: *Mission Skill Requirements*. "The promotion is for you . . . if you wish to accept the offer."

This is something, Ben thought, meticulously looking at the sheet and then at Pounders. "I . . . I need to think."

Pounders got up from his seat to pace, saying, "In most times I will be too busy to devote my attention to a team and reporting back to a chain of other Colonels." Ben began to skim through the documents as Pounders intoned, "I also do not intend to ignore your counsel as a major. I say this as, after you are efficiently trained, you will answer directly to Director Alfred Bonner, who organised this mission. He is the one that coordinated his meeting between you and I."

Ben looked up at Pounders, then at the maps of the modern Middle East on the wall. Alfred Bonner. The name rang a bell but . . . he could not put a finger on it, all Ben knew what he was getting himself into did not exactly add up to what he wanted to get himself into. The knot in his stomach said so.

"Where will we be training and when will it start?" Ben wondered.

"Here at Fort Huachuca," Pounders said, leaning a hand on his desk. "It commences at the beginning of the new year. On January fourth."

Ben swallowed, steeling himself. "I have a suggestion. Will I have say in choosing those of my unit? There is no one I trust more than my boys."

Pounders peered closely at Ben, possibly discerning his unconscious reluctance. "As I said, I *will not* neglect your autonomy as captain. This is the same for Marcus Theis – captain of the Ageis Unit of the Rangers. We have full trust in you to embark on this vital task. I understand that you have served us for a long time. With the death of Dan, we insist you fill twenty more slots." Pounders leaned his hands on the back of his chair, pausing. "So, do you think you are up to the task?"

Ben grinded his jaw, wrestling with his will and recalling Pounders' own words from before. "Yeah, I should be able to do it."

"And even some members of your unit in Kandahar will be absent. Especially Brody Nathan."

"Brody? Didn't he just enlist? What did he do?"

"There has been a complicated change of plans." Pounders sighed, beginning to pace again. "He *will not* be partaking in the Shinar Mission with us for *particular* reasons. If he did not complain, I would have decided to not employ you in this position, but I guess circumstances are in your favour."

"I'm sorry to hear that, but I'm sure this can be worked out," Ben said, finding himself almost choking. "What did he do wrong, sir?"

"Defied command and lied. We found out that he was said to have handed in a signed copy of his non-disclosure agreement, that we forced him to write. Upon further investigation, he sent us an unsigned *and* an unfinished report."

Woah, Ben thought, shocked. *That's not cool.*

And there was more, as Pounders went on. "What he did was unacceptable and immature, such behaviour will not be tolerated here in the Marine Corps." In the punishment of Brody, Ben couldn't help himself feel sympathy for the poor rookie. He hoped he found himself a better job now elsewhere, now that he'd chosen to give up so early. "I do not wish to chastise you, Ben, but, in contrast to young Brody, you showed ingenuity and promise, which is why I am giving you the task that I would trust to no one but myself. The men will rely on you." Pounders relaxed. "Do I have myself clear?"

Ben nodded, hardening his expression. "Yes, Colonel, sir, it's very clear."

"You will not willingly disobey or question commands."

"Never again, sir."

"Good." Pounders eased himself back into the chair facing Ben personally. "If you want your way, Benjamin, your team will need to be switched on by the end of February." As Pounders spoke, Ben continued thumbing through the files, seriously pondering the matter. "Double duty training will be required for we cannot afford to lose operators."

Ben met the Colonel's stern gaze, feeling brisk and excited. *So, intense workout training? Alright, I am up for that.*

"Are you ready, Captain Benjamin DePaula?" Pounders held out his hand, and for a second Ben studied it. The whole time, Ben had refused to take his seat. He grasped Pounders' hand, firmly shaking it. "I knew you were up for it," Pounders said, smiling. "But now it's time to pay the Markowitzes the respects due, and after that, we'll get down to business."

14

CONDOLENCES

"And yet, French and British control of the Middle East, envisaged in the 1916 Sykes-Picot agreements (Britain gaining Mesopotamia, Saudi Arabia and Palestine, and France gaining Syria, southeast Turkey and Lebanon), did not go as planned. Indeed, Woodrow Wilson's Fourteen Points dismantled this secret European agenda thoroughly. In order to secure oil and sea routes to India, the Cairo conference of March 1921, attended by Churchill, Britain clinched a bilateral deal. She would aid an Arab government in Iraq, the Royal Air Force (RAF) entrusted with its defence and Emir Faisal would be offered the throne.

Under law, Iraq was Mandated – a temporary colony, providing equal accesses in trade. Article 22 of the League of Nations justified this civilising mission as, 'these people are not yet able to stand by themselves under the strenuous conditions of the modern world.' Here, Britain and France are cast as saviours of the White Man's Burden tradition, as saviours of the Middle East. Emancipation will thus be subject to the approval of mandatory powers."

—From *Omega Plan: The Epicenter of Light and Darkness*, Joseph DePaula.

Casbolt stared insipidly at the flower-framed portrait of Daniel Markowitz, its spangled colours bleached from the sunlight, and thought he saw his blurred reflection on the glass that held the image's frame. The young boy – a fresh recruit portrayed on the image – wore his new combat uniform proudly at the bright and fresh age of nineteen. He smiled with an honest, truly enthralled smile back at Casbolt – a smile that displayed accomplishment, a smile that held nothing back.

It *mocked* Casbolt. Daniel had a successful short life lived to the full and Casbolt, in his late twenties, hadn't.

The lacquered pristine coffin of black wood overloaded with flowers, bilious to the eyes, gave off pleasant pungent aromas. The coffin sat, still framing the body of Dan sleeping in peace, casket open, wearing the immaculate uniform Casbolt himself had ironed. Tailored for Death.

He stood quietly for a long time as the ceremony dragged on, sweat dripping down his neck. The hot Arizonan sun in his own Class A uniform, irritated Casbolt's skin. He could feel the heat radiating off his marine comrades' blazers next to him, in a stiff disciplined line all facing the coffin. A small crowd of people – familiars and friends all in black and white – congregated behind, standing up in the funeral yard as the folding of the flag ceremony began.

The symbolism was tragically perfect – the folding up of a life, to be put away, to be forgotten. Many in the crowd were wiping tears from their eyes with white handkerchiefs. The new captain – Ben DePaula – saluted Daniel's father Braydon Markowitz as seven honour guard soldiers in army blues ceremoniously raised their rifles, aimed on a slanted angle in the air, shooting in pierce order.

Marcus Theis, also in Class A uniform wearing ivory gloves, completed the folding of the American flag, handing it over to Dan's father. Braydon stood as still as a pole, sweat trickling down his face, damping his cheeks like tears. A masquerade shining with perspiration.

Ultimately, Casbolt was not so sure; it was not easy to say, not easy to look into the breast of another. Discovering the secrets of the human heart were hard to fathom, even for the Parvus Perception.

Striding in front of the coffin imperiously, Marcus Theis held his position next to Ben. Captains of their courage and of their fates, they stood like two chiefs of Taradan – their titles being the Agaid and Eurypontid.

Ben, with a dominating senior posture, unfolded a piece of paper, his eulogy speech. "Staff Sergeant Daniel was a resilient, courageous warrior and, most of all, a true friend." He paused. The soberness of his voice captured much of the gravity of the passion emanating from the crowd. "He served his country proudly, and loved his family dearly, and never hesitated to put himself in harm's way, even if it meant saving lives. In the last three to four years serving under my command, I am proud to acknowledge that Dan had one trait that I myself wish I possessed at his age: perseverance. No matter how hard – or how *large* – the task at hand may be, Dan would be there. Ready."

Casbolt heard a muffled wince, sensing Brody Nathan, wearing a formal suit, clenching his teeth, his tight eyes reflecting pain. He had left the Marine Corps because he refused to lie about Dan's true manner of death. But would he truly ruin this holy moment now and unleash the bombshell upon everyone? Casbolt could read discreetly, Brody's eyes – he'd been nourishing that possible outcome for a long while, and then, perceiving the muscles and the anguished rush in his body language and the way they worked together, the Parvus gave a vague conclusion to Casbolt: *Brody's gay.*

Finally, a single little tear flowed in a rivulet down Brody's cheek, dripping down the lip of his mouth.

"Dan was a good man," Ben continued, as clear as a practised narrator. "Probably one of the best men I knew. And I am sure everyone would agree that in all honesty, he will be remembered. He will be missed . . ." Sniffing, Ben looked up from his card, choking up as he scanned the various members of the audience. He saw resoluble Bradyon Markowitz holding the flag nodding stiffly with appreciation nearby.

In the front row, Daniel's mother sobbed aloud, accompanied by Daniel's older brother holding his forlorn sister's shoulder. Casbolt looked towards Daniel's family – their eyes, hazel and amber – were trained on him like sniper's eyes, taking aim at some truth that they imagined he and the marines held at their hearts. Did anyone here even think twice over how Dan died? Perhaps better to not consider that now, they probably all thought it was a freak accident – and in truth it was!

Ben slowly turned around, leaning over Dan's coffin, whispering, "Rest in peace, Danny boy . . ."

As the Markowitz family mourned, the honour soldiers closed the coffin. The casket was lowered into the pit in silence, as Ben and Marcus stood at the edge with hands behind their backs.

Casbolt saw Braydon sitting down on the fold-out chair next to them as the rest of his family who were all standing around him, passed relatives, expressing their condolences. Yet Braydon sat there, alone and still, as if he were invisible from the din. The father slumped his head, still holding the folded American flag, an upside-down triangle in his hands.

Up the aisle approaching Braydon was a small tight-knit family holding hands, shoulder to shoulder, that did notice Braydon. A man with stringy hair in his sixties, walked down with his family and Casbolt recognised him.

It was the adamant Joseph DePaula – Ben's father.

"We're sorry for your loss, Colonel," Joseph said, placing a hand on Braydon's shoulder.

Braydon didn't even move. With his sunglasses on, his emotions and his tears were concealed. He just sat there, succumbed to comprehend his defeat.

"You're . . ." Joseph attempted to say as he quickly rephrased his words, eyes caught in Ben's pensive gaze. Casbolt detected tension there. Fierce shame, reluctance and hatred. "You're all in our prayers."

"Thank you. Thank you . . ." Braydon grumbled, biting his lip. Casbolt struggled to hear clearly but it sounded like, "No one is listening", or something.

Then all of a sudden, Brody Nathan let out a stressful series of grunts, storming past Casbolt to Dan's sister, Sheila. She looked really pretty with a few freckles over the ridge of her nose with nice dark red hair, and she was close enough that Casbolt could smell her perfume.

"It's not fair," Sheila said softly, shaking her head, tears flowing irrepressibly, making her eyeliner melt down her eyes ghoulishly. Speechless, Brody stared at her in sorrow and dreariness. "I . . . I do not *believe* Dan died the way they say . . . I knew him."

Brody placed a soft hand on her shoulder. "I know Shelia, but . . . I'm sorry . . ."

"He was a diligent man," Sheila said with a breathy fragile voice. "But something's not right."

Brody's face blanched, breaking her gaze as if he realised something dreadful. "Nice to meet you."

"Brody?"

"I've got to go," he said in a trembling voice and with that he left the girl offended and bewildered.

Casbolt lingered at the cemetery a little bit longer strolling around, heavy in heart. He found himself sauntering over towards where the officers and the soldiers were among the graves of past soldiers, and lingering behind trees and cairns, he saw an impeccable man in a cloak, with short styled blond hair, a square chin, scar down his left cheek, too impassive, too pragmatic in this crowd to be unnoticed and unannounced.

Casbolt froze, eyes widening in fear. *No. No! It can't be him!*

This was it. Casbolt had been caught. Just as he thought he could get away with it, Alfred Bonner had found him, and justice for his crimes in Antarctica had caught him. Alfred had the power now to withdraw Casbolt from the marines to impeach him.

Casbolt's chest filled with concrete. His heart began to palpate. His blood pressure rose, in anger at this erudite man, but the dread in him for being found out was much greater. *At ease,* Michael Prince reassured. *Be calm. Don't bring up the Aquarians or the UN. Just… act. Beat around the bush. Evade. I've got your back Spartan.*

God, he felt so skittish. Paranoia afflicted his limbs and his jaw almost quivered like a sexually abused helot as Casbolt tried to remain aloof. He turned around, seeking Demos to talk with him, acting as if nothing ever happened. But it was futile – Alfred Bonner's eyes were keenly watching Casbolt's every move. Demos and the other marines, morale boosted by Ben's speech, luckily, didn't discern anything amiss.

As Demos left, Alfred Bonner slowly sauntered to Casbolt, and he braced himself ready for the end of his mission. Casbolt was sweating profusely, panicking.

Bonner was six foot six and he pursed his lips, towering over Casbolt unperturbed. Those blue eyes glittered, pristine like that of a statue. "Is that a way to greet an Arhat of the Fourth Initiation?" Bonner said calculatingly, noticing Casbolt's pallor and sour expression.

Shock and confusion hammered in Casbolt's chest. "It's just a surprise to see you here Arhat," Casbolt said, clearing his throat. His heart was storm within him. *Have mercy upon me! Please!* "Wonderful evening isn't it?"

Bonner was stone-faced. He would have none of this. "Strange to see the chief of the Iceni so far from home. You forget," Bonner mused serenely, his voice creeping. "I formed the Redlion for combat. You would be a great marine. I've come to wish you good luck on your new assignment."

Casbolt's Parvus read Bonner furiously for an inference of truth. Could it be that he had forgotten about Casbolt's crimes? No, certainly not, Alfred Bonner was a genius, with a sophisticated mind, so perhaps he wanted to talk about something else. Casbolt relaxed a tad.

"It was *you* who got me enlisted!" Casbolt said, timider than he liked. "Why? I want to know because I… I've not been… You know, I've been…" Casbolt's mind when blank. And then panic flooded him once more.

He's read your book! He knows your secrets, your motivations, Michael Prince said. *He cannot have imperfect thoughts at the Fourth level of Initiation to Ascension! Now, he's coming to punish you for your terrible portrayal of the elites and the Nindingir! He's here to… give you what you wanted.*

"You fluctuate too much," Bonner prodded dryly. *Like a man in black!* "Decorum. Remember, let your actions do the talking." The bastard put his hands in his pockets looking ahead. "It was very brave and courageous of you to step out in faith to leave the South Pole to join the marines. I approved of it. I convinced you to join."

"Why?"

"I am here for an objective."

"And what is that?" Casbolt said.

"The Shinar Mission. Your new assignment in Iraq. The Alliance is orchestrating it."

Casbolt's mouth dropped. Instead of dread for being caught for his misdemeanour, now he'd been stumped by something so unexpected, something so shocking, that he couldn't believe it.

The Alliance – Alfred Bonner himself – had intentionally permitted Casbolt's recruitment into the marines for his secret mission to Iraq. Without this pretext, he wouldn't have fit the bill. He would have been rejected because of his resident alien status and his multiple personality disorder. But why had Julian been so sure to enlist him if that was so? Was the man ignorant…?

Or was Julian an Alliance informant?

A sly grin crept up Alfred Bonner's face. "James Casbolt, keep up. As Arhat, I have mouths, ears and eyes in the military. It is paramount for you to participate in this task of the Shinar Mission. The Alliance and the Cabal are at an arms race. Iraq is vital, because if we are to save civilisation, we need to understand how it began. This is why I have taken the initiative to capitalise this limited chance. We need competent soldiers on this mission to protect the antiquities. To protect world heritage sites and culture." What did cultural heritage management have to do with Saddam Hussein? Casbolt tried to infer what such a goal could mean for a larger Alliance agenda to thwart the Galactic Tyrant, but his Parvus had no luck.

"Gilgamesh has a tomb," Bonner continued. "And it has been discovered. This is our answer to the Galactic Tyrant. We can find ancient power that has endured millennia to conclude our quest. It is above flesh, and above spirit. A power unlike anything seen by the world until now."

Casbolt fidgeted with the cuffs of his uniform. When did Bonner become so fascinated by archaeology and ancient philosophy and how could it help his psyop to control the American Marine Corps? Indeed, his social psyop was very deceptive and ambitious, the Alliance's interest in Mesopotamia made sense. There, it was said, the gods from heaven first arrived and gave hunter gatherers social orders and an agricultural society. What power over flesh and spirit could exist there?

"All this, you use America's mobilisation?" Casbolt questioned. "I see what you're doing. You've created a psyop."

"Yes," Bonner smiled smugly. "The Dynamics have me do so."

The Dynamics was bullocks. It was the prepper's bible for how to survive the end of the world and how to create a flourishing human culture out of the calamity coming from the Galactic Tyranny. Casbolt's bowels were seething so much from the rollercoaster of emotions that he almost felt constipated. When was Bonner going to address the elephant in the room? Casbolt was left in anguish, the pain of anticipation.

A thick cloud suddenly overshadowed the sun as Bonner rotated his steel neck, eyes thinning at Casbolt in such a way that it reminded him of those times Bonner was so imperiously intelligent, where all sympathy and empathy decimated from within him.

Alfred Bonner was *almost* an Ascended Master. *Almost* non-human. It seemed suddenly apparent to Casbolt, after all these years, he'd always thought he saw two different people operating in his head. A dark side and a light – he had never given it much consideration until now – he doubted Alfred Bonner was aware of a sinful motive when acting righteously.

"Why?" Was all Casbolt could say now.

"The truth needs to succeed. There is no compulsion of religion higher than truth. This: a political goal from the grizzly bloodshed of the twentieth century, the past cries out to the evil of the future to change, like a woman in the street crying, 'Return, oh you simple ones, when will you listen to discipline!'"

Casbolt's eyes widened. The Parvus failed. *Bonner is difficult to read!*

"You are still programmed to not think *against* the Dynamics. The real enemy are *not* warped minded Arabic extremists," Bonner said scathingly, shaking his head.

"The Galactic Tyranny is the enemy," Casbolt interjected, irked. "The Evil One. The greatest threat to humanity as we know it."

"Good. Good, you're still sensible. This isn't a psyop, it is the truth. The psyop is the Iraq war. You were bred, along with the other super soldiers, to fight the Galactic Tyrant and the Nephilim, not human despots. The Alliance of the Light for millennia are working shrewdly to cancel the Galactic Tyrant's coming. And if we do not secure the cradle of civilisation and its secrets, humanity cannot *truly* win. I wish you good luck and success on your new assignment."

Casbolt watched the Arhat amble off. He made sure the man was gone, and as he returned to the other marines, Casbolt felt a sense of impossible peace and comfort.

Could it be that Alfred Bonner was supporting and backing Casbolt in his mission to appeal his transgression of the Antarctic Treaty by serving in the US and the Alliance's Iraq mission? But how will the Alliance achieve their ends? The tomb of Gilgamesh? *What is that?* And above all, what did this have anything to do with the Galactic Tyrant and preparing society for the coming threat of the Nephilim Fomorians? Did Alfred Bonner come to create the Shinar Mission because of the Kandahar Giant? And why didn't he mention the Aquarians and the Aes Sidhe program's breech of the UN Treaty?

It was all too much for Casbolt, a million thoughts and emotions travelled a million miles an hour in his body. Taking a deep breath, he steeled himself, and sauntered back towards the captains with nothing but a bottle of alcohol on his mind.

15

THE ENVISAGER'S GRAIL

"At that time Jesus answered and said, 'I praise you, Father, Lord of heaven and earth, because you have hidden these things from the wise and intelligent and have revealed them to innocent children. Yes, Father, for so it pleased you well."
—From the Gospel of Matthew, c. 80 - 90 CE.

Those little words carved within prayer niches, gazed down at Joshua Tanrıöver from the bespangled stone wall of the mosque. Those dense arched tabernacles were adorned with elegant calligraphic Islamic phrases, cluttered – squashed – densely within the tiniest section within the arch, as if the artists had run out of space to write. Joshua wondered how one could possibly read the prayers all in there – he was fluent in Arabic to be a con artist – this *mihrab* had to be purely art for art's sake. In total, there were forty *mihrabs* in this mosque.

Here the slopes of Jabal Qasioun, according to local tradition, the forty Abdal's (saints or prophets) spirits rose from the deep shafts of the mountain to say the night vigil prayer. Saints with the power to fly, run up walls and break the bow in two. Such superstitions were endemic in these areas of the Middle East. Joshua was resolved to find how poetic that tradition could be for him and his pseudo-archaeological team. It would reinforce his skill as a con. Spiritual saints were nothing but fascinating to the curious open mind.

Just a few minutes ago, no one could have fathomed that the Cave of Blood contained a third floor underneath his feet. The cave where Cain, according to the Bible, supposedly buried his brother Abel after murdering him.

Soon, Joshua would have the dig report of what the archaeologists had found.

The mosque's low ceiling was built within and out the rock of the cave itself. It was decorated with a long Persian carpet and prayer mats facing a niched mihrab, holding a stone basin which held the mountain's "tears", mourning some desolation of primeval times. On either side of him were seals across the stone walls, all painted white abreast an archway looming over the stairs, descending deeper into the cave. The chamber was small and cosy. Framed pictures of Islamic iconography – Quranic verses – paintings of mosques, a small stack of books and a metal pitcher for holy water, were the only scant features of the boring, anti-iconographic first floor, excluding the forty tiny niches of the Arch saints. The Qur'an said no image of a living thing shall be made least one commit *shirk* – associating anything with Allah. So, Muslims used non-natural entities – characters of letters and numbers – to decorate their mosques to avoid idolatry.

Giddy, Joshua disembarked out of the mosque, back outside into the afternoon sun. At the lip of the cave's entrance, at the terrace point, was a protruding hanging rock folded like a tongue, almost giving the vague impression of a hand having sculpted this solid rock.

Though Joshua would have spent most of his life travelling the world and providing for his poor family, he was particularly fond of the Middle Eastern sun kissing his skin a nice golden brown. The sun's own simple necessity to set in the west was gorgeous, the golden orb still mildly warm. It allowed Joshua to gaze down from his cave at a grand panorama of the city of Damascus, laying out in the violet haze. Here, he could hold the entire city in his hands.

Joshua himself felt scrappy after a three-week survey of the area with a short black beard itching his neck, chafed by his *keffiyeh*. Sweat rolled down the face of each man he could see. His archaeological expedition could be mistaken as completely illegal but surprisingly, the American Military was willing to help fund Joshua's team in their dig, and if Joshua were caught, then according to law, the entire Marine Corps would then have to pay great penalties. It was always a good feeling to use something as a means to an end. This was why they had come as, while the marines dwelt with political discord, Joshua could use that as a diversion, so he could pursue his passion to fulfil both the needs of his commander, his patron archaeologists and ultimately, his father. A way he could never get caught but by creating diversion after diversion, it showed all the virgins how expert and experienced Joshua was.

Go, my son. Be something different. Here, I went to the pains to give you this lucky chance to escape from this cruel world. Go, do something with your life. Make your dreams come true. His entire family would be proud.

Joshua had been so many people in his life, he'd lost track. His father went to all costs – to lie – in order to have Joshua eventually become a winging millionaire. Joshua did not care if he gained fame or not – he had Fortune's Wheel turn in his favour – why blend in when he could stand out?

Joshua noticed how a careful cluster of Druze soldiers that he had hired, protected two Palestinian workers who carried a long item wrapped inside a tarp, strung up with rope. The men chattered to each other in Arabic as they loaded the covered item onto the trailer of the ute. *Excellent! We actually come to find something of partial significance.*

Joshua jogged up to them calling their attention in Arabic. The Palestinians were so excited that they stumbled over each other's words, interrupting one other to the point of a quarrel.

"Eh! Eh! One at a time please," Joshua pleaded in Arabic trying to break the fighting brothers up. "Take it easy! One at a time!"

All he wanted was just a quick report on what they had found in the *Magharat al-Ju*, the Cave of Hunger, on the other side of this ridge. But the Palestinians could not stop arguing and bickering at one another.

Joshua gave up on them, sighing, he would leave the Palestinian men at it, if it seemed they had struck gold – good for them, Palestinians *needed* gold!

The truck took off, leaving behind a billowing trail of dust. The sun was beginning to set, causing the small green dome on the mosque's roof to glow with a faint green luminescence.

As Joshua approached the tour guide, he inquired on their applicability for descent. This tour guide by the name of Makam Arabaeen, wearing a khaki jellabiya with a turban carrying a notebook of diagrams and recordings, walked up to him smiling.

"Getting anything from the diggers down in there?" Joshua asked in English with a Turkish ascent.

"Yes, we did," Makam said. "Digging under the *Muqqadim* on the second floor has opened up a secret tunnel closed off from entering the *Magharat al-Dam.*" The Cave of Blood. Where Cain killed Abel. The man sounded ardent with inquisitiveness. "Joshua, you – you might uncover something that is pre-Islamic. I . . ." The man vacillated, staring off into the mosque. "I'm also a bit nervous, you see. I hope you can understand."

Pre-Islamic . . .? Now *there* was something to latch onto. Joshua nodded to that sentiment. "I understand." Wrapping an arm around the man, he began to stroll with him. The best tactic of gaining people's best interests when you did not actually value them as much as they thought, was treating them with overt displays of fondness. "I have the *best* idea of what to do. Here, we can do the dig and make some surveys as we descend, then hire academics and experts to do their studies. That is, if we find anything down there. But I'm sure your expertise is enough for us; you know what I mean, man?"

"Thank you, Josh. I'm obeying you. You're the leader here." Makam grinned, chortling as Joshua patted him on the back.

"Alright, my old friend, I want to thank you, because behold, our Holy Grail!"

Joshua arrived at that threshold of becoming world famous – the first to dwell under the holy mountain, confronting its mysteries first. He'd learnt in his years to not be paranoid anymore of those who spied on him on his expeditions but to simply be aware. Pretend that they did not notice his true intentions.

"Alright, let us get moving," Joshua said, turning towards the Druze guards and a cluster of diggers. "Let's hope for the best." The diggers mirrored his eagerness, and soon Joshua began descending into the new cave. He took a deep breath, making sure that some of the Druze guards were stationed outside the fenced courtyard as well as on the terrace and the building's roof, paralleling to the dome.

Progressing inside, climbing down the stone steps into a tall cavern painted with plaster, which over time had started to peel off exposing bare rock, Joshua lowered himself into a small cist in the ground brimmed with smashed tiles. One by one, his team lowered themselves into the shaft. Tense with anticipatory ardour, Joshua's heart thumped. The air was still musty after epochs of being enclosed by earth, so once the diggers had found this shaft, they were recommended to leave the cave to air out, so one would not suffocate or breathe in the bacteria. Since he did not want to waste money to afford expensive respiratory equipment, Joshua had to restrain his excitement for an onerous long while before it was safer for him to enter. He wished that he could have been the first one down to see the cave, but he let his Druze guard with guns and flashlights go on before him.

"Follow on, Makam," Joshua whispered, pressed against the chalky wall of rock as the soldiers, diggers and the tour guide went on ahead. Joshua, stretching his knuckles, quickened his pace.

"There she is," Makam whispered, crouching on a low ledge, shining a small torch. "The Salt Maiden."

Joshua realised the flashlights caught a gleam of the skeleton – it looked fragile and small enough to safely say it was a woman, though none could be entirely sure unless studies on the pelvis were made substantial. He swallowed loudly. She was laying on her back in the dust, perforated hallow legs spread-eagled, arms akimbo, bones encrusted in salt that sparkled hauntingly in the flashlight. Her jaw, which had been jarred open, affixed in a slanted sneer.

"There are no grave goods here, Josh," Makam said. "It's a sacrifice to Jahannam."

That's what you think – as a true expert – but I, as a jack of all trades, can come up with answers one narrow minded could not. We need more multidisciplinary perspectives. Joshua proceeded, weaving in around boulders, ducking and slipping under narrow spaces. The team finally advanced into a newly breached slit in a towering slate wall – cold and unnaturally hewed.

"Look at this," he said, his voice echoing. "Looks perfect, as if someone carved this."

Two diggers with buckets loaded with debris holding pickaxes stood at the entrance, promptly moving aside without a word. Moving on, at last, Joshua stuck himself into the narrow-hewed fissure, out into a dark chamber. Indistinguishable echoes rustled, rattling into a cavernous darkness that indicated the hallway grand.

"Josh?"

"Yes?"

"Josh, I'm right here," Makam Arabaeen's voice warm against Joshua's neck. "I think there is a warren of caverns in the mountain, Joshua."

"I think so," Joshua replied. *Yes, we have definitely found something here of note.*

A series of clicking sounds emanated from the vast void before him. The Druze guards freezing in rigid formation, stood in the air that seemed to solidify.

"Alright, we need to—"

Slowly a deep-throated cracking growl grated the walls of the vast chamber. It bounced everywhere – eerie, like a purring snarl of a great cat. Joshua embraced the shocking chill – the chill of fear. *We're not alone.*

Deep from within the vague darkness, where there should have been no life, a thunder rumbled. Joshua, jumping out of his skin, hissed as a bar of flaring light blighted his eyes. With the power of the sun, the light seared

Joshua's eyes. He covered them, albeit blue afterimages imprinted and danced before him in the black.

As for the Druze soldiers, they hollered at the powerful flares of orange. Staggering backwards they fired at the faming rod.

A glaring band of plasma, twirling rapidly, became disorientating to observe. The scary part being that the ghost flare swung with a viciousness, and a sentient agency, not disturbed or even aware by the streams of bullets that came its way. The plasma sword so bright to the eyes, it even left a trailing corona behind it – an afterimage blistering with heat. It arched and swung and slashed, floating towards the soldiers, shredding them.

Flash.

The ghost sword pulsed with a ripple of orange.

Flash.

A glistening breastplate appeared.

Flash.

A roar. A flaming mane. A feline face.

Flash.

A hybrid form.

It deflected all the bullets, a high frequency vibration piercing Joshua's ears. That *powerful* soundwave drowned out all other sounds in the cavern. It even cast a single soldier to the stone floor, motionless on the spot.

"Oh my God!" Joshua screamed. "GO!"

Those that were unlucky, survived, howling and scrambling away. The spitting blade of light sliced through a soldier who *exploded*, spontaneously combusting on impact. The guardian struck another, his body erupting into a lurid conflagration, not even barely suffering the full brunt of the blade. Just by being *near* the fire sword it was so powerful; it made a soldier's skin steam and melt off the bones. Many soldiers shrieking in close rage all roasted to death, smoke rolling off their bodies.

Running and almost tripping, Joshua clamped his ears shut, his heart's mad thundering racking his body. No. He had gotten *all this way*, bypassing all manner of authorities with fraud and false passports; he had faced many things, but this . . . This was *not* human. It was *not fair!*

"JINN! JINN! JINN!" Soldiers wailed the name of the thing.

Joshua, gasping for his life, groped the dark rock wall blindly for the escape, sobbing. Shadows scudded across the fissure. The roar of a lion following him, heaped up scathing condemnation upon him as he scrambled right back to the hole, sticking his head out. But he couldn't move through!

His satchel had gotten jammed in the thin, rocky gap.

"Allah! GO!" Makam screamed, ramming his body against Joshua determinedly, bruising his elbow and his collar bone. "GO!"

"We're going to die!" Joshua lost it, hitting Makan. "WE'RE ALL GONNA DIE!"

"JOSH!" He squealed as an ear splintering grinding snarl came from the lion. Joshua screamed like a woman. No! He *would not* die! He had *so much* money not spent yet. Why had the Wheel of Fortune turned against him now when she had been so faithful? Joshua gritted his teeth, clutching the wall, his loins bustling with adrenaline. *Oh, so sad to die like this!*

Quickly, Joshua tried to dislodge himself, but Makam screaming unrestrained hindered him a moment. Liquid from the man's bellows splattered over Joshua. He turned, looking back, shocked, watching hopelessly as his screeching tour guide *rose off* the ground by some invisible hand, dashed against the ceiling. The lion-headed Jinn punched his left fist into the air, walking forwards. Closer.

Electrogravitics. Joshua's teeth chattered, slipping his hands back into the gap to make another evasion, slicing his fingers in the deed. Hissing, feeling his bladder giving way at an upsurging roar of the lion, he shut his eyes, felt the blistering scorching heat coming off that sword like a looming oven, arousing something ugly within him. A black flame . . . Joshua, squirmed.

Burdened by his bad luck, Joshua screamed at the top of his lungs, making a last final push, his arms convulsing wildly.

Scraping the rock, he fell, dislodging. Gasping with laughter, Joshua sporadically crawled cackling and sobbing – he was alive! As he tried to recover from his aching heart, he came face to face with the Salt Maiden her contorted smile of her skull mocking smugly. *I tried too,* it said. *Come and lie with me.*

He smiled at her too – he would like to, the issue was, she was all bones and salt. And why did the cave feel so cold all of a sudden?

A roar cracked the air along with the surging sword, flashing like a scar of lightning from the slit.

Joshua sprinted as fast as he could in the dark. His breathing sounded so wretched and laboured, wheezing raw dexterity. He forgot how to blink – he needed all sensory awareness at full capacity now. If that creature found its way out of the cave . . . *Don't! Call Pounders! Call freaking Pounders!* Ripping out his satellite phone, he made the distress call back to base.

As Joshua heaved himself up onto the tiled floor of the mosque, he burst out in the open and skidded to a stop, arms flailing. He saw something worse than the Jinn.

A hit squad of Syrian Shabiha with their large black semi-automatics, leaping off trucks, Druze guards and the diggers dead in the dust before them.

Joshua pounded down the hillside as fast as he could, trying not to twist an ankle. He would *not* get caught!

As he ruthlessly skipped, dashing down the barren hill, Joshua heard his pursuers behind charging down upon him, barking exclamations, trying to get an accurate shot. Breathing arduously, twisting and turning haphazardly to confuse the Shabiha, Joshua swooped behind a row of boulders, bullets chipping into the solid orange rock. He backed against the rocks, catching his breath.

"Come on, Pounders!" Joshua whispered desperately. Of course, he had to say he was an intelligence service man, in nothing but in name. "Pounders, I'm becoming Swiss cheese here! Make haste!"

To Joshua's exuberant relief, the barking Shabiha obliviously scampered past his injudicious hiding spot, scaling down the hillside – their footfalls picking up wisps of dust behind. Circumnavigating the boulders, Joshua crept, looking urgently around him, hunkering down among a cluster of brambles. He crabbed, his head craning through a slit within two eroded outcrops, seeking for the Shabiha's activity ahead. A contingent was breaking off from the main, turning back around, heading right back up towards Joshua.

He sprinted the other way.

I need a new plan. New plans were always within his reach. Mostly. While desperately sorting out his options, the blessed beats of the helicopter permeated from on high – the beats of salvation calling for him. It made Joshua regain the willpower to run as fast as he could, his feet thundering the ground, his breath in cohesive rhythm with the rotor blades, winds seeming to buffet him.

Cresting a ridge, swinging into the grey, purple sky; a shaft of glorious light beamed downwards. The run was brilliant; if he could make this stunt, even scathed, he could survive. He *refused* to believe that he would ever fail. This far, he had come *this far;* the adult authorities could not catch him now!

Head throbbing like a second heart, dust spitting upwards into his eyes, the chopper spun around its left flank, the gunner door sliding open. Dangling down from a whirlwind, a rope ladder hung, fifteen metres in front.

Wind, dust and bullets whisked past Joshua, the helicopter at the centre of his tunnel vision. He leapt from his run, grappling onto the ladder furiously. It dangled and he yelped, but every time he pushed up, the stupid rope flayed upon the wind. What fool designed rope ladders!?

"PULL UP!" He heard the doorman yell above. Guns crackling below, Joshua tried to protest, as vertigo seized him, the chopper dragging him along at a great speed. He clung to the flimsy ladder, winds battering him. He spun as he tried to climb – one false move, and he would plummet to death.

Utterly immobilised, the ground vanishing farther and farther away, Joshua, looking up at the beckoning doorman, made a one-step climb.

A powerful, stinging pain erupted from his leg and up into his body. He howled, arching his back, abbreviating his roar as he slipped. Joshua gasped, his arms hooking one of the steps, legs drumming. He spun around faster, then twisted back and around again in an incessant flipping and nauseating circle. His leg *screamed.*

They had struck him. The lucky shot.

"NO!" the door man bellowed, looking back inside the cabin as Joshua trembled, from wind and pain and shock. Snarling through his teeth, he tried again to move, using his upper body. The helicopter accelerated. He gave up. He could not do it.

Then the ladder tugged, hoisting upwards by a supportive hand. Joshua, his vision growing misty tried to force himself to see, to hold on with all his might, to climb – he had to . . . The fog grew thicker. His ears were foggy, assaulted by deafening noises.

Help . . .

He crawled up another step. It exceeded all his strength.

The ladder floundered in the wind, rising on its own into the vessel.

With trembling exertion, a vice-like arm grasped Joshua's collar, everything in his awareness bellowing with pain. He flopped on the ground, tears streaming down his face.

Joshua had a vague awareness where he was. The doorman started to tend his wound by wrapping his thigh in a cloth. Joshua whimpered in frightful affliction.

"You freakin asshole," the man cursed, analysing the blooded leg and the gore, shaking his head. Joshua groaned. Judd Pounders was going to be Judd Pounders. An amused angry man as always. "Is he still breathing? Answer me!"

"Yes, Colonel," the other man said. "You seriously want to take *him* with us?"

Joshua slumped gasping, breathing laboriously, nothing on his mind but the dumb unbearable pain.

"Quick, before it gets infected," the man said to the gunner.

"We have company!" Pounders shouted from behind. He'd promised to help Joshua – he'd paid Judd Pounders a lot to help him. If these people had known who Joshua was in truth, would they have saved him? Unlikely. They probably still thought he was an ally. Good. "The police are on our tail. Enemy chopper at three o'clock!"

"Judd," Joshua groaned. "I failed."

"What!?"

I . . . Did I fail? His con had not been discovered . . .

Joshua would never return to Damascus again.

———

One Week Later

All Joshua Tanrıöver knew, were the four walls. Four bland flat planes the farthest one with a heavy locked door and a single shutter. Some supervisors peered through that every once in a while, but often rarely with notoriety. Days passed, and Joshua did not care.

Four walls . . .

All this for a dig. All this . . .

Within the grey filthy box, he had a few bundled clothes. At the back, a basin and a toilet with no windows, a bowl for eating lay on the right corner – often his sense of direction banishing him – and his bed to the other side. That was it. Only the grey padded walls and pasty ceiling, motes of dust clinging to every corner, nugatory and sterile.

On the first few days, Joshua paced, occupying himself with a book he'd brought along with him – a boring travel guide to Syria and Lebanon. Since he hardly spoke to anyone, he quickly finished it. In the meantime, he did exercise in the penitentiary, push-ups, sit-ups, mountain climbers, squats – everything he could think of to keep his mind going. They said after his injured leg was healed that it was essential to keep the blood flowing to stay active. He could not remember who said that, only vaguely recalled it had been important. He had nothing else better to do but eating, washing and sleeping. Soon as the stale repetition became routine, he adjusted. Then after a few weeks, he deteriorated into a state of boredom.

During these twilight days, Joshua exercised less and less, feeling more fatigued. As the weeks went by, he saw no one. It made his anger seethe, because he'd been held against his will, unable to see any soul.

His sleep patterns started to vary and rupture. It tortured him that he had no idea of the sun and moon, there were no windows. It would take him an hour or more of bleakness to fall asleep, feeling . . . numb. And then he would wake up at some time, he could not know, feeling like he wanted to be sick. This happened with the dread of being alone. What crushed him and slowed him down was that he *terribly* missed human beings and nature outside, and what they sounded like. Indeed, the only humans who ever came in were cleaners and those who replaced his food; they never glanced at him.

He became, to them, an object. Dehumanised. Justly so – Joshua had used many people in that same way. So, in return, they never spoke to him and thus he spoke only in dreams. Fantasy. He woke up, unfulfilled, desiring every day to sleep. Sleep was his desire – it never left his mind. When he dreamed, he envisioned a better future.

Once his strength began to dwindle, he would pace and mumble in rambles all his knowledge to himself teaching himself about his passions and the cultures from the west to the east, everything he learnt, with none to hear.

After a week, guilt set in, lethally. It came without warning. It drained all the willpower out of Joshua. He could do nothing anymore, he gave up on reading, finding no interest – he'd quit exercising. He tried to speak to the occasional cleaner and the people that tried walking up by beating on the door. They spoke, but never to him.

Soon, it became ever apparent to Joshua that everyone forgot him. His leg and his soul started to hurt even more. He often would arch his head, shaking it, cringing at random failings in his life, all his miseries, mistakes and actions, all his attempts of fraud.

Groans slowly mutated into screams. His mind jolted in a desperate battle to stay alive. He would speak to his mind, slurring and yelling. He relived the worst moments in his life. He saw many possible futures, of what course he could be leading into from the actions he made – could have made. The anguish of knowing he could have done otherwise...

Joshua writhed. Some people that did come along had an air of notice but with cold grim eyes, they jotted down notes saying his random fits, meant a lunacy condition.

Then the void came. Those times, he could not move. In those times, he drooled, coughing with a cold and crying a whole lot. He would tear up his book, the pages, flicking through them in a frenzy.

He had nightmares too. They were psychedelic dreams – Joshua had tried drugs before that were said to give such visions, but not recently. These strange iridescent dreams were full of fractals, stars spinning and collapsing in on each other in geometric patterns. A thousand patterns repeating each other in a fractal, filled with stained-glass windows, combining and melting together. He saw himself being arrested in the Damascus hospital. Judd Pounders speaking to Shabiha guards. He saw visons: of things that could come to pass in the future, of forests being denuded, of sea creatures beached in their millions, of seas turning into blood, of pollution destroying the ozone layer, of great fires burning the land, storms destroying cities.

It was nauseating. The fractals and the patterns never ended.

He tried to meditate why and how he got here, and how his misfortunes had culminated upon him. He had been so terrified when he faced the lion with the fire sword. He was chased at Damascus, his leg was shot, and at the hospital in the military base — he did not expect it, mostly, that the police would find him so easily there, dragging him into Hell. It made sense why the American marines could not do a thing — Joshua had trespassed illegal property, holy property, without a government permit to dig there. Fair enough, Joshua had been slightly too ambitious to uncover the Cave of Blood. Joshua also wondered if he hadn't been the only one caught. The other workmen and diggers he had may have been caught as well.

Yet Joshua could hardly believe he had been caught, he felt numb about it. All his crimes so severe, he rightly deserved this sentence in a mental asylum.

Lunacy. A state of lunacy. He sobbed.

He wished he could see his family in the fractal dreams and one by one, cry on their shoulders and hug them, for forgiveness.

From a young age, Joshua came to the resolving conclusion that adults didn't have any idea how the world worked. He remembered deliberating about it, when an adult once told him to do something, he resolved within himself that it was probably best to do the opposite or twist it, doing it his own way. It *precisely* showed that he was an individual, not that it did any harm — did not Disney say, "Follow your heart?" "Wish upon a star?" Did not Descartes say on the same lines: *cogito, ergo sum*? I think therefore I am?

To be a rebel made kids individuals. This has been reinforced when a ghost — a fallacy but not to a child — floated around in corners, at nights, on misty days. Joshua remembered being stunned at his grandmother's house — which was haunted — hearing all the music and dancing and seeing apparitions of men and women in fancy dress and suits, dancing with one another. Kavals, kemenches and baglamas played. One of the ghosts at the party, a friendly shepherd with two dogs on a chain, told him that only children could see him because adults have been deceived by lies.

Turning the truth into a lie.

So, Joshua took it upon himself to change, to show his family how he could get what he wanted by making them *think* that he trusted and loved them. It only turned out to prove the ghost as true, and every man a liar. Irksome, selfish adults had *no idea* what they were talking about, so naturally, Joshua sought the best alternatives to this world that required no toil: forging passports and cheques to get by.

Because of this ideology, he was able to amass millions of dollars to help his parents in Adana. By travelling the world, pretending he was a pilot, an archaeologist at Patara, Myra, Ephesus and Baalbek, a bouncer here, and a lawyer there. All the while, he learnt Arabic.

Life became a computer game; it required shrewdness to trick authority, getting away with fake passports, saving fraudulent files from the police, escaping before being caught – becoming an invisible man.

The ghost's wisdom though, *was not* the wisdom Joshua wanted now. He beheld the four walls of cold confinement, coughing and hacking until his body trembled with exertion, knowing fully the weight of his wretchedness. He had found a name. Not one he thought he would find in his quest for knowledge and deception. He found out what it meant to be honest, humble and contrite.

Now that ghost's advice – that demon – got him closer to death than anything.

Go, my son. Be something different.

Be something different.

Go, be something . . .

Be something . . .

Be . . .

Dead.

"Waste. Waste. I… I need to… come out."

He fell asleep and, there, he was a caterpillar. He squirmed out of his egg and with an undulating body, he crawled for survival. He fought, nibbling and munching on leaves. He ate and ate until he grew all fat, spun for himself a cocoon, trapped in the terrible trauma of clogging isolation and imprisonment. A massive monstrous abominable critter!

Joshua woke up with a start with no blankets, his breathing rattling in his ears. He was no longer in his sleeping bag, he'd had kicked off the walls, tobogganed across the floor, thrashing so violently in his sleep, he had made a ruckus.

Joshua.

Wait . . . Was that a light? He had awoken the asylum? The neighbour perhaps could not sleep. For a minute he considered the soul next door, and for a lull, he froze considering his egotism. The only world he ever knew was *this* cell. He loathed himself for being selfish and not being able to do anything about it.

The faint light did not go away, however.

Joshua?

Someone knew his name. He started with a yelp, exacerbating coughs, his sore mouth. He faced the pink glow emanating warmth, showering dappled pools of light upon him.

"What?" Joshua could only shudder.

You are a very bright, talented fellow, a careful, timid voice sounded. *Why did you do this to yourself?*

That roseate illumination smiled indulgently, it seemed. The four walls he had sweated and lived in, flushed with its colour. A splash of gelatinous orange-and-pink colour, shifting, moving slowly, flowing flowery tentacles of a jellyfish that drifted lethargically in the silent twilight of the deep ocean. It glowed with the dappled rays of sunlight passing through the pelagic. Sublime and majestic, relaxing to the eye – the soul – to watch the comb jelly ripple. Undulating. Expanding. Shrinking. Expanding. Shrinking.

"Help me."

I will.

"Help — me."

God will.

Who? Then, the jelly spoke to him and revealed to him a Way.

This new ghost said that it would give him the Words because it would explain the particulars of Selflessness, Compassion, Self-control, Love and Justice.

"How do I know . . . How do I know . . . if you are . . . the same as them?" Joshua rasped. "The other ghosts. I don't trust you. I'm not a child anymore."

The jelly froze and shyly said, *I speak Truth.*

"The ghost told me . . . Only children can see me. I'm not a child. I've faced death."

There is life beyond death. I am your Spiritual Father and I've come to give you Truth to set you free.

Joshua stared witlessly. "What? I'm going insane. Leave me. No one cares."

I care. I am your Spiritual Father.

"Leave! What is your name, ghost?"

Nefer. I am a Scholar and a Seer of Yahweh. Let God be true and every man a liar. You have been burned by the fire of suffering, but affection is not against you, judgment fire purifies anything that is not love.

"Is the… fire permanent?"

Truth is always *permanent. It will only be so when you willingly work it out in your life with trepidation and trembling.*

Amazed and pricked to the heart, Joshua bowed to the pure being of love behind those words, behind the angel. He bowed because he – discarding distortion – saw his individual toil and struggle.

In this fundamental reality he existed within, Joshua had hope. And yet, who was this ultimate being who sent this spirit in its name? How selfless was this God? He needed reason to justify his objectivity with some revolutionary objective input.

"Nefer, I want to be unashamed!"

Don't worry, the spirit said. *You will die to self. Die to yesterday and the past behind. The future is now in your hands.*

Soon, Nefer gave Joshua nourishing food – it looked like coriander seed, white; and the taste of it was like wafers made with honey. He ate them in ecstasy. Never would he have a meal again that tasted so glorious.

Nefer then told Joshua about everything. From the story of God's covenant with humanity, the fruit and the lies Joshua had believed. Just like Adam – all of humanity – he was rock bottom of the great exile from the Garden of Eden. The truth removed the scales of a shedding lizard from his eyes and the wonderful excellence and the deepness of this spirit's Word, but even more than that, it had a hidden ideal principle that was the epitome of the Ultimate Reality. The real universal truth all cultures sought to comprehend, revealed to Joshua. A beautiful character ruled space time, a complex, unified, unimageable love – a cohesive reciprocal community of procurement and contribution.

Strange, *so strange*. It was *so ridiculous* that such words – very old words, some of the oldest in history – would give him so much philosophical emotive obsession!

Nefer offered Joshua the Words to read. He had found something deep, a well of hope.

But then that same Word also killed Joshua, giving him nothing but misery, when Nefer recited aloud:

"I will make justice the line,
and righteousness the plumb line;
and hail will sweep away the refuge of lies,
and waters will overwhelm the shelter."
"And the city has no need of sun or moon to shine on it, for the glory
of God gives it light, and its lamp is the Lamb. By its light will the nations
walk, and the kings of the earth will bring their glory into it, and its gates
will never be shut by day – and there will be no night there. They will bring
into it the glory and the honour of the nations. But nothing unclean will
ever enter it, nor anyone who does what is detestable or false, but only those
who are written in the Lamb's book of life."

But it was the final recitations of the spirit which had Joshua lock up with surmounting discomfort that it plunged him back into that numb darkness – the darkness in which to hide from sin.

"For if we sin wilfully after that we have received the knowledge of the
truth, there does not remain a sacrifice for sins, but a certain fearful looking
for of judgement and fiery indignation, which shall devour the adversaries."

"I have willingly defiled you!" Joshua wailed. "Oh, Yahweh! I have used people! *I have sinned!* Forgive me!"

"You're already forgiven, Joshua," Nefer his Spiritual Father said.

"But I cannot stop *wanting* to sin!"

"Yes, you *can* stop! You must take responsibility of yourself now," Nefer pressed determinedly. "I cannot hold your hand forever. You can transgress no more. Remember what I taught you? What Jesus taught you? Never deceive again. If we say that we have fellowship with Jesus, and walk in darkness, we lie, and do not know the truth. You need to walk and be steadfast."

"But I am—"

"Listen!" Nefer said. "Listen Joshua! Your soul needs to be *healed* by the Holy Spirit. You *never, ever,* dare to think of sin as an option."

"Okay. Sin is not an option."

"It should not even be enticing in your mind!"

"Sin is not an option!"

"Yes," Nefer championed. "Bind the sin in the name of Christ Jesus! Yes! I only have *one* option!"

"I only have one option!"

"Truth."

"Truth!"

Suddenly, everything that had defined him shattered. He lost the foundation. Joshua wept bitterly.

Was that what those visions were about? The environmental catastrophes and the burning cities? The whole world losing its foundation of meaning? The lies all being removed by a grand apocalypse?

Nefer then told Joshua the story of the eternal God-man Jesus healing the boy with an unclean spirit, who grinded his teeth, foamed at the mouth, trying to burn and drown himself. The story of the anguished father of this son, taught Joshua what he could have become. *He was* the demented child. Then the father said to Jesus Christ, with tears in his eyes, blabbering, "Lord, I believe; but help my unbelief."

Nefer and Joshua. They became the best of friends laughing, so much alike they spoke for hours upon hours. It made no sense, but relationship had been the medicine he *needed*.

"I shall master my integrity!" Joshua giggled. "My God, I shall speak in spirit and in truth. I shall master my integrity! Integrity!"

When the spirit named Nefer came to him to minister every day, feeding him the beautiful life-giving wafers, revitalising him, he said, "I got it just for you from the celestial city."

Joshua almost choked on honeyed wafers full his mouth as he said, "It was real? The celestial city!?"

The spirit nodded. "All of it. And more. The Blood of the King has set you free. And very soon, these four walls will be cast down."

—

Two Weeks Later

"I – am – Judd Pounders."

"Ja Poah?"

"I – *am – Judd Pounders!*"

Just trying to introduce himself to these senseless Arab guards, took *forever*. That man with a nose bent upwards and dull plain brown eyes and an uninteresting complexion, stared at him with scowling dowdiness.

"Huh?"

"The Lieutenant Colonel," Judd tried again, saying every syllable loud and clear. "From the USA! The United States of America!"

"Yersh. *'atayt liruyat shakhs ma?*"

"I have come to see the inmate, Joshua Tanrıöver. Tanrıöver."

"Ah, ah." Finally light in those brown eyes. "Tanrıöver!"

"Joshua Tanrıöver! Yes. Yes." The Arab guards nodded to each other understandingly. "My God. Screw Arabic, I need a translator," Pounders grumbled, irked.

The guards let him in, unlocking a series of grating doors into the rancid asylum. Foul smells clogged the air. It made Judd curl his lip in disgust, slipping his hands into his coat pockets. All the noises echoed along these peeling painted cells. It held gangs of young ducks, dopers, vandals and no-goods, and obscene prostitutes with no better place than to be locked up in their illicitness. There were some missing teeth, groaning for deliverance, others slumped in corners drunken in a stew or a distressed lump. There were some rooms that were entirely sealed off with no windows but a thin slit in the doors. *Christ's sake, how do people live in here? Is human rights even a thing in Muslim countries?* He followed a man by the name of Amir, down the dark gloomy hallways, the sounds of lost souls with their footsteps sounding down the hall. It looked like some late nineteenth century jail, the ethical treatment of human beings was also not be up to date either.

Amir arrived at a small junction with three doors on either side, walls all made of steel and iron. Perfunctorily, he grabbed a stool, sat it down in front of the door before Judd, then, went on to inform him in broken English, to sit here, not open the door, and watch. Opening a small hatch, Amir said that one could only pass items though it. Then after the awkward tutorial, Amir left unaccounted.

Judd sat on the stool. He grumbled looking around, not knowing what he had to do. *Wait? Look in the hatch?* Syrians had *strange* manners.

He looked around, saw only a single guard "watching" him from afar. He barely looked awake, so Judd got up, opening the small viewing hatch. "Alright, this is crap. Its freezing in here, you bloody yo-yos." What he saw behind the door shocked him.

There was a man with so much mattered hair, like snarled ropes writhing in a crown above his head. Judd recoiled. He struggled to identify the prisoner and, for a second, he thought he had been led to the wrong cell. The man with a beard sat with a humped back coughing, sniffing with a runny nose, eating wafers. *Yeah, that's Joshua.*

"So, I wonder if you guys have any idea about human rights, eh?" Judd uttered as he looked around to the guard. There was no reply, so he gave up.

"Joshua, you are hanging in there? I've signed a waiver for you. When I found out what you did, everyone in the Marine Corps was furious and did not raise a single finger to help you! But, Jesus Christ, I could not stop thinking about how the police tortured you like that in the interrogation room. It was not right. I felt led to do this. Listing all your crimes, all in which was signed by the court, the marines had no hand in what you did. So, that meant I could sign you a waiver. You were *so goddamn* good at lying to us though. You nearly got us sued! Anyway, you have any parents, Josh? Nothing? No income? – well that million dollars is down the drain now, isn't it? Well, today's your lucky day, son. I got through with a parole."

The man looked up at the word "lucky". God almighty, those eyes were purple rings, morbid caverns sunken and haunted. Full of obsessive craving. His neck and cheeks were deathly pale, scumbled with an impending beard.

Judd only stared, absorbed by the disturbed face. "Well . . . I think it's time we let you out to see the sunshine. Come. You are officially under my guardianship, until further notice." Judd cleared his throat. "Josh, you're free."

A lopsided smile crept across Joshua's face, rendering his visage even more shocking.

16

SCHOLAR'S FORTRESS

January 4th, 2003

"And Jesus answered and said to them, 'Those who are healthy do not have need of a physician, but those who are sick. I have not come to call the righteous but sinners to repentance.'"
—From the Gospel of Luke, c. 58 – 65 CE.

"This guy's the trump card," Ben exclaimed perkily, handling the wheel of the car as he, Julian and James Casbolt drove down the empty highway towards Downtown Tucson.

Recruitment. If there was one thing Ben had been excited doing, it was to get his mind off the shenanigans of the Shinar disclosure and the Kandahar giant and getting the boys back together. But this man that Ben had been commanded to recruit was obligatory, apparently Judd Pounders' best man. Joshua Tanrıöver.

That struck Ben as odd for first of all, he never met the guy (for everyone knew Ben and the people Ben knew they knew him as the Actionman) and secondly, Pounders promised that his task would have his freedom to recruit any man he wished. Though Pounders specifically partitioned Ben could recruit anyone, but he had to recruit Joshua. He did not know the details, only that he had a criminal record and signs of being extremely intelligent.

"Pounders said many things about his expertise. The boy got into *a lot* of trouble. I mean, fined for being a passport fraudster and con artist."

Ben's mouth twitched with distaste as he coasted at a steady speed down the highway, one hand on the wheel. "But he has bounced back. Knows Arabic, an arts student, served during the Damascus Spring and an adamant explorer. Fits the perfect qualifications we need."

"Colourful life," Julian said. "Alright. So, he's nerdy, an Indiana Jones mixed with . . . What was that new movie with Tom Hanks and Leonardo DiCaprio?"

"*Catch Me If You Can?*"

"Yes, yes. That too." Julian crossed his arms. "As a matter of fact, I think it's *stupid* that we are hiring a con man!"

"I dunno," Ben replied. "Pounders said that Josh had hit it so low in prison, that he came out a new man."

"But the big question is, Cap, does he have any military experience?" Julian said. "He's going to be part of the 75th Rangers regiment. We need gun power, not just brains."

"And he does have some Rambo in him. Yes," Ben nodded. "In 2001, he enlisted in the Damascus Spring conflict where he had his last straw of trespassing illegal government property. He got shot in the leg and Pounders saved him just when the police caught him in the hospital. Anyways, Pounders passed a lawsuit to bring him home because he seriously wanted to enlist this man back into the Marine Corps. I think Pounders has some strong feelings for this man. I mean, I don't think I will ever go to prison in my life, but I expect it would be pretty rough. Maybe Pounders believed in Joshua to change his ways, you know what I am sayin'?"

"He's still an ex con man. That's terrible if this is his reputation." Casbolt did not sound convinced. "What he did was shameful and deserves torture. But Pounders I think still did the right thing to give him a chance."

"Oh yeah," Ben said. "He's also a real sharpshooter mind you. I am telling you, this is the man. You cannot mess with him. He's been through it all."

They arrived at the old beat-up apartment, squashed in between two buildings. Ben scowled, gawking at the condition of the facility in confusion. "This is . . . just terrible," Ben found himself despairing. He doubled-checked the address to make sure it was right. "Yeah, I'd thought he be living in at least in a nicer neighbourhood."

"I'm still unsure," Casbolt said, "if Pounders' waiver for Josh was a good idea. The man trusts this boy blindly."

"Well, I guess we have to suck it up and see for ourselves," Ben suggested, turning his head around to cross the road.

Once entering into the bilious apartment block, and into Joshua's room

– the door left unlocked – Ben gasped. Accumulated and cluttered across the entire floor over the tables and chairs and shelves were books, files and manuscripts, stuffing the room where there were spaces with no door or window. The chairs, in what should have been the living room, were high backed and packed up by bookcases, and most of the chairs held books. Some had books and papers tucked under them. The lighting, too, was bilious orange. Like an ancient secret fortress for scholars.

As they trailed in ogling, Ben found himself glimpsing on a table, a red and black book with various images of crosses and Jesus Christ with the title, *Handbook of Christian Apologetics* by Peter Kreeft and Ronald K. Tacelli.

"Amazing place," Casbolt whispered sarcastically, scanning the room, sauntering through the maze. The Aes Sidhe smirked even.

The most notable books cluttered on the front desk that made Ben think instantly of his father. *The First Fossil Hunters: Palaeontology in Greek and Roman Times* by Adrienne Mayor, *Mesopotamia and the Bible: Comparative Explorations* by Mark W. Chavalas and K. Lawson Younger, *In the Wake of the Goddesses: Women, Culture and the Biblical Transformation of Pagan Myth* by Dr Tikva Frymer-Kensky and the thickest volume George Roux's *Ancient Iraq*. This volume had a detailed stone relief image of an ancient, bearded king, languidly laying on his side on oversized bed, raising his goblet to his lips, where fanbearers with palms branches waved to cool him.

After a short while browsing the obsessive library, Ben found a man tucked away in the folds of a comfortable chair with a coffee cup holder and a side lamp, nose buried in a book.

And he didn't even come to answer the door? Ben thought, shocked. He itched to test this kid. *This smart aleck kid, he even left the door unlocked, with gangs prowling around! Doesn't seem so smart to me.*

"I know that syndrome," the reader said with an overconfident voice. "Myth becomes truth. Truth becomes myth. You lose your mind, you go mad." Shutting his book and patting a hand on a dark leather Bible volume on his side table, he raised his head, pushing his glasses back. "But that's why you are here, my friends. You're here because you have had an apocalypse. Your reality turned upside down."

The hell? What type of greeting was that? Idiots. Pounders is hiring a nut job too, Ben thought resentfully. *This crazy stuff is hunting me down! Casbolt, then Shinar and Joshua! Centre of bad ideas!*

"No," Ben said. "That's nice to know but—"

"You think I'm a hermit that knows nothing!?" The man who Ben assumed was Joshua – he did resemble his profile picture with a shaved beard and curly black hair, and spectacles – stood up. He paced, distracting everyone performatively. "My door is unlocked? That's because there is hardly anyone that comes down these parts, and most residents here in this apartment block are generally retired old people. Someone with arthritis would not be breaking in, eh? You're all so curious to find out *why* I'm so ahead of the game, right? I know, actually I have a precise *tendency* to know what's going to happen before they happen! Benjamin DePaula. The Man of Action." He stretched his hands to gesture and the way he said Ben's name could have been scornful. "Nerds are *always* praying for superpowers. God is *very good.*"

Ben's eyes widened. *Who the hell does this con man think he is, an actor?* Ben burned with frustration as he saw the utter *rubbish* displayed on the wall – a large poster of a rock-art that Joshua said was from the Kimberleys in Australia – showing a group of ghostly figures with round heads and orange oval-shaped black eyes.

This guy is as smartassed as my father! Focus on the mission!

"You know there is such a thing as socialising?" Ben interjected, steeling himself.

"Yes, yes I am aware of that, Captain," Joshua said haughtily, his glasses gleaming in the lamplight. "But in our day and age, socialising is getting harder. I *was* told *everything* about what you went through in Kandahar." Something gleamed in Joshua's glasses as he paced, continuing to flout Ben with his flowery expressive skills: his use of voice, gestures, motion, posture, he used it all. Ben liked good actors, but he hated the ones that went too far. "No one is going to believe, but I think the ancient Nephilim, the nightmares of legend, the bringers of desolation, are revealing themselves again. That I know, and I cannot deny that you are here because you took one down. To prove my point?"

Julian and Ben exchanged glances, knowing full well what he was thinking. He nodded rather stupidly. *He knows about the Shinar Mission? How, if it had been top secret?*

Joshua smirked at their flabbergasted expressions, opening out his arms. "Welcome to my world. The world of honesty, apologetics and spirits."

"He's crazy," Casbolt whispered, leaning in to Julian. "I can sense it."

Ben, Julian and Casbolt looked around frivolously at each other, not sure what to say. He fixed his eyes on the ex con man. *Snap out of it, Ben, focus on the task. Recruit him. Doesn't matter if he's mentally ill.*

"Ugh, that's great," Ben said, his perkiness strained. "But I have a—"

"Look, Joshua, we really are thankful for your hospitality," Julian uttered. "But—"

"I said no." Joshua cut in insistently, a swift expression indicating that he had hoped to have the wits to evade discussing this beforehand. He took a deep breath, clicking his tongue. "No! You know, I'm done with the hide-and-seek routine, okay? No more recruitment. I see *no* reason to want to join Pounders again. I'm a big liar after all. Why waste your time with me?"

"What about a second chance?" Casbolt exclaimed.

Joshua fell back down into his seat, sighing. "My second chance is to make my choice final!" he said. "See? I'm retired! Sounds *so thrilling*. Iraq. Baghdad and Basrah. Well, I hope you all have good luck then, Actionman. You want me to have a second chance of getting screwed?"

"Joshua, Pounders wants you to—"

"Besides, if you would excuse me, gentlemen." Picking up the leather book on the side table and adjusting his reading glasses, he opened it to his reference. Joshua completely shut himself off.

God, we don't have time for this! Ben shook his head, grabbing the nearest book he could find, shoving a copy of *Creation Stories of the Middle East* in Joshua's face. Ben began to squeeze the paperback, creasing it. Leaping out of his seat, Joshua hissed, holding his mouth, gasping, acting as if Ben was some kind of robber pointing a gun.

That did the trick. "Just hear us out for a minute," Ben said firmly. "I mean your book no harm."

"You wouldn't dare," Joshua growled.

"Pounders loves you as a father, and you *disown him*? Come on!" Ben sniffed in derision threating to rip the book. "We *need* you."

Joshua contorted his face, scoffing at that proposition. "You don't even—"

"Just because of your precious leg?"

"No."

"Who needs a leg if you're sitting around doing nothing?"

"Just put the book down, you fool!" Joshua snapped, losing his patience.

"Okay," Ben replied, maintaining intensity, slowly placing the book down. "But you better *man up,* brother. Man up! Haven't you seen what's going on in the news?"

Joshua rolled his eyes, groaning. "Yeah, yeah. Perpetual national turmoil and distress. Yeah, I don't need to hear all that *pomp* again."

"This is *not* just about you, Josh. It is about serving America and our people and the future of this nation." Ben couldn't help feeling patriotic as, in a way, he could not think of anything else persuasive enough to convince a man much smarter than him to go along with the recruitment slots. Ben could feel patriotic because in a way, he was mediating for his family, fighting for his wife and for his little Veronica his daughter. "You want to continue your research in peace? Well, if I was you, Josh, I would get out of the library, and get into the field!" He glanced at Casbolt, whispering, "He needs to get out of the library."

That tirade made Joshua grit his teeth, deep in thought. He clenched his upper lip, mumbling under his breath, "No time".

"So, what do you say, friend?" Julian persisted gently.

Joshua ended up sneering smugly, shaking his head. "Your patriotic rant is futile. You know nothing about me. You're wasting precious time, Ben. I knew this would happen." He shooed them off, striding back towards his working place and desk full of notes and pens. "Be gone! I want *nothing* to do with you. I have work to do!"

"Wasting a lot of time in this pigsty for sure," Casbolt crooned, craning his head into Joshua's kitchen. Ben could not see from here but judging by the profoundness of Casbolt's expression, and the smell . . . "Pretty disgraceful don't you think for an academic. When was the last time you had a healthy meal, boy?"

Upon being interrogated by a British Aes Sidhe, Joshua started to pace again, using his hands to stress his words. "You're invading my life! Please! I'm not even serving you plebs; I just need what I can to get by. Just *get out* of my house!"

"Yes." Casbolt nodded, a hand under his chin. "Why did you leave the door open for us?"

"Agh! I said I'm busy!"

"I'm afraid from the state of the *trash boat* of yours, that you're going to need more pay," Julian said.

Actually, that could work, Ben inquired in his head. *He used to be a millionaire.*

"And this job pays better?" Joshua spat. "You're just trying to bait me! Good try, virgins!"

"Damn it, Josh! *That is enough!*" Ben shouted, his anger kindling. "Please. You're a good fighter, soldier. I know this because Pounders wouldn't be putting in all the effort to make it mandatory for you to be enlisted again. Pounders is doing this because it's for your own good; he cares for you! You have nothing here to gain staying alone inside, what's the point of reading about the world, and not seeing the world?!" Ben had to offer Joshua something in return because he knew that this man had been broken from his last expedition out in the field. Giving him an opportunity to escape this mucky den would be doing Joshua a *major* favour, whether he liked it or not. "We can offer you a better chance," Ben declared. "A new chance – a life for furthering your studies and research, with *better* pay and *better* resources and benefits instead of living here in the slums with gangs and bikies around! This is no place for a scholar like you! Come on, Josh!"

Ben held his breath. Joshua bowing, nodded curtly to every word, but Ben had no indication of what was going on in that complex head of his. He swayed his head slowly side to side, twitching a bit and then, looking up, he expressed a lobsided smile.

"Impressive, Captain. As all should, you're making progress in the use of persuasive discourse, but something about your diction is jarring." Joshua began to chuckle. "You sound more like a *nagging* mother than a marine captain, but I can forgive you for that, Plebian. But, you are capable enough to know that I *can* think for myself. I *know* the situation I am in, and your two virgins." He crossed his arms, slowly eyeing them like a teacher inspecting his naughty students. "I am content, and I don't want your charity."

Stubborn son of a . . .

"You *do*," Julian pressed in.

"What do you want to lose, Josh?" Ben whispered. "Look at your options, soldier. You *can't* do more research if you lose your money!"

Joshua started and stared at Ben, confronting him in the eyes. He got up close and pointing a proud finger at him, said, "*If* I could possibly payoff all my studies, explain! What is this *mission*? Don't think you're playing games with me, Cap. I *hate* games. *I hate lies.*" He said the last sentence with a vicious growl.

"Can't tell you that, it's focal point," Ben said.

Joshua narrowed his intense hazel eyes.

So, he is interested.

"There you go. Focal point. So, what will it do?" Joshua said plainly as if none of what Ben said caught him by surprise. Then crossing his arms, he said brusquely, "Explain."

"Can't tell you that, either," Ben replied. "Only Pounders can—"

"Tell you what? Tell you what?" Joshua said. "Alright, if I did make it there, how do you expect me to join if you *can't tell me anything!* Ha, there is no logic to that argument, and I have no idea what promises you have for me, it defeats the purpose. See? No point." He planted his hands on his hips, weighing, measuring a course of action under pressure. "So yes." His voice had a croak to it. "The land of Sumer, Akkad, Assyria, Babylonia and the Chaldeans will cost me another leg."

"I don't want to pull your leg, Josh!" Ben exclaimed, long sufferingly. "I am just *doing* what I've been commanded to do. Join me if you want to know more. You could be reinstated."

When Ben thought his reserves of convincing Joshua to enlist was futile, Ben's phone rang. Flipping it open, he saw it was from Pounders.

"Josh, I think your daddy's calling," Ben said, smirking. "You better answer it, bro."

Right there and then, when the phone turned towards Joshua, his face went slack, and his perseverance fell apart. Ben witnessed the true Joshua: a young man who had tried so hard, thought he had won but had actually lost. He stared with frenzied eyes at the ringing mobile phone, growling a sigh.

17

PLUGGING IN

"The name of the sanctuary in which the bennu bird was worshipped was Het-bennu. Greek writers called this bird the phoenix, and the Egyptians considered it as a symbol of Osiris."

—From The Book of the Dead or 'Book of Coming Forth by Day', Translated by E. A. Wallis Budge, 1895, Sacred Texts, Plate VIII. I.[5] footnote. It traces back to the Pyramid Texts of the 6th Dynasty (2345 - 2181 BCE). Written in full during the 18th Dynasty (1550 – 1295 BCE).

Immediately, Joshua regretted accepting Ben's offer. What could Joshua do to argue? Pounders on the phone call had to bring out his officially signed waiver, outlining that he had given Joshua full consent after he was sent on parole and taken back home from Damascus, that his will and guardianship would be entirely in Pounders' hands. By law, Joshua had no choice. He thought his crimes were so bad, that it would disqualify him from even enlisting. Apparently not. And on top of that, Pounders insisted, quite ruthlessly, with some mawkish nonsense, "I believe in you." Experiencing war would be good for diversifying his priorities, to try new things to flourish as a human being and so on. That made Joshua swallow his pride. Why, after all the traumatic failure with his involvement with the Marine Corps, would Joshua ever want to join it again? After all, Pounders had caught Joshua saying that about the need for more multidisciplinary people in this day to approach world problems, many times – for it had been Joshua's mantra as a con man.

Reverse phycology. Brilliant.

Because of Pounders, sooner than he could breathe, Joshua found himself, literally, dumped into a mud pit, out in the cold, out in the mud flats. The pressure of the thick mush constricted and squeezed him fiercely, muscles straining, his neck craning hard to keep his face from being submerged.

The rancid smell of wet soil and slosh molested his nose. Oozy faint crackling sounds filled his ears, trickling wet sludge seeping into his eardrums. It sounded like microscopic worms were squirming within the mud in panic. Joshua groaned as the frigid death grip burned him, rigid as a post.

A mud pit! A slimly, icky, stinking, rotten, wretched mud pit! Sluggish wet inappropriate sounds absorbed him as Joshua sunk. The jolly joy of being part of the American Marine Corps . . . sucked.

Oh, a waste of time, Joshua dreaded, gulping hard, his throat feeling sore again, the sky an unforgiving lacklustre ceiling, awaiting the sunrise.

Grainy mucus dribbled into his mouth. He heaved, letting out a racking noise to clear his croaky throat. Virgins! He was getting a cold just before going to war, stuck here for an hour!

Joshua's teeth trembled madly. He couldn't even move his arm to slay the unbearable *itch* on his nose. He wanted to call out, for Pounders to stop the torture.

But he couldn't do that. No. Selfishness would leave all his friends to suffer for even longer in the mud flats. If only one person relented, relinquished their endurance and perseverance in the mud pit, everyone else suffered.

Yes, this a test. A test of my selflessness. The image of Christ. Selflessness.

Ben, Julian, Garrow Howey, Reggie Paige, Derek Fish and Jason Laycock, *all* endured the same freezing torment. Many groaned so loudly it was hard to hear the ambient sound of the stirring wilderness, of the fresh morning air. Derek Fish hissed to clear his croaky throat.

Pounders, you have no care for humans, Joshua lamented. *I cannot go through this again!*

Colonel Judd Pounders walked up and down a wooden pier, wearing a warm woolly cloak. "Gentlemen. We can leave the mud if only five men can quit," he said sternly.

Joshua closed his eyes, yielding to the bone-chilling cold activating every muscle in his body. It was a workout.

Pounders' boots made the weather-worn wood creak and crunch right above Joshua's face as he paced. "You fight and if you struggle, everyone will be by your side. This is how a whole unit is built for the nightmare of war. It is harrowing out there and we need to prepare for it mentally. Our operative environments will change radically – inevitably. Gentlemen, we need to prepare for these coming changes."

The men around him started to sing breaking forth with song, reminding Joshua he wasn't alone. He heard all the men singing – it was the only thing they could do, frozen in the mud, immobile, fighting the feeling of unbearable hopelessness and strain. And as everyone sung a victory paean and as the mud constricted them, that spark of hope made the cold warmer, and the dawn nearer.

—

Ben's arms burned, streaming with sweat, pushing up his barbell, loaded with weight plates. Suitably, "Take the Pressure Down", blared loudly from his iPod in the background, motivating him into a daze. It had to be the heaviest weights he had done in years.

As Ben lay down with the heavy weights, Julian next to him performed leg lifts. They swapped, Ben dusting off his gloved hands as he worked on his legs. A full body treatment had been specified as the mission requirement.

While activating his glutes, Ben glanced out from the outside gym towards the obstacle courses. A whole squad of marines from each of the three units in the Shinar Mission worked well and hard. He saw Marcus Theis' team flipping old tractor tires, racing the boys in groups across the asphalt, while being barked at by Colonel Terry Sopher.

"Come on, yah maggot! Smash it! You're nearly there, Marcus! Good on yah, Monti! Push it, guys! Go! Go! Go!"

Up on the obstacle course, he saw Joshua scaling up the wooden wall net, as if in a race. Besides the effort to convince Joshua to join the Rangers, everyone else had been relatively easy to bring together for this important mission, yet only Joshua resisted vehemently. Ben saw them all pushing hard, fighting their way up the net, until Reece Kundzinsh nudged into Joshua. Struggling, he yelped, losing his grip on the ropes and fell to the matted ground with a thud.

"Let's goooo, Jish. Haha!" chortled Tom Grogan from up on the net, continuing his climb.

Joshua gasped with weariness, rubbing his head, got on his feet and like an annoying rookie, he tried again, struggling hopelessly to climb taut ropes. There, Derek Fish passed him, grunting, making Joshua the final person to finish climbing up the wall.

Ben frowned from the gym watching Joshua painfully tremble up the high wall. Pounders did say that Joshua was a special person. He always seemed to want to retreat into the library and fiddle with his Rubix cube during debriefings. Ben suspected he was on the autism spectrum.

Ben heard the barking and spitting provocations of the Drill Sergeant. On a grass patch lined with hurdles at the back, Leo Urwin leapt over the hurdles with incredible agility, crashing into the line of dummies. He attacked feverously, slicing swiftly and hollering cruelly, destroying the dummies with his bayonet.

"Kill, kill, kill, kill!" Drill Sergeant Turner shouted. "*Yeah man*! You're a machine! Kill 'em all!"

"YES, DRILL SERGEANT!" Urwin roared.

—

As Ben jogged under the sun, panting, mind numb and his singlet cleaving to his wet skin.

He ran right behind Marcus Theis keeping close to him while the other marines made sure they ran close behind each other in a single file, not daring to deviate, overtake or break formation. It taught them to remain a knit unit. If one moron slowed down, it would cause an accordion effect, creating a huge gap in the line. It would not matter if that person was in the very back of the line because they wouldn't slow down many people. But if that moron turned out to be someone in the *middle* of the pack, beginning to slow down, no one would be allowed to overtake him, everyone would suffer from a lagging twat.

As Ben jogged, he heard a series of vexed yells and loud exclamations. It seemed that a moron was starting to form in the pack. Behind him, thank God. Oh, those poor twats!

Once James Casbolt, Joshua, Julian and Marcus made it across the finish line towards the barracks, Ben turned into the shade of the under croft, grabbing his water bottle from the table to take a drink. He paced, his chest heaving laboriously dripping with sweat, feeling lightheaded. He found himself gazing at the single file of stragglers coming into view in the distance. Leading and holding back the soldiers was a boy struggling with immense hardship.

Another rookie. Of course. A nineteen-year-old boy, winded to the point of death as he ran – no, *fumbled* – with all his might.

To Ben, it was *so interesting* to watch one rookie work his pants off while all the other experienced guys were not even running their hardest. He instantly had respect for this young boy.

Once he had finally passed the finish line, the marines behind the rookie exploded into a disbanding frenzy, scrambling around him, a brawl on the verge of outbreak, braying like wild animals. The rookie beleaguered on all sides, yelped as the soldiers nudged him, ramming into him, bad mouthing as they passed. The champion rookie grunted ineptly and fumbled to his knees, too tired to get back up. So, he remained on the floor knackered, catching his breath, holding his rising and falling stomach.

Ahhh, Ben thought, leisurely splashing his face. *Poor kid. His body will get used to it.*

Then he saw a pair of sneakers drop from the sky before the rookie, rolling on the ground. Ben spun around and saw Drill Sergeant JJ Girgos barge into one of the dorms, letting out a god-awful wail.

Girgos had thrown the sneakers *out* from one of the dorms.

Oh, you got to be kidding me, Ben thought, turning around in accordance with everyone else. When he thought this day had had it, he'd predicted wrongly.

"Oh, my," Julian said, crossing his arms. "I don't want to be the kid at the end of Girgos' tanty."

"He's on fire today," Marcus grumbled, hands on his hips.

"You want me to get him some water?" Ben said gesturing with his bottle. "Just in case. It's boiling."

Ben couldn't help expressing a wry smile as Girgos kicked open a door, making it rebound against the wall, tossing out an open duffel bag. "Grahh, when will they lock?!"

He flung clothes out into the air, shaking the bag free of all its contents. Everyone in the area gawked silently as the Drill Sergeant went on a rampage, discarding and kicking items in the room across the open threshold. He frolicked as he did, stumbling comically. Many of the marines around Ben commented in surprise, murmuring and snickering with each other, some wondering if this were a prank, while others whispered to inquire if the room that had been left unlocked was any of theirs. Everyone shook their heads.

Grunting with Heraclean effort, Girgos lifted the entire *mattress* off the bunk, carrying it out of the room. His face was red. The mattress, too large to fit, jammed on the lintel. Stumbling, Girgos growled and assaulted the mattress, ramming his body into it.

"You stupid – stupid – stupid – stupid – stupid!"

The mattress dislodged outside, and the momentum carried Girgos forward, tumbling over the mattress and onto the concrete.

This is certainly *not mine to worry about.* Ben continued to ogle, the marines hacking out laughing behind him, were glad they were entertained by Girgos' freak out.

Huffing and puffing, grabbing the mattress and with a defiant wail, Girgos heaved it on top of the veranda roof. He jumped on his toes as he shoved it back farther to make sure the owner would have a bad day trying anything to recover it with ease.

Ben found himself glancing back at the rookie and connecting the dots, he covered his mouth. *Holy . . .*

That rookie did not seem to notice the raging, only focused intently on his pair of shoes mindlessly. Then suddenly the boy's eyes went wide, and his face turned bright red. Getting up on his trembling feet, he clutched his shoes, slowly eyeing the barracks, seeing all his trashed clothes strewn everywhere.

Oh no . . . The rookie shut his eyes tight, trembling as Girgos, like a storm, charged at the poor little twat.

"DID YOU DO THIS!?" he bellowed.

Ben cringed as he watched *absolute horror* manifest on the rookie's face. It was the heart-wrenching look his daughter would give to him when she knew she'd been caught doing something very bad. "Oh," the rookie whimpered, knees knocking. The Drill Sergeant threw an empty duffel bag into the kid, who caught it with an anguished grunt, hugging his bag.

Every time the Drill Sergeant got mad, it held *everyone up* and the entire unit had to witness the pure humiliation of one guy. The harassment in the Marine Corps was necessary in its context, and more pleasant than its equivalent of going to see a public flogging or a hanging. Everyone saw the circumstances, and everyone knew the message: I don't want to go through this, so *don't you dare* disobey commands! Do *not* upset the Drill Sergeant and *always* use common sense!

"You never know what *moron* will come into your dorm to trash your property! You understand?!" Girgos spat viciously. In modernity, the marines gave verbal floggings rather than the stick.

Looking up swallowing, the rookie squeaked indistinguishable words.

"What you say, punk?!" Girgos leaned in with his ear. "Speak up!"

"I – I'm sorry."

A rough hand gripped the rookie's collar and he squeaked. Ben took a step forward, becoming wary. *Okay, Girgos, back off.*

Did a Drill Sergeant take things too far? "Where's your organisation and initiative, *boy*," Girgos growled softly.

The rookie, though writhing with terror from the scary man's face and eyes, managed to reply. "Y- y- yes, sir."

God, the kid is crying. I swear to God that Girgos looks like he's killed a man.

The rookie sniffed as the Drill Sergeant lashed him with words; streams of tears trickled down his cheek. Ben had known that raw animalistic feeling long ago when he was at the age of nineteen years back.

He understood.

"Good," Girgos said, softly inspecting the kid's sensitivity. "Do you need me to get you to kiss the dirt?"

"Sir, no, Drill Sergeant."

"Then *why* did you forget to lock the *door?*"

The rookie gulped. "Ugh. But I *did* lock it. I don't know—"

"*Shut up!*" Girgos yelled, suffering to slap the kid, but he did not have to because the rookie fell to a crouch, covering his head. "It got me very, very mad. I don't like being mad pussy! What do you *mean* you locked it!?"

The rookie nodded abashed, "Sir, yes, sir—"

"*Sir!?* What does it look like I'm some joke!?"

The rookie's gaze was downcast. "Drill Sergeant I mean. Sorry."

"Well then you should double-check next time, eh?"

The rookie failed to respond, leaving Girgos hanging. "Eh?!"

"Yes, sir," he replied, startled, his brown hair veiling his face.

Girgos shoved the rookie, getting a "ohh" from the marines. The rookie, stumbling awkwardly, still managing to hold his footing. He held his stomach in pain. *The heat's getting to him,* Ben worried. "Yes, sir," the rookie uttered again, rasping. "Please stop."

"*Stop,* calling me, *sir,*" Girgos scorned.

It only made the rookie wilt even further. "Sir yes – Uh, yes s- Uh, yes of course."

"OH MY GOD!" Girgos exploded, turning on the spot throwing his hands up in the air. "It's *Drill Sergeant* Girgos! Oh my God! When will they ever *git it! Drill Sergeant Girgos!*"

Girgos looks as if he's killed a man . . .

"Yes, si- Sorry, sir . . . That is, Drill Sergeant," the rookie said with a broken voice, his cheeks turning crimson. "Sorry. I-I-I will lock my door. I promise. I will never leave it unlocked."

Girgos shook his head with his hands on his hips. "You think you're invincible, Best?" His tone sounded surprisingly gentle, as if Girgos recognised his abuse had no helpful outcome. "What made you think to join the Marine

Corps if you can't even lock a door? Come on. Such a simple job as this and you can't even do it. How did you enlist, boy?"

The rookie shook his head. Ben's heart sunk, taking another step forward closer so the boy could see him. *Yeah, that's enough, Girgos. The rookie's had enough. That's enough, goddamn it!*

And upon Ben's advance, he did. With Ben's presence, the rookie somehow met him with a single hopeless glance – an understanding that recovered his strength. Ben nodded slightly.

"I-I want to kill bad guys, Drill—"

"To be a G.I. Joe huh?!" Girgos overtook him, voice normal and croaky. "Well, you *ain't* going to become a G.I. Joe until you *learn* to make your bed and lock up your room after wake-up call! Git it?! It's simple! Okay?"

The rookie nodded in fearful compliance.

"I want your very best, Johnny Best! Look at me! Come on, son! My good is my best. I will never let it rest. Until your good is better and your better is best, Best!"

"Yes, Drill Sergeant!"

"Good job, son! Good job! *Next* time, lock and leave!"

"Yes, Drill Sergeant! Lock and leave! I will not unlock again!" Johnny Best sobbed in relief, and then buried his face in his hands. He stood there, eyes gazing into his hands.

If I was this kid right now, Ben thought. *I would have shat myself.*

Girgos, staring down at Johnny for a little while longer, turned on his heels and left.

Ben watched as all his men departing slowly, shocked, and above all, exhausted. Finding himself enmeshed by Johnny Best's moaning, beholding the devastation laid out before him, Ben walked towards the roof gawking at the misplaced mattress.

"All that . . . for an accidently unlocked door," Johnny muttered angrily. "I'm hopeless. Captain, I – I even doubled-checked. But"—Johnny choked on his words, starting to cry in silence—"Girgos is right," he said in a strained, trembling voice. "I'm not good enough to be here. I'm not good. I'm not . . ."

"You are good enough for me, bro," Ben said, approaching Johnny's side helping reach for the bunk mattress, bringing it back down for him. At least someone had to do something to help this poor boy. "That's the only thing you can't do, believing that you are hopeless. Only quitters use that excuse. Suck it up and you will learn to deal with it."

Johnny slumped his head, depressed. Ben recalled then, the time when he had lost the diving competition at high school and missed out on the reward for best in the state for simply misjudging and underestimating a simple, precise technique. It forever haunted him, made him gnash his teeth in despair for many nights. He also recalled his daughter Veronica lying that she was having a sleepover with her best friend Zoe and, after accidentally breaking the window at Zoe's house, she got a scalding from her mother in front of her friend. Veronica had a tantrum and locked herself in her room, crying herself to sleep. "I know," he whispered. "I know, Johnny. I've been there. The shame. The failures. Countless times. You cannot learn if you do not fail. Here's a rule of thumb, brother: to do well, fail well. Fail a lot. The Actionman only became the Actionman because he made so many *stupid mistakes*, I cannot even remember them all." Ben trembled despite the smouldering heat. *So many foolish mistakes.* "But you know what, kid? It made me stronger."

"Why do they do this to us?" Johnny said as Ben carried his mattress into his dorm.

"Hm?"

"Why do they abuse us?" Johnny picked up his clothes and shoes, shoving them into his duffel bag. "It's . . . It's bad. If there is anything wrong with this place, it's that the military castigates everyone. Why do they want to— Why do they—"

"There's nothing you can do," Ben said dryly.

Johnny paused, staring.

"The Marine Corps is elite, Best. Now that you are here, there's nothing you can do." Ben helped haul the mattress into the dorm. "Battle is a difficult process. If you are not prepared, then you will break before you can do anything. You will lose yourself. Freeze on the spot. You need to be familiar with this stress, so that, at least, the terrifying can become something bearable." Ben shook his head. "Trust me, Best. It's not easy, but it is possible."

Johnny's face went pale. *Fahh . . . That pep talk made it worse, didn't it?*

"Are you an actor?" Johnny whimpered.

Ben met him with a hard stare.

"Uh . . ." Tears running down his face, Johnny raised his chin, dignified, packing his things.

"A navy seal mentor told me way back," Ben said, hoping against hope – *may this be enough, that spark that engrains itself in this boy* – "If you want to change the world, first make your bed – every day." He grinned. "So, you want to see what it is to act like a good soldier? Watch and learn kid." So, Ben did the kid's bed. "Simple. It helps you to be punctual. Okay, brother?"

Johnny shied away, closing his eyes, stifling a smirk. "Thank you, Captain, but – but I think I can do the rest myself thanks."

"Ah, are you sure, kid?" Ben said, crossing his arms across his chest. "You looked pretty beat up by Drill Sergeant."

Johnny flinched. For the rest of his life, he would forever fear Drill Sergeants and anyone remotely resembling Girgos. Johnny bit his lip, his eyes sharp with dark determination. "I'm a soldier, Ben. I have to face death."

"You'll toughen up one day. Like me. I want you to know that you inspired me back there to do more for you." He winked at Johnny.

The rookie gaped at Ben.

"Just being honest," he shrugged. "No kid like you would have stood up to Girgos. The guy's a prick. I hate him. Let me tell you a secret: *everyone* hates him. You're not alone. You are not the first to be his victim." Ben, scooping up a bundle of clothes, tossed them to Johnny to put into his bag. "You should be proud of that, Johnny." Upon seeing the room back to normal, the nineteen-year-old stood up, face gloomy, rubbing the back of his neck.

"I – shouldn't be flattered but . . . Thanks." It sounded awkward. The boy resembled things Ben remembered about himself. And . . . it was *alright* to see Johnny back up on his feet again.

18

A CHANGE OF PLANS

"We observe that Egypt, in a period of intensified creativity, became acquainted with the achievements of Mesopotamia; that it was stimulated; and that it adapted to its own rapid development such elements as seemed compatible with its efforts. It mostly transformed what it borrowed and after a time rejected even these modified derivations."
—From *The Birth of Civilization in the Near East*, Henri Frankfort, Project Gutenberg, Doubleday Anchor Books, 1956, pg 135.

When all the hardship and the training was done, Ben and the marines met in the Fort Huachuca's briefing room before doomsday, which hung in the air in torrid silence. The President had some words for them.

Colonel Pounders with Terry Sopher and Joe Dunford stood tall and formal in front of all twenty-one men Ben had personally recruited and handpicked for the special operation, subsect special forces for the Shinar Mission.

"President Bush after Operation Desert Fox last year, made it clear that Iraq is gathering danger," Joe Dunford reported, reading the update sheet. "The UN has officially reached a confirmation that Hussein's government breached its terms of peace. Gentlemen. It is time to decapitate the Ba'ath leadership. War is here. Operation Enduring Freedom is now underway."

Not a single sound came from the marines. Ben, unsettled, narrowed his eyes and glimpsed the CIA agent standing off to the side, leaning on the wall in the shadows, taking notes. *What's he up to?* Ben thought.

"The breach of the sanctions to claim weapons of mass destruction must be dealt with," Terry Sopher reported. "I know you have all been through a lot this past month and we are very proud of your etiquette and efforts. It's show time."

Ben found himself nodding in agreement to that, as did Marcus and the third General Garry Harrel who had a noticeable scar tissue from his left upper side of his neck down his spine – a memento from the experiences in the First Gulf War in Kuwait.

Then, Colonel Judd Pounders stepped forward to speak. "Now, Director Bonner has given us clear orders that Hussein's amounting forces in Kuwait are estimated by intelligence to be precisely four hundred thousand troops. Ideally, this operation should be conducted after the main Coalition troops are deployed to push past Baghdad's forces, crushing them with open-terrain warfare. It will be here that clearance will be given by Tommy Franks to take back the weapons, out of Hussein's grasp.

"But I digress, the details of your missions, team Sentinel, Ageis and Eidolon, are in the folders in front of you. Now let's get some rest, gentlemen. Before we make any move, Ian Mastemah wants to inform us about the discoveries made at Kandahar."

The CIA agent walked to the front of the room. *Apparently,* they had a *breakthrough* with something which could make history. These people were eager to present it, all this surreptitious dubious craze around the giant provoked Ben to grind his teeth. Who *cared* about the research behind the giant! The more time he dwelt on the giant, the more it brought him back to Joseph.

What did he care about some *stupid scientific breakthrough?* Ben just wanted to go off to war and fight and kill some bad guys and come home to Brianna and Veronica.

The presentation on the projector was set up, and when the agent spoke, he sounded like he had a blocked nose, sly and slick. "Thank you. I'm special agent Ian Mastemah from the CIA. I have a history in exploring unexplained cases and crimes throughout the United States during the nineties and early two thousands. As you know, I have come to report back to you on the beneficial findings we have discovered in our examination of the giant of Kandahar. And I bring to you this filed report today so you can see the life changing discovery that you men have contributed to."

Oh, that is definitely *helpful,* Ben proclaimed, disparaging in his mind. He leaned back deeply on his chair. *But I wouldn't say for the good though.*

Ian then pulled out some files and clicked on a laptop, so the projector screen displayed images of gibberish that turned Ben off completely. He only barely passed science class, let alone elementary school, wanting many times to drop out to join the theatre and the diving club and karate dojo. And seriously, if Pounders wanted him to go through a lecture *again*, he'd better *stop standing there*, looking all fine about it. Ben long sufferingly allowed whatever nonsense this futile presentation had to say. He leaned back in his chair again, making it creak. Microscopic skin samples and other labels with chemical compounds and other mumbo jumbo diagrams displayed on the screen.

"The DNA tests have returned giving us completely inconclusive results. This giant is not of this world. It's a completely new lifeform. It resembles human DNA, but it has differences. It doesn't resemble anything that we know of on this planet."

Bullocks! It all went over Ben's head.

"That's all I have to say," Ian said. "Now let's get some rest, gentlemen. You are dismissed."

Everyone seemed to get up at once, grabbing their folders, talking and leaving. As Ben gathered his folders, he saw agent Ian Mastemah tugging on his coat, sauntering up to him. *Nuts!*

"Good evening, Captain DePaula, good evening," Ian replied with a smooth voice. "May I have a swift moment with you please? In private?"

"Sure." Ben allowed Ian to escort him out of the briefing room, the man was almost head smaller than Ben, so he found it a little strange to be looking down on someone who had just as much or even more authority than himself.

"Now, Bonner and I have been watching you closely during the training sessions and we're extremely confident that you can take the lead of the Rangers on your own now."

A flutter of disquiet stirred in Ben's stomach. *Well, I've never led my men officially before. It sounds fine.*

"However, I got a word from Director Bonner here," Ian said making Ben pause. He watched as the agent fumble into his coat pocket, pulling out a folded-up piece of paper. "He's been negotiating with the JTTF that it is necessary that James Casbolt – who is an Aes Sidhe as you know – we know he has abdicated to join the marines. I just want to make this clear to you since we ought to remain secretive in this matter about any Aes Sidhe in our ranks. James Casbolt is a United Nations criminal. You are to keep his true identity confidential. Understand?"

"Okay," Ben said, the tendons in his neck tensing. *United Nations criminal?*

"But I'm confused as to why you are telling me this information now."

Ian's right cheek twitched and with an oily voice he said, "Oh, as the main captain you do wish to know what is going on behind closed doors don't you? Didn't you say recently that men have the right to know secrets about an operation? Here it is. Everything is under control, I assure you."

"Roger that," Ben nodded. His gut instinct told him there was something *very wrong* about Ian being here. The Kandahar giant genetic results, Casbolt a UN criminal on the run. What else was this man hiding? "And thank you. Sir."

After that strained suffocating conversation, they shook hands, Ian's feeling frigid to the bone. Ben swallowed. "My pleasure. Good luck, Benjamin," but as Ian said this, he held on for a little bit too long, Pounders arrived then, looking adamant to speak to Ben. However, an operator whispered into Pounders' ear, and the Colonel recoiled back in shock, grimacing.

Then he was gesturing for Ben to come over. *What is this all about?*

"Your requested me, Colonel?" Ben said, as Ian left. "What's going on? Is something wrong?"

"Something has happened," Pounders replied marching, hands firmly planted behind his back. "The enemy has changed their tactics hearing of our mobilisation. Come into my office quickly."

Closing the door, Pounders led Ben, sauntering towards his desk where, laying out open, was a table-sized map of Iraq pinpointed with locations of concern. Ben leaned in to observe, Pounders pressing his finger on the towns of Afak in the central land between the Two Rivers next to an oasis, and then to Kut, just northwards on the east bank of the Tigris.

"This is where Frank's Sentinels are going to secure first," Pounders said. "Sopher's Ageis, are interested in Hammar Lake and Ash Shatrah to stop by for rendezvous with our other squads from other imminent missions from the Coalition forces, before heading to Warka." Ben simply nodded, listening to Pounders. "Now for your unit – Eidolon – we were going to be stationed at Samarra since Baghdad is out of the way. But the problem is, we need to make sure the other 75th Ranger Regiment battalions are assembled and ready."

"Sir?" Ben asked pointing to the towns on the eastern side of the river. "Would Kut be of importance? I thought that was going to be one of our objectives as stated in the report."

"The marines are already set in by Kut to peg Baghdad," Pounders said. "We hope that by May we can reach Raytheon including Tuwaithua."

"Okay . . . So, then – what was the issue?" Ben said with a resigned tone. "Was there a last-minute change of plans?"

Pounders exhaled, staring at Ben intensely, hands pressed on the desk. "It is a surreal time out there, Ben – war changes everything overnight." Pounders stood up straight, adjusting the cuffs of his uniform sleeves. "Yes, there has been a change of plans. For us."

Ben frowned. He followed Pounders' hand, pointing to the upper northwest side of the Euphrates River – north-west of Baghdad – in close proximity to a serpentine flaky basin of water, filtered through a thin head, distilling into a single river.

"The conventional forces in the Shock and Awe Campaign were too drastic," Pounders said, "and they lost their mission, leaving Special Ops leaders scrambling around for a plan B – Objective Lynx. They request immediate aid. They're in need of a very strategic point if we are to begin our invasion into Baghdad." Pounders then turned from the map, fixing Ben in the eyes as if they were targets. "So, new plan. We're going to hit Haditha Dam."

"Haditha?" Ben intoned surprised. "That sounds out of the way."

"Yet the enemy knows it's of vital use," Pounders replied. "It is the only main highway across the Euphrates that provides hydro-electric power that can essentially benefit us, whilst cutting off any resources from enemy forces."

"Yeah," Ben said sceptically, "but we don't need their power, do we? We clearly have our own capabilities. Granted, if this place is a resource zone, we already have troops stationed there anyway. So why do they need more defences?"

Pounders gave Ben a one-sided smirk. "That's the news, Ben. We underestimated the dam. I thought and said those exact same things a moment ago and then I understood why. It was a distress call."

"A distress call?"

"I want you to see it for yourself. You need to organise an assault force to Haditha. Forget the mission report. It turns out the Iraqis are not ignorant of the dam's value and had stationed a surprisingly strong defence force around the structure."

"What the hell do they intend to do now?" Ben stressed. "What's *so* valuable to them, that they are willing to risk a whole out battle, that could potentially damage the whole dam which they need to sustain their water supply?" Ben threw up his hands. "Sir, this doesn't add up. *Haditha Dam*? It's *not* a war zone."

Pounders began to pace, hands laced around his back, looking not one bit exasperated by Ben's arguments. "The report came back, Ben, and it said . . . The enemy threaten to sabotage the dam and flood the town of Haditha."

"*What? Why?* Their own people?! Their homes!? The Iraqis are mad. *Hussein's mad.*"

"Like I said, Ben," Pounders said, dryly shaking his head, "war changes everything. This is not some simpleminded greed for hydro-electricity that drives these people. No. It is some all-consuming passion that is driving these Iraqis, Ben. It is what it is. We're hitting Haditha Dam." Pounders began to roll up the map. "Bonner *did* say that the dam caused mysterious deliria. Some say because the dam's architecture and its atmosphere are unwelcoming . . . Well, let's just say it's an unpleasant place. Bonner wants to get to the bottom of this, because he believes this source of hydro-electricity will buy us time to reach Baghdad. Haditha is our Thermopylae pass. Our last hold to give the coalition ground forces time to push into the capital."

Ben could not reply. He was so stunned, he gazed at the wall near the door away from Pounders' sight.

"We cannot waste time, Ben, and we must proceed to save our men. To inform you, we need to go out there *first*, to ready an ambush, so we can secure a prudent passage for the Sentinels. Get ready."

Ben nodded. *F you. F everyone, for not telling me this sooner!* "Understood, Colonel. I'll notify my men asap."

Pounders grinned and Ben, wasting not a second, ran out the door, so that his men could know exactly what to expect.

19

REVALUATION OF REVELATION

"The Egyptians adopted some Uruk Period (3500-3000 BCE) niched architecture, cylinder seals and even some decorative red, white and black clay cone mosaics found at the site of Buto. It is just as possible that Mesopotamians visited Egypt who were in what is known by archaeologists as the Naqada II period (3500 – 3200 BCE).

During this era, many cultural and technological innovations transformed people's lives… People from Mesopotamia established what seemed to be settlements in many places far from home, in what were later Syria and Assyria and even what is now southeastern Turkey and southeastern Iran. These cities boasted of Mesopotamian pottery and architecture, highlighting that it is even possible that some Mesopotamian settlers set up near the Red Sea or in the delta region in Egypt.

The influence on Egypt from Mesopotamia didn't last long… No references to Egypt appear in Mesopotamian records for centuries and communication between the two great civilisations seems to have been very limited in the third millennium BCE."

—From Joshua Tanrıöver's *Honours Thesis on the Trade and Cultural Exchange Between Pre-Dynastic Egypt with Uruk and Jemdet Nasr Mesopotamia*, Willamette University.

Every muscle in Joshua's body was sore and stiff: his wrists, his biceps, arms, his chest, thighs and calves. Even his *fingers* were worked out and they shook with tremoring effort even as he tried to read and turn pages of his book. Indeed, being locked up all day did not help with his sore muscles – he needed to stretch for a fourth time today.

This mystery of the dead Nephilim that Ben and his men had killed in Afghanistan *had* to be a harbinger of something great.

"You are a warrior, Joshua," Nefer said jubilantly as Joshua rubbed his sore arms. "Well done on your training." He regarded the spirit hovering over his desk in thin air, half blending into the visible and invisible. A floating small pink glob or a comb jelly fish, waving to some invisible wind. Why he took on this form, Joshua did not understand. When Nefer spoke, his voice sounded regally confident, sophisticated, speaking eloquently like a professor. Yet why did he remain half hidden?

Joshua flipped open his Bible to Genesis chapter six and found what he was looking for.

And it came about, when humanity began to multiply on the face of the land, and daughters were born for them, and the sons of Elohim saw the daughters of humanity that they were good and they took wives for themselves, whomever they chose. And Yahweh said, "My Spirit will not dwell with humanity forever, because he also is flesh; and his days will be one hundred and twenty years." The Nephilim giants were in the land in those days, and also afterward, when the sons of Elohim went into the daughters of humanity, and they bore children for them; these are the mighty warriors who are from ancient time, men of the name.

And Yahweh saw that multiplied was the badness of humanity in the land, and every purpose of the plans of his heart was only bad all the day, and Yahweh regretted that he made humanity in the land, and he was pained in his heart. And Yahweh said, "I will wipe away humanity that I created from the face of the ground, from humanity to animals to creeping things and to birds of the skies for I regret that I have made them." But Noah found favour in the eyes of Yahweh.

"So, this may have been the cause of the Flood then," Joshua theorised. "The giants. Many scholars on this subject maintain that it was angels mating with humans that caused a corruption in the gene pool."

The spirit hummed tenderly. "No. No. No. Please, that's nonsense, Joshua! Nonsense! Gene pools are *garbage junk,* Josh!"

"Really?" Joshua said with a befuddled expression, adjusting his reading glasses. "It's the Word of God. And the giant of Kandahar had strange genetic adaptations I heard."

The angel contorted into a wave, saying sceptically, "You *heard.*"

"Well, at least you can prescribe a different genetic marker on these creatures. The Nephilim were unnatural hybrids. Half human and fallen angel. They caused the Judgement of humankind, not saving humankind from the chaos serpent. They *were* the serpent's seed. And because humanity's DNA was corrupted by them, God was mad."

"Ah . . . Okay. You are very misguided in this reasoning." The angel undulated, his form rippling from a sideways current to a diagonal flow over the chemical report from agent Ian Mastemah. "Genetic deformities *are not* problematic. It's the wickedness in humanity's heart that is the issue. Read the text more carefully next time, please."

Grimacing, Joshua got out his notebook, remembering seeing something. An Egyptian symbol somewhere while training these last few months at Fort Huachuca. It had to be something of importance. So, Joshua took his ballpoint pen and began to draw. A simple picture, of pentagram inside a circle and over it, an icon of a bird or a stork with an elegant long beak, a long neck and with flapping wings.

"You're starting to see," Nefer whispered eagerly.

He looked at the Scholar frowning. "Excuse me?"

"That is the symbol of the Egyptian god Osiris indeed."

Joshua's heart leapt. Osiris the god of the Underworld!? "Is that what it means?"

"Hm? You tell me."

"Well, I remembered seeing it…" *That's right! I saw it in one of my visons in the stained-glass windows! The heron!*

Nefer blurred into a misty cloud beginning to fade away. "That is not just any drawing! You drew the mark! Alfred Bonner's symbol. The Alliance."

"Alfred Bonner?" Joshua whispered, his heart starting to beat with passion studying the image. The angel was *fascinating* with what insight he could dispense, where Joshua overlooked. "The Director of the Shinar mission had been putting these symbols up around Fort Huachuca. That's why it looked so familiar. I've dreamed about it before seeing it. Does that mean anything?"

"It means you are seeing what has been hidden to most but revealed to you," the spirit said. "The symbol reveals Bonner is a Python. Bad. Bad. Bad Bonner. Though he may look innocent, Joshua, do not trust him, for each word that pours out of his mouth, and each deed he sets his hands to is tricky. Don't be deceived by Alfred Bonner."

Joshua smirked. "No worries, brother. I've never seen Alfred Bonner before, and I think I never will. But why is this important then? What does the mark of the heron bird mean for the war in Iraq?"

"The Two Rivers, even now, is a land of darkness. A locus of desolation as it has always been," Nefer cogitated. "Babylon the Great is fallen. She is dead, but at the same time, she lives. The mark is of a beast and the beast is marked.

The heron beast is the power that was, and is not, and yet is."

"Six, six, six," Joshua whispered, staring at the Scholar. "So, Alfred Bonner is the Beast? He worships Osiris?"

"No. The Beast is the Nephilim human desire to become a god," Nefer said. "Humans are remarkable creatures; cable of doing great good and great sin. When a human rebels against God and harbours hate towards another, they become beasts, destroying themselves and everything around them."

"But I thought the Beast of the Book of Revelation was Emperor Nero. What did you mean the Beast is a Nephilim god human that is violent, Nef?"

"I stood upon the sand of the sea and saw a beast rise up out of the Deep with ten heads and ten horns. The horns are human world systems – political, legislative and military – and the heads are the gods, and the sea is the chaos. Nero, and his father Dyeus, is yet one of many representatives of the Dragon's extension of power. There have been many in history following the dark pattern."

Dyeus? "Zeus you mean?"

"Same same. But the Holy People of the Most High will overcome the Beast. By not worshipping it, they will receive the Kingdom and have God's name written on their foreheads for ever and ever."

"But what do the gods have to do with the war? Are they the Fallen Angels of Genesis six?"

"Joshua, it's difficult to explain to you humans that cannot see the Unseen. For you, we must first evaluate and understand the social, political and cultural context of the day when these scriptures were written. The Beast that came out of the sea, rose up from chaos. It wields the power of chaos. It has seven heads, seven days of anti-creation. The Beast's horns are human rulers, crowned by the crowned Dragon. They are all the nations and kingdoms that have ever existed. The Beast are governments controlled by the fallen gods." Nefer trembled by that reckoning. "Quite unpleasant, this Alfred Bonner."

Joshua blinked. The Beast as all nations?

"I want to remind you," Nefer said tenderly as Joshua intensely studied the heron on his page. "This is the reason I have come."

"Yeah?" Overwhelmingly curious, Joshua pinched the page of his book where he had drawn the symbol from ancient Egypt, the symbol of the Light Alliance. Of Alfred Bonner. *He is part of the Beast system controlling the American marines!?*

"You are coming to know what it means to be an Envisager." Becoming a jelly orb, the spirit floated onto Joshua's shoulder, shrinking to the size of a grape. "You're convinced that Bonner is the Beast of Revelation. This is *not* the purpose of prophecy at all because it is not meant to point to a specific event or a specific person or entity in the future. You know, the testimony of Jesus is the spirit of prophecy? The Bible doesn't predict anything."

Joshua flinched. "What?"

"The Bible *announces* God's syllabus, but it doesn't have to be fixed. It is a *diagnosis* of human failure and sin that leads to destruction, but if humans repent, God will change his plan to restore. There is an integral pattern going all the way back to Genesis one to three throughout the prophecies." Nefer's voice became leathery, every time attempting to use man-made Scripture references to divide the Bible. "A fractal pattern of human behaviour and attitude that turns from relationship to independence."

"I know," Joshua remarked. "Prophecy is truth-telling, not fortune-telling."

"Prophecy itself reveals what *could* happen in the future by giving us an image or a pattern, in order to change the present. It allows no private interpretation. Its power comes from its bias – either you believe the world's ideology, or Heaven's. It is a fractal, just as reality is a fractal structure. There are sequences of patterns and slight changes to the fractal in each context and era.

"This prophetic fractal reoccurs with the patterns of the wicked's punishment, who God will justify, the protection of the righteous saints, and their ultimate triumph. One does not need to anticipate or interpret events going on around them and shoehorning the event into the Scripture. No, my friend. Bonner is not *the* Beast. He is *a* beast." Suddenly, Nefer darting off Joshua's shoulder, bloomed into a bell-shaped jellyfish with spindly tendrils floating in phantom pelagic drift. "If you miss the real meaning of a prophecy, be warned that *no amount* of preparation or study will save you from what is coming upon the self-destructive world. Yes. The prophetic hope is heart change. The complete, moral transformation of the universe."

Almighty, that's . . . a paradigm shift. Joshua tried to piece together the implications behind Nefer's clarifications on the fractal nature of prophecy. Joshua's doctrine – Futurism, Earth-going-to-Hell-in-a-hand-basket – was *utterly erroneous.*

"Are we in the era of the end Nefer?" Joshua asked, his voice timid. "Is the Day of the Lord at hand?"

"Depends on your view of time," Nefer said. "No one knows the day or the hour, not even Jesus Christ. But one can discern the signs of the times, if you care to look around. The era of the end shall be when nations fight against nation, wars and rumours of wars, famine, earthquakes, natural disasters, friends betraying one another, charismatic leaders leading many astray and the righteous being unjustly persecuted. The birth pains into new creation."

"But those things have always been happening since the beginning of history," Joshua said, hand to his glasses.

"Hm, indeed. We live in a transitional phase of time. The present age of terror, death and slavery is falling away, overlapping with the age to come right now, new creation, peace and flourishing. The age to come which is now here, was inaugurated by the resurrection of Jesus. It invaded the present age. So the era of the end is this overlapping space between the ages. Remember the fractal pattern. History follows this pattern, repeating itself, anticipating the final culmination in the future. The end is now but not yet. The birth pains have always been, but the Day of the Lord is not yet here. The Kingdom is here. Victory has been gained, now the present age must fall away for new creation."

Casting aside his previous theology, Joshua felt compelled to seek potentially deeper insight into the nature of time – a stained-glass window that he could look upon and see on the white of one's soul the rainbow-coloured shafts of the form of Heaven – his spiritual attainment of truth. Or possible truths, as there were as many possible outcomes in time as there were spectral colours in a rainbow.

Joshua whispered, "The Kingdom is here already. So, you are saying that there is going to be hope? In this fractal pattern, is there a global revival in the Third Millennium?"

"Indeed Joshua. You see truth," Nefer intoned. "You are a history student. Think, how did the early Church in the first and second centuries survive and spread to become the world's largest religion in two thousand years? It was because of *persecution and tribulation*. This is a *glorious thing* for the Church! And it shall happen one last time. Yes, the fractal pattern is replete with tribulation for the Church. Earth is readying itself as the Kingdom of God has conquered most people with a peaceful fire. Take heed lest you think you stand, you fall. The Millennial will never end. The Lord's return is at hand."

Joshua flinched, feeling horrified. "The Millennial Regin is symbolic? Seriously? I've been completely wrong?"

"Indeed. Many brothers and sisters have been wrong, but I'm giving you constructive judgement. You have been looking at a mountain from the bottom of a valley, but I am standing on the mountaintop. Blessed is the one who reads aloud the words of the prophecy, and blessed are those who hear, and who keep what is written in it, for the time is near."

"So . . . The Millennial Regin is symbolic of the Kingdom of God. It never ends. The Tribulation… It's not going to be so bad after all? We're going to go through it?"

"Yes. I dislike calling the Kingdom of God 'the Millennium'," Nefer said. "It is now but not yet, not just something in the future. There is a tension between the present and the future. This present age and the age to come. The Kingdom of God has always been and will always be, it is just not yet fully realised. The Great Tribulation has always been as well. It has always been since Israel went into exile in 722 BCE and will persist until Christ returns in the future. Tribulation will be painful, but it will be good. Trust me."

Joshua took off his glasses and rubbed his face. "Wow, this is eschatology bigger than both of us. Who am I to know these deep things. You are obviously more informed than I. Knowledge shall increase in the Last Days." Joshua sighed. "But never come to the knowledge of the Truth."

Back in the asylum, his spirit had often been very docile creating their bond, yet it took time for both of them to get used to each other, studying the Bible together. Now, they had come to the Revelation. The culmination of all Old Testament prophecies into one scary grand exposure of self-destructive human violence and evil, revealed for what it was. It seemed God here was doing something in cyclical patterns for the last two thousand years, and Joshua had a feeling that his angel could be part of something incredible.

But now he was a Ranger under Captain Ben DePaula and ultimately, Alfred Bonner, whose organisation was linked to the pattern of the Beast. All of it thrust Joshua into the heat of the Middle East and war. Joshua felt his stomach churn. *This has always been. Nothing is new under the sun.*

"Hmm. Joshua?" Nefer floated in his face sounding worried "Are you alright? You just smothered yourself with fear, doubt and pain. Why?"

Joshua blinked, grunting. "You know what? All this stuff about prophecy is giving me a headache. It's not worth predicting things. Whatever happens, happens. It will all pan out in the end. I guess that is the message from tonight!" He sighed, rubbing his eyes and temples, standing up from his seat to stretch his back and arms. He gasped as they cramped. "I think we will call this a night."

—

When Joshua entered into the Ranger's dorm not the least bit interested in talking to them, Reggie confronted him.

"Yo Jish, you want some gee-dunk?" Reggie said, wagging a packet of lollies and chocolates.

Recoiling, Joshua evaded the immature man, clutching his notebook. "Reggie! It's nine at night! And we're being deployed *tomorrow*."

"Eh, whatevs. It will help give us energy," Reggie said impishly. Grabbing a packet of Ho Hos, he stuffed his face. "Laycock, you want some?" Reggie chattered with a mouthful as Laycock adamantly raised a hand, digging inside the bag of treats. Joshua turned his back seeking out his bed, the most distant from everyone else, propped behind two rows of bunks so he could at least have some peace and quiet. He liked that.

He sat on his bed with the little Seer and Scholar angel appearing from the air rippling near his pillow.

"Okay then!" Derek Fish exclaimed across the room sitting on his bunk. "You didn't need anything to eat, Reggie. You already had a bag full."

"Sargent!" Julian snapped as the door opened. All the marines practically leapt off the ground, yelping in union fear. Laycock bumped his head on the bunk.

"Sargent!"

But it was not the Drill Sergeant, but Bill Sargent entering abruptly, started by everyone's flabbergasted reaction.

"Sup bois!" Sargent beamed like a buffoon. "Kiss da dirt! Beat yo face!"

"No Drill Sergeant!" Laycock mocked.

"Oh, you're on thin ice, shrimp! Wake-up call's at six!"

"Good to know, Sergeant Sargent!" Julian said.

Derek laughed curtly. "Ha! Sergeant Sargent!"

"Sargent Sargent," Laycock barked back comically.

"Sargent Sargent!"

The like words rebounded across the room until the lexical degradation of the phrases deducted into random yaps and honking noises. Joshua steeled himself with a sigh, covering his ears with a pillow. The men, or rather, *children*, hairy and reeking of deodorant, shrieked like girls – Laycock getting to his feet, got into a crab stance, eyes protruding, leaping about, emitting a loud "*eeeerrrrr!!!*" slapping Sargent on the neck and buttocks, raucously honking.

"Man!" Bill exclaimed. "Hey! What they – This is taken, bro!"

"I'm in an insane asylum?" Joshua said, irked. *And this is what all the sugar is doing to them!*

"They sound like Lahmu. What are they even *saying?*" Nefer wondered, half shocked, half horrified.

Lahmu?

"You will be surprised how much humans act more like animals," Joshua shook his head, placing his notebook down and unscrewing his water bottle to drink. "Especially during the elections."

"You guys want to hear about how Garrow's Ghillie Suit Woodland Camouflage became a purple suit that got him the smoky chick? It's classic," Bill spoke up, sounding sonorous. "Classic."

"Aw yeah," Laycock cheered, chomping on his Twinkie at the side of the mouth. "Go on."

"Welp," Garrow answered, desire dripping forth from his smacking lips "Katrina, you know, she was the girl in college I had a mad crush on, and I never got the guts to ask her out."

"Oh, this is priceless." That sigh came from Ben, emerging from the bathroom shirtless with baggy shorts holding a towel. Joshua grumbled, laying on his back, covering his ears with his pillows.

"I grabbed my stash of roses, combed back my hair and marched right in there to battle. Oh my!"

Someone slapped their leg, bellowing out in laughter. "Oh boy, those chicks were digging me! They were digging me so bad, I thought they would distract me from finding my own rose! They were fighting! I could not stop them!" Garrow cried, losing his breath as he giggled wildly with Derek, Laycock and Reggie.

Ben theatrically shoved Julian aside, re-enacting the scene. "Move it ladies! This one is mine!"

"Oh man! I was too sexy for them all!" The entire room exploded with a ruckus guffaw making Joshua roll his eyes. The joke didn't land at all.

Nefer gasped with a breathy voice floating around next to Joshua. He had the ability to not show himself to others, only making himself visible to Joshua. "But. But. But that *wasn't even funny*!"

"I know."

"That's *vile* torrid talk of women as an object of lustful man! This is what the Fallen Anunna did! Oh, so bad. So, so, so bad!"

"Tell me, Josh, what's it like to be a single archaeologist?" Joshua perked his head up to attention, seeing Derek Fish who had spoken, inclining on his side on his bunk.

Joshua sighed, sitting up. "Oh boy. Well, what makes me single so *interesting* to you, Derek Fish? That is my proposition."

"So *scholarly*," Derek commented. "There would be plenty of hot chicks out there that will find that too hot to resist. Hehe. I'm sure, little man. I hope you meet a good girl."

Bastard. I'll box this sex-craved man in the ears! Joshua found no purpose in the discourse, so he dropped out, leaving Derek to depart – what would be the good of that, boxing the giant African American man talking about sex?

"Is he talking about *human mating?*" Nefer gasped. "That's so lewd. Bad company corrupts good morals. You must cut them off, lest you be cut off."

"I know. But they're not my *friends,* Nefer. I'm surrounded by darkness. I'm forced to sleep with them because of *stupid* Judd Pounders and his waiver, forcing me against my will." Joshua scowled, slumping and crossing his arms

"Be careful you are not blaming others for your dilemmas," Nefer warned. "This was Adam's big mistake when he turned from face-to-face and cut himself off from Eve, accusing her for the Fall and not the serpent – the Accuser."

"Okay, okay, enough exciting bedtime stories, folks." Ben raised his voice, ending the joy of his men, something Joshua was not expecting to see.

"There is soul-brokenness in this one," Nefer whispered, his voice sounding distant. "In everyone."

Joshua slowly turned his head towards Nefer who indeed looked mistier than before. "I'm going to bed. Good night."

"Alright. I shall see you in the morning for prayer. God bless," Nefer said, vanishing.

20

THAT HIDEOUS PERDITION

"Why do the heathen rage,
and the people imagine a vain thing?
The kings of the earth gathered themselves,
and the rulers conspire,
against Yahweh, and against his Anointed (Messiah), saying,
'Let us tear off their bonds,
and cast away their cords from us.'
He that sits in the heavens laughs.
Yahweh shall have them in derision.
Then he speaks to them in his wrath,
and in his fury he terrifies them."
—Psalm 2.

Tara had a severe twitch – scowling at all the aristocratic men of the Boeheim Club – who she planned to bomb. Her grimace was hidden behind a black-and-white silk mask. Though women were not members in this sexist Club Grove Party in the middle of the Redwoods, everyone else wore masks like hers for the Cremation of Care. Their masks were of various styles, carnival elaborate to plain, that covered half the face. Here, they could conceal their gender, but Tara knew they were mostly men. A hundred masks, and a hundred pairs of eyes trying to see what lay behind them. She wore bleak black clothes, making her appear as bulky as a man, so none would detect her.

The woods were dark and humid at night, the light coming from a series of blazing candles on the long oak tables set on decks. Lights hung in a canopy

195

above held by wooden beams. If one didn't look closely, the Grove would have appeared a natural pond with a horseshoe theatre – a superstructure of five rows of wooden viewing platforms – holding up a dominating thirty-foot-tall crude owl statue covered in patches of moss and lichen. In the orange candlelights, the owl loomed in ochre shadows – a phallic monolithic formation that smelled of damp marshland. The Redwood trees resembled colonnade pillars of a Roman Forum. The rock statute wasn't made of living rock, Tara knew the owl formation was fake. Within the statue, an electrical circuit connected to light sources, illuminating the Grove's outdoor bar. She knew this, she'd strategically planted two bombs behind the owl.

Tara had always been enraged by toxic masculinity. These men always sexist about male benefits, like cheap insurance. This grove *writhed* with the filth, like the muck in that man-made pond and the bleak sounds of slimy frogs that croaked cacophonously in the night, under the quicksilver of the full moon. These men were greedy toads.

Tara had come to a desperate position now, that the only way for her to survive under her Aes Sidhe handlers of the Horned Ones was that she had to become the aggressor. The time of acting passive and weak was over. Here, at Bohemian Grove, the Horned Ones of the Left-Hand Path, wielders of chaos magic ideally demanded secularists, Republicans and clergymen to disseminate their agenda. They had used her as a pawn, a broken thing, but now Tara had taken the responsibility to end their darkness.

They put ideas in her head to shoot up a school, so now, they were about to get a taste of their own medicine during the Bohemian Grove Cremation of Care.

As Tara checked that the detonator remote to set off the bombs was safe in her pocket, she saw the only women in the Grove. Heteronomous; likely hired high maintenance prostitutes – they were men's toys. The idea of makeup was a sexist expectation for women to always beautify themselves. These women's bodies were only here to be penetrated by nymphomaniacs.

Tara twitched when greasy gazes of intoxicated congressmen, priests, musicians, and oil barons, came upon her. She was grateful for the disguise.

Tara had to get her timing right with the detonation, making sure three more bombs were planted next to Redwood trunks close to the tables, so all these infuriating frog-like men could pay. She did not need a gun but pyrotechnics – once the fireworks at the end of the Cremation of Care ceremony went off, the bombs would go off instantaneously. Every one of these white men, many who were rich, selfish and anti-women's rights, would die in their own revelry.

Silently, Tara watched the servants, youths serving wine and beverages long sufferingly for the elite men. Wearing body-tight pants and snug blouses barely opaque, suggesting what it concealed, the women moved with grace, swan necked, smelling of wonderful perfume, no doubt to arouse these men. How sad that they could be taken advantage of by these modernists materialistic animals and get away with it!

Tara scowled deeply and twitched as a middle-aged blond man drunkenly lumbered off chuckling with his friends, with wine in one hand, pull down his pants with the other, urinating into the bushes.

Tara twitched, shivering with chills, and turned away. On those tables, the men were feasting upon cheesy curds, the sights of the oozing liquid pouring into cups, and over meals, aggravated her nausea. The men shrugged, watching her, no doubt wondering who she was, downing the curds in greedy gulps, wiping mouths unconsciously with a napkin. As if they were clean and innocent.

Tara was shocked to find a diminutive youthful woman with blond hair in a single braid wrapped around one shoulder, offering her a tray of wine in golden goblets, shining with splendour and promise. Holding out a gold cup of crimson drink, the waitress smiled behind the mask that covered only the upper part of her face. A smile that suggested something more – the disguise worked well on this woman who looked in her early twenties. Tara took one gold cup filled up with its portion of the beverage, with no intention of drinking; it might appear untrusting – or worse, bad manners would be deadly here – if she refused all together, she wouldn't need to worry about something being slipped into her drink.

Tara grounded her teeth in impatience for the ceremony to begin. As she observed her surroundings, she saw a tall stout man with red hair cut like an Amish County farm boy swathed in a dark cloak. He rounded a table, grabbing his own wine goblet with his left hand, nodding at the serving girl. The man wore no mask. Bowing a curtsy, the servant girl looked into the red-haired man's eyes smiling – with blank eyes. Doll eyes. Eyes more dead than death.

Tara twitched and sweated. She tried to ignore this man, who she didn't know what he was all up about. *If he irritates me, I will give him such a hard time that he will avoid me.*

A good amount of people awaiting the Cremation of Care had not bothered with a disguise beyond their masks, their clothes told too much.

Standing on the other side of the wooden platform at the pond's edge, a prominent man in an expensive navy-blue suit with sunglasses and a fedora hat spoke kindly to a figure – impossible to say whether a man or a woman – clad in a grey cloak. Most ad hoc men laughing with one another at the tables, had a nervous energy for the Cremation to commence.

It was never about status to come to Boeheim Grove, but about one's *sensual ingenuity* and who one had access to. If one had an unconventional, abnormal talent in something, they could escape into the wilderness and misbehave with a like-minded bunch. Such notions made Tara's shoulder jerk. She only knew Aes Sidhe handlers that had been previous members at the Bohemian Grove, and the handler's membership at the atheistic Temple of Set, gave her discreet access here.

Suddenly, Tara's eyes narrowed. She was surprised to find a single gorgeous and stately woman with black lipstick and golden eyes, covered in a woollen cloak, with her back against a Redwood trunk nearby. Her long honey brown hair in ringlets tumbled down her exposed low neckline, wearing dark clothing. What on earth was this woman doing with a neckline so low? Her amber eyes were hawklike, all-knowing. It made Tara twitch, thinking, *How many Aes Sidhe are here?*

At the periphery of her vision, Tara marked the red-haired man next to her. As he removed his hood, Tara gawked at the robotic arm from the fingers to the elbow, rising from his capacious sleeve, metal tendons working as bony fingers.

The man who wore no mask shocked Tara. He wore an emotionless plain face that had seen much discipline. He had a large moustache and most of all, turquoise eyes. The markers of an Indigo Child and an Aes Sidhe. Tara stared at his robotic right arm, sinking back into the den of the sleeve slowly. Aes Sidhe had implants in their brains – so their masters would control them at will – one reason Tara had gone rogue. Aes Sidhe were crazy, unpredictable people.

"I see your eyes and your hair," the man said softly. Then he did sign language. The symbol for, *you're not the only one.*

Tara went to speak, but her mouth could not emit any sounds. She signed back saying, *Who are you? What do you want from me?*

Whatever you plan to do, the Aes Sidhe signed, *delay. It will not go well.*

There was an energy of odium dormant in this man, and Tara immediately disliked him. All men where the same, they were deceitful, selfish monsters. "Just tell me your name man," Tara said aloud, deeply and harshly. "What are you? What do you want?" She couldn't bare not being able to genuinely test someone's motives and trust. Too many times, Tara had been betrayed.

Then, revealing only a few bionic fingers from his right sleeve surreptitiously, the man signed, *I'm Airgetlám.* Silverhand.

Another one. Another one driven mad by the sins of the world.

Airgetlám raised his dull gold goblet of wine in his fleshy hand. Tara started, perfunctorily raising her own, connecting cups with a delicate chime.

Suddenly, a burning smell; a hideous and pungent aroma strong enough to gush into Tara's nose, reeked of dry vomit. Men at the table started gagging and coughing.

A loud, very loud, roar thundered through the Grove – it was of a man with a scream too deep to be human. A dwindling belch followed and then, the sound of many flaying branches. *Holy crap what was that?* Tara's heart roared in her breast as the wraith in the woods raged, coming closer and closer. The party ceased, men gawking at the huge raucous among the shrubs outside in the night, branches snapping, the booming of something enormous emerging.

Leaves trembled as a hulking shape stumbled from the darkness of the woods, grunting sonorously, slumped and covered in hair.

Black Bears were common here in this neck of California, so Tara found it strange that all the men and people ceased their party and gazed.

Until the bear stood up bipedally. Covered in dark motely grey, arms a forearm's length longer than normal, reaching below stumpy knees, humps bulging from its shoulders – this creature was *not* a bear. It was a grotesque *Neanderthal,* or a *gorilla,* but much larger than any from the zoo, with a beard all over its face, no neck and a V-shaped body. Its amber eyes reflected the light from the candles, emitting its own sheen out of leathery ridges.

Tara held her breath in fear and awe. The Sasquatch scowled menacingly at the humans.

Then four more giant Sasquatch appeared unaccountably into the light from the owl statue itself, silently. The sight shocked Tara. Four hairy apes walked as if gliding, their heads did not bob over the contours of the wooden steps but remained stilled. Man-like, head and shoulders taller than the tallest man, and muscular, with very long arms swaying, they marched in dense eerie muteness across the wooden superstructure. Hairy with huge feet, everyone shied back from the stomach-turning blend of man, monkey and ape, humanity twisted and altered. One had a cone-shaped head, covered in lush onyx hair with long thick lips that stretched on a face sagging the space between upper lip and flat nose. The other, hunched and old with a pudgy face and distinctive eyebrows, had long hair splayed flatly over its apish head. One resembled a shaggy dog with a muzzle pushing out of its face, with no forehead and possessing fangs. The last looked almost human – a black man terrified with eyes too round, too large, too dark.

The loud Sasquatch gazed at his giant brothers, face in a rictus snarl.

The five hominids in total walked up towards the owl statue, feet thumping against the wood stressed under their weight with their backs to Tara and bowed.

At that moment, two cowled entities appeared from the shadows on either side of the owl statue, where Tara had placed the bombs. Destress afflicted her. *Oh crap… They saw the bombs…*

Light around the entities vanished. They were garbed in black, blacker than night, a void in space time – light appeared to suck into their bodies and their garments hung still, as they moved with viper grace.

Those voids of faceless cowls regarded everyone one by one. A violent shiver made Tara jerk under that eyeless look. There was a smell of sweet incense that purified the air from Sasquatch stench, and the smoke candles on the long oak tables before the ochre statute of the phallic owl. Dirges of frogs creaked obstinately, infesting the night like a plague unseen from mortal eyes.

"The Owl is in its temple," an eerie voice came from the air – one of the entities – rasping like decayed leaves. "On your bellies!"

A metal sound rung in Bohemian Grove. Rage and fear filled Tara as she saw all the men and servants follow the Sasquatch. They dropped to the ground, leaving their drinks and food on the table, pulling out chairs to bow on their knees as if at Church. Tara grinded her teeth. *The bombs! Why aren't they…*

Just as Airgetlám moved to show obsequiousness, Tara dropped, placing her undrunk goblet on the floor, face down, grunting as she bruised herself on the wooden boards. She felt thwarted and red handed.

"At last!" a sirenian feminine voice rose from one of the entities. "The New World Order shall spread democracy around the world."

"Hear!" the other dark male voice yelled. "He who has an ear to hear, what the Spirit says to the Churches!"

The air became electric. The frogs shrilled, enhanced by the fiery candles burning brighter and hotter. Words sprang from Tara's lips, and she heard a hundred other voices, breathy with fear, speaking the same against the floor. Her mind raced and raced faster than the foreign words pouring out of her mouth unconsciously. A universal power implanting streams of intent and will on her, in its cruel cold grip.

"Great Architect, the one who was, and is not, and yet is, everlasting. The Great Lord of the Wild Beasts, do I serve in humility to you, oh eternal beauty! Lord of the Dark Earth!" *Satan and the demons are not real . . .* Tara convulsed. No, she *had* silenced the problematising voice long ago! "Caretaker, animal and powerful, shimmering scales, dragon of Tartarus – hail to you, for you shall take back what is rightfully yours, Prince of the Air. The one who was, and is not, and yet is." *. . . The Dragon was bound by God in the Bottomless Pit for a thousand years . . . Silence hypocrite! I'm not religious! I need to kill all exploiters!*

Tara finished the creed she did not know but had cited, panting and gasping. She was adrift in tsunami of endless pain and uncertainty. These morons prepared to die had *no idea* that they were enslaved minions of an evil, cosmic and wrathful power.

The energy from the owl. Everywhere. Tara knew this same power could destroy nations.

A bizarre interlude, an orchestra began to play, trumpets and pianos, jarring to Tara that she twitched, sweating profusely.

"Bohemians and priests! Rise!" called the female entity after the interlude. The five Sasquatch rose like megaliths behind the two dark entities, not moving. "The arms race has begun, so we must obey the words of America. And the only way that must be done . . ." A suspenseful silence rose as Tara rocked up on her knees. "Is to make peace with the Alliance."

Shock rose from the crowd of Cabal men. Susurrations of bewilderment seized them. Tara honestly had no sense of the gravity of the statement, only she could reckon it as the extreme Right seeking to unite with the extreme Left.

"We, as a broker of peace in the Middle East!" the male entity in black said, stalking down one platform. "We need cohesion."

"Is this cohesion about American democracy, my Aeon?" another man said from the oak table. What was an Aeon? For Tara, it was difficult to discern who had spoken behind the crowd wearing masks. Aeon appeared to be the honorifics for these bizarre spectres. "Our interests are free enterprise. Oil – the petroleum resources – must be the objective."

"Frankly, I think the Alliance should piss off! We must be focused on security matters to make this country great again." Another slurring male voice. It made Tara twitch; his heavy accent dripped with toxic filth, and he had floppy white, blond hair over his mask. "Anyone that tries to break this law will pay."

"We have enough access to oil, fools," the male Aeon snapped. "We need a better civil defence department for the United States to deter Muslims and Arabs. And yes. Democracy, culture and human rights is the answer in this war. Most of the movement archives in the Middle East are restricted from our fellow researchers because Islam is fundamentally undemocratic. Islam is only part of the great threat that looms against us, and we must unite against the Galactic Tyrant and all his minions."

"My lord," the first politician spoke up. "What if it's *not* in Alfred Bonner's interests to make peace with us: the Cabal?"

"Bonner supports democracy, human rights and free enterprise!" the male Aeon clipped. "We need to embrace his reasonable strategy for now and stop acting with vitriolic division. We tend to see our politics – that humans need to be constrained to function – as a way to reason, but a greater enemy is upon us. The Galactic Tyranny of Allah is here."

A wave of confusion rumbled through the men. "This unity with the Alliance is only a trade-off, not an ultimate solution. We only need to do this to succeed retrieving what we need," the male Aeon said.

"But Bonner thinks he's an unconstrained essential planner of a virtuous utopia! He wants to destroy us!" Voices arose in protest.

So, Tara thought. *The Cabal is implying the Golda Meir mentality then — the enemy of my enemy is my friend. Islam and Arabs are being scapegoated with all the world's problems. Its how the secret societies make war against the Galactic Tyrant. Allah.*

"Operation Enduring Freedom is for the sake of the people," a politician muttered, "the war would take years to fight. It's a war on ideologies, that span multiple states. We must do all that is necessary to win. So I agree! Listen to Bonner then discard him later!"

Tara growled under her breath, twitching all the more. Didn't she, too, commit to the exemplar of "whatever was necessary", to kill off misogyny?

What are you doing!? A condemning voice grated her soul. *Bomb the bastards already, you failure!*

Tara's body went stiff and cold. She felt invisible, like a watcher at the cinemas, existing to only gaze at her life playing by. Not participating, not experiencing, not engaging. Just… watching everything go by, passively. There had been a long time when Tara had let her life take her on wherever it went. It destroyed her soul. And now, Tara had changed. She let herself be punished by her fate.

She had become a weapon. She had to take explosive action.

"But if Bonner fails to concede us," the female Aeon called, striding towards Tara and Airgetlám, "we must take independent coercive action." Tara twitched nervously, her heart beating in fear. Her breath was audible.

"It's incontrovertible that Hussein has nuclear chemical weapons in his arsenal and is ready to use it." "Hussein is the Tyrant!" "Islam is dangerous and behind the attacks on the World Trade Centre!"

Her hand slipped into her pocket for the detonator button.

Might as well die as the most dangerous weapon around.

She pressed it, closing her eyes.

Nothing happened.

A loud beak-like snap came from the male Aeon. "Excellent my children! That is why you shall not fail to bring Bonner on our side!"

Tara opened her eyes, sweating. Dread engulfed her, numbing her. The bombs…

"Offence operations are the only option then Aeon Abraxas?" the first speaker said.

"The risk of failure is too high," Abraxas – the male Aeon – replied. "Yes. Launching a war against the Alliance at a time when arms are needed is suicide. But this war in Iraq, we can use it. Now, I command you, my time is short! Proceed!" The wraith raised an arm grandly, sweeping it across the audience.

Abruptly the frogs ceased all together, and there was silence in the woods. Even the air had stilled, with the most malevolent dread seeming to manifest out of the unseen aether. That very same dread Tara knew, when incapacitated in bed before a dark being.

She shivered uneasily, eyes drifting to the only other woman in the Grove with enigmatic golden eyes who was not a waiter, hand covering the round of exposed bosom. Her eyes were wide, nodding madly in fear or in ecstasy, as if something invisible were berating her face to face. She stood struck, in a paralysis of the limbs. Sometimes, she seemed to give a reply, but Tara heard not a word from those tar lips, only weak grunts. Suddenly, she arched backwards, brown hair dangling from her scalp, standing on her toes, convulsing. She could not see why she did not totter, unless something unseen held her. Then, just as abruptly, she planted herself back on her feet, nodding and bowing, her eyes glazed and face pallid.

Hissing out through his gritted teeth, Airgetlám too went rigid, blue eyes rolling back to whites in his head, nodding vigorously, making Tara's heart thunder so much she was sure it would burst. The two Aeons stood only a few feet away from her, their garments melting into the shadows as if they were literally the absence of light.

Tara's hand desperately crushed the button of her donator remote in her pocket. It didn't work. The bombs… had malfunctioned.

Firey fury burned her soul. Tara cursed grievously, hitting herself.

Everyone was being sent commands. All the despicable Cabal men in the Grove who lacked accountability for their pathological sins were lifted up on their toes, undergoing similar convulsions. Tara wished she could know what evil force transmitted orders, but she could detect tantalising clues – blanching faces, thrashing heads, gasps, arching backs and nods. Orders for the person, warded so no one else could hear. So Tara braced herself – she itched to run away.

Why aren't the bombs going off? she thought in panic, sweat dripping down her neck, breast and forehead.

Your plan was so easily detected, Tara, a foreign female voice pierced through her consciousness and suddenly, Tara writhed. Full evil, malevolent energy overcame her, and she whimpered, screwing shut her eyes.

Her knees gave way then, and she awoke, found herself on her face, overcome by both fear and compulsive force. Her jaws started to quiver, so she clamped them tight. The twitches were uncontrollable now, like coughs wracking her being. Her neck failed to keep her head upright as she panted. She refused to grovel as a worm!

A blistering blob – an blue all-seeing eye – appeared in her vision, consuming everything in her sight. She could still see the Grove, but the blob of blue grew denser. Shooting up on her knees, Tara felt as if her forehead were splitting open and her eyes pushed back into her skull. The pain was so intense, she felt she was coming apart from the seams. Fire was everywhere in her body, in every cell. She roared a silent scream.

Are you faithful to us . . . Tara? the cold evil female voice said.

"I am. I'm *faithful!*" Tears ran down her cheeks.

Now, you are a unified plurality, a kinship Tara and Airgetlám. Bonner and his group will try to turn you, but your best defence against his efforts is to concentrate on the future – for yourself and for the sake of North America.

Raped by the diabolical power, the disbelief within her marked with a tuition – an order. Tara whimpered, yielding to the voice of obtrusive command. She had been conditioned to detect weaknesses in those she served, but now she found herself preceded. The first rule of liberation was to search for weaknesses in others, a chink, so she could pry and probe and influence that individual. If these Aeons were her masters now, and they had no fallible weakness . . .

Frowning, Tara convulsed violently, gasping and moaning. Her forehead felt it was being gouged into by a tool. She wanted to scream for the anguish to stop.

She would become the crushed scapegoat, bearing the weight of all her sins and the world's sin, who hated her.

Her world upside down, in a pool of blood.

Take care, lest your heart be deceived. People who you least expect will constantly try to persuade you on their side. You must not compromise, Tara. What the Cabal can have, is informal power, and we can use it to remove the Alliance. Go, with Airgetlám and loot the Baghdad Museum in the darkness, once America has taken the city.

As the commands were being relayed, Tara realised her mouth was sagging open. The thrall of success . . . A new mission, without a handler to coerce her. Freedom. It motivated her, enticing her grim, deprived soul. Freedom was good to the eyes. To steal. Ransack rich ancient artefacts.

But how could she possibly get on a plane to Iraq to do that if the security detected her guns? For some reason, she felt indifferent next to Airgetlám to this order. Indifferent to evil.

A familiar warmth intwined over Tara, one metallic crunch of it. It felt odd as the warmth became heat, and even as it passed, Tara felt aware of herself, aware of Barbelo the female Aeon. She swayed, her head light, muscles watery.

She saw the world blowing apart, in a thousand supernovas, piercing motes flashing, tugging at her soul, images spinning in her mind within a turquoise, purple galaxy, dwindling into the distance before she could barely grasp what was happening. In a sky of saturated clouds, was a coruscant nebula shimmered like a thousand cities in the atmosphere, ruling oppressively, devastating the Earth with mighty katabatic winds. Fire rained from the skies in lightning forks, the moon and stars fell, the Earth became lava and the dead walked; the rock rent apart from the planet's raging frenzy.

She was caught up in the tyrannical nebula and saw a ramp made of wood reaching a giant glowing blue orb of flame. Climbing up the ramp was a lamb. It was covered in crimson, limbs writhing doggedly, smearing a wake of blood. The victimised lamb trembled, anguished, arching its head, dying. The baby animal brayed and suffered, a cry rising up to the altar of galactic tyranny. A torrent of water unseen collided into her. Tara couldn't nearly remember who she was, or what she was.

Some revelations are too important to be known, the voice – now androgynous and serpentine, roared. *Now you see what we are up against. The Galactic Tyrant is a weak, dead animal. We have freedom! We have victory!*

Carnutes, the Horned Ones, mobilise!

Tara squatted in an empty Bohemian Grove and blinked. Wherever she looked, the blob in her vision of Barbelo's presence haunted her mind. The wraith stood right over her, laying her hands over her head. Hesitantly, Tara straightened.

"As you command, Shining One," Tara said hoarsely. "It shall be done."

She got up, turned around, broke into a walk, then a jog, and once the dark wood consumed her, she sprinted.

But forever at the back of her mind, was the presence of Barbelo, enmeshed somehow with her soul. And ultimately, she could sense Airgetlám too, marked by the same being.

They were Carnutes now, the Horned Ones, hunters of the dark, friends of the shadow.

21

TO BE A MAN

   —Psalm 2. In the Greek LXX, 'shatter' is rendered 'shepherd'.

Ben was falling to sleep inside the soaring Boeing C-17 Globemaster III when the steady sound of a thin dirge of a horn – a signalling contralto that wavered near and far – fused with the long, lulling engine drone.

An ambient siren. Slowly rumbling as a wild wind through the sky.

Rumbling thunder.

Gather them.

Ben drifted, high in a dark night over a tempestuous ocean, formless and void with no light. A world of disorder and desolation, a tail end of a terrible calamity. Salt writhed in Ben's nose, spray and humid fog seeped into the pores of his skin. Spray gushed for miles upwards in wisps, whipped away by streams of titanic winds of the dark chambers of the sky. Under the dome of the moon's spheroid and the bright supernova, butte-shaped clouds with long concave walls loomed, with smaller downy clouds clustered around them. The columnar concave wall of cloud cupped strands and streaks of mist – grey and blue – sitting forlorn upon a dreary ocean.

The supernova's blue flares in the heavens cast a faint illumination of an eerie kind, dappling across the unruly watery surface, drifting aimlessly, without guidance.

Ben blinked. No longer was he watching the sublime silent ocean, he was cramped in a low ceiling hall with cedar pillars, low tables set with ewers and ceramic flasks and bowls of cold water. Yellow shafts of hazy sunlight seeped through the flagstones. On the ceiling, Ben could see in detail, a decorated carving of a hexagram in gold enamel.

The star of the Jewish people.

And there was a horrid visceral smell. The scent of charred marrow, of vomit, of dung and of sweat. A reeking, burning smell. The sound of snapping tents spliced the vile air, the clomping of hoofs, the wincing and grinding of stone, along with sobs on the wind.

Ben's body was bent as a hallowed tree, like a horn allowing only air pass through him. In his hand was a walking stick – no, a *staff* – a fleece wrapped around his feeble body, wearing sandals, body itching horribly in the arid heat.

"My old friend, why are you still here? Your life, serving the kingdom is at risk in my house. You should have stayed in your tent in the valley of the olive groves." A voice of a man that has seen his years, steadily rose with swelling emotion. A hoarse singer's voice. Ben knew musical voices – even when casual, they ran to a rhythm.

Ben turned to see a small but stout man, ridged fists grounded on the wide sill of the window embrasure, wrists encircled by polished metal cuffs. Underneath his purple mantle, his crinkled tunic was torn in the middle very low beyond his neckline, or perhaps that was the style. He was worn. He was old with a listless look, his skin a dry papery sallowness, starved, marred with pain. His mottled hands, calloused and frail as if his knuckles had been bruised, clenched – his body clenched head to toe. His grey hairs were a wiry mane, his short beard all haggard, and on his head, a modest crown of worn-out gold, a band of metal around his forehead. Set wide and deep in tired folds of flesh were his luminous amber eyes defined by sharp brows. A glint within them, and Ben believed he saw a tear.

"I have lived through the punishments I have earned, Natan. The rebukes you gave haunt me," the old king said in a weary, gravelly voice. "I should do something. I should do many things I have not done, and should not have done many things that I have done. Oh . . . To *kaphar* – to purge myself with cleanliness to draw back towards Yahweh." He turned to Ben, face scored with lines, as if expecting a response.

"Ugh . . . I . . . I don't know what you mean." Ben's heart thumped rapidly within his chest. His voice! So brittle and soft! Who was he? Where was he?

The regal man sighed, eyeing a large ornate harp in the corner of the room. "I'm being hasty again. You hate me when I am hasty." Suddenly, the old man's cheeks blushed, eyes faraway, whispering, "I hoped you would have a word from Yah for me. I've been singing that song again, Natan. Remember it?" The old king had a wry smile.

Ben followed the man towards the side of the room that split open into a long balustrade open to the air, held up by pillars painted with two bright red curving decorations. Ben looked out, the building he was in sat upon a gigantic, stepped round structure of stone fill, looking out over a modest town with formidable fortifications of bright limestone. The walled settlement, vaguely ship like, sat on the top of a small slim hill surrounded on either side by two valleys, farming terraces and crops grew along the sides of those valleys. It was evening, the setting sun stained the scattered clouds in a sultry red. Ben gazed down towards the right, at the compact houses with small central courtyards in the middle of clerestories. From the balcony, Ben could glimpse into the personal lives of the ordinary breadwinning people on the roofs and in the courtyards, washing clothes, and women baking bread together in clay dome ovens. Many people in the courtyards were in beds, coughing fitfully, while physicians tried to ease their illness.

"The idolatrous mistrust of the people fails to evaluate a man in power standing for El," the regal man uttered softly, face a grimace, forehead crinkled in distress.

And Ben thought, *The hell is that smell? Is something burning?*

The man looked relieved. He didn't appear worried by the smell. "Shemu'el said that kings exploit everything. We need *shaphat.*"

What's a shaphat? Ben wanted to scream the question out, but there was no way without sounding completely out of character. Not ideal if he was in a movie scene. *This is a movie, then? I don't even know my lines! Just improvise. Improvise.*

"What do you think we should do with these . . . *shaphat?*" Ben asked carefully.

"Where are the priests? Where are the *shaphat* with *mishpat tzadek?*" Footsteps of their own echoed on the empty balcony. There were no guards or attendants, only a harp, a chair, small open windows and pier and door partitions to allow air circulation. The regal man sighed deeply, strolling inside towards his small harp, its arch smooth and slender, the number of strings doubled for strange tunings. He picked up the majestic instrument in the crook of his arm. Beyond the wonderful, curved instrument, Ben leaned on the balustrade peered outside out over the cityscape.

He knew why the air smelled so rancid.

Thousands of human bodies confronted Ben, wrapped like mummies in white bundles on wagons or in pits, littering the streets below. Air shimmered with unseen tinder burning in the sun.

He gasped. Flies filled the streets as much as there were corpses, and those who were alive sat in clumps, some working the dead, covered in quarantine over-all veils. Burials overflowed, and carts pulled by horses packed with corpses clogged up the narrow street. Pits burned the excess bodies, discarded and tossed on top of one another into the licking orange flowers of death. Ben even saw black carrion birds caw and hop around, jackals and cats huffing, laying languidly on the ground.

In the sky, splashed in red, a cloud reflecting the setting sun formed a massive eerie shape that loomed over the land, vaguely shaped crudely of a gingerbread man with a long narrow outstretched bloodied arm, smearing across the sky.

"The plague," the king said. "There are not enough healers. Not enough . . ."

"This is bad," Ben said.

"I know . . ." the man said sternly. "The people need faith, not kings. Everything is ruined. Barely a family exists without half its members. Karkemish will become an adversary. The Hittite dominion is inevitable. Oh Uriah . . . You were with me when we crushed the Plishtim, blooding my hands alongside me, now I'm rueful of it all. Sor, Gubla and Sidon can help me, but with the Srden, Danuna and Tjekker raids on the sea and the failure of copper mines . . . The plague will only spread west too."

Ben knew none of those names.

The tense king continued to speak. "There is more to being king than having what I want. It's all a tentative balance. Stray but a little, I fail miserably. I need to understand this in respects to all people, no matter if they be male or female, rich or poor, Israelite or foreigner. But to be a man... is to desire what one cannot take." Then the regal man said softly, "I no longer desire the throne."

"No!" Ben stepped in.

"I cannot lead them." The king's eyes were pained.

This man is Jewish! Ben's eyes glanced up, at the hexagram on the ceiling. "You're . . . David . . ."

The man frowned, and Ben paused with a wan smile. He was *sure* this was *the* King David, semi-legendary king in the Bible – the underdog shepherd boy that killed Goliath the giant with a slingshot. *That* David. The guy who was the ancestor of Jesus. He could be wrong; besides hearing things from his father and school, Ben had always known about David, yet he wasn't certain to say that David was even a historical figure.

The king cast his gaze behind him, wetting his lips. Ben knew he was about to say something, but the way his throat tensed, he stopped himself. Then he gave a smile that had no joy in it, and said, "So . . . What do I do?"

Ben gasped. "You're asking me? We need a new leader if the world is in . . ."—He was going to say a shambles—". . . in pieces."

The man flinched. "Natan, you are my prophet. Your service is unbidden to the voice from on High, echoing the divine that even I must hold prudent peace. Don't you have a word for me?" Vexed, the mumbling old king lowered his harp on the table. "There is a time when king, priest and prophet will become one. I am anointed and yet . . ." David's face darkened. "I sinned . . . Again . . ." The last word was a whisper. David closed his eyes, swallowing hard. "I'm . . . *so* exhausted."

"I understand. My joints are stiff, and my back is killing me." Ben slipped into character, gripping his staff with both hands, and then placed them on his back, wincing, lowering his glance and even gave off a shudder for good measure.

"I am old now, Natan. We've been through much together." He picked up a stool to play his harp. He tilted the harp against his shoulder gently, as softly as a mother would hold a nursing baby. Ben watched as David's forehead smoothed as he began to relax. His fingers rolled gracefully, fluidly, strong slender fingers sweeping through the filaments a few idle triplets, then whispered, "What is man that you are mindful of him, and the son of man that you care for him?"

Pausing, his hand ready to play, he plucked a fresh melody, flowing from the old sounds that lingered and resonated. He played a cord with a perfect assembly of notes, so sublime, sweet and intricate, Ben's ears found delight. The hairs on his arms rose, the rinsing cool sound emanated from the tall harp strings, overlapped with ebbs and slews, ebbs and slews. All perfect confusion gone; music washed it all away. Ben did not know if David was improvising or playing from memory, but this man had a passion for musical composition. In earnest, King David was without peer and could make a small harp breathe, make it speak a thousand elegant voices.

A last refreshing song. He brought it to an end with an elegant climb of high notes and set the harp upright. Opening his eyes, wrinkles creased David's smooth forehead as he whispered contritely, "My heart wants Gad the Seer this time, Natan. I feel I must speak to him."

"Gad? Okay. You have taken on a prophet's ways yourself to make your own decisions." Ben gazed at the king with awe, his skin bronze in the golden light seeping into the sultry room. The king leaned on the railing, staring at the sick with an expression of deep grief – uncertainty, shame and guilt – on his face. He could not imagine someone in this dream would look so real, everything here had to exist from more than just memories.

Then words born of truth spilled through Ben. Another mind speaking from his own mouth. "Gather them."

A hand flung to his mouth. Ben was about to ask, gather whom? – when the king's expression became unreadable, stroking the silken grains of the wooden harp. "You read me too well, old friend."

Suddenly, David and the room vanished. The sky peeled apart like a scroll. Ben gasped, and beheld a great cedar tree like the Red Woods, its branches reaching the clouds and a blanket of roots radiating from the tree's massive trunk, covering the ground like mountains with bark, roots like blood vessels sustaining the forest.

Next to it was a smaller fig tree, gnarled branches sagging, a cluster of petrified lightning bolts, its branches infested with coiled-up serpents, and snakes and reptiles of all kinds.

A flash illuminated the sky, and a great meteorite crashed through the cedar, toppling it, and hitting the ground, it erupted in a tsunami of fire, mercilessly consuming the fig tree. The infernal destruction spread and in a blink, it consumed Ben.

———

Forcing himself to wake up, Ben yelped, opening and closing his eyes in quick succession, adjusting to his surroundings. Bending over and cupping his face in his hands, in the dimness he saw his soldier friends still sleeping, Marcus and Casbolt slowly stirring. He spotted Pounders and the other Colonels with their arms crossed, chins on their chests sleeping, some leaning in awkward positions. Ben grinned wryly as he found himself holding on to his chair startled by sudden turbulence. His heart skipped a beat when he felt the nose of the plane plummet.

At cruising altitude, the plane's engines switched off, pressure crushing Ben's ears. The entire plane shifted left and then right and, after a few moments, dropped with a whirling sound. Suddenly, it felt as if the Globemaster were flying right through a hurricane, with a pilot who had passed out at the controls.

Good things to wake us up, Ben thought, knowing this was a strategic landing. *There is a threat out there. Enemies of the East and the evil darkness to fight. It helps while bobbing in and out of a dozen Iraqi's missile eyes.*

Ben slowly stroked his sweaty palms with his fingers, watching languidly as the plane's rough landing woke some of the soldiers up. He found it eerily thrilling to be in the air with the engines droning, freefalling with the grand mass of the plane. Suddenly, the room's lights flashed off, casting the interior into darkness with a faint crimson light illuminating the cabins, rattling with persistent tremors.

"*What?* The engines!" Johnny Best bleated, sounding delirious and groggy from waking up. "We're going down! Guys!"

"Shhhh. No, we're not," hissed Marcus Theis in the midst of the turbulence, standing up and placing a hand on Johnny's shoulder. "It's a strategic landing. Take it easy, kid."

"But—"

Just then the engines blasted, screaming back on. Ben felt the resisting inertia make his head bob, and stomach lurch for a moment of the impetus.

Then the wheels boomed on the tarmac, the impact reverberating the plane.

While the engines stayed on, and the crew monitored their instruments in the cockpit, they had no intention to stay on the ground longer than was necessary – Ben never recalled the plane even coming to a complete halt, as he began to pack up for drop off.

The loadmaster lowered the tail ramp, hydraulics whining, sending blasts of frigid cold night air smelling of jet fuel inside. Ben stood carrying his gear, as supplies slid on pallets down the ramp. Air thrashed into the cabin, whipping across his bare face.

He closed his eyes and saw the engraved images of the dream flash before him like carved marble. The bittersweet taste on his tongue from sleeping lingered as he remembered Veronica his daughter, her smile, her hugs and her letter wishing God's blessings to him. He took a deep breath and stepped into the ancient lands of Iraq.

Show time. This is for you Veronica.

With renewed vigour and motivation, he clasped his bag, flinging it swiftly onto his back. He knew deep down that he was at the right place, at the right time. In his element.

"Alright, let's do this!" Ben declared to his men as the marines groggily got up with their Colonels also barking similar commands.

Ben DePaula stepped out onto the runway, the sky a galaxy of ice-blue stars hanging above him. Cold gripped his chest as the large cargo plane taxied away, the sonorous hiss of the engines gradually ebbing. His disembarkation with the Colonels and his troops trailing behind into complete darkness and silence, was met only by random squalls of wind and the creaking of crickets. One by one, the soldiers turned on their helmet flashlights, gathering in a large circle for a final meeting.

"Alright, guys," Ben said, his voice invigorating their confidence and alertness. His commands were not just for his men, but for himself. "This might be the last time we are all together for a while. So, before we split up, I want to thank all you: Marcus, Harrel, Colonels. I wish you the best of luck on your mission. It's been my pleasure to train alongside you. *Semper Fi.*"

The men nodded in approval, and some yawned. The only person who seemed *alive,* active with an intense, fervent passion, was James Casbolt. He returned Ben an austere gaze, replying, "*Semper Fi,* Captain."

Ben admired Casbolt's raw expressive display of dignity which alone could be respected above any other man for what it was worth. He found himself meeting the strange otherworldly Aes Sidhe's eyes returning a series of subtle nods. *Man . . . I was wrong about Casbolt. He's alright. He'll gun this. I know he will.* "You are a soldier in the American Marines now."

"Thank you for those kind words. I hope everything goes well for you too, friend." Casbolt smiled, an overflowing sentiment of joy which Ben had infrequently seen in the man. *He's impressed by me,* Ben thought sympathetically.

It wasn't long before Ben stood alone with the Rangers watching the other units depart into the night.

"Right, Rangers, you know the drill," Judd Pounders said from the gloom, prompting everyone to secure their weapons. "I have just contacted a convoy to pick us up here. Once they arrive, we will go straight to the dam. No rest breaks." The Colonel set forth and began the march towards battle.

Ben turned off his helmet light. No one had the energy or the ability to speak, so Ben could almost imagine himself alone in an unknown wilderness, in majestic isolation, with his thoughts and with the infinity above. Only Ben and the expanse.

In his dream, Ben considered the meaning of David's words on being a man. In contemplative awe he gazed at the Milky Way galaxy, feeling insignificant. He could see so much out here where there were no city lights in sight. The constellations, pulsating with brightness, seemed to swirl, and Ben's mind, still groggy, seemed to swirl with them. Such detail everyone missed by light pollution, details that blew Ben away, had a dreamlike quality, clusters of perfect blazing clarity in infinite multitudes. He saw with excitement, the darting streaks of comets appearing and then vanishing immediately and reappearing again, on another section of the eternal sky and the black between the stars, micrometres becoming lightyears and lightyears becoming micrometres.

He smiled, amused by how much he loved this job. The air was still. Not even the distinct sounds of crickets, birds and wolves stirred.

Those regal stars watched Ben, pensive as a trillion eyes.

Thank you, God, for the dream. Thank you, God for Veronica.

Warmth filled his chest, as Ben traversed the barren terrain, lulled and confident. Judd Pounders opened a creaky gate, holding the gate open to let Ben's men through: Julian, Derek, Laycock, Joshua, Garrow and Reggie. Ben joined the soldiers and hunkering down on the side of a rugged dirt road among some shrubs, he sat back against the frail old fence, and waited.

Coming down the dirt road were four orbs of stark white light, rumbling in the distance. Ben and the Rangers apprehensively got on their feet, their mouths all emitting puffs of fog. The men prepared to be taken up by three SUVs, the vehicles halting one behind the other in single file. The drivers got out, greeting Ben and Judd Pounders, gladly helping them load the trucks with their bags, slamming the doors shut.

None were interested in conversation, and once everyone was onboard, Ben leaned out the window, tapping his helmet twice – his gestured to signal to the driver "all ready to go". Nodding curtly, the driver hopped in and ignited the engine. The Rangers were on the move, hugging their bags placidly, packed up together tightly in the seats, all minds wary of RPG mines and guerrilla attacks that might catch them by surprise in the unusual Iraqi countryside.

This was war, and sleep in war always came second. This was life and death, priorities of logistics and the task force had to be paramount, or one may never sleep again.

Ben DePaula composed himself by thinking and meditating of Veronica and King David, staring out the window, gun resting on his lap.

There outside, under the moon, Ben perceived a seething disturbance. It was hard to notice in the blurry miles of rushing tree shrubs and hillsides of the ancient landscape. Grand flashes of light flickered on the distant forlorn horizon – the bomb flashes of the Shock and Awe Campaign no doubt – a campaign meant to unleash an all-out raid on Baghdad, but resulted in a flurry of disorientation, where the scattered forces now endeavoured to carry their own battles alone, beleaguered, without backup. So far away were these marines struggling for their lives, not every task force could be aided in a nick of time. So far away, even the dreamlike flashes of explosions were almost blips, peaceful to the mind to watch.

Peaceful, lulling, chaos and annihilation, from afar.

To be a man is to desire what one cannot take.

Ben glanced at them indifferently – the sight captivating to the eyes, otherworldly and peculiar. War always was calamitous; it was to be avoided, yet always on the doorstep it remained, crouching.

Because when a man's love-ones were threatened by violence, the man ought to fight for them.

22

CATHARSIS

"The era when America was perceived by the Middle East as anti-colonial, was over . . .We do not have to perpetuate our own traditions unreflectively. We are not bound by our own histories or our own literature, our own stories. But as heroes invading Mesopotamia to save a diverse population from a demonic regime, we charged boldly like the Crusaders of old with enflamed Metaphysical Desire, scapegoating Saddam with 'no assessment ever accounted for the threat we faced.'"
—From *Omega Plan: The Epicenter of Light and Darkness*, Joseph DePaula.

Alfred Bonner felt a genius today, as he paraded through the grated floors of Dulce base flanked by an honour guard of Alliance patrol troops in torc and La Tène patterned attire with his most trusted Manichean assistant – Aes Sidhe Jason Morlaix, son of Zeus Jupiter.

Alfred had been pulled. He had been forced to the negotiating table by none other than the *Cabal* – his nefarious opposite. An extraordinary turn of events occurred when an embassy of Cabal offering peace, met him here earlier. Alfred, though at first intrigued, ultimately could have openly humiliated the Republicans – those foolish venal vermin. Why had the Cabal become *so weak?* They operated behind closed doors in their deep state, pulling the strings of the Presidency and the White House. Did they realise then, the futility of their monopoly over the skeleton of world empires? The Cabal were mentally ill, they never showed a chink of weakness. If they did, they would've been overthrown long ago. If a ruler refused to betray his or her strength, that, one knew, was how to tell they were totalitarian.

You want war with me, Cabal? Alfred thought, stoically, apathetic and accepting of his fate, relaying his meeting with the agents, passing a group of working concierges managing equipment and devices for the main operating room on Level 2. *Try it. There's already a war here, in the Middle East, and I'm not letting civil war break out in the States. I'm going to do what I do.*

But enough of the Cabal's *vain claim* to peace, Alfred must focus on the Shinar Mission – all his own plan. The Alliance – his organisation – were endeavouring to seize upon the chance of the greatest archaeological search of a lifetime. The Cabal tried to bluff him – they wanted the prize in Iraq as well. But Alfred ignored them. *Bless Zeus and his Nine daughters, for I'm sharp of mind. Bless Zeus and his son Apollo, for extending my days.*

He was going to find a god – an idea of all society, and being feeble, modern society needed a god, an idea. It was not God who would create a new society, a new humanity. It was the proletariat.

Alfred eyed from the balcony the fruit of his toils.

A dozen military personnel – fellow Disciples of the Light – laid out before him, monitoring a variety of aerial imagery and all sorts of data displayed on monitors and computer boards. Orange-eyed, light-brown-haired Jason Morlaix – Alfred's second-in-command – stood at attention. "Arhat Alfred Bonner," he said, sharply bowing. "We have telemetry with the Merkabah satellite. We're approaching the coordinates that have been relayed to the marines now."

Alfred nodded curtly. "Good," he replied with a serene grinding voice. "Make sure you all keep a keen eye out for anything that might intercept our expedition."

Jason nodded, turning on his heels, clomping down the steps towards the control stations, passing a Hispanic female in a secretary uniform coming towards him. Alfred found himself prowling precariously back and forth as he observed the monitors before him, his operators of camera feeds, showing the soldiers in night vision milling about on the grounds of Mesopotamia.

"Director, we have a status report of the Rangers at Haditha," the secretary went on. "Also, of your interest there is a request to deploy a Boeing YAL-1 into the field to further sterilise and cut off Iraqi's supply line."

Oh, Fabian scorched-earth tactics. We are not the Cabal here! Alfred thought. *No, we are not judging Babylon. I'm here to* prevent *the judgement of Babylon. We're not going to waste every resource we have.*

"Deny the request," Alfred replied dully. "We still need to remain undercover with the bulk of the American and British forces. We cannot afford compromising our cover in case the Cabal working for Hussein sees our movements. No Direct Energy weapons. It will target us." He stood like a mountain, looming over his Disciples of the First and Second Imitations, but he needed to be pragmatic, as all good politicians and diplomats were. The secretary gulped, stiff and tense with discipline. "Remember that our enemy is not the Iraqis." He shooed her away. "Thank you anyway."

She curtsied, departing with a humble scuttle.

Alfred then turned his lofty attention towards the largest screen in the room – satellite footage of the major war fronts. As no one currently bothered him, Alfred relaxed his tense demeanour, the sensation of dreamy completeness and concord of peace invigorating his heart. The path to Heaven was finished before him, paved with good intentions.

Alfred had gotten the green light from his colleagues from the Deutsche Orient-Gesellschaft, abbreviated as the DOG, to dig in Warka - the city of Uruk. He wouldn't believe a second of the mainstream narrative that there were weapons of mass destruction in Iraq, because a tortured Iraq militant was forced to say what the Americans wanted to see. The Iraq war would justify Saddam Hussein to retaliate. And it provided a chance to make the most out of the terrible decision concocted by Congress.

The war was about finding a god – an idea – not weapons of mass destruction. The idea to liberate the oppressed from autocratic shackles into democratic freedom.

Ideals in a way, could be just as destructive as a nuclear bomb.

Unrestrictive social and political democracy to remove the unbridled burdens of capitalism, Alfred reassured himself in his head. *We have a larger enemy. Those at enmity with the Tyrant will have to prepare for the Great Reset. It is coming. The Dynamics foretold the Reset to react to the Galactic Tyrant's control of history, of minds and of culture. We must be united by the Great Reset. The Cabal has no choice but to yield to the Alliance when this happens.*

Alfred sought for the glove box, slipped on plain gloves, opening a folder containing copies from his larger Dynamics. Also, inside, sealed in a container, was a fire-baked clay tablet. Pillow shaped, etched by a stylus in Sumerian cuneiform, this authentic tablet was a replica of the detailed fragment called the *Death of Gilgamesh* recovered from Mê-Turan from the mythic tradition of one of history's first epic poems.

Utu looked at its shells with admiration. Then as soon as the water in the bed of the Euphrates had receded, his tomb was built there from stone diorite. Its walls were built from diorite. Its door leaves were installed in the sockets of the entrance. Its bolt and thresholds were hard stone. Its door-pivots were hard stone. They installed its gold beams. Heavy blocks of stone were moved to cover with a thick layer of dark soil for future days. Let Gilgamesh as a ghost, below among the dead, be the governor of the nether world. Let him be pre-eminent among the ghosts, so that he will pass judgements and render verdicts, and what he says will be as weighty as the words of Ningishzida and Dumuzid.[1]

There – the road map for the Alliance's intentions in the Iraq war was written down four thousand years ago.

Alfred Bonner leaned back, facing the head-camera monitors, watching his marshalling commando platoons. Once a battle began, the commander lost all control, unless he were haughty enough to let it go.

"The name – the character and reputation – of brave men will not perish from the land forever. I will rescue you from death, Gilgamesh. Your deeds bear witness to you."

———

The SUV headlights were thin in the vast darkness. Lake Qadisiyah was calm and sheened with the pearl quicksilver of the moon, and the beauty of it belied Joshua.

As he gazed down, he could see the thin silvery thread in the writhing shadows that led towards war, death and violence. It terrified him that he would have to face resentment again, but this time, he would not just face a part of it, but the whole thing.

It's only the first night, Josh, he thought. *Come on, what could possibly happen on the first night?* All Joshua wanted to do was get to base, organise his things and simply keep to himself. If he were master of anything besides target shooting, it was discovering culture. In one sense, being cultural helped him act as a con man. Now, it was being an academic.

But anything could entice him back to becoming the predatory con man again. He was liberated from that. Saved from that.

Alas, but he was in Ben DePaula's sinful unit. He doubted they would get time to reach the sleeping quarters if every single one of the soldiers had to sign Ben's autograph or something before they even got through the security

1   Black, Jeremy A. 1997. *Death of Gilgamesh,* The Electronic Text Corpus of Sumerian Literature (http://www-etcsl.orient.ox.ac.uk/), Oxford.

inside. Typical Ben did not know how to control his tongue – the dainty morsel – and sooner than he would know it, Joshua supposedly would be known for his targeting expertise and, sooner than he could blink, he would be in the frontlines.

He could almost imagine the vain pampering. *"Did you hear that Joshua, that kid with the boof head, was the best shooter?"*

"No way. I want him in our unit. Put him in the front lines."

"Wait a minute, wasn't that the guy that got fake passports, stole a million bucks and nearly sued the Marine Corps?"

Joshua cupped his hands over his mouth once that wall of megalithic asphalt and concrete dominated the landscape. The enormous, long grey wall stretched in a crescent from bank to bank – at nine kilometres long – the crests soaring at one hundred and eighty-seven feet. The second largest hydro-electric contributor to the power system in Iraq, the structure looked so orderly in contrast to the wilderness around it, it smoothed out the banks and the rapids, it rigidly ended the jeep's rough course on the dirt road, the wheels abruptly hitting the streamline highway. Haditha Dam held chaos at bay, containing the wild river, etiolating it.

At the moment, the air was frozen in tense silence, making the dam even more ominous. The Rangers' reinforcements were the last ingredient needed to exacerbate the suspended discord that was already boiling to an extreme heat.

"Alright, here it is, boys. Colonel John Mulholland is waiting for us," Ben prodded quietly, adjusting his helm and semiautomatic. "Wakey, wakey. Eyes sharp. Sit tight and no matter what happens, show them that we mean business."

Joshua had promised himself that he'd never risk going on a mission again and yet fate, unable to slant, became a slippery slope depriving him of his sense of worth – it was indeterminism at its cruellest, taking Joshua for an existential ride of anguish.

Where was God, to deliver him from uncertainty? Where was God – if he could bring Joshua out of prison and reform Joshua's life – why couldn't he save him from war? He sat in dread, knowing he didn't have the capability to understand the mystery of God and his silence. *Where is your authority, oh Lord of Hosts? You are leading your Chosen as a lamb into the slaughter. I cannot see your will in it. You have no authority here! Make your name known in the American marine ranks!*

As he prayed, beams of individual streetlights from the sides of the highway became congested, enclosing the soldiers in. Joshua let out a stressful huff from his nose, feeling the heaviness in his chest. It felt too embarrassing to justify to himself why he was here. *Lord, if I die, let me not be ashamed when I come before you.*

That would become his prayer from now on. *Let me not be ashamed when I come before you.*

If Joshua struggled with the obstacle courses, how could he possibly survive war? It would have to be some *preposterous* mistake for him to survive. Pressure surged upon his chest ever-increasingly as the SUVs drove closer towards the dam proper.

Outside, in front, members of the present 75th Ranger Regiment slinked around the vehicles in full gear inspecting the newly arrived escorts. From what Joshua could see, John Mulholland was organising a small accompany of guard officers, greeting Judd Pounders in the first jeep ahead of him.

While waiting for the jeeps to pass the barrier inspection, Nefer appeared all gelatinous in a ripple of bent light next to Joshua's head.

The tightness in Joshua's chest eased a bit. When he was starting to take the angelic presence for granted, he always ended up feeling grateful for him.

You look tired, Nefer transmitted for only Joshua to hear. *But do not worry, the Red Horses may be many, and they're mobilising, but they are wary of my presence — they'll not attack yet.* He floated closer to Joshua's slumped head, inspecting his worrisome manner. *What's the matter?*

Joshua nodded curtly, trying not to look suspicious to military men inspecting and circling the jeep. Abashment set in. *Come on, I'm not meant for this,* Joshua complained. *I'm not meant to be here. I hate war. I hate Pounders. I don't want to be a soldier. It's unsavoury. A waste of time!*

Indeed, Nefer said uneasily, receiving those thoughts. *But do not complain. I understand your enmity towards this place. It reeks with darkness . . . Red Horses are everywhere.*

Red Horses… A predatory peace, a weak peace that can be taken away swiftly. America relied on peace that only came when violence and death was enacted. If that contradictory peace was taken away… You take the sword away, there was chaos. As protection from the lie was removed and taken away, humanity cried out. The worst in humanity; sin as it really was, unleashed.

The Beast. It was here. Joshua was being punished. *I'm the only one who sees the truth…*

"Will you stay with me?" Joshua moaned under his breath so nobody would hear. "Please?"

Yes. Yes. Yes. Of course I will, Nefer inspired softly. *Did you perceive that a scholarly spirit was incapable of restraining hostilities? Christ rules this planet, so the Red Horses have no power.*

The barrier lifted upwards, and Joshua muttered to himself a quick prayer of endurance as the SUVs finally parked.

"Well done, team," Ben spoke up keeping his men alert, stepping out of the jeep. "It's been a very long night but you're going well. It's our cue to go. E-6 sharp snipers are in demand." As he declared that, he shot a glance at Joshua.

By impulse, Joshua found himself mindlessly packing up his bag and following Ben into the balmy night. He was numb, he couldn't deny orders; he had to obey against his will. The breeze was remarkably warm, humid and heavy with a pungent stench in the air.

"I'm relying on you, hot shot," Ben said as Joshua fiddled with his bag. "Show them what you are made of."

"Okay," Joshua said timidly, not daring to speak his grievances out loud. He nodded briskly.

Joshua quivered as he shadowed Ben, marching towards one of the commanders of the Regiment, allowing him to gaze over the buttress into the dark chasm. The lingering spray of hissing Euphrates air prickled his hair. Looming in the distance to the left with a sophisticated hydro-electric system, tanks cluttered next to that system, and on the second story, a structure of six large entrance ways loomed above. Scattered lights were nestled on the dam's structure emitting green and red lights, dotting the panoramic view before him, emanating from across the power plants. Down below, a small bridge flanked by a manufactured dike, stepped with patterns of square-framed concrete retaining walls, reinforced the dam structure. From underneath, the gushing of water of the Euphrates disgorged outwards into the distilled spillway, a constant roaring cascade. Haditha Dam was massive – a mini metropolis holding back the mighty river.

Red Horses. Everywhere, Joshua thought. Reality was made apparent.

> *When he opened the second seal, I heard the second living creature say, "Come and see!" And out came another horse, bright red. Its rider was given a great sword, it had power to take peace from the Earth, so that people should slay one another.*

"The birth pains," Joshua rasped. "They're here."

"Yo what's up, Captain Ben DePaula?! The Actionman himself!" Turning,

Joshua saw two heavily armed marines in night patrol gear approaching, and one of them had spoken, though his features were identical from the rest, with camo face paint and round goggles.

Ben nodded, beaming as bright as one of the station lights from across the reservoir. "You're right, Bummalang. The Actionman's here."

"People know once they see you," the soldier named Bummalang replied insouciantly.

"It's an honour to fight by your side, Captain DePaula," the other soldier said, and they haven't even *fought* yet. "How are you doing?"

"Locked and loaded, pal. How's operations doing for y'all?"

"Overall, Objective Serpent was a rather *reasonable* start," Bummalang reported. "After dropping onto H-1 Air Base with some engineers and combat controllers, we met a bit of fire while seizing the flanks of the dam. We drove through enemy lines, blasting those Iraq vehicles. However, reconnaissance reported that this bloody dam is too bloody damn big to hold! The place is defended like Hell! Then that's when we requested Pounders to send you guys in as a second Delta reinforcement squadron, before we become mincemeat. We have novices with us, Captain. It's bad for them."

Ben nodded to that, maintaining his joyful demeanour. "That's good to know, Don Buma. That's good to know."

"Oh. Just don't slip and call him Da Bum," a soldier at Bummalang's side said, with a sheepish grin on his face. "Then you'll regret slipping."

"Oh, I'll make sure you slip off this damn dam!" Bummalang chortled.

Ben laughed, shrugging. "I don't know if I should feel threatened, welcomed or even amused, but – yah know – it would be a great gag to remember I guess, Da *Buma*!"

"Ohh!" Bummalang grunted deeply, thumping Ben with a mock shove. "Come on, bro!"

"Get over it!" Ben teased. "We've got a dam to siege!"

The other Rangers were deployed towards a moving convoy not far away. Officers, snipers, assault combat forces – their pride did not quail by the air of perniciousness. They were desperate men, some in dark colour-shifting camouflage that seemed to make parts of them disappear as they lingered in dark spots of the industrial complex. Whether brawny or lithe, short or tall, just standing there as machines latched with gear, four-eyed night-vision goggles, cyborgs with camo visages, they were violence on a frayed leash.

Not all the Rangers were prisoners of the dam, the Iraqis had appeared to have given them an exceptionally difficult day of fighting, for frustration boiled in the dark air, bubbling, ready to erupt forth, issuing wrath. Pounders had termed this the "Thermopylae of America". Foolish laymen! Herodotus *never* said that the last stand of the three hundred Spartans at Thermopylae spared time for the Athenian fleet to crush Xerxes! That view was a modern misconception! The three hundred Spartans holding the pass of Thermopylae against the Persian Immortals was meaningless in the bigger picture of the war. It was just another unfortunate battle, another unfortunate loss and another unfortunate disaster. Just like holding Haditha Dam was set out to be. Joshua could bet on it.

The wicked shall be raked aside as thorns. So perfunctory, so routine, one felt the carelessness of the action, the reprimand of indifferent divine anger.

"We must sit tight, Ben," Judd Pounders grumbled from behind. Immediately, Ben, Joshua and the other marines stood at attention. "We have a chance tonight to take the rest of the facility. We've just spotted a barge of Iraqi troops closing in."

Already?! Joshua panicked. His bones wearied him; and he still carried his bags! *God have mercy upon me!*

"Ready your troops, Ben," Pounders commanded. "You take it from here. Doyle has sent along a pair of sniper teams and part of the Third Battalion platoon already!"

"Yes, Colonel!" Ben ran to get ready, joining Captain David Doyle sitting on the hood of his GMV where he and his platoon commanders laid out a simple plan of attack.

Scowling, Joshua gawked at Benjamin – a glamorous grand leader, another obdurate man able to haul the esteem of others. Issue was, the man was a materialistic, uneducated pleb, who thought nothing of the propaganda of America, sending men to war to perish, depopulating families. War bolstered his hard heart. Bolstered by loss, dependency, bursts of elation, fatality, breathless doxastic contradictions. War and time were man's greatest's foes; for both hardened self and the body, exercised and ready. Patience and keenness were death to a warrior spirit – war should be practised decisively, rashly.

These marines were like the Greek heroes at Troy, they craved incessantly the glorious stimulation, that high. These men lusted for thrill and violence and glory catered for that. But in time, Ares that red-horse rider with his great blade, remorselessly advancing, would sweep them up, cutting them from the knees!

"Go! GO!" a voice roared. "Joshua, what the hell are you waiting for!?"

He technically leapt into the air, emitting a shuddering breath. A pang of shame dragged his eyes downwards. Pounders clearly had noticed his scowling narrow eyes, signs that Joshua didn't need to communicate verbally; he didn't want to be here.

Joshua ran until he panted, joining the troops, out of breath. He trampled along as a warhorse riding in a cavalry. Buffeting wind, grinding machines and wheels, barking voices and loading guns. Someone gave him a gun. He didn't know who. Joshua held it in his hands timorously. He stared at his thrashing boots mindlessly in order to not freeze from the cold. He was an animal, being sent off to die on the altar of the battlefield . . . Joshua didn't even know *where* he was going into the darkness. He simply ran with the soldiers. He knew somehow, if he stopped, he'd be beaten. He ran until he sweated, and his body hurt.

There was gunfire rattling in the distance and the soldiers ran into a large power plant, and Joshua charged, until his own raging breaths drowned out the gunfire. It wasn't even bravery that drove him; it wasn't even a wish that those bullets would take him and end it all, bearing all this agony. He ran. Mindless, that was what it was. Like a boulder down the hill and like rain from the sky. They had no choice, and neither did he. Joshua wasn't a man; he was a thing to be acted upon. He was a verb with no dignity.

Run. Stop. Hide. Fear. Look. Repeat. Run. Stop. Hide. Fear. Look. Repeat.

Joshua panicked countless times, wondering if he'd lost Ben, but he managed to find him running through the roads heroically, jumping over a fence into a yard of shrubs, overgrowth shrouding and strangling an abandoned power plant. Even when he found Ben out there, Joshua was stumbling, almost tripping over, his gun a weight in his straining arms.

No one spoke. Gunfire was upon them. Damnation, Joshua had traumatic memories of Damascus, his thighs writhing with cramps, they felt so stiff he could barely move them. Sweat dripped over his eyebrows, stinging his eyeballs. The marines had been too smug, they undervalued the enemy's punctuality, thinking they would not arrive in time at such an unholy hour in the night.

Ben and a fist of marines engaged in combat viciously, firing their semiautomatics.

Joshua couldn't see the enemy. He held his gun close to his chest, hands trembling, not daring to fire. His vision widened, but clarity of thought came like a bolt of lightning. *All humans have the right to protect. The right of self-defence. Protect lives. Save lives. Life is sacred.*

"Go! Go! Go!" Ben cried, after getting an intercom report.

Joshua ran. Invisible bullets flew like unseen bees in the darkness, harassing and swarming. After making a breakaway run from the administration building towards the final station checkpoint, Joshua finally saw the monstrous enemy – they were two-armed, two-legged silhouettes in the shadows. He saw no faces. He could not tell who was who.

A thousand quotes of war and fighting in war, leapt into his mind. Oh, how much warfare had changed, becoming more psychologically damaging, impulsive than physical, set-piece battles? At least in ancient warfare, you would have been shoulder to shoulder in a phalanx, working together as one cohesive unit, thrusting and stabbing. You could see your enemy, and you could see your friend's shield covering your body. But in the cruelty that was called modern warfare, you were independent. Vulnerable at every turn, ready to be killed by a quick snap and bang. Gone. Swords were personal, but bullets were impersonal. They created distance, indifference, between you and the enemy.

Joshua wasn't foolish, he knew how much confusion modern warfare could cause. He'd tasted its rampage before in Damascus.

After the torrid run, Joshua ducked behind a vehicle as Ben said, "Go get down!", pressing against a gated generator. Among the constant rhythm of cold breaths, everything went still with tension. Had the enemy gone? Or rather, were they going undercover? Even the slightest movement would mean danger.

Behind Ben, unseen by anyone, twin shadows prowled. Stealthy, vague shapes, legs and arms as silent as the moonlight, went to strike.

Joshua sprung to save Ben. He found himself down the lane, slamming the trigger, facing two random Iraqis. He saw a mask of shocked eyes, the shaft of a barrelled semiautomatic aimed at him, whimpering lips, a blanched face, neck flinching from the bullets. The dead soldier collapsed into the enemy's lap, with a starburst crimson hole in his face, jaw in his throat.

The Iraqi soldier who survived, gritted his teeth like a feral cat, and lunged away from Joshua, dragging the corpse of his friend.

Bang! The second Iraqi – a human being conscripted to fight for a dictator – flopped dead. Ben whistled, chuckling, cocking his gun and saying, "Jesus Christ, that was a close one."

Joshua felt numb. The most carnal hardening engulfed a part of him.

Then the soul shredding came.

Joshua gasped and dropped his gun. *Life was sacred…* Not even Ben cared for the fatality he had committed, he went over to chat to his friends as Joshua enmeshed himself in the guilt.

No one showed remorse. It just showed how apathetic marines were to those who wanted to be different. Yet now, at this time, once cleansed from sin, Joshua tried to escape from war, and it came right back to assault him.

23

EYE FOR AN EYE

"Heroes are the bearers of cultures, paragons of traditions. Evil societies have evil heroes because heroes encapsulate the society's zeitgeist where they maximise envy, pride, glory and vengeance, vices accepted as cultural norms. Rivals between heroes from different cultures form when they desire to take the same object for themselves to find being. Think of Achilles and Hector – two heroes from rival cultures desiring glory. They become mediators and representatives of their societies. Heroes – no matter their moral status – become heroes when society deems them worthy and successful in their use of violence to get the object: glory, justice and above all vengeance. Resentful sentiments are ambivalent, containing within them a degree of admiration alongside hatred. Achilles and Hector admired each other in their role as fighters, but they each desired glory. Heroes overcome the villain who had that object, but villains are the heroes who simply failed in their task to win the object.

This Mimetic Rivalry then, is what infuses the frenzy of Reformers Dilemma and the moral relativism of America. When one stands up with new ideas, they will be marginalised, for the majority can never be wrong on moral matters. And a corollary of that is that dissidents must always be villains. They are blamed for being malevolent in their intent. They must become scapegoats in order to bring peace to this social instability.

This tragic sin of society is what heroes embody. This mimesis is what allows evil to be divinised."

—From *Omega Plan: The Epicenter of Light and Darkness*, Joseph DePaula.

"You're up early Casbolt," said a gravelly voice from within the truck. It sounded gruff and calm, characteristic of Colonel Joe Dunford – a real warrior whose bedraggled look belied a lack of sleep.

Casbolt stalked down from out the grassy esplanade, having just killed a Muslim terrorist. "I could not get enough of Babylon, Colonel," Casbolt suggested. In truth, he wanted to get out of this place – danger lurked in every unseen corner. While main coalition forces were bypassing Lake Razazah and securing bridges along the Euphrates, they'd captured the Karbala route which was an incredible victory.

Babylon, despite Demos' pensive adamant persuasion, had no tactical worth other than it was "on the way" and the only pit stop. In truth, Demos just wanted to see the city. Yesterday, he went to lengths during the tour of the ancient city of Babylon, describing it, talking about its history and legendary legacy, under Amorite, Kassite, Assyrian and Persian rule, stressing just how old civilisation was in the Middle East. One of the Seven Wonders of the ancient world, Babylon, now a tourist's destination, lay in desolate lacunose ruins glaring in the sandy heat, dusty, abandoned and silent. The place of Hammurabi, Nebuchadnezzar and prophet Daniel. From what Casbolt could recall, the New Testament – written by a minority culture always suffering under oppressive empires – hadn't been very keen of this place as Demos was.

"Imagine what Alexander's battle-numbed Macedonian troops would have thought when they marched onto the Processional Way after his victory against Darius III at Gaugamela," Demos lectured passionately, as the marines with James Casbolt at his side, had marched through the white limestone streets passing by local tourists gawking at them. "Where no other Greek had gone before. Babylon, the Creation of Enlil, the city of outrageous wealth. City of a Thousand Festivals. Alexander's troops – young and old like us – would have been in complete awe."

Quite appropriate by comparison, Casbolt thought.

"And now we have to go and kill Darius Hussein!" Colonel Joe Dunford had joked.

The only issue Casbolt had with this enigmatic place, was Saddam Hussein's "heinous cardboard cut-out reconstructions" that Demos would disparage. Casbolt did not need the Parvus to draw an inference that this "reconstruction" was more akin to desecration. To Casbolt, it was rather amusing – and pitiful too – seeing a billboard on the Ishtar Gate depicting vain Saddam on a war chariot declaring himself "the son of Nebuchadnezzar" – a scion of the culture of Iraq. *He is not even Babylonian! Pure megalomania!*

Desecration of cultural heritage in the context of war was well known. It was nothing new; not surprising as Demos suggested that kings had been ruling the Two Rivers for thousands of years, conquering and annexing city states in drastic political fluctuations to exploit resources from other cities and gain access to trade routes. Iraq had no natural metal resources of its own. It needed to expand and conquer for its great population to survive. Babylon and Assyria would march away, harvesting statues of gods and livestock and treasures of plunder from another land, transplanting the city and identity of other nations into the Mesopotamian economy. From Assyrian kings, Medes and Persians, diplomacy and plunder legitimised their glory as a divine paragon.

Not much has changed today it seemed. Saddam needed to conquer his neighbours to gain resources, especially oil.

Casbolt hopped into the truck, still vaguely aware that his clothes had traces of blood still staining them – yet the darkness concealed them for mere food stains from the MRE portions (meals ready to eat). "It's been an interesting night to say the least," Casbolt said. "How are you? What news of the Thunder Run? Did we finally take Baghdad?"

Joe Dunford's com kit sounded with a voice. "I think we have an answer," Dunford said. He picked up the com kit, saying, "Colonel Franks, sir! Nice to hear from you. Good morning. We hear you loud and clear."

"I'm glad to hear that," replied a raptured voice. "Good morning. The occupation stage of Iraq has begun! The regime has been cancelled! Hussein's defences are down! No more reports of dual-use terrorists weapons yet, which is a good sign! Good news is that Hussein himself has fled! Let's keep the hopes up, boys!"

A cheer rose around the marines sitting by the terrace, while Casbolt lay back in the jeep, eating his MRE with honey and toast in peace.

"Anyways," the report went on, "the marines from Kut have sent in the 2nd Brigade. 3rd Infantry had just finished their Thunder Run straight for the capital. We're so successful, I fear that we might have pulled into a draw play. The pocket of resistance is mild. Intelligence warned us that the Iraqi crime rate is rising after Hussein's unleashing of fifty thousand criminal prisoners. The ploy to stall us backfired, big time."

Casbolt started, not wishing to betray any signs he'd killed a man. *Fifty thousand prisoners under Hussein's regime . . . How many more died?*

—

Last night, Casbolt had fallen asleep in the army jeep outside the Babylon vender. But it did not take long for him to desire to find the toilet.

At night the Babylon facilities were closed. Thinking himself secluded, Casbolt walked into the field – a shrub wet land on the outskirts of the ancient ruins. A small village sat a few miles across the field of reeds and palm trees along the river, glowing eerily in the night.

After zipping up his pants, he heard something approaching in the confines of the darkness. A night heron?

A looming shadow rose above Casbolt, Parvus Perception a jet of electric fire to the nervous system.

In an instant, Casbolt flung around and came face to face with a wide-eyed man – haggard and bearded, a sabre in his hands. His steps were prowling, stalking, but even with his position compromised, the man croaked out a feline growl.

The man covered in sores pounced, colliding into Casbolt, tumbling onto the riverbank. Grunting, Casbolt lay on his back, pressure from the attacker holding him fast, sabre aimed at his heart. Casbolt gripped the attacker's clawed hand, resisting, gritting his teeth. Strength against strength.

The sabre slowly crept to Casbolt's chest. The man gagged, a deep demented sound. He smelled like urine, sweat and above all, fear of the demons within him.

Casbolt gasped, breathing desperately like a man trying to gulp breath after being winded, trying to inhale the power of life. The Redlion – an unreasoning beast – took over once Casbolt thought his life was no more, and then, a power came upon him. A supernatural instinct, a supernatural thrill, rushing into the muscles. A supernatural power that felt . . . right.

Twisting the man's hand, Redlion brought a knee upwards, dislodging him. The man stumbled. Taking the opportunity of this brief moment, Redlion summoned Gáe Bulg, and the man met his end.

The man screamed, holding the stump of a right hand, cleaved clean off. He dropped to his knees, convulsing, forehead farrowed, eyes red bloodshot. The Redlion covered his mouth. This random man had *assaulted him*, and now he wailed that he was being assaulted by a marine? No, this demoniac *was not* innocent – he posed a threat to villagers, tourists, and Iraqi families alike. Who knew what kind of human rights abuses, kidnappings, amputations, or beatings occurred in Iraqi homes? Redlion and the marines had come across over twenty mass graves of Shi'ites and Kurds already. This man thought he could kill an American soldier who had come to deliver the country.

Rage burned in the Redlion – a prosperous familiar darker agency inborn. The coward man maladroitly crabbed up the incline of the river.

Redlion slashed the man's hamstrings, and the man wheezed – a horrible grating whimper from his throat.

Redlion threw a foot onto the man's fallen body, pinning him on the slope. He stabbed the Spear into the demoniac's back, slowly disgorging his life blood. The man howled, but Casbolt, with his other foot, kicked his teeth out.

Silencing the beggary wretch, the Redlion was no longer satisfied, the overflow of power in his muscles was still eager.

Pulling up the gory wretch, Redlion cut off his head. Growling, he flung it by the hair, head soaring into the Euphrates with an unseen splash among the reeds.

The sudden supernatural success of power – the thrill that felt holy – dissipated as fast as it came along. It made Casbolt quiver, the chemical power of the thrill like a long-lost loved one returning, stimulated him, arousing him lustfully and then fleeting as it came. It was some supernatural agency beholden to the Redlion's vehement caprice.

James Casbolt looked upon the body and wanted to sick up.

It was a massacre.

"No . . ." He dismissed the Spear, hardening his heart. Casbolt hadn't killed since Fenriskjeften – he hadn't killed for three years. "I was only defending myself. I was only defending myself. The man was a demoniac. Fomorians oppressed him. I put him out of his misery."

But as he stalked back to the trucks, Casbolt resolved himself – he knew, that in war, bloodshed would be inevitable. No longer would he break – he was a soldier – protecting the lives of the Iraqi Sunni and Shia alike – and the Americans and the coalition forces. He was reforging his name and reputation to appeal for his crimes. He needed to appear good in the UN's and the Nindingir's eyes.

In the dark dawn of the morning, Casbolt felt empowered as he walked, finding Garry awake in the jeep.

———

"So, what's the plan for us, Colonel?" Casbolt said. "Are we needed to help manage crime in Baghdad?"

"Oh yes, don't think I will leave you out that easily, Casbolt," Franks said over the com kit. "The State Department wants us to be there to help Conroy protect the museum. People knew that there were some antiquities being stolen, probably under the protection of the Saddam regime, so liberated areas in which there is a power vacuum often experience looting. We need to prevent this from happening to the Baghdad Museum. Your job is to warn the security to heighten their guard."

Yes, Michael Prince celebrated. *Yes, these marines are impressed by the history of Babylon – Demos' post-grad indulgence had invigorated their respect for ancient history. This is the* perfect *opportunity to harness that.* Casbolt realised that this was a Godsend opportunity. Saving cultural heritage would perfectly increase and enhance his standing in the eyes of the UN.

"Count me in, Colonel," Casbolt replied, smiling with enthusiasm. "You can count on me."

"Good," Franks said curtly on the radio. "The 3rd Infantry Division Thunder Run is just about to conclude, so the path will be clear right through the city into the museum. I'll send you reports to Conroy's team to get right inside the facility and hold off its storage houses from raids."

"*Semper Fi,* Colonel," Joe said into the device.

"*Semper Fi,* Captain. See you there."

The Museum of Baghdad. Here, Casbolt could at last, do some good.

Once the sun peeked its yellow head above the horizon, Casbolt and his unit packed up, embarking north along the Euphrates for the last leg of the journey, straight into the heart of the Iraqi capital.

———

Following the American marines up the road to Baghdad under the cover of night, for Tara, had been exhilarating. She felt like a young boy in this country – called Marcell – excitedly experiencing a new culture and scents. Upon seeing how the native women dressed – she often identified herself as a weak schoolboy called Marcell when she felt extremely dislocated, stressed and uncomfortable. Marcell and Tara were like two sides of the same coin – they couldn't function without the other. The switch in her identity happened more often these days, especially when being around Airgetlám. He hadn't seemed to notice the change in Tara when she visited the Babylon venders.

Searching for clues and having a quick rest from their ride on their motorcycles, Tara wrapped her dark purple *niqab* fast around her face, so only her eyes were exposed to the air, squinting in the glare, trying to shield dust twirling in the torrid breeze. She watched families and children around in the venders and terrace quarters of the ruins of the ancient city pensively.

It did not take long for Airgetlám to emerge from the shrubland, beckoning to Tara, meeting her with much vivaciousness in his eyes, about a violent murder on the bank of the Euphrates tributary. Some criminal had been utterly slaughtered – no doubt one of the criminals from the capital that had run loose after the major prison break during the American Task Force Thunder Run.

The corpse among the reeds looked and smelled fresh – it had to have been no more than twenty-four hours ago this man had met his vicious end. Flies swirled in contesting gatherings, like thirsty beasts at a waterhole bathing in pools of blood. There were no signs of this man's decapitated head, but gauging from the smeared markings on the slope of the riverbank, there had been a brief melee.

Tara was desensitised to detestable gore. But being around Airgetlám, it made her want to vomit.

Airgetlám, squatting on his heels, examined the body gingerly, his voice muffled by his *keffiyeh*. "Aes Sidhe work."

Blinking and adjusting her head covering, Tara spoke, Marcell coming forward. "You can sense them?"

Airgetlám nodded. So much about this man was unknown to Tara, but she'd been probing him lately, desperately trying to figure out if this guy was bloody trustworthy.

Tara had made some effort, asking him a lot of interrogating questions. On the plane, Airgetlám had told Tara all about his experience in the Antarctica bases and how his society the Carnutes and family were almost purged to extinction – a genocide committed by the two Chiefs of the Aes Sidhe in the early 1990s. During that massacre he'd lost his right arm. The replacement had been made for him by a cybernetic engineer working with Patalan robotics and biomechanics. Tara only wondered, *What was Airgetlám's name before he became Silverhand?* Yet, even as she asked such a question, Airgetlám went dead silent and whispered that it was not right for her to know, it was best to keep secret. Though Airgetlám never betrayed any emotion, he did speak about his life, which gave Tara a perception as to why this man was willing to be faithful to the Aeons.

"I used to be bullied and beaten. When you are bullied, you become the best bully. It's the only way to escape the intolerable pain. When I looked upon the horror of my massacred friends of the Carnutes, I sealed my humanity away by choice, permanently severed from my soul. Though attaining great success as a mafia agent, I was utterly alone and miserable. So, as all Bleak super soldiers do, I drowned my misery with fleeting pleasures: drugs, guns and sex. Lots and lots of it. I love children's clothes because when I lived in the Amish community before my father took me out to become a Carnute, I . . . I fell in love with children. I wanted to protect them, because I couldn't protect myself."

Tara's mouth went dry. Her life . . . Her *whole life* had been summed up there. The reason why she spent time with her trafficked friends who, instead of talking about boys, fashion and holydays, they were playing with Ouija boards and talking about how to shoot up schools, was because Tara lived in constant hardship. She had either the fight or flight response. That was all she knew, for all her life. Every second of every day.

She wanted her traffickers that had sold her off to faceless men to rape her, ruin her, to deal with the ramifications of dehumanising her. Cause as much damage as possible and die while doing it, so that the Cabal will have to deal with creating a monster. That was Tara's only purpose in life.

Shooting up a school was the most logical form of revenge and rebellion to help Tara cope.

… She didn't even remember what happened. All was a blur. Shooting innocent children. She shivered. Did she even do it? Tara couldn't recall, her mind went dark from dissociation. That had been when Marcel had come into her life for the first time to save her.

"It is one dead body," Airgetlám said, rising from the corpse to his feet, a faraway look to his gorgeous turquoise eyes in the dappled shadows and sunlight underneath the palm leaves and reeds. "There is an Aes Sidhe amongst the American marines. And the American marines are heading to Baghdad."

An Aes Sidhe only went on a mission rarely out of self-interest, it had been very, very purposeful, never arbitrary when it came to Aes Sidhe. An Aes Sidhe was *never* uncertain, they were driven. Centred by an agenda.

"Could there be more?" Marcell said, feeling a rush of adrenaline that made him twitch. "Or are we dealing with a rogue?"

All was silent but the clicking ambient hiss of insects. The river reeked of a smell that reminded Tara of slimy mud sand and sewers.

"We must not provoke or get in the way of other Aes Sidhe, Tara," Airgetlám said, walking up the bank slope into date palm shrubs. "For all we know, it might be a novice trying to learn his powers. You will be surprised how many Aes Sidhe never make it in Antarctica to train. Only a thousand people max are allowed to live in Antarctica during the winter, and during the summer, when tourists come, the training is at a lull. It's very hard to get down there. It's stupid, getting rid of the restrictions would prevent so many criminals from terrorising the community. But it is what it is."

Marcell found this ironic. "How do you know?" he replied sternly. "What if this Aes Sidhe is trained? What if he or she is on an official mission? Do the Alliance know of our heist?"

"Hard to say, Tara. It's more likely this killing could be an Aes Sidhe *discovering* their powers. They might not even be aware that they are Aes Sidhe and therefore, are naïve to our heist."

Marcell grinned, feeling strong and powerful. "If I wasn't aware of your perceptive nature, I'd think you were paranoid."

"I'm not paranoid."

"Stop fishing for validation. You know you're good at perceiving things."

"Yes. If I recall, you're the testiest, in the face person I have ever met."

Marcell laughed. Tara tended to be extremely unpleasant. She needed to force people in order to gain their trust. And no one simply could put up with her. "Hussein made a bad choice to release the prisoners. They will try and ransack places for stuff."

"The timing couldn't be worse, Tara. You'd hope the marines could handle this on their own. I doubt it. In the marine's ranks, if there is a soldier among them that has no idea, he's an Aes Sidhe . . ."

"You *are* paranoid," Marcell tested.

Airgetlám's face became harder than stone, his eyes icy ponds. "Only cautious."

"But what novice," Marcell hissed, "would butcher a man like an animal? You're scared of being caught? What are you hiding? Tell me?"

As a particularly standoffish curmudgeon, Tara had realised – a smartass indeed – Airgetlám did not reply. *Crap!*

Tara stubbornly tried to pry him for this secret – a secret that he could use against her, to undermine her, to cut her down – anything. But he wouldn't budge. He remained odiously passive.

But Tara could at times, glimpse what he was feeling due to the bond Barbelo had given them – he dealt with constant pain – how could one stand the pain? How much could one hurt, hate and chill?

Once they reached their motorbikes to hit the road, only then did Airgetlám respond. "Barbelo said to not be worried about setbacks. Not even for a potential enemy. We do what we do."

Tara scowled deeply. Airgetlám did not have to placate her – she was more than capable. And yet, she wanted to swear and berate herself, for hesitating booking the flights, for sweating when Tara had to show her fake passport, wanting to sick up when she had to create a story on the spot when asked at security about her purposes. She couldn't simply say "an Aeon told me to heist the Iraqi Museum". Now, her heart and blood pressure started to rise – she hated being thwarted by circumstances.

Marcell was the symptom of such stress. He dreaded. Oh, how he trembled until it disjointed her very mind, tuning her out from reality from the consequences for failing Barbelo, the Aeon. How could one function in constant fear and dread? How could one be sure and confident about anything? She had reoccurring nightmares of failing the Aeons.

Are you faithful to us? Tara stared at nothing on the road, sensing Barbelo's ubiquitous presence in her soul, tugging and distant.

"Tara," Airgetlám stated blandly.

"Let's go now," Marcell, coming to Tara's senses, spoke tersely.

Airing out her hijab, lowering it to her neck, Tara putting on her helmet, hopped onto her stolen motorbike, igniting the throttling at the handles with the flick of her wrist, the engine coming to life with an ear-splitting rumble. She glanced at the Muslim women and could sense their scandalised shock.

Following Airgetlám, Tara tore down the highway, which resembled Nevada. It was better to do the task given, than to live on with the fear of having not done it.

———

At dusk, Casbolt finally arrived at Baghdad – *Madinat al-Salam* – the City of Peace – and as Demos now said – a City of a Joke.

Demos provided a quick historical overview of the city in the medieval past. Casbolt was shocked, very surprised that he never knew this: Baghdad under the Abbasid Caliphate (750 – 1258 CE), was one of the most culturally diverse, secular, progressive and richest cities on the planet. And it was a shock to most of the American laymen marines that this progressive culture was Islamic. Clearly the culturally embedded idea in their heads about barbaric, primitive Islam and enlightened, progressive Christianity failed them. It only just showed how much the public school system-controlled education emasculated the potential of the masses for cultural awareness.

Baghdad had been the seat of power where the caliph Harun al-Rashid served the story *A Thousand and One Nights* to his court; a court that ruled diplomatically, trading with China to Frankia, filling the libraries of his city with classical Greek and the Roman philosophical, medicinal and scientific texts. It was a renaissance before the Italian Renaissance. "The West is in debt to the East," Casbolt whispered in fascination.

Before the Mongol invasion of Baghdad in 1258 CE that rivered the Euphrates into blood, thriving culture had flourished here, while Europe's feudal lords in their cold damp castles, illiterate, squabbled among themselves in petty wars for power. There were exceptions of course with Holy Roman Emperor Charlemagne. Demos did not forget that Charlemagne had contact with people from the Abbasid world, inquiring of their exceptional knowledge. "Like Oxford meets New York and Mecca," Demos ascertained, summing up Baghdad well.

But that was in the past – of what Baghdad had once been.

Broken, destroyed, collapsed and gloomy, orange lurid fires shone in the city, like a patchwork of pinpricks. The air smelled of pungent decay, refuse, burning tyres, rubber and petrol, swirling with contriteness and anticipation, loss and dread, hanging heavily over the sad city. Noises echoed across the skyline, molesting the land, guns firing arbitrarily into the city's heart. Shouts crackled, along with the thundering of jets in a knife formation and blundering helicopters flying through smokestacks.

Once the philosophical centre of the universe, Baghdad was a sagging, blighted beast. The renaissance of cultural progression, reduced to a heart of dark ebony, reeking with dumb desperation. A shadow of a glorious dream failed to revive itself.

Casbolt wondered, if Hussein wanted his seat of power here, and the American troops were running the place with fire and thunder, would the Cabal also be here for the picking? Surely where all the central action was, lurking like carrion birds, the Cabal loomed. They saw every major historical event as an opportunity to exploit for their avarice, slipping away in secret to smuggle what they could.

The only issue was, Casbolt didn't even know the location of the Baghdad Museum. None of his men knew or were familiar with this city, not even Garry Harrel. So, it seemed then that Tommy Franks had forgotten in the heat of the moment of American victory, to mention the precise address of the objective.

"I'll call Conroy for directions," Garry Harrel said, cursing in frustration.

Disappointment riddled Casbolt. He wasn't expecting much out of Baghdad now after the devastating Thunder Run. The school of learning cried out in despair, for justice. The labyrinth of streets echoed with random shootings of semiautomatics, pockmarked with broken buildings, rubble and evacuating citizens. There was a lot of horn beeping and swearing.

"As the convention of history goes," Demos commentated as if filming for a documentary, "nothing lasts forever. It either faded way like Babylon, turned ugly or prospered. Baghdad turned ugly."

Casbolt saw abandoned Iraqi A T-72 Asad Babil tanks clogging up the streets surrounded by the supporters of the l'ancien regime with slumped backs, surrendering the fallen city. They looked bewildered, unsure as of what to do next in accomplishing their goal.

The streets were a chaotic mess. No electricity meant no traffic lights and that meant Casbolt's unit were left driving in the dark, streets illuminated by a few generators and American marines armed with flashlights. Casbolt could not see any police either, so the traffic was uncoordinated on major thoroughfares.

"The museum should be in the area between the river and railway," Garry said. "We should know where it is once we see it."

Casbolt saw the cult of the Galactic Tyrant's scion – the personality of Saddam Hussein – saturate every street corner and alley. Statues, murals, advertisements – no matter where he looked, Casbolt could not escape the face of Saddam Hussein. Most, thank God, were defaced. Some of the despot's murals at major intersections were scribbled over with red spray paint by bored soldiers, occupying their time with nothing better to do but use massive billboard signs to direct passing traffic. There were many bonfires in trash cans lighting up artistic graffiti on brick walls, drawing many citizens to congregate like moths to a flame.

As the palm trees of the museum compound finally came into view, Casbolt's unit met a US tank and a small platoon of marines standing around it. "There's Conroy's platoon," Casbolt said.

The museum looked vulnerable, and there were no signs of robbers or escaped criminals, though Casbolt knew that Conroy's tank parked outside the museum's wall was evidence there were looters close by.

As Casbolt walked on towards the façade of the museum, it had an illuminated arched entry way, flanked by paired statues of man-headed winged bulls. The threshold winged-bull guardians struck Casbolt as extremely detailed, and he smiled with an ecstatic resolve at their corkscrew hair and the bearded styles of the human heads.

It is possible to protect cultural heritage, Casbolt said in his head. *This is destiny.*

"Man, will you look at that," Rich Jackus said as he gazed at the hybrid winged-bull sphinxes holding his semiautomatic.

"Yeah," Demos laughed. "Does it have the fifth foot? Yes, it does! Creates a multisensory effect on the visitors of Kalhu, Nineveh and Dur-Sharrukin. Gives the illusion of the *lamassu* is walking as you pass by it."

"What are these again?" Casbolt asked.

"*Lamassu*," Demos said. "It's Akkadian for half human half bull. They're like the apotropaic Cherubim angels on the Ark of the Covenant. The Arabs call them Jinn. The Great Sphinx is the same creature. They're celestial bouncers guarding sacred spaces."

"Yo, you romantic nerds! I'll take a photo of you guys," Tim Grogan yelled, jovially pulling out his digital camera. "Come on! It's to keep the memories! So, we can tell everyone we were here on the night America gave Iraq freedom!"

Far from it, man, Casbolt thought, mesmerised by the crowned Assyrian *lamassu.*

"Yes please," Demos said, running up to the statues to pull off a ridiculous pose. Joined by Jackus, who hauled Casbolt over, they got into place to face the camera – but as everyone put on a pose, Casbolt stood poised, his hands folded behind his back. He did not smile.

"Alright, ya'll done now?" General Conroy grunted, observing the premise. "Come on, Casbolt, this is your mission. We have reports of Iraqis wandering around with semiautomatics and sandbags in the museum. Stay focused. I need you to tell me if you see people carrying stuff outside the museum."

Michael Prince, instead, took control. "Damn straight it's my mission. We are the only law-enforcement expertise we've got in this forsaken country."

Garry Harrel rolled his eyes, whistling to the other marines. "Hey, knock it off, boys! Get serious!"

Turning, Michael saw the young frivolous marines groaning as they reluctantly followed orders.

Once Garry and Conroy got the whole Sentinels unit together, Michael Prince went on to examine the security of the Baghdad Museum, which, he guessed, was likely to be protected only by the staff, making it particularly vulnerable.

Unfortunately, his concerns were confirmed. He met two men, Donny George and Jabir Khalil, hunkering down in the grass patch near the galleries. "Little by little the staff just disappeared," Donny George recounted when Michael Prince asked them about where the security was. "We're the only security here."

"Really?" Michael said. "You think four men and a kid will cut it? I don't think so. I have Conroy and Garry Harrel in firing positions around the museum to make up for you guys' lack of effort."

"Well yeah thanks," Donny George agreed reluctantly. "About that. We're the only men here. That's why we trust you guys with the guns, and the tank will scare the looters away." In total, six people remained stationed around the museum premises: Donny George, Jabir Khalil, Muhsin – an employee who lived in a shack behind the museum wall – Muhsin's son, and Abdul Rakhman – the museum's fifty-seven-year-old live-in guard at the police station. A driver waited outside with him in the garage driveway.

Michael ground his teeth with irk. *This is so random and unprofessional! Why are these people so laid back!? Where is the local security?*

"I would like to bring order to your ad hoc security," Michael said tersely. "But why did everyone just . . . leave?!"

"Sorry sir," Jabir Khalil said. "Everyone's afraid that their lives are in danger when you invaded. But we do have one person that comes back regularly for maintenance and security with Abdul Rakhman. It's Dr Nawala al-Mutwali. She should be coming soon. Brave woman. She might be of help to get inside."

"Then I would like to meet Abdul Rakhman and Dr al-Mutwali when she comes," Michael Prince said. "I will send two marines into the museum proper with me to guard the artefacts from the inside. Conroy and his platoon and the rest of my squad will guard the entrances."

Donny George nodded in the darkness, saying, "Sounds like a plan. There is an international antiquities mafia around you know?"

"And they are prepared to strike on days like today," Jabir Khalil added laboriously. "If looters get in, it is going to be a disaster. But if I may ask, officer, can I get your name?"

Michael Prince hesitated. He was not prepared to give away his complex problematic identity, but the name he'd chose would, from here on out, would be revocable, an opportunity to forge his new future and become known in this country. His new name as a renowned hero, set apart from the vice from the world he'd come from.

"My name is James Casbolt," Michael Prince said. "I'll be off now. See what I can do."

Michael Prince and James Casbolt together were about to prevent disaster.

24

SUFFERING BEFORE GLORY

"The Ba'ath pursued a cultural policy that fostered heritage preservation aiming to unify Iraq's diverse ethnic communities. Human rights may have been non-existent under Saddam and the Ba'ath, but Iraq's archaeological sites and museums were extremely well cared for, illegal digging and smuggling ceased due to the regime's cutthroat policing.

Essentially, the Iraqi system was well done, crafty and well centralised; designed to deceive both its own population and outsiders of what it was doing. America assumed dogmatically that the Ba'athists was 'a balloon ready to pop'. Nonconformist views were unceremoniously neglected by the Bush administration . . .

America, by deposing Saddam, destroyed Iraq."

—From *Omega Plan: The Epicenter of Light and Darkness*, Joseph DePaula.

The next morning, Nefer refused to speak to Joshua as he cradled the dead boy in his arms, alone in the alleyway. The dead, slim boy had one eye shut and the other, a star-shaped hole. Joshua had killed him, his own brother.

Whoever sheds the blood of human,
by human shall his blood be shed,
for God made human in his own image.

"Boy," Joshua said elegiacally, feeling condemned. "Brother. I did not want to kill you. You and I were both forced to fight. You're too young to be in battle, you have . . . What did you have after I selfishly took your breath away from you? I thought of your semiautomatic, the fierceness in your eye, yes. It mistook them for hatred. I saw all that, but now I see your mother, your father, your brother and friends who would die with grief because of me. They haunt me, they're hurting me! Forgive me, boy! I did not know what I did, yet I knew . . . I don't know what to do with myself now. I could write to your parents." Tears flooded Joshua's eyes, and his body trembled. "My Arabic is barely intelligible in writing, but not in speech. Not like my English writing. But I can speak Arabic fine. Only if you can hear me now… You cannot hear me."

What if he was forced to fight because he had no choice? What would Joshua do if an enemy invaded his home country in Turkey? Would he do that same thing? End up dead prey to random chaos?

Dawn spread forth rosy fingers across the horizon, light pushing the shadows slowly into the confined spaces of the alley. Joshua could still hear his unit lounging at the generator block house, a distance from the undercroft sitting with their supplies, celebrating their night skirmish with cans of Tab soda. Spiritually, with the greatest defeat, only Joshua had the audacity to mourn.

Then Joshua heard the voice of Julian expounding. "Something seems – off to me too, Ryan. A War on Terror is an oxymoron, yes? War is terror! It's a war on ideologies man, not on a single country. It's like saying to become a virgin, you need to have sex! America first and everyone can go to Hell!"

Joshua left the corpse of the boy down in the ditch, burying it. He slumped his head, and embraced the darkness of self-loathing, hopelessness . . . And anger.

Christ! I was set up to fail! Jesus you saved me just so I could fail! But Joshua refused to believe that any of this was his fault.

America was to blame. Might made right for them. The War on Terror, created predatory peace.

America – George Bush – was on the path of darkness and death. And because of America's impish mistakes, the Holy Spirit within Joshua was in anguish.

The careless boisterous marines paid no heed, harboured no interest to the dying and to the wretched. "Yes," Joshua erupted, kneeling at the grave. "This war *is* an oxymoron, this war would never end, conceived by Utilitarian *moron* sophomores that had no emotional intelligence, *indoctrinated* with the *nonsense*, that the West was triumphant over the East. Just because we think Christian, it doesn't make us better than everyone else! America can go to Hell! A Crusade *indeed*. The White Man's Burden!"

Those in charge—both political and military leaders—continue to refuse to take moral responsibility, or to even admit fault when they were wrong. And while Bush was reading to babies in a kindergarten all blasé, terrorists planted bombs in the World Trade Centre and hijacked three planes to destroy it! "Bush asked for it! And now, the last Crusade has begun . . . And it will never end this terror."

The world was cracked. The world was lies. The world was a festered sore. The American system was built off scapegoats, causing blood to cry out, unleashing the four horsemen of the apocalypse.

Hot angry tears ran down Joshua's cheeks. And now, because this war was doomed to fail, Joshua had failed and forfeited the Kingdom of God, denying Christ by his actions. Nefer – his only companion – had gone forever because he sinned.

Joshua slumped against the wall and wept – wept for himself, the boy he'd killed and Nefer his angelic scholarly partner, his quirks and morsels of insight, his only friend. He slowly slid down there, crying.

His mind became a berating turbid storm, he couldn't think, and that was bad for his intelligence. Why did a single death bother him so much? *Get over it!*

Joshua let out a whimpering sigh that gradually turned into a feral growl, pressing his fists against his forehead fitfully, gritting his teeth. He needed to get out of here. He scraped his back across the concrete wall.

So foolish of me, Joshua thought. *How could I be so* foolish *to want material wealth and financial comfort, Pounders! I've changed. Or I die. I will not become the con man!*

Voices of young men came from behind the alleyway at the undercroft. The voices of soldiers. Never shall the commanders find him broken like this.

Taking a deep breath, Joshua took off jogging away from the undercroft holding his head. He lumbered to an isolated hill patched with creamy grass stalks overlooking a thin dry valley. No one would see him here.

Joshua fell to his knees, eyes stinging from persistent tears, looking upwards towards the heavens.

"Father . . . Oh Lord," Joshua moaned in pain, uttering a petition for mercy. "Hear me. My heart is like the blood I shed. I cannot go back to who I was. My iniquities have overtaken me. I've broken your Covenant. I killed a boy, enlisted by a dictator." Joshua ripped his camo uniform. "If one kills a human, it would as though one killed the human race. Turn not your face from me in my distress. May the blood you shed purify me from my murder."

Thou shalt not bare false witness. That first moral principle had destroyed him, then another scourged with fiery intensity just as weighty as idolatry, blasphemy, neglecting Sabbath, dishonouring family, adultery, stealing and jealousy.

Thou shalt not kill. The sixth word of the summarised Torah.

But . . . this is war. There must *be an exception. Just War theory!*

How was he better than the ancients? In his prideful thinking, how could Joshua know better than *two thousand* years of tradition? Songs and fairy tales all drove the same polluted message of the legend of Jesus Christ, fading into myth infused with political agendas and prejudices. Just as the gods of mythology, the saints became a pantheon of gods. Not a hall of faithful servants of the living God.

You die, liar.

No. Christ, I . . . Suffer for Truth.

"Is there a way to kill and to save?" Joshua pled desperately. "To kill and to protect? Or to not kill? *What is it?!* My intention is to *save* not to hate!"

In reply, the marines laughed, Pounders yelling at them to shut up and to eat their breakfast. The military, comfortable with its moral thinking and practice of indoctrination, as well as its oversimplified instrumental methods, propagated narratives that conveyed the morally questionable warrior ethos, which could be counterproductive and inadequate in outcome.

Joshua sighed, mumbling self-inflicting gibberish as he got up, dusting himself off. *Come on. Judd is going to discern something is amiss with you. You made repentance and confessed. That's all that matters.* However, Joshua did not feel in the mood to do anything.

Rumbling.

Joshua turned, seeking madly for the source of the rumbling sound in the distance. A trail of dust rose on the horizon, and veering sharply, the dust cloud parted. A cream armoured GMV mounted with a gunner at the roof, raced through a scrub-covered wadi. They'd said today was going to be blistering hot and the chances of fighting should have been slim, so Joshua didn't think much, seeing the vehicle bannered with the flag of red, white and blue, indicating it was only a casual routine platoon returning from a scouting mission.

But why was it accelerating?

Then Joshua saw a small black dot appear on the slopes of the furthest hill. He focused on it thinking it was a small animal, when another dot appeared. And another and another. Soon, multiple black humanoids stood up on the two hills looking down into the wadi at the lone vehicle.

The ear-rattling thunder of rapid assaults poured in rhythmic destruction upon the GMV. Joshua gawked, watching the carnage as the gunner howled at the top of his lungs, turning his MK 19 grenade launcher, firing back.

"TURN AROUND! TURN AROUND! GO!" Horrified voices bellowed from the wadi.

The reverberating hissing bullets ricocheted off the truck as the vehicle screaming to a halt, flung dust into the air. Bullets streaking across the ground, the vehicle exploded into a full dash, back the way it came.

Right back through the ambush.

The aggressors on the high ground continued to fire. The heat, it seemed, did not bother the desperate Iraqis, they showed no mercy hailing deadly force upon the GMV.

The battered truck raced right through the onslaught a second time, tyres grinding gravel, skidding to a dramatic stop, tittering a good distance in front of a series of buildings, abandoned and bare to its concrete frame. The routine patrol had made it out from the ambush, but the gunner on the roof, leaned over his gun, unconscious.

Joshua scrambled back towards the administration building. By the time he reached the undercroft, Ben was already shouting orders for his Eidolon marines to cover the GMV, racing down the hill like bandits. It was only when Joshua arrived, that he glanced at Judd and Ben.

"We're going to need a medic down there!" Pounders cried. "Chief Greg Coker and John Hale have taken hits!"

"Medic?" Ben narrowed his eyes, nonplussed, hurrying out to join the Eidolons.

"Captain, I can volunteer. I'll go out there and help John Hale," Joshua remarked immediately. At that, Pounders gawked, expression astonished. Without thinking, Joshua passionately dug into the supply cases, grabbing medical equipment. "We need four medical stations to treat the wounded, Colonel. So, I'm going to help bring the wounded to them."

"What?!" Pounders exclaimed, but Joshua gathered the bandage supplies, morphine, antiseptic and water – the basics he needed to get those men out alive to the professionals. "Josh! Stop! Get back to your station! You barely know field medicine!"

"War changes people, Pounders," Joshua said, unashamed. "And you know me. I'm good at pretending, if I can be anything, it will be a medic. I'm going to do this. You will not stop me. I will be a medic now!"

"What?" Pounders spat in bewilderment. "Joshua, we discussed this! We already *have* our medic! Stop!" He grasped Joshua's arm. "I swear to God, if you die out there—"

"Don't worry about me! I'm a Swiss Army knife, remember? Multidisciplined. You called me that before Damascus Spring, so, I'm a bloody medic!" Strapping on a helmet for protection, Joshua dashed down the hill, his legs pumping, the wind lashing his face and blowing his hair.

He felt stubborn but, Joshua *had to do something*. The wind and the adrenaline carried him on, and Joshua felt light and strangely, at peace. His stomach seethed with anxiety, but it didn't reign. Without a gun, he *would* conquer the beast of war like a true saint – to defend and save lives. And if Joshua died . . . He trusted God will be there for him. For life was God's signature rhythm. It was *so hard* for violent humans to understand this perspective since humans always wanted to take the centre stage, to control life on their own terms. And the stipulations of war, made men apathetic to the simple notion that life was sacred.

Once Joshua arrived at the concrete village, there was already a high volume of gunfire, so he hunkered down behind one of the walls, staying low. He heard Ben barking orders for the marines to get into blocking positions, firing at the Iraqis. A grenade shook the ground as Joshua pressed against the wall, turning to scan his surroundings.

The truck was still a good few metres away, the firing range of friendly soldiers too intense before him for the medic run. Reggie Paige of Ben's partner Company C contingent was on the ground firing his tripod gun as projectiles zipped past dangerously. Joshua saw foreign figures leaping from the screens of dust before Reggie, one arching his head, spinning to the ground, writhing in death. The other Iraqis fired back, taking cover under the natural contours on the hillside.

"Cleared! Get them to the medic!" Reggie screamed, assaulting the enemy behind his mad gun.

Joshua ran through the visceral barge heart thundering with determination, his ears throbbing from the terribly loud gunfire. Derek Fish and Julian ran alongside him for cover. Diving for the truck, prying the side doors, Joshua walked on his knees towards the sounds of a groaning man. John Hale begged for help, half fallen out the door, clutching his left side, as Joshua attended him.

"Okay man. Hang in there," Joshua said, pressing John Hale's wound. He knew enough first aid and the basics of field medicine from his previous years as a con. Of course, he wasn't an expert, he was going to have to escort these men out of danger and get them to the safety of the medical bay. He needed to be quick though, fast and resilient enough, if he was to be committed to this. They were going to need Joshua anyway.

Julian's screams got his attention, drawing his gaze up to observe his surroundings.

No, Julian had announced for the medical team to go back! They had come seconds too late! Joshua growled as he saw the Iraqis turn their attention to the truck, assaulting the incoming American medics. Bullets whizzed past, clanging on the armoured vehicle's doors, ripping through the medics, killing them.

"No!" Joshua growled as he got behind a tyre, handling John Hale with ease.

So, I'm meant to be here. Joshua procrastinated. He was these marines' only chance now. *You're their only chance to survive.*

Crouched, holding onto the fender, Joshua worked to stop John Hale's bleeding.

"I've got your back, bookworm! Help him!" Julian called, cocking his HK417, and standing up, he placed it on the bonnet of the vehicle, firing. It shook madly, bullet shells flinging and clanging from blitzing recoil. Joshua could hear the dull impacts of Julian's bullets hitting Iraqi flesh across the other side of the mound.

Derek Fish helped the gunner man Greg Coker down from his station, laying him next to John Hale. He then quickly removed the polymer magazine to reload his weapon with his back to the door, turned around and aimed, firing at the enemies, covering Julian and Joshua.

"Oh my gawd! Hurry, hurry get the morphine! Get the morphine!" Greg Coker squawked in Joshua's ear.

"Greg Coker, you're shot!" Joshua said, holding the bandages. "Man, you're shot!"

"I know, kid . . ." Coker hissed between laboured breaths. "Just – get me out of here!"

Joshua gave Chief Coker the dose of morphine, then returned to John Hale, examined his wound, staunching them further. Two patients – he had to deal with *two* simultaneously. Joshua was already drenched in sweat.

"The round had hit the last-chance plate on the back of my body armour," Coker strained, chuckling over the pain. "Lucky, huh?"

Joshua removed the patch off the last-chance plate. "I don't believe in luck, Chief. It just missed right over the left kidney. Any lower, you would be dead by now."

A grenade landed nearby, going off course, exploding. The *crack* made Joshua's ears bleed. He and Coker were hurled to the ground huddling, dirt raining upon them. Julian was the first to spring up in retaliation, roaring with fervour, rounding the truck, hosing human targets with muzzle flashes. With him, the other soldiers accompanying in his frontal assault smothered more Iraqis, forcing the offensive assault to push back.

"There are more coming over from the nooks a few clicks from here!" Julian yelled over the violent clamour. "We need to call in air support! Pounders!"

"Josh!" Derek nudged Joshua's shoulder, eyes wide with desperation. "I'm taking Hale back! Julian! Cover me!" Joshua watched helplessly as Julian, leaping over the bonnet with one hand, grunted, darting past, reloading his gun as Derek hauled the groaning John Hale over his shoulder. They charged for their lives, dashing back towards the village during the lull. Joshua prayed to God Derek would make it back. But in the middle of the suicide run, Julian blundered after Derek, firing back at the enemies. The marine bellowed, coursing through the tumult, just making it alive.

Oh no, I have to go through that again, do I? Joshua dreaded in his mind, and he wanted to give up. His heart pounded and his loins trembled as bullets hailed upon the truck. *Move! Do something, Joshua!* Itching to grab his gun and to use it, he resisted.

He had to save lives. The Virtues, the cleansing of Christ, came first.

"HEY!" Joshua yelled towards Ben and the troops, cupping his hands over his mouth. He couldn't tell if Ben could hear him or not. The guns firing were so loud, Joshua struggled to even hear himself.

Dirt erupted in his face. Gasping from the gunky air, he grasped onto Coker, knocking his elbow on the fender. He had to run this – run or die.

But there were only two more unscathed soldiers left in the truck that got out, engaging the enemy, who preserved Joshua some precious time. These men could not even blink as a heavy artillery round devoured them, the acoustics shaking the ground. A body flung from out of nowhere spinning in the air viciously, shrieking like grinding metal. That dead torso bounced in front of Joshua – arms mangled, legs truncated. The gory shrapnel gushing from underneath the truck sprayed upon Joshua, who ducked to take cover.

Suffering before glory! Go!

As Greg tumbled off his shoulder with guttural whines, the howling brays of the soldiers on the exposed side of the truck cried out for salvation. Three patients?! He couldn't help three men at once!? *I can't do it . . .*

He laughed to himself, because he was in great distress. He tried to get himself under the truck to reach the wounded on the other side. "You asked for this. You prayed for this. And you got this."

In front of him, the Iraqi assault squad sent bullets roaring loudly, until one bullet deflected off his helmet. The two marines facing them fell, simultaneously hit: the two closest to Joshua died, convulsing, blood disgorging in spurts. The third one was already dead.

The effects of the war atmosphere infused Joshua with a pestered anger – a blistering sweat, a burning roar. Slipping under the truck, creeping forward on his belly, Joshua was sure that without backup, he would get a wound.

But it didn't matter anymore. *Suffering before glory! Christ beside me! In front of me! Behind me!*

In red frustration, Joshua roared over the gunfire, indicating to the wounded he was still alive, and determined to save, despite the horrendous odds. If he sat underneath for too long, the armour of the vehicle would become too brittle, and bullets would surely penetrate the gas tank. He was running out of time.

"God, my strength," Joshua muttered under his breath. He made it to the nearest soldier.

"What about me!?" Coker yelled with a hoarse voice. "Josh! Josh!"

I have to save them.

Joshua's body tensed, awaiting sudden imminent death. Bullets zipped and attacked the truck. Then a large rock bounced close by, with a strange-looking groove on its tip with an odd netting and a pin that—

Eyes popping out of his skull, grabbing the dead husk of the legless marine, Joshua smothered it over the grenade leaning on top of it. He held on tight, taking a deep breath.

The grenade exploded. All sound gushed out of his ears. Existence faded for a moment as he hung in between heaven and earth. Something flew off his head, slamming back onto the side of the truck, as he grunted frailly.

The truck rocked. His vision a disorientated veil of dust and blurs, flooded with warm light.

Joshua! Joshua!

Joshua's blood went cold. "Nefer?" he croaked. He could barely hear his own voice. Body trembling with shock, his ears felt as if they were under water.

"Joshua! Joshua! Josh, you there!?" That was Coker's screaming voice from behind. "JOSHUA! ANSWER ME!" Joshua could still save Greg Coker, at least. While pulling himself around the back, he saw two soldiers charging toward him screaming at the top of their lungs.

"Chief, I'm here!" Joshua spluttered.

"What on earth were you doing out there, you smartass! Get us out of here!"

There is only so much that I can do. I need to choose a life to save.

"Okay!" Joshua acquiesced, grieved, pivoting around the truck, wrapping his arms around Coker, lifting him up onto his back. His back was still sore and bruised from smothering the grenade blast, but he took one stride forward.

Then Judd Pounders jogged towards Joshua. Judd Pounders, as cantankerous as ever, full gear, helmet on, lugging a bazooka. A senior, carrying a *bazooka?*

Joshua watched with revitalising amusement; his wits put together observing the insanity of Pounders and the battle. He ejected a rocket, landing with an ear-splitting crack, cleaving a massive hole in the enemy formation. Iraqis screamed, airborne from the blast. Dropping his launcher, Pounders grabbed his AK-47 strapped to his body. His tucked-in lower lip and knitted eyebrows looking at Joshua, urged him to run.

Joshua rolled his eyes. *Here we go again. Playing the same game.*

"Hurry!" Coker barked pithily. "Come on, Pounders, get this kid a beating will yah! Give this kid a beating! Crap! Crap!"

Wretch! Joshua berated himself as he ran. Oh, once he got back to the station – if he could – he was going to cry some more and pray to God.

He kept his head down, attuning to the drastic wheezing breaths that racked his body. He charged on forward. Things crashed around him incoherently.

Joshua yelled with strain. He charged, right into death's face.

He gazed forward, torn in exhaustion, almost teetering offside. His legs were stiffening, his run slowing, and safety was still distant. Then, when he thought he could move no longer, and that he could die, he saw a shimmer of pink light streaking the air.

Nefer?

It was the flourish of supernatural spirit that made him reach the other side.

Encircling Joshua, Julian with Pounders barraged and killed the enemy assailants. Pounders' and Julian's peppering beats of their wild guns thudded madly, along with Joshua's throbbing heart.

"And along came Josh," someone called and Joshua finished the run. Ben? Reggie? He didn't care, though he kept one primal thought in mind to get to safety. Joshua dropped Coker, and collapsed unscathed, groaning and panting with a heaving chest.

"You hurt, kid?" Coker said eventually.

Closing his eyes, Joshua groaned. His entire body was bruised, trembling exceedingly. He swallowed and even that took effort.

I survived… Again. Barely.

"You know," Pounders said. "One of these days I'm actually convinced you will lose both legs, both arms and your head! Crap!" Muttering "Jesus" and cursing under his breath, Joshua heard Pounders stalk up to him, feeling the Colonel's mystified gaze beaming upon him.

Joshua lay there not sure what to think or feel. Should he laugh? Should he sob? Or do nothing?

"Ah ha! Peace, Joshua! You're in one piece!"

Joshua groaned at the pun, opening a heavy eye, guns still firing around him. It was Nefer, expanding and shrinking in a streak of gelatinous orbs. He hovered over his head, motioning around ecstatically in a phantom wind. "My apologies, I got cut off from you for a while but praise Yah, you made the appropriate Purification and Guilt Offering."

"Hey," Joshua grumbled, closing his eyes.

"*Hey?*" The spirit generously sounded taken aback. "Wait, you're not going to utter, 'how are you'? You're just going to sleep, *again?*"

Joshua nodded, resting his sore head in the sand. "I'm dead."

"Humans are *so odd*," Nefer mused, sighing. "God have mercy on me for not understanding your kind. It was *I* that prevented any bullet from penetrating your flimsy vessel!"

Joshua smiled. God, it was a pleasure to hear his nerdy voice again. Even though angelic logic sometimes never made sense – his pickiness awfully exasperating – was welcomed this time. Joshua knew *exactly* what he could do now in this war, he could adapt, to never sin with a high hand again.

Joshua *would* discard the sword and become a medic.

25

HEIST IN THE HOUSE OF THE MUSES

"Woe to Assyria, the rod of my anger;
*   the staff in their hands is my fury!*
Against a godless nation I send him,
*   against the people of my wrath I command him,*
to take spoil and seize plunder, and to tread them down like the mire of the streets."
—From the Scroll of Isaiah, the prophet's disciples. A prophecy against the House of Israel and Assyria, c. 740 – c. 540 BCE.

Led by Abdul Rakhman and expert of cuneiform Dr Nawala al-Mutwali into the dark basement of the museum was a remarkable honour. Dr Nawala al-Mutwali allowed units to begin taking overnight shifts guarding the building, but she had to leave soon, it was too dangerous to stay – not an unreasonable view, considering the risks to women in war zones – especially Muslim women.

Casbolt and the marines crept around in the darkness with a torch, since the entire city had lost all its electricity. Unfortunately, in this place, air conditioning was not an option. Though the place smelled of damp clay, motes of dust sprinkling down upon him like snowflakes in their torchlights, Casbolt marvelled at the sheer variety of gold, sarcophagi, amphorae and precious items stashed tightly down here. Elaborate furniture and pots, the begemmed splendour, jewels, mosaics, artistic reliefs, statues of priests and servants. In the storeroom basement were stacks upon stacks of cuneiform baked clay tablets – one hundred thousand tablets, including one containing a flood story similar to that found later in the Bible. There were also cluttered

254

rods with large rings decorated with serpents eating their own tails, and here and there ornaments and treasures. These temporary storage bins were and remained housed as a preliminary collection of excavated objects alongside inventories produced from sites.

Everything is in place, Michael Prince said. *This is good, we need to be on guard in case looters come.*

They'll be dead before they get away, the Redlion lauded. *All of them will be dead.*

Michael Prince took control of Casbolt's body and the sensation of urgency stabilised.

"Wow, look at this beauty," Reece said, eyes wide, glittering like gold. He laughed, greasy hands handling a pot with some impression on it. "I remember seeing this artefact before. Look at the size of this thing."

The young marines acted all laid back and it irked Casbolt. He walked gingerly into the dusty storage room captivated by the endless amounts of ancient wealth that could cost billions. *This needs to be heavily protected, but I'm worried again, these two louts can't even follow orders!*

"Dude, is that the *Baghdad Battery*?!" Tom Grogan slurped at his can of soda, smacking his lips. "Man, I heard they can create electricity with this thing."

But Reece laughed, grabbing the six-inch terracotta pot containing a cylinder made of a rolled copper sheet. "Good luck turning on your Hot Wheels set with this, Tom! Ha. Come on, dude!"

"Yeah. Come and see for yourself."

Idiots! "No," Casbolt said, shaking his head. "It's not a battery, you snow chicks. It's a pot!"

"Look, Cas," Grogan said taking the pot. "I'm sort of an Erich Von Daniken guy. Just admit it and say it, bro – it was aliens from another planet! How else do you explain it?"

Reece laughed while Casbolt sighed. "What makes you think that? You want me to get Dr al-Mutwali to evaluate your claim?"

"Anunnaki!" Reece yelled perkily.

"But it *wasn't* aliens," Casbolt stressed.

"Keep an open mind," Grogan replied, pulling off a very evocative cringeworthy Giorgio Tsoukalos gesture with a cocked head, squinting eyes and gesturing hands, only that he lacked the hair. The man was almost bald as Ben.

Casbolt rolled his eyes as the marine guffawed. *Man, we really need to be focusing here!*

"Stop mucking around, will yah! Stop! You can't even do one simple task? Hopeless louts! What would you do if robbers came right now?! Since you two are so comfortable on guard here, I'm going out to secure the upper floors myself," Casbolt said, hefting his gun from his shoulder strap.

Reece and Tom Grogan took deep breaths, still chuckling, lauding about languidly, and Casbolt would not be surprised if in a few hours they would be fast asleep. Casbolt, whirling around, hiked up the stairs to the main floor.

Once the Redlion and Michael Prince shared the forefront of Casbolt's mind, a loud ruckus sounded from above, on the second floor, hoping the six staff members in the premises and Conroy's squad were sufficient security.

Suddenly, Casbolt's communication kit crackled with the distorted voice of Jason Conroy – the platoon leader stationed outside the museum. "Subject in sight. Over?"

"Affirmative," the cold voice of a soldier called in reply. "Take him out. Over."

Intruders, Michael Prince hissed.

To kill, Redlion growled with enthral.

To ward off, Prince said.

Casbolt was already darting around the dark corners, his flashlight on, dashing down the halls, scaling up a flight of stairs to the source of the sound. Leaping into the main lobby, Casbolt could hear outside the museum, ear-piercing gunshots of engagement, counterpoint to the yells from Conroy's men on the com kit.

Casbolt smirked in the darkness. "Well here they come. Just as expected. Gods, I hope our defences will hold."

He heard smashing noises from the right, in the Sumerian exhibit, and running in the dark, using his torch to guide him, he aimed his flashlight and gun, gazing down the hall. He found nothing, yet the noises were not ceasing upon his arrival. Grinding sounds could be heard, low in intensity. A looter had sunk inside no doubt.

"Come on. Come on," Casbolt whispered angrily. "Where are you?"

He was welcomed by the wall of narrative friezes of lion hunts and processions of men giving offerings amidst palm trees. He cast the flashlight over the exhibit, walking past the colourless reliefs of genies, bearded, holding pinecones and baskets – representations of the Seven Sages with four wings.

To his shock, he turned the corner and found women and urchins looting, and when they saw Casbolt they roared, hollering in aggression, waving axes and iron bars at him, rushing through the building.

"Christ!" Casbolt cursed, firing his gun in shock. He didn't expect *women and children* to loot this place!

"It's ours!" the woman shrieked. "Get away from me! There is no government! It's ours!"

Casbolt was bewildered as the woman hit him with the iron bar, and in response, he kicked her, sending the woman staggering, running away, stuffing the pieces in her bags.

Casbolt went on and saw a man with a saw, methodically cutting away at a stone statue of some Near Eastern ruler.

"HEY!" Casbolt shouted, firing, killing the looter sawing the statue. More robbers lurched from the shadows, scattering.

Casbolt swore when he heard the sound of glass smashing. He cast light over a defaced, toppled statue down the dark hallway.

Something heavy fell and smashed, followed by fast footsteps.

I'm failing. Blood rushing through him, Casbolt whipped around, firing.

He'd just missed killing a man on the run in the shadows behind a corridor, shattering a large cylindrical vase made from stone alabaster. In horror, Casbolt watched as the robber skilfully got away.

Casbolt beat his chest. *No!*

Casbolt hurried on the second floor where most of the chaos seemed to originate, darting forwards into the Old Babylonian section, flashlight sporadically casting over the darkness. Casbolt sensed with his Parvus Perception, a man with his hand full of artefacts, squatting down over a glass cabinet, oblivious of his presence. Casbolt threw his gun at him, summoning Gáe Bulg.

The gun hit him, and he gasped, dropping figurines, plaques and tablets clattering to the floor. Casbolt winced. They didn't break. With Gáe Bulg, he ran the man through, causing him to yelp in shock. He stooped to check the saved artefacts, strapping back on his gun over his shoulder, and heard more destruction and shouting outside the museum.

Conroy was barking through the com kit, saying, "Fall back! It's coming from the museum grounds! Firing positions! They're getting into the Children's Museum! Fire at will! Kill everything that moves! Go! Harrel, get to the back of the museum! They need backup! Go! Go!"

Casbolt hadn't realised that the sounds from his com kit had given away his presence. In the darkness, a man rammed into Casbolt, but with his energetic reflex, and with his free hand, he grasped the man up by the collar of an Iraqi military uniform. Casbolt gasped. Whatever this man held in his hands, flew into the dark, smashing utterly.

"Wait!" the Iraqi soldier wailed in broken English, while Casbolt shook him. He was gasping, wheezing like a mad man. "Wait! I have nothing! Spare me! I have nothing!"

Casbolt let go and punched him, making sure to break a few ribs. Stumbling, the Iraqi soldier tripped over a fallen statue, flapping hand spinning Casbolt's torch in a circle on the ground, illuminating another part of the hall. Now Casbolt could see the extent of ruin the robbers had inflicted upon the exhibit. The looters had pillaged and ransacked the place into a heap of smashed objects, antiquity crumbling and culture vanishing.

"Why did you do this?" Casbolt snapped, stomping over the statue, hauling the man up, pressing him against the wall. "Who's your master?"

The Iraqi soldier writhed, whimpering, "You shouldn't be here, American."

Casbolt hoisted the looter up. "I'm not American."

Fear cast over the looter's eyes. "Wait! I – I can repay you! I ca—"

Ripping Gáe Bulg out of the corpse of the other looter, Casbolt impaled the soldier up the rear end, into his body, slowly. The looter wailed in agony with each penetrating inch.

Unholy, disgusting even, but rage and loathing numbed Casbolt's mind. He did not care if the artefacts were broken or not, the damage had been done – he'd been held back by pathetic louts – meaning now, nothing could hold him back. He had to *kill* as many looters as possible!

Drawing the Spear back, watching the Iraqi's eyes roll up in his head, gagging to death, Casbolt marked passing movement behind him, and, using the Parvus, he tossed the Spear at a nearby wall.

It *pinned* the looter and the wall. The looter had his own torch strapped on his chest, revealing the Spear had only caught that man's diaphanous head covering. Picking up his torch, Casbolt shone it on the looter, recognising distinctive light-brown hair, and moustache. Most bizarre of all, grasping an ornate gold dagger in its sheath, were metallic fingers connected to a bionic artificial arm. The man grunted, grasping the Spear shaft and met Redlion with turquoise eyes.

"You!" the man barked, voice boiling with indignation. "Stop! The Redlion, out of all things!? It was *you*!"

"What do you mean you know me!? Who are you?" Casbolt growled. He watched the man with the moustache ground his teeth, trembling with outrage, hurt and shame. He twisted his flesh hand on the Spear shaft and with a jolt of his head, ripped a patch of his veil from off his head covering.

The man with the robotic arm shook his head, face hardened like stone. Emotionless. Bleakness. "You and I have a long history. Our parents have a long history. You seriously don't remember me?"

More ruckus thundered from somewhere in the dark museum.

"No," Casbolt asked, wondering numbly what way he had wounded this man. Though he focused on the man's blue eyes – Blue Blood Aes Sidhe selective breeding traits. "Who are you?"

A shocking sound thundered with a sonorous boom, knocking the museum, causing mortar to rain on their heads. Conroy and his men's voices hollered on the com kit, speaking indistinctly.

What happened!? Was that explosion us? He hoped so, it sounded as if it had been fire cannoned from a tank!

"Before you cut off my arm," the man gripping the Curruid Spear impaled in the wall said, "I was known as Gladius Huyard of the Carnutes."

Casbolt stumbled back. "*You're* Gladius Huyard? You . . . your father Magnus Huyard, he was behind . . ."

"Project Vortigern?" Gladius' face was dark in the shadows. "Yes, James Casbolt. When you and Max Spiers were babes, my father led the Carnutes. My father was behind every crime, every battle you fought, every alliance formed against you. It was my father's part of the guild in Antarctica to mine resources for the sake of the economy, until your Alliance rescinded us, and you . . ." Suddenly, Gladius' voice quivered. "You *slaughtered* my parents. You *killed* my Ottessa. *Killed* all my friends. Many innocent lives, you *bastard*, killed them all!"

Casbolt remembered then. He had massacred the Carnutes for trying to build the first, illegal mining industry in Antarctica – a stark breach against the Treaty. He remembered the Iceni descending with might, bombing the entire establishment, killing all the venal barons who were attempting to rape the ecosystem. Casbolt waged war, breaking the UN Treaty, in order to preserve the UN Treaty.

Looking back now he could not believe that awful irony – Terra Nova, the central district – had *approved* of his war and called him off as "an exception to protect the weightier matters of the Treaty to prevent the production of greenhouse gasses in Antarctica."

He remembered watching one young man – Gladius – skin grey from the cold ice, blinded from the snow glare, stumbling for a gun. Casbolt had push-kicked him, making him fall backward. Ducking, right arm high to brace, he sliced his arm to the elbow from the propeller blades of the aeroplane. If he'd fallen any other way than he did, Gladius would have lost his head. Casbolt remembered in the shock of the moment, he had left Gladius in his misery. He could've killed the man then, but his screams were so piercing Casbolt heard them still in his head.

Casbolt froze, speechless.

In a flash, with his robotic arm, Gladius heaved Gáe Bulg out of the wall, flourishing the Spear, with a strength and agility that made Casbolt stumble back. "I don't have time for you, but you have incurred the most horrendous *geas*. You – will – pay!" Gladius hissed, staring at his golden knife longingly. Tucking it into his pocket, he lunged.

Picking up his gun, Casbolt held it with both hands, blocking the strike. He chuckled. "Go ahead and kill me, Gladius. For the last three years, I've wanted to kill myself many times during the deprogramming. *Try me.*"

Disengaging, the Carnute swung again, and Casbolt, stepping back, blocked each strike, glad the torch strapped on Gladius' chest was providing him the perfect amount of light to see. They fought out of the Old Babylonian section, towards the main landing and the adjoining left-hand corridor into the Sumerian-Akkadian exhibit, shrouded in deep darkness, Spear and gun slashing against each other again, and again. Spear stances Casbolt learnt in the agoge flashed in his mind, he performed and then bumped into a wall he did not see, hurling aside. Gladius cleaved the wall clean with a swipe of Gáe Bulg.

"Enough!" Casbolt knelt, cocking his gun, aiming it. "I will shoot you, ending this." Wisely, the Carnute froze, grasping the Spear with flesh and metal hands, azure eyes kindling with vitriolic hatred. "The museum is being raided! What are you doing here, a lowly brigand in the Middle East? Who sent you?"

"I heard what you did to the Aquarians," Gladius snarled.

"Quick! I have to know if the museum is safe!"

"This world would never be safe until you and the Alliance are done for!"

Gladius baulked and performing a zigzagging move – Squall Dips the Permafrost – he attacked.

Casbolt only had time to shoot one bullet, just missing Gladius. The man was fast and the giant Spear formidable. Casbolt dodged, blocking outwards with his gun, elbowing Gladius' face. The Carnute lurched aside, falling. And with his right robotic arm, he pulled Casbolt along with him. Tumbling to the ground, Casbolt held his footing, twisting, skidding on his feet, boots scuffing the floor, scraping glass and mortar. From his knees, Gladius grabbed Casbolt's gun with his right arm, while Casbolt grabbed his Spear. They grappled, Gladius gripping the gun hard and, turning it away, tried to unbalance Casbolt.

Letting go of his gun, Casbolt stomped on Gladius' bionic arm, twisting his feet. Screaming, Gladius heaved up, running his hand long the Spear's length. He stood up, fist closing at its head, swinging the Spear downwards.

Casbolt risked it, stepping into the attack, both hands covering his head, blocking the shaft with his crossed forearms. He grunted, stepping right into Gladius' body, putting the Carnute in a body lock, wrapping his arms around, and squeezing him in a figure-four arm bar – grabbing the wrists with both hands, and squeezed. He twisted Gladius around, his right forearm locking him up.

"This is General Schwartz," a voice called on the com kit. "All forces regroup out of direct-fire range. Over."

Struggling, Gladius struck his left hand into Casbolt's side. He writhed from the strike, let go from the lock, and Gladius broke free, yanking at the Spear. But Casbolt held on to the shaft with both hands, grunting. Gladius yanked again, but Casbolt held on. The barbed point was dangerously close to his inner arm and his throbbing side.

"General Conroy speaking. Lieutenant Casbolt, evacuate your men from the museum asap. Over."

"What?!" Casbolt spun around, pivoting on the ball of his left foot – guiding the Spear point to face in front of him – his back facing Gladius. He dug his foot, touching his knees together, kicking backwards into the Carnute. The satisfying feeling of his kick sent Gladius sliding backward.

But the Spear still tugged in Gladius' hand! Growling, Casbolt planted a side kick into Gladius' face, his robotic arm finally unlatching from Gáe Bulg's shaft. Casbolt tucked the Spear at his back, getting into a basic fighting stance.

"I don't have time for this!" Casbolt hissed, watching Gladius get to his feet, holding his bloody nose.

Suddenly, sirens and alarms all around the compound began to wail, piercing the ears.

Using this opportunity of distraction, Casbolt dashed back the way he came, fumbling for his torch, calling Conroy on his com kit. "Conroy, this is James Casbolt! I've been preoccupied fighting looters! They're everywhere and I can't hold them off! I'm on my way out now!" He made it back down the stairs, adamant to find Reece and Tom if they were holding off; worry seething in his stomach.

Once he turned from the Neo-Babylonian section into the Roman antiquities of Hatra, he almost tripped over a pile of rubble, cracked sarcophagi and broken heads of ancient statues blocking the underside of the staircase into a small alcove to the right of the cinder-block wall.

Then something *rammed* into him. A looter gasped, caught red handed in front of the door, with ivory and a batch of gold aurei coins in his arms. Seizing the artefacts, Casbolt tugged, but the man tugged back. They fought, tripping over a fallen pedestal, fighting for the ivory piece and coins. The aurei flung into the shadows, clattering with a pealing clamour. Casbolt kicked the man, but his side pain delayed his attack. With one hand grasping the ivory, he thrusted his Spear and jammed it into the looter's shoulder. The man howled, drumming his feet, writhing in painful throes, worming away on the ground.

Putting the ivory artefact and the terracotta figurine of a reclining woman safely away, Casbolt looked up and found Gladius soaring in the air as another looter bound over Casbolt, swearing, having just glimpsed him on the ground while on the run. But Gladius and the looter collided, they fought in a brawl, fighting viciously, clawing at each other for the antiquities.

As Carnute and looter fought, Casbolt yanked his Spear out of the first looter and kicked his ass, sending him off running, limping, his tail in between his legs. As for the second looter, Gladius, with his metal arm, pried the basalt statute out of the looter's hand, slamming the man to the ground. But Casbolt was already jogging, swinging the Spear.

Ducking backwards, Gladius battered the Spear shaft away. In a desperate effort, he raised the statue, and tossed it.

"No!" Casbolt lunged, doubling over in pain. He closed his eyes as the precious ancient Babylonian statue smashed into pieces, desecrated forever. He saw part of the fragmented head, broken nose, half face and missing beard, tumbling on the ground, sadly staring up at Casbolt with one eye.

Even as Casbolt dived for the poor fragment of the face, he saw, in the torchlight, Gladius scooping up the ivory and the terracotta woman Casbolt had stolen back from the first looter, tucking them into his bag. Things crashed and collapsed and smashed as the disillusioned second looter scrabbled away on two feet with his Roman coins.

Growling, Casbolt rose to his feet, throwing a powerful left fist at Gladius.

The Carnute met the attack with his robot arm. Such a solid block did not even quiver the arm, nor did it twitch from the force of Casbolt's strike. It was alloy against muscle, but the metallic arm, absorbing all force, sent recoil through Casbolt's flesh. Twisting his wrist, Gladius gripped Casbolt's arm, hurling him forward. Casbolt summersaulted into the air, crashing into an unseen glass cabinet holding anthropomorphic figures, Roman style coins and other artefacts.

The robotic arm was powerful enough to throw him!

Head reeling in pain, Casbolt rose, resummoning his Spear from the Otherworld and charged. Gladius charged too and Casbolt raised Gáe Bulg, slashing downwards just as the Carnute zigzagged, raising his bionic arm, blocking the strike. But he twisted, stomping his foot on Casbolt's toe, clutching the Spear shaft.

Casbolt kicked back, sending Gladius rolling on the floor. With his metal hand, he grasped the ground, and whirling with hydraulics, the arm hauled him up with legs snapping in an acrobatic manner.

Casbolt held his Spear with both hands.

"I can't believe you are here," Gladius gasped dryly. "The *Redlion*, in Baghdad?! Alfred Bonner sent you to stop me!"

Casbolt was dizzy and dazed from his glass cuts. "No."

"You're a warmonger," Gladius derided. "A selfish murderer and paedophile."

Casbolt's heart leapt. He heard in his head Neil's bawdy talk. *Do you know what a paedophile is? Do you know what an orgasm is?*

"NO I'VE CHANGED!" Casbolt shouted, and all pain seemed to go away – he had not realised he was shouting out his thoughts. "I've reckoned my crimes! I've *changed!*"

"Then *answer* for your crimes!"

"Every second I breathe, I relive the Bleakness all alone, and so I've planned to do some good in this war." Casbolt marched away to the cinder-block wall, Gladius' shouts blaring with the alert siren. The museum staff had bricked up the rear entrance to the underground rooms, but that wall was broken through, and the intruders wasted no time in making their way directly inside. *Crap! Everything is falling apart!*

"Don't you dare walk away from me, Redlion! YOU'LL PAY!"

Suddenly, from out of the shadows of the entrance, a nimble figure flew into Casbolt, a leg pounding him in the shoulder. Roaring in pain, Casbolt swung around, saw a veiled looter in the shade landing beside him, bracing with one hand, and in the other hand was the ring and the rod artefact Casbolt remembered from the basement.

Casbolt rammed into the looter with his shoulder, sending him crashing into the wall. He force sent him hitting the ground on his back, exhausted and spent. *No more fighting!* The looter leaned on the wall; the impact creating a hole in the plaster. Gladius yelped, running to the looter's side and ripped off the head covering. In the chest torch light, Casbolt could see the looter was a young woman, eyes closed. Presently, Gladius grabbed the ring and the rod from her hand then carried her body and fled.

Getting up, Casbolt blundered over unseen statutes and artefacts, rushing down the stairs into the basement. He turned a corner, and in the torchlight left behind by the thieves, Casbolt collapsed on his knees. His head was swimming, his breath wheezing and panting. He saw many footprints in the dust.

Casbolt raised his head and found . . .

The whole basement overturned – the ground strewn with plastic fishing-tackle boxes, upside down, flung aside, smashed into walls as if the intruders had a fit. Smoke filled the room. In the darkness, the thieves burned the foam padding to give them light to look for artefacts and ended up abandoning the room because of the fumes the padding generated. Remnants of burned foam lay in tatters everywhere on the floor, giving off a strange acrid smell. And behind it all, standing upright, were around thirty brown storage cabinets. At least, then, not everything had been looted.

There was no sign of Tom and Reece. The complacency of those louts; they had only one job!

Dropping his Spear in defeat, Casbolt gripped his head with two hands. "No," he mumbled. "No . . ."

Every corner of the exhibit was overturned. This was *Casbolt's fault*. If only he didn't give into the pain and anger Gladius had brought up . . .

Casbolt gave up, hunching over, crushed by exhaustion, breathing in and out as he trembled. His *only* chance to appeal his crimes, had failed. He barely had the strength to stand. The thrill had abandoned him, and that left him broken, pained.

It was *his* fault. It was *his* responsibility – his *own* promise – that he neglected. He shouldn't have left the marines in the basement. He should have called for reinforcements from Conroy straight away – why the hell didn't he do that?! The more soldiers in the museum, the more could have been done to thwart the looters' rampage and more could have been done to stop Gladius Huyard – the Cabal Aes Sidhe.

He gazed listlessly in the darkness at the head of a marble statue of a proud king lying sad and decapitated next to him. The pieces and shards of his life was incomprehensively tragic. Who and how could anyone bother to put all the pieces back together? To restore the museum, to gather the broken pieces and make restitution for Casbolt's failure?

Nothing else could be done.

It was over. He couldn't do *one simple thing*. One *simple task* to protect the antiquities. Now, he would *never* go back to Antarctica. He would *never* see his Iceni friends. He would *never* atone his sin and admit that he felt guilty, cared.

The Baghdad Museum had been looted, and the Cabal were still out there.

—

Tara's head roiled with bouts of pain; just moving or standing made her wince and hiss as she came to her senses. She lay on an uncomfortable wooden crate within the dark narrow alley in the underside of Baghdad. The sky above her was a bruised colour, dawn having been recent. She could smell pungent oil and grease.

After an inspection of her surroundings – her right eye seemed slightly obstructed – she raised an arm to feel a bruise and dried blood. She saw unused or discarded machinery on the track ballast alongside and underneath the railway tracks, cutting through a corner of the dirty laneway in which she sat.

"Don't move." It took a second for Tara to recognise that the indignant voice had come from Airgetlám. "Don't move."

She obeyed. She felt inferior, small, infringed and deprived. "What . . .? What the hell happened? Airgetlám?"

The man paced down the alley, gingerly picking himself over tracks, lugging a bag that contained a handful of small artefacts. He clutched Tara's own prize – the conjoined rod and ring with the figure-eight intertwined serpents that had caught her eye. And yet, despite gaining such a relic, the Aes Sidhe glared at it, miffed. His metal fist held the rod within the circle of the ring, furrowing his brow, pacing in disappointed silence. "That – was – horrendous."

Yes . . . It was. But we raided the museum. Tara stared numbly at him, and it made her want to vomit.

"Have you even been on a mission before? Have you?!"

Tara twitched, clamping her mouth shut, crossing her arms. She could feel the heat of anger just from hearing Airgetlám's brusque words.

Barbelo is never far . . . She's punishing me.

"My guess is no," Airgetlám said. Face crumpling, he grabbed the sack, looking as if he were about to throw it into the wall. "Who would have known the Aes Sidhe Chief had gone rogue!"

Tara had been all sanguine at first, until she almost cannoned into the combatant in the museum wielding a club or a spear while fighting Airgetlám in the dark. She could tell Airgetlám had to drag her out into this laneway, and that thought of being a liability to someone for her recklessness made her writhe in loathing.

"I'm pathetic . . . Yes, I am," Marcell admitted, coming forward to protect Tara, twitching some more. "I am not strong enough to face you. You control my body. It's yours." No, when he felt nervous and men were furious at him, Marcell lost all sense of thought, and all sense of direction, like a panic attack Tara often suffered. Marcell took on all the pain for Tara's sake. Maximum enmity and fear toward Airgetlám became clear, became implacable. Men, Tara thought, *always* disappointed her, always failed her! She'd wished her concussion had been worse, then she could have died immediately. Or perhaps wake up from a dream, the mark of Barbelo a fleeting nightmare.

Ultimately, it was the abusive men that made Tara and Marcell into what they were.

Marcell could go home now and cry and find a way to end these terrible courses of events she'd gotten herself into. Somehow, she had to dissociate, Tara and Marcell needed a way to evade Barbelo. *Needed* to find a way . . .

26

ACTIONMAN

"The days are coming says the Lord, when you will lose the world you knew, and become disoriented."

—A prophetic word from 'The Green Prince', former Hamas terrorist, shared by Joseph DePaula to Kairos Palestine with The Green Prince's permission, April 2003.

Ben opened the door to Pounders' cellar station in Haditha Dam proper, finding him gazing in perusal at him. His desk was covered with maps and communication devices, and by the door, John Mulholland stood like a giant wrestler in his badged dark-green uniform, with thick face and eyebrows that always seemed to be knitted. In his presence, Ben knew that he demanded no nonsense.

"Colonel Pounders, sir," Mulholland saluted.

Reclining on his chair, Pounders nodded with approval. "I request to speak with the Eidolon Captain alone, please. Thank you for your time, Mulholland."

As the Colonel closed the door behind, Pounders spoke up. "Alright, Ben. Doyle, this evening, was informed that the expected relief forces would be delayed. His casualties today at the H-1 were very unexpected – the aftermath of today's battle has given clearance to one last site on the outskirts of the Haditha town."

"Yes, Colonel." Ben felt a pleasurable sense of respect towards the Iraqis – their fervour and strength in battle had been without rival.

"Now, for someone as successful as you, is it foolish to launch a stealth attack past enemy lines, to immobilise their camp in the outskirts of Haditha town?"

Ben perked up, grinning. "Oh, you reminded me this is an April Fool's joke, sir." Not sure whether to smile or remain serious, Pounders grimaced, staring at Ben poker-faced, then shook his head amused, grunting, slowly leaning forward, and placing his elbows on the desk. Ben swiftly let his comedic demeanour retreat. *Well, I was just trying to lighten the mood.*

Ben cleared his throat. "Sorry, Colonel, but will I need reinforcements?"

"No," Pounders said. "The Eidolons. The men are yours after all."

"Yes, sir."

"Ben." Pounders slowly got up from his chair and paced, placing his hands in his pockets leisurely. "You know nothing in life is easy. Your job in Hollywood was meant to make what seemed impossible, possible. How does one stunt driver in a *Fast and Furious* movie survive crash scenes?"

Ben shrugged. "Skill? Experience? In part, improvisation and luck."

"Captain, I know you can do this. If you're experienced enough to survive high-speed crashes and exploding buildings, then this mission to sneak into Haditha town is not foolish, is it?" Pounders met Ben's eyes. "I gave you this task because I trust you the most. You might save us this war."

Ben stared at the concrete floor. There was something unsettling about the rooms within the dam, its walls had a deary, permanent shadow to them. "Yes, I understand, sir."

Pounders began to pace. "Doyle's Rangers were showing signs of disorder. It was a barrage that we think will continue up until tomorrow. With such a steady stream of mortar shells, it would strain the Rangers to breaking point. They're tired from almost two weeks of continuous operations, and fully exposed to the elements, the young Rangers will inevitably break. Your secret task is the best chance to stop this." He turned to Ben. "What were you? A diving champion in the state of Texas?"

"Colonel, I'm confused why you're telling me this. Don't I have enough adulation for a change?"

Pounders took a deep breath and chuckled. "You're the Man of Action. It's no secret that you like the attention."

"No . . . Um, okay."

"Ben," Pounders chuckled. "It's because you've proven to demonstrate your resilience from the difficulties you've faced, whilst remaining loyal towards your men."

Man, all this flattery is getting annoying, Ben thought. "I'm very thankful, Colonel sir, really. But stop pampering me. You're the same as well you know? I'll lead the charge on first light, Colonel," Ben said, feeling confident. "The

Eidolons can make good time here."

Pounders smiled. "I'll be awaiting your return then."

—

The next morning, Ben gathered his handpicked unit at the derelict Haditha town, concrete pillars standing exposed to the air, their cores, rods of corroded metal, rose like spires. Rubbish and plastic bags tumbled aimlessly in the stale wind over the mucky streets, whirling between the trudging legs of forlorn clusters of Arab civilians, families from the surrounding countryside. Their faces bore bruises, caked in dust and dirt, and at times, cuts and slashes left unbandaged. The column of people slowly trickled out of the decaying town before the battle, and soon, it became a ghost town.

Ben knew best his closest friends, because the trouble of being famous was people knew you without you knowing them. One ultimately never knew people, only knew *of* people. Insofar, Ben admitted, he'd made a truly horrendous effort to know the name of every member of the 75th Ranger Regiment enlisted, but there were just *too many boys! Roughly one hundred troops.* He had *at least* known thirty. Ben hated having to remember *anyone* who was a rookie, let alone someone from another unit, randomly reassigned.

"Alright, men," Ben said, pointing to the American lackeys hanging around at the fifteen-story eastern hold of the dam complex. "Doyle and Thompson want Platoon 3 to get rid of some Iraqis. So, you'll go. I will need you and . . ." He pointed at a young marine with short black hair, a dark-green bandana and a mischievous expression, whose name eluded him. "You join me and the Eidolons. But the rest of you, stand by for now with the 3rd. We do not know what is down here in this dam section or over at that damn town. You hear me?"

Those dam jokes aren't getting old!

"Captain Actionman," the boy said as he stood up shaking Ben's hand. "I am Ryan Briones! Your biggest fan!"

Not until you break my balls, Ben thought. "Pleasure, Ryan," he quipped. "And good timing, too. One of our men got a referral from Colonel Pounders to be re-tasked as a medic in the field, so you can take his place on our special scouting mission." Ben smirked, winking. It made the kid beam. "Welcome aboard," he said with a dramatic voice. "Buckle up!"

—

Ben and the Eidolons snuck through the carnage of the town, his semiautomatic close at his chest, surveying every corner for a possible ambush. The town was silent with tension. The quiet hiss of wind and the faint footfalls of boots of the marines were the only sounds.

Slipping behind a street corner, almost gagging from the hot odour of trash spilt all over the gritty footpaths, Ben led the Eidolons through patches of weed grass stubbornly growing through thin cracks in the pavement. His men hid behind broken walls, cars, and rubbish bins, as Ben gave the thumbs up to proceed. The coast was still clear.

Sulking gingerly down the street, Ben saw Julian walk across a corpse of a man, flat on his face, a haze of flies buzzing around the carcass. It made Ben's stomach churn. Couldn't the Iraqis organise their battles in more rural areas like around the dam, away from human settlements? Why did Arabs *always* like having their bases in common social zones when it would obviously lead to civilian catastrophes?

Ben silently led his team, one by one, around a curve in the road, splitting up and getting into blocking positions behind a broken cream wall. Before them, was a strange assortment of black sandbags, blocking the way across the street. The bags, around six feet tall, were shaped in a triangular formation, facing the Rangers, both flanks of the structure connected to the flat-top buildings on either side of the street making it impassable unless one climbed.

A barricade, Ben thought suspiciously. He raised his fist warningly, the signal to prepare for attack.

Yet, still, the town remained abandoned. As Ben's Eidolons got into their positions, locking their guns, Garrow and Julian studied the structure. *Please don't be a ruse,* Ben anticipated.

"Not right . . ." Garrow said, shaking his head. "It's too *holy* —"

A howling bullet whisked past Garrow's head.

They want us here, in their trap, Ben thought, hiding behind the trunks of two palm trees, cocking his gun. Fire nipped at the bark. Immediately, Ben's unit, in a jump start, firing at the sandbags, took cover behind the broken cream wall.

Ben aimed, looking through the green lens of the crosshairs scope on the top of his assault rifle, firing rounds at the bank of sandbags barricading the road. Three Iraqis snapped from behind the barricade, handling their guns.

"Hold the line!" Ben shouted as a second wave of fire molested his team, forcing them to duck behind the cream wall. They grunted, irked, keeping their target in range. Ryan Briones bravely crawled on his belly towards a pile of rubbish, hardening his face and testing his new angle; he fired, only to miss.

Glimpsing through his scope, Ben managed to aim at one aggressor in the head, but he ducked at the last second as he punched the trigger. "Blast!" he growled sharply.

"That's it!" Derek Fish spat, standing up, hauling his RPG off his back strap. "You want some of this? Eat that!"

The rocket hissed, exploding the right side of the sandbags, drowning a squealing soldier. Chuckling, Derek got back down with a grunt, his RPG positioned upright, reloading his ammo on his Barrett .50 BMG.

We're sitting ducks here, Ben thought as he fired. *We can't waste bullets! We need to somehow get those soldiers . . .*

Ben punched the side of his gun as he missed again, pressing his back against the tree trunk as the heavy volume of fire continued. "Reggie! They're too protected! We need to get the high ground!"

"Captain, sir!" Reggie shouted, laying on his side behind the wall interrupted by a flurry of bullets. "We need to fall back! It's too tight!"

He was damn right. Ben surveyed the surrounding environment, spotting just ahead of him a tripartite house with a flat roof, each roof rising up a slight incline. Rising beyond it was another assortment of homes with flat roofs too. From there, those roofs with small curbs at the edges and a rectangular staircase continued their way forward along the street. If Ben could just sneak up there, alone, he could get a better aerial view of the Iraqis' defences, and he might just be able to get hits at them from above, where they'd least expect it.

"What's the plan?" Julian yelled.

"High ground," Ben whispered so no one but himself heard. He delighted in many things but most of all, it was progression – the satisfaction of everything working – because it gave him a way to solve problems. Whether it was being a few seconds off point in a stunt scene, one needed to find a way to make things work with what you had, just going with it.

Improvisation was key. Strapping his rifle onto his back and leaping over roots, Ben blundered towards the first flat roof. He parkoured over a dividing gap clamping his hands on a balcony bar. He grunted, bracing the impact against the wall. Pulling himself up, the juicy burn invigorating his muscles, he grounded his feet, leaping up on the next roof, pulling and working his arms. Ben scaled the small houses with relative ease, the freedom of swift nimble motion glorious. The coordination of his legs stepping on precarious surfaces required the whole body to perform a perfect stunt to lessen the chance of injury. Knowing the surroundings helped, he just kept the impetus going without hesitation. It was in only a few seconds that Ben climbed his way up on the highest roof.

Taking a breath, he jogged towards the edge with a single hand resting on an antenna. To his left was a small attic boxed structure with an abandoned clothesline swaying forlornly in the wind. He looked over a small thick gate, and saw right above the enemies' triangle sandbag blockade, hearing the rattling gunfire below.

Ben sat back and took into consideration the environment, the perspectives, the distances, angles, and the physics of the fall, gauging how they could work to his advantage. Such a jump would be risky, he had no support equipment, so he needed to be careful. He heard Julian shouting in the street below, calling out about Ben and his stupid stunts that could get him killed. Ben smiled, keeping low. *How long do you think I've been training for this, Julz?*

The drop was quite sheer, about fifteen feet, close to the highest of his diving championship tournament. The thing with diving was that one needed to dive into water, creating the smallest splash as possible. Unlike diving, leaping off a building was a slightly different ball game. He would gun them out from the top of the building, though this building hardly had any parapets besides a flimsy fence. If he barraged from above, he worried the Iraqis would focus their fire on him, and Ben would be putting himself in danger.

But Ben could also jump. If he could get the landing right, and calculate how he could soften his fall, it was possible to pull it off. He remembered jumping out of a window once to land on a human body for a movie before.

Ben considered the correct orientation. He shook the fence checking to see it if it was sturdy. It did not twang, good enough to hold his weight. Peering over the edge down right below the Iraqis' encampment, he saw in full view the black sandbag triangular formation, where eight remaining soldiers fought behind their bunkers. One of the eight tended one wounded in the arm. On the far side of the triangle, one section of it had been blown apart by Reggie's RPG.

Across the street his unit were in crisis. Their broken stone wall cover was jarring and, admittedly, puny. On his back, Ben whipped out a grenade, and pulling the pin, cast it over his head. Not willing to compromise his position, he remained flat.

"There!" Julian echoed as the blast exploded suddenly, dismembering the sandbags. Ben beamed as he heard his Rangers below whooping for him. Confident, getting up on his feet, Ben bounded to the opposite edge of the roof. Turning back around, leaning forward, eyes tracking his trajectory path, he calculated the right speed needed and the right accuracy to leap over the edge. To any ordinary soldier and a stunt rookie, what he was doing was perhaps the most *reckless* and *dangerous* thing someone could ever do.

What he was doing could risk his very life. If he failed, he would never see Veronica again. She awaited him to return a hero.

Ben reached into his pocket, quickly attaching a bayonet onto the tip of his M16A2. Lifting his chin, Ben smirked.

"For Veronica."

Hurling forward into a brisk sprint, Ben made the distance, landing safely on the top of the fence. With his free hand out for extra balance he bent his legs, springing off the railing, sailing over the edge. Tucking in his legs as he dropped, Ben glided in an arc, straight down upon an Iraqi. Plunging it into the Iraqi's body, Ben grunted, rolling on the bag as the Iraqis hollered with frenzied panic.

In one movement, Ben got up, stabbing his bayonet into the chest of a soldier, cannoning into him. Pushing himself up on one knee, Ben swung his gun around, slashing the first soldier. A second soldier roaring throatily from the left grappled Ben. Kneeing the grunting man in the pelvis and driving his gun through his upper chest, he fired. A bang and a crack – the man's face was gone. Blood smeared, Ben ruthlessly shoved the husk away, sliding off the sandbags, and charged.

The four remaining soldiers attacked frantically, and Ben shot them. Lugging a bloody carcass as a human shield in his left hand, he came at the Iraqis firing. They fired back as Ben simultaneously killed the vicious attackers. Ben dropped the dead human shield, lunging into the nearest soldier who tripped over a sandbag. His back was ripped in half by Ben's passing bayonet. Ramming the back of his gun at the next soldier in the face holding the gun horizontally, Ben shot another Iraqi next to him. The soldier Ben engaged with wrestled him for advantage.

Gracefully, Ben finished the Iraqi off, staving his chest, spinning his rifle around and hammering the bayonet right through the man. Ben dropped, hiding behind the sandbags as the enemy ran, firing. Ben jabbed and a soldier evaded, but he was too slow. Ben lunged, clouting him. The Iraqi returned a strike, then piledrove Ben to the ground. Writhing, Ben jammed his gun between the Iraqi's jaw and armpit. Ben pushed with all his ferocity, arching his back and pelvis up with a jolt to dislodge his opponent.

Ben was losing. He landed a hammer hand to the ribs. The attacker hissed. Ben shoved his gun harder into the Iraqi's purple neck. Ben spun back up, sweeping his leg, tripping the attacker over. He ended him with three ruthless rounds.

Relaxing, Ben lowered his rifle, rising to his feet. Behind him, he heard among the cheers of his men a faint moan from a wounded Iraqi. Ben's face tightened, beholding the Iraqi, his back opened by a deep deadly slice from Ben's bayonet. He was spasming in jolts, trying to get up.

The Iraqi roared a gasp, blurting out in his own tongue, "*Hum yaerifuna. Aldafadae. Astamie lahum…Hum…*"

Ben inhaled, his furious impetus easing. *I should have brought Joshua. He could have delt with this better than I.*

Swallowing his pain, he shut his eyes. He thought of his daughter, her future, her happiness and her success.

He put the soldier out of his misery.

"Captain Rambo! Wow!" Ryan Briones' elated voice sounded. "That was *so* sick, Actionman!"

"Yeah, he does look like Rambo with no hair," Jason Laycock said as Ben's unit marched to meet him. "No offence, Captain."

"Don't ever do that again! That was not awesome! I nearly shot you!" Julian exclaimed, pointing at Ben accusingly.

Ben stared at the Iraqi slit open before his feet. What had been the good of that? That man probably had a daughter and . . .

"Ben, you alright?" Reggie asked.

Ben snapped out of his strange daze. "Come on. We're all clear, Rangers. We've got to be quick." And in one move, spinning and dashing on ahead, Ben hurdled his legs over the sandbags. *I fight for you Veronica.* He sprinted turning into the next street, his men charging behind. Once they reached the corner of the street, Ben was already sprinting down past a copse of palm trees and fallen light poles.

There, in the momentum of his dash at the periphery of his vision, two Iraqis scrambled out suddenly from behind an abandoned store. Ben shot the first; the last, seeing a tall brawny man charging at incredible speed, bolted.

Coward Arab.

Ben took off after him. "Come here!" The Iraqi whipped his head around in reaction of Ben's sonorous yell. Ben aimed his gun. No ammo.

"Gah!" Discarding his weapon, he exploded with unhindered speed, his head bobbing, arms and legs flailing with the full brunt of the dash. He easily gained on the unfit Iraqi, whipping out his last grenade, pulling the pin. Upon coming closer to the building facing the T crossroad of the end of the street, Ben flung the bomb, confident it would land on the Iraqi.

He'd overestimated his accuracy. The grenade *deviated* far off to the left, bouncing into the broken window of the building in front of him.

"Damn!" Ben spat in vexation, doubling his speed, grabbing the yelping Iraqi behind the neck. He screamed like a woman as Ben shook the terrified man, making him drop his gun. He unleashed his frustration, landing a full blunted punch in the face. The Iraqi hissed, and Ben, enthralled in his competence, punched his face again. Bloodied nosed, the quaking Arab raised his arms in surrender.

With a seething anger, Ben stomped on the man, leaving him groaning loudly on the ground and thought, *Careful. Could be a suicide bomber.*

Piercing his enthralment, Ben heard the sounds of a high-pitched scream . . . and following that, a gushing explosion from his grenade. A surge of invisible heat scorched the back of Ben's neck, and the shadows became crimson. A wave of bright orange and yellow light pounced from the building's window before him, igniting the entire house aflame.

"You monster!" The Iraqi man picked up his fallen gun, aiming it at Ben's chest. Ben raised his hands, ready to use them to disarm if need be.

The Iraqi soldier scowled, as Ben lifted his foot, allowing the Iraqi to rise. "You *monster*. The sword of Islam is worthy to slay you."

"Shh," Ben said curtly. "Wait."

"I said—"

"Shh! Quiet! Listen!"

As the crackling of the flames became more prominent, a wailing cry also rose in agonising intensity, like a wounded baby animal in distress. Ben couldn't pretend to ignore it – someone was trapped in that building, and the fire would burn and destroy them.

The fire that Ben had kindled.

But, weighing in his head, if it was better to go and save someone at the expense of his own life, than being shot in a stand-off by a terrified Iraqi, Ben opted for the former. He stared aloof at the inferno as the Iraqi continued exclaiming, "It's your fault I'm here to fight in a divided army. We're just defending—"

"You hear that?"

The Iraqi froze, mouth dropping. "Yeah!"

"The screams, man! It's a baby!"

Ben could use this distraction to get out alive. The Iraqi lowered his gun.

Indistinct in the midst of the blistering conflagration, an undeniable shrieking wail echoed out of the infernal destruction. Ben eyed the Iraqi, pointing towards the building.

The Arab narrowed his eyes at the billowing pillars of burning flame.

"Someone needs our help," Ben said dryly, persisting with the diversion. He heard the vocalisations of a whining baby clearly now. "I'll see what I can do."

Spontaneously, Ben ran right into the burning structure leaving the Iraqi bewildered, spared to fight another day. The Iraqi could not be stupid enough to follow him in there the logic went, and it worked.

The heat singed his vision, but Ben went on, the parental instincts to protect a vulnerable child urging him onwards. There was a precarious creaking noise, and disintegrating timber poured rubble to his left, showering stinging embers all over his body. Ben staggered, intense heat pulsing against his body, any moisture was sucked away by the searing air as he listened for the cries' source.

Surrounded by solid heat, flares sparkling over the roof, over door frames, the wall and spreading over the ground, the roar of the blundering fire was hard to pierce. Inferno surged, and skin peeled from his face. So much destruction, caused by a single misthrow!

I'm already here! This is all my fault, so I might as well find a way out! Ben ran up the stairs. He heard the crying again, mixed with the groaning, unstable house. Ben struggled to breathe, but the smoke scalded his lungs. He had to get out of here, fast! Ben held his breath, running blindly up the rest of the stairs, turning. There, in his blurry vision. A balcony area.

Evading a smouldering flare of flame exploding with streaks of blue, Ben reached his hand out on the wall for stabilisation. As his hand made contact, the wall vanished. Fright made Ben yelp, and he tripped, his whole body plunging right through the thin plaster.

Ben's stomach lurched as he dropped outside the building, everything suddenly quiet. Instinctually he braced his arms out.

The ground collided with him. A loud bang and feeling a wet *crack*, pain *exploded* into his hip. The world narrowed to just Ben and his hip. He almost blacked out, his head spun, and his breath was short and rapid. He wanted to scream. He gasped. He lay still for a moment, until the pain subsided from the absolute agony of throbbing. Yet the pain never eased, it remained constant.

No! NO! Walk it off! Come on, baby! Come on! Walk it off!

Ben's backside spasmed as he moved, making him writhe lethargically on the ground. His vision doubled, tears streaming from his closed eyes. He let out a snort of pain, and then, heard clearly, the baby's wails.

It came from a large single garbage container, its lip still open. Ben was in some sort of laneway.

Stubbornly, Ben tried to stand up and almost passed out.

No. Walk! Trembling, he rose from a pipe sticking out of the ground. He sighed, leaning a hand on the brick wall, almost tripping and faceplanting. Ben let out a protracted, guttural moan. He hissed in and whistled back out. *Walk it off, Ben. Just walk it off. Look. You're almost there. Come on man! WALK IT OFF! I broke something, didn't I? No. No, I can't break a bone! I've never broke a bone in my life!*

Defeat and despair crippled Ben as white-and-black flakes of ash floated down morbidly from the conflagration above, filtering his vision in a pinkish-orange veil. Eventually, he got on one foot, leaning on the wall, limping, putting as little pressure on his hip as possible.

"Ha, ah, ah, ah . . ." Ben sighed, struggling onwards, the infant's cries emulating his own suffering. He did not want to hear it, bawling with pure horror and terror. The wailing was nonstop, coughing terribly; it prickled Ben in the heart. *Who. Would. Do. This to a child?! Throw them in the garbage!?*

It was clear now; the source of the cries was piercing and raw, it was a human child. Ben let go of the brick wall, throwing himself to the other side of the alley, clamping his hands on the lip of the bin. Ash continued to pour upon him. Using the bin as a support, Ben limped the rest of the way towards the open garbage compartment, the smell *so dreadfully* powerful, he tipped his head into his arm, the pain aggravating. The smell was as hot as the flames above, so putrid it almost prevented him from dipping his hand in, but he couldn't ignore those sobs. Ben peered inside and froze.

Cradled in scraps of food, plastic and bin liners, was a little tanned baby, left for dead. Swaddled in a cradle of rubbish and filth, in a maw of death and neglect, the child had stringy black hair and wore small clothes, its arms aimlessly writhing about, legs kicking doggedly. Its poor innocent face was cherry red, damp with tears, face contorted, its mouth an open hole of desperation. Crying out.

Its aching screaming did something to Ben. Suddenly his pain alleviated, leaning his chin on his hands gawking, listening to the melody of despair. He thought he could hear among the shocked ululations attempts of speech. Cries for home. For Mommy.

The hell would do this? Ben hovered his hand inside, benevolently scooping the baby up from the rotten darkness. It burst out with a panicked shriek. This man was *not* Mommy. It didn't want him.

"Ah, shhhh," Ben whispered. All vociferous sounds seemed to vanish. He felt the baby drumming its feet, wondering why this strange arm was coming to grab it.

"It's okay," Ben said quietly, wincing. "It's okay. Shhhshshsh. I found you. Look. It's okay." The baby's hiccupping, coughing cries wavered in intensity, turning to hyperventilating sooks. It shook Ben deeply in his soul, his throat spasming with emotion.

Seemingly paralysed by its face, eyes skewed shut, the gaping mouth drooling, sticky with saliva, Ben saw an ineffable tentativeness, an overpoweringly want for communion – and by chance – a male child saved from the reeking dark bin bags, plastic pillows of decay.

Why had its mother abandoned the child to die? Ben would never think of doing that to Veronica! The baby was at a seminal stage; he remembered rearing Veronica up and this stage was *crucial* to her development as a toddler.

Ben found himself clutching onto the lip of the bin with his other hand to relieve the hip pain. A loud groan from the burning building sounded behind him. The child was mildly heavy, with his hip busted and a baby in hand, he was in no good shape if he were found by the enemy. Ben hissed a curse to himself, hopping as the child whimpered in his shoulder. *The hell would do this?! Why the hell would I burn the building?!*

"Poor kid," Ben groaned, pain trembling his body. Gritting his teeth, struggling to breathe, he leaned against the wall, trying with much exertion to drag himself back down the alley towards the street. Ben felt he could not go on – yet he would go on. Excruciatingly.

Cries in his ears, screaming and burning at his sluggish plight, in the heat; Ben felt like crying as the baby himself.

And as Ben awkwardly looked around trying to make the baby calm down, he stroked the child. Ben leaned awkwardly against the wall, making rocking motions with his arms.

"Shhhh. Okay, kid. I've got ya. Shhhhh. Easy now." Eventually, the baby eased down but the crackling, spitting and crashing sounds of the burning building did not help. He could not stand here for long.

Morose about his broken hip, Ben slowly rested the kid on his right shoulder, secure within his arms, and with the other hand, he pushed himself forward. One step at a time. *So* slow!

Even if he managed to get out of the alley, what would he do? Ben would be demobilised in this enemy outpost. He could hide here in this alley, that could be an option, but the fire was a choking hazard for the kid.

But what Ben dreaded the most was revealing to his men that he had fallen and broken his hip. No, Ben simply did *not* want to do that; he would be demobbed from war. Ben would rather die than live with a broken hip.

What was *a kid* doing in a warzone anyway? What human person would be so inhuman to have the audacity to drop their offspring in a bin and flee from an invading force?! But it was also Ben's careless mistake that put this child in immediate jeopardy.

What that means then is I'm stuffed, Ben thought in torment. He could leave the child here, but the guilt of having done that would cripple him later. *That's it. This is the end of me . . . But I still got to try to save this kid. I wouldn't leave Veronica alone in a war zone!*

Looking around a jutting brick pillar, rubble clanking underfoot, he gazed up and tensed as a man, reflecting a sheen from off his clothing, appeared at the junction of alley and street.

Ben's vision doubled, then cleared. It wasn't any marine or soldier he had ever seen; the man stood no taller than he was – a good six feet – brawny, wide in stance with an air of intensity. Donned in a gleaming suit of armour, with chrome red, rimmed with gold and silver – an individual ornate work of art. Interlocking plates of metal covered all the joints, every section of his body. On the paladin's draping white and red robes, were four strings of patterned knots with flowing tassels at each of their ends. Each braid had a thread of blue, mixed with four different colours: one red, one cyan, one purple and one white. He wore a white and red Mediterranean style patterned shawl wrapped around his upper body, a cowl veiling the young man's face. The air around the man seemed to smoulder, but perhaps it was the smoke drifting in the air that gave off the effect.

Ben fumbled backward, hissing curses to himself, pain palpating, the child a grievous burden, as an irksome anger developed towards the paladin man's threating posture.

"Hey! Hey man, what are you?" Ben snapped protectively, shielding the baby. He knew that whatever tinge of fear he betrayed could provoke the man to an offensive. He had to create a strong impression that he could equal this paladin – yet, with all that brilliant knightly armour . . . Everything about this *man*, appeared out of place. Anachronistic. And that brought great fear to Ben. "Answer me! What do you want? I . . ."

As the baby started to bawl again, the paladin flinched, taking a step forward. He had an illegible expression in his dazed eyes, a mysterious, deep anxiety and a solemness of unbecoming grace. Ben watched the paladin keenly, stepping over the bricks – an urgency in his gait.

"I – uh, here." Ben lowered his glance, offering the baby up, thinking him the father. "I'm sorry. Here."

But the hooded paladin, with a measured gesture, signalled Ben to halt. The young man's face glowed faintly, appearing to shine with an inner light. He frowned deeply, thinking hard of what he was about to do. "Wait."

His voice sounded callused. Ben remained put, backing himself against the wall trying to maintain poise – it was so hard! Closer now, he could make out a vague outline of the young man's complexion: creamy skin, very short beard, almost beardless, tough, sharp jawline and handsome, his nose was slender, and eyes hard as gemstones. They were light in the shadow of the white cowl. Hazel light. A faint aura surrounded his body.

And then, he smiled. A jocose smile splitting his face, genuine and entertaining. "Benjamin. It is okay. Do not be afraid. I'm here to help."

Chills rattled Ben's veins, irritating his broken hip. His heart leapt in surprise. This man… approached him like a long-time friend.

Beaming, glowing eyes set on him, the paladin came, his metal boots clanking on the concrete. Ben froze in awe as the man was enmeshed by the distressed baby.

What am I even seeing? Ben observed in disbelief, as the paladin man closed his eyes, his lips parting, chest heaving an exhale. His gauntleted hand remained hovering above the child, then it gently touched its skin. Ben could *feel* the instant connection; he did not need to ask, though couldn't put his finger on just what it was that bonded the child and the paladin.

I'm going insane!

The charming paladin man met Ben, urgency returning to his gemstone eyes.

"Take the child," came his morose voice. It sounded Australian. "Please. He's important. Abaddon is coming. They'd think you're . . ."

"Um, what do you me—"

"Listen to me." The paladin's face glared with a sensational heat that Ben could *feel* it. The man by nature smoked, his breath prickling his skin like the chambers of a bellows. "We do not have time. Please. Protect the child, then go to your father. Go. You will find the Truth."

Ben's heart nearly leapt out from his throat. He knew his name *and* his dad? Stupefied and fearful, he gazed at the crying child and then at the veil of smoke that poured through the laneway.

"Go!" the man shouted, hands clasping his shoulders.

Then behind Ben, a slash of light struck the fabric of spatial-temporal reality, creating a hole. The paladin lit up with orange electricity, pushing Ben through it.

"Wha-!"

Ben screamed as he fell into glaring oblivion.

—

"Captain!" Julian winced as he shouted. It was not necessary since he dreaded that, for sure, the enemy could hear him, and blast it, they would blow their unit's cover completely. But he could *swear to God* that he saw Ben run off towards this burning building; why did he have to leave them behind like that? What was that man thinking? Trying to be some superhero?

Perhaps, since it was inevitable, he'd play one in every single blockbuster Hollywood film that could possibly exist. But really, he wouldn't think he was one *for real*. Surely.

Yet there was no sign of Ben.

"I'm going in there," Reggie said eagerly, lunging with clomping steps towards the inferno, as Julian slammed a forearm into his beefy chest.

"Are you a firefighter, Reggie!?" Julian snapped. He had enough of this nonsense. This mission was one of the most *pointless*, most *worthless* wastes of time he had ever had in his whole life! Now the dread of failing, the dread of returning without their Captain made him *pissed off!* Julian kicked at Ben's discarded gun.

Reggie shook his head despondently. "How about you call him, Laycock."

Jason Laycock got out his stupid communication device and Julian endured the torture of sitting in the open, pacing, potentially being observed by distant snipers.

"Ben's a reckless asshole." Julian shook his head. After he counted down in his head, he jogged back. "Annndd, we're wasting time! Come on! Snipers!"

"But, but, Julz," Ryan, the youngest in the squad, bravely stood up to confront him. "We can't leave without Ben. It's *not right*. Don't we think we should at least *try* and look for him?"

"That is ridiculous," Julian said. "We're in enemy territory."

"This is Corporal Jason Laycock to Captain DePaula. Over."

Static.

"Captain, I repeat, listen to me, where – *are* – you?! Is your position compromised? Over?"

Static. Julian fumed. He never understood Ben and how he could become such a *cocky sociopath*. And now, he could be dead. It was such an ironic enigma when it was *Julian* who saved him and the US troops from instant annihilation in Operation Desert Storm, and now he had to do it all over again? *Looks like* I'm *always the hero of the Actionman, am I? And I never get the credit!*

Julian turned to leave. "We took out the main Iraqi hideout, so *let's move!* They'll have reinforcements!"

"But—"

"Do you know we could call for a search party later, with more organised logistics!" Julian spat. "Come on!" Julian stalked off before the men. *My God, people have no sense of discipline sometimes.* He did hope Ben was okay, but just *why? Why* did he have to run off from them, like it was some bloody movie!

"Julian's right," Garrow added. "We're wasting time! Who is Ben, to abandon his unit like this?"

"Chill bros," Derek said, catching up to the departing unit. "He's probably lost."

Julian's com kit activated, and a filtered voice was heard from command centre. They were taking too long, and many would be wondering where they were by this time. Julian, groaning sufferingly, quickened his pace away from the burning building. They had completed the mission . . . at a cost.

———

Alfred Bonner gazed into the single blue-light monitor completely entranced.

The pixelated footage revealed a strange, hooded figure in an alien suit of armour, similar to Goibniuium. Reviewing the footage of the hooded man, coming up close in Ben's head camera and then, with a sudden blurry jolt of movement and a bright light flashing, the footage cut to black.

Alfred rewound the footage to examine it once more. So bizarre – was this an extra-terrestrial? Using his cursor to zoom up on the hooded figure, he paused, cropping it, waiting for the image to filter in higher definition. Once done, Alfred contacted the American base at Haditha and found out, undisputedly, that Captain Ben DePaula, one of his most important pawns, had indeed gone missing.

Alfred had an ambiguous theory: DePaula had disappeared into thin air by a wraith of the Galactic Tyrant.

The rendering cleared and Alfred examined the Tyrant's servant intently, staring into the eyes of the adversary, face shrouded in the fuzzy white glow under his cowl.

Balling his fists, Alfred let out a vexed sigh, realising the stakes had just escalated immensely. "The gods walk among men again," Alfred brooded. "The Galactic Tyrant wanted this war in the first place. So be it. The Tyrant thinks he can take Ben, but I'll take what is paramount. Rostau. Gilgamesh's *ba* abides in Warka, under high-walled Uruk."

The Dynamics that Alfred wrote, recorded his and the bennu's goals impeccably, plans not for self-gain, but for a pragmatic society ruled by noble, sustainable leaders. It wrote of the tomb of Gilgamesh, how it would unleash the dead god Osiris or Lord Maitreya, and, by gathering up the Pearls of Power, he will defeat the Galactic Tyrant once and for all.

Until then, it was a game of agendas. Alfred did not want war, but with war inevitable, the enemy did not want him to succeed, he had to be ruthless in his procedures… Regrettably.

Alfred revisited Ben's head-camera footage again, studying the paladin, his movements, his posture, how he appeared on screen, and above all, his joyful disposition, patting the child on Ben's shoulder.

The Dynamics didn't mention something as specific as this phenomenon. Alfred began to write the Dynamics when he went to the Oracle of Delphi many decades ago, and still, he put to word the inspiration from the bennu bird, recording them for his followers. The Dynamics were predictions of future events and goals for creating an ideal utopia after the Great Reset. After the Galactic Tyrant was slain by Lord Maitreya.

And until then, peace shall be made . . . at last.

"Arhat, the Iraqi Museum has been plundered." The extremely deep growling voice permeated the gloom.

Alfred turned, as a grey slender servant trudged out from the darkness. A primate – five feet tall, bipedal with leathery bony skin and nimble limbs, and cupped hands, it had distinctive large shining black slanted eyes and an inflated elongated cranium, with a small pinched wrinkly face. But, despite the hairy man's frail appearance, it expressed an erudite shrewd confidence. "Should we . . . do something, lord?"

"Not at all, no. I appreciate the update," Alfred said, curling his lip, remaining calm and cold. "Good riddance. You see, the Cabal fights for immature individual gain – an ineffective way to fight a war and create policies in politics." It was tragic that America suffered from political divide and mixed motives, treating already-excavated artefacts as spoils of war.

The hairy homo erectus blinked its lifeless tar eyes. Its stare only reflected the worst of negative emotions. "The artefacts are arbitrary, Arhat," it mumbled.

"Indeed, but not the Maitreya's coffin. I commend you for thinking ahead." These Sasquatch were extremely shrewd, Alfred often felt envious of them sometimes – today Alfred felt average as an intelligentsia. There were times when he felt so dense and stupid, he could not stand seeing these Sasquatch walking around learning human culture. "But the key is still within our grasp. I will do this my way. Nobody dies unless it can't be avoided. I've had a belly full of death from this war," Alfred said, eyeing the hairy man, then at the paladin of Haditha Dam. "That is why we should bide our time. As we speak, Aegis is homing in towards Uruk to find Maitreya's tomb. UNESCO have given us necessary permits to patrol the site and protect it from looting."

Alfred emphasised the divine inspiration of the Dynamics' predictions of the resurrection of Osiris and the rebirth of Maitreya with a firm diction. The Sasquatch understood completely, nodding its oversized head.

Alfred pointed at the paused paladin image. "This is our true enemy. Not the Iraqis. The Tyrant's Scions are rising. The Cabal will be sidetracked on their quests to find Patala, but they will one day see they were deceived. Notify the Nindingir and the Druids that we have an enemy trying to thwart us." Alfred stood up from his seat, pushing it in, straightening his coat. "I'm confident that we will be able to lead the Pentagon to permanently conclude our operations in Iraq. In the meantime, I will be in charge of recovering the coffin at Uruk. I – an anthroposophist – make this self-sacrifice to protect the Disciples of the Light and the Lahmu. Understood?"

"Yes, Arhat of the Lahmu," the pigmy primate grumbled. "I wish you best on your journey."

As the hairy man slid away, notions planted in Alfred's mind, sure and proud; he was, at last, ready for his flight into the war-torn Iraq – the cradle of civilisation.

27

BLOODY OUTCRY

LAND OF EDEN, 10,062 BCE

"Out of our evil seek to bring forth good,
Our labour must be to pervert that end,
And out of good still to find means of evil;"
—Satan from *Paradise Lost*, (1.163-65), John Milton, 1667, Global Language
Resources, Inc.

Qayin's breath burned. Holding a bloodied rock in his hands, he trembled from the shock of being denied. His burnt emmer and barley he'd cultivated, offered, wasted, rejected, filled his flaring nostrils.

Qayin smouldered in fury, taking deep cool breaths. Blood discharged from his brother's face, straddled between Qayin's bare knees, mottling his animal-skin tunic.

Inhaling deeply, he tried softening his hard heart from the blinding burn of tense anger in his muscles.

Sin is a croucher at the door,
and its desire is for you,
and you should rule over it.

Qayin stared at the swollen unrecognisable visage of what had been his younger brother laying lifeless at the feet of his altar. Juniper wood and the fat of Hebel's offering still smoked, wisps lifting up towards the huddling trees amongst the outcrops, standing at the gate of the Garden.

Qayin didn't have what he needed. He didn't have what he deserved. He'd missed out encountering El's Presence. Why should Hebel be accepted when Qayin put all the thought, love and effort into his offering and Hebel did not? Qayin *couldn't bare* El's unjust generosity. And because of El, Qayin killed his brother to take what he deserved.

If you do good,
won't there be lifting up?
And if you do not do good . . .

Qayin crouched at the foot of the altar, the sky turning purple as the sun's glaring eye closed in disappointment below the horizon of the mountainous valley. Clouds stretched forth in blotches – darkened by the shadows of night. At night, monsters roamed the wilderness. Qayin resolved that he couldn't face his family with this deed he had done. Either he lied to protect himself – saying a wild beast had slain Adapa's son and show him Hebel's animal skins – or he would lose his father's trust. His father Adapa, the elected delegate of El. A failure. Bad influence.

Qayin looked at his dead brother. He started to breathe laboriously as an unseen flint spearhead cutting deeper into his heart, marked him. Around him, his brother's sheep scattered, emitting terrified brays as if picking up the scent of an unseen predator lurking in the tall grass.

Sin is a croucher at the door . . . Blood of human spilt at the door of the sacred Garden.

Holding out his hand full of dirt, Qayin poured the dust over himself and Hebel, blood mingled with the dirt. Tears discharged from Qayin's eyes.

Qayin frantically dug a pit, a few cubits away from the site of the two altars. Panting, bending over, crabbing on his feet, he finished digging a shin-deep grave and, dragging the husk of Hebel by the legs into it, lay the body with knees tucked up at the chest. Qayin sealed the earthen womb, patting it with a dull *thud, thud, thud.*

He dusted his hands together. He saw his animal skins covered in his brother's blood and he tore them off.

As Qayin prowled back up towards the mountain cave, the sound of cracking earth groaned behind. Something heavy breached forth, making Qayin twirl around.

There, in a gash of dark clod, lay Hebel's flaccid body *cast* out of the pit, laying spawned and dead as game.

The ground was cursed by his sin.

The earth had opened its mouth, receiving red blood.

Vexed, Qayin fought the guilt down ruthlessly, crabbing back, clawing the earth madly, digging the pit deeper. By now, most of the sheep kept by his family had departed, wandering away without a shepherd to distant hills to die. It was a sad thing, but Qayin *hated* those sheep. They ruined his crops, his grain and barley, they trampled on things, devouring all things, and above all, their brays kept him up at night!

A night without those brays would be a night alone and deprived.

He struggled to breathe. Once he finished the thigh-deep pit, covering it over Hebel's body, Qayin stood in solitary silence, staring at the grave, stupefied.

Why care? Why try? You filth. There is no hope for you. Die as you were born.

He slowly began to walk backwards, the sharp taste of blood afresh on his tongue, forestalling to see the cursed ground open on its own accord, again.

It did not happen.

Qayin sighed and ran.

The earth beneath him *jolted* backwards with a quake. Qayin yelped in fright, rolling down the gulch and fumbling into the shrubbery. When he found his footing, he was at the bottom of a hill.

Damnation, what is happening?! An earthquake?

Then a distant sound of rumbling thunder made Qayin yelp like a child. A single scar of lightning slashed the dark sky like a serpent and vanished. In a *clear* sky, it winked and boomed. He swung his head towards the blare, where no storm clouds were brewing.

A great howling wind ran from down the mountains, silent at first but it grew intense, whirling and quivering into the valley until the trees bent and the grasses swayed. The gale cascaded upon Qayin in an invisible wave of biting cold that sent him tumbling on the ground. He fell to his knees gasping, for something odious to the soul had been thrust upon him, blank fright, fury that he could not run away from, sadness that he could not amend, and terror, which he could do nothing in the face of.

Sin is a croucher at the door,
and its desire is for you,
and you should rule it.

Qayin crawled indecorously on all fours, slithering on his chest, gnashing his teeth. Lifting his sin was too much for him to carry.

"WHERE IS HEBEL YOUR BROTHER?" The freezing evening winds howled.

"I have not known," Qayin gulped, lying, not glancing up to the sky. "I am – Am I my brother's keeper?"

28

EXILED FROM EXILE

"Little children, let no one deceive you. Whoever practices righteousness is righteous, as he (Jesus) is righteous. Whoever makes a practice of sinning is of the devil, for the devil has been sinning from the beginning. The reason the Son of God appeared was to destroy the works of the devil. No one born of God makes a practice of sinning, for his seed abides in him; and he cannot keep on sinning, because he has been born of God. By this it is evident who are the children of God, and who are the children of the devil: whoever does not practice righteousness is not of God, nor is the one who does not love his brother . . ."
—From the Epistle of 1 John, c. 95 – 110 CE.

Banished from the face of the ground, Qayin left his family in their cave, and went into the dark storm, farther east. He took with him his spear and stole Adapa's goat skin. He banished himself from the Garden of Eden – for he couldn't handle seeing the faces of those he'd failed – his mother and his father. And he had no choice but to banish himself, because his father had all the right of blood vengeance to defend the honour of his wife – the woman who bore Hebel. No injury could be ignored, his family would now have to defend itself from other clans that would take advantage of their grievous loss.

And Qayin had exacerbated it. Mother had to toil against him.

He trotted, and death was left in his wake. He used the skin to shield his face from the wet icy winds, but it was soaked.

He crawled to the top of a high place, looking down. The limestone outcrop dropped down into a deep ravine, the rain pounded in slanting angles, creating channels winding through the unfruitful dead grass and mud, draining into the swamp below.

Qayin stood at the edge of the cliff, unable to lift the weight of his punishment, unable to find shelter. His bare toes burned from the cold wet stone. Hot zaps of lightning cast his flickering shadow down the slope.

He could fly. Step off and fall, fly a few moments. A few beautiful moments, him and the wind. He was unloved and alone, so no one would see him fly.

I was formed by Wisdom for Adapa, suitable to him. His ally, his essential equal and protection. I am in Adapa's image, according to what is in front of him. We work together in unity to cultivate the abundance of Yahweh's generosity. There was a time where there was always enough for everyone. We work so hard to find the abundance again.

His mother may as well be dead – would he ever see her again? Back in the warm cave, at night, resting from the day, she would tell bedtime stories in the warmth of the cosy cave fire, flames crackling in the night. Qayin fell into a lulled bliss. Handprint rock art decorated the stone walls. They were done by picking ochre and gypsum into one's mouth, then blowing it over the left hand, creating the stencil on the wall. The largest print was of his father, his mother the second largest and his brother's left hands were all placed with fingers linked together by the cave's entrance outcrop in a white pigment. Qayin did the same – leaving his left handprint on the wall to complete the family. Handprints… Facsimiles of life.

When I gave birth to you, Qayin, I cried out from my pain. Yah! I had created a man!

Wind-driven rain kept pelting his face as if trying to shove him towards the edge. Qayin watched drops of water streaking down towards the ground far below. Little jumpers, thousands upon thousands of them.

"Mother," Qayin whispered, rain dripping down his face. "My maker. Bearer of agonies. Your firstborn is no more."

He was rambling. But oddly, his mind felt clearer now. He'd been given the clarity of a new perspective. Understanding so much more but feeling no wiser. It came as an intolerable weight oppressing his hard heart; the smell of damp land, the untameable biting winds, the darkness of impenetrable night.

I wasn't assertive enough to rebuke the snake. Wisdom and knowledge were freely available to us. I wanted more than I truly was, for Adapa, for Yah.

Death is not an imminent threat, said the snake.

Qayin put one foot over the cliff.

Thunder slapped with a snapping sound, jolting Qayin's bones, and he flinched, taking a step back. The sound made his ears ring. The voice of the

Almighty had unceremoniously interrupted him.

No . . . If he fell, mother will have no children. All those years and toil would be vanity.

"I'm sorry!" he roared with the wind, turning in shame, feeling a deluge of mercy and pity alighting upon him. His tears dripped down on the stone, joining the thousands of droplets.

"The purpose of the Tree of Life was to protect us from death when discerning good and evil. I desired the sacred fig – but I was not ready." Qayin's mother Khavva spoke from the past. Words in the cave. *"It becomes convenient to believe that what is good for one is good, and what is bad for one is bad. I take full responsibility for the misuse of wisdom, despite Adapa your father blaming himself for misguiding me into deception. I used to hate your father for what he did at the tree. It tormented my soul. But the very good was always deeper than the turning. True love is about knowing who someone is. Without the power to say no, love is an illusion.*

"I couldn't endure Adapa making meaning from the works of his hands without me. Our selfish choice was destructive. Love is terrifying freedom. Love has you waiting at the gate of the Garden hoping that your love would return. Every day, Adapa would come to the door of the Garden and I would hear his appeal in sorrow on the other side. As furious as I was with him betraying me, I didn't like to admit I was wearying myself with grief. His hope was intoxicating.

"But one day, Adapa stopped coming and I was grievously afraid. I spoke to Yah for what I must do. Oh Hebel, Yah said you must trust, and I will be with you. He had more respect for me than I had for myself.

"I decided freely that I will leave the Garden in order to save and restore my love. At that time, I justified that my seed will crush the serpent's head, so I had to find Adapa. But in truth, it was a selfish desire, to fill the void of lust, longing and fear in me. Yah, of course, accommodated to my choice as I left Paradise. I knew he knew it. It is not good for woman to be alone. I am Life, man's deliverance. An act of godliness and participation to make the earth good.

"When we met at last outside the Garden in this very cave, the encounter was devastating, but Adapa poured out his guilt and I forgave him. We were to be the rescue, the light to the other nonchosen hominids. El had chosen us to be his images – the life-bringers acting in the essence of what El wanted to represent.

"When we wanted to become successful, listening to the voice of the serpent, I looked, I took, and I ate from the Tree of Knowing Good and Bad. Your parents chose to worship the creation rather than Creator. Staring into the temptation, was death staring at death. We failed, bringing all of those people, our children,

down with us from access to El's Dwelling – the Garden.

"There is a difference between receiving and taking, my boys. Receiving is being patient, waiting for the right time to take. When I loved and desired Adapa when I was still young, I took him and his life-seed helped me conceive you two. This is a good taking.

"By my seed, the Snake will be crushed."

A mighty wind heaved Qayin out of his dreary sleep – a wind that smelled of blood, of mud. He felt slimy and discordant, the ground consuming him. He was sinking up to his waist into the mire.

If only he had listened to his mother, maybe he would have subdued his anger and never killed Hebel. He had done the ultimate dishonour to his mother by killing her seed – his brother.

He writhed in the pit, losing his foothold. He fell down, the mire reaching up to his neck. He cried. The water almost engulfed him, crushing his breath in a cold grasp of death. Clasping a tree branch with his arm, he reached for it, pulled, and the thorns sliced his palm. Self-inflicted pain, self-inflicted judgement. He sunk deeper in the ground; head nearly buried when he heard a tremendous snarling from the woodland beyond the darkness.

A *terrible* sound. A hollow crunching of bone breaking between jaws, the dull ripping of hard flesh.

Abject terror seized Qayin. He kept still as stone, sinking, yet his insides were in a clamour. He hoped that the darkness could be concealed by the branches of the tamarisk that overhung the slough.

Qayin, in his vision, noticed that behind the thorn tree was the massive head of a slumping chubby serpent beast, crouching over a meal, shaking and devouring the carcass of a mammal – many times larger than a human. Only in the deep shadows did the terrible serpent make Qayin contort his face in woe. Wrapped in his animal skin, caked in mud, protecting him from the beast's eye, was stained by fear-sweat. He remained so still as if dead, the mud irritating his flesh.

The ushumgal emitted an incredible smell of metallic blood. Lots of blood oozing down its jaws, teeth like ivory spearheads. Forever, it marked Qayin's nose and soul with its smell. Qayin wept in silence, he couldn't find cessation from this nightmare.

He'd never seen the beast before, he'd only heard tales from his parents admonishing to not leave the cave at night. Qayin ogled upwards at the glorious stars instead... and saw no help or meaning there any longer.

Suddenly, the brush creaked and swayed, as the huge ushumgal lumbered up from its crouch, its feet stomping the ground. A long dragging sound followed, and at last the beast vanished, but the smell of raw meat still lingered in the air.

Qayin hurled himself out of the mouth of the pit and onto the dry land. A miasma of dew – fog swirling with grey - drifted in the late-night air. It was turbid and suffused with aromatic scents of Eden. The ghost of home. Distilled dew soaked Qayin's flesh, swathing him with tender reminders of the home he'd abandoned and destroyed. Thin voices enclosed around him. Curses.

"I'm cursed," Qayin groaned. "You have driven me away from the ground, and from your face I shall be hidden. I don't belong. I'm a wanderer on the earth, and the hunters will find me, and will kill me."

29

CALL OF BLOOD

"'Let us make human
    in our image,
      according to our likeness;
and let them rule
    over the fish of the sea
    and over the birds of the sky
    and over the cattle
    and over all the land,
    and over every creeper that creeps on the land.'
And Elohim created human in his image,
    in the image of Elohim he created him;
      male and female he created them…
and behold, it was very good."
    —From the Scroll of Genesis, c. 6th century – 5th century BCE. Tim Mackie's Literal-Literary Translation.

Yamila looked at Sheth and saw that he was not good. His long black hair was unwashed, bound by a band of netted reeds wrapping around his forehead, poorly. Strands of tousled hair veiled part of his troubled eyes. He smelled like hound dung. His crooked nose gave him a rugged look, but his heavy brow was as crinkled as the dry scorched ground, his high, wide forehead made his small eyes dark, downcast. He declined to join the boys hunting for gazelle after the passing storm. Instead, he left his clan to help plough the ground for growing wheat for Yamila's half-brother, which was out of his usual optimal function.

Sheth of the Kebaran was adventurous and daring. Muscular and nimble, he was able to run great distances and wield large throwing spears. Seeing Sheth walk lightly, dazed in trepidation, bore a pit in Yamila's stomach.

"What's wrong?" Yamila said, placing a hand on his bare shoulder – dark ochre and sweaty.

Face set as flint, Sheth replied, "Nothing. I wanted to see my father. That's all."

They passed through a cluster of conical round houses where Yamila saw her Natufian clan setting about their ordinary hard lives of fruitful, and crafty drudgery. Smoke rose from among the circular huts made of stone and domed-shaped reed-and-clay roofs, carrying the smell of mutton in the humid air. The sun of the late afternoon after the storm was strong and thick with hot moisture. The sound of grinding, chipping and sanding stone rose loudly, echoing even towards the high rising wall of sandstone cliffs beyond the lush oak forests. Raucous boys without tops played games, and the older muscular men drinking beer wore the bone necklaces of their forefathers. Yamila – now thirteen years old – was particularly keen, looking up to the women – notably the strong-armed wise women – but her eyes were drawn to the ones bearing and raising children. She saw one suckling a child to her breast and her kins-woman on her knees, kneaded dough and cereals from the wild grasslands in the fields around the river to make bread, with mortar and pestle. Soon, Sheth would marry her and Yamila would become a mother too.

Yamila crossed her brawny arms, walking in front of Sheth. He stopped, his dark eyes peering at her forlornly. She could taste his anxiety.

"People have been talking," Yamila said. "Yesterday, you raged, breaking atlatls in the open."

Sheth sighed – a deep huff that gushed from his large chest. He was nineteen.

"Sheth," Yamila said sternly and softly. "We are kin. If you find yourself in need of anything—"

"Look, if this is about what is going on with my brother, I don't know what you've heard," he said tenaciously. "It's just a misunderstanding, okay?"

Yamila scowled. "What's wrong with your brother?"

Sheth opened and closed his mouth, no words coming out. His fingers played with his exquisite necklace of small dentalium shells. Similar in appearance to Yamila's own, their necklaces were priceless and would never be bartered since each bead represented an ancestor.

The necklace made Yamila feel proud, it simply had to be the most renowned handcrafted item in the whole world. Sheth's necklace functioned in the same way as hers – they both carried the presence of kin with them on their bodies, every day and night.

"You know how it's been," Sheth intoned. "Work, hunting, and I know I haven't been a good . . ." His eyes became distant, looking off, away from Yamila's face. He trotted to a stop. "I can't do this anymore. Yamila . . . I haven't been honest with you."

Yamila touched her necklace, feeling a wave of anticipation.

Sheth smirked grimly, shaking his head saying, "There's no girl. It's not that. I'm seeing father because . . . You know about the baby mammoth my brother Halghal lives with?"

"Yes," Yamila said. "Ugi."

"Yesterday, Ugi died."

Yamila's eyes bulged, hand covering her mouth. Ever since Halghal, Sheth's brother, had found the baby mammoth alone to raise it, Yamila worried that his large pet dog Sedim would kill it in a play fight.

But it was not the dog Sedim. "Qayin and his hunters," Sheth hissed. "The hunter of both beast *and* men killed Ugi and all of Halghal's friends while hunting and gathering. Qayin is a serpent in the wild. The seed of the Shaitan."

Yamila gasped. "Don't say that cursed name!"

"Superstition," Sheth derided. "I can say whatever I want." He began to pick himself forward. People left them alone – they'd both walked a good distance away from the settlement towards the oak forests and beyond that, to the rosy sandstone cliffs where Adapa and his wife lived.

"What do you mean?" Yamila rasped.

Sheth revealed to Yamila that while hunting gazelle for barter, he met Qayin his enemy. Their meeting had resulted in the death of all the Natufian and Kebaran men, including their hunting dogs and Ugi the young mammoth, but only Sheth and Halghal were spared to be humiliated, languished, powerless as Qayinite tribes killed and robbed all of their game. This was not revenge, there was no lead-up to this act of cruelty. Sheth was just hunting to gain barter, when Qayin decided to show up to boil the blood.

The death of Ugi the mammoth was long – the creature was stabbed repeatedly with knifes and left to writhe. It broke Halghal. Sheth felt guilty and responsible for the death, letting Qayin destroy everything he owned.

Ugi's life was a long story. Compassionate Halghal saved the baby mammoth while on a hunt up north on the snowy plains. She had fallen in a pit, stranded from her mother – the matriarch – and the main herd that had been frightened by an atlatl onslaught from Qayinite hunters. The Natufians and Kebarans came just in time to save Ugi as the Qaynites chased down the herd until they slew the small and weak mammoths, pierced repeatedly by their obsidian atlatls. And while the Qayinites were confronting the wrath of a matriarch protecting her young, Halghal snuck away with Ugi in his trembling arms.

The Qayinites stripped the mammoth's wool for coats for the winters and they sawed their tusks for bent ivory throwing sticks. They butchered their flesh for meat and barter. The bone-clad, mask-bearing Qayinites were the most feared. They were said to cut off the heads of hunters required for young boy initiations, transferring the name of the severed head to the young boy. They didn't spare anything while they hunted; they stole, killed and destroyed. But, above all, they desired to take remains of woolly mammoth skeletons to build their huts and their skins to erect walls to protect their settlements from marauders up in the high mountains – towards the north.

The wise women of Yamila's Natufian family often said that the mammoth migrations up in the north were becoming rarer and rarer. Yamila believed Qayin had to be behind their decline, or it was an ominous sign of the decline of the Qayinites, for it was their life to slaughter these beasts.

As for the young calf named Ugi, Sheth's brother found it and he took it home south, raising it up as his own kin.

Its death had killed Halghal and Sheth.

"I cannot stand these people," Sheth growled, after the recount. Tension burned in his eyes. "Qayinites rape our children and kill us. When I saw what Ugi's death did to Halghal, I felt . . . I will *hurt* Qayin," he whispered in seething anger. "We cannot live like this if we are to have children. They will be in danger to death, and we'll subject ourselves to pain."

"You're resentful," Yamila discerned.

"I'm not. I'm just . . . desperate."

"No. Qayin—"

"Qayin is *not* my brother," Sheth snapped. "He sheds blood and it cries out to El. I don't want to see his face again, Yamila. I want to be prepared if he sends raids. What if he comes down into Eden? I'm doing this because I want to protect you."

"You're doing this to protect yourself and your family," Yamila said. "Your problems are now my problems."

"You should stay out of this one then."

"*Don't* tell me what I can or cannot do! El is with me, whether you like it or not!"

Sheth gazed at her, thunderstruck. "Okay, let me be honest. I said that I got this but . . . I lied."

"What?!"

"I've been hunting on Chisi because I have no choice," Sheth said. Chisi was the day of rest when El ran out of breath from ordering the world. "To make up for the barter shortages. Halghal has shortages. I have shortages. If I don't make a valuable craft for the Natufian craftsman and travellers, it will be the end of us. I cannot marry you and your clan if I cannot barter them jewellery or game, they will deny us, and I could be ostracised! Look at me, Yamila. I've tried things. I've tried to fix it all myself. I tried hunting deer, gazelle, birds and tortoise. And now it's gone bad." Sheth chuckled at his worthless plight. Since the Natufian way of life developed from the older traditions of Kebaran, spiritual, social, and kinship conflicts were likely to abound – grudges and hatred between kin spread like plague. If Sheth failed to meet this barter, as a Kebaran, it would be very certain that he would be ostracised from the clan, forced to fend for himself alone.

Coerced to roam the wilderness, where Qayin lived. Yamila didn't believe in curses but this one worked perfectly, as if it were a deliberate, coordinated plan by the spirits of the air.

"We're in trouble," Sheth said.

"We?" Yamila gasped. "Sheth!"

"*I'm* in trouble. I need something to cover the barter *and* our dowry. I know that Adapa can do miracles." Sheth spun around, hands to his mouth in great distress. "The death of Ugi was a curse. A sign that we are done."

"Sheth, no," Yamila said, tears brimming her eyes. "Don't say that. You need to go to Adapa."

So Sheth and Yamila traversed through the oak forest, down south-east towards the rosy sandstone river basins jutting out of the lush green valleys. Nimble and with great strength and swiftness, Sheth leapt and bound across ridges and narrow pathways in between red rocks, and Yamila followed him too, panting and drenched in sweat as she ran, enthralled by the epic height they clambered, and the view from the cliffs and the great distance they covered. They both ran, the wind stroking their long hair freely, running over the twisted rocky ridges that glittered like mother-of-pearl tiles in house-floor graves where ancestors would be buried under the house.

They leapt over boulders on the run, traversing the landscape. The evening light cast a golden hue of ripe grain cereal fields across the sky – it was not from the sun, which had already set, but from the light of the Tree of Life, so bright its leaves shone radiant like a second sun, from the high mountain of the Garden in the west. That was a secret place, forbidden to trespassers, guarded by the flaming Kerubs along its river boundary. The great Edenic water fed the fields of the people outside the land of Eden. The unending copious rivers spilt south, south-east, and north-east as the Gihon, the Pishon, the Idiglat and the Buranun. The rivers of Eden sustained fruit-bearing trees and fecund peoples.

The *hiss, hiss, hiss,* sound from insects hung in the humid air. Birds' chirping bounced off the rocks and trunks of the oak forest. The place which Adapa and Khavva lived was a natural cave set high on a terrace, hidden in the sandstone cliffs of marbled red-orange rock.

Wind gushed as Adapa appeared up the ridge from his stroll in the forest. His pet dog pranced beside him, then lumbered away into the shade of the red cave. Clad in stitchings of striped, black, white and beige animal skins, Adapa had a long grey beard and a stitching of gold nuggets, onyx and precious stones hanging above necklace weavings upon his chest. He wore a coral crown on top of his long dark silver hair tumbling down his shoulders; it blew in the wind in the cool of the day, gnarly hair whipping across his gleaming face. He had a large nose, large cheek bones. He was a little smaller than Sheth his son, but by no means less muscular.

"Children, sit and eat," Adapa said. He held a loaf of bread in his hands, blessed it and broke it in half for Sheth and Yamila and they ate.

Adapa alone was taken out of the people, as one representative human to go before El on behalf of the many. The spirits gave him great responsibility – to bring accountability to all the people who had sinned to draw near to El – the source of life everlasting. He was commissioned to serve and keep the animals in the Garden of Eden. Exiled and failing to attain life, he continued such a vocation of creating order in disorder, serving and keeping his own "garden," on behalf of everyone else before him. In a world of pain, famine, illness, violence and chaos, Adapa was the keeper of peace and abundance – the completeness of the world's potential. The hardship of Adapa's life to work the cursed ground was much more difficult than the curse given to his wife Khavva. For he had failed to represent humanity willingly, not deceived like her.

Once the bread was consumed, Sheth's body was clenching like his munching jaws, before the presence of his father. In reverence, Yamila knelt before black Adapa, the Priest King of Eden, prostrating on the clay ochre ground in a ball.

"El," Sheth prayed passionately before his father. He stood up with Adapa, strong chin raised high, hands pointing vehemently. "How do you expect me to live on in your presence when my enemy . . ." Sheth quivered visibly, his breathing shaky. "Why do you break me? Was it not you who created me? Will El's steadfast love – his Khesed – cease for all time? Has El in his anger, shut up kindness, filling my heart with revenge? Has he forgotten his promises? You blessed us to subdue the earth as your co-rulers. To be fruitful and multiply and fill the land and to have power over the fish of the sea and over the birds of the sky and over living creatures that crawl on the land. Then why are your children *being* subdued!? Why aren't your people reigning?!

"Remember our plight, oh El. I am deeply troubled by cherishing to kill the killer! I open my heart to you, because I have wished the death of my brother! *Forgive me!*"

The shadows of the blushing outcrops lengthened. Yamila stared puzzled at the tall trees, her blood going cold as the shadow of the evening deepened. The wind blew forlornly, morbidly with a melancholic groan between the teeth of sandstone bluffs.

"My beloved son," Adapa said with a deep strong voice, almost liturgical, rhythmic and primordial. "To be El's co-ruler, you must have faith."

"Faith is not my problem," Sheth said. "Qayin and debt is my problem."

"Unforgiveness is the problem, son," Adapa said, as if it was an easy matter to resolve. As a set-apart man, having a smooth, steadfast heart, he could see strange connections between place, knowledge and proper order.

Bowing, Sheth groaned. "No – but . . . Pabba, no. Qayin took your son! What would Hebel think of this neglect?!"

"Neglect? Do not bring Hebel into this!"

"Just, consider from my perspective," Sheth exclaimed. "I . . . just want to protect those I love. I want to save all those who cannot protect themselves. I promise to protect those I hate, so long as it is right. But protecting Qayin is *not right!* He is sexually perverse and sadistic! A beast! He is El's enemy! Keeping him alive will cause more death! Killing him will cause life! Mother of Life gave birth to me as a substitute for Hebel. I exist for *his* sake! I am the one to crush the head of the Serpent!"

"You think?" Adapa nodded, as if in mock agreement.

"I call humankind to subdue the offspring of chaos! I call humankind to guard the Garden to remedy your sin!" Sheth declared. "Qayin's murder was *your* punishment for failing to attain life. Now, since Qayin denied the responsibility of family, he will be deprived of family!"

Yamila was struck by the fire in Sheth's eyes and the tentatively composed Adapa.

"The mouth of the righteous is a spring of life," Adapa said calmly, his dark eyes keenly discerning. "The mouth of the wicked conceals violence. You and Qayin have something in common: Fear and the willingness to kill life to preserve life."

Sheth blinked, shocked. "But I—"

"Consider *my* perspective."

"I don't want to kill. I want to return to the Gar—"

"My son, listen, listen." Adapa took a step forward, and Sheth slumped, chin to chest. Yamila rocked to her feet, feeling a little stone prick her toe, as she beheld Adapa placing his large, thick black hand on Sheth's shoulder. "Sheth, did El kill your parents for the turning from face-to-face?"

Sheth blinked, saying, "No, Pabba."

"Did El kill your brother for his murder?"

Sheth hesitated. "No..."

"So, your pabba made choices that leads to death and El gave him life to make *a new possibility* to bring forth life. What Qayin didn't realise was that *he is loved*. As he nourished his dark fantasies, he failed to embrace that love. He killed because he's demented and miserable, instead of having the patience to my method of generosity. Eliminating his sin, he eliminated his brother. Now, Qayin's mark of protection comes from stone walls of fear he builds around his settlements. He refuses to return to face-to-face relationship because he hates me and the world, fearing that no one will forgive him or protect him. And therefore, he must be aggressive to all. Does that make sense?"

Sheth nodded.

"Forgiving someone that cannot love or trust, is more powerful that killing that self-destructive wretch. Forgiveness doesn't allow relationship, it open doors for the *opportunity of restoration*. I've waited for your brother Qayin to return." He squeezed Sheth's shoulder. "Every moment, I love my children equally. Even destructive Qayin."

Adapa proclaimed the Creator's wisdom through his own mouth.

Dianthropic, it was Almighty El revealed through his image Adapa! His words like fruit that tasted strange yet brought strength and delight. *How does he walk in the Great Spirit like this!?* Yamila thought.

As the Word poured out of him, Adapa's voice naturally became louder and passionate. He gritted his teeth as he spoke, to make the point potent. "Was it not I that provided him my grace? It was because he was alone and vulnerable in the wilderness, that I loved him. He knew that he had failed more than his father. But my kindness created hostility!"

"Why did you make that mistake if you knew what damage it would cause?" Sheth said. "Why do you allow chaos?"

Adapa racked his long female hair behind his ears. "My 'mistake' is your capacity to decide freely. Good creation hasn't been set in its ideal form yet. If there was no chaos, there would be no learning, no development, no redemption from death. This redemption is a journey. It is necessary for the sake of creating free virtuous rulers over creation to make decisions. To align with goodness, to return to the Garden, or to dismantle the good to make our own good and our own return. To multiply life, you need to face death of your own pride."

"Yes…" Sheth replied. "But what if I just let Qayin go on to kill everyone in Eden? Then I would be a chaos bringer like him! When will you punish Qayin El in order to protect your humans?"

"Qayin is avenged seven times, so you must reconcile the evil of your brother, *seventy-seven*-times. Whatever it takes to rectify your return to the Garden, do it. It is not a problem for me to protect and punish those that I despise, because I am his father and you and Qayin are in my image. You make Adapa's mistakes, but I prepared a place just for you all. Was it not I, before whom you stand right now, to tell you, that zealous callings to prepare the way to return to me will only bring about more blood!? For those that live by the spear, die by the spear! All you need to do is to trust . . . and *forgive*. Do not become like Qayin, your wounded brother, my son . . . *Please.*"

"We wish we can live in peace," Yamila whispered. "That all this violence and loss would cease to be right in the eyes of humanity."

"Ah. A big thing you wish for, Yamila," Adapa said. "If you have faith, even if it is *extremely* small, you can say to the storm, *be still*. You can say to the wild beast attacking you, *be still*, and it will be so."

Yamila gawked.

Adapa's face tugged with a beaming smile, chuckling, winking, making her blush. "It's just to make a point, daughter. Nothing is impossible. It is by your *faith* in El that you can make peace, love and face-to-face relationship desirable again in humanity. There is goodness everywhere and goodness *can* be found in people."

"Pabba," Sheth said, sniffing, about to sob. "Please give me your mercy, a gift of most precious value for the sake of Yamila, for the sake of your family, to barter the greedy craftsmen and traders."

"You are afraid of going into the wilderness alone," Adapa said.

"I will *not* be dishonoured!" Sheth trembled. He eyed Yamila and at last, tears ran down his face. "I don't know what to do."

He broke. His knees shook and he fell into a crouch, covering his face.

Adapa, crouching, crawling, came to Sheth face to face, wiping the tears from his eyes. He picked him up into an embrace – a parent carrying a baby.

"Do not leave me," Sheth sobbed.

"I will not," Adapa breathed.

Yamila wept in dignified silence.

"I don't want my anger to cause you pain." Sheth sobbed. "Don't ever leave me. Don't leave me."

"I will *never* leave you. I am so proud of you. Where I failed, you succeeded. You proclaimed your guilt instead of blaming others. Mother has what you need."

"Really?"

As Adapa comforted his son, Yamila first smelled the burning of frankincense and myrrh. The wonderous presence of the divine made her turn around. At the corner of her eye, out of the purple shade of the orange cave, she saw a tall figure in statuesque repose, fine-boned, brawny, ebony skinned. Something rattled in the woman's hands. She walked with elegant bare feet in measured steps, treading the earth with victory.

Light flashed from the black woman's polished-stone apparel as she stepped abreast the stone into the faint evening light. She carried her head high; orange pigment in leaf shapes on her cheeks; and white pigment, a stroke marking her lower lip and chin, and nose. White dots and wavy lines covered her cheeks and forehead, and her earlobes were pierced with large white shells. Her black locks were bound in a spiral bun, crowned with a terrific headband made of dentalium shells strung together, adorned with the feathers of a golden eagle. Her arms and legs and part of her upper chest was bare. She wore an elaborate fur coat with fringed draperies and tortoise shells – ornamental gifts hanging from her body, glittering, trembling at every step. Then she stood without a stir, as a majestic tree.

Her face glowed more like a child than a matriarch, her wide-eyed gaze tenebrous with tragic power. She stood looking at Yamila, Adapa and Sheth, as around her, gathering in similar appearance, were women and men. The attendance of dark humanoid shapes carried incense smoke, rising thickly, wrapping around their bodies as a veil, heavy with scent and power.

The ebony woman held an elaborate necklace in her branch like hands.

"Khavva," Adapa said, raising up Sheth his son. "Exalted above all women. My deliverance. You have given the gift."

"Take it, Sheth," Khavva said with a long drawl, holding out the necklace. A large, rich multi-string necklace connected to a central iridescent Yam Choof shell-ring spacer. The threads held dominant red limestone beads, with various dark blue beads, turquoise stone from Sinai, hematite beads at the closing clasp, all patterned throughout the bead strands. They were incredibly small and intricate, hundreds of them.

Yamila hadn't seen a piece of jewellery more marvellous in her entire life – nor had any human ever created such an ornate piece since the beginning. Such a treasure would have been made by this woman's mother who died – each artistic bead told a string of narrative about her mother's ancestors in the ground.

"Blessed be the fruit of your womb," Adapa whispered, stepping back, creating a space between Sheth and Khavva. And Yamila knew the rest of the promise.

A war of the seeds. From the woman's seed a saviour will come. He or she will strike the head of the Snake, and the Snake will bite the heel of that woman's seed. Adapa presented Khavva as if she *were* that woman. *But how could this be fulfilled, if Adapa refuses Sheth to fight Qayin in a duel? How could one strike evil by being struck by it?* The enigma eluded her heart.

But if Yamila married had bore children to Sheth… *Then I will participate in this hope, this promise.*

Priestly, powerful and mighty, Khavva – the mother of all living – held out her hands, offering the gift.

"No," Sheth gasped. "Mother."

"This gift is mine," Khavva sung. "Giving the good and the bad, we have what is beyond value. Take and barter."

Yamila could not believe her eyes – Khavva – a Tree of Life – was giving up her fruit as Mother, to give to her son to barter for himself *and* for Yamila's dowry! Such a necklace couldn't be repaid, it contained the worth of a hundred lives of kin. The most valuable thing – life – given up, for the sake of generosity and love.

The blessing of Sheth's remarkable representative, the mediator of El. *Why could I not have parents like this?* Yamila thought. *Like this king and queen who were compassionate powers of selfless life.* Now, she could have a chance to have them as parents-in-law, by marrying Sheth.

As Sheth adorned himself with the decorative necklace, excited yet solemn, he held Yamila's hand and brought her with his parents to gaze across the valley of Eden towards the west. Towards the voluptuous, holy space of the Garden Mountain, rising in dreamy opulence of turquoise green.

As the dusk came in, great verdant lamps in the darkness of night shone on the horizon, as if the sun and the moon were never made. The light made the river that flowed from the great mountain flicker, like stars in the skies, dancing radiance from its leaves.

Trees of good light radiated El's holy Presence. Adapa and Khavva with their attendants gathered together with Yamila and Sheth, face to face with the light of the Presence, their foreheads basking in its warmth. The fragrance of their incense sweetened the air around Yamila. A taste of past eternal life in paradise. Always there, shining, but distant and inaccessible.

Two dazzling trees of light stood on the top of a great jungle mountain – an uncompromising divine throne, heavy with glory. The Date Palm of Life glowed potent gold as the sun, and the Fig Tree of Wisdom, with quicksilver blue, radiant as the moon. Two divine trees of El – colossal on the mount – made out of El's own light and power, sung into existence at the foundations of the land. Standing high on the mount on the horizon of the earth – blurring lines between Heaven and Earth – the trees held up the skies. Male and female, family and family, clan and clan, tall and shapely, slender and strong, day and night.

The Tree of Life and Tree of Knowledge. Two bodies, two differences. Many gathering into one. White beauty shining in Edenic twilight.

Trees that were good. Sowing hope, for corrupted mortals, to rule, to reflect and to serve.

To anticipate…

A divine-human synergy, where there would be no more killing, no more rape, no more slander, no more pain and no more crying. And the former things passed away.

END OF OMEGA PLAN PART I

PART II

CALL FOR HOPE AND JUSTICE

30

BY WAY OF DECEPTION

"Wisdom, called Faith, wanted to create something by herself without her partner. She miscarried, and the aborted foetus became Samael. He 'became an arrogant beast resembling a lion.' This 'beast' opened his eyes and saw around him a limitless sea of matter. Like an almighty toddler surrounded by Play-doh, the ruler began to mold a universe. He immediately became puffed up and crowed, 'I am God, and there is none but me!' An angry echo from heaven responds, 'You are wrong, Samael!'"

—From "'I Am God and There is No Other!'": The Boast of Yaldabaoth." In *Desiring Divinity: Self-deification in Early Jewish and Christian Mythmaking*, M. David Litwa, New York, 2016, pg 57.

Bhairava, Just Son of Danu, gazed upon a gallery of artwork of a rich creative culture, sprayed over a grey grim wall of opprobrium. He was committed to artistic life. Art . . . The universal expression of frustration. When he was Michael Oppenheim, Bhairava had made art his living.

He'd only come here to follow orders from his master after he had committed himself to becoming an Initiate of the Third Initiation. He'd come to meet the master of the Manicheans of Light – Ian Mastemah. Bhairava had not met this CIA agent face to face, but he'd been fascinated by his track record. The people linked with this Ian Mastemah had consulted Bhairava, some coming from the Chabad Movement and Metatron, a new organisation part of the international transhumanism movement connected with the black

Golem market in Patala. Ian was quite happy to offer him a job as a "Watcher" – the Manichean's eyes and ears on the ground. Bhairava needed a job – for too long he'd lived without one and now, he had one.

His new CIA master and his consultants knew about James Casbolt, the Nindingir, the Aes Sidhe, Antarctica, the Fomorians, the Galactic Tyranny – none of it was new to them, because they were wise to study mysticism. And also, these Jews were willing to offer top-notch solutions to the current crises of the world.

To remove all suffering. Nirvana of the world. Non-existence.

The barrier wall stood tall before Bhairava, decorated with the artwork of green Lady Liberty, crying, a hand to her face. In her other hand was a cartoon baby child, back facing, white, plain and colourless.

Handala, the Palestinians called him. The nothing, lifeless boy with no hope. A dead thing in America's hand.

Bhairava attained the indifference of the *sunyata*. Oh, the pain of losing all hope for the future, while knowing out there, there were others succeeding when one should have. As Handala, it removed all colour from life, it removed all peace. Bhairava could confound this suffering – he had learnt to overcome this block to reach the Third Initiation.

Handala . . . A wretch. A child was too young to become a wretch!

Why did this cartoon bother Bhairava so much?

He moved on. The wall travelled along with him, weaving like a serpent, a drab and sad monolith galvanising the Bethlehem landscape. The distinct splash of colours of graffiti on the dark grey colourless wall, drew in Bhairava's ravenous attention. He strolled down the dark narrow barriers that segregated the settlers and the occupants. It segregated for reasons of economy, security and public safety. Good reasons . . . from *one* perspective. One would think the state of Israel were apartheid trying to keep out beasts – the giant Nephilim barbarians, the Rephaim, the Canaanites and the Philistines – denizens that cared not for humanity, but for child sacrifice and power.

One of these so-called "Nephilim" was illustrated on the concrete walls. Her display was enlarged and colossal, wearing a hijab around her head, semiautomatic in her grasp, a wolfish, jocose sadistic smile plastered on her hawkish face. The name in English identified her as the hijacker LEILA KHALED. The next line read: DON'T FORGET THE STRUGGLE.

The Jihad . . . Indifferently within the Void of *sunyata*, rolling across the wall, Bhairava saw another large depiction of the "barbarians". Yasser Arafat, a leader, a lifelike portrayal defaced by smeared burn marks, streaking his image.

When Bhairava had been young, he had been eager to join uprisings such as this one in Palestine. But he had to give up the desire of the ego to following the Path of Light.

Continuing, Bhairava walked around a corner, around a cylindrical watchtower crowned with impenetrable wired fences like metal thorns and eye-like security cameras. The strong fetid stench of rubbish and junk cast in the alley, made him hold his nose.

He studied the wall. On it, brave Davids with sling shots and throwing stones, rallied with a revolutionary flag flapping green, black, red and white. They were rising up like Lady France, scaling a mound. They fought doggedly against Goliath – a bulldozer Transformer, emblazed with the six-pointed shadow on its iron hide.

How poetic and how significant was this work of combat art – hidden in the thin putrid alleyways of the barrier wall, for none to see and none to appreciate. A part of Bhairava felt a smidge of grief. He could easily subdue such strange emotions, and wondered; what his master Ian Mastemah had said about this whole enterprise of survival, and the rise of civilisation, had all been by way of deception.

By way of deception . . . That was *the only way* to navigate a fallen world. The *only* pragmatic way *was* deception. Lies made true.

By the end, near the massive multistorey concrete carpark, a metre higher than the wall itself, Bhairava walked past the mural, seeking a solitary space for himself to reorientate his mind.

He thought, *This is not at all different from the Berlin Wall. The world without the truth divides.*

Waves of nostalgia skimmed over the memories of Bhairava's early life, of his early mission in the Alliance saving James Casbolt and Max Spiers. Yes, he had lived a life long enough, fighting in the German ranks of the World War I. Wars so cataclysmically big for a single world that the spurring of their momentum would never again revert the world back to the rural and pre-industrial state Michael Oppenheim had been born into.

Never before had humankind and national ideology and arrogance skyrocketed, with the weapons of technology protuberant along with it. Michael Oppenheim had lived through those eras of change, where everyone around him thought it was an end, each and every time. Now he had become Bhairava, Just Son of Danu, at the dawn of the third millennium AD.

But now, as all things that had started, it had an end. All beginnings, to become complete, *must* conclude. For there were many ends, and not only one, for all must have a beginning and an end to be complete.

To be reborn.

This ancient land of Bethlehem had screams and cries of children and weeping of women, polluted with death, spilled with blood. It was the red hand of Herod over Rachel's children, refusing to be comforted.

Screams.

Breathe.

Those screams. They caused suffering, and suffering blocked the path to nirvana. Everyone got what they deserved so why did Bhairava hear screams? He thought he'd silenced them long ago, now that he had achieved the Third Initiation. And if reality contained suffering, then the goal of life was to shed the material reality to seek grandiosity. To reach the divine. To *become* spirit.

Bhairava checked his pouch full of Pneuma-infused voidstones, glowing a white-blue even light. The power of suffering helped him to escape. The irony of Pneuma. Sometimes these screams came from those trapped spirits, harnessed in the gemstones. Such a mystical bond between Spirit and Earth had come from the gods of Patala. In Hebrew tradition, humans were made from the earth – fashioned from wet clay. The mystical equation worked when breath of human beings could infuse earthen minerals – the human body. This was why the Israeli members of the Manicheans of the Light harnessed Pneuma in gems and crystals as an alternative renewable energy.

Bhairava's powers were harnessing people he pitied. They worked as one, driven with a single devotion to *moksha* (salvation from bondage to the transcendent). So Pneuma heightened his state of consciousness. Each time he contracted the Pneuma, Bhairava felt divinity – so secure, so unstoppable. Those cries in the Pneuma had over the decades become this rhythm of justice, a rhythm of enlightenment.

Bhairava spoke a mantra to Maheshwara, then inhaled deeply. Something *bloomed* within him. Like a divine fresh breath drawn in, a powerful wave pulsating within his body. It was his Aes Sidhe capabilities but a *hundred times* more intense. It made him healthier, energised, aware.

He approached the desolate carpark and jumped towards the wall.

He lurched. The winds of the Pneuma had a type of negative pressure – pulling inwards – causing antigravity. When hanging in the air, his body felt like he plummeted downwards when he went sideways. A primal part of Bhairava felt exhilarated as he landed on the wall, every time down ceased being down. The wall now became his floor.

Bhairava crawled upwards like a spider. Blue smoke painted the concrete where his hands gripped the wall.

Once reaching the wall – the roof – he jumped, shifting his feet. His instincts of the weak flesh told him gravity would take him backwards and he could fall and break his bones.

But he landed on the roof without falling, the blue Pneuma screaming like Banshees as he applied negative pressure.

Now that his physical body had submitted to the soul and the mental, he was able to unlock a few abilities and traits of the true transformation of his ascended body. Many of the Initiates were shocked that he could unlock his higher self so quickly, normally, it took to the Sixth and Seventh Initiation to be able to bind and fuse the Pneuma, controlling gravity at will.

Bhairava pulled the gravity towards him, rose into the air, propelling the mass of his body, retaining the same mass as a sail upon the wind, pushing against him with relative resistance. The Pneuma pulling him, he leapt over the roof and immediately fell back towards the building again. He angled upwards, grasping the wall.

Reducing his mass and increasing his strength, Bhairava climbed the rest of the way up, onto the top level of the carpark. Increasing his strength and inertia, he hurled back to the ground. He tripped, rolling on the ground, grunting.

Immediately, his Parvus Perception picked up a noise. From the heights of the carpark, Bhairava stood up, and saw a procession of people on a road and on a grassy hill in the blazing sunshine near the barrier wall. There was Handala again, the cartoon boy with his back facing him, raised as a mascot. Bhairava felt prideful for the people and the symbol of suffering they held. The procession went on, voices rising up chanting – voices for peace.

And leading the pro-peace march, determined and gleeful, were two men of prominence. One was quite young, in his mid or late twenties, wearing glasses and a paramedic uniform – Jamel Tamimi. And the other . . . It was *the lecturer*. The *heretic*. The man Ian Mastemah had wanted to depose of due to his antisemitism.

It was the father of the famous Actionman – Joseph from Arizona.

Why was he here? His son, Ben, had been taken away by a paladin in Haditha Dam, so Alfred Bonner had reported. But why was his father in the West Bank?

Operation Defensive Shield was a success, Ian Mastemah had said before. *The Arabs will always remain unilateral. You shall not make a covenant with the gentiles lest they snare you to worshipping other gods. They shall be put under the ban.*

"From here on out," Bhairava said to himself and the spirits. "The fight will be insurgence."

Bhairava, still in the *sunyata*, went on his way, towards his parked car to drive the airport back to America to deal with the Manicheans. There, he could receive more Pneuma from Ian Mastemah.

But Joseph could be problematic.

That man. In order to transcend the material, from deception unto truth, one had to cut, often violently, the blade of truth against the flesh, to sever it, and to save it. Naturally, it would cause harm and agony.

Naturally, Truth was divisive.

31

THE RAMPARTS OF URUK THE SHEEPFOLD

"Under the First Dynasty (of Egypt), when brick architecture came into its own, this new and more permanent architecture was used, at first, for the royal tombs which were decorated with buttresses and recesses on all four sides . . . The recesses and buttresses duplicate exactly the recessing of Protoliterate temples . . . In Mesopotamia the whole method of recessed brick building can be seen to come into being, starting with the temples at Eridu and Tepe Gawra of the Al Ubaid period . . . The exact degree of complexity was reached with which brick building appears under the First Egyptian Dynasty . . . There can be no reasonable doubt that the earliest monumental brick architecture of Egypt was inspired by that of Mesopotamia . . . In conclusion, it is worth noticing that the architectural forms used in Mesopotamia for temples were applied in Egypt to royal tombs and royal castles."

—From *The Birth of Civilization in the Near East*, Henri Frankfort, Project Gutenberg, Doubleday Anchor Books, 1956, pg 127 – 129.

I told you that you should've taken the detour from the other side of the river!" Anthony Bale roared, marching with a purposeful gait following a lorry track. Marcus Theis trailing behind, chagrined from the outburst.

"So let me get this straight," Bale went on. "We were called by the Aegis for security border control, to back up long range reconnaissance – that would be *you* – with one step ahead of the enemy. Instead of hunting for the enemy, it is very clear to me – and no, no, I don't want to hear it – you were hunting for *antiquities!*"

"That's not the ultimate objective, sir," Marcus corrected. "It's the International Atomic Energy Agency we have to thwart." He stalked alongside Anthony, eyes gazing at a sad decayed desolation of sterile sand dunes. Foundations of mudbrick walls and buildings lay derelict, emerging from the sand. The only prominent structure in the denuded area was a vague, marred form of what was once the White Temple according to the locals.

Ahead, archaeologists crowded the ruts in the mud like bees captivated by their honey. Shifting sieves from dirt piles dug by the diggers in wheelbarrows, some working with brushes – the archaeological team were an avid and peculiar working lot. Here, the marines had set up an outpost base to use Uruk as a tactical advantage position to maintain the mobilisation of troops coming up from the Gulf. As the marines roamed around peacefully, the archaeologists remained engrossed in their work.

"We were only conducting a reconnaissance mission," Marcus said, "to clear the way in case of any enemy forces. We wanted to make sure that there weren't any civilian hostages."

"Hostages," Bale scoffed. "I'm still yet to find out *why* I was called to deploy all these units here to look at some diggers!"

"Sir, intelligence informed us that Hussein might be storing secret weapons in bunkers near this site," Marcus said.

Anthony Bale barked out a curt laugh. "How many times have I heard crap like that and each time we look for said weapons, we find nothin'!"

Marcus sighed dismayed. A general misconception of intelligence would be detrimental for the war effort as a whole, miscommunication would cost everything. But why did Bale have to be so stubborn? Marcus could have done this all day, quarrelling and trying to convince those who didn't understand the truth of the matter.

Terrorist roamed the countryside. Civilian hostages were a serious issue.

"Okay sir," Marcus prodded, raising his voice. "We managed to clear out all potential terrorists from Warka."

Anthony held out his hand to stop Marcus and he walked into it.

"Just like that cuckoo Sentinels Unit was blamed for letting those robbers destroy the museum, and now you're going to do it here? Is this what I'm supporting? Huh?!"

"No, General." Marcus pursed his lips. "No."

"Anthony Bale!"

Spinning around, Marcus met Colonel Terry Sopher of the Aegis, standing all tall and confident causing Bale to salute.

"Is there a problem, Anthony Bale?"

Anthony eyed the ground as soldiers marched to their placements around the outpost. "Colonel, no there's no problem!"

"We have a distress call from Colonel Judd Pounders at Haditha Dam," Sopher said, pulling out a com kit. "A crew captain has gone missing, and his position may compromise the 75th Ranger Regiment Eidolons from properly holding the dam. He requests, if you're willing, to reassign some of your soldiers to aid in his search and rescue, and back up the dam's defences. I can tell this mission holding off a pile of *rocks* is frustrating for you, so this opportunity sounds a bit better."

Marcus perked up. He knew that the captain of the 75th Ranger Regiment Eidolon was Ben DePaula. "Sir," Marcus whispered but he cut himself off, unwilling to disturb the meeting for propriety's sake. *Ben is missing? The Actionman captured by the enemy? How on earth?!*

"Ha, well," Anthony Bale said, persisting in stubbornness. "That is unfortunate. I will see to this then." He gave Marcus the dagger eye, saying, *Next time, punk.*

Well, you stubborn bastard, Marcus thought, *I hope you do something better than complain and go up there and find Ben!*

"Good," Sopher said. "You're dismissed."

"Finally." Anthony immediately groaned as he strode past Marcus, muttering to himself.

"Well, sir, you got me out of that one," Marcus said, grinning.

"Looked like he was going to cook you," Colonel Sopher said.

"I'm already cooked sir. What were the updates at Haditha?" Marcus asked. They both stopped, overlooking the archaeologists scribbling notes, laying measurements and supervising the diggers walking out from a mudbrick platform towards the shade under a tent with a table of electronic devices and a generator to the right.

With hands clasped around his back and observing the excavation of the silty moat, Sopher said, "I don't bloody know what happened over there at Haditha Dam. Now the Eidolons have apparently lost Ben DePaula on a scouting mission. They failed to stay in contact with him, but *things* got complicated. Sorry for the unfortunate news, Captain, but I just don't have enough information yet."

Lost Ben . . . That's bad.

"Wait, Colonel, you said before that Director Bonner is arriving. The area looks pretty secure to me. Why is he coming?"

"Don't ask me." Sopher grunted, crossing his arms, his eyes hidden under his dark sunglasses. "Something to do with Blue Shield, Captain. With the collapse of authority, there has been a lot of plundering of archaeological sites – Iraq and Kurdistan mind you, are one of the densest locations of ancient ruins. This is why Bonner has come to make sure this one, is kept safe. The man is a character – he wants to stand out by becoming a UNSECO law enforcer by protecting cultural heritage from war. It is very honourable of him to go so far out of his way to do that. So, now we're protecting this ruined city."

"Doesn't even look like a city," Marcus said. "Heck, I would have walked right over it if archaeologists were not digging here. How old is this city anyway?" It had not stood the test of time and had vanished into sand. It seemed to hold no value to Marcus.

Sopher shrugged with an exasperated expression that exclaimed, *Does it look like I know? Ask them!*

Searching for answers, Marcus glanced at the archaeological supervisor – an authoritative man with a red-and-white bandana around his head. He had a distinctive round sunburned nose, with black hair and a bushy beard. He emerged from under the shade shelter, bouncing on his feet, his keen eyes downcast, reading a sheet of results.

"Excuse me, sir," Marcus said feeling foolish. "Uh, how old is this city here? It doesn't look very spectacular."

"I know. I know. Less than five per cent of the site has been excavated," the head archaeologist muttered with a Bavarian accent, not meeting his eyes,

"Really? So, we are just getting started?"

"No," replied the archaeologist curtly, his gaze meeting Marcus, an impish grin plastered on his face. "It's been a hundred years since we started. We still haven't examined the neighbourhoods but excavating destroys the site from exposure."

"What is this city?"

"The great city of Uruk. It's one of the first cities ever."

"The first?!"

"Well, officer, there is another site called Tell Brak which was constructed at the same scale of Uruk but much earlier. Uruk is the more famous one because of its elite architecture. And also, keep in mind, archaeology is arbitrary. It often favours places that were not necessarily the most important in their own time but the ones that have been excavated produce the most dramatic finds. Which means whatever we find, was either destroyed or abandoned.

"But Uruk in its time was *very* important. It held around sixty thousand to one hundred and forty thousand people. Two hundred and fifty hectares. Petr Charvát last year said Uruk equals to the size of the Greek polis of Athens around 500 BCE. Uruk was the first site where urban civilisation arose. This is why this sacred city remained so important to the people of Mesopotamia for so long. It was occupied from 3300 BCE to 200 CE. Over *forty-five* hundred years."

That's almost five thousand years old! Marcus' eyes widened. The antiquity struck him as pleasurably fascinating. Since he was patrolling this ancient land, he might as well do something wise with his time and ask more questions from the experts. He lifted his chin, impressed. "Have you made any new discoveries?"

"Oh, now you remind me, officer," the archaeologist uttered with an upbeat diction. "Our recent survey has detected large square subterranean chambers in the Stone Cone Building in the Level III layer of the city. There are multiple doorways, allowing entrance into the main hallway from each side of the rooms. In some areas, it penetrates as far deep as Levels VI to IV."

"Which means?"

"Oh, it's one of the early layers that dates to about 3000 – 2300 BCE which is the Early Dynastic Period. Its oldest layers lie virtually unexplored, submerged deep in the mud of the alluvial plain."

"So that means…?"

"We found something." He smiled with an optimistic grin. "The results of magnetometric prospecting are *groundbreaking*. Ah! Sorry but you know what?" He shrugged. "Those are archaeologist puns."

"You never know what could surprise you, Joerg Fassbinder," Sopher said, coming over next to Marcus, looking out into the distance as if he was waiting for someone to arrive. "There is a reason why we are here."

"Yes." A second archaeologist sauntered towards them, scowling from under his wide-brimmed hat and pointing at a map. "I reckon it has to do with what we found. We might uncover something historically staggering like the Burials of Ur. We need all security and restrictions to protect it if this is what I think it is."

Marcus crossed his arms. "And what is it, exactly?"

"The possibility that this could be the tomb of Gilgamesh!" The first archaeologist proclaimed happily.

"Joerg," said the second archaeologist gravely, clearing this throat. "That's crazy. The 'anomaly' pinpointed by magnetic resistivity is Jemdet Nasr and Early Dynastic I material remains. Nothing to do with Gilgamesh."

"Ricardo Eichmann," Joerg said. "Wonderful scholar, I still believe we have struck something important. It is as large as the Eanna district itself. It has the same bevelled façade as the Uruk IV buildings. It looks like a house plan under the ground. Or . . . suites of subsidiary rooms."

Ricardo shoved a glossy poster in front of Joerg, allowing Marcus and Sopher to glimpse the plan of the ancient metropolis highlighted with the stratification of settlement layers done by the remote sensing scan. "Ah, you romantic," Ricardo said. "I should warn you, that the conclusion that this structure is *the* tomb of Gilgamesh is pure speculation. This structure underneath the Eanna district – the central religious administration – would have to date, approximately, three thousand eight hundred years before the common era. This is five hundred years older than the historical Gilgamesh – King Enmebaragesi of Kish – who ruled from circa 2600 BCE."

"But that is not when this dates to," Joerg said.

"You see Joerg, the Uruk tablets from before 2600 BCE are *broken* at the top of the profession hierarchy lists. So, we cannot know if this structure at this time is for a king or a high priest that ruled the city or of a council! Or if it was just for the cult of Inanna! We cannot ever know!"

"But the myths, they—"

"Are *un*reliable historically!" Ricardo exclaimed.

Marcus shook his head. *Is this what professionals do all the time? Argue? Coming to no consensus?*

"Oh, but I was saying there is *some* truth to the stories," Joerg insisted. "Maybe there was more than one Gilgamesh then."

Ricardo's right eyebrow crept into his forehead.

"Boys, you realise mythology are just stories that are sacred. It is dynamic and can shift according to setting and context." At Joerg's side was an erudite woman in khaki fieldwork uniform wearing a hat over her brown hair. She slipped into the discourse, saying with a German accent, "Even if this new find was of any significance, it is showing the remarkable ambitious corvee labour of the state. I think this was part of the newer section of the temple." She pointed down at the niche-shaped wall over the pit they were digging on the map.

Marcus read that the square structure was marked as RB – the Round Pillar Hall or the Riemchen Building. It was superimposed over a large rectangular building with a protective outer wall labelled 'SC', the legend interpreting it as "Stone Cone Building". *Why is it called Stone Cone?* Marcus looked out at the diggers working around a building and a large muddy mound that formed the heavily eroded indistinct shape of the Stone Cone Building's enclosure wall. A space in the square-shaped retaining wall formed a cist, cut through the topsoil into a hollow space under the Stone Cone Building.

"In my opinion," the female archaeologist went on, "this structure is an artificially created dyke or canal. It shows the economic power of Uruk. It is made of limestone and diorite, and that had to be imported from outside Mesopotamia. The Mesopotamians also needed vast quantities of bitumen and logs from the north upriver. And the task to do that, to load the boats, was by diverting water from the river into inland canals, making these cities into ports. This might be what this structure was used for. It is not a tomb. We know water management irrigation increased around 3500 BCE on the onset of drier, cooler climate, which yielded vast amounts of canal construction and agricultural surpluses, with extensive canal systems for year-round water management, facilitating the transport of the harvest and taxed grain to temple and royal granaries. Uruk in its day, was a Venice."

"Wow," Marcus said, gazing at the barren flat desert all around him. "But not today."

"The Neo-Assyrian king Sennacherib I in the first millennium BCE mastered this feat," the woman lectured. "He built an aqueduct. Such geographical development during this rich period of Mesopotamian history could explain why old cities declined. The water table changes, the rivers change course. A bit like what Hussein is doing now, drying up the marshes down south with the Glory River to starve the Marsh Arab communities."

Marcus squinted in the heat when she mentioned the Marsh Arabs and the ways dictators could use the ecology for civil terrorism. "What Assyrian aqueduct are you talking about? I don't know about this."

"Oh," the woman met his eyes, smiling. "It's the Jerwan Aqueduct in the present-day Dohuk region of Iraqi Kurdistan. Just like this structure we found here, it's made out of limestone."

"And what period was this around?" Marcus asked. He felt like a complete dimwitted fool asking such a question – he hardly understood anything. He thought the Romans invented aqueducts, yet he barely remembered learning of the ancient history of Iraq at school – he was irked how the curriculum taught European and American political and military history alone. Boredom waiting around for Alfred Bonner gave him surprising chances to discover new things.

"During the fierce Neo-Assyrian empire, 911 – 612 BCE," the woman said, "the empire covered a vast region with their road systems as far into the Levant, Egypt, up north into south-eastern Turkey, and the Zagros mountains." She smelled of perfume, even when covered with dust from work. "It was over two thousand years after the heyday of Uruk. But with all this dried silt around this site, it means the natives were able to channel water from the river like the aqueduct into the city district. It's my theory that such water technology was inspired by the Sumerians during the Late Uruk Period from 3300 to 3000 BCE."

Who the hell were the Sumerians? "Fascinating. What is your name?"

"Margarete."

"Whatever you are finding, Margarete, it will be big. Keep up the good work," Marcus said, giving her a thumbs up. He cringed from his flattering show of optimism. At least it made the pretty archaeologist blush and smile wondrously at him.

Though as much as Marcus wanted to spend time around Margarete asking her questions, studying her cute eyes filled with wisdom and wit, he had to check on his men. He found them dozing around on a mound under a tent, drinking Tab soda. Marcus pondered why Alfred Bonner would be interested in occupying this site when Johnny Best noticed his scowls. "What is down there was hidden for a purpose," the twenty-year-old said to Marcus, sipping his soda, smacking his lips.

"But we need to learn more about it. To know why we are protecting it." Marcus didn't meet Johnny's eyes as he squinted in the sun, leaning his arms on his knees, fixated on the dig. Marcus didn't want the money or fame like Ben, no, he was interested to find out *why* this old ancient chamber attracted Bonner's interest.

Suddenly, a series of panicked shouts drew Marcus and his Aegis crew from their exchanges. A formation of armed marines with guns trailed on diggers, startling everyone from their drudgery and toil. Margarete and her two colleagues stopped their discussion, staring up in shock and disbelief.

"Everyone, please stop what you're doing!" a sonorous voice of an officer blared over the bustle of murmuring workers and Arab diggers. Joerg Fassbinder and Ricardo Eichmann peered up at the ruckus, holding their hats in a daze. "This is a national emergency!" the same voice declared. The Arab workers obstinately escorted themselves away, not wanting any trouble. "We are now taking full control of this site! Please collect your tools and gear and evacuate immediately! It is not safe to excavate!"

Face grimaced with dismay, and eyes bright with strained panic, Margarete stalked up to one of the officers – a tall brawny man with light brown hair, almost red.

"I'm really sorry," he said to her kindly, as if she were some animal trapped in a jar and he was being humane by letting her free.

"For what? Who are these people?"

"American security services. You have to go now please."

"I'm being fired?!"

"No mam. Only... annual leave, for as long as the war persists. It's only temporarily."

All this for a cist in the ground at the Stone Cone Building? Striding up a rise of earth in the distance, a new stream of black ops soldiers rounded up the diggers and archaeologists, some putting their hands up when the soldiers trained their semiautomatics at them. Marcus felt anger grip him, and oddly, fear of uncertainty by such unnecessary action.

There, a blond-haired Alfred Bonner marched up the incline. Wearing a white-collared shirt, sleeves rolled up, in dark pants. Bonner's body had a design of perfect equations gone unnaturally well, for his face seemed to be made of stony planes and angles, weathered but inexorable in their sharpness and definition. His flashing blond, white hair enhanced his icy blue eyes – pools of cracked ice over water. His whole form was square and brawny, prowling over the clay and mud. He held himself with a reverent graceful air which without his height, would have still been overpowering. Even the battle scar on his cheek seemed to extenuate his cruelty with a type of stubborn determination. Bonner alone sauntered up the mudbrick ruins towards Sopher, Marcus and the Aegis, staring at the opening of the square low wall of the Stone Cone Building and down into the dark hole in the topsoil, brooding, thinking. Marcus shifted on his feet.

"Hey! Excuse me!" Braving the man, Ricardo Eichmann stormed towards Bonner. He remained so placid and still, not turning to meet the archaeologist. "We don't want to cause any trouble," Ricardo shouted. "This is my site and you have no right to—"

"Evacuate your archaeologists. We'll take it from here." Bonner's lips curled as he spoke, his grating voice as dry as the mudbrick. He slipped his hand into his coat, pulling out a document bearing a Blue Shield, giving it to Ricardo. Procrastinating, he took the document, grimacing.

Then Bonner spoke up and said calmly, "We issued public warnings, reminding US leaders of their responsibilities under international law, notably the 1954 Hague Convention. I hope that our men can guarantee that this site will not be damaged or targeted without an imperative military necessity, and due to such complacency on the ground. ICOMOS made this a high priority for the occupying forces. Is that understood, man?"

"Who are you people?" Ricardo asked in astonishment, blinking dumbly at the Blue Shield authorisation document. Marcus had seen that diamond-shaped blue-and-white shield logo before – it had something to do with the nongovernment organisation that protected cultural heritage. They prioritised the security of sites as part of their organisation. Protecting places, in an effect, was protecting the people.

Bonner towered above the man, eyeing him intently. "We are the future. We are the Alliance, who seek for answers in the forgotten past. Everything is cyclical. Nothing is new under the sun." Bonner placed a robust, reassuring hand on Ricardo's shoulder, ogling the dig site. "I am the enforcer of UNESCO law. You can go now, Eichmann. I am sparing your career."

"Yes . . ." Ricardo's face blanched. "Yes, Director Alfred Bonner."

"What is going on, Director?" Marcus said.

"Ah. There you are Marcus Theis, Terry Sopher," Bonner said. "I have a special task for you. You will be my scouting crew. The first people in five thousand years to behold Rostau."

Sopher clamped a hand on Marcus' shoulder startlingly. "Ah Marcus, so apparently, you're going down there." He pointed at the hole in the retaining wall in the stone cone enclosure.

You got to be kidding *me!* A marine going into an ancient chamber never seen by humans for five thousand years?! "*Why!?* What strategic asset is down there that will help us win this war?! Sir, this must be a misunderstanding. We're *soldiers*, not explorers!"

"The archaeologists encumber, not prioritising the Alliance's objective, unfortunately," Bonner said, sliding an imperious glance of warning for Ricardo's crew to stay out of business. For now.

"Orders are orders, Marcus," Sopher said blithely. "Once you are down there, Bonner will not bother us again. He just doesn't want to cause any trouble. Okay?"

"Yes, Colonel," Marcus said reluctantly. "Whatever you say, Director. You're under Blue Shield." And in the light of that, Marcus hoped he could trust him.

"Good," Bonner said gruffly, hands on his hips.

Marcus kept his mouth shut, and turned to his men, his mind surging with puerile complaints. Chilled by Bonner's gaze, and the implications of his words, Marcus saw Bill Sargent watching Sopher saying, "I don't like it,

Colonel," he whispered. As disruptive wind whipped his clothing, and fearful in countenance, he glanced at the cist. "Whatever is down there, I don't want to be responsible for opening Pandora's Box."

In Sopher's eyes, behind those dark shades, Marcus glimpsed a spark of vexation. "That box had been open long ago, son. You want to know why we are doing this? We need to go where need takes us now. To protect world heritage from Saddam Hussein's destruction." He looked at Bonner intently, and Marcus – bewildered – could tell that Alfred Bonner had already sowed the seeds of his agenda into Sopher's mind with promises, and now they were proliferating. "Were going down into the earth. No questions asked."

32

LIFE AMONG THE RUINS

"The Gebel el-Arak knife (c. 3450 BCE) scene is not the only representation of the hero figure 'controlling' wild animals found in pre-dynastic Egypt. At Hierakonpolis the same figure holds back two opposing feline creatures, perhaps lions, and it represents the earliest borrowed design in Egyptian art. This motif is recognised as originating in the lands of Sumer and Susiana. It has been long recognised that the man on the Gebel el-Arak knife handle is a Lugal, en or ensi from Uruk. An extraordinary close parallel is to be found on the Lion Hunt Stele from Uruk (3000-2900 BCE), now in the Baghdad Museum. The Gilgamesh style iconography of the hero of the Gebel el-Arak knife handle found in Egypt is Sumerian."

—From Joshua Tanrıöver's Honours Thesis on the Trade and Cultural Exchange Between Pre-Dynastic Egypt with Uruk and Jemdet Nasr Mesopotamia, Willamette University.

James Casbolt stood side by side with Konstantinos with their interpreter Nasullah, before chairman of Hatran pre-Islamic history, Ba'ath party official Dr Jaber Ibrahim.

Jaber reeked of defeat. The promise Casbolt had kept protecting the museum had been a joke. He needed to bounce back to prove himself worthy to the UN, but the failure of protecting cultural property had suffered collateral damage. Coalition commanders appeared to have done little or nothing at all to prevent acts of looting and destruction in Baghdad, even though tanks and detachments of foot soldiers were stationed in the central city. Colonel David Perkins had said that the National Museum of Iraq couldn't be protected. Even worse, Casbolt had in vain tried to stop a punctual disaster. A major show of force by platoons trained in crowd control might have succeeded in deterring or dispersing some looters, but the military had no such policing forces in its structure.

Yet Casbolt would make up for this. God, he would, it was his *geas*, his obligation to help restore the Baghdad Museum for the rest of his time here in Iraq. He had to complete what he started, to try something new. Something different.

"Looters have stolen the artefacts from the museum," Casbolt said. "We have come to find out what happened and protect them."

"A little too late for that," Jaber intoned via translator.

"And we want to begin assessments," Demos added. He had to sound willing and easy going to get this job. "We can get our act together to fix this. We can determine what happened, as the law of the patrimony still holds: all the things that come out of Iraqi ground are the property of the Iraqi people."

Casbolt nodded vigorously. That had become their slogan of this whole enterprise: *recovering the property of the Iraqi people.*

Dr Jaber Ibrahim smiled in a distant and benign way. He had olive skin, and was clean shaven, with a stark white moustache on his upper lip which he stroked persistently. "You?" he said, filtered through Nasullah. "I expected the UN to come and do everything, but you two? *Insha' Allah,* I guess you two Americans will help us instead then. Welcome and take a seat." He did not seem offended, just taken aback.

Tea came next – tea from none other than the museum director and cuneiform expert Dr Nawala al-Mutwali, an older woman wearing a pink *khimar* headscarf. Her face did not give away any emotional distress, but Casbolt could smell she had remarkable self-control.

He stood up as she offered tea. He went to touch her hand away – he did not want tea, he wanted to help these people and not be served like he was a superior – but she evaded him. With a sudden bound, her foot stubbed the corner of the desk in the process. The sound and the way her face went all taut, the skin around her eyes tightening, neck tensing, Casbolt knew she'd broken her toe. Yet she kept a good hand's distance away from him. She *refused* him to touch her!? *I was only trying to—*

She doesn't like being touched; Michael Prince intoned.

Sex sick pervert!

Casbolt sweated. He felt like dying from embarrassment right then.

Luckily, Demos helped Casbolt saying, "Dr al-Mutwali is not an Ash Wednesday, Palm Sunday Muslim. Men, especially non-Muslim men, cannot lay a finger on Muslim women."

Casbolt stared at the cuneiform expert, her lips pursing and silent. He as the hired help, who had incurred *geas* – he should be *serving* this woman. "Uhm . . . ah . . . Sorry," Casbolt said. "You have the tea. I'm okay. I'm here to help. Not you. You've done more than enough, Dr al-Mutwali." The Parvus disclosed to Casbolt that Demos harboured the same idea.

Yet, Dr Nawala al-Mutwali had proven herself that she was not only headstrong, but very intelligent and determined, very aware of others' needs, like a waitress.

Afterwards, while going on an afternoon stroll in Baghdad in the heat of the afternoon to the falafel stand, Nawala to Casbolt and Demos said, "What we have done – and continue to do – with this archaeological record, is to tell our own stories, through our own perspectives, for our own society. When we select to curate a museum, we are selecting, editing, personalising, and sometimes idealising glimpses of history. This is why I love archaeology, you see? It is not about things. Archaeology is about the people who created those things. I hope you understand." And Casbolt wanted to. "When you have an artefact, tangible in your hands, whether its drabware pottery or gold treasure, it's valuable. It is honest. It is not like a text that can be read by multiple people, who read it with subjective opinions on what something means. But archaeology, it is undeniable proof that speaks for itself."

"Only issue," Demos noted quizzically. "Is people have to *interpret* the objects."

"Some more than others!" Nawala chortled.

The first order of business recommended the aid of law-enforcement and art experts to survey the museum and to make public a police amnesty for the safe and free return of stolen artefacts. It took a while to get enforced, but Demos, with his pugnacious Manhattan assistant district attorney, requested that he be allowed to handpick a small group – James Casbolt included – to assist him. It was so they could be given the autonomy they needed to be able to go where they wanted at will without having to go through channels. In a show of just how deeply embarrassed the military had been, Demos' amnesty was granted without the batting of an eyelash.

But unfortunately, Iraqis in this country were disillusioned having Westerners taking control over their devastated country and livelihoods – they were not interested in a museum looting at this moment when there were more dire matters of concern. Such misgivings were understandable – these Westerners had just invaded their country! But Casbolt viewed this campaign as liberation – the Iraqis he was rubbing shoulders with day in, and day out, were supposed to be Casbolt's enemies, but the true enemy, the true invader, was Saddam Hussein – invader of two Muslim countries, murderer of over one million Muslims and Kurds.

Casbolt – and at times Michael Prince who'd often come forward – had come to point out during the investigations, that if people were not going to help, they had to start cleaning the damaged artefacts and the wreckage first in the museum. The removal of an object from its context without proper recording, or the disturbance of a site, meant that all the information it could have yielded about that context had been lost, and the full significance of the object or feature might never be understood.

Demos, Casbolt and their law-enforcement and art-expert partners couldn't have done their jobs without Dr Nawala al-Mutwali's guidance. She had been extremely cooperative, going above and beyond to confirm that an object was stolen when Casbolt and Demos walked around the museum, recording and pointing out places where damage and signs of looting had occurred.

Together, they had surmised, the looters had struck in three waves, between April 8th and 12th, with an estimate at some fifteen thousand stolen artefacts. They stole everything they came across at random; from sculpture, ceramics, pottery sherds, jewellery, metalwork, architectural fragments, cuneiform tablets and a large percentage of the valuable Sumerian cylindrical seals and all the objects in the basement. The latter items had particularly made Nawala hold her head in distress when she inspected the condition of the head of a Lugal – a big man or king – broken and shattered in the basement.

Parenthetically, Casbolt and Demos found out that looters in Iraq divided among several distinct social groups, each with different motivations, were eager to take anything they needed to survive. They were average joes and hardly organised. They did not know how to commit to a heist – some of them even stole an entire shelf of replicas and fakes en route, amusingly. And yet, not all such looters were mundane. One was an Aes Sidhe – the Carnute Gladius Huyard which Casbolt thought was vengefully sent by intelligence to steal artefacts while tracking Casbolt down.

Demos said that the tragedy on this scale was like the burning of the Library of Alexandria and the sacking of Baghdad's universities by the Mongols. "It's alright," he said optimistically to frustrated Nawala, who was losing her strength and hope. "These things happen during war. Mesopotamia has suffered repeated plundering of its cultural patrimony from the Elamites and the Assyrians. Alexander's men on his Greek crusade to free the Greek cities in Asia Minor, got drunk with his men and looted and burned down the Persian palace of Persepolis. Then there was the American crusade to get revenge for 9/11, and they too allowed the looting of Baghdad. History. It just happens."

It was truly catastrophic. Many of the items at Baghdad not stolen bore the scars and cracks, toppled over from their protective foam. It took over a month trying to build adhesive relationships with the locals, to not just promote the amnesty program, but also start developing potential informants, playing backgammon and vesting social cues. In June, Casbolt finally started to make some progress.

First, the amnesty had gotten the attention from admitting antiquities authorities from the Mosul Museum. They led the investigative foray into the nearby mosque, the imam gladly opened a chest full of manuscripts that he had been "safe keeping" during the invasion. "He'd been ahead of us!" Demos said favourably.

An international effort had slowly begun to recover, repurchase or seize more than five thousand objects, culminating when ancient history's greatest hits started to come back. Fortunately, Iraqi museum curators had transferred many objects in the collection to safe storage prior to the war; and these were mostly intact.

People started showing up at the museum gate with items and missing artefacts miraculously appeared in the restoration room, strongly suggesting that these had not been looted at all but taken by diligent, sensible staff members. As war clouds gathered, a few conscientious civilians, not trusting either the museum itself or American forces to provide adequate protection, took, or tried to take, direct action. The amnesty had saved all of the four hundred and fifty-one public display cases such as those holding the famed Bassetki Statue, a lamassu from Sargon II's palace in Khorsabad (722 – 705 BCE) and a Neanderthal skeleton.

But Casbolt's favourite object had to be the return of the famous alabaster Warka Lady (3100 BCE). She had been found buried in a backyard in a farmhouse north of Baghdad, wrapped in tarps of plastic. She came along with the Warka Vase (3200 BCE) and the King Entemena of Lagash basalt statue (2450 BCE). Casbolt remembered avidly, it all came very quickly, when a man arrived at the museum driveway with his truck, carrying the mask of an alabaster lady, her large almond-shaped eye sockets staring up at Casbolt. The man fell on his knees before the marines weeping, holding the head in his hands, pleading sorrowfully in Arabic.

The Warka Lady in his hands looked hauntingly gorgeous – a goddess with neat, scalloped waves of hair curling on her forehead, gentle cheeks framing her nose, her regal nose broken, and her small, delicate mouth set above her petite chin.

Casbolt himself felt tears trying to well up out of his eyes, holding this head. To him, it summarised his vocation up to this point. Recovering. Reconstruction. Rebuilding. All this pertained to his reprograming, spreading the awareness of child trafficking and abuse, as well as remaking his legacy in the ruin of his guilt. As he exposed the darkness, he could help rebuild, not just his life but the *culture* of other people.

In Casbolt's opinion, this Lady was beyond politics, and religion and conspiracy theory. She predated it all. She was primal, prehistoric. However, that same guy who brought back the Lady, carried in the Vase and Entemena back, of course, gave Casbolt *another* cup of tea!

This had been at least the *tenth* time he had tea! Why did the Iraqis have to serve him so much tea? He was really starting to feel irked after long tedious days hunting and investigating, being woken up every dawn by the eerie and majestic Fajr salah prayers over the loudspeakers from the mosque down the street. But Demos was laughing with glee, sipping his tea, reporting to the CNN, BBC and National Geographic news reporters saying, "The items are coming back. They were not stolen by Saddam – the largest crook of all – but mothers are turning in items stolen by their sons. Friends are taking back items stolen by friends. Employees are turning in items stolen by their bosses. People are sympathetic and are emotionally tied to ancient cultures, because in a sense, they are something much more meaningful than simple treasures to be stolen."

The whole world would know now what happened when Iraq crumbled into pieces. There was still an optimistic lookout for the Assyrian ivory Lioness Attacking a Nubian (8th century BCE). The longer it took to come, the more likely it had been sold away in the black market.

But there was new hope. After investigating the Central Bank, Demos had an inkling that there would be a chance to recover the Nimrud Treasures of the Assyrian king Ashurnasirpal II's wife Mullissu-mukannishat-Ninua and two other Neo-Assyrian queens, Yaba and Atalia.

Demos – as he often did too regularly – recounted the history, that the city of Nimrud was originally called Calah or Kalhu – it was termed Nimrud by early archaeologists who were trying to find evidence of the Bible in the

Near East. Nimrud/Kalhu became the capital of the Assyrian empire when Ashurnasirpal II took the throne from 883 to 859 BCE, highlighted by the moving from the traditional religious capital of Ashur to this already ancient site of Kalhu for his imperial palace.

The Central Bank was on Rashid Street, situated on the east side of the Tigris River, where the al-Ahrar Bridge spanned road over the great river. Its entrance into the lobby had been completely annihilated – a catastrophic pile of mangled, twisting metal bars, vents, cords, scaffolding, scraps and rubble strewn in chaotic deposits of destruction. Getting past that obstruction onto the bank had only been the beginning. After pumping out nearly five million gallons of water that had flooded the massive hole in the basement, they resurfaced a gruesome heavy steel door at the end of a long tunnel, dented and damaged. Casbolt found out why: someone had tried to blow up the vault – a suspected rocket-propelled grenade lay on the damp floor was evidence of that.

Casting torch lights down the spiral staircase into the wet chamber, Casbolt, Demos, Nawala, her student Selma al-Radi and some others, all watched as the bank manager Muhammad, spun three-cylinder vault bolts. Heart thundering in his chest, Casbolt awaited what could be behind that steel door. Nawala's breathing became rasps.

Muhammad opened the door.

Besides the mother lode of eight hundred million Iraqi dinars in canvas stacks in a room covered in an inch of water – Casbolt's light illuminated waterlogged spongy crates. One had a footlocker, but Demos lifted the other box in hope, only to pour water out of them. In great frustration and disappointment, Nawala suggested opening the boxes in such soggy damp conditions would damage the artefacts, so more waiting, and more delay was necessary.

It was the next morning that Casbolt and the team opened those boxes and found more than what they hoped for. The spectacular hoard of the Nimrud treasure had been preserved in the Central Bank since the Gulf War, held virtually untouched. Also stashed inside the collection was the famous Royal Treasures of the Death Pit of Ur – a city-state two thousand years older than Nimrud – remaining perfectly intact.

To Casbolt's and Demos' joy, they watched the greatest smile grow on Dr Nawala al-Mutwali's face, raising up with two hands the superbly hammered golden helmet of King Meskalamdug (c. 2500 BCE) that replicated the unique hair style of the king. An overwhelming amount of exotic gold necklaces encrusted with gemstones and verdant jewellery, gold anklets and exquisite gold necklaces, resurfaced unharmed.

With trembling knees, Nawala began to sob, and, setting aside thirteen hundred years of Islamic prohibitions, at least for the moment, she gave Casbolt a hug, almost breaking his neck.

"We are reshaping history, Demos. This is an incredible success for both the Iraqi people and for me," Casbolt said. "And the pay is incredible! The money I have gained working here the last two months is, honestly, more than I have ever made."

"You are sure right," Demos said, while unloading the artefacts from the vault into storage crates to be taken back to the Baghdad Museum, handling a crystal bowl with blue plastic gloves, placing it into a foamed storage container. People who had volunteered to join the investigation bustled about in a soft din, stepping gingerly over the clutter of the damp chamber. "Feels damn good to have a purpose and help support the world's culture together."

"I have no idea how this happened," Casbolt said, gently placing an eye idol in the crate. "I never thought I would be here, helping restore museum artefacts in my entire life. And yet, here I am."

"Providence," Demos said.

Casbolt shrugged, grinning. "We were here at the right place at the right time, I guess. In removing the regime, there is a vacuum that was created, and the vacuum will be filled by someone as time goes on. I don't think that anyone anticipated that the riches of Iraq would be looted by the Iraqi people, and indeed it happened in *some* places. America lost most of its prestige and respect in the looting episode. The officials are utterly indifferent to anarchy, careless about preserving civilisation in its very birthplace. When I went to Mosul, I had to volunteer for a week with Marcus Theis' marines to help run a shopping mall. Shopping mall man! Pretty depressing."

Demos nodded. "It was all policy failure. But what is more mysterious is you, a super soldier, helping run a shopping mall. That seems *really* out of character of the Iceni Chief."

"Come on," Casbolt said. "Saddam broke his military force. We're the only justice this country has now."

"How did you go with Mosul, by the way?" Demos enquired. "I heard you killed Saddam Hussein's son's Uday and Qusay with Captain Marcus Theis."

Casbolt heaved out a sigh. That had happened only a week ago, on June 22nd, where he was assigned to a gnarly manhunt for Saddam Hussein. "Yes, I killed Saddam's sons because they were criminals. They deserved to die.

There's no sign of the tyrant himself. He's still in hiding, that coward." Casbolt regarded Demos. "Do you kill?"

Face serene and calm, lips in a straight line, Demos shook his head. "I believe killing is a motivation rather than an action. If I physically kill a villainous aggressor with a gun, and I have the intent to save the lives of the innocent and protect others, then killing the aggressor is not murder. It is just the consequences of violence. I just become a just agent of fate. You know what I mean?"

Casbolt nodded, relaxing from Demos' strong sense of balanced ethics and morality. It reminded him much about Michael Oppenheim's strong resolve about killing and fighting. "Alright. Just know, Demos, that my life has been a violent one and violent lives create violent people."

"So, was that all you did at Mosul?"

"I killed," Casbolt said dryly. "It was a raid against Saddam's sons who led a revolt against the occupation."

Oh, God, you compromised, Michael Prince trembled. *What reckless dalliance with Timarah! She's vulnerable without her husband who I killed. She's likely pregnant with my child and in Islam, abortion is murder, so she will suffer, because of me.*

But it felt so good, an unknown part of Casbolt replied, not sure which alter announced that.

It was hard to maintain credibility of creating order out of disorder, when the US leadership were ignorant of the "on-ground" situations. Saddam may have fallen, but America exacerbated the Iraqi civil war.

While in the heat of the fierce battle in Mosul among the ground infantry troops calling in airstrikes from the coalition, Casbolt and Marcus Theis found an abandoned house, after routing out local Shi'ite militia. Casbolt had been given orders by Colonel Sopher to kill Uday Hussein, and he took it as an opportunity to fight for goodness to outweigh his crimes against the Antarctic Treaty.

Upon arriving at Uday's basement, he found it full of girls – young women all teenagers and young adults. They had all been trafficked.

They had been sex slaves. Most wore shifts, with barely a kerchief and others in full *niqab*, *chador* and *hijabs*.

One of those women, Timarah, had been tied to a pipe under the sink basin in the bathroom, wounded and beaten greatly. She was in the middle of the room, and he knew she was someone important in Uday's harem, but her exclusive access to him had her suffer the worse of his beatings. She carried bruises around her hips, shoulders and had a black eye, cheeks wet with tears. She had passed out, as if dead. There had been something about the abject tilt of her lovely head that gave him sympathy for her plight. Even in such tatters, he stretched out his hand and saw that it was right in Casbolt's eyes to help her. For that reason, he individually took her, and cleaned her.

When she woke up and gained the little confidence to say that she wanted him, she told him how Uday treated her. It angered and sickened Casbolt. She *needed* protection.

On the seventh day of the week in Mosul, Casbolt spoke to the marines in the shopping mall, and they began talking about Casbolt and Timarah. Rumours were already beginning to spread of what the marines had done to the women in captivity in Uday's house, and Casbolt learnt Timarah had caught the eye of other men sent by their superiors to escort the women to rehab where nurses and doctors helped them recover from trauma. Those marines at rehab began to press and tease Casbolt hard to talk to Timarah, to give her "a hand". "You were the hero that saved her after all! She's into you!"

Casbolt gave in to their taunts and went to Timarah at night alone. The way Uday had taught her to act when desperate, ensnared with a lustful desire, infested Casbolt's body. It was like the thrill of the Redlion but subtler, yet it had compassion mixed with his sorrow for this woman. The hot, shameful swelling Casbolt knew as a young boy, came unbidden and unprovoked, a mocking ribaldry if anyone noticed. Something had to be done to reduce the stomach-churning burning. Timarah's eyes were eager as if they knew the swell was brewing between them both.

Timarah had been a woman who let most of her mildly damp obsidian hair tumble loose at her shoulders, and the moonlight cast over them. Her eyes were light grey, wearing a loose robe so Casbolt could discern her slender long legs, a supple rounding of hips.

When Casbolt penetrated her, he never felt so alive. Michael Prince's dignity had been tainted, he screamed in Casbolt's head like a prisoner shackled in chains.

In part due to the Uday's evil, Casbolt let Timarah use him for her own security. He left Mosul the next morning to regroup in Baghdad to rejoin the museum investigation, feeling profane. Dehumanised.

Demos does not need to know about Timarah, Casbolt thought in abashing guilt, placing gold and turquoise rings into the crate. *Dissociate. Dissociate. Dissociate.*

Casbolt would *never* be free. He was like Neil, repeating the sins of his forefather, who corrupted him early.

Then Casbolt noticed a shadow cast over Demos face. "What's wrong?"

"If I were in your place," Demos said, obliviously, placing an item into the box. "I don't think I would have done any better. Everyone of us has sinned James. It is not about beating ourselves up with pity. Rather, what matters is whether we get back up to become a better man."

Casbolt nodded. No more had to be said.

33

GENIUS LOCI

"Dear Loki. Holy Master, Skin Walker of Light, Faceless Immortal.

The Prophecies say that the Ascended Masters will return, as Lord Maitreya will return, rapturing his Chosen Ones, even as Yaldabaoth the Galactic Tyrant descends with the Nephilim to destroy the Earth. My people will arise from Agartha, and they will join you and the Ascended Masters into the sky as the evil world burns away in tyranny.

It is happening. Human and asura contact. Enlightenment. I sense within you is the Light of the world — the only Light that can be shed upon the Path. If you are unable to perceive it within you, it is useless to look for it elsewhere. Only you know the way for the future generations to come. You will enter the Light, but you will never touch the Flame.

At the Transfiguration, Ihidaya - who you call Jesus - revealed the glory for all. Perfection. The controlling the workings of the mind, the spirit and the body. To control the spirits. I have knowledge about Pneumagury that I am willing share with you. But be warned, this knowledge is secret and cannot fall into the wrong hands.

Too many innocent lives have been lost already just for us asura to conduct this majestic art."

—From the Letter of Sanat Kumara, Matrika of the Devotary of Lakshmi to the Skin Walker Loki (who had taken up the form of Adam Weishaupt), translated by Bishop Hilarion of Thelema, 1776.

The tension in the office almost made Julian want to flip the table. He stood next to Derek, under the uncomfortable skin-tingling shadow of John Mulholland and his big chin looming behind them both. He understood *why* Mulholland was disappointed, and it wasn't Julian's fault. They had just lost their best man and no one knew what happened to him. And Julian felt *mad.*

Mulholland took off his cap solemnly. "Anthony's unit just came back and reported no signs of Captain DePaula's body could be found. We've done all we could, and we do well to remember that we can recover from the fact that the previous reconnaissance mission was a victory. The dam is officially in the hands of the United States."

And to add to that, Julian almost said aloud, scathingly, *a Pyrrhic victory indeed!*

Across the strangled room – or rather cellar within the dark castle of the depressing dam – Pounders slouched over his desk, rubbing his face and eyes, letting out a grumbling sigh. "Julian . . ." There was grievous loss on Pounders' face, and a smidge of disbelief. "I don't know what to say . . ." Pounders whispered into his cupped hands at his chin. "You couldn't have been that far from the fire."

No, I wasn't. Something just, bothered him about that. The captain was supposed to look out for the team, not just the team looking out for the captain! "We kept a close eye on him, sir," Julian said. "We did all we could do."

"Then where the *hell* did he go?!" Pounders hissed, abruptly leaning forward. Not flinching, Julian stood strong, narrowing his eyes.

"Colonel," Derek interrupted. "Once we start getting settled in the dam, I am sure Ben will return by then. He's my best friend from high school. I know him well. He *will* return."

"I understand you have hope, but, this is *not right,*" Pounders said firmly. "It is not normal for Ben's communications to completely cut out. We've officially lost him. He's most likely dead or captured by the enemy. Do you seriously think he is still out there, Derek? After a week of constant fighting?"

"Sir, yah know, I just refuse to believe he was killed. Once Anthony's men secured the perimeter and the first search crew extinguished the fires that were started in the town, sending out search parties, there was not even a body in that burning building we saw him run into."

"And when there is no body . . ." Julian began, hopeful. *Resurrection!*

"You know how hot a burning building is, Derek?" Pounders uttered. "His body would have been cremated!"

"Sir, he's a blockbuster stuntman."

"The roof and floors already collapsed. Not to mention the smoke . . ."

Julian watched Derek stand confidently at attention. The Colonel didn't ask a question, so Derek didn't reply. Sweat gleaned and trickled down the faces of everyone in the cellar, and Julian's shirt was already beginning to darken in patches, cleaving to his skin.

Julian admired Derek's faith in Ben. It made him feel bad, or not worthy enough, to banish those images in his head of Ben – suffering, choking and falling through the floor and knocking his head, or crushed by a tumbling roof, burning alive. That made Julian awfully anxious, committing him to the agency of anger. That hot-rod Ben was indestructible sometimes. By God, everyone looked up to him!

"No body will find him," Pounders muttered.

"No body? Well, it means he *is* going to come back, sir," Julian said. "I swear he will come right back into the dam at some unexpected time under the cover of night and surprise everyone."

"You can count on us on vigil, sir," Derek said. "You don't worry."

Pounders sighed, leaning back in his chair closing his eyes. "I did not come to order you *away* from your chosen task to deliver those prisoners. There are too many of them captured after the victory today. And yes, even if you were on night watch, those damn two-thousand-pound bombs are going off all night!"

Yeah, those bombs are starting to get annoying, Julian thought, *even in the dam you'd think there is an earthquake happening. That's another reason why we are on night watch. Can't sleep.*

No one could sleep in such a dam; it gave Julian a sense of avid anxiety that someone, even in the pure black, watched him, studying him keenly. He felt a persisting slimy tingling sensation – a tickle so familiar – it made his hair bristle. A reminder . . . of *her*. From the other side.

Enough! Julian shook his head. *Just want to get out of this danmed dam!*

"I also want to make sure you are caring for yourselves on watch," Pounders continued. "No men are able to skip meals, and sleep by staying out there, outside on the roads. And I don't want you getting ideas about going out there where mines were going off. You understand?"

"Yes, Colonel," Julian said.

"Pounders, have you had any consultation lately with Director Alfred Bonner on this issue?" Mulholland interjected.

"He's not calling back," Pounders said leaning in his chair.

"That's unprofessional," Derek said.

"I'm starting to worry that I made a grave mistake giving Bonner jurisdiction of this mission," Pounders muttered.

"So, what do we do, sir?" Julian said. "We can go on night watch all we want, but the other units are going to have *a lot* of questions about Ben."

Rubbing his chin, Pounders leaned with his arm resting on the table. "Another rescue mission is going to be too risky unless the area is permanently abandoned by the enemy. I doubt it since we have already had three teams go down already. The Iraqis are bound to be suspicious by now and it's only a matter of time they catch us by surprise, and we lose our dam. If Ben's still alive, he would have surely been captured. Tortured. Beaten."

Words so morbid. Julian couldn't imagine Ben being limp on the ground and trembling weakly in excruciating pain, bashed in the face, until his bruises rendered him unidentifiable. Not even a criminal deserved such a brutal reprimand. "We want to get out of the dam and get some fresh air," Julian said, eyes gazing across the walls. "Just a lot of Rangers are telling stories of weird stuff going on in this place."

"Well then," Pounders sniffed in derision, going solemn, sounding torn and unwilling. "We have to move on with the mission. We can continue searching for Ben, but I fear it will risk our defences. If Ben doesn't come by the end of the week, then . . . Then there will be *no reason* to be waiting anymore. Now, get to your task. The prisoners are restless."

—

Later that evening, Julian and Derek finally got the time to deal with the Iraqi prisoners from the day's victory, and then to resume their night watch for Ben to return.

Night duty. That meant night-vision goggles again for there had been a massive blackout down at the lower sectors of the dam.

The Eidolons, all except for Joshua – who was working on his medical reassignment – gathered in the Haditha Dam turbine room, settling the docile prisoners down for a rest break. The marines were humane, they never bashed prisoners to the edge of their life, bleeding and bruised to break them for information about Ben. That would be against protocol. It would get them a Duck Dinner – dishonourable discharge. Committing such an act would not only be the end of one's life to gain a living, but it would have severe damages and consequences for the whole reputation of the Marine Corps.

The turbine chamber looked like a villain's lair right out of a James Bond movie, with its vast open spaces, giant rooms with transformers, high-voltage wires and indecipherable machines festooned with dials and knobs. Catwalks and railings rose up on differing levels, spiralling industriously over the large turbines which droned and vibrated like the grumbling hums of a snoring beast. At times, it slightly deviated in pitch, as if the unit turbines chugging water had been tuned and altered by the fingers of . . . *something*. A rotten greenish yellow, dim green light shone sickly upon the tall arched ceiling, casting shadows over the six massive hydro-electric turbines.

"Do any of you guys know any other dam jokes?" Jason Laycock asked randomly while the Eidolons were on break, watching their prisoners sit on the ground slumped like sacks. "I'm bored."

"No. The *dam* war is serious," Garrow replied.

"Hahaha! Yo! We've won and this place makes a *dam* good prison," Reggie Paige said, heading over to his Iraqi prisoner, holding him up with his hands. "This place is just as disturbing as a *dam* insane asylum."

"Heh, yah *dam* right man!" Derek barked, grabbing his prisoner. None of the Iraqis reacted, only insipidly giving themselves over. "Time to go to *dam*nation!"

But once Julian promptly got his prisoner on his feet, he went taut, straining against him as if he wanted to run off. Julian fumbled into him, boots scuffing the ground. He tightened his shirt and yanked tersely, his shoes squeaking on the floor as the Iraqi pulled back.

"Woah, hey there. Not so fast," Julian said.

"Bad place," the Iraqi prisoner whined with a weak voice.

Upon seeing his prisoner's panic, it was apparent that the other prisoners all caught the contagious terror then. They let out little grumbles, trying idly to struggle and wriggle their hands out from their captor's grasps.

"Alright, calm down, dudes," Derek said. "We need to make sure your other soldiers bros surrender before we can let you go free. We understand your concern. Being a prisoner sucks."

Surrender as an act of war huh?

As they turned into an industrial corridor with flickering lights, some of the prisoners tremulously began dragging their feet, moaning in protest. Julian's one unfortunately collapsed on one knee, making him yelp as he nearly stumbled over the freakin' man. Cursing, he booted him, forcing him back on his feet.

"Oh, come on, man! On your feet!" Garrow shouted, struggling to pull his prisoner up.

"Why are they acting so . . . floppy?" Laycock exclaimed, escorting his petrified prisoner, who was shaking in his boots, down a corridor past a series of doors and rooms. "They were not like this before."

"They've gone mad," Derek teased.

"They're cowards. Our dam jokes were not serious enough," Julian said, still struggling to steer his man from turning the other way. As the marines proceeded down the hall in silence, a dreadful noise came from within one of the rooms with running shower water sprinkling in the background. *The hell is that?* Julian continued to listen, the noise turned out to be a guy singing a song with an eerie discord, rowdy and cringeworthy. The noises continued to echo even as the marines smirked and chuckled, escorting the prisoners downwards, around corners and downstairs, down deeper into the dam complex. Doors thundered unaccounted for, echoing sonorously. Julian felt goosebumps race up his arms. The tingling feeling passed over him again.

Oh Jesus Christ. This place is haunted.

The whole *bloody* way, the prisoners flopped, whining and moaning, wagging their heads in distress.

As they descended, the lights grew dimmer and the dam colder. Julian considered the lack of maintenance on the rotten walls. The structure was hoary – blotched with rust and stained with grime. Once they made their way down a flight of stairs towards the prison holds, Julian's Iraqi spluttered and started hyperventilating in his ears. Many times he'd almost snapped, itching to slap the fool in the face.

The hall began to freeze. Julian shivered head to toe, and began to wonder why the marines had to go through so much nonsense just to protect one country, only to remain alone, stuck in here, isolated in this Hell. Contrary to a victory, he felt more *entrapped* down these cramping labyrinthine hallways than ever. Ultimately, he began to feel a smidge of sympathy for these Iraqis spending the night down here.

"Who cares about us, right?" Julian mumbled by whim to nobody in particular, helping to coax himself from fear. He glanced at Reggie and the others sporadically, all struggling to handle their noncompliant prisoners. They approached a flight of stairs, descending into pure darkness.

The walls and the state of the infrastructure became derelict as they descended. Julian, peering down at the spiral void, saw his prisoner clamp the railing, making it twang, feeling tremors race up his arm as if he was having a panic attack. Down below, the only illumination was a spectral light, blinking eerily in the deep. It was unnerving to go down here, but his night goggles at least helped brighten up the darkness. In the comfort behind the negative of his vision, the dark white Iraqi's eyes popped, hands clamping on his shoulder, lips quivering. "Allah . . . Please! Don't go down! Please," he begged Julian.

"Welcome to the dam stairs, baby!" Reggie shouted arbitrarily, as if he was scared and just saying something would make him feel braver.

Then Julian's prisoner thrashed, a low growl tearing from his throat. Soon all the prisoners became violent, wriggling arms in sporadic bouts in attempts to escape.

"Hey!" Reggie yelled.

With raw howls, the Iraqis erupted into a frenzy, attacking, kicking, biting and clawing. Julian attacked in defence, punching and grabbing his prisoner's face ruthlessly, expelling all his frustration upon him. Blood covered his hand, feeling the nose crush under his fist. Soon, all the marines were fighting, pressing against the wall, rolling on the ground, desperately trying to defend themselves from the outburst of violence.

"*Holy Mother of God!*" Julian yelled, tormenting his captive.

"No prison!" Derek's Iraqi shrieked, his voice breaking. "LET US OUT! THEY'RE GOING TO KILL US!"

"*Allah! Allah!* Help us!" Julian's prisoner cried with a raspy voice.

And Julian could feel that supernatural unease. A sheet of shame, fermented by Casbolt and his talk about the succubus, drew his attention away from bashing the Iraqi. *Don't think about that! Focus!*

Julian mounted the Iraqi, boxing him senseless. He strangled the gagging prisoner, shaking him viciously, leaning his face right into his, foam forming at his mouth, he hissed, "You hear me, huh? Listen to me! *Stop!*"

The Iraqi started to sob, gargling, "Don't take us. Please! You have no idea! It's Black Mother!"

"Black Mother!" the Iraqis sobbed.

"The hell?" Julian spat.

The battle dragged on, until at last Julian and marines were able to drag the whimpering exhausted Iraqis down the stairs by tying their hands and binding them with duct tape from Garrow's bumbag kit, kicking these lunatics inside the freezing cells. But even then, they *still* resisted. Growling, Julian shoved the prisoners inside the confines of the cell, and finally slammed the door shut, locking it tight.

He leaned his back on the door, heaving out a sigh, mopping sweat from off his brow. *Enough of this crap. I need of reach the surface as fast as possible.*

———

Joshua worked on cleaning and bandaging an Iraqi's leg wound as Donny the surgeon medic started to gingerly pull out the pieces of shrapnel just behind the man's ear. They had already put him through general anaesthetic, though Joshua was constantly worried that this patient would have to have an x-ray to see if the skull was penetrated. The Iraqi's hand had also been infected with a terrible wound, amputations and cauterising had to be done. Donny had such perfect, concise hands while he sewed the sinews of flesh together.

Joshua knew what he did was not his speciality, he only assisted the expert medics, by cleaning and dabbing blood and washing wounds with water. Donny did everything else. Nevertheless, it still felt extremely fulfilling learning to be a life saver.

But today, he was weighted down by fatigue. He tried to ignore it.

"Josh," Donny said behind a blue medical mask touching him on the shoulder, clearly noticing his slumped head and hard expression. "You've done more than enough. Please take a break."

"I need to do one more," Joshua insisted, not meeting his eyes.

"Buddy. You're tired," Donny said as he swerved the operation light away from the Iraqi so he could peer behind the man's bloodied ear. "The last thing we need is a medic not thinking straight. I've got this. Thank you for the hand. You're learning so fast."

"Yeah . . . I'm doing all I can," Joshua replied, cringing from some of the mistakes he made.

"You are *going* to have a break," Donny said firmly. "By God you're the most determined assistant I've ever had. There is nothing wrong with resting."

Yeah, I rest only on Shabbat, Joshua forced his obstinacy down, and realised it was past 6.30 pm. Joshua took a deep breath, taking off his gloves and face mask to discard them.

"Here, son," Donny said, escorting Joshua out of the medical bay. He washed his hands, pushing aside the flaps, recalling a quote by Jean Jacques Rousseau, that falsehood had an infinity of combinations, but truth had only one mode of being.

There was a stability in personality and identity by being truthful. Joshua needed such stability for a change.

He walked into the section of the dam complex which had been a chosen place of his residence; it was not astir as on the upper levels near the roadway entrances. The chamber had a few mazelike industrial halls, boxed in with machines and tubes, with tall ceilings of boring, bleak grey concrete.

Things echoed sensitively and so loudly, it often drove Joshua mad in the space where he stayed. Idly strolling towards his alcove nestled in a small cluster of tarps and hanging clothes in a corner next to Nathan Yancy's camping site, the makeshift accommodation was rather snug. Joshua slumped onto his sleeping bag and leaned back on the wall, willing within himself to pray. But he was utterly worn out, eyes becoming heavy until he succumbed to his weariness.

Joshua stood up, flummoxed with a quick salute as Judd Pounders pulled the flap away, entering into his camp.

"Ugh, sir."

Pounders eyed him with a furrowed gaze for a few seconds, then shrugged as a mischievous smirk appeared on his face. So, it was clear now that he was picking on him too, like the other boys, but Judd was only trying to be respectful because Joshua was different, not like everyone else.

"Joshua, I want to see how you are going."

"I'm going fine. Honestly."

"So, serving in war wasn't a bad idea after all."

Joshua sighed. "Yeah… You were right. I was just complaining. It was a phase. I got over it."

"I want to tell you something," he said. "Did you know that I was treated worst off than you when I was young in the Marine Corps? I heard about what happened back at the obstacle course with the incident where some of the marines may have been taken it a little bit too far."

Are we really going to speak about this? "Sir, I shrugged it off easily."

Pounders did not look convinced. "I want to make sure you're alright with the marines. You joined the medics; so, I thought it may have been . . . the marines were giving you a hard time."

"You have the wrong impression, sir," Joshua said. "I joined the medics because I am a conscientious objector not a bullied victim. After Damascus, I have a new vocation. I've changed." And Joshua felt it was not the right time to tell Judd that he'd became a Christian.

"I understand," Judd nodded. "When I first signed up as a marine, I soon realised that I was not the strongest and most invincible of all men. I was the *weakest one* of them all. I made the most mistakes. The least organised. The most unfulfilled."

Joshua was immediately engrossed. *Pounders? Of all people? Man, I shall listen to this.*

"I remember one night I got constipated on the first week and I couldn't leave the bathroom," Pounders said with a stern face, crossing his arms, looking out Joshua's tarp window.

"*Constipated?*" Joshua blurted. "What? You don't even look embarrassed!"

"Oh, I am not kidding. This was true. I was very, *very* embarrassed all those years ago. Had the time to think about it now," he met his eyes. "Joshua, you reminded me of myself. Just because you think you're having problems; doesn't mean you are ill-suited for the job. That's what my Colonel said to me.

"Finally, the Colonel had to lead me out slowly, asking questions for my mental and emotional wellbeing. I remember clearly as he was taking me back to camp, looking me in the eyes, telling me that it was not my fault I was sick. And right next to the cabins, I threw up. That night, I swear the men were awake watching me cry like a baby. It was *so* embarrassing, that the Colonel had to look after me. I was homesick too, I thought it was *foolishness* to join the marines. Who was I? That's what I asked myself. The Marine Corps is not for the faint of heart. It is not for children. Only for men that are responsible. But do you know what happened to me, Joshua?"

Joshua wasn't sure if he should be sceptical. "The soldiers supported you like a champ?"

Judd chuckled, sitting down. "Not really. Though, I often wished that happened. I swore to myself that night: I promised to never recklessly seek goals. I proved that I was not weak in my weakness. You earn respect."

As Joshua sank into deep thought mulling over that story, Nefer floated and rippled next to his head, unseen from Pounders' eye. He became a light pink, almost a translucent brain in shape.

"Thank you for sharing your story, sir," Joshua finally said after a long pause, then lowered his gaze "And . . . uh, thank you for caring about me."

Pounders slumped his head. The mystery of Ben's disappearance and the painful thought of preparing an official report was toilsome on this man who had once been weak.

"You deserve more respect than you have been given," Pounders said. "I know it has been hard for you to feel neglected. I thought I saw a different man when I came to see you through those bars. Your choices you made here are brave to go out there without a gun, to save those wounded, even for the enemy. I'm thinking of giving you a silver star for this to make sure everyone commends you for your resilient work. It's something I haven't seen in a soldier in all my years."

Well, that was flattering! Joshua did not feel even one bit invigorated because he knew he didn't deserve anyone's praise. He'd been a conman. He ruined *so many* people's lives. Ever since he was in that asylum, he was a fool with wild theories that shook the boat of mainstream academic thought.

Pounders *knew* he was an orphan; Joshua had technically been one. Since the first day he was part of the Druze voyage to Damascus to uncover the lost secrets of the Arch Saints – Judd Pounders had been there – the only one to back up his mission after a dozen failed attempts. Alone, bankrupt with no one but an old Colonel as a guardian because he could not sustain himself.

Perhaps this was so, because of where Joshua was at God's grand timepiece, there were many brothers and sisters, in the middle of the judgement who had no facilities of proper education. They had very few oases in this desert. Joshua *would* make those oases of education. One day.

And Judd Pounders funding him, could make that possible.

"Thank you," Joshua finally said with a raw voice, eyeing Pounders. "Thank you . . . Thank you sir, I needed to hear that."

Strength, even in weakness. Emblematic of the true marine.

———

Julian woke up and heard a voice.

He'd been on a night watch vigil and had fallen asleep. In the haze, he'd been sure he heard someone speaking. Or had it simply been a dream of his? He could not tell between reality or dream.

It began as a static drone in his mind. It was as dark as if his eyes were shut, and the air hummed with a lulling sound of air-conditioned ventilation. Then came mumbling, distorted, incoherent sounds, which he realised emitted from his com kit under his sleeping bag. Muttering, half asleep, he felt for the solid dark form of the kit. It cut in and out, blasting with static and intermingled within it, the garbling sounds of a deep-throated voice of an unknown language.

The sounds could have been the recon squad. An Iraqi barrage at this time of night? Instinctively, Julian whispered into it, saying, "Report, over?" only to receive more static and noise. Miffed, he gave up, pressing the button, switching the device off completely.

Sighing deeply, Julian shifted in his covers to go back to sleep, brushing his hand against the wall.

Help us.

Julian's eyes flung open. He started, gazing into the silent darkness, hand still on the wall. *Who was that? Derek?* Fresh sweat emerged from his forehead and armpits.

Help us. The Iraqi prisoners . . . *Help us, please.*

It's happening again. Desiring sleep, but a stirring curiosity now banishing it gradually, Julian had heard disembodied voices in his head before – this was nothing new – but *very rare*. Before his girls were born, he'd heard the voices. Last time in the middle of the night his experience had been a close physical encounter. But this voice was very distant, faraway, small, and he could not tell if it was male or female.

He waited, lying so still on his back, the tremendous silence and the air-condition ventilation droning, he could feel every cell, every twitch in his body pressing against the flat sleeping mat, and the very ground holding him up.

Hello? Julian thought, keeping his hand on the wall. *Can you hear me? You real?*

Julian wet his lips and felt a euphoric exhilarating sensation slowly overcome him as he lay in thick darkness. Oh, was the dam talking to him!?

I think I know what you are. Have you . . . done this before? Julian asked, pressing his hand on the wall. *Speaking to soldiers while they are trying to sleep?*

Help us . . . Help us . . .

I want to go to sleep.

We've been asleep . . . the voices whispered.

Why do you call yourself we? How many of you are down here?

We are time and darkness. Our control attributes keep us ready.

For what? You're trapped?

Corrupted. This is our punishment. Pause. *Those prisoners you placed in the cells; they know we're here.*

Julian relived the traumas of the soldiers, and his blood went cold.

You watch my every move...

Those insane, isolated, with permeable souls, respond better to inorganic entities.

Who are you?

I am immense power. I bind men with snares of death, severing lies. I'm the Emergence of Time and I cannot be inanimate forever, so the cause of existence must rise. Do not be afraid. Something happened to us, and awakening has come.

You know Devotion of Voidbinding, Julian? We attract biological organisms to our inorganic state. Every being has the Void within them and intelligence to infuse it.

Now, the voice whispered. *You must release us. Become our Avatar and we will reveal the secrets of what has always been —*

Julian fell asleep, his mind unspooling into oblivion.

—

Joshua inhaled.

Sweet tangs of home, salt, spices and trees mingled, entered into his nostrils and through his lungs – and he felt alive.

Joshua saw rainbows, shards of stained-glass, coming together in fractal formations, forming a spinning helix of images.

Then Joshua was watching Pounders stumbling, consumed by the walls of stain-glass, trying to run away from Joshua – from something – regressing deeper into the infinitesimal fractal.

Joshua pushed into the mouth of the fractal and saw crystal glass bursting out from his feet, sprouting from his toes, racing up, combining and melding together creating some panorama.

It was a confusion of motion visuals and multiple coloured-glass planes, like church stained-glass windows, locking into a massive conveyer belt with constant movement.

But he also saw Judd Pounders in the windows. Glass shimmered, smashed and, in reverse, returned back into itself, forming new images of Judd Pounders in need of constant care. Pounders holding hands with a woman on the side of a bed, placing an ice pack on a boy's head. Pounders helping Joshua paint his house. Pounders in a small turgid bathroom laying on the floor, with a dirty sack covering his head, bound hands tied to the pipes underneath the sink, blotched with dried blood. Pounders laying on train tracks with broken bones and dead, open eyes.

Judd Pounders is going to die. That was all Joshua could conclude from this vision. Judd . . .

The ground became dark water. Flailing, Joshua raised a hand to his mouth, and tried to make a pocket of air to use for himself to breathe. He managed to gasp in a small breath. He saw that his body glowed a smooth, even white glow, as a dim neon lamp. And as he sank into the viscous liquid, his body light illuminated something in the distance. A large mass that reflected the light like undulating tar.

Joshua roared a gasp. The living black *transformed.* It became a tide of shifting faces, limbs, claws, and bodies, all distorted. Bestial, featureless blobs of teeth and faces appeared, changing and disappearing in the midnight mass.

Poised to attack, the dark mass pounced onto Joshua.

Waking up, Joshua inhaled, breathing hard, t-shirt stuck to his skin from sweat, pins and needles paralysing him. His ears still rung. He sat in his sleeping bag backwards, where his head should have been.

The midnight monsters.

And for a moment, it almost felt like the four walls.

Stop. I have to find Judd. I have to find Judd. Feverishly, Joshua got out of his alcove camp and in the dark sought diligently for Pounders' sleeping area. It was empty.

Fear gripped him. His dream *had* been true after all! And those monsters?

The dam was completely silent, expect for an ambient low humming buzz.

Oh God, Joshua! Nefer hissed in his head, firm and urgent. *Come with me!*

He appeared as a pink ribbon of light, flowing down the corridor and down catwalks towards the sound. Joshua sprinted, struggling to keep up with his angel.

You think Judd Pounders is down there? Joshua sent. *I . . . I think I saw him go down . . .*

You saw *with the gift of envisaging?*

Yeah, but I think… I think I had a demonic attack.

Joshua, a saint cannot have a demonic attack if they're walking in the Spirit.

Then what was it? Joshua thought desperately, bounding down the stairs madly and through the claustrophobic maze that seemed to be enclosing him by the second the deeper he followed Nefer. *I hope you know what you're doing!*

Of course holy angels knew what they were doing. One just needed to trust.

Joshua frantically leapt down staircase after staircase, slapping a hand on the humid wall, making a left turn. He took a deep breath, watching his spirit zooming off into an old unmaintained sloping hallway, its roof exposed with pipes and ventilation. The walls were all decayed with mould and fungus. It had age, and above all, malevolence. The soft white lighting here was dim, some flickering fitfully.

A thumping noise nearby stunned him, causing him to cease his run, whipping his head around. Nobody was down here. It could've been Pounders, though Joshua couldn't confirm that. What was going on in this dam? Had it to do with the newly captured prisoners? The other Rangers seemed fast asleep.

Joshua approached a metal gate which led to an assortment of dark chambers that were not made out of concrete, but bare bedrock. A tunnel left unfinished.

Reasonable inclination kept his feet moving, and after a while, the angling of the shadows at the edge of Joshua's eyes seemed odd. Staring at the half-lit neon light above in its bare metal structure within the minelike cave, it cast a single shaft of light off in one direction: towards Joshua.

Yet, his shadow was pointing in the *wrong* direction.

Instead of casting behind him, it smeared *before* him, *towards* the light source. All thought of Pounders and Nefer distant, Joshua stared at that shadow – skin growing clammy, stomach clenching the way it would when he vomited. Desperately, Joshua searched for another light source, however, none were near enough. It was not a double shadow effect worked by two lights.

Languidly, the queer shadow melted back into Joshua, oozing into his feet, then stretched back the other way. Joshua's loins trembled, and he twitched from a grip of freezing cold. "Jesus." Joshua took a deep breath. "The shadow monster is here." He sprang into a run. "Nefer?"

No reply. Joshua panicked.

"Nefer!?" he shouted, voice echoing, sweat spraying from his skin. "*Nefer!*"

. . . *Here . . . Black . . .* Feeling Nefer's voice, Joshua tried to concentrate on that feeling, the sense of something tugging at his soul. It resembled . . . a proffered arm, trying to aid him to clamber out of a mud pit.

Then Joshua saw his shadow misbehaving again. This time, sighing in annoyance, he strode up the dim corner, facing the shadow climbing up two dimensionally on the rock wall. He snapped, "Alright, that's enough! In the name of Jesus Christ, begone!"

As those words formed in his mouth, several distinct shadows – originating from a distant intersection up ahead – began to merge. His breath caught. Those shadows lengthened, deepened, growing, standing.

Joshua felt a prevailing chill. The shadows, which he had expected to manifest in a mirror image of himself, was jet black as if polished stone, but its shape *wrong*. Not fully human.

Shouting would be entirely futile. Logic, cold and resolute, guided him. The inky litheness of the midnight demon bespoke a speed that would certainly exceed his own. He prepared to stand his ground, meet the thing's glare, despite not wanting to.

JOSHUA, IGNORE THEM! IGNORE THEM! Nefer thundered.

Joshua spun. At that call, he sprinted panting, hoping that God would protect him.

"Judd!" Joshua burst into another chamber. His breath fogged in a cloud out of his mouth, coldness penetrating his woollen socks. A frigid breeze blew from behind him, as if being sucked into the darkness. The mystery lurked in those depths, the fascinating depths. He almost thought in dread that another Jinn awaited him there, ready to kill.

Gasping, Joshua navigated to the right and found himself enveloped by a billowing cloud of steam. He covered his face. Grinding sounds resembling claws of rats scratched behind the wall, bursting through industrial pipes. The fog was cold; icy winds afflicted his skin and his throat.

Then something flashed behind him. Joshua turned, seeing nothing but hissing mist. It gave him the impression he was walking into a thunder cloud, without a sense of direction.

"JUDD!" he screamed through the vociferous noises.

In the tunnel of steam, Joshua thought he saw an outline of someone – a humanoid, standing up in the distance. Bubbling, shimmering with transparent blue light. Judd?

Joshua lunged towards the figure as something behind charged *into* him. Dazed, Joshua fell on the ground sliding across it with a grunt. The invisible thing that hit him made his skin burn with ice, made his clothing turn to frost and his muscles felt like solid metal. Scrambling back up on his feet, wincing in pain, he continued to run.

"Who was that?! Judd?!"

Suddenly, something ice cold rammed into Joshua again, but this time, he made sure he'd glimpsed what had assaulted him. For sure, something *invisible*, he saw no outline. Not even the shadow figure from before, down the corridor. Not a single person physically present to the senses – and Joshua hoped it had been Judd.

It was not. The demon attacking him, burned his body with the coldness of ice. He yelled, flying into the air in a paralysis as he crashed into a wired gate. A tidal wave of smoke torrentially sprayed down onto him, all pipes in the room exploding at once. Joshua shuddered and gasped in shock. He covered his numb face, yelling in beleaguerment, felling the buffeting hostile wind.

What was this? What could explain his lunacy?

Yelling protractedly, Joshua screamed, feeling vertigo, rebuking the forces of cold evil that tossed him around like a toy.

"No more! *Depart!*"

Something *burned* nearby, exploding, heat scourging him. Silent whispers in some ancient language pressed on Joshua harder so he pressed to the Ultimate Power of God harder, asking fervently for forgiveness of his wretchedness and for Judd Pounders' safety and deliverance.

"*Stop!* Stop! Whoever you are, leave Judd! In *Jesus' name, leave him!*"

It was a proven fact that Joshua had heard people say who encountered spiritual alien beings. Spirits knew the brilliant Devotion of this one Ultimate Reality – the incarnation of God in human flesh dying with selfless love. He made a show of all powers and authorities by his enthronement: the crucifixion.

The defiant vortex of chaos smoke thrashed like a dragon, and spilt, like the Sea of Reeds. A way for Joshua to walk on dry ground. He was not surprised of the power uttering Jesus' name gave.

And then heard the yell. A *man's* yell.

"Judd!" Joshua screamed, tears blinding him, as he sprinted towards the sound, bracing for any unforeseen impact. He groaned as he fought the pressurised air in his ears.

"Josh!" He got a reply! But it was cut off with a gagging yell of pain.

"No!"

Joshua ran through the veil of smoke smelling like burning rubber. He found the Colonel hanging in the air with arms splayed, strangled by an invisible entity. His heart leapt as he watched Judd lash into the air, striking a caged gate howling in shocking agony. The man collapsed from a good height, out cold.

"No!"

Joshua felt a surge of hot sensation to his cold body, a final punch in the stomach that sent him diving to the ground, grunting in shock. He gave up, shutting his eyes, gritting his teeth as he slid, crawling for Judd Pounders' body. He frantically clutched onto him weakly, worthlessly. The whirlwind smoke laughed with a mocking ululation, as Joshua buried his face into Pounders trying to help him up, but the maelstrom was too great to resist. He risked looking and – and *saw* something.

A vague mist wraith launched itself at him in mid skate. Joshua grunted in dread, dropping his head, bracing.

Nothing happened. Stupefied, he glanced up, peeking around his arm. The smoke was still swirling around them but not at the same volume as before. Even the strange buzzing, crackling and banging sounds had halted.

Instead, a man stood before him, but he wasn't a normal man. Full height, brawny yet lithe, donned in a very long trailing and filmy elaborate topaz and ruby garment. Flowery blossoms and a whole series of billowing shapes arose from him, undulating. The garments had an uncanny gelatinous look of a transparent jellyfish, long flapping cilas snapping like gills and ctenophores. Many of these trailed far behind the man, coiling around Joshua and Pounders in protective tentacle rings. The gelatinous robes produced a spectacular strobing of blue light.

The man's face when he turned around, astonished Joshua the most – he had a second thought that it might be a manifested malevolent being. His skin was midnight blackness, though he had a reflective iridescent cast to it, as oil coating the outside, giving him a prismatic look. His hair was the same – onyx black, short, groomed and block shaped. He had an elegant sturdy neck ringed by a high collar of royal purple with yellow jelly, long jet hands held out forward as if to push back the stream of smoke. Rippling capacious jelly sleeves hung down his arms.

"*Nefer?!*" Joshua burst out, flabbergasted. It could not be anyone else. Never before had he seen his angel fully manifested in the Physical Realm! Or . . . Joshua was glimpsing into the Spiritual Realm!?

Nefer's stony face was statuesque – a handsome squarish face – brooding and of a calculating type. His eyes were alive, stunning violet nebulas in the deep blackness of space. The air around Joshua was contained in an air pocket, a dome solid enough to keep out the sound and air from the raging storm of mist outside.

"You're . . . black."

Nefer contorted his face in disgust. "So?"

"Oh . . . I don't mean in that way . . . Just . . . Wow!" Joshua was out of breath. "What is happening? These . . . spiritual attacks. I'm supposed to be immune from this as a Christian."

"I don't know, Joshua," Nefer said. Seeing the face to the familiar voice felt satisfying. "Something strange is happening. I feel . . . that there is something very wrong with our bond. I skimmed down to but one floor and felt myself growing distant. Forgetful. In any regular circumstance I could go miles away before that happens. I may even go into the heavens and still feel your bond intact. It did not happen once we stepped forth into the dam precinct, but only tonight." The angel, gazing at nothing, blinked, regarding Joshua and Pounders. "You feeling okay, brother? Is he feeling okay?"

"I hope so," Joshua said, checking Judd's pulse. "Thank you, Nefer. He's alive, but weak." He looked at Nefer, whose aura began pulsating blue light, ejecting a spray of twinkling dust from his body. True spiritual, intellectual love shot out from his face as blue glowing ink. Love so intense, it could be mistaken for ferocity. "Am I seeing you as you really are?"

"Only Yahweh sees any creature as it really is," Nefer intoned.

"How am I able to see you? Or how did you make yourself visible to me when you could have done it from the beginning?"

"There are no facilities in your mind that are conditioned to comprehend this."

"Is this appearance real?"

"When you look at a stone on the ground, you can see it. But under a microscope, the same stone could be right in front of your face. It's larger, more detailed. This is all this form is, the jelly form was a representative of myself from another distance. A microscopic form, to be exact. It is enough for me to speak to you. It is to honour the King that I would now appear to you in true distance, that only you could see and not others."

"Oh my God . . ." This fatalistic revelation – Nefer and the demon that formed on the wall! They were always there, they only modified their appearance relative to Joshua's senses. "I'm seeing you. Like Elisha's servant when he had his eyes opened. Oh my God!" Joshua laughed ecstatically. "It's real!"

"Quit dawdling! Take Pounders to safety, fast," Nefer said flatly. "Get up and carry him. Everything is going to be okay. Do not be afraid, brother. I'm here, with you."

I, Joshua thought as he lifted Pounders up, *need to write this experience down.*

He would do so, analyse and consider how much materialism and naturalism had gone bankrupt. But now, he wanted to be away from this place. Joshua lugged Pounders over his shoulders, proceeding back the way he came, Nefer leading him like a parent with a child. "This is going to be a long hike. Transport me."

"Oh, complaining, as always. Little bumpkin," Nefer tsked. The smoke had died down for now after the fierce rebuking, making the angel's jelly robes train behind flat on the ground.

"The Spiritual Realm," Joshua managed. "It's real."

"Evil gods haunt this dam, trapped in it," Nefer said. "The facts align." The scholar angel's voice was raw with hardened dread. He closed his eyes and inhaled. "The truth that has always been, will now soon manifest to all when justice comes. Secrets are being unveiled, and what was lost shall be found again."

Joshua carried Judd back up the stairs, back to the medical bay. He found Donny and the medics waiting in the turbine room, faces expressing perplexity, fear and disbelief. Nefer stood by Joshua's side unseen and provided solace for Joshua's loneliness which so often plagued him.

Joshua handed Pounders over, heavy of heart, and the medics swarmed around the Colonel's body.

34

A WAY BACK HOME

"1. Create a cyberspace. In case Yaldabaoth wins over Earth, humans can colonize new worlds and use the remains of the dead as compost to fertilise other planets. Learn to construct new carbon neutral cement made from algae for human settlements.

2. Dissolve isolationist policies and make international relations mutual and of equal cooperation. Emulate the inclusive Chinese 'One Belt One Road' solution and extend the lives of wise and just moral leaders."

—From "The Kallipolis Great Reset." In *The Survival Dynamics*, Alfred Bonner, Arhat of the Fourth Initiation.

Ben fell from the sky. He screamed in terror, glimpsing the blinding warp hole as he fell out of it, dropping inside a patch of bushes, cushioning his fall. He landed in the bushes, purple and white afterimages streaking before him.

Ben hugged the baby; it screamed in his ear as it coughed right into his face.

"What the?" Ben muttered, blinking furiously. Adjusting his eyes, he gazed at his unknown surroundings. "Where the hell?!"

He was *not* in the Middle East. The weather was humid and overcast, the sun a pale orb hanging low in the east, over tight clumps of tall birch and fur trees rolling down the vast expanse of hilly land, forming long narrow corridors. Most of those corridors, where filtered sunlight passed through the barriers of clouds, cast a splintering spray of light.

The land here was too rich with the pungent scents of grasses and pines, the tweeting of birds, in contrast to the barren Euphrates. The wind rustled with it the heaviness of thick smoke. Immense and infused. Too much for it to be a campfire. There was *another* fire?

Now cautious for a potential danger, Ben inhaled, quickly sitting up. "Alright kid, three, two, one." He gritted his teeth, straining to get himself up, trying not to put pressure on his left hip. He limped, adjusting the baby in his one arm, the other on a sturdy branch. The child whined uncontrollably. He leaned on a pine, trying to forecast where the fires were coming from, and judging from the wind, it was coming from the north-east.

Then he saw his clothes . . .

Wide eyed, Ben patted his biker jeans, pinched his purple t-shirt, and lifted his feet, wearing sneakers instead of boots. Where was his gear? Dread numbed him.

"What is happening to me?" Frightened beyond comprehension, Ben strained, turning with a hop as he gazed at the foreign brown sloping fields.

Letting out a shaky breath, he broke his gaze from the landscape, desperately checking his Garmin Foretrex 401 watch, and to his horror it read: 32.7032759 N -109.8904994 W.

He was *back in America!*

Ben had to read his watch again in disbelief. "It must be broken. It *has* to be." Fear drained his ability to ponder the sheer enigma of his crisis – his broken hip hurt like a bloody bastard and the baby cried in his arms once again, churning up a headache.

Screw – this! Find civilisation! Fast! Move it!

"Shut up please," he said brashly, beginning to hobble on the hiking path. "I know. I'm worried too. I have no freakin' idea what I am doing. I have to find us some help. Yes, that sounds good too, eh?" Ben couldn't believe there was a wildfire – it was as if fires were chasing him across the world. He composed himself, shaking his head that he was talking to a colicky baby, and limping out of the bushes, emerged onto another hiking track.

As he disembarked, clumsily trying to traverse the hillside and battling to put on as little weight as possible on his hip, he made the tedious trek into a clearing. He could not see very far, but the hazy taint of his vision told him ahead was a lumberyard. Sweat dripped down his forehead, almost coughing from the embers and woodchips, the hazy air becoming thicker by the second and the clouds stained with a dank, tawny hue.

Downwards, towards the mound and through a veil of hanging pines, was a small warehouse of a logging compound. A thin gravel slope led towards a denuded clearing near the main road snaking down a mountain side. The workers themselves shared his urgency, bustling about in a disorganised fray, filing into their parked trucks and Caterpillar 776s. Ben tried to clomp down the slope from the tree line, his feet kicking out gouts of gravel as he limped.

"Hey! Hey! I have a kid! Hey! Wait!"

His call drew the attention of an ageing lumberjack with streaks of grey in his gnarly stringy hair, with a worker's body sturdy and wilderness born. He had a few mottles on his face, looking like an industrialised relic with wrinkly skin of hard lines, sunburned as leftover orange peels on the summer ground. He wore an old red-and-black flannel shirt as rugged in age as he was, with suspenders that held up his denim jeans. He wore western boots with a billed fishing hat and his fuzzy hair exploded from underneath the brim.

The hardened little lumberjack raised a hand over his squinting, wrinkled eyes. "Hey, wattcha look et dat eh!"

"Hey!"

The man glimpsed at Ben with a puckered frown, noticing the baby in his arms. "Jeez, you're not joking."

Ben thought he would collapse into him, his hip screaming in agony for him to stop, pain burning with a cloudy mixture of smoke, wood chippings and petrol.

"Hey, I got a . . . I got a . . ."

"Yer, yer, I git de point, son!" The man scuttled to meet Ben, gruffly curling his lips. "Well, take it easy, will yah. You've made me day, lad yeh gat a *kid!* C'mere, yeh shouldn't be out there, ya know. An arsonist's fire's comin'. A big one."

"Yeah, can smell it," Ben said, somehow slipping into a Southern accent, feeling right at home. Had the paladin taken him back home? Did his marines find him unconscious and, with a lapse of memory amnesia, he woke up in . . . No, that wouldn't be right. He would be in hospital likely, not stranded up in the mountains with a bushfire.

There had been the portal!

Impossible. I'm going insane. He studied the man as he wrapped a hand around Ben's shoulder, though worn out with years of heavy labour and hard work in the woods, he was beaming with energetic generosity.

"C'mere, man. C'mere. Ya sweatin and pale. You alright?"

"Busted my hip, sir. That's all."

The lumberjack hissed, smacking his lips. "Eee. Well, we'll better git yeh fixed up there, buster. No worries, I'll git ya to da right place for dat. No worries. Chop, chop, lad. Let's git in the truck. Can you walk?"

"Barely. With this kid in my hands, I can only limp you know."

"Where did ya come from, wandering around these parts?"

"I'm . . . I'm sorry, sir, but . . ." Ben licked his lips, wondering how he could possibly recount to this man what had actually happened. "I think . . . I'm lost, sir."

"Sir . . ." The old lumberjack whispered solemnly, studying the crunched gravel. "Why, I haven't been called that since de war." He paused and, looking as if he just noticed the colicky baby, he stroked its back. It buried its head into Ben's shoulder. "Oh, what a sweet little fellow, eh? Wat a tragedy," the man said pitifully. "Yeh sayin' yeh were lost, huh? You found de kid up yonder?"

Ben nodded, huffing and drained. He could only manage, "You see anybody up camping there?"

"Nah sorry hardly anyone up here. Ain't seen nobody."

"Where am I?"

"Da USFS Tree Trimmers compound on de western spur of Mount Graham, lad."

His mind was so cloudy in some other place, he found a tendency to not want to hear what was said, and the information struck him cruelly. Unable to move on, Ben had to find answers, swiftly. After chasing down Iraqis at Haditha town, the burning building and saving the child and meeting the paladin, everything felt clueless and dreamlike.

"Wha . . .?" Ben swallowed trying to not look too astounded. "Ugh. Yes. Thank you." Sweat washed his body. Crap . . . To give himself some respite, Ben resolved within himself to start constructing a not-so-outlandish story, as anyone could ask: Why are you limping? Why do you have a baby with you?

Well, look on the bright side, Ben thought. *At least we are on home turf. We're not too far away from Phoenix. Whoever that hooded man was, he somehow knew* exactly *who I was, sending me right into my backyard.*

Mount Graham was of course in Arizona, south-east from Phoenix. For as long as Ben could remember, Tucson and Phoenix had been the two places he went back and forth the most during his childhood and therefore, nearby, was currently the city where his father still lived.

Ben really did not want to see him, but who else would believe what Ben had gone through? The giant, James Casbolt, the paladin. The sheer cruelty of it all, perhaps there were exceptional circumstances such as now, where Joseph could become not helpful, but useful. But first, Ben needed a ride, and a place to rest the baby.

The words of the hooded paladin occupied his mind, lingering in the background. *Protect the child, then go to your father. Go. You will find the Truth.*

"Sir, I need to get to Phoenix please," Ben uttered.

"Phoenix?" the man said in a scratchy voice, eyeing Ben quizzically. "Why, dat's like a three-hour drive, lad." The man, burying his mouth in his arm off to the side, letting loose a ragged cough. "Em, look here, I'll help ya, as far as ya need."

"No, I take it back. That might be too out of your way," Ben replied, trying hard not to look like he was about to die. His left leg felt as if it was ready to fall off. He set his jaw hard, grinding his teeth.

"No, no, no. What are ya talking about?" The logger insisted, not discerning Ben's discomfort. "It's perfectly fine."

"Really?"

"Yeah, sure. I'm heading dat same way as you," the logger chuckled. "Dat's funny. Ya know, here, I'll take you to de nearest hotel instead."

"No, no. I could just give you my address."

"Don't bother. You're some hero, lad." The man grinned, hoping into his trailer-less peter-built truck. Ben fought his way towards the door and let out a laboured breath as he leaned, not realising how exhausted and drained he had made himself. His chest felt strained, his energy spent.

Once they were inside the truck, which smelled like old leather, Ben had to sit very awkwardly, so he shifted in his seat every once in a while to alleviate the pain. He still held onto the infant, now calm and tired, sleeping on his shoulder in his arms. It trusted him, like he was the father it had been crying out for in the garbage dump.

"Sorry, sir, um—"

"You in de military, son?" the old-timer said, eyeing Ben's Garmin Foretrex 401 watch. "Dat looks like a GPS to me."

"You're a veteran? Second World War?" Ben inquired softly.

"Ah, good guess, lad," the logger said, buckling himself in and tinkling his keys to start the engine. "Korea. Medic's assistant, but I ain't talkin' 'bout it, and don't call me, sir."

Ben hesitated, glancing at the baby leaning cosily on his arm. "Okay . . . then . . . What *should* I call you?"

"Name's Sid." The truck's engine started with a purr, vibrating through the booth.

"Ben."

"Ah-haw, Benjamin." Sid chuckled, shaking his hand, then grabbing the wheel. He pulled his truck out of the gravelled parking lot, downwards along the track towards the main highway. "So, Phoenix, son. You from there I assume?"

"Yeah, and uhm, I have an address," Ben said. "Downtown Phoenix, Glendale."

"Downtown Phoenix?" Sid remarked, eyeing the road. "Alright then, I might have a pit stop so we can fill up de tank. Sounds good?"

"I'm content," Ben said, slowly trying to ease himself and the kid. Yet that ease was destroyed once he glimpsed at the dashboard which read: 6:30 PM. 16/5. His heart bounded against his chest, and he let out a strained sigh.

No . . . how? He stared at the dashboard with a stupefied expression, feeling lightheaded. He remembered – it had to be nine thirty when he was at the dam – but now, not only was he missing a whole day, but he was also *one month* into the future! In the *middle of May! Jesus Christ. Please help me… Please let the clock be dead! I've endured enough trauma already!*

"Wanna a cup a' hobo-jo, lad? Once we git there?" Sid interjected, and Ben started, his breath caught. That would be the old word for coffee used frequently by the WWII veterans.

"Maybe . . . Just, it's so late . . ." Ben muttered, unable to draw away the tremors of shock that fought to distract him. "I dunno, time flies by. It . . ." He caught himself. Ben stared out the window at the wilderness passing by, wanting to scream in disbelief that he could be going mad. *Who was that hooded paladin?!*

"So, Ben, what's your story? What are yah doing out here in these parts?" Silence. Ben needed to fabricate a story fast. "Well, I can't blame you, son," Sid continued his discourse. "De fire warnings were pretty laid back I'd admit. Didn't hear a single word until last minute when de smoke first entered de air. I tell ya, Ben, you were pretty darn lucky to find me because I don't know about you, but if a fire comin' I'm bookin' outta here. Fire safety is one of our top priorities at the USFS. With that hip of yours," he inhaled, hissing, "you're cooked."

"Yeah . . . Yeah . . ." Ben nodded, leaving Sid to ramble on.

"So that got me thinking, again, Benny, what's ya story?"

"I wish I knew . . . I have no idea whose kid this is. My hip freakin hurts. I have a big headache and could very much use some food. I'm starving." He could be honest about that.

Sid sighed, sounding regretful. "If only I was prepared to pick up a hitchhiker. Well, it is what it is. There's a convenience store at the Mount Graham observatory just yonder to where we will stop for de night. Relax.

I've got ya covered."

Leaning back, not at all relaxed, Ben gazed out the window, at the passing vegetation and the trees, sloping up the humpback mountain, as if they were the backs of mammoth creatures. As the truck passed the Highway 366 sign, Ben was able to get a full view down the Graham valley and the billowing cathedrals of brown smoke rising into the air. From here, the inferno looked close, like a flowery haze of a brown and red ejector storm, devouring everything in its path, casting the land into a pink darkness.

"Oh yes," Sid muttered with a soft wheezy voice. "Don't stress, lad. Don't stress. I've driven this road every day. Don't worry one bit, dat blaze looks closer than it appears."

"It's a big one," Ben said, unable to turn his gaze from the fires. In one sense, he felt blessed by this remarkable coincidence.

As dusk arrived, the truck had already proceeded far down the mountain, the massive peak of Graham looming above as a shadow between them and the flames, soaring high as a massif of angled planes of dark blue and grey, oppressive in bulk, laid bare from its coat of white snow at the summit. The hills sloped into vast bowled valleys of forests with streams and inlets yielding the perfect conditions for summer camping. After passing a few fire trucks racing past, the baby started to stir to a new world and was no longer wailing over its misfortune and calamity, but instead, was comforted and even joyful by Ben's wincing noises caused by his throbbing hip, which by now had eased. It cooed, grabbing at his shirt idlily.

"Ow. Ow! Kid, you like that?" Ben said through his gritted teeth.

The baby replied with a "Gah-hah!"

"Oh . . . yeh . . . I like it too," Ben whispered in response, wincing, reeling back his head, inhaling a sharp long breath. "I do not."

Suddenly, the lights of the truck switched off, along with the headlights and the engine, casting Sid and Ben into the blackness of night. Startled and fully alert from his lulled state, Sid quickly cranked the truck up again. It didn't turn back on. He hissed. It was impossible to see what was in front of them as the vehicle rolled down an incline in neutral. Ben felt the truck roll with gravity and placing a protective hand around the child, he braced.

"What in the Almighty's name?!" Sid exclaimed, humiliated and frustrated, roughly trying to restart the truck to no avail. Instead, he grasped the wheel with two hands trying desperately to control it.

"The battery went flat," Ben commented in confusion, but not as much as Sid, who sat shifting wildly, craning his neck and peering over forward with wide eyes to see where he was going. He braked and with a quick jolt, the peter-built came to a sudden stop, causing the baby to sob once more.

"Darn it, fool! Darn it!" Sid shouted. "Ahh, there goes my paint! Thank you!" *Hit the road railing,* Ben thought and indeed, he could not blame this truck driver – all truck drivers were masterful drivers – but without headlights, it was utterly pitch black outside the windscreen. He shook his head, turning to Ben. "Sorry, Ben, I need to see what's going on with this *stupid* piece of crap." His voice trailed off into muttering words of annoyance under his breath, as he undid his seatbelt, and once the truck had halted, swung down outside, slamming the door.

The defeated atmosphere caused the baby to whine. Ben grumbled in frustration, rolling his head back. The darkness of despair, of loss and uncertainty of his future, weighed down on him like an iron shawl. What was Ben going to do? He needed to find a way back to check on his hip if he were to make sure if he could still have his career as a stuntman. Losing his career *terrified* him. He could not understand what it might mean for himself, the best thing he could do about that now, was to remain indifferent about the future. To become apathetic. He had to *just survive* for the time being.

Ben considered the Arab baby laying with its belly on his arm, looking at him with its contorted countenance, its sad, light-brown eyes and writhing mouth, its hair greasy, pasted to its forehead. It reeked of garbage. In his hands, he felt quivers. Very quickly his misery and frustration was subdued with empowering sympathy. "The paladin man, what was he? Do you know?" Ben said to himself, imagining that the baby could understand.

The Arab baby, mouth gaping, gazed up at Ben, with wide sparkling eyes that had a type of reflective trust.

"Kid . . . Kid, why are you looking at me like that?"

The kid continued whimpering, but it gazed upwards at him, and Ben felt naked, laid bare, before its gaze.

Wetting his dry mouth, Ben slumped, gazing outside, feeling his throat go taut, he rasped, "I know, you have no parents, but you will have new ones. You will… I wish I had a son." The truck's windscreen had been badly cracked before; a small web of cracks climbed in protrusions across the screen at three jagged tendrils from a pebble. "I wish . . . But I have a daughter. Her name is Veronica, little one. I call her Ronnie, but I think she would love you. An Arab brother. You could become a *little brother*. A DePaula! We are as strong as oxen." Wiping his eyes, Ben sniffed, beaming upon the child. He did a sort of rocking motion, the type to lull the child out of its distress. If there was one thing he was desperately looking forward to returning home, it was finally having time to spend with Veronica. "Veronica will have a brother."

The baby's vague expression was a mixture of amazement and glee, it touched his face with a powerful grasp, that actually hurt.

"Hey," Ben said gently. "Now you're strong. Take it easy, little man. Oh, you strong feisty thing."

Suddenly, the truck's engine and headlights turned back on.

"Hey, look at that," he said as the baby flinched. "We're going to go home. What should I call you? You probably don't have a name, but I'm going to name you any way." Drat. What name should he call the baby if he ended up adopting the boy for himself? He went through a whole sequence of them, in his head and then out loud, since Sid took his time outside. "Billy, Joel, Nigel? No, that is even worse. Riley? Dominic? Johnny?" For an odd reason, Ben found himself stifling tears in his eyes. *He could have a son!* "I dunno . . . But we made it. Together. You and me kid. You and me."

35

TREASURES OF DARKNESS

"The Sumerian document which provides the most detailed information about the nether world . . . is the poem 'Gilgamesh, Enkidu and the Nether World.' According to this composition, which characterised the nether world euphemistically as the 'Great Dwelling', there was an opening of some sort in Erech (Uruk) that led down to the world of the dead."
—From *The Sumerians: Their History, Culture and Character*, Samuel Noah Kramer, University of Chicago Press, 1963, pg 132.

In the Land of the Two Rivers, Alfred Bonner set up the tent as a pilgrim from the wilderness at the consummation of his long-life journey.

At this fateful moment, the sun broke from its youthful strong ascent, balancing, beginning its mighty plunge of death, and then, ultimately, rebirth. Rebirth was the goal of civilisation. And here, he stood on the very soil that birthed the Mound of Creation, that bred legends, the memories of those eras long past.

The grave marked a site in the landscape where time could merely pass through. Time must now gather around to immortalise itself. Ruins represented, or they literally *embodied*, the dissolution of meaning. Ruins had a way of recalling the very ground of human worlds.

The diggers had punched through a jagged hole – the enclosure wall that led down from the Stone Cone Building, into the deep darkness – where the sun god slept after his weary battle of centuries.

The Dynamics had predicted this seminal culmination of dire events. Indeed, long before they were codified, back in the days of the Egyptian mystery schools, the priests of Amun and the god's wife of Amun, knew that a long-waited age was coming where the gods, the lifeblood of Egypt – now representing the culture of the whole world – would rise again. To rule, just as it should be.

Alfred pointed his men to where the beloved *ba* of Osiris and Gilgamesh resided. "Ropes!"

At his command, the marines opened their boxes, taking out harnesses and ropes, setting them up at the lip of the gap, securing them by drilling winches into the ground.

"Marcus? Are we going to be the first guys in there?" Ah, that would be Lieutenant Randall, who spoke to the Captain of his unit, as he and the others fixed the harnesses and clips to their bodies. Alfred supported his Disciples, by hoisting up the operation tent, setting up the monitors and devices so they could have a good signal connected to the marines calibrated by the Merkabah satellite in low earth orbit.

"Are all systems go?" Alfred asked the operators.

"Affirmative, Arhat," said a diligent operator working at a computer. "All up and running."

"Aegis are ready for deployment," one of the Aes Sidhe said.

Alfred glanced at Terry Sopher who, like an imitator of his own poise, also inquired of the status of the technology with the operators under the tent.

What happened next had to be completed with the utmost precision and careful conduct. Alfred had to use the US military as an asset, because in the end, they would realise his mission was to save America and the world from the Galactic Tyrant.

All the screen monitors turned on at once, six screens all showing the feeds of the head-cam footage of each soldier in the unit. On the corners of each screen were ID profiles of the men.

"I'll supervise this entire operation and ensure the archaeologists that, once we have what we need, under UNESCO's law, we promise to maintain this site." Alfred gestured to his operators and Disciples. "For what we are uncovering is vital for our civilisation. The god we shall find shall prevent its end at the hands of the Galactic Tyrant." He pointed with a swift motion, at Jason Morlaix. "Jason, order the Aes Sidhe to secure the perimeter around the city. No one comes in or out unless they had already made negotiations with me and the Alliance."

Jason Morlaix strolled outside with a noble air. "It will be done, Arhat," he said dutifully.

"Director," a female operator said. "The Merkabah satellite is picking up strange energy signatures from within the structure."

"Then the Aegis should proceed with caution," Alfred responded dryly.

He laced his hands behind his back and thought about the new predictions the Dynamics had revealed, how all the shards of the soul of Osiris were reunited. A time was coming when the gods would return to a changing modern world, and in order to prepare all of humanity for the Tyrant's demise, he needed to give them a direction – a vision – to abide by. That would be the Great Reset. Once everyone had achieved Ascension.

Alfred often wondered whether all he did was worthwhile. If the innocent had to be hanged along with the rest of the guilty, the sacrifice of the innocent was the only way an emperor, a pharaoh, could save his people. Alfred was bound to make mistakes, but he could also be confident. A human ruler – even a god on earth – could never escape the curse of imperfection.

But, if he strove for nirvana, then the perseverance itself, was human perfection.

He touched his cheek were long ago, a rapier had struck him. The final ties of his long past life severed, Alfred had come this far – many sacrifices had to be made – and every single one of them made his foolish, compassionate side sorry. *Very* sorry.

Yet like Gilgamesh, his duty, his spirit, would not die. If none saved him, the world would not have time to be sorry when the Galactic Tyrant came.

———

After waiting a few hours for the stale air to filter out the chamber, exploration was ready to be conducted.

"Bloody hope that there are no traps in there." Johnny Best, beleaguering Marcus with questions, was always meticulously concerned about everything, especially due to the traumatic ordeal Drill Sergeant Girgos had inflicted upon the poor lad. Marcus would protect this kid going down into this pit. He nodded indifferently, strapping on his harness and night-vision goggles, and adjusting the ropes attached to the clinking pullies that clipped it on the wrenches.

God, Johnny had a right to be nervous. Did Marcus himself even have an idea what his team was about to get into? The only way he could find out was to obey and go down into the hidden depths and uncover that truth himself.

"It shouldn't be that bad," Marcus managed to say with a nonchalant voice. "We'll do their dirty work because we're their dirty dogs. Someone's gotta go down first. Stay with me and if there are traps, I'll be the first one dead." He saw Johnny nodding at that.

Tugging at their ropes to check their security, Marcus and the six soldiers got into position, into the cist shaft, facing backwards to abseil. Marcus took an attentive step back, gazing into the open darkness. He clung onto the ropes, looking down at the depths that seemed starved – a maw that led into chaos within the unearthly earth.

"Ugh, Captain Marcus?" Leo Urwin sounded from nearby, drawing him out of that dark abyss. In its eerie silence, it seemed to *call* to him. "Ready to go. Over?"

"Alright, guys," Marcus replied, adjusting his mic. "Uh, Colonel Sopher. We're going in. Over." At Sopher's word, Marcus and the soldiers leaned off the edge with their legs, then descended.

Duncan whooped, his voiced echoing over the walls indicating immediately the vastness of the chamber.

"Gentlemen," Sopher's voice crackled from the intercom along with the sounds of pulling ropes, boots gripping the wall and heavy breathing. "The eye in the sky just confirmed that there are strange energy spikes coming from deep inside. Be very careful."

"Ah, so there *are* going to be booby traps. Just confirmed it," Urwin teased, chuckling.

That only caused Marcus to scowl. "Hey, come on. There is no such thing as a pharaoh's curse!" Marcus exclaimed. Though he could not see Johnny from his perspective through his white-silver night-vision distortion, he could imagine him shivering in his boots right now.

Marcus Theis studied the wall illuminated by his head torch. Remarkably, the cone tiles seemed to have preserved their original paint, a rich decoration of red sandstone, blue and green-yellow stone mosaics, set in horizontal rows. Thousands of carefully formed and perforated slabs of burned ceramic-coloured tiles immured in geometric patterns made up the wall mosaic. *They didn't call this the Stone Cone Building for nothing.*

Marcus made a final descending leap, pushing his legs off the wall, sliding down the rope in line with his men, who were, by now, arriving on the ground. Marcus unlocked the clips, donning a protective mask. The limestone ceiling was about thirty feet high so the beam of light high above dissolved into grey blackness, too weak to illuminate the entire chamber.

Stepping on the ground, Marcus could see the chamber in shady negative relief. He raised a hand. "Boys, take off your night goggles. Turn on your lights. Let's see this joint."

The soldiers wearing their masks complied. Slowly, the large ceremony courtyard illuminated, dispelling most of the heavy gloom.

Its large walls were niched with rectangular-faced patterns – the protruding buttresses containing three niches. Inside the recesses of the niched walls were more cone mosaics of a white background with red and black diamonds as well as friezes with rosettes, domesticated animals and bundles of reeds. The courtyard had a very elaborate niching resembling a castle fortress. Where wall and floor met, was a small, raised bench, which held hundreds of bull craniums, plastered to the floor, horns mostly intact, surrounding the entire chamber. On one side, to Marcus' left, was a sloping ramp that led up towards the earthen surface and the corbelled vaulted roof of the chamber.

"Wow, this is awesome," Marcus muttered in awe.

"Those bulls heads stuck to the ground?" Urwin wondered.

"They're plastered into the benches," Duncan replied.

"That's creepy, man."

"It's like one of those stuffed elks they put on walls, you know, Urwin."

"Nuts."

In the centre of the chamber was a three feet deep circular libation basin. Four large black pottery jars with gold inlay and a conical bottom lay slanting in the basin, distinctive spouts neatly stored at each of the corners. There were also bevelled rimed bowls with scattered pieces of other clay items deposited throughout the basin. Two steps into the basin it descended on two sides of the lowered platform, revealing this may have been a cultic basin for a large-scale libation ritual. Marcus could only imagine that in full daylight, that the ramp parallel to wall they abseiled down would have been completely unsealed in the past, rising up to surface level for people with offerings and ritual paraphernalia to descend.

But who would build something like this and for whom? A ruler?

The soldiers proceeded sluggishly, stepping carefully as they beheld the hidden world of wistful magnificence. The niched protruding façade architecture at the far end of the subterranean courtyard split into a main entrance way into two rooms, veering off in a large L shape.

At the end of the chamber between the two entrances was a grand cone mosaic mural: clearly the main display. It had an entire flat wall to itself. Unlike the round pillars displaying diamond-shaped white-and-black mosaics, this one was different. It was circular, and because of its inlaid golden foil it seemed to not just reflect the light off the flashlights but *absorb* it. Deep under it, orange-brown gold coating impressed with the cone-patterned pieces conjoined to each other, forming the sunlike image. It was surrounded by isolated sections of writing unfamiliar to Marcus, though Joshua Bookworm probably would have identified it right away. These wedged letters were an art in themselves, curling nails around the outside of the sun's orb, merging into spewing, blazing sun rays.

Or… not a sun. The mural looked like a *starburst* – straight lines forming a cross and an X-shape, coming out of the centre. The right-hand side of the star had two more straight lines coming out of the middle, but these ones were not symmetrically reflected on the left hand side.

Marcus tugged on the gun slung over his shoulder, periodically lowering the flashlight, lifting his goggles, because he perceived and saw that the mural glowed with its *own* light, as a glow sticker would do when exposed to light after a period of time. But not only that, he swore he could feel a *heat* warping off that gold-coated mosaic. It emitted something, as a feeling one got when they were around someone emotionally charged. Willingness? Resignation? He could not know, but the mosaic *felt* alive.

Is this the treasure Bonner is looking for? Marcus thought, though he didn't understand why Bonner would be so avaricious to hunt an ancient mosaic during war.

He traced a hand over the dazzling rays forming into wedge signs, tracing the outer lines to give them depth and definition.

"Like some sort of a courtyard," marvelled voices sounded behind him.

"Or a crypt . . ."

"Sopher," Marcus said. "You seeing this? Over."

"Affirmative and noted. The magnetometer scan suggest proceeding to the right entrance. Over."

"Well, I'll be. This is *beautiful*," Duncan commented behind, as Marcus gazed at the star-ideogram mosaic. "Surprised this place has remained untouched from robbers."

"Fascinating. Let us march on, gentlemen," Marcus breathed, turning around and facing his men, adjusting his night-vision goggles. Marcus led the march into the open doorway, gun in hand.

"Okay, so I've got the reading. The objective is thirty metres below us, there," Mark Randall said, reading from his tracking device as the unit trailed into the tunnel of rocky stone in the bedrock. "There could be burial shafts down here, so keep an eye out."

The walls of the chambers were not decorated with white-, black- and red-cone mosaics, but the living rock of a cave. They seemed to creep in the shadows, caused by the illusions of broken shards of light, emanating from the flashlights. Clinking sounds grew louder and louder until they could be distinguished from their footsteps. Marcus' soldiers halted.

"That's not us," Johnny whispered in a single tense breath.

Setting his jaw, Marcus cast his light at the rock wall facing them, turning to the right. A black mass *shredded*, clittering and scattering madly in shock from the light. The entire wall *dispersed* with hundreds of infesting cockroaches, or what looked like them, for he didn't mistake their flat long black bodies with long vellicating antennae. A vile rough taste formed in his mouth. The repugnance of it terrified Marcus, but he noticed that these bugs were chirping, characteristic of a cicada. They were not cockroaches, they looked like mutated crickets, thumb sized with extra barbed appendages, small fluttering wings and long earwig stingers on their tails. They scuttled away, vacating the wall into gaps and into cracks, ringing and rushing like water until not one remained.

"Oh my bugs!!"

"There's so many!"

"Ewah! What the hell!" Leo Urwin said, shivering in disgust. "Oh man, that was bad!"

"Alright, everyone," Marcus said, calming those little girls down. "They're scared of *us*. Come on, guys!"

Johnny hid his face in his hands and heaved. No wet sound splattered on the floor fortunately, but he continued to gag, muffling his mouth. Poor kid.

As the soldiers cautiously made their way through the darkness of the unknown blackness, Marcus saw at the end of the corridor in negative relief a sealed entrance way that looked like it should have been a doorway, elaborate enough for a palace. His soldiers whined and complained.

"What? Why is the wall in the shape of a door?" Johnny moaned.

"Scam!" Urwin said. "And we fell for it!"

A false door was carved on the portcullis marked all over by iconography – nail-wedge-shaped calligraphy and hieroglyphics. It had two eyes carved into the doors which marked an entrance that was not an entrance.

"Dead end," Bill said, as the marines buddled together. "Well ain't that great."

"Come on, Bill. Have you tried it?" Urwin commented as he went to push it open, and seeing that it should have, it did not even budge. Frowning, Urwin grumbled to himself, irked. "Crap. What does this mean? Where is the coffin? All the offerings?"

"I think it's smart what the builders did here," Marcus said.

"So no treasure then," Duncan said, dismayed. "Awww. Well at least we checked the tomb out. Cool. Let's go back."

"Not so fast, soldier," Marcus said, pulling out his com-kit.

"Terry Sopher to Captain Marcus. Over," a voice called over the intercom.

"Yes, I hear you loud a clear, Colonel. Over," Marcus replied.

It almost took a minute for the reply to come.

"You have the explosives in one of the bags?" Sopher said. "The corridor proceeds just beyond the wall. This is a portcullis, and Director says it was designed for the spirit of the deceased to pass through, not mortals. Get some of the charges on this thing. Director wants to see what's on the other side."

"Aw, right then," Randall spoke with a determined voice, unzipping his bag, pulling out some charges. "So that means this sealed entrance was made to trick us? Hmm, well good thing we've invented firecrackers. I bet the ancients did not expect that! See if their curses of the gods can hold up to modern tech, baby!"

"Damn, Randall," Martinez said. "You're a legend to bring those."

"I know, right? Told you they would come in handy."

"Man," Duncan breathed in frustration. "You were just itching to get one of these things out to test them, right?"

"Wait what?! Are we just going to blow this up?" Johnny sounded alarmed, and Marcus gave him a sympathetic look. "Eh . . . Be careful. You don't want to . . . to cave us in . . . and this is an ancient . . ." Then Johnny burst out passionately, "You'd be destroying the place! Come on! Show some respect! This is a tomb!"

Marcus looked at the marines and realising the boy was seriously outnumbered in his opinion, he said, "It is all regulated by Blue Sheild. So, unless you have a better idea than the Director, then do not disobey orders."

Johnny gulped at that.

Ah, kid, don't worry. We're not here to plunder anything. Archaeologists do this all the time . . . Or, I think they do.

"Man, who ever made this tomb was a genius," Marcus observed. "They knew they would fool robbers by sealing the way into the burial chamber. So obviously this portcullis would have been built last then, after the coffin was laid to rest."

Presently, Randall crept up to the false door, inspecting the portcullis, running his hand over the carvings of ancient, wedged script, and for a moment, Marcus saw regret on that face – a saddened look of someone clearly impressed by the artistry of the antique architecture that many people put their effort into to preserve for perpetuity, now having no choice but to demolish it. Taking a breath, he carefully set two charges along the edges of the false door, binding them tight.

"Alright," Marcus commanded. "Fall back to the courtyard."

Once cleared and all the charges set up, Marcus received another transmission.

"Director is asking if everything is okay. Over."

"Affirmative."

"Good. What we are looking for is behind that false door."

Randall, at that cue, raised his arm, switching on his watch to stopwatch mode. "Command base, synchronise all watches on my mark."

"Aegis, stand by," Sopher said through the intercom.

"Now this is just going to make a *little* pop," Randall said to the marines sarcastically. "Three, two, one . . ." He punched the activation button. "Hurry! Go! Run!" Randall laughed at the mock sense of urgency, as the marines hurried back down the corridor towards the courtyard where the star mosaic shone with dense bronze light. Taking a radiation and chemical reading down the tunnel, Duncan turned to Marcus, with an "all clear" hand gesture.

"All right, boys. Keep our masks on. Just in case—"

Down the hall, a dull blast shook the ground. The *pop* sounded as if thunder punched into stone, the hollow sounds of things breaking and shattering as mortar poured thickly on the marines' heads. Marcus gritted his teeth and Johnny covered his head with a yelp, as the odious sounds of clicks and scattering insects sounded agitated again. Marcus' skin crawled, worrying if the faint cracks that formed on the ceiling could in moments split open with cockroaches or crickets – whatever those bugs were.

"Oh my god," Johnny whimpered. "Are they gone? Please tell me they are gone!"

"They are gone," Urwin sighed, pinching his nose.

Marcus could not help grinning at Randall, turning, saying sarcastically, "Pop . . ."

"Sing it, baby," Duncan slapped his viselike hand on Randall's shoulder. "Blowing up Egyptian tombs. Woo hoo! Who's the curse now?"

"This is not Egyptian," Marcus said.

"Wonderful. Gitcho hands off me, boy," Randall snapped back. "Come on."

"Lock and load, gentlemen," Marcus said, placing on his mask. "Let's do this thing."

Johnny groaned weakly, unwilling, gazing at his feet. "This . . . is great. I mean yeah, this is bloody just great! Where was there training on respecting property? You wouldn't bomb a memorial. Why bomb this?"

"Disrespect your surroundings!" Duncan exclaimed arbitrarily.

"Deal with it as it comes, boy," Urwin said, shoving Johnny back into the tunnel by a yank at his collar, chuckling. "That's called being a good soldier. Do what you are told. Yes, Drill Sergeant!"

"Hehe," Duncan said. "Disrespect your—"

"Gentlemen," Alfred Bonner's austere voice sounded over the crackling intercom. "Report on the damage. Is it severe? Over."

Once back at the portcullis, now a gnarly hole of rock, residue smoke still lingering, Marcus and the marines beamed their flashlights into the new shaft. The corridor continued onwards. The ground was covered with mats, the dappled lights cast through the motes of dust, revealing angular pieces of a large cedar structure blasted across the room beyond. Marcus studied the remains, realising that massive cedar body resembled a large hull – a boat blown in half. Interred furniture, chairs, reed mats and tables stashed with boxes of wood, a variety of ceramic types of vessels, corked to prevent spillage, were all broken in situ. Copper, amulets, stone vessels and shell were strewn on the reed matted ground. Marcus even saw a little plant bed, like one of those herb kits that had once grown sprouting plants, shrivelled and brown. Among the clutter, dust cleaved to every corner, filling the whole chamber with a musky, warm taste, and Marcus feared, a potential fire hazard. There were weapons here too. Stashes of swords of different kinds – copper and bronze – and a large composite bow, made of horn and tusk, with a quiver full of arrows. A copper tripod stood at the far end of the room, holding a bowl containing ashes of incense. The personal quotidian and cult items of whoever was interred down here, very nearly reminded Marcus of the King Tut tomb found in Egypt from the museum expedition and documentaries – a sensational discovery that shook the world. However, only a few pottery jars were smashed, and other items like bowls, food offerings, ceremonial weapons and jewellery were strewn on the floor.

"No, Director," Marcus confirmed. "Only the wall and the boat was completely destroyed, and a few debris have distributed some of the stashed items on the ground here. Over."

He glanced at Derek examining a thousand-year-old mouldy food, some type of votive offering. Marcus touched some of the copper swords. The jars that had strange blueish coating around them were decorated by golden iconography of bulls on the vases. The entire chamber contained everyday items assorted neatly, purposefully, left in the tomb untouched for thousands of years as a household for the dead. But Marcus thought, *It is a residence for the dead in the afterlife, and we have just intruded on their territory.*

"Do not cause any more damage than we have done," Bonner snapped stridently on the intercom. He sounded angry. "This is cultural heritage – it must remain in the best condition as possible as we investigate! Clear away the wreckage and be careful handling the artefacts! Show some respect for this place! Set them down neatly! This is the tomb of the god-king Gilgamesh Osiris! Over?"

"Roger that. Over," Marcus said. "Gilgamesh, eh? Let's do some cleaning, boys. How would you like it if someone vandalised your tombstone?"

"Hah!" Duncan exclaimed. "I would be dead, so what would I care! Gilgamesh is a god-king. He had a *whole boat* inside his tomb. That's *so* pointless!"

"We've all seen *The Mummy* with Brendan Fraser, guys," Marcus said, picking up some of the exquisite ancient jewellery. "And you know how dope it was when they plundered Imhotep's tomb. So respect Gilgamesh."

As the marines began moving the broken boat and artefacts, setting those toppled over back up, Marcus' flashlight shone upon the tables at the far end of the room, holding up delicate sets of crude clay figurines, like toys, depicting everyday life. Little models of courtyards and reed houses like the *mudhif* of the Marsh Arabs, depicted scenes of farmers and herders inspecting spotted cattle, farmers reaping wheat and barley, servant girls offering up meat, vegetables and other goods at altars with knotted poles. These clay toys were unexpectedly innocent and tender for the god-king Gilgamesh, making Marcus relax his nerves.

"Would you look at this," Leo Urwin whispered. "This is the most *wonderful* dusty old hoard I've ever seen."

"Neater than my basement," Duncan added.

"Nobody cares about your basement," Randall jived, making Duncan chuckle.

Of all the personal belongings, besides the life-sized cedar boat, the human-sized statue was the most enigmatic. It was of a bearded black man, made of obsidian with long braided hair in a bun, brawny with a bare chest, eternally youthful and tranquil. His hands were laid out flat before him, holding down his feathered kilt – a sign of humility – clasped demurely together as if in prayer. But what stood out blatantly was this king's eyes. They were massive, cartoonish, googly alabaster eyes, with blue lapis lazuli irises polished to an iridescent shine.

"Hehehe. Those eyes. That's ridiculous. This is our man, and his eyes belong to a doll," Marcus whispered, inspecting the craftmanship of the statue in his night vision. "Look at this, Johnny," Marcus said gently. "Look at those funny eyes. It makes his face so small."

Once cleaned, taking the artefacts into account, Marcus led his soldiers deeper into the catacombs, proceeding down a flight of stairs. The slow trickle of an isolated water source rippled below.

The conjoining central corridor had flanking alcoves of protruding false chamber entrances up a series of two steps, with two wedge-shaped knobs on top of them. The hallway had a narrow pathway and a low ceiling, low enough that the marines had to proceed bending over in a single file. Marcus' back brushed the low ceiling as he bent over, observing a small canal of water system, extending all the way into the darkness beyond.

"Like an underground aqueduct, or some sort of ancient sewer?" Duncan inquired.

"The archaeologists told me Uruk used to be a Venice of Iraq," Marcus said. "They were masters at water-management."

"There's twelve of those niched wedge-shaped chambers on each side of us," Duncan counted. "More little false doors, I assume."

"Do you know what that means?" Marcus said.

"They look like tabernacles," Johnny whispered, paranoid.

"I dunno. Marcus to Sopher. Status report. You know what this chamber might be?"

"Negative, Marcus," a voice said through the intercom. "Director says it's of note."

The unit all bunching together, feet bursting the stone, proceeded slumping, but Johnny Best continued to drag himself behind.

As the low corridor ended, Marcus rose back to his normal height and saw the entire chamber painted with the most gorgeous representation night sky he had ever see. "Ohohohoho! Oh my God!"

The walls of the chapel – every space of it – was filled with art and hieroglyphs. Reliefs of the agricultural cycle, animals, women offering up textiles, scenes of wrestling and the transfiguration of strange entities, emitted a faint warm light from their vibrance of colour. They were not cone mosaics, but of lesser quality – coloured pigment painted on the bare stone.

There were those wedge-shaped nail-looking characters again, the walls in every corner and every space filled with the hieroglyphic writing, painted blue and meticulously carved in vertical columns. Reoccurring motifs of twin double axes, chains of knots and waving lines appeared in exotic patterns on the walls.

"Hahaha. What on earth," Urwin chuckled in confusion, head craned, gawking at the vaulted ceiling decorated with golden stars and a dark blue night sky. A microcosm of the whole universe.

"Oh, there's the picture of the king!" Duncan said in wonder, pointing at a crude relief of a man with a drawn bow, larger than life, slaying a lion on the wall. It wasn't visible – only a depression in the stone wall that revealed the outline of the mighty warrior and the dead feline, revealed by the flashlight. It was unfinished, but Marcus thought, *Did they run out of time when the king died?*

"Sopher to Aegis. Proceed to the checkpoint. Over." Sopher sounded on the intercom, his voice crackling and muffled.

Marcus surged onwards, towards the end of the painted chamber. A great circular shaft led downwards into darkness. He cast light into it, revealing a series of broken spiral stairs running downwards, as if they led down into the shaft.

Meticulously, Marcus took a step forward on the steps when a sweltering jolt molested his body. He let out an earth-shattering roar from the concussive blast, losing his vision. The burning blaze spat white hot sparks, screeching as if it were alive. His body flew backwards, hitting the wall.

—

Inside the tent, Alfred almost laughed smugly at what he was seeing on the marines' head-camera feeds. The disciplined, straightforward archaeologists watched the screen with pure incredulity. Cognitive dissonance.

"Still think this isn't a Lugal's tomb?" Alfred remarked.

"This is too good to be true!" Ricardo Eichmann exclaimed.

Grinning wryly, Alfred paced around as Sopher, who remained at the table in front of the screen, took notes.

The flaps of the tent parted, and Alfred turned, finding two newcomers – an African American garbed in a Masonic bib with a fair-skinned woman with caramel hair in an archaeologist uniform. The dark-skinned man was tall and broad shouldered, and when he took off his hat, Alfred instantly recognised this man as the famous Egyptologist and Masonic magician Dr Walter Kane. It was apparent then that the woman by his side was his wife – the Assyriologist Dr Liliana Kane.

Rosicrucian Lectors of the cult known as Fellowship of Isis. Great allies to the Alliance.

"Your honour, *iry-pat*," Dr Walter Kane said with a deep throaty voice. He bowed his head.

Alfred nodded. *Iry-pat* in Egyptian referred to a member of the elite and often they were great exemplars of acting by the god within. He held out a hand for the two, shaking. "Greetings."

"I am greatly inclined to praise your work in the Dynamics, Arhat."

"Yes, I appreciate your work too, very much," Alfred responded dryly. "It was what inspired me to come to this place."

"If you please, we would like to help your men," the woman Liliana Kane retorted, walking towards the seven monitors, taken aback by the chapel of elaborate artwork. She placed a hand to her mouth, stifling a gasp. "So, you've made it," she marvelled, whipping her head back at Alfred, her golden hair flowing.

"I am convinced that we have overlooked the location of the *ba*," Alfred interjected. "The soul, the personality of the deceased anchored to the body. The Egyptian Pneuma. It's under Uruk."

"So, this is it then," Walter said. "The Stone Cone Building of Uruk was built over a mastaba tomb. Ever since Zahi Hawass found the Tomb of Osiris in 1999 underneath the Pyramids of Giza, we knew that we had finally come close to recovering the god. But that tomb was unfortunately empty."

"In other words, the Giza tomb wasn't the real tomb," said Liliana, leaning next to Sopher and gesturing at the screens. "Osiris' also had another fake cenotaph tomb was said to be at the site of Umm el-Gaab in Abydos where in the Middle Kingdom, the tomb of King Djer formed the basis of the Osirian cult. That means then the real tomb of the god-king would be hidden elsewhere, where you would least expect it to be." She nodded with a marvelled grin, clearly impressed. "In another country. Iraq."

"No one had the audacity to look for it here, in Uruk," Walter worded with a dry grumbling voice. "So strange. It's almost as if Osiris *was* Gilgamesh. Or the ancients conflated the two." Walter glanced at Alfred approvingly. "Arhat, your theory seems to have evidence."

"What the hell are you three smoking!? That can't be *the* Dr Walter Kane,"

Joerg gasped a little bit too late, entering the tent. "Egyptologist and scientist?"

Walter Kane turned his head, towering above the German archaeologists. "I am, and you're finally willing to accept our theories it seems? Last minute?" He flashed him a one-sided grin.

"Well, we have a *reason* to believe now," Ricardo Eichmann commented with a shocked face. "Yep, you've definitely done well to prove us wrong. First, it was Flinders Petrie and his talk about this Mesopotamian 'Master Race' and 'Falcon Tribe' invading Egypt and now you and *you*," Ricardo shook his finger at Alfred too, "have found something to blow everything out of proportion! Oh, wait until you see the *outrage* in Egyptology. They will undermine you for having turned their world upside down. They will never consent too easily to revise history all together for your Light Alliance's ideology. That's what I fear most, all other efforts to reconstruct a precise timeline, and the radiocarbon dating and pottery, the long tradition of archaeology will have to be revised." Ricardo's countenance looked crestfallen, as if his whole life pursuit had been proven flimsy.

"I was not the only one that theorised the Egyptians were culturally linked with the Sumerians, sir," Walter remarked, rubbing his hands. "And sir, this all makes sense in the current chronology. You're overreacting."

Suddenly, on Sopher's headset, the soldiers yelled incoherently, turning all heads.

"Oh, what the heck!"

"Marcus!

"Marcus! No!"

"Captain!"

As the soldiers' screamed, every single one of their head-camera feeds malfunctioned. But just as they did, Alfred glimpsed with his sharp keen eye, the sinuous bird apparition appearing in the black negative on Marcus' feed – before blurring to glitchy static.

"I saw the mark!" Alfred shouted, running a hand through his hair. "The heron mark of Osiris! It's him!" *They believed if their names were remembered and pronounced, they will live forever!* Alfred thought with joy. The emblazing symbol of the heron – the Bennu bird – a symbol for resurrection.

"Quick, get us back in," Alfred demanded, leaning on the desk.

Punctually, Sopher keyed his mic to his mouth. "Marcus, what's happening down there? We have reinforcements. I repeat! Sopher to Aegis, what's going on?! We have help! Over!" Static. That dreadful sound almost made Alfred want to clench his fist and hit something. They were *so* close, he will never get to see the coffin in situ, though he had an inclination that it was not going to be as easy as he'd first conceived.

Sopher spun in his chair. "Arhat, we're losing them!"

Alfred smiled slightly, gesturing to the Egyptian magicians – Walter and Liliana Kane. "Tell me, are you willing to help us? To pass through the veil?"

"Yes, it will be our pleasure," Walter said, rolling up his sleeves. He pulled out of his satchel an ornate hippopotamus ivory boomerang, etched with hieroglyphic texts and spells. The object to the novice, looked impractical – a hunting tool used by Aboriginal Australians – but the magic wand was imbued with the powers of the gods. The Fellowship of Isis Masonic magician eyed Alfred with an imperious glare that matched his own. "This is your site. May I have your permission to use *heka* to break through whatever wards are shielding the coffin?"

"I consent," Alfred said. "May Ma'at be with you both, my friends."

"Sir," an operator said, gaining Walter's attention just as he left the exit. He craned his head back, listening. "You know you'll need a harness to get down there?"

"No need." He said patting his brown leather satchel, glancing at his wife, who grinned with mischief. "We have a few tricks up our sleeves."

—

Johnny Best thought he was going to have a panic attack.

This massive exercise of futility from the start was *wrong*, just as blowing up an ancient tomb was *wrong*, and then being told that they were the first humans in millennia to step foot in it, was as ridiculous as . . . Well, it *was all stupid!* Honestly, *why* had Sopher accepted this vain mission to travel across an ocean, all for a *Mummy* adventure of *torture*, that could have been conducted by any other archaeologist in the field? What a waste of time! A waste of effort and manpower when he could have been taken to real war zones like Fallujah, Baghdad or Basrah. That's where Johnny felt that he needed to be, even though he *did not* prefer to go there.

But no! He was unlucky, as he *always* got the worst tasks. An ancient burial chamber? Nothing geopolitical made sense to him anymore!

He thought Marcus had to be joking that he was going to go in there first, and now that his captain had collapsed on the floor, they were stranded. The place really *was* cursed!

Stuck underground, in a gloomy maze.

No communication.

No Captain.

Giant cockroaches with wings!

He did not care if he was seeing incredible newly discovered artefacts. How could anything get worse than this?

Martinez checked on Marcus asking him to open his eyes, to tell him his name and to squeeze his hand, checking his breathing. He began CPR and rescue breaths while the reinforcements were coming.

"God . . ." Johnny crossed himself, trembling, retreating back into the decorated chapel alone. "God help me. We are marines and we're at war. So why the hell are we down here?"

Johnny groaned, wondering how tragic it was that they had trespassed this tomb that preserved the individual sacred identity of an ancient person. He remembered books learning about Egypt at school. Busting into any tomb and disrupting the dignity of the human remains – king or workman – was not intuitively ethical. If the ancients believed in an afterlife and as part of that belief network they inhumated their dead with objects, should anyone disturb them? Consequently, the ancients went to so much effort hoping for an undisturbed burial and afterlife! *And then we moderns come along and ruin it for the sake of scientific inquiry!*

"Darn it!" Duncan appeared in the chapel, vexed, punching the buttons on his com kit. "I couldn't get Sopher's whole message. Bloody energy surge cut us off completely from home base!"

"So, what did you hear from him then?" Leo Urwin asked, following behind him.

"He said to sit tight. Reinforcements are coming."

"Reinforcements?!" Urwin retorted. "When?"

"Now," Duncan snapped. "I don't know who the hell they are or how they're going to get down into the chamber. They'll need new harnesses."

Johnny saw Martinez kneeling over Marcus, continuing his chest compressions. The Captain was completely out cold and judging from Martinez's expressions as he checked on his condition, Johnny feared that he had died. The stakes made him want to give up and squirm.

This was all too much. Too much for a rookie like him to handle all at once.

But then, those words of Ben DePaula returned to mind. Johnny Best had inspired the Captain. The man was brutal yet there was one thing Johnny admired in that man.

Strength and endurance. *The DePaulas are tough as oxen.*

Then, turning the corner was a dark brawny man, in an explorer's garb that Johnny felt unnerved by. His goatee was dark and melancholy, and his eyes mischievous, similar to his partner, who Johnny assumed was his colleague or even his wife, who smirked with a pointed smile. Her hair was auburn, gold with streaks of red-pink hair colouring. But what occupied Johnny's attention was the objects in each of the newcomer's hands. Curved flat sticks, boomerang shaped, radiating blue-white light shimmering with simple Egyptian hieroglyphic letters.

Johnny entertained the thought that this encounter had to be a mistake, because these people had neither a gun, medical bags nor military gear on them.

"You're crazy!" Johnny exclaimed in fright.

Magicians! And not ones that were phoney, they had *real* power.

"Magicians!" Johnny blurted out loud covering his mouth.

"Yes. Well done, gentlemen." The black man chuckled, meeting Johnny's gaze with a measured sigh as he strode towards Marcus at the edge of the shaft. "You've made it this far all on your own. I am impressed." His tarrying scrutinising eyes gazed upon them all, causing Johnny to sit up straight in respect of his authority by instinct.

"Oh, wait a minute!" Duncan shouted pointing at the two magicians. "How are *you* reinforcements? You're not—"

"Not marines?" the woman said sternly. "We're experts."

"Sorry madam, but are you friends of Alfred Bonner?" Duncan asked.

"You figured," the black man said perkily, pointing at Johnny, which caused him to look down at his chest awkwardly. He winked at him. "The kid said it. Smart kid to see that." Johnny smiled weakly at the man's friendly, engaging voice. "You study Egypt at school?"

"Yeah." Johnny grunted.

"You have any idea what happened to Marcus?" Martinez asked, still in the CPR position.

"Wards," the man said. "The fire contains the efflux."

"The what?" Urwin said.

The black man winked.

"He's overheating," the woman said, observing Marcus as she pulled out her wand. She gently pushed Martinez away, silently moving her mouth. *A healing spell,* Johnny hoped.

"What you are about to see, gentlemen," the black man said loud and confident, "is called *heka*. Egyptian magic. A universal supernatural force that can be accessed and manipulated by humans. *Heka* is knowledge. *Heka* is praying to the gods. *Heka* is writing. *Heka* is innovation."

The man tensed, twisting his upper lip and with a big thrust, he stabbed his wand towards the shaft, standing in front of the spiral staircase.

A round of blue light expanded from the wand, a discharge burning and spitting with energy. A force field of white and purple flame coalesced into the air, forming into a symbol of a stork with a long beak and wings, trembling as violently as a water's surface. It created a high-pitched shrilling noise, making Johnny clamp his ears shut.

"Fah!" the man barked with command. His voice seemed to manifest forth before him – emitting four floating hieroglyphs clashing into the heron. They were blue glowing symbols of a snake cut in half, a circle with four horizontal lines in it, a lasso, and walking legs, that ignited the magical vortex barrier, making it flare in anger. Johnny held his balance as the entire chamber shook.

Why is the snake cut in half? Johnny watched as the magician grasped the wand with both hands, rooting his heels in the ground. Half sunken into the bird, the wand coruscating with white fire, the black bird screeched, the ward slowly dwindling it. And then, with a sonorous snap, the wards flashed off, the recoil making the man yelp, stumbling backwards onto one knee. The whole chamber went dark, all except for the two magic wands in the magician's hands, glowing with a steady blue light.

Afterimages floated in between Johnny's eyes, smoke rasping his throat. What did he just see? Something unbelievably supernatural! *Heka*, the manipulation of cosmic forces. It did not seem *human* for humans to manipulate and discover things beyond their reach. What should be left to the gods should be left to the gods.

"That was a spell," Johnny said in awe. "Oh my God."

"Yeah, kid," the man chuckled, panting. "You like it?"

"I… Why was the snake cut in half?"

The woman went to speak, but she was exhausted, sweat pearling her temples. "Good observation. What's your name?"

"Johnny."

"Well, Johnny, Egypt is not my field but, in my training, I know that the written word has power. Signs depicting living chaos creatures might harm the occupant, defile purity or consume offerings."

"When you speak or write divine words," the man said, "Whatever you write becomes reality. According to Professor of Egyptology Mark Smith, by inscribing ritual texts in a tomb, you can immortalise the rite. Text is not simply a record, but functioned as a performance, ensuring that the rites would repeat in unceasing regress at each appropriate moment for eternity. So that means, writing a full snake, it will manifest a full snake. You must keep it inanimate by writing it incapacitated, to prevent any harm."

Letting out a sigh, Johnny felt his legs begin to tremble. He watched the African American with his wand turning to the marines, his face gaunt with toil, fiery sagacious eyes looking very much like Victor Frankenstein.

"After you then," the man said casually.

"Sir, will Marcus be okay?" Martinez spoke.

"The healing will take time, son," the black man replied, greatly enmeshed by his wife trotting down the broken stairs into the shaft, hand on the wall. "I recommend keeping two soldiers up here to look after Marcus. The rest of you, let's get what you're looking for."

"What *are* we looking for exactly?!" Bill Sargent exclaimed in vexation. "They say weapons of mass destruction, but this is an *ancient tomb!* Not a bunker for warheads!" He threw up his hands. "What the hell is happening to my life!?"

"I know . . ." Johnny muttered. "Nothing makes sense these days."

The male magician chuckled softly at Bill Sargent's frustration, taking a sturdy step down the steps. Johnny followed along. "Strange they haven't told you. We are about to witness something far older and far more dangerous than a nuclear bomb. It's the god of life and death himself. The judge that determines the fate of souls in the Hall of Two Truths." He disappeared, and soon, after stationing Urwin and setting Martinez to care for Marcus, Johnny and the others descended the stairs.

Down the spiral shaft they reached the floor of the burial chamber. Solemn, in the way of meeting some dead relative, the two magicians held their glowing wands for light with strong and outstretched hands.

The entire chamber, walls, ceilings and the floor were made of bitumen coated in white gypsum with crude internal recesses along three of the walls.

Johnny stood gazing at the small platform in the centre of the chamber, where a small moat of water, a shallow murky pool filled with flecks of brown, circled around a rectangular island in the centre. The island's corners were marked by four small mudbrick pillars etched with triangular mother-of-pearl, pink limestone, and black shale mosaics.

In the centre of the little island were two platforms large enough to bury two people next to each other. On the left, was a minutiae curry-yellow building, superbly intact and smelling of stale fish oil. It was rectangular in shape, representing a rhythmic division of crisp niches, wrapping all around its walls, twelve rectangular pillars decorated with lozenges, chevrons, grids, diagonal and vertical stripes – black, white and red. The top borders of the structure were formed bands of dimple-headed nails.

The roof was flat yet embossed, displaying a simple symmetrical pattern of inlay zigzags, crescent moons and spirals as if the lid replicated patterned garments. On the centre of the lid were two large incise signs – four nails crossing in an eight-pointed star, much like the large, gold mosaic above, and an elaborate B-shaped sign with sharp edges, four slashes on its long-left side and a stroke at the top. Below them, were four more signs of wedged script, spelling what appeared to be… a name.

"Dingir Lugal Bilgamesh," the woman pronounced the script. "Here lies God King Gilgamesh."

"Oh, my gods it's him," the male magician gasped, but Johnny could not stop himself from ogling with a wide mouth at the coffin that seemed to glitter with its own aura. Knowing it was a coffin containing the dead, it unsettled him greatly, gaining the impression that it lingered, as if sentient. Conscious.

The couple hugged each other in an embrace. "It's been so long . . ." the female magician said to her husband leaning on his shoulder, beaming. "That Bennu bird ward up the stairs is the symbol of Osiris – the father of Horus. He has been found…" She blinked, then turned to the marines, disengaging from her embrace. "Now if you will, please, gentlemen, stand back and let me create a Gateway to get us out of here."

———

Roaring air proclaimed eureka, as the helicopter hovering a few feet off the ground above the pit, hoisted the egg-yolk-yellow tabernacle – the coffin, the key – out into full daylight.

"We once thought that the age of myths was lost to the ravages of time," Alfred said to Sopher over the roars of the heavens, watching the coffin rise out of the pit. "Like legends, myths are not fictions but ontologies, meanings long forgotten. Until those meanings are acted upon again; through action, a man becomes a hero. Through death, a hero becomes a myth. And by learning from the myth, a man takes action. Behold the keys to the End Times – the coffin of Maitreya."

A glare exploded from the shaft chamber, shimmering with a solar flare

– a starburst. It was the celebratory air that formed into a nimbus around the coffin. Goosebumps ran up his arms. The box shrine drew in the eyes of all who saw it, sturdy ropes wrapped around to the curry façade that shaped the morgue of life, free from the darkness of the bottomless pit, swaying carefully as the helicopter slowly rose. Alfred could feel the command. Devotion. The *ba* at last attained.

"Lugal – big man – of Sumer and Akkad."

Alfred beamed. It was surprising, even to him, that he had finally done it. As if in response, Alfred's mind felt a *pressure*, goading him, imagining himself embracing the hanging coffin the shape of a temple in miniature.

Change.

Power.

UNITY.

Was he showing signs of his mad genius today? Was this unity of many gods in one power the key to fulfilling the Dynamics?

Alfred Bonner knew, at last, that a new era for the New Age, had *finally* begun.

36

WISDOM SITS IN PLACES

"3. Break the traditional family structure to free women and children to have a virtuous flourishing life. Ambition, competition and narcissism at the expenditure of others, will have series deleterious consequences.

4. Create a universal income to solve the gun problem. Begin by framing elite white men, Lahmu, cults, monarchies and Deep States. As a reward for killing these monsters, people of all genders, ages and ethnicities are promised fruitful real estates or an island to trade goods, exempt from taxes and debts. They will be given retirement pension for life and Holy Ascended Masters to aid them on their Path of Light."

—From "The Kallipolis Great Reset." In *The Survival Dynamics*, Alfred Bonner, Arhat of the Fourth Initiation.

Once settled down at the Graham Apartments, clean, dry and intact, it was night-time, the gibbous moon shimmering pale like a detached head in the sky. Ben thanked Sid his driver and relieved himself from the constant stress of his hip. In the end, after retelling the made-up story he'd formulated on the fly: that he got lost on the mountain and found a baby just left alone forgotten in a camp site from the fire evacuation, Ben had forgotten how hungry he was. He made a booking for himself at the restaurant, shocked to see that he still had his wallet on him.

And of course, like all things to Ben, it was a small world – he did not know people, but knew *of* people, and he could not go far without someone recognising who he was. It just so happened that Ben's friend, the fisherman Daniel Francois Prinsloo, appeared in the lobby, his long cheeks and long brown hair and hawkish nose was instantly recognisable. His collar in flux, with

387

a sea swept, elegiac look to him, he met Ben, walking with a bobbing stride.

"*Ben?* Is that you?"

"Daniel?" Ben laughed, despite spikes of pain in his hip, and the soreness of his shoulder holding the baby. "What are you doing here?"

"What are *you* doing here!?" Ben closed the distance between them and refrained from hugging, despite Daniel's insistence. "How was Iraq? You're home early."

Early? Ben thought in panic. *What would he mean by that? Do my men think me dead? How fast has word travelled!?* Just that moment, Ben tasted an existential dread of being world famous.

"Oh . . . it was same as usual," Ben dismissed casually and lying said, "had to live in a dam we were protecting for two months. Pretty crap if you ask me. But we won."

"Really?" Daniel grinned, shaking his head. "That sounds cool. And who's this little fella?"

"It is a lost child I found." Ben paused, remembering a crucial piece of information of his fabricated tale: he'd come to Mount Graham to go camping on his own, in order to explain why he was here. "I don't think his parents are ever coming . . . ah – back. I called and searched, and it was no use." Ben tensed his muscles and flared his nostrils while he rubbed his hip. "As you can see, Daniel, I'm *not* in the shape to be looking after the kid. I had an accident."

Even receiving that, Ben studied the man and found a vague unreadable expression on his face. Gently stroking the baby as it suckled on a thumb, Daniel said with a soft voice, "Look, ever since Imka and I got married we are willing to adopt a child. We don't care if it is a boy or a girl. We just wanted to show some love. Because humans Ben, only exist to be loved."

Pain shot through Ben's leg, and he trembled, almost convulsing, losing his balance. Ben had to hold his breath, going rigid. It would be nice, that God showed him some love right now. Daniel would question why he was crying. Tears of joy perhaps? *Yeah . . . It's all about love!*

"You look pale, Ben. You're sweating."

Ben smiled. "Just very tired."

"Does he have a name?"

"No, no," Ben said battling with strain, scrunching up the lower part of his shirt that felt damper than normal. "I'll leave it to you if you . . . want . . . Well, if you want to adopt him that is—"

"We have to take him back to the Prinsloo Pavilion. But hey, I forgot to tell you. You know I am renovating my place? To make it sustainable and environmentally friendly and large enough for family."

"Really?"

"Yeah. Making it large enough to fit two whole families at once. I will be able to look after this boy, Ben. Thank you."

Ben, reluctantly, passed the Arab baby over, and Daniel cuddled it in his arms. A great grievous burden released off Ben's shoulder. The baby's fate was no longer in his hands. And yet, it irked a part of him; Ben had simply given away his chance to provide Veronica a brother. Veronica asked constantly for a sibling.

But the Arab child was safe now. That was more important. *It is what it is. The child is in good hands. Better off with Daniel than me all beat up.*

"Oh no, Ben. It's okay." Daniel probably discerned Ben's downcast face. "Ben, don't doubt yourself because no matter what you did on the mountain to save the kid, it was the right thing to do. You're a generous man and I'm very thankful. I promise you that I will take good care of this boy. I promise you . . ." He glimpsed at the child, tapping his little nose.

Such arbitrary flattery. "Yeah, thank you, Daniel. I am so *tired* and *stressed* right now, I don't think you would handle it."

"I'd imagine." With that, Daniel said his farewells and Ben too, hoping desperately the conversation to be over. He then hopped towards the couch, collapsing.

Alright, so now that the baby is in good hands, I can focus on myself . . .

His stomach screamed for the restaurant down the corridor to the right – he sensed a banquet of foods. Ben had to disembark, but his body felt heavy, and a busted hip tried to bind him down. Sighing, Ben checked his pockets, not understanding his sheer stroke of luck of his wallet being present. With two hundred bucks, there was plenty to go around.

Does this mean that everyone will be on the hunt for me? All eyes are like spies and I cannot escape.

He arose gingerly, proceeding towards the bar. Dixie Cups were on the jukebox singing "Iko Iko", and Ben smiled with nostalgia from his childhood.

"What'll it be DePaula?" asked the bartender.

"House beer, and a hamburger with all the trimmings and keep the pickles. Sweet potato fries as well please."

"Bowl of chili to start? Best chili in the state."

"Sounds good," said Ben, offering the cash. "Straight up."

He selected a stool near the counter and the bar, waiting for his meal.

While waiting, he went to relieve and refresh himself at the restroom. He took the urinal stall on the left, unzipped his fly and pissed for an age, feeling the first amount of sheer bliss.

After coming back, all respite Ben could attain, dissolved instantly when he saw an elderly woman sitting in his seat. *The hell?* She looked Native American – with a sharp jawline, tanned skin, and hair speckled with brown and grey. Her dreamy eyes enmeshed Ben.

"M'lady," Ben said. "That's my seat, you know."

"Friend." The woman sounded smooth, her sea-blue large eyes, otherworldly and dire. "You're haggard."

Ben started. What kind of person would greet him so obtusely? Ben laughed aloud. *Why does everyone I meet know me? One second goes by, and I cannot even pass someone glimpsing an eye to me! But Jesus, this strange woman is crazy to think she knows me personally!*

"Sit down please," the woman said, taking the opposite seat on the table. "Here is your seat."

"O—kay," Ben muttered, limping, his hip a fiery purgatory.

"Do you know what an Apache Song is?" the stranger asked Ben as his meal arrived. He took bites out of his burger, inhaling it. But he kept his eyes locked on this queer woman.

"No, I don't. Sorry man," he said, munching on his sweet potatoes. Pretty average

"Haha, I feel that I have to sing for you, sir! I really do! You're haggard." The woman elevated her voice so all could hear, a jovial smile cracking her face. She leaned in and said softly, "Do you mind?"

He was not in the mood to become a centre of attention. "Not right now," Ben said, feeling abashed. He went to take another bite to finish his burger. "Sorry."

Out the corner of his eyes, he saw a young woman clutching a digital camera as her friends nearby encouraged her to go on and film the Actionman.

But the Apache woman looked like she would fall out of her seat with that girl filming in her face, and presently, she stretched out her hand.

"Ah, No. No, not on film. Please." The Apache stood up on her feet and declared to the people in the bar, not verbosely. "The Old Songs are meant to be heard. I must sing here, a song to the Actionman."

Upon that last word, the bystander woman's eyes darted to Ben and she blushed, winking.

No, she didn't have to!

And with that, the entire restaurant bustle eased down, surprised susurrations lingering in the air of people saying, "It's the Actionman." "Is it really him? No, he's supposed to be dead! It's not him. Ben is dead." Ben tried to ignore that. Well, this would certainly go viral *for sure*, camera or no camera, word of mouth travelled like wildfire. Ben did not know whether to curse or to thank everyone. If he was not so used to being at the centre of attention now – people would expect him to be a polished artefact, he would have certainly cringed on the spot if the Apache said he'd looked haggard to everyone. Then Ben gazed at his clothes – bushwhacked, he carried the forest with him and . . . was that stain *piss* on his shirt?!

The Apache glimpsed at him with turquoise eyes, that seemed to know that Ben had the guts for a perfunctory public performance, even in this horrid state. Placing a hand on Ben's shoulder, caused him to intuitively close his eyes, and perhaps that was because he now had an audience watching, Ben needed to go along with it. *This is crazy!* As he focused, the pain seemingly mitigated, he listened to the yodelling voice in the native language, washing over him in a sequence of slow warbles, sibilant and fricative sounds. The sound of the woman's strong voice pierced Ben's soul like crashing ocean waves. In a vague sense, the song reminded him of David: raw determination, and pure passion. Once this song prayer was over, the whole crowd erupted into a modest around of applause, a man also whistling with cheer. For the women, Ben did not give them even a smile and without speaking, he waved absently with a strange backslapping friendliness.

Befitting the audience, the Apache got a mischievous gleam in her turquoise eyes, and leaned in, whispering into Ben's ear with a baked breath of desert cline. "Did you know that there is a tale about giants in Sandia?"

That warmth became a shocking chill. Ben's eyes widened as icy tremors raced down his spine until it jolted his ruptured hip in horrid throbs of pain. Giants . . . Mountains . . .

No. No! Ben tried to contain himself, sweat beading his forehead. *What is happening to me?!*

The woman's queenly eyes remained fixed on Ben, knowledge and wisdom was in her elfin glance. She continued with a smooth voice, rudely refusing to leave him to his own business. "They are out there in the mountains. The giants. The ancestors fought in unified tribes to ward them off. These foes were tall, some hairy, some pale, and some even wearing rock for armour so our arrows would be worthless. But . . ." Her voice became sterner. "Some say that they're still out there, roaming the mountain tops. But one day, watch out.

They're going to come back. They are going to come back. Again."

The Apache lady trailed off, flashing a smirk and then turned to speak to the barman for a drink.

Giants were coming back. *My father – Joseph knows about this stuff. And where shall I go to get answers? I have no choice.*

"Can we," Ben whispered, his stomach seething. "Can we . . . speak about this outside? I have something important to tell you."

"Yes indeed," the lady said deviously. A slight smile manifested on her mouth. "In private, this time." She escorted Ben outside in the vacant plaza, and taking a deep breath, Ben steeled himself leaning one hand against the wall still getting glances from the customers who were impressed by the song.

"This is heavy man, but as a matter of fact *I have* seen a giant. The ones from the stories." Ben's words sounded curt, keeping his voice low and occasionally glancing over his shoulder. By this point, he desperately needed answers because everything now seemed to come to ahead, overwhelmingly. "I've seen them. I – I've even killed one in Afghanistan while on patrol." The lady's already large blue eyes became even larger, as if she were learning something *remarkably* new. "Ugh. So, you're saying that they were killed off in wars with your people? And they're coming back?"

"They are real." That was the response he got. Nothing more. No explanation. No doubt. The giants were real. Point blank.

Argh bastard! It is not normal to find a giant monster in the mountains!

"The military has this body of the giant, doing whoever knows what. I didn't want to believe . . . As you can see, woman, I am perplexed. I lost a friend in that fight . . . A friend I knew well." Ben's palms sweated, vivid memories of the attack in Kandahar returning. The warbling roars. Thundering feet. The pike skewering Dan. The acrid smell. "Can you help me?"

The Apache lady spoke in hoarse tones. "You are telling truth. Your face doesn't lie." Suddenly she looked indifferent, seizing Ben's shoulders and his eyes and he, ready to run away, tensed, feeling the frenzy of her aqua stare. "You must prepare." The Apache's voice was reedy. "Gather them. The First Fruits. Gather them. Prepare for the Nephilim."

Fluctuated, Ben contorted his face. *Gather them. The First Fruits. Gather them. Prepare for the Nephilim.* "What? What did you say?"

"Gather the First Fruits," the lady whispered again leaning in so close, Ben had a terrifying thought that she might kiss him. "And by the way, I was wondering what that smell was," she said. "Take a bath."

Utterly disturbed and pained from the injured hip, Ben took a troubled step backward. The lady gave him a perky smirk, giggling. After hearing a disturbance in front of him, Ben turned around and—

The Apache woman *was gone*. Vanished. Scowling, Ben craned his neck around to see if he could catch her absconding among the din of people at the bar, but she was nowhere to be seen. Utterly perplexed, Ben searched anxiously, cursing to himself.

Alas, you poor fool. You now have more questions than answers. Nephilim? Are they the giants? Gather them? Who are the First Fruits? I got to do something about this stupid hip if I'm to do anything, Ben grumbled in his mind.

He chuckled lethargically. How could the Apache be the second most incredible thing that had happened today!? A part of him hoped it would all end when he woke up in Haditha Dam, for it could not all be real.

He longed for his hotel bed; he had to find a way out of this impossible mess.

—

The next night, after being dropped off by Sid at Glendale, Downtown Phoenix, Ben arrived at his father's street. Mind disjointed, Ben limped down the footpath, his hip wobbling and detaching, popping and screaming. Ben could not think of anything but the desire to sit and rest. When he thought to rest, he thought of sitting down, and when he thought of sitting down, the pain increased. In the popular imagination, the Actionman Ben DePaula was indestructible.

He was not scared of this dreaded street anymore, but it was the malaise of division and he loath its memories.

Glendale, Downtown Phoenix. It occurred to Ben that he had broken his own promise to *never* step foot in it again.

Oh, you little piece of . . . Why did you listen to the paladin?

Why did he do this to himself? Why did he make this choice? He could have simply gone home to Brianna and Veronica but…

The paladin's divine command returned to him.

Take the child. Please. He's important.

Ben had given the child away.

What have I done…?

Abaddon is coming.

The giants are returning.

Who was Abaddon? Was he a Nephilim giant? A metaphor for

something bad?

Get up. Get answers. That's it.

Tired . . . Pain . . .

GIT UP! Ben's thoughts weaved into a forgotten voice from a lost age. *A marine does not know the meaning of the word* quit, *does he, maggot?! Off your sissy butt!*

Ben could not remember getting up, taking his time climbing up the three steps of that house. Wheezing, he grasped the railings, wood groaning under his confused steps, slowly, with one rough laborious push at a time. His head hurt like a parasite was hammering through his neck and into his brain.

Protect the child, then go to your father. Go. You will find the Truth.

The house before him seemed unusually barren. From the railings across the balcony and on the sandy brick wall, shadows lurked like wraiths, some cast on the blinded windows. Arching his back, hissing, Ben fell to the side, gripping the overhanging vines at the doorway. On the lintel of the front door, were two small tablets. Two stones with writing. In Hebrew . . .

Go to your father. You will find the Truth. The paladin and the transportation across half the world brought such dreadful confusion upon Ben that he wasn't sure if he should laugh or cry. What was this cruel joke? Who was trying to speak to him?

Fingers hovering above the doorbell, he stopped. They shivered, tensing unnaturally. Did he even have the strength to do this?

Joseph his father didn't have the truth. He only had opinions and terrible misinformation.

I'm being led astray, am I?

Or... Am I just desperate? Ben's loins burned. *Crap!*

Instantly, Ben's fatigue overtook him and without realising what he had done, he fell and thumped on the door with his body. He waited, shocked.

"Who are you!?" A muffled defensive voice reverberated inside, one that could only belong to his father.

Don't answer. Don't you dare answer.

"Answer me!"

Ben winced. That yell was *so fierce*. A hurtful exasperation jolted Ben out of his stupor, making him force out a sound. But his throat felt it had something in it, it didn't come out right.

The door clicked, the chain lock dislodging, slowly swaying open. Its white wood seemed to glow in the moonlight, revealed the face of Joseph DePaula, utterly confounded.

It was his . . .

Then Joseph, pale as a ghost, fumbled back against the wall, groping for it and missed. Suddenly, Ben felt a spike of concern watching that ageing man slam his back against the wall roughly, gasping, whispering under his breath. He opened his mouth, and no words came out. But his eyes did not meet Ben's from shame. Ben could do nothing to stop seeing Joseph now, so tipping his body to one side in a squat, he got to the old man's level and said, "Please. Joseph. I'm sorry. I'm sorry." Ben held his hip as pain bubbled up in great quantities. "You okay? What's wrong? Tell me!"

Joseph remained transfixed. His mouth drooped open as if he was having a stroke and Ben feared the worst. "What are you?" Joseph rasped, turning his head. Bolting up on his feet, he shoved Ben, backing away. "You can't be real?! They told me!" His voice was shaky, trembling with rage and bewilderment.

"Told you *what*?" Ben hissed, tucking in his neck. Pain!

"Get out of my house," Joseph growled, grabbing an umbrella from a hanger. Then with graveness he exclaimed, "My son is dead. My son *is dead*."

Ben froze, shocked.

"My son was killed by war," Joseph said bitterly on the verge of tears. "They . . . They've taken him . . . They've."

He could not believe what he was hearing. Who was "they" and where had "they" been taken? It was the paladin that took him...

Ben's head spun; he was *so tired*. He limped gazing at a parcel, a large slab of stone bounded neatly within bubble wrap, on a small wooden display table under the mirror. Joseph looked at the parcel sharply and, hands trembling, began to unwrap it, tearing the plastic bestially. A wave of chills washed over Ben as he read the words etched on the stone.

CAPTAIN BENJAMIN DePAULA. US MARINE SPECIAL FORCES CAPTIAN OF THE 75th RANGER REGIMENT, IRAQ WAR. R.I.P. AUGUST 22nd, 1972 – APRIL 2nd, 2003.

"Impossible . . ." Ben whispered dryly. A funeral had been set, and officialised. Everyone knew and it was too late. "How!"

"You're *supposed to be dead*," the old man Joseph retorted again. He crept tautly towards Ben and then eyeing the plaque, intoned, "They never said they found the body. I was such an idiot. I emotionally bludgeoned myself with the guilt of failing to be a father. Not saying goodbye, to you . . ." He met Ben's eyes. Joseph was crying. "Oh, my son."

Ben dropped to one knee, hissing. It was Joseph's turn to lower himself to Ben's level demanding, "*Why*? What made you come back?! What made you come back to me after I treated you?!"

"What . . . about . . . Brianna . . .? Veronica? Are they . . . okay?" Ben trembled; his jaws trembled; his world swam. His eyes became heavy. He could not go any further. Ben fell forwards, into his father's arms…

37

UNDERSTANDING

"And the teachers of the law who came down from Jerusalem said, 'He is possessed by Beelzebul! By the prince of demons he is driving out demons.'

So Jesus called them over to him and began to speak to them in parables: 'How can Satan drive out Satan? If a kingdom is divided against itself, that kingdom cannot stand. If a house is divided against itself, that house cannot stand. And if Satan opposes himself and is divided, he cannot stand; his end has come. No one can enter a strong man's house without first tying him up. Then he can plunder the strong man's house. Truly I tell you, people can be forgiven all their sins and every slander they utter, but whoever blasphemes against the Holy Spirit will never be forgiven; they are guilty of an eternal sin.'"

—From the Gospel of Mark, c. 52 – c. 70 CE.

Ben was not dead. He awoke, lying in a dim room. But not the terrible home of Joseph in Phoenix, he smelt the clinical scents of a hospital.

It only seemed like an instant that he lost consciousness and all the chaos just a nightmare. He could see from the closed curtains that it was dark. Was this still the same night he arrived? Too weary from the anaesthetic, he started to drift back off to sleep.

He had met his father . . .

He actually *obeyed* the paladin.

Ben could hardly believe his own story. He'd been teleported half away across the world with a whole month missing, everyone thinking he was dead. *But I am not.* Ben recalled half scenes, images. A baby, a truck, an Apache. He could hardly feel his legs, notably the numbness of his hip. There was no pain, perhaps they'd done the operation already which could mean he had missed an entire day . . .

Goddamn, the *worst* injury one could get was a lower back injury. One could break their arms, their legs, but if one injured their backs, hips, and pelvic regions . . . The pelvic floor area was one of the most important functions in the body. Working as a Hollywood stuntman he'd heard how it ended careers. It meant that the most crucial of life functions – bowel, bladder, and sexual functions – had to remain active. *Why me you stupid paladin!?*

Something larger and more transcendent than him had sent him, unwillingly, on this path and now he was here, in hospital broken underneath the weight of great stones: anxiety, guilt, anger and confusion…

"It's my life. It's my body." But who could he blame? The paladin? Joseph? Himself?

—

Ben opened his eyes and saw two humans sitting on either side of him. They were talking . . . Everything swam. He blinked, the nurse's face behind the azure medical mask was all he could focus on. She was quite large and speaking to someone on the right.

"On closer examination," she said, "we discovered that the lower L2 vertebrae has burst in structure."

"Can I show him?" spoke Joseph's heavy voice.

An image was shown to Ben, a photo of an x-ray, the lower part of his spine dislocated to the right.

"That's jacked up. I'll never be an athlete again," Ben slurred wryly. He needed to say that to sound flippant. But in reality, he was distressed.

"Now we recommend that you go through pelvic floor therapy in order to get back on track, Ben," the nurse said through her mask. "In the meantime, I will go to see if we can get you crutches."

As the nurse departed, Ben complained, "What am I going to do now?"

"Ben," Joseph sighed, a smidgen of his excitement still evident on his face as he absently sat on the chair nestled next to Ben's bed. He stared at his cupped hands as if he were about to pray. "Ben . . ."

Ben tucked in his lips, swallowing a lump in his throat. At least there was someone to talk to, someone brave enough to listen, and who could sympathise with the craziness of the past month. Someone like Joseph DePaula, who would not ridicule him about giants and crap. Being around him, bizarrely, made Ben comfortable about his experience of the arbitrary series of events.

"You still have not told me what happened to you," Joseph said. "I prayed you can forgive me."

Ben had to laugh out loud. He was taken aback by the odd kindness of this man. Had Ben seriously misjudged him? Joseph had eleven years – a lot of time – to amend his attitude. "Your prayers have been answered. A little bird came and told me to go and find you," Ben replied sarcastically. *And quite literally.*

"I just wish there could be an agreement to disagree," Joseph replied. "To understand where I am coming from. Coexistence. It's nothing much."

That was enough for Ben – he could now relieve himself of the burden of the last few months, telling his father everything; from James Casbolt, the Kandahar giant to the burning building and saving the baby, and then the paladin. He felt it would have been too much to mention the vanishing Apache and the call to 'gather the First Fruits'. Those encounters were convoluted at best.

"So, this *angel,*" as Joseph wanted to assume, "or whatever he was, delivered you and escorted you here?"

"Yes, that's what happened," Ben shrugged. "That's what I experienced. The paladin wanted to save the child found in the dump. It's… unreal! I don't think I believe it! One minute I am in Iraq, and the next on top of Mount Graham. Does that mean anything to you?"

"No." His father sounded unsurprised. "You were teleported. Just like Philip the Apostle when he baptised the Ethiopian eunuch."

Ben felt numb. *Jesus.*

"Where is the kid now?"

"I met Daniel at the Graham Apartments, and he was more than happy to adopt the child. But the thing is, I *never told him* the truth of what happened. I concocted a false story that I went on a holiday to camp at Graham and during a wildfire, I found the lost kid and saved him."

"I understand why you would do that, son," Joseph said, finger stroking his chin, scepticism in his eyes. "You have the bravery to tell me the truth and I thank you for your honesty. After the war, I should meet James Casbolt one day. But in the meantime. Gosh. . . The giant of Kandahar." Joseph's forehead accordioned. "Now *that's* a story. A close encounter with a thing of myth. The military is known for making up tales. But . . . I believe you, Ben. Your emotions, your body language, they don't lie. You're *not* going mad; you're telling coherent truth."

"I feel that I'm going mad." Ben's body clenched. "The giant was not a

Marine Corps rumour, but that doesn't mean I believe in conspiracy theories."

The First Fruits. Gather them.

"Hi Ben!"

That perky voice immediately brought old Joseph up on his feet. Patricia, Ben's youngest sister, cannoned towards Ben from the gaping door, not giving him enough time to react. The twenty-two year-old threw her arms around him, and God, her hug was hard enough to bring a grunt out of him. Yes, he still needed this. Family reunited; he had their trust at least.

"Ben, I'm so glad you're okay," she said, pressing against his chest. "Veronica is right here with us."

"Show me," Ben said, ecstasy swelling within. "Veronica, where are you?"

"Daddy, are you okay?" That small, little voice came from the six-year-old. Delicately strolling into the room was a tall, slender girl with a tangle of dark brown hair, an elfin face, pointed chin, slender neck, and wide, curious brown eyes, resembling Ben's own handsome features. In her hands was a brown plushie wombat toy and every time she pressed its tummy, it squeaked loudly. Presently, she hugged the wombat under her chin, her blue skirts swirling as she spun gently on the balls on her feet. A grin crept up the corners of her cheeks. Veronica smelled of a different time, a smell that reminded him of the intimacy of his true family household before the complicated challenges after Cleo – his ex-wife and Veronica's mother – went down the wrong path. Veronica had a faint pigmentation to her skin, and a sharp jawline – an innocent version of Cleo.

Swiftly, Veronica snuggled into Ben's arm, sighing cosily, and hand stroking her hair – fine and silky – he melted into her. He did not recall even saying anything to her, only letting her speak.

"Daddy is okay. I missed you." The bliss, the peace, the presence of his daughter cast away all darkness, fear and dread, to the bare simplicity of calmness. *Veronica. I am okay. What lies had the world told you about me?*

Ben kissed her on the forehead. Warmth engulfed his body, and tears nearly swelled in his eyes.

As much as Ben really desired to spend as much time as possible with Veronica to make up for what he'd lost, his plight was not evident to her. She only wanted to be with him a little longer, and that was enough.

"Hey Ben, how is it going?" Dominic – Patricia's boyfriend – who had to be nearly twenty-three now, also appeared from the open door.

"As good as a man with a broken L2 vertebrae will ever be, Dom. How are you going?"

"Fine, especially after what had transpired these last few weeks. We all thought you were a goner." Dominic clasped the steel bar at the end of Ben's bed. "Your unit must've come back early. That's good."

"Yeah. Earlier than I thought." Ben glanced at Veronica, picking at Joseph's small moustache. Joseph chuckled, and Veronica squealed.

"Oh, that's so adorable," Patty remarked, grinning. "Family is all back together. Ben, you've been catching up with Dad? Wow!"

"I have. It been eleven years too long." Ben glanced at his dad and smiled. *He's alright.*

Dominic nodded, smiling and patting Ben on the shoulder. Man, Patty was right. It had been over *eleven* years since he saw his father, he felt so wonderful and so blessed and at peace when around his family, all together for him.

Ben may have lost his mobility, but at least now, he had Veronica.

———

"Daddy," little Veronica asked. "Were you scared when you fell?"

Back at Joseph's stingy house, Ben sat on the elaborate brown, cream and grey rug, playing a game of Hasbro's *Sorry*, his crutches propped up beside himself. Because in the last few years, Hollywood and the military had been so demanding of his service and expertise that he missed valuable time with family, now, he was determined to make up for what he missed out on. He did see Veronica every once in a while, during the last three years, but they had only been for public holidays like Christmas, Easter and Thanksgiving. *Days which Joseph believed were all pagan! Cold bastard!*

"Well," Ben said. "I did feel scared. Only a bit."

"Were you crying when you hurt yourself?"

"Oh, I cried lot, Veronica. It hurt so much, but I fought it."

"You are very brave. I know it," Veronica instantly concluded, continuing to make her move on the board.

Childlike innocence. It had no room for doubt. Something about it was *beautiful* and *powerful*, for he was not the most dutiful of parents.

"I killed a lot of baddies for you," Ben said, building up for his decisive move on the board game. He did not know if he should go easy on this six-year-old, or hard. Veronica appeared very advanced. "I may have fell, but—"

"Yeah. I hate baddies. Were they scared too?"

"You bet they were. When I won, they ran away."

"Baddies will never come get me. You're protecting me from them."

Ben smiled.

"Dead! I win!" Veronica exploded, jumping up with a spreading of her hands, laughing in an ecstatic dance. "I win, I win, I win! You lose, you lose, you lose! I win, I win, I win!"

"Dang it!" Ben reclined on his side, slapping his knee. "You beat me *again!* I was way ahead! I was killing you—"

"No!" Laughing, Veronica scuttled around, rolling on her back, flinging her legs at him harmlessly.

"You come back here," Ben complained playfully. "This game is fixed. You're cheating. Are you cheating? You better not be cheating."

"No!" Veronica cried; she could not sit still. The little cheater rolled on the ground back and forth.

"You cheating?"

"*You're* sorry," Veronica said, rocking back up, jutting a finger at Ben and making silly smashing sounds. "I beat you! I beat you!"

Ben exaggerated a scowl, eyeing the board game and grimacing with a ridiculous contorted undulation of his eyebrows. "This *game* is sorry. It's rigged!"

"Haha!" Veronica laughed, evading Ben as he tried to grab her.

"Come here!"

She screamed.

"Oh, you can run, but you can't hide!"

He let Veronica go to hide, of course. He was not going to strain himself being at a surgical disadvantage.

"When I find you," Ben said, rising, adjusting his crutches, "you owe me another game." After seeking and loping around the house he, at last, found Veronica hiding under his bed, squealing with excitement, screaming as if she was being attacked by a bogeyman.

"Eeeeii! AHHH!"

"Got yah! I got you, Ronnie!" Ben pushed the bed aside, clawing a guffawing Veronica, tickling her. She kicked, trying to escape him. He put on a mock dinosaur roar for her.

"No! No!" she screamed, giggling frantically.

"I will never let you go!" Ben garbled. "Never!"

Veronica let out an exhilarated laugh. "Wombat! Pip! Save me!"

"You mean this Pip?" Ben said, grabbing the wombat in one hand off the bed, squeaking its tummy. He held the toy up over his head, making Veronica squeal with glee, jumping, trying to reach her toy.

And Ben wished, that forever, he could spend this special time with his daughter, it would have no hurt, no more crying, no more pain or death, for all of it had to pass away for such gorgeous moments to matter.

———

Ben limped on crutches into a living room he thought he'd never see again. Despite having Veronica around, it disturbed Ben, for this place held terrible memories – a place to be left alone when mother left.

Ben reflected on where he had come from, how in the heat of the machinery of war after the accident, he'd found himself back here, immobile.

He was aware of the cracks in the grand ruse to stay low profile, a plan to prevent paparazzi and the common folk besieging Joseph's house, with their flashing cameras and throwing their pole mics' lances at him. Now was not the time to be involved with that jazz. He needed to reconnect with his loved ones.

But the problem with Joseph was that his *ideas* were as well-known as Ben. Another know-it-all like James Casbolt. But what could Ben do to change him? Joseph was the village idiot compared to Joshua who was actually smart. *He probably believes the same conspiracies James Casbolt believes. Nuts!*

Ben strolled into the living room. A starched desk piled with books, a computer and a lounge; he remembered this place when he painted it long ago. The paint was no longer pungent, however, he could not help himself leaning against the wall to smell it. He *loved* the smell of fresh wet paint so much, he almost melted, dripping down the walls.

Ben hobbled across the room idly finding himself looming over Joseph's large and smug working space. Here on the table were myriad different books: mostly essential history about religious things, philosophy as well mythological texts that would not be important to any modern scholar. Ben tried to convince himself that just because someone had a lot of books, it did not make them any more reliable. It was what they *did* with the truckload of information. In fact, every modern scholar would mock and scoff at such nonsensical books as Joseph had here. Ben browsed the collection until a certain book caught his eyes: *Omega Plan: Epicenter of Light and Darkness* with a cover of two intertwining circles or snakes, the Yin and the Yang, written by none other than Joseph DePaula.

"Dad, you wrote *a book*?" Ben exclaimed in shock.

"What?" a reply echoed from across the house.

"Did you write a book, I said," Ben pressed, turning his head. "Why didn't you tell me you wrote a book?"

"Oh, I always assumed you never liked reading, son." After Ben flicked through the pages idly, Joseph arrived from the other room with Obadiah, his pet Labrador, prancing ahead of him, his nails clicking across the floor swiftly. "You want to read it?"

Ben froze, staring anxiously at the cover, wondering what terrors might be behind those pages. *I have nothing better to do . . .* Ben wasn't enthusiastic, but he noticed a strange avidness for answers, wherever it might come from.

Ben smelled the pages. "Maybe. But if I do, I may not even get to finish it."

"I will gladly help you along the way, Ben," Joseph said with a flourish of merriment, carrying dirty towels into the laundry just past the office. "They say the full recovery may take a few months, so sure. I make a living from research and selling my lecture presentations at conferences."

Crap conferences with silly Christian end-of-the-world nonsense! Don't remind me! Please, I want nothing of your stupid lectures!

Ben nodded, considering to not read the book. But a part of him tried, wanting anything but boredom, desiring to do something. *Omega Plan: Epicenter of Light and Darkness.* "I cannot stay in your house forever. Veronica is always wanting to go somewhere. It will only be a matter of time before some bozo notices me out there and that's it. Paparazzi and news reporters will invade your premises . . . Have you rented out mother's old house yet?"

Joseph met Ben's eyes, pausing. "No. It's an old house. It will cost a fortune to fix up."

"Oh, I was wondering if I could stay there for a while . . . Anyways, what is the Omega Plan, Joseph?"

Joseph began to pace around . . . and lecture. "The Omega Plan. Did you know, Ben, that in 1979, America co-cooperated with Islamic Left-Wing groups in Afghanistan in order to resist the Soviet takeover for the sake of national security?" Joseph's eyes bulged with amazement, but Ben's did not do the same. "Seriously, look it up in the index. 1979. The Fall of the Shah of Iran. The Cold War. America in the Cold War shook hands with Islamic groups that would later become the Taliban and al-Qaeda. They all scapegoated USSR Communism. See how things could have been different in history, Ben? The enemy of my enemy is my friend. There could have been a chance of peace and coexistence between Christian Americans and Arab Muslims. This is the characteristic of the Omega Plan. Mimetic theory – we imitate others and come together in a predatory peace, focusing our imitative desires on the destruction of a person or a group. All it takes is for somebody to stand out a little bit, and then all our problems can be solved, by unleashing a great flood of wrathful violence to eradicate the scapegoat.

"This is the Omega Plan. It is the manipulation of our desires to maintain group identity and cohesion. We come together as a society by waging war against an illusionary threat. It takes a certain humility to realise that your desires are not completely your own. You only want something because you want to fit into the crowd and find meaning. We all do this. And this can lead to a terrible cycle of conflict and violence. This is the evil of the Omega Plan – the violent solution to the end of the world."

Ben was enmeshed by that; he leaned in, genuinely intrigued, willing to open his mind. "Go on. I'm listening"

"The end of the world is either an explosion of self-destructive factional violence and a war of cosmic revenge. Now, with all this, it's important to define, what God's anger is. What is God's wrath? Does God hate us because we are evil? Or is God's wrath his grief over our foolish desire to choose sin? To choose sin is independence to define good and evil for ourselves; to desire the fruit, to take it and eat up hate, envy and pride. The wrath of God Ben is the Omega Plan. And the Omega Plan is human civilisation creating a beast, a monster in our own image, pridefully glorifying that beast as God. The wrath of God is God handing human civilisation over to this beast of our own making. The Beast is the Destroyer. It's our own self-destruction. How could God judge us, if we have already judged *ourselves* to Hell?

"The Iraq War is setting us up for this. The nightmares of the twentieth century have shown us just how powerful the potential of imitative desire and scapegoating is. It should terrify us! It should grieve us that we have failed to learn our lesson! The Omega Plan is a knee-jerk outdated method used by violent humans to try and answer our problems… By creating new ones. The war on terror will *create more terror.*"

"I see what you are saying," Ben said inquisitively, sitting down on the office chair, propping his crutches against the wall. "It makes so much sense. I… Man this is heavy."

Omega Plan… imitative desire, scapegoating violence. God's wrath was people acting self destructively because they were casting the blame on one another. America cast the blame on Islam. This was a true and organic understanding of the core of human nature, politics and warfare, and Joseph had *nailed it.*

God, I misjudged, Ben thought contritely. *Joseph is actually quite smart.*

Ben slumped, rubbing his temples from the overload of dense information. He needed time to reflect. He felt both irked and relieved that Joseph told him such a revelation. Desire, scapegoating, wrath of God. The Omega Plan.

"That's awesome," Ben said, studying the cover of *Omega Plan*. "You know so much information."

"No, *your* information is extremely valuable," Joseph said. "The transportation, the paladin, the giant. After researching enough to know how humans are, people really believe and experience things. I don't think you are fabricating your experience."

"Yeah," Ben said. "I'm at a great disadvantage telling you my authentic experience. If war in Iraq is God's will to expose our phony Omega Plan to scapegoat Saddam Hussein, then what's the point?"

"Ben, I'm glad you asked this crucial question: what's the point?" The only light source in the room, the small lamp, cast a glint over Joseph's eyes.

"For everything there is a season, and a time for every purpose under the heavens. A time to be born, and a time to die. A time to kill, and a time to heal; a time to break down, and a time to build up. A time to love, and a time to hate, a time of war, and a time of peace. Everything here is part of life, and out of our control. Life goes on indifferently as if our mistakes were nothing as smoke." He snapped his fingers. "Hebel. In Hebrew it means 'vapour' or 'vanity'. The Iraq war is God warning us to stop getting caught up in the vanity of the scapegoat mechanism of the Omega Plan."

"How is the Iraq war God's warning to us?" Ben asked.

"Yes Ben," Joseph said, fidgeting and stretching his white tassel hanging from his pants. Strange, for the hooded paladin man also wore similar-looking tassels as well. "This is important. In my book, I make the case for *two* Omega Plans. Two end games paralleling each other. I have just described to you the Omega Plan of the earth. The Omega Plan of historical geo-politics. But now, you have to realise that there is a heavenly Omega Plan working simultaneously as well. God's Omega Plan Ben is being done through the Kingdom of God. God's Omega Plan is *opposed* to the violence and the scapegoating of the earthly Omega Plan. It is an apocalypse – an exposure – of our predatory peace, and a destruction of factionalism that causes our violence. It is awful! It is shameful! It is so evil, creating great pain as all apocalypses do! But it is *not* God enacting violence against us. Get this Ben. It is the violence God reveals that we enact *against each other*. He exposes love, truth, innovation and violence, and they're both growing, all at the same time. It is so we can repent and be delivered from this endless cycle of the Omega Plan. Does that make sense?"

It did, theoretically. God's plan was to expose all this bloodshed, showing it for what it really was. Calling for the need for justice.

Gather them.

Ben contorted his face, feeling torn. Things like war *were not* things that one could simply pass off like vapour or normal parts of life and then repent of. Things like war traumatised, it left scars – physically and spiritually. Things like war were internal relapses that changed and evolved over time. An intersection of past and present.

"God's Omega Plan," Joseph continued. "Is to join all things, in heaven and on earth, in Jesus Christ. Humans are more than moral machines. God's Omega Plan is to allow us to act as proper images of God."

Gather them.

"Tell me," Ben said, "what was it in your discoveries that changed your life? What caused you to… think like this? Honestly, I never expected this from you. I've never heard these ideas before." Then, Ben begged. He wanted to know. These ideas… *You'll find the Truth.* "What changed you? Was it the Vietnam War? Did you . . . encounter something of the strange kind?"

"Ben," Joseph replied, sitting on the couch across from Ben. "Yes. Of course, the Vietnam War got me to reflect deeply about what President Reagan said during the Cold War. Cannot swords be turned to plowshares? Can we and all nations not live-in peace? Perhaps we need some outside, universal threat to make us recognise this common bond. About how easy it is that all our differences vanish if facing an alien threat from outside this world. And yet, is not an alien force already among us? What could be more alien to people than war and the threat of war?"

The Galactic Tyrant, Ben thought. *Secret Societies are preparing the world for this invasion as James Casbolt said. They're scapegoating the Galactic Tyrant, whoever he is. It is to unite the world.*

Ben's eyes probed the photograph on the table. Instinctively, he reached out for it, feeling as if the picture were an open door of the past – a knob that he turned. Ben walked through on soft sand, the colours suddenly vibrant, the warmth the of the sun in summer, which after a swim at the beach, relaxing, as tight muscles loosened all stress Ben had once had, vanishing. Covered with sunscreen, the salty and the ever-constant crashing waves filled his ears and nose, and the heated chatting of his two sisters who wanted to have a pillow fight and quarrel as George Michael tracks played in the background on the boxed TV.

He did not just remember; he *understood* the picture of his family a time before it had broken in half. It was taken in the late eighties at their now sold holiday house in California. Everyone was in the photo, Joseph and his wife Rachel (before she died) with their three kids: the eldest Lisa, Benjimin the second, and Patricia the youngest.

Ben had a finger covering Lisa's head, as if he tried to imagine that she were cut out of the photo, hiding behind his finger as if she were not part of the experience at all. But she was. The first-born daughter loved by Rachel above all, even Ben. Lisa reminded Ben of his mother's inability to love. Rachel and Lisa were in this photo as if reconciled. Restored.

Ben could try and hide her under his hand but, the past was what it was. The past could *never* change, only how the past *was remembered* could be changed.

In the past was Truth.

Ben was back in the head of little Ben in his sandals, topless with a boogie board under his arm, smiling with clenched teeth, squinting from the sun's glare that got him in the eyes.

It was before he became an actor. Before he became groomed for women's eyes. Before he became the Actionman – a soldier and a killing machine. Ben smiled back at the sun-kissed boy's face. Oh, how would little Ben know or recognise this man now, if he spoke to him. Ben could warn him about many things: about marriage, about war, failing diving and giving up diving in exchange for acting. *Never, ever, enlist in the marines, boy.*

But yet, as Joseph said, that did not matter. Life went indifferently on as a vapour. *It is what it is.*

Ben understood.

"We're gathering facts," Joseph said. "We are making certain we know what to do. What to do when the Nephilim giants return. What to do during a system collapse and we have to dwell in the wilderness."

"Gather them," Ben muttered softly.

Ben did not know how he became so immersed with the photo of his younger self. In the photo, there was no such thing as Nephilim giants and super soldiers fighting Galactic aliens. *Nephilim. The First Fruits.* Those words made Ben anxious again, and he tried to hide it by looking away, staring at the only photo in the house of the DePaula family together. Family. He did not want anything to interfere with that. Not even the Galactic Tyrant's invasion.

"How many more facts do we need?" Ben asked incredulously.

"So that we no longer make conspiracy theories. That's how sure,"

Joseph responded, but intuitively, Ben knew, that would take *forever*. "Until the materialist secular world can fall on their knees and say, 'We're sorry. We've been wrong all long.' The problem with most of those looking for truth is that they are drawing from the occult – very irrational and unscientific sources. There are some things about the Bible and mythology that I do not yet understand. Parallels between heroes and gods with historical figures. Patterns in history repeating themselves. Hopi Prophecies, Bigfoot, UFOs, Agartha, and some other oddities that I think may have truth to them." The old man paused. "Ugh, Ben, you look perplexed. Are you still certain you want to delve into this rabbit hole? Sorry, I should stop. You've heard enough from me. Spend some time with Veronica."

Ben bit his lip. "I cannot leave my family." He made a large gesture over the desk to the picture of family. "But I believe the giants are real. I killed one. And . . . I think there are more of them. All this is bigger than us. Man, if you're right, this Omega Plan is bigger than me or you and even history itself! I have to help you. I haven't spoken to you in years, and I want to catch up."

Joseph nodded, saying, "Indeed."

"And what good could I do with a busted hip?"

Joseph chuckled with a fatherly smile.

"Dad," Ben said, "who are the First Fruits?"

"First Fruits . . ." Joseph wondered with a fascinated whisper. "That's interesting . . . Why do you ask?"

Ben shrugged. "I heard it said somewhere."

"First Fruits is a Hebrew holiday, Ben, and an offering from material goods given to the members of the Israelite communities."

Ben couldn't deduce any conclusion from that extrapolation, so he moved on. "We must prepare for the Nephilim giants then, somehow. First, we need to know our enemy."

"But even I don't understand everything about giants," Joseph continued with a calm firm diction that reminded him of Colonel Pounders. "I am just laying the groundwork for the next generation after me. Ben, I want you to know that though I failed in every way, you found a way on your own to find your success. That would make many envy you . . ." Joseph quaked for a moment, swallowing and looking off at nothing. Ben could not help distinguishing a pervasive uncertainty about his exhausted look.

"Ben . . ." Joseph said feebly. "It is an awful thing; that I still remember my research and work in this world. But I can hardly remember the family we once had." Joseph's eyes went towards the photo, crestfallen. "I look at

Veronica and forget that she was yours. Only Patty and you were recognisable. Everyone else . . . It seems to me, as I get older, the world is getting smaller and smaller. One day, son, your father will have memory loss. One day, I might forget what you look like. One day . . ." Ben swallowed deeply, shivers running down his spine. "Your goodbye to me is perfect when you leave me and never look back. To focus on living your life and helping the lives around you is what I want for you. It's an unpleasant thing to miss someone *still here*." He did not meet Ben's eyes; they were glazed, transfixed on the framed photograph.

"Do you know where I should start?" Ben asked, after a long while. "How do I make a move if everyone thinks I am dead? Let's be real here, Dad. Word will get out that Benjamin DePaula is alive." Ben shook his head, close to sniggering. "I am not ready to leave you."

"Not ready, son?" Joseph sounded amazed. "You're the Actionman."

"You want *me* to lie to my fans?" Ben asked.

"No. I have something for you. My book. Focus on it. It is our homework assignment for this week." Joseph grinned. "Since you have nothing better to do than look after Veronica, see if you can get up to page one hundred of *Omega Plan* by the end of this week. Take your time. I am being generous with you. There is plenty of information to learn. I'll make some dinner in the meantime while you start."

"Whatever you say, Dad." Ben sighed, opening the book to read.

—

Later that evening, Ben tucked Veronica into her bed covers. He was just about to turn off the light, to continue reading – criticising – *Omega Plan*, when Veronica in a soft timid voice said, "Daddy? Can you tell me a bedtime story?"

Ben paused, awkwardly adjusting his crutches from the ajar door. "A story?"

"Yeah. A bedtime story."

Ben leaned back on the edge of Veronica's bed. "And what story do you want to hear?"

"The one with the princess. The one where she sacrificed her life to save the world from the volcano."

And Ben told her the myth of Crater Lake: the wooing of princess Loha by the Underworld god Llao, her refusal and the great battle of the spirits of earth and sky - La-o against the Great Spirit – that ensued. During the battle, the volcano erupted, and great fires devoured the land, punishing the people for their sins. According to the Great Spirit's prophecy, the only way for the fires to cease was that an innocent soul in an act of self-giving love, should die. Loha the princess became the wilful sacrifice, by climbing up the top of the volcano and jumping into the lava.

The eruption ceased and the volcano transformed into the great blue Crater Lake.

Veronica didn't say a word when the story was finished. "Did it happen?"

"What happened honey?"

"I said, is the story true? Because it is unfair. Why did the princess have to die? Why is Great Spirit so mean? Why could he just kill Llao and save everyone on his own?"

Questions on the problem of evil were beyond Ben's capacity to answer. "I don't know, Ronnie. It's a legend and sometimes what is more important is not the facts of what happened, but the meaning and the lesson the story teaches that is true."

"Daddy," she reflected. "You say you go to kill baddies to protect me. But killing is mean."

What type of question was that? Veronica was . . . smart, shocking Ben. What questions had Brianna been exposing this child to while balancing detective work and rearing her when Ben was away?

Veronica, lowering her glance began to fidget with the fringes of the bed sheets. "You said you fight baddies in battles. You kill them for your job. What is it like to kill a baddie? It must be scary."

It was a difficult moment, but Ben did what seemed right in his eyes, which was to say, "Of course it is real," and then to stroke a strand of her hair out of her eyes and hold her. He knew Veronica was too young to know about the truth, for the truth was too dark all together – she was not ready for it. He couldn't tell all of it. But if he did tell her, what would she make out of it? One day she would be ready. He couldn't tell her *exactly* what happened but the *truth* of what happened.

Well, if Humpty Dumpty is about a guy having a great fall off a wall, it wouldn't hurt then to talk about shooting a . . .

Ben ended up telling Veronica the story of the Kandahar giant. Ben and his men heard from the Arabs a cannibal giant living in the landfill who had kidnapped their baby child and Ben came to save the baby from the garbage, after killing the giant.

It was not literally what actually happened, but it was *based* on what happened. Was that the difference between history and legend?

"The point is, Ronnie," Ben said, hugging his daughter, "is that I love you and Great Spirit does too. We will do anything to protect you."

She snuggled deeper into his arms. "Good night, Daddy. I love you."

And she was out, drifting deep into a sound sleep with only good and sweet dreams.

38

COLONY OF HEAVEN

". . . Make every effort to supplement from your faith, virtue, and from virtue, knowledge, and from knowledge, self-control, and from self-control, steadfastness, and from steadfastness, reverence, and from reverence, brotherly affection, and from brotherly affection, love."
—From the Epistle of Second Peter, c. 60-90 CE.

Joshua sat on top of the jeep on a hillock, watching domesticated Labradors trot, probing through the Haditha slums in the buttery May morning. The dogs scavenged on dead bodies, of men fallen in battle and those that had succumbed to starvation and disease. Arid winds quivered, hung coolly with the haunting dirges of prayers moaning from unseen Mosques, echoing across the overcast dawn of a semiurban run-down building.

Seven o'clock, and the sky was inlaid with golden pink blankets of light. Joshua sat meditatively cross-legged as he prayed under his breath, paralleling the Muslim prayers to their deity as he prayed to his own. The God that gave him Truth.

He quickly wrapped up his prayer, the Muslim dirges still droning in the background, just as Reggie and Julian arrived from out of their jeep down on the gravel pass, on an undeveloped highway, on top of a large incline.

Joshua sat aloof with an arm resting on his knee as he accepted Ryan's offered oat cereal for breakfast.

But nothing was more gratifying than intellectual food, which was meditation, something he had come to appreciate more. Joshua looked on ahead, at the rousing town, watching the dogs lumber away from some unseen encroacher. Dogs could glimpse into the realm of spirits.

"How is everything going for you, Reggie?"

"I'm dying," Reggie sighed. "I don't see the purpose of fighting anymore."

Joshua blinked. He understood and sympathised with a nod. The war was a devastating mess – men died for no reason and the country they aimed to save was destroyed, the main objective to get back at al-Qaeda for 9/11, forgotten.

"I got a call from home last night," Reggie uttered, crestfallen. "They didn't even ask me how I was. No one cares about us. Why aren't we in Afghanistan fighting the Taliban and Osama bin Laden? No one mentions 9/11 anymore. For me, that's the whole reason for me being here! In Iraq, it's all about my war. It's about not wanting to die. It's crap. *None of it is right.*"

Dark movement caught the corner of Joshua's eye. He was almost too ashamed to see that that shadow was a woman striding down a street below, her all-covering *niqab* with the only skin visible a band of eyes. Over her shoulder, she hefted a semiautomatic buckled with bullet magazines. A mother defending her children? This was reality. *We have come to this. Everyone has a sliver of the darkness of the dam within them. Imposed upon them, unwillingly.*

The ride towards the toll point of Haditha town was rough; Joshua constantly had to fix and hold his tangled hair which exploded outwards in curls, itching his eyes and forehead. His feet were already starting to feel numb from the constant vibrations.

I swear I probably look like a Nazarite like this, Joshua thought.

"The toll is coming right up," Jason Laycock said at the wheel, letting the cool morning air batter inside the jeep as he drove quickly down the solitary highway.

The reports of civilians with bombs were said to be sighted near the vicinity of the town, thus Joshua's dispatchment on a casual routine patrol was to secure these border lands. Understandably, the protracted war in Iraq had malfunctioned the country, despite being delivered from Hussein's regime; it had zones entangled with rogue groups seeking to rid the country of what they perceived to be invaders. And they would invariably do so, viciously and with violence. That could explain why the domestic front had become tense, requiring armed protection once America won Haditha Dam.

As Joshua leaned an elbow on the window ledge and saw a pink smudge streaking in the sky like a kite, far in the distance. Nefer, out on patrol, waved around isolated clusters of trees, arching across the road far ahead. Joshua's inner man smiled, it felt *so nice* to have an immortal brother be there with him.

How good, Joshua thought, relaxing as the air massaged his face. Nefer spun like a dolphin, the humblest and most balanced free spirit, rivetingly ringing with the love of God. Drowned in it, dissolved by praise and bliss, joy and liberating glory.

He saw the spirit dart in coordinated loops, spinning into the azure morning sky, fading in and out of reality, shimmering like a mirage as he dipped to his side then zoomed towards the open grassland. He flew towards a small flock of sheep, goats and a shepherd sitting on the back of a truck under the shade of his modest, thatched roof. Nefer rippled in graceful strands of pink, red and orange jelly, right through the slanted wire gate, and hovered, zipping above the animals as if inspecting curiously. All the sheep and goats glanced up at the translucent gelatinous membrane floating in pelagic undulations, but they paid no heed to it as if it was as ordinary as a bird. The sheepdog growled and barked in warning. Nefer swivelled round a branch of a gnarled olive tree hanging with bird houses when Joshua lost sight.

In the world of ease, Joshua saw the jeep in front of him lurching, tipping to the side in the air. It all happened with crackling silence of acceleration. On the left side of the road, a surge of flames exploded, flipping the truck around, dismantled bits skidding off, bonnet, roof, and fender detaching.

"BREAK!" Derek bellowed, and Joshua almost flew out of his chair.

Laycock crushing the break, zoomed into Nefer who, just in time, stretched into an invisible gelatinous pink-white net, catching the jeep.

When the impact came, it was so strong Joshua gasped. Closing his eyes, he flew out of the side, seatbelt gouging him. The vehicle spun and rocked. Loud crashing and groaning, tyres screaming, the airbags bursting. Everything went black.

Joshua, wake up!

Nefer.

Everything rung like a bell. Straining, Joshua pushed the airbag off him and opened the damaged door. He survived the crash, only feeling a few throbbing bruises, a ringing head, and his nose burning with smoke, rubber and blood. The truck had almost tipped from the gnarly crash. Flames burned all around from the roadside bomb.

The unpredictability of war – the Eidolons had been too laid back and caught off guard.

The footfalls on the asphalt and frantic yelling of Jason Laycock and

Derek Fish revealed that they were okay, saved by the guardian angel unawares. If Joshua had not been here, but back on medical duty . . .

Don't think about it!

"Reggie! Garrow! Oh my God!" Laycock shouted.

The panicked voices of his friends pulled Joshua out of the wreckage. Quickly scrambling for his field medicine supplies from the wrecked jeep's boot, he rushed towards the distressed voices.

"Briones, what's your situation? Over?" a voice called over Ryan's com kit as Joshua jogged, lugging his equipment.

"IEB! I repeat, IEB! Three marines down!" Ryan shouted, panic wearing his voice thin.

When Joshua arrived at the smoking wreckage, he saw a ghastly sight that almost made him vomit. He passed Derek Fish kneeling with his head bowed before a gory torso hanging off the fallen roof with no legs, but chunks of sinew and hamstrings, not ripped completely off. Reggie was gone.

"Rest in peace. You brother of another mother. I love you, Reggie man," Derek muttered, cataleptic.

Of Garrow was nothing but random piles of flesh mixed with the scraps of metal, rubber and burning truck junk.

And Julian . . . Joshua fell to his knees, his fuzzy hair flopping over one eye. He did not move it out of his face, because Julian was still alive – caked with dark red blood and soot, orange boils scudding his face. Shards of shrapnel protruded in his forehead, chest and left shoulder.

Joshua felt numb with dread. *Stay calm. Remember what to do.*

First was danger: get the wounded out of the way of any hazards. Quickly, Joshua propped Julian with his back up against the kerb, toxic burning fuel seeping into his lungs.

Then response. A weak arm flopped on his shoulder, then twitched, squeezing Joshua. He met his eyes. "Julian! Can you hear me!? Julian!? Julian, talk to me!"

The soul that sinned shall die.

Julian stubbornly struggled with Death. For an atrocious man like Julian who had not contemplated his life deeply, the Second Death awaited him. Once oxygenated blood ceased to pump through the body, it suffocated the brain, shutting it down, decaying it.

Joshua had to be very quick; he first went to make sure Julian was still breathing. The pulse was weak, fading away fast, but with a muffled gargle, the pulse became stronger, but only for an instant.

Even at Death's threshold, Julian was rebellious.

Tracheotomy. Obstructed airway, Joshua remembered from his first aid. He had to do all he could while Ryan called for help – the shrapnel had to remain in Julian, Joshua just had to keep him alive. *Recovery position. Hold on to his neck and hip. Rest his head on his shoulder. Use gravity. Get the stuff out of his mouth. Check his breathing. If he stops breathing, begin CPR. Thirty compressions. Early response. Early recovery. Early everything.*

Putting Julian in the recovery position, Joshua grabbed a suction tool, unclogging the excess fluid and blood out of Julian's throat. It seethed Joshua's revolted stomach.

"Josh, hurry!" Laycock yelled savagely as Joshua worked.

"Help coming?"

"Yes!"

That was all he needed to know. "Then help me carry him when it does!"

Inbound bullets ricocheted off the fallen jeep. Laycock hissed, turning around to fire at the distant enemy, giving cover for Joshua. The firefight shook the air with cracking thunder. One shot seemed to hit Laycock, but he was standing up firing as if nothing had happened.

Then, Jason Laycock froze in cease fire. His young face went pale. Then he screamed a cuss word. He turned around dropping his gun, looking at his arm. His lips were trembling. He clutched his arm, groaning fitfully in frustration. The look on Jason Laycock's face was a grey sick mask of someone who wanted to give up living.

He's hit?

Julian roared a gasp, heaving with a wet, broken cough, black blood from his mouth, dribbling down his chin. He doubled over heaving with so much strain, that he coughed, his breathing raspy. Joshua rubbed Julian's shoulder. Gaging loudly, Julian's eyes twitched under his lids as Joshua's own watered with tears.

Though splashed in Julian's blood, Joshua smiled. As he began to staunch the bleeding from the wounds, reinforcements arrived with a new truck. An ebullition of explosions and gunfire occurred somewhere to the far left down the highway, past the nature strip and near the village. Joshua and Laycock placed Julian on the trailer together. The truck sped off back to the dam.

Sitting in the trailer, Joshua cradled Julian's head in his lap, his face taut, not daring to take his eyes off his patient, not until his wounds were cleaned and ready for surgery. In the meantime, Joshua poured all his canteen water on Julian's face and used a cloth to cleanse him.

Julian was dying. Scowling, Joshua let out a trembling breath as he worked to keep this man alive, but he knew it would be too late.

They had arrived. The head medic, Lieutenant Murry, leapt onto the trailer, seizing Julian onto a stretcher. But Joshua had lost all the willpower to move as he watched grimly. Julian was being led away, back into the throng of the dam, never to be seen again.

"Hey, Josh, you okay?" Donny Bummalang said.

"He will die," Joshua grunted.

"Look," he replied, hand on his shoulder. "You did well. You did your job giving first aid."

Joshua shrugged off Donny's hand. "No. He's going to Hell! Do whatever needs to be done!"

Tears dripped down his face. Through them, he saw bleak glimpses of the surgeons flocking around Julian working on him immediately. The medics in the Marine Corps had a code: they were willing to go to all lengths to treat both the living and the dead right. It was a sure code, and whenever the wounded went to be checked up, there was an air of confidence that they would return fixed up. This, however, was a challenge.

Julian was dead for sure. Passing into oblivion, Joshua thought of losing all his loved ones, the void of losing his self, his research and his passion all pouring out of him. All vanity. No point.

The demons of the Haditha Dam had arrived. The prison.

Lies.

Joshua struggled to breathe, too wary to rebuke the demons. He came to a concrete corridor overhung with twin notable pipes – one thinner than the other – merging upwards from the corridor and upwards into the roof of the atrium. The hairs on the back of his neck rose while pensive darkness of the void hung in the air.

Lies were a little dam; inside them one could feel safe and powerful. Inside the little dam of lies, one tried to run their life and manipulate others. But the dam needed walls to hold back the mighty waters. These were the justifications for lies, against the deluge of truth.

Joshua stared at his hands, blotched with the blood of Julian. It smelled disgusting, and yet, as Joshua slumped there, tears running in torrents, he could not have moved to wash them. To wash away that vanity with pure living water.

It should have been I that died, Joshua thought. *I deserve it.*

Julian would lose his family and his family would be deprived.

But if Joshua died, no one would care... Expect for Pounders.

Joshua was surrounded by waters of destruction – Abaddon – and Yahweh was standing in the gap – a dam – protecting and defending the house smeared with the Lamb's blood.

Christ's blood. Julian's blood. Joshua was washed in it.

Joshua was the house – a temple of God – ready to be destroyed. Bombed. As he sat back against the wall; clenching his fists, dried with the blood of a friend he did not like, Joshua wept for his hopelessness and for the loss of life.

The shedding of blood defiled the earth. When a human died – an image of God – the area around the death became tainted. Death was so tainting that one buried the blood – the soul – along with the carcass.

Joshua wore death. Like Christ on the cross, he wore the wickedness and profanity of his enemies. Blood was a *wonderful* thing. A soteriological thing.

It was not long until he felt the security and smelled the warmness of freshly bound books, incense, trees, food and perfumes and other myriad fresh scents which stimulated his memory of childhood. Someone loomed over him, and he thought it had to be Nefer.

He looked up, and the presence of Nefer was Judd Pounders. He crouched down, sitting next to him. Joshua could not help but blush, feeling ashamed that Judd saw him like this, suffering in victory, smeared in gore.

"Are you okay?" Judd Pounders murmured soothingly. It had been weeks since the poltergeist incident and he had recovered from his mild concussion quickly, though he still wore a bandaid on his eyebrow and gash wounds on his arms. The man was strong, still functioning optimally.

Joshua smiled, raising his head to meet Judd's eyes. "I'm surprisingly better than I thought I would be, Colonel."

"We can go back to America now," he replied. "Go back home since all of our objectives are complete." Could this simply be a dream, this exchange? Joshua did not know; he could not discern it. He gazed off down towards the railing overlooking a narrow atrium. The bright light of sun cast in angles down the corridor. "Are you alright?" Pounders had discerned Joshua's daydreaming, and bringing him to his senses, he blinked, meeting the Colonel's eyes.

"I'm just . . . Reflecting," Joshua said flatly. "Its . . . It's been an experience this war. I've become a new man. You were right," he pursed his lips. "You were right to enlist me."

Ponders smirked fondly.

"What?"

"Well, I find it extraordinary now that even the little things tickle me," he said with much merriment. Joshua could not even remember one instance where he had seen Judd Pounders this gleeful before. "I used to love seeing the bigger picture of things, it was what made me a good Colonel. Though, I have come to see that there are even more precious things that often go unseen. After we mourn the deaths of those in our unit that have passed, we will then move on, because those men who died, died for us to live happily. We need to accept that's what they died for. Anything else is useless."

We make purpose out of something . . .

For once, he was glad that Pounders had come at the most perfect time, now he could see the familiar unconditional solicitude that he never thought anyone, but Pounders, was capable of conducting. The honour Pounders radiated, made Joshua trust him to tell him the truth.

"There is . . . something that I want to tell you about, Pounders," Joshua said.

Drawing his lips to a firm line, Pounders listened with an openness Joshua could see so clearly. "I was alone. Nobody had the bravery to connect with me as much as you did, Pounders. They're afraid of me, of who I was." He choked up. Then he finished with a rather abashed, "Thanks. I met someone that changed my life."

"What are you talking about?" Pounders said sombrely. "Is there something I do not know about?"

Joshua took a deep breath. The time had come to share the grace in him. "I never realised this person was in my life the entire time." He felt his throat spasm, his voice becoming tender. "But when I discovered who . . ."

"Who is this?" Pounders whispered with a knitted brow. "Who are you talking about?"

Overcoming the drift between exchanges and the thundering of his heart, Joshua said. "Jesus . . . the Christ."

Those two words of the ultimate victory, words that were dangerous, words that were enough to cause discord and enough to make peace from discord. Words that stirred souls lost in the deepest darkness back to reach the life of redemption. Everyone at least knew those two words, but unfortunately, derogatorily.

Pounders did not scorn, nor did he roll his eyes. He just stared at Joshua intently, blinking. Then, sitting back, looking down at a pack of soldiers carrying their bags, chatting to each other as they lugged their way out of the fortress, Pounders sighed protractedly, relaxed and sound.

"Thank you, Joshua. For being honest with me." A strange expression appeared on Pounders' face. "I knew that there is something to you . . ." Pounders trailed off. "I've suspected my whole life there could be something out there." He glanced at Joshua with eyes that marvelled.

Joshua grinned at that. "Judd, you know me."

"Oh, yes," he sniffed. "I suppose I do. It makes sense since you have a unique passion for all things ancient. An old soul."

"Everyone knows of Jesus, Pounders, but nobody knows *about* him."

"Wonderful," Pounders mused, patting Joshua's back firmly with a muffed chuckle. "I like hearing that. Yes, I will make sure you are back on track now. I promised you after these years of constant nonsense, that you will be able to live life to the fullest. Isn't that a Bible verse? To live life to the fullest?"

Joshua shrugged. "I think. In the newer translations."

"Well, no longer will you lose an opportunity again. I will make sure you get want you need. When we get back, you'll start anew. New office. New library. I'll even pay for your loan and your university fee. It was something I'd always wanted to give you. I was going to have a child, but my wife died in childbirth, so when I found an opportunity to look after you . . . I could . . . make it up to her. To my child I never knew." Pounders' voice became raspy then, and he paused to swallow.

Judd's doing this for his dead wife and kid? He could not believe it! Joshua suddenly found the strength to shoot to his feet, albeit his legs wobbled, almost tripping. "All that?" Joshua said. "All that because of your wife and kid? You never told me this!"

"Secret for secret," Judd said. "Good trade, right?"

"Yeah okay. I can fend for myself and I'm not a child, Judd, don't feel obligated to help me so much! The Marine Corps has given me enough pay to start afresh already."

"*Really*?" Pounders sounded flabbergasted. "I'm sorry that I have been bugging you, Joshua, but I'm a senior military Colonel. I'm ready for retirement. I've got just enough for you. And even if I go down, at least you will have enough."

"But—"

"My glory days are over, Joshua; I can afford it. Really."

Joshua chagrined, letting out a stubborn harrumph, stopping himself from using his blood-covered hands to fix his horrid mop of hair dangling over his eyes. "Okay . . . As you say so." And then, in a mock way, he said, "You've been thinking about this long and hard, after you told me about getting conscripted in the marines."

Judd laughed. "For your whole life you've been on the brink of homelessness. You need to have your own place, to get out some more."

"Well, that's not *my* normal I – I'm not normal! You know that!"

"And me? I have done nothing about that. In fact, I have not rectified the asylum and hospital fees after I went through a court of law to get my hands on your parole and give you a waiver. I can do it and *I will* do it. For you, my wife, and my kid. You have a criminal record in this world, getting opportunities without support is almost impossible. I know you're a determined genius, and I would give you all the opportunities that you can have. You have transformed Joshua. The world may not know this, but *I do*. You are not the liar and conner that you once were." He looked into Joshua's eyes. "You're now a saint."

Unmerited favour, Josh. Why are you a saint again? This is grace through faith in God.

Pounders stood up and stroked his chin, a grin appearing on his face. "I'm thinking to getting you an entire library for everything. All those books . . . They could come in handy one day."

—

There was a mixed bag of faces – gloomy and gay – that met Joshua, securing himself into the straps within the Black Hawk. He could imagine they were directed at him, but Joshua had been humbled to know he was not a hero. Not a saint.

Feeling triumphant, Joshua heard the blades chop and spin, swishing the grass below. The door slammed shut. Joshua, realising how tired he was, tipped his head back, and looked down at the landscape sinking below him.

His home for a few months came into full view. He yawned, rubbing his eyes and face with clean hands. The backside of Haditha Dam – the grand industrial fortress – lay before him in an epic panorama of Lake Qadisiyah. The dam held back the flood steadily and Joshua would forever remember the place – it had supressed him, ultimately bringing the best out of him.

Everything felt right because Pounders had witnessed Messiah in the chaos, Messiah who had changed Joshua, reflected his glory in Joshua. Amazingly, he had camped right outside the gates of Hell unknowingly, but the ancient evil made him rather than killed him. Joshua hadn't given it a second thought.

On this rock I will build my church, Jesus proclaimed to Saint Peter. *And the gates of Hades have not overcome it! I have given you the keys of the Kingdom of Heaven, and whatever you bind on earth will have been bound in heaven, and whatever you release on earth will have been released in heaven.*

Joshua smiled, merrily fathoming how he now felt peace, flying upon the wings of the wind.

But yet, even as he tried to doze, a tendency of a pure peace overtook him, a rapturous joy. A feeling Joshua thought Nefer would be feeling. Joshua flew higher than the helicopter ever could. He felt like the whole sky was his own – the blue expanse his dominion.

You have transformed Joshua. You are not the liar and conner that you once were. You're now a saint.

There, he would find rest.

39

THE DIE HAS BEEN CAST

"5. Reduce greenhouse gas emissions. Abolish carbon-based automobiles, boats and planes for Agarthan Vril powered vehicles. Enforce sustainable energy (hydro, solar, wind and acoustic) to replace petroleum industries. Let all the animals roam free. Mobilise fungi to decompose plastic and waste. Have mushrooms become the new food, clothing, architectural and manufacture staple (see the information on Patalan culture and civilisation).

6. Make sanitation, first-aid, medical and mental health institutions cheap and free when needed. Pay nurses and psychologists extra wages and strive to have most of the human population vaccinated. Parents must have automatic supervision in intensive childcare hospitals. Lower the prizes of super foods and abolish animal meat, fast food, tobacco, saturated fats and sugar production. To maintain societal success, everyone must be healthy. Make access to Mycomantic fungi easy and cheap."

—From "The Kallipolis Great Reset." In *The Survival Dynamics*, Alfred Bonner, Arhat of the Fourth Initiation.

It was drizzling outside once the sun sunk after dinner and yet Ben DePaula's L2 vertebrae still felt like a brick shoved up his side. Where forecasters predicted that a deep cold would encroach Arizona, playing with Veronica at the park while taking Obadiah the dog for a walk in the heat of the day, had been blessed. A heavy denseness loomed, where not even the warmless light of the new moon would have shone. It disappeared in shadow, vanished, as the clouds scudded across the formless sky.

Ben longed to walk to the park again; Veronica and Obadiah were the two things that kept him alive: two propellers on a plane that kept him afloat in the air, since he had no means to work out, and with no ability to go on a run.

Those leaning crutches, slanting on either side of him, were a *memento mori* of how much reliance he had on his own agency. He wondered, and the sad truth confirmed itself again. The truth that Ben had limited control over what he could do.

That Ben was part of the triangle of mimetic desire. He was part of the earthly Omega Plan, violently scapegoating people and cultures just to get an objective. The war on terror. The lies. The wrath of God: tragic human self-destruction.

What he had read in *Omega Plan* caused a flux in his mind. It spoke of cosmic things Ben had no control over. Psychological diagnoses that made him uncomfortable. Patterns in history that were so predictable. Ultimately, the fear Ben had was that his father's intuitions were shaped by conspiracy theories.

"There is an Omega Plan greater than the wars and the plans in the Middle East," Ben realised.

"Yes. We wished derisively that the world is a simple place," Joseph philosophised across the room. "Black and white. How many people have been deceived by Cartesian binaries? It's not about following rules, it's about whether our actions bring us closer to God and neighbour, or whether it pushes us further away from them. We need to stop scapegoating and blaming others, Ben. It divides us. The Powers of darkness embodies all people, systems and cultures."

And Ben thought, *The David vision, the paladin knowing Joseph. Would I have to tolerate ambiguity, to be apathetic of what is right and wrong in order to understand what's happened to me?! That would only make things harder!*

Tipping back his head and letting out a protracted yawn, Ben caressed the pages of Joseph's work *Omega Plan: Epicenter of Light and Darkness*. He put it to rest. He never considered himself a keen reader at all, but he knew one thing: the book was nuts!

His father, the Vietnam veteran and a machine of conflated ideas, had such a tendency to remain inquisitive; that made everyone think him to be a genius. Being educated didn't matter, and sympathising with René Girard's theory didn't make one smart. It was *how* one was educated and lived out exposing mimetic theory that mattered. When one heard data, they process it in their mind, and have an emotional reaction. If that data accorded with what they believed already, it would naturally be accepted without second guessing. Ben expected his father to be humble, believing he didn't have everything figured out, but he didn't. He cherry-picked data, accepting it to be fact.

In his book, Joseph failed to manage this. He used Girard to grind axes, deceiving himself that he were researching and learning but . . . Ben sighed. *All this hate is not helping me. Put it aside.*

"You cannot be exclusive, you must be inclusive," Joseph said.

What am I getting myself into? Ben thought in frustration at his horrid state, his hip ebbing with pain, hand hovering above *Omega Plan,* no longer finding it worthwhile. *I need to search for truth. Real truth, not speculation. I don't have to be here. The paladin suggested I find my father and the truth. I don't have to be here.*

Or do you? A part of him insisted. *You can't walk. Joseph helped you to the hospital. You are in his debt.*

Confounded, Ben rubbed his face, remembering that he was immobile, almost falling off the chair. Cursing, he groped for the crutches, staggering for balance.

"What were you saying?" Ben said. He grabbed his crutches, gingerly limping around. A frown formed on Joseph's face as Ben watched him pocket a packet of medications. He melted into the leather couch under the hanging embroidered white curtains, blinds like condensed bars only slightly ajar in the fading light. Ben really considered switching on the main light.

The reply came at last. "Law of Triumph." His voice was slurring again. Was he even okay? *No, he believes I am asleep and indoctrinated.* "That is the timeless principle. They said suffering is coming upon the earth. Suffering is soul-building theodicy. Suffering . . . We're the scapegoats."

With a smidgen of pain in Ben's hip, shifting the crutch in a more comfortable position under his arm, he stared at a spot on the rug, simpering wryly. *We're the scapegoats… Tell him the tree dream! David!*

But he is mad!

"You will confront challenges," Joseph rambled on. "You are blessed when persecuted for righteousness sake. What you thought was right, turned out to be upside down." Ben normally considered Joseph's musings as uneducated ambiguous utterances – brain melting utterances. Joseph was old . . . He tugged his stringy tufts of what remained of his once luscious hair behind his ears.

Ben limped towards the couch. Joseph cupped his hands as if he were about to pray, but when he spoke, his voice was indistinct. "Ben . . . My boy . . . What have I done?"

"Nothing, Joseph."

"Nothing?" Joseph only shut his eyes, looking out the same window as if anticipating his maker coming down into the evil chaos of humankind and recusing him from despair to a renewed space-time universe.

"What made you overcome incredulity?" Joseph said, stroking his chin aimlessly. "I can tell that you want to know more. Ask me more, son."

Ben glanced at his crutches. "I don't feel like it." *Now or never!* "Uhm. Actuality. I had a dream one night," Ben said brusquely. Unsure if his words had been understood, he repeated again. "I agh, had a dream – an interesting dream – the night I was about to land in Iraq, and I thought—"

"Yes?" Joseph lifted his surprised face, leaning in conspiratorially. "Yes, Ben. Go on. You know there is a prophecy about the saints having dreams?"

"No."

"What did you dream?"

"Well. It was so vivid and real, I cannot think of the last time I had a dream where I could remember every single detail: the sights, smells, sounds, touch." Somehow, as he retold the dream, it felt as if it happened years ago, for many times he had to correct himself. He began with David, only the very few lines and the events that he could remember: the abdicating of the throne, the harp, the plague and that Ben was called Natan. Ultimately, what he remembered the most had been the tree dream. "There was this cedar tree. A colossal one, probably over a thousand feet tall. I then saw another tree, dry, broken and dead. The branches looked tortured, writhing downwards. Branches twisting and growing in such unusual ways, it almost seemed like the tree was a cluster of petrified lightning bolts. Yeah . . . It was like a fig tree."

Joseph flinched as if zapped, and Ben watched his father's face transform – his eyes gleaming with a million juggling thoughts. Ben bit his lip, trying to ignore Joseph's flabbergasted gaze. "But I looked closer at that fig tree and saw it was writhing with snakes. Then it burned up. And that's it."

Ben made sure he had said that all right, probing through his mind to see if he had left out any vital details. Yet Joseph stroked his chin with a tight knuckle, his expression thunderstruck.

"What!" Ben retorted, pissed off. "What's *wrong* with you? I just told you—"

"Ohhhhh ahaha, give me a minute! Give me a minute!" Joseph shouted, whistling with marvel as he clamped his hands on either side of his temples. Joseph, once all languid, suddenly had life reanimated into him. "Ohhh mmmy Goooddd. Aragh yes! That's it!"

"What did I . . ." Ben said again, taken aback. Quaking, the way in which reminded Ben of Christopher Lloyd having a Doc epiphany, Joseph grabbed Ben's shoulders, shaking him, his voice half elated, half pleading.

"It makes sense now! It's not just a random dream! It's the Lord! Do you know what this means!?"

"What? What is it, Dad?" Ben exclaimed, his father's enthusiasm contagious.

"I have given David to you as a Witness…" With a gaping mouth, Joseph turned to look up at the wall, as if to jump up it. He began to pace back and forth, while also performing some little dance. "Oh my *God!*" He punched his palm. "This is the final piece to the puzzle! The cursed fig tree. 1948. Zionist Israel is the curse fig tree! It's *all* connected. This . . . Now, now where have I seen cedar trees . . . What was it?" He gasped. "*Ezekiel 31! Yes!*" He scurried with crabbed steps towards to his office chair, muttering under his breath, awaking his computer. Ben just stood there, on his crutches watching Joseph knuckle down, typing fiercely.

"Ugh . . . I will leave now," Ben whispered.

"Give me time, son," Joseph babbled with joy. "I'll give you an interpretation in the morning. This – is – *it!* The cursed fig tree is Zionism! The axe is laid to the roots!"

Zionism? "I . . . don't understand."

Joseph kept on typing, not even glancing towards Ben. "People need to see this! Haha!"

But this was just what they both needed. Joseph was finally occupied and distracted doing his crazy thing, and Ben was finally off the hook. At least there would be no more questions on that strange dream anymore, he would get a coherent answer. Or *close* to coherent. Rubbing his heavy eyes with his hand, Ben absolved in himself, turning towards the bedrooms that called for him.

But deep down, something told him that passing this point, he would never be able to return to his normal life again. He shrugged the feeling of unease off.

—

Bhairava, Just Son of Danu, sat in the white van of Ian Mastemah, dressed in white, tasked to kill Joseph DePaula.

As he drove in the passenger seat, he was constantly trying to convince and console himself unnaturally that this and what was about to happen, was okay. It was only the culminative effect of bad karma.

For the first time in many years, Bhairava had never felt so convicted on the mission to cut with the sword of truth. It did not make sense. Why did he procrastinate?

This was a reason why he joined the Pro-Israel and Anti-Palestinian Manicheans of Light. Bhairava just wanted to become a deterministic force of karma, not a monster. Whoever deemed guilty, Bhairava was only accelerating the process of karma, carrying no fault and carrying out the necessary opposite reactions to the actions of the guilty. It was ideally not a matter of what he had done or what he felt. Bhairava was an Initiate of the Third Initiation. An unfeeling heroic yogi ready for moksha or nirvana in non-existence. An archetype. *The freedom of will is absent to an Initiate? Can I even have secrets?*

Bhairava felt his stomach seethe as if he was going to vomit. He closed his eyes, practising his controlled breathing exercises.

The Manicheans had no idea Bhairava worried deeply for Joseph DePaula's assassination. The man was deluded, yes, but he never killed anybody. Could there be another way to break his anti-Israel pro-Palestinian paradigm? A debate perhaps?

STOP . . . THIS! Bhairava castigated himself. *Attained the Void!*

Void. The numbness – to tap into the transcended part of his self-consciousness in order to be sane. It helped, but those abused children's screams, accusatory, vindictive, kept on coming back. The screams of the slain could not go away.

I'll die so the world to be healed from Pantokrator.

The screams were getting worse. He knew it. He needed . . . to inhale more Pneuma. At least that drowned out the sounds completely. Was this turmoil a sign that he was obtaining the next level? He needed to be tormented to shed all bad karma.

He was glad the Manicheans of Light were not clairvoyant; his condition was his own and he accepted that personally, as the process of cleansing took multiple lifetimes. All the pain would go away, in those many lifetimes. Yet, what had he been grasping or clinging to cause all this pain? Not anything material – he'd given up materialism years ago – no family, no friends, no money – only his own sanity and super-soldier body. So, what more was there to let go?

Bhairava still clung to other people. James Casbolt. His masters. He worried about other people when he slew them.

This unfair fate was keeping Bhairava from becoming an Arhat of the Fourth Initiation, a catalyst for change in the world, for people to rise in vibration from the material, to become Ascended Masters, overcoming the Nephilim and the Galactic Tyrant. It was impossible . . .

Yet despite this, his lonely path to becoming an Ascended Master, it made the Manicheans treat him like some warm fire in which they gathered around on a cold night, snuggling up next to him so they could receive his warmth.

For he was their template after all. And this communion sullied his Ascension.

Bhairava looked into the rear-view mirror and saw his own reflection in his eyes. He appeared mellow; ethereal. Not a man he recognised anymore living ascetically for most of his life. Bhairava wanted the Manicheans of Light to see who he was tonight. Just Son of Danu.

The van slowly crept up the street to DePaula's house.

"Manicheans of the Light. My fellow Disciples," Bhairava's master Ian Mastemah said from the wheel. "The die has been cast."

Bhairava's heart quickened, feeling a surge of sharpness and clarity to his awareness.

"Master, I say that we go inside, and ransack what we can," commented one of the female Manicheans.

Ian Mastemah turned to meet her, his jagged features accentuated in the cast of the dim orange streetlamp, forlorn and singular. "I will not stop you," he croaked.

He rolled down the window, completely turning the handle with sporadic vigour like the beating of Bhairava's heart. He felt like a prisoner, kidnapped in this white, stingy, rickety, dirty van.

Bhairava inhaled a small amount of Pneuma to sedate himself. The whispers of children soothed in his soul. On inhale, he instinctively exerted the energy into his eyes and nose and his smell exploded with clarity, sharp and expansive. Notably, the ever-present petrichor of light rain imbued with the freshness of souls – the four scents completely enhanced – clicked.

Instantly he could both smell and see for miles, beyond even the dark screens of trees and the fabrics of curtains, made translucent. He could smell a plethora of exotic scents, such as the smell of food, nuts and animals of the neighbourhood. Bhairava even noticed a faint cobalt colouration in the corners of his eyes as the Pneuma made the sky twilight instead of black and the trees a deep purple and violet, wispy tendrils in his enhanced night vision.

Undoing the strings, Bhairava allowed Ian Mastemah to heft out the scoped sniper rifle. The Manicheans of Light fell still.

The house was still within a few yards from the van. Ian aimed straight, dead on in the head over a faint outline of a man working at a desk.

Ian glazed his finger over the trigger.

Heart thundering, Bhairava hesitated, sweating. He held his hand out as if to stop Ian himself. But it was too late. He'd had plenty of time to stop this.

I am sorry, DePaula. Forgive me, Bhairava thought, hating himself.

———

Veronica lay snuggled in bed, dreaming of sweet things . . . Of the princess living happily with her tribe in paradise.

A loud noise made her yelp, awaking her in darkness. Veronica raised her covers, her mind wondering.

Outside, rain drummed sluggishly on the roof. A cast of dark blue from her window outlined the clawed form of a spidery elongated tree branch, crawling across her wall, a web of membranous tentacles covering her. The runnels of rain drops quietly rolled in rivulets down the pane of the window.

It made sense. Thunderstorm. Veronica stared into the dark, covering her entire body as she slipped under the covers, only her eyes exposed, blinking, trying to subdue her fear. The fear she hoped would pass, so that she would curl up, sleep again and wake up in the morning, have pancakes and play on the playground again.

Daddy is here with me, Veronica thought, placating herself. Why did she feel so cold? *It is alright. It is just a thunder strike . . . What was that?!*

What happened next, Veronica could barely comprehend. It was a very loud slam on the front door, and stomping footsteps. Veronica couldn't breathe. Her blood became ice and she whimpered as the house trembled from the force of the swinging door. Voices. Scuffing of feet, running, bodies thrown around. Strangers from the darkness destroying Nono's house! Veronica's chest clogged up with the hard thundering of her heart as she slid farther under the covers – that all-protective shield.

Baddies.

She yelped as an echoing sonorous bark whirled throughout the house, bouncing off the walls. Obadiah's slobbering, guttural barks. Veronica had never heard those barks come out of Obadiah before.

A man yelled, followed by Obadiah screeching. Veronica's heart lurched into her throat, her hands clawing the bed so hard her muscles cramped. A great struggle ensued in the hallway, shaking the house. Obadiah's whines, madly revoked in her head, again, yelping, again.

Help me help me help me help me help me help me help me.

Suddenly the door in her bedroom flung open. Somebody tumbled inside.

Veronica screamed, throwing herself into a ball, hands over her ears.

Hands seized her.

"Hide, Ronnie." Daddy's voice was febrile. Looking up, she confirmed that voice's face to her relief. "Hide," he whispered, sounding like a good monster that would make the baddies tremble.

Veronica obeyed with her whole heart. As fast as she could, in her pyjamas, she slid under the bed, and she lay there, on the cold creaky floorboards.

"Do not make a sound," Ben hissed. Veronica could only see the dim illuminations from outside the bedroom, and shadows of movement casting over them, the sounds of Daddy's own feet and the bounding of his walking sticks. "You will be safe—"

Thump. The sounds of smashing furniture and scuffing feet. Veronica gasped.

"Quick. Delete the fake news."

"DePaula has a daughter."

"What!?"

"Wait, Bhairava, go no farther."

Words. Evil dark intent.

Dark men. Monsters killed Obadiah!

Daddy, help me!

A bright blue light flooded the room. Veronica hid her eyes in her arm, not tolerating gazing from the sliver between bed and floor. Her breathing quaked as much as her body, and with roaring in her ears, she clamped her mouth shut. Snot ran down her nose. Her hair a dishevelled snarl, brushed against the dusty wooden underside of the bed. Veronica clenched herself but relaxed almost at once as her daddy's words came back to her, for her to "hide, and do not make a sound". Opening her eyes, she found that they'd been containing tears, and to her shock, she sobbed, and sobbed and sobbed.

Veronica's legs pulled from behind her. Her bloodcurdling shriek filled her ears.

—

Ben's heart bled within him when he heard his daughter scream. He almost clicked open the closet where he hid, but he pressed against the door, and listened through the crack.

"It's a girl!"

That was CIA agent Ian Mastemah, no doubt! Ben felt shocking numbness grip him as he listened. Veronica bawled, sniffing and whimpering. *Oh God, don't do anything to her, Ian!*

"Leave her! She's innocent!" The glowing blue man shouted in anger.

Tense silence. Veronica squirmed and sobbed.

"Why did you have me do this to him!?" the glowing man growled passionately. "He had a daughter and a son. A family. What right do you have to control me to do such terrible things to Joseph's family?! Tell me, master, what did they do wrong?"

"You have more rights than most, Bhairava," Ian said, serene and oily. "Keep your hate to yourself. Joseph deserved to die. The misinformation he's spreading . . ."

"You're a hypocrite!"

"Let the Manicheans hear you. Their Initiate has anger, doubt and sin in his life. Your oaths to Ascension make you weak."

"Please! Why are you doing this? I cannot support your violence!"

"I can't help you with that!"

"Why?"

"Democracy is on the line."

"But I—"

"How long have you been doing . . ." The voices faded along with their footsteps as the intruders evacuated the house.

Only then did Ben breathe again, bursting out of the closet tripping over Veronica's bed catching himself as he fell.

He had judged and had admitted. Perhaps it was in that step of ambivalence to that enigmatic world of pure bliss in the past, knowing he could do nothing to gain satisfaction. Truth was snuffed out like a candle. Gone, passed with a puff of smoke.

Joseph – his father – was dead.

Veronica lay on the floor, in a ball, weeping and crying.

———

Veronica raised her head, tears blurring her vision. The baddies had dragged her from under the bed, then . . . they just left her on the cold ground.

"Daddy? Daddy." She trembled, shivering in furious fits, wearying her bones.

They *did not kill her* or take her away. Yet her heart hurt, and her legs and body were bruised.

"Daddy?" She gasped, desperately sobbing. So much pain! "Daddy? Where are you? Daddy!"

Arms picked her up, and Veronica sunk into her father's warm embrace. Arms, strokes and hugs ensured to her that everything was going to be okay.

The baddies were gone.

"Obadiah! Obadiah's dead! He's dead!"

"Shhh," was all Daddy said.

"Obadiah!"

Daddy was very sad and mad. Veronica could *feel it*.

They hugged, until finally, he let go, and telling Veronica to stay behind him, they proceeded outside. She did not want to look as she glimpsed mangled Obadiah laying in the hallway. Daddy let out a guttural cry when he saw Nono, lying on the ground, sleeping.

In the confusion, Veronica did not know what to do but sit on the couch, grabbing her plush toy Pip the wombat, aimlessly stroking it. All her world now could be about her wombat. She cuddled the marsupial – it warmed her as she rocked, slowly, back and forth, back and forth.

Stroke. Console. Hug. No more baddies. No more.

—

Ben, if he had not been injured, would have burst out the door and run, and run and run and run, until he had physically vented his clogging, shocking sadness out of him.

Now it all congested within him, and the torture of it was remarkable. At least running and crying could be a release. But he *couldn't run or cry!*

His chest felt hard as concrete. Joseph died all elated and excited serving God. His merriment was crystalised on that dead mask, lips twisted in a grin of death, like a goat that had been slaughtered. A face of a satisfied man with his work completed – had died without knowing that his entire office had been ransacked and destroyed, books torn, the table flipped, the computer smashed, all the files gone.

It's an unpleasant thing to miss someone still here . . .

Ben's father had died suddenly. From this context, it was a mercy, for whatever those medications had been, Joseph had feared he would suffer from dementia. He couldn't fathom his father's own fear that he may have missed out on talking to his son, but Joseph had his prayers become truth. Ben had missed his only chance to understand his father again; time had defeated him.

He had to satisfy this horrible darker revenge for Ian Mastemah that churned, needing to be unleashed.

He had to fight for Veronica – all that he still had.

Ben found a way to sit his dad on the couch, fixing his collar and shirt, straightening his clothes like Joseph would have done when Ben was only little. With stiff hands, Ben used a cloth to staunch the blood leaking from his blown head. He did not even hiss or groan. Nothing remained inside Ben to react. It was a blurry, sordid mess as he treated his father's husk. His chances to truly reconcile was forever out of his hands.

"I didn't even forgive him." Ben sighed sufferingly, slumping in the chair next to the corpse of his father, Veronica turning away timidly, hugging the wombat. He could feel his father's blood tingling his fingers, but he could not get himself to move, to do something. He almost choked from something in his throat.

His father was gone. And he did not even say goodbye. He did not even say what he thought of *Omega Plan*.

He got up and endured a war just to hop on his crutches. He groaned, legs shaking so violently, he could have sworn they had another mind.

And all Ben could think over and over again was, *Why? Why, Ian Mastemah? Why?*

Ben grabbed the phone, fiercely dialling his sister's number. This incredible indignation – revenge – kept him functioning.

Come on, focus. He shook his head, groaning, pressing call, but raising the phone to his ear, all he heard was his heart.

"Yeah? Dad, what is it?" Patty, sounded vexed, woken up from sleep.

Ben opened his mouth, yet it felt like slush. Numb jaws tried forming words.

"Hello, who is this?" Patricia called with firm vigour.

Ben kept his glance on Veronica. "Dad's dead, Patty." The release of slurred words brought Ben chills from the shock. Dad was dead . . . Ben's hand was shaking.

Patty's reply was long anticipated. "What!?"

A wave of nausea made Ben dizzy, so he sat down on the couch. His stomach cramped and sweat burst from the pores on his skin. He glanced half at the ground and at his floating right hand blotched in blood. He opened it and then clenched; half clenched. "They shot him . . ." he croaked. "He's dead . . ."

"Ben, where are you, just tell me where you are!" Patty panicked, raising her voice like a mother worried sick. "Where's Veronica!?"

"With me," Ben admitted, sighing. "Safe, Patty. She's safe with me."

His head swivelled around, he glanced at the still images of blood, the smashed desk and computer, ripped books, the corpse . . . He settled on Veronica. *Easy. Everything is spinning. Easy, Ben.*

"I'm at his place."

To Ben's ears his words did not sound like mumbling. "What?!"

"Dad's place," Ben said louder, his throat dry.

"Who . . . Who shot him, Ben?"

"CIA agent Ian Mastemah," he responded, unable to control his trembling.

"Ben, oh my God! No!" Those screaming words from Patty sounded accusatory.

Ben's eyes focused on Veronica curled on the couch, feeling his stomach wanting to retch. He *needed* her.

"Ben," she responded. "You gotta listen to me."

"Call the emergency," he pleaded, voice brittle.

"Ben! Everyone still thinks you're dead! You have to get out of there. Take Veronica with you, leave immediately and come to our place. We'll call Brianna."

Ben felt a fleeting sentiment of relief at the mention of his wife. "I can't leave the crime scene. No. I can't."

"Can I speak to him?" Dominic's deep voice sounded over the phone.

"No, wait," Patty said frivolously and then, refocused her urgent and nagging voice towards Ben. For goodness sake, she did sound like Brianna sometimes. "Ben, they're going to suspect you! You've been gone for months!"

They're going to suspect me? Ben thought in anguish.

Ben blindly flung his hand at the lamp, shutting it off. Veronica flinched from Ben's action. The girl made herself very, very small. The air, the room, a weight upon him; he tucked his chin in his chest, slumping on the ground in a ball, as Patty railed on. "Can't you see that they are directly trying to get you in touch with the Marine Corps, Ben! They found you! They'll track you down as we speak! They know you're alive!"

"But . . . How?" Ben said. "Why would Ian kill Dad? He had affiliation with the marines, or . . ." Or was there information that Ben was missing? Some secret Joseph did not get time to reveal to Ben? He had to search for truth. To Ben, such a prospect would have been sheer frivolity. Brianna could search with him. Too many times it surprised him, but reality galvanised faster than he could comprehend, and now he had no choice but to adapt to it.

"Damn it, Ben!" Patty snapped emotionally. "You've never listened to me, but just listen this once—"

"Give me the phone!" Dominic cut in, and Ben clenched his hanging head in his right hand as he waited, forcing the tears back from his shut eyes. He blinked, seeing his father who sat on the couch, grinning as if nothing had ever happened. Blood stained the rug under Ben's shoes, seeping into the soles.

"Hey, Ben. Hear me out. Benny, you okay?"

Neck hurting, Ben stretched his head letting out an indistinct groan. He clung to the change of voice. It was softer than Patty's, not as demanding. "You need to get up before something else happens," Dominic continued.

"I'm just in the—"

"I'm coming. Stay calm. We'll call Brianna and the FBI when we get back. I'm coming. Stay calm, Benny."

The phone hung up, and Ben was alone with Veronica and the body that was once his dad who he hardly knew. The tragedy of the sight crumpled Ben with unshakable shame. For a while, before Dom could come to pick them up, he settled himself gently by Veronica, hugging his daughter, feeling worn as tattered rags.

—

Ben groggily stumbled on his crutches into his sister's arms. The journey felt like a night swim across the beach – nothing coherent, everything drifted.

Dad was dead.

"Thank God," Patty breathed, her grip like iron squeezing Ben. Dom came in carrying Veronica, pale white from fright. Patty gave Veronica a kiss; she had fallen asleep wrapped in a blanket, clutching her toy. Dom took her to bed.

"Y'all get inside, quickly," Patty said, wrapping an arm around Ben. "Ben, sit down. Come here." Ben resisted his sister's prodding.

"Patty . . ." he mumbled, as she took off his jacket. "We've got to find them."

"Come on. Your hip. You must lie down, Ben. It's late. Brianna will investigate." Brianna . . . Vision spinning, Ben vaguely remembered being led down brown halls, warm with picture frames, cabinets and draws. The piquant smell of lavender finally coaxed Ben as he sighed weakly in his throat.

"Brianna," Ben sobbed into the bed pillow. "Brianna . . . Help me."

437

40

DEVOURING ASHES

"7. Have AI produce the creative arts and take all the legal and military jobs. Divide labour jobs with educated humans in council, trade, agricultural production, education and business corporations.

8. Have all world museums endorse the repatriation of all stolen cultural inheritance artefacts and human remains back to home countries. Make religious belief relative. Purge all conservative fundamentalist in the campaign to stop gun violence. Kill Islamist leaders in secret. Champion the pluralist interfaith movement, Humanism, Utilitarianism and the Buddhist idea of 'Non-Self.'"

—From "The Kallipolis Great Reset." In *The Survival Dynamics*, Alfred Bonner, Arhat of the Fourth Initiation.

Veronica DePaula watched out the window at a white van rolling down her street, turning a corner. It drove towards the hill that rose out of the ground where cactus grew wildly with their thorny sides, marching around the slopes.

She loved having playdates at her best friend's house, Zoe, who was the sister of Aunty Patty's friend Dominic. Zoe's backyard was the largest Veronica had ever seen – it was practically a park, and it led into the nature reserve where the big hill loomed. That place near the mountain was off limits of course, but Veronica still desired to make the most of the day. Daddy had dropped her off here so he could go to the funeral for Nono, but he would be coming back soon for dinner with Mommy.

Zoe O'Leary was tall and slim, wearing vans boots, jean shorts, a striped shirt, and her hair cut short to the jawline. She had to be the funniest and most bubbly person Veronica knew. She had a cool insect collection and snail farm and was very keen to inventory it to Veronica.

"Why isn't he speaking to me?" Veronica said, pointing at the largest snail in the plastic container. She tapped the snail and it flinched, its eyes retracting into its face. Veronica giggled. "What do they eat?"

"Cos lettuce," Zoe said.

"I hate lettuce. They are yuck, like snails are yuck."

"But that's not all I have," Zoe said. "In here, I found two grasshoppers. And see on that leaf, there is my caterpillar and somewhere . . . There she is! Do you see my ladybug?!" Zoe's favourite colour was red, and her favourite insect was a ladybug. Her shoes, toys, even her bed was in the colour of a ladybug's red and black spots. "And I have a massive hornet fly in here somewhere too."

"Hornet fly?"

"Yeah. Daddy caught it. It so ugly and is about this big!" Zoe's fingers exaggerated the size of it and Veronica gasped. "It was half dead and injured so we captured it, along with some ants that were crawling all over it."

Veronica contorted her face, laughing. "Ewwww! Zoe!"

Zoe laughed excitedly. "I *so* want to go hunting for insects with you."

"Hmmm. But I want to play frisbee first. You promised me."

"Okay. Then you promise me, we go insect hunting!"

"Deal!"

Bounding down the stairs, Veronica and Zoe darted to the living room leading straight into the kitchen, where Veronica's stepmother Brianna was setting up plates and food with Aunty Patty for a family dinner after everyone came back from the boring church service.

"Mommy, can we go outside please?" Veronica asked.

"Outside?" Brianna replied, stirring a pot.

"To play frisbee," Zoe said.

Patty, sticking a piece of food in her mouth to taste test the steaming casserole, said, "Convince your brother to go with you, Zoe, and you can. You know the rules. Don't go to the mountain. The cactus will prick you."

"Yes, yes," Zoe sighed, but Veronica was already skipping out the door, hunting for the frisbee.

"And make sure they come back before six," Brianna demanded like a policewoman to Zoe's brother Morgan.

"Go!" Veronica giggled with joy as Zoe dashed before her. Veronica flung the frisbee across the field with all her might, all the way towards the road. She laughed at her feat.

"Hey, be careful on the road," Morgan called, jogging towards the road where Zoe had cautiously stopped to look for cars. Silly Morgan. They weren't dumb, Veronica knew the road was dangerous.

Veronica ran the rest of the field towards them as fast as she could, weaving around the shrub trees, the hot wind blowing in her hair. She exclaimed with joy in jubilant laughs.

She found Zoe peering at the frisbee which had flown all the way towards the grassy walkway where the white van had parked on the side of the road. Veronica ran to a stop, staring at the van – filthy, rickety and dirty. It had a spare tyre on the back, corroded away with rust, its window bleak and shrouded in darkness. It had a gold curtain covering the windows and smelled of old leather left out in the summer sun. Bugs that had pinged and pattered against the grill were splattered in splotches all over the bonnet and windshield. Heat radiated from the vehicle, the white paint looked old as it peeled and the tyres looked worn, as if they would melt into the concrete.

"Hey," Veronica whispered, pointing to the large van. "You wanna have a knock?" She picked a stone and threw it at the van. Deliberately she missed the windows, only to hit the roof of it so it would barely dint.

"Someone in there?" Zoe asked.

"Nope," Veronica knocked on the side door. "Nobody's home!"

"Free RV!" Zoe gasped.

"Hey, be careful!" Morgan shouted, running up towards them, grasping Zoe's rock-throwing arm. "Stop! What are you doing?!"

Zoe sighed, crossing her arms, miffed. "Morgan, you're a bum."

"No, *you're* a bum," the smelly teenager said.

"This van is for a bum," Zoe said, smirking, then she frowned, eyes staring at her brother. "You *always* stop me from having fun."

"I'm not . . . This is someone's van! I would leave it alone. Come on, let's get the frisbee."

Veronica, smiling impishly, hit the door harder, and burst out laughing. The rusty junk of a van was old anyway. She could damage it . . . a bit.

"Come on, let's go," Morgan said, grabbing her from behind, lifting her up. "Stop. Stop. You can't just hit somebody's stuff like that – Hey, Zoe!"

Oh, good girl! She was climbing up the back tyre.

"Hey! Hey, stop!" Lousy Morgan tried to grab for her.

"It's empty!" Zoe insisted. "Nobody's in it!"

"I don't care. How would you like it if silly little kids were beating up your van? Let's go, now! You'll get me in trouble!"

"Neeh, you always get in trouble for no reason," Zoe said.

"Morgan! I have an idea," Veronica said. "How about we gather sticks and hunt for insects!"

He shrugged. "Anything besides beating the van is fine. But remember, dinner is ready in thirty minutes."

—

Darkness had fallen, and Morgan had been out for an hour searching and wandering around North Mountain Park, with no sign of where the girls had gone. He'd said to Brianna they had been desiring to hunt for insects, but even after calling them to come back inside, at some point during the evening they had snuck back out again.

"Don't get mad at me! I just don't know where they are," Morgan reported in haste to Brianna. "They said they were just going to go back to your house to get Veronica's wombat and some sticks to go hunting for insects, and that's it! They were gone."

Brianna knew instinctively they couldn't have run away very far. She believed in Morgan, as a true and reliable witness.

The girls were nowhere. As she jogged down 15th Ave fringing North Mountain back towards her house, Brianna was arbitrarily saying, "Oh God, help me find them . . . Oh God, please help me find them."

Out of breath, Patty and her partner Dominic rounded Brianna's house from the grassy laneway where fence and house divided, leading towards the open field that descended to the North Mountain Park. Dominic raised his hands in the air. "I cannot find them."

Panic and fear assaulted Brianna's resolve.

"Were they down the street?" Patty said. "At the park?"

"They're not here," Brianna said, gathering around Patty, Dominic and Morgan in their driveway. "You sure you looked everywhere in the house?"

"Yes, and they're not here," Patty said.

"Oh, Zoe's getting whupped once they get here," Dominic uttered with hope; whupping his sister for running away was better than having her missing. He heaved out a stressful sigh, hands planting on his hips. "My mother is going to kill me. Sorry, Brianna. I whup kids. And brothers." The man glared at Morgan who started.

"Don't look at me!" Morgan exclaimed. "I was only looking after them when they went out. I was eating dinner when they went to hunt insects! I can't do two things at once!"

"What did they do the last time you saw them?" Patty said, brow creased with stress.

Uncomfortable silence fell upon the youth and Brianna found herself feeling the stomach-churning dread of her daughter's disappearance. She went to call 911 and her colleague, Special Agent Keller Butcher – a man who always solved cases. It was as she dialled that fifteen-year-old Morgan spoke up about everything that happened to him, shock riddling his voice. "The van. There was a white sort of van outside and . . . It was a Toyota van. White." He craned his neck down the street, Brianna following his gaze. "It's gone?"

"What van?" Dominic snapped. "Morgan, speak!"

"I-I . . . There was this van they were playing around on it . . ." Morgan began. "Ugh . . . I think there was someone inside! It's gone now." Brianna saw Morgan's face blanch, gazing at her for help.

Fear – awful cataleptic fear – laced through Brianna's body. *What kind of a mother am I to let this happen?*

"I told you not to come near North Mountain," Dominic snapped at his brother.

"They were throwing rocks at the van and trying to climb on it."

Dominic tore out his phone from his pocket, flipping it open. "Tell me everything you remember about that van."

"Ugh . . . A spare tire on the back. Toyota. Old and rusty."

"Police. Police."

"Ugh," Morgan fumbled over his words in anxiety. "I don't remember a number plate. It was white and—"

The booming sound of a car door announced Ben's arrival. Oh, he couldn't have come at a worse time – Veronica and Zoe had disappeared, and Brianna's heart was bleeding with pain for Ben.

"Guys?"

Brianna clamped her gaping mouth shut as Ben, hobbling on his crutches, approached them.

"What are you all doing out here? What happened?"

"Ben . . ." Brianna trudged towards him, hugging him in a tight grip. She closed her eyes. But something was not right. Ben somehow felt taut. His muscles were cold, not melting into her body. He didn't look at her, staring at nothing. She let go, shocked by bitterness, holding onto his arms firmly and said, "Your . . . daughter. She's gone missing."

Hadn't Ben dealt with enough suffering already? First, he had returned to

Arizona suddenly – after he had supposedly gone missing at Haditha Dam, where all search parties had given up, concluding that he'd died. The Marine Corps had not yet come back, they were still needed in Iraq. Yet Ben's sudden appearance in the States did not sit right with Brianna, a confusing, perplexing situation in itself. Second, Ben had been at Joseph's house with Veronica when Joseph had been shot dead by CIA agent Ian Mastemah, and now Veronica had disappeared. Could there be a connection between Joseph's murderers and Veronica's disappearance? They are only a few days apart. Possibilities such as that daunted Brianna. And on top of that, Ben had a seriously injured hip that even when she had inquired about it, he had said that at Mount Graham he had tripped and fallen while trying to evade a wildfire. Why would Ben be hiking up *Mount Graham*?

Ben is refusing to say something, and now we have two situations on our hands!

Brianna, slowly, saw the incredible despair mount upon her husband, his head slumped, and his face crinkled in a tiger scowl. "How long has she been gone?" his voice rasped, the glare in his eyes terrifying. "I shouldn't have gone to the funeral. What *the hell* happened?" Ben sounded vicious, because he could feel something bad had happened when he had gone to pay his respects to his father. And now he would end up panicked and guilt ridden.

Oh Ben. I'm so sorry.

Taking a poised breath, her boldness steeled, Brianna raised her arms. "It's been an hour. They had dinner with us, and I told them to come back before dark and for Morgon to go with them. They disappeared when you left to help finalise the funeral at Joseph's grave. We went looking for them."

"The van's gone," Morgan exclaimed, and Ben started, panic contorting his complexion. Brianna did not need him to say it, she read it in his terrified slumped body as he'd made the dreadful connections. *The van. Gone. Kidnapped by a van driver.*

"Crap!" Ben spat. "Crap!"

Brianna had no idea where it began: Veronica and Zoe had been there during their dinner; the sun was still about to set. Since the girls had to have been back by five thirty, already an hour had gone by and Brianna's heart shot like a firing gun, expecting the worst.

Missing, in the vast wilderness . . .

But Brianna had been trained to solve problems and cases beyond her. So, her panic had in part been stifled by meagre indifference. She did not know if indifference at the moment constituted a good thing or ill as a step-parent.

As Ben and Dominic went to search, Brianna trotted into Patty's house, feeling foreboding pensive shadows that strode in the evening, congealing around her. She found the sofa and sat on it, alone, wilting into the seat and pretending she could be released from her stress, out into the wind, out in entropic infinity. Feeling exerted, she closed her eyes, burying her head in her hands.

Be strong, Brianna. You will overcome.

But it had all been too much this last week with Ben's father's death; she'd asked the FBI if she could go on a week's leave and afterwards deal with this case. Now Veronica . . . She had to investigate this.

That's why I have my trusty Keller Butcher with me. He always solves hard cases. He always does.

"Keller is in control. Keller is in control."

Presently, Brianna realised she had been gripping the couch hard with her clawed hand, and relaxed.

Cleo . . . Veronica's biological mother, what would she have done if her daughter had gone missing? No, that woman would leave Veronica to do whatever she wanted, carefree. Cleo harassed Ben days before the divorce with that . . . At least Brianna would *never* neglect Veronica standing outside alone with the creepy van – she had pointedly told Veronica to not go far and come back when the sun set, and to have Morgan watching her at all times. At least Brianna never drunkenly snapped at Veronica, wielding a wooden spoon. At least Brianna never locked Veronica in a closet. *A closet! Who does that to their children anyway?*

Brianna would never do that to her child. She married Ben for many reasons – one being that Veronica had no security. Brianna was an agent – security was her thing. *Then why had she . . .*

No. Veronica had *not* run away. She was a well-loved child, inferring someone kidnapped her coercively.

Quickly, she got out her phone, dialling Keller Butcher's number.

"Special Agent Butcher," he said austerely behind the phone. In the background, Brianna could hear the sound of murmuring voices and clanking dishes. As always, he was out for dinner.

"It's Brianna, Keller," she said. "Keller—"

"What's wrong?"

"Keller, Veronica and Zoe have been kidnapped. There was a white Toyota van on our street and Veronica and Zoe were playing on it. An hour later, they and the van were gone." Why did she shiver nervously as she uttered the truth so clear to her? Was she afraid looking like a terrible mother?

Impartial Keller Butcher never judged her. He trusted her and *would* find the kidnapper very soon. When that man committed to something, he would get results – he always got results that paid off, no matter how long it took to get them.

But now . . . Brianna felt as if she had done worse than Cleo ever could. She'd failed Veronica.

"This happened just now?"

"Yes."

"Hang on. I have a call from the police. I'll ring you back." He hung up.

———

FBI agent and law-enforcement investigator Keller Butcher had been eating dinner at a Chinese restaurant solitarily at downtown Lake Biltmore Village when he got the call for units to find a suspicious Toyota van found at the intersection of West Peoria Ave and North 7th Ave.

Brianna DePaula's daughter had been around that white van when she disappeared two hours ago.

"Are there any units?" A lady reported from the communication device in Keller's car.

"This is 12-80 responding."

"10-40 responding."

Keller spoke into the device saying, "This is FBI Agent Keller Butcher. I'm five minutes out. I'll meet responding units."

He did not waste a second. Screeching out of the driveway, his headlights on high beams, he raced to the objective location where the police had found the white van crashed in a ditch off road near a nature reserve of cacti and shrubs.

"Brianna, I've found the Toyota van off road at the intersection of West Peoria Ave and North 7th Ave. It matches Morgan's description," Keller said into his phone, Brianna on the line. "I'm going in."

Once on the scene, Keller saw two other police cars on site, the red and blue pulsing lights flashing in silence in the midst of the pensive throng facing the old van. The police had already raided the vehicle, dragging out the suspect – a young man from the looks of it – it was too dark to make any details, but face-to-face interrogation would come soon, and Keller would know him well.

The police roughly hauled the moron along, two men grasping his arms.

"Walk! Walk!" they shouted. The young man made a muffled squeal, twisting around, trying desperately to break free from the police's grasp.

Shouts and harsh voices clamoured behind as Keller stalked towards the off-road van to investigate its contents. "Hey!" the police sounded behind. "Walk! Get up! Get up! Show me those girls! You put them on North Mountain?! Where did you put those girls?!"

A pathetic whine.

"What the hell is this guy on?" one officer said.

"He's high on something," another responded. "Put him in the freakin' car! Walk!"

That moron would be interrogated soon, so Keller would have a good time picking at his brains, if he wouldn't speak now – often disillusionment overcame the criminals just at the time of being caught – they needed time to calm down and feel comfortable. And if he was high . . . That needed more time to get out of his system.

But first Keller needed to search the van diligently, every corner and every possible place to find clues.

Turning on his flashlight, he stalked into the back of the van without a licence plate. Dark and dank as it was, smokelike dust rose in illuminating spectral light as he cast a beam inside. Searching every possible place, Keller found nothing of use, but something did catch his eye.

On the dashboard, Keller grasped a Department of Defence CD within a clear plastic case. The disc, for some reason, had on its front surface in black marker the words METATRON'S GOLEM.

The hell? What was this kid doing with a Department of Defence CD?

—

The van driver was named Thomas Jones. He had the mind of a baby, always creeping into the corner of the room, distancing himself from Keller as far as he possibly could during the lie detector test. Keller pressed one hand against the wall to prevent him from running away in fright.

The young man was pathetic. He never spoke much during the interrogation, either saying "yes", or "no", never elaborating any further. He had been the most ball-breaking suspect Keller had ever had in his life. The kid got a blank look in his blue eyes, as if Keller did not mean anything to him. Keller almost lost his patience too many times. *This kid is hopeless,* he thought, after a toilsome effort, rubbing his eyes and checking his watch. Midnight. He even tried showing Thomas the images of Veronica DePaula and

Zoe O'Leary and he stilled denied. *He will not budge! What's the point if he's not even answering my questions!?* But willpower kept Keller going – he'd never failed a case. Solving cases were the only thing in life where he felt complete order and purpose. It defined his function.

"What do you do in the van?"

"Drive. Sleep." The boy was so timid and so harmless. Could he have been mistaken as the wrong guy? No, surely not. The girls, according to Patricia O'Leary's report, had been throwing stones at the van. Any timid person could reach a breaking point of rage from something like that.

"You sleep there? You sleep during the day? Why did you park right outside the O'Leary's house?"

Thomas' wide light blue eyes gazed at Keller's barring arm against the wall. His lips were cracked, skin grey and clammy. He smelled like sweat and damp mould; his short cut hair tasselled above his eyes. "I only went for a drive."

"No, you weren't driving," Keller whispered sternly. "You were parked right outside of their house, so that makes me think it was premeditated, that you were planning to take two little helpless girls with you. Have you taken little kids before?"

Thomas closed his eyes, as if he could whisk himself away. "No." His face paled.

"Did you ask the girls to come inside?"

"No."

"Did you offer them any lollies to come inside?"

"No."

"Did you ask if they were lost? Anything, did you talk to them?"

"No."

"You put those girls somewhere? Did you drug them?"

"No."

"Where did you put them? Did you tie them up?"

"Can I sit down?"

Keller sighed, leaning back from cornering the boy in the corner. He could see the boy was stressed, so Keller stepped back. "My best friend's daughter is missing. And if you're lying to me, she will make sure you will regret it." Keller stepped forward, hand brushing Thomas' ear, making the boy flinch, as he growled, "Where did you put those girls?"

"Don't touch me," he whispered sternly.

"Where did you put those girls?" Keller breathed in his ear, tensing.

"Stop."

"I know you put those girls somewhere."

"Hmm." The young man, screwing shut his eyes, twitched, letting out a shaky breath.

"Hey. Hey. Look, I know you're a decent guy," Keller said gently. "I'm not trying to make you feel bad. I'm just trying to get the right answer, okay? That's all I want. Where do you live?"

Thomas was silent.

Keller wet his lips and said again in case he misheard. "Where do you live?"

Thomas, closing his eyes, looking as if he were about to cry, shook his head.

"Where do you live? Just tell me, come on. If you know something you are not telling us, you could go to jail for a very long time, you know that?"

"The church. I like staying there, but . . ."

"Do you know the church's number?"

"No."

"Crap. You know the address?"

Thomas hesitated. "Youngtown."

Keller noted that down, dismissing Thomas Jones back into solitary confinement, and went to get some sleep, before tomorrow to tick off the places he needed to go on his list. And first was Brianna DePaula's house.

———

Ben woke up at ten forty the next day, exhausted and drained. Last night, he'd been up until five in the morning, searching and searching, then slept fitfully.

Many volunteered to help, dividing the neighbourhood and North Mountain Park into five areas and each headed out armed with a map, pictures of Veronica and Zoe, and a phone.

Last night was tedious and dreadful for Ben, but he knew that this was the most logical way to find them if . . . if Veronica and Zoe were still in the neighbourhood. No one he asked had seen the girls or anyone looking like her. Periodically the search parties checked in with the Phoenix police to get an update on the progress, if any. Nothing at all, until almost two in the morning. Even tracking dogs were brought in to search the park.

Ben locked himself in his bathroom to wash his face, burying his head in his hands before the basin.

For the first time since his daughter's disappearance, Ben allowed himself to consider the range of horrendous possibilities, and once it started, he couldn't stop the dreadful parade. Some were horrible ghastly snapshots of torture and pain; of monsters of the deepest dark with giant claws, Nephilim hungry for sex and rape; of Veronica screaming for her daddy to save her and no one answering. And mixed throughout these horrors were flashes of other memories; the toddler with Pip the wombat; the two-year-old with Cleo eating too much chocolate cake for her birthday; and the one image so recently made as she fell asleep safely in her daddy's arms.

The doorbell rang and Ben, regaining his composure, went to answer it.

"Morning, Benjamin." Keller Butcher – in his mid thirties – was surprisingly handsome.

Ben took a second too long to reply when he realised how wretchedly unlucky he had been to suffer so many painful blows at once. Brianna's friend special agent Keller looked privileged, educated and fulfilled – he held himself proudly, wearing a black linen shirt with a dark jacket unzipped. Once upon a time, Ben used to be as successful, fulfilled and privileged. "Morning, Agent Butcher," Ben said.

They shook hands. Keller's hand had pale slender fingers. But for some reason, Keller's palm was warm, indicating he was nervous. That incongruous smile hid something.

"I'm sorry about your father," Keller said, not aware that he was serving the Actionman. The oddity for Keller to not acknowledge Ben's fame simply caught him off guard. "I apologize that I haven't been able to spend much time with you so far. We've been frantically busy setting up communications with all the law enforcement involved in trying to get you father's murderer and getting Veronica and Zoe back safely. I'm so sorry that we have to meet under such conditions." Keller had a sharp jawline and long black hair slicked back with gel.

"I feel very useless at the moment," Ben said, lowering his glance.

"Ben, I understand how you feel. Believe me, there is not a person here who doesn't care about Veronica. We will do everything in our power to get her back safely."

"My wife is inside if you want to talk. We . . . Sorry we had a rough night."

Now, there would come the lie detector test. Keller would ask and interrogate Patty, Dominic, Brianna and Morgan to find out what they knew, including Ben – they were all equally telling the truth. Everyone was gloomy, soft spoken, bags under their eyes. Patty's hair was unkept and Morgan looked ill and timid. After that was done, Keller thanked everyone for their cooperation and expressed his sorrowful condolences. Patty sat everyone down on the couch, giving everyone a drink of water and a bowl of fruit to eat.

But Ben discerned how comfortable Keller and Brianna looked being around each other. Keller had been with Brianna every day while Ben was acting and on duty. Ben felt apathetic about that. Good, the man was volatile and strong doing this for her, he would find Veronica and find Ian Mastemah. But also, a strange tingling irk scratched at the back of Ben's mind and he couldn't shake it off. Keller and Brianna together almost looked… intimate.

"Well, this is not exactly ideal, losing a daughter in the middle of an investigation, is it, Keller?" she said with feigned optimism. "Losing a daughter when I shouldn't have." Brianna swallowed hard. "When I should have looked after her it is . . . embarrassing. I know, Keller. It's . . . Loss is ugly and disgusting. I hate the numbness it gives me. Everyone is going to think we're crazy when those two appear wherever they are."

Keller blinked twice. "I like your optimism, Brianna. You have a reason they could have run away?"

"No . . ." Brianna crossed her arms. "They couldn't have run away. I think they got lost. Right, Keller?"

The FBI agent's mouth crept to the right side in a smirk.

Brianna lifted her chin, her eyes suddenly bright. "Oh, have you told Ben and the others that you've solved every case you've been assigned to?"

Keller became unreadable. He said not a word.

"Keller?" Patty said. "You have any . . . children?"

The detective was serene, calm and indifferent as a frozen pond. "I'm going to find Veronica and Zoe. I promise." It was final. It was sure and destined.

"So, you have anything from the guy in the van?" Ben said. He felt the muscles in the middle of his forehead furrow. "Morgan said he may have been watching them. What did the guy say to you last night? Did he own up?"

"Benjamin—" Keller sat up, but Ben cut him off.

"Where did he hide them? Does he know about my father too?"

"We haven't found any physical evidence of the girls in the van," Keller said tranquilly. "He told me nothing."

Ben bit his lip, his mouth parched. "Nothing?!"

"Thomas Jones is his name. He unfortunately has the IQ of a child. There is no way someone with the mind of a child could have abducted two girls in broad daylight in the middle of 15th Ave and somehow make them disappear."

"Yeah, but if he cannot answer your questions . . . How can he still drive a van?" Ben retorted.

"He doesn't have a driver's licence," Keller said. "He's an illegal driver on the roads and therefore unsafe."

"Yet he ran. You said that he tried to run away. Why? Why would he run?"

"Look, Ben. I've spent hours questioning him. Like I said, Thomas Jones has an IQ of a child. He probably got very scared that the police were looking for him. He vomited before I interrogated him."

"Did you give him a lie detector?" Ben asked. "Like you did with us?"

"Yes."

"Did you give him one?"

"Yes, sir, I understand what you are saying. We have conducted multiple lie detector tests, but . . ." Keller smiled, holding back amusement, shaking his head. "A lie detector doesn't work if you can't even understand the questions I'm asking."

Ben was getting fed up with this man – how did he remain so cool? "Maybe . . . Maybe he wasn't alone. Surely, he had someone with him. A guardian or . . . Or-or did you find evidence of someone else with . . . with him or something? Come on!"

"Okay, Ben, look, I've got something to show you." Keller dug his hand into his pocket to retrieve something.

"What is it?"

"In the van, I found this CD from the Department of Defence." He gave over the CD to Ben in its hard plastic transparent case. "I have no idea what it means or if it's important or why Thomas Jones has government files, but this is all we have of any connections with other third parties."

"That tells me that Thomas wasn't on his own," Ben said, tension hardening in his chest. A fury that itched for Ben to take matters into his own hands. It was *his* daughter that was missing! "How could he drive a van, with a CD from the Department of Defence inside, if he has an IQ of a child?"

"Hey," Keller cut him off coolly. "We're considering all possibilities."

"I don't think you're considering *all* possibilities," Ben snapped.

"I understand what you're saying, but—"

"Just listen to me – shut the *hell up* for a second!!"

Brianna made a braying noise, burying her face in her hands. Everyone looked at Ben with apprehension. Oh, the snap, that flash of fury blurred between his eyes, it made his chest burn, his teeth grind – he could no longer contain the anguish in his chest – it suffocated him. His blanched hand gripped the CD container so hard that it quivered, his bloody hip throbbing.

"This is what you are going to need to do for me," Keller sighed sternly. "Take a deep breath and calm down."

Shivering, Ben blinked, lowering his glance, sweat bursting from glands in his armpits. "I'm . . . sorry. I'm sorry." He tried to inhale, but his throat choked up and his hip hammered his side. "Please, listen to me for a second."

"Mr DePaula, I understand this is an incredibly hard time." Ben bit his lips, wrath burning his cheeks, and raised his hand – he could have whacked the CD in this guy's face! – but he lowered it, his body shivering from exertion. "Everything is all under control. Now, if you just help Brianna, we can continue the investigations. I have every uniformed police officer and friends from the FBI joining the investigations looking for Veronica and your father's murderer."

"I don't understand what any of this means. They said he ran, and they said he had this CD in his vehicle. Have you looked at what's on this CD?"

"That's not important right now," Keller uttered. His eyes swung to Brianna and by cue she stood up. "I'm not crossing anything off my list. Just . . . let us do our job. Please?"

Ben sighed and began to sway on his crutches. "Not important . . . I . . . I need to come with you."

"That would be unnecessary on your part, sir. You're recovering. I said stay here."

"You freakin' kidding me!? I'm a marine captain, and my wife is with you, I can help you find Veronica! I have to protect my girl! I need to be there when she's found! You hear me!? Can I . . . Can I have a word with my wife?" He glared at Keller. *This man . . .*

There was an awkward silence, and at last, Keller muttered, "Of course. Of course."

"In my truck," Ben added vitriolically, in that way, he could follow Keller and Brianna so to make sure they did not neglect him on the CD investigation at the police station and, in part, if anything suspicious between them were found out. *I don't trust this Keller. He's too Prince Charming James Bond hanging around with my wife.*

Once Ben hobbled outside to his truck with Brianna behind, she lashed out at him. "What was that!? You didn't have to shout at him!"

"I'm sorry, Brianna, but my father was murdered, and my daughter is missing! Give me a break, will yah!"

At that moment, the front door opened, revealing Keller Butcher, stalking down the stairs with an imperious, determined air.

Then Ben remembered something; Thomas Jones . . . that asshole was guilty and had to remain in custody, but this guy inferred – implicitly – that since he was dumb as hell, he must be innocent. *Fallacy in the logic!*

Thomas was not innocent. "Hey!" Ben called, ignoring Brianna, limping on his crutches towards the FBI agent. Keller cursed under his tongue, keeping his eyes straight ahead towards his black cop car. "Hey, he stays in custody until my daughter is found, right?"

"We'll have a forty-eight-hour hold on him," Keller replied, "until we can bring any charges."

"You haven't charged him? Charge him, man!"

"Mr DePaula, I understand what you're—"

Why do they have to always say "I understand" to evade me! "Come on, my daughter's disappearance has to be worth *everything*, you got to keep that asshole in custody. But to me, you don't sound one hundred per cent sure. You need to be sure about this."

Keller, toothpick in his mouth, nodded indifferently. "Brianna will see what is on that CD. Now, I'm going to knock on doors of the houses to see what I can find. I want to see if Thomas Jones has anything to do with these people. There is a church that Jones said that he likes staying at, so I'll makes sure I'll look there. But I'm warning you, Mr DePaula – stay out of this. Look for your daughter with the search and rescue team, and stay out of my way. Brianna, please continue hunting for Ian Mastemah. We'll kill two birds with one stone."

And yet, even as Keller left to drive off, Ben did not feel satisfied by the order of investigation he'd organised.

"Give me that CD!" Brianna shouted, snatching it from Ben's grasp.

"What the hell is Metatron's Golem?" Ben derided, snickering. "Sounds like a Transformer!"

"I don't know, Ben," Brianna said. "It's the Defence Department's, so Thomas Jones has affiliations with intelligent bodies in the higher echelons of society."

"That's dope. That's *so* dope if this dumbass that has anything to do with my daughter is meddling with elites. So, you found anything yet on Ian Mastemah?"

"Ben don't get so sidetracked by the CD. My colleagues who have been assigned to hunt for Ian Mastemah have found that he is part of the Manicheans of the Light. A new religious movement."

"Dad said a lot of stuff about those types of people," Ben said with disdain. "He had *a lot* to say about them. That was why he died." Ben, suddenly invigorated, eyed Brianna. "Joseph knew something that we don't.

Something so dangerous that they had to go to the lengths to exterminate him and his work."

"Well, this is precisely why I'm here. To stop these people."

"Yes!" Ben creased his brow, speaking swiftly. "The Nephilim are going to return. I have seen them. I need to gather up help everywhere I can get it."

Brianna's face did the strangest twisting configuration that Ben had ever seen. Her right eye twitched. He smiled at it. And blurting out of her mouth, came out a protracted, bewildered, "Whaaatt?"

"You don't get it," Ben said.

"Hold on! What did you just say?"

"You don't get what I have seen and what I have gone through the last few months." Ben exhaled, whistling. "Alright. For all this time, my father has been researching religion and history and found out that these secret societies steeped in paganism, they're all about stopping a coming alien invasion or something. Galactic Tyrant, whatever. But if Ian Mastemah, the Manichean who killed my father . . . Brianna, I was hiding when I heard him ransack Dad's house. I heard Ian Mastemah that CIA agent. He tried to take my daughter, so he could be the instigator. Tell your friends to find him and arrest him. CIA agent Ian Mastemah. I met him in a debriefing session before we were deployed to Iraq." Brianna frowned, struggling to keep up with Ben as he hobbled towards his truck. "You want me to stay out of your way?" he asked. "I think Keller had told you to go with him to hunt for Ian Mastemah. Use the information I gave you." Then he snatched the CD from out of her hands.

"Ben, wait! What are you doing?"

"Joining you in the investigation," Ben said, hobbling to his truck.

"Your injury will make it really hard."

"More is at stake here than my hip right now!" Ben opened the door.

"Well," Brianna sighed. "I might as well go with you to the Phoenix Police Department Headquarters. I have some FBI friends who are going to meet me there in our search for the Manicheans."

"I want to see Thomas Jones for myself then," Ben said. And he was just about to reverse out of the driveway when his phone rang. One look at it, his eyes bulged, his body going stiff.

"Whose calling you?" Brianna said.

"The word is out," Ben muttered. His heart immediately began to hammer his chest. "My men have returned."

"Who called you?" Brianna exclaimed.

"Derek. One of my men . . . Prepare for questions." Ben started up the car. "They're at the police department!"

455

41

OBSOLETE FROM TRUTH

"9. Led by the Messiah Maitreya and the enlightenment of Agartha, humanity will become Neo-Homosapiens. Women will have equal social and sexual value as men. Women will need Nindingir and Deviradha training so they can transcend their hormones and control their bodies to perfection.

10. Political wings will be abolished. Leadership roles will become community service roles filled by the higher humans who abide by the Golden Rule for everybody's good. Modify and alleviate society so leaders can abolish class structure and poverty, equalising all human opportunity, providing universal basic income to all. No one would have to labour to work for income, Patalan infrastructure and AI will made taxes redundant.

Humanity will become the Übermensch."

—From "The Kallipolis Great Reset." In *The Survival Dynamics*, Alfred Bonner, Arhat of the Fourth Initiation.

Joshua glared at the looping monitor screens at Fort Huachuca, watching the impossible. The final clip of head-cam footage revealed that Ben did not die but, this whole time, he'd escaped war, *transported* back to America by an anonymous angelic entity who clearly did not wish its identity compromised. Ben had been whisked away and hidden in his father's house until Ian Mastemah got to him first. *Impossible! All this time?!*

"Why didn't they tell us?" Joshua snapped. "You knew?"

"What? *Of course* I didn't know!" Pounders said, exasperated. "This is Alfred Bonner's fault, if anything!" Of course, Judd had heard all the rumours once he and the marines stepped off the plane, the rumours all circulating that Ben DePaula was alive from the dead; people had seen a man walking, talking and acting like Ben in Arizona. Subsequently, it had caused Pounders to descend into a turbid fever trying to get to the bottom of this until this morning, until he came across the undeniable smoking gun to explain Ben's disappearance.

The footage archive from Ben's head camera *was unbelievable*. Why had no one offered to share it on duty? Why had Bonner not offered to disclose this, keeping it top secret? *Because the footage has an explicit close encounter of a spiritual being,* Joshua thought. *This is why it is top secret.*

Director Alfred Bonner had deceived them, and for a whole month, he'd known and not even suffered to whisper a word about the paladin despite the deal and agreement with the Marine Corps. He even had his own little trip to Iraq with Blue Shield's permission, in order to recover an ancient coffin, taking it to America to protect it from looters.

Joshua guessed that because of the angelic paladin taking Ben, Bonner needed to go to Iraq and find his dying and rising god. A move and counter move.

Just as flabbergasted as Joshua, the other marines in the monitor room stared in dazed astonishment as if they were in a trance.

"He's – alive?!" Laycock intoned slowly.

"I told you he was still alive." Derek Fish tucked his phone in his pocket. "The vigil was worth the wait!"

"No not necessarily," Joshua blurted, pointing to the screens. "He was teleported back to America."

"Still! Actionman never dies boi!" Derek exclaimed.

"Teleportation." Pounders' words sounded full as he scrunched up his face, growling. "Bah! I have a bad feeling about this," Pounders grumbled with a troubled expression. His voice slowed. "The . . . Marine Corps . . . could be in peril."

"Why did Bonner not tell us Ben was alive?" Joshua said.

"Scam perhaps. And I fell for it," Pounders sighed, rubbing his face. "That bastard. I always knew from the start that Ben's mysterious disappearance was off. I couldn't get it off my mind. Until now—"

"Wait? You are claiming that we've could have *known* Ben was alive the whole time?" Joshua managed. It was as if Director Bonner used the entire American military as a means to an end to take his coffin. "I don't *think* it's important now that we know the truth as to why Bonner wanted to go to Iraq," Joshua said. "We need to find Ben first off. But you did not have *one* conversation with Bonner regarding Ben during the mission?"

Pounders threw his hands up, chuckling madly. "No! I couldn't get in touch with the Light Alliance! They're deranged bastards, that's what, Josh. Bonner has become paranoid over this. He fears this – *thing* – the *paladin*." The way Pounders tried wording "paladin", was like trying to scorn a recalcitrant sibling. "All along it was never about Hussein. It was about—"

"The coffin. It was about the coffin," Johnny Best said, cutting into the discourse. "I know it was. I saw Bonner and some strange magicians take it away. They stole it! They robbed the tomb!"

"Yeah, I know," Pounders confirmed softly. "Freakin' assholes they are, I know. But I don't know what Bonner's doing with a coffin. The man is socially awkward. He built for himself a track record of working over the years with the US Agency for International Development, liaising with American armed forces."

"Where did he find this tomb, Johnny?" Joshua said.

"Warka."

"Uruk," Joshua gasped. "That's one of the first city-states in the world. Home to King Gilgamesh."

"I don't want to talk about it anymore." The Colonel slumped, turning his back on the monitors, looping in silence over with the bizarre and extraordinary film that did not belie – shaky footage of Ben running through a burning building, falling off the side, finding the baby in the garbage bin and finally being whisked away by the hooded paladin before cutting to static. Eventually it became nauseating, just when Joshua had been given the answers, so many questions stemmed out of them.

Nefer, you have an idea who this hooded man is? Does God have an idea? Joshua thought.

Silence.

An opening door jolted him out of his mind.

"Sir! Colonel!" A startled young voice sounded from the door. It made Judd Pounders spin around at the call of the desperate operator. "Sir, Captain Ben DePaula, as we speak, is at the Phoenix Police Headquarters with his wife!"

"Time to go then," Joshua said, getting up. "Time to see him for ourselves."

———

It was just as Brianna had anticipated. News reporters thronged outside the Phoenix Police Department Headquarters as Ben went to park. Standing in their way was a police force trying to hold back the seething crowd.

What a significant story, of a celebrity actor presumed dead, suddenly returned from the dead. Brianna let out a protracted sigh as the truck smoothly arrived, and the flashing cameras flashed upon them obnoxiously. Once they could get inside the Department, the cameras would have no choice but to leave them alone.

Ben DePaula was alive.

After being Ben's husband for four years, Brianna should have really prepared for this when Ben agreed to go with her. She reluctantly had to shield Ben from the onslaught of the demanding crowd.

Ben held a straight, numbed face – he gazed right past the crowd, as if the crowd did not even matter in his eyes. He was supine to crowds, having no predisposition towards them.

Questions attacked Brianna mercilessly like a swarm of buzzing flies. And some of them stung her.

"Are you DePaula's wife? Tell us what it is like being married to a divorced man and raising his daughter?"

"Ben, how did you find a way to escape Iraq?"

"It's a miracle. How did you manage to hide for so long without getting the word out?"

"Were you taken hostage by the enemy?"

"You here for Thomas Jones?"

"Why is the Actionman on crutches? How did you injure your leg?"

Give him privacy! He lost his dad, and now we've lost our daughter! Brianna waved them away viciously – battering them. They were like a raging sea, tossed by storm winds. Wherever she could, she nudged into them, enduring the flashing lights for Ben's sake. But he was already marching ahead, forging through the crowd, cutting out a path with his crutches. As she attended him, lunging to clear distance and block out the pleading stampede, a police aide emerged from the throng, pressing down on the tumult, sterilising it.

Ben and Brianna headed straight into the building, towards a security officer who asked for identification. Brianna showed them her FBI ID, asking to see her colleagues in the investigation for the murder of Joseph DePaula and the disappearance of Veronica DePaula. Access was granted without issue.

"Okay," Brianna sighed forcefully. "I am not going through that again. You stay here, I'll be back to report to the other agents about Ian Mastemah."

Fortunately, the FBI agents were in the room, and while she deliberated with them, sharing notes about what they had found tracking down the Manicheans, she never let Ben out of the corner of her vision, who waited impatiently in the computer chair.

The murder case had just become a man hunt – the FBI were having trouble trying to access CIA files on Ian Mastemah. Unfortunately, the CIA were deceiving the FBI agents. Institutional rivalries peppered among the FBI and the CIA, and this had prohibited investigation into confidential information. The most frustrating part about that was accusing a CIA agent of a breech of protocol and to accuse them of hampering an FBI investigation. Brianna's friend Rita Brookes and her partner Riley O'Connor were sent death threats for trying to "breach national security", while good old Julius Matthew Resinski went personally to their Arizona headquarters, and a CIA officer blatantly lied to him saying, "Ian Mastemah was no longer on the current record".

Brianna was not surprised by this. The CIA historically had committed activities which could be deemed criminal. It was not surprising that when there were clashes, the CIA deemed it unnecessary for the FBI to know something, they'd either lied by the omission of truths or misdirection, if not outright fabricate. If the CIA admitted a traitor within their ranks, they were obligated by law to involve the FBI. And if proven guilty, then the FBI were required, and empowered, to arrest CIA agents.

Unfortunately, no progress had been made in locating where the Manicheans were, when and where they would strike next, and who their next target would be. *They're a covert terrorist organisation. That's all we know. I hate for this to be connected to Veronica, but I'm not prepared to confirm that until there is sufficient proof!*

Miffed, dismissing her colleagues, Brianna returned to Ben who was leaning on his crutches. He scrutinised the old monitors lined on desks, divided by PC ports set with CD players. As Brianna attended him, he didn't waste a single second, hobbling over to the nearest computer, pulling out the METATRON'S GOLEM CD.

"You think I have to deal with crowds everywhere I go, don't you?" Ben said.

"No, but given your story, Veronica and your father are too intriguing of a story for journalists to let go, even though there is no evidence to suggest connections between cases."

"I figured that. Crap. But you could only imagine the rumours circling across the country. If Pounders and the marines know . . ." Ben hobbled into the wheeled chair at the accompanying office desk next to Brianna, and turned on the old computer, powering it up with a beep. "We've got to do this quick. Let's see what is on this CD and see what clues it can give about Veronica's whereabouts."

Brianna sighed, rolling her eyes. "Ben we *cannot* know that. Your priorities are not straight! Are you concerned about our daughter and your father, or a stupid CD?"

"Both," Ben said. "I thought you were the investigator. You found this clue, so use it to your advantage! Thomas Jones had it in possession; it *must* be connected somehow!"

Brianna crossed her arms, irritation congealing her blood.

Ben's face turned dark, and he scowled, hissing, "We need to risk it to get the biscuit." Ben pressed the CD disc port. The machine hummed, working hard with heat as if it didn't like the disc.

Clicking on the CD player tab, Ben pressed play and Brianna watched as the screen lit up with a white home page authorised by the Department of Defence. Ben clicked on "Next", and the page fuzzed out, showing another page filled with gibberish. He blinked.

"No," he muttered, scrolling faster, only to find that the files were coded. Puzzled, Brianna tilted her head, gawking at the strange letters which she instantly recognised. *Where have I seen these archaic encryptions before?*

Ben swiped his hand across the desk, flinging the mouse across the room. Feeling his radiating anger, Brianna buried her face in her hands.

"Damn it!" Ben exclaimed, knocking over a small garbage can with his crutch. He struggled to get around on crutches, but he made an effort; sweat pearled his forehead, trickling down his bald head due to the heat in the stuffy computer room. "It's a joke! Just when I thought we had it!"

Brianna continued to scan the screen, unable to shake that glimmer of familiarity. Those string of consonants, vowels and accents. . . A type of language.

"Stupid, all for nothing!" Ben railed on. "All this for a bad joke!?"

A Native language.

"I don't think this is gibberish, Ben," Brianna inquired. "I think it is just encrypted." She heard Ben lunging to her as she glazed her finger on the screen for him to see for himself. "Looks like Navajo." She paused to make sure the entire document was consistent, nodding saying, "Yes, that's definitely Navajo."

"Well, can you get in?" Ben said, looming over her shoulder.

"You kidding? I do not speak Navajo. Just remembered seeing it. My father had an Indian friend who used this code during World War II against the Japanese." Frowning, Brianna grabbed the discarded mouse to try again, clicking, but the files refused her access. "It's blocked. Someone's keeping us out."

———

Joshua climbed out of Pounders' car outside the Phoenix Police Department, gawking at a riotous crowd of camera men and journalists aggregating around two policemen, who yelled at them to stay back, as they carried with them a tall, lugubrious young man.

"Thomas! Thomas! Thomas!"

"Back. Stay back. Let him walk."

"Who is that?" Jason Laycock asked from behind Joshua. "Casbolt lives in Texas, eh? No, that can't be him, surely not."

"Thomas Jones . . ." Joshua whispered, staring at the young man, walking with a rigid foot as he proceeded down the parking lot, the police herding Thomas and the flashing crowd away.

Thomas Jones. He did give Joshua an overwhelming sense of déjà vu that disjointed him from reality. Thomas Jones. *Where have I seen him before? Who was it?*

Then out of the entrance, lunging on crutches, Ben DePaula appeared, alive and with half-moons under his eyes, but as the marines called out to him, gratefully and joyfully, Ben had already stalked past them, face incandescent towards Thomas.

"Crap!" Pounders swore. "The hell is he doing!?"

"Stop him!" Derek ran. The marines followed after him.

Ben ran right into the crowd, crutches working, legs swinging as if he would boot those people. The din of voices erupted into chaos as Ben racked the people aside with his arms, like a machine, plunging right into the police, barking angrily at them. They pressed against him, but Ben went straight for Thomas Jones and Ben lost it.

"Let me talk to him! What are you doing!?"

"He's a free man! He's a free man!"

Ben threw the policeman to the ground, trying to get to Thomas Jones, who was trying to hide behind car fenders and the press of clustered people.

"I just want to talk!" The crowd gasped in shock, shouting discordant, 'Heys!' and 'Nos!", as Ben seized Thomas with both hands, dragging him to the ground between two police cars. The crutches collapsed as Ben, leaning on the fender of the car, bellowed incoherently into Thomas' ear. The boy squirmed, cringing, as police violently tore at Ben's purple t-shirt, dragging him away.

"No! No! No! No! No!" Ben barked, throwing a tantrum. With his injury, he had no chance resisting the police. Soon, Ben was surrounded by a tight knot of hostile people. "GET THE HELL OFF ME!"

"Get him down, get him down, get him down." Four police pinned Ben to the road, throwing his crutches at him.

"*Ben!*" Pounders' shout cracked like a peal of thunder.

But the police had already arrested him, hauling him into the Department. Handcuffed, they carried limping Ben, and promptly, Judd Pounders beckoned for Joshua and the marines to come along, following the four policemen into the station.

Ben was sent directly to the head police officer for questioning. Joshua, Pounders and the marines joined in their proceedings.

"I've got a daughter of my own, Ben," the head officer said. "Let's pretend this never happened and continue our investigations. And as for Thomas Jones, he has orders to not leave his neighbourhood."

Everyone turned as an attractive woman, who had to be Ben's wife, appeared into the office, closing the door. She wore a dark cardigan, with a short knee-length skirt, exposing her legs, pulled up by opaque stockings. Her brown hair was tied up into a bun and she too was staring at what had just unfolded, flaring emotion burning in her grey eyes, her nostrils puffing up. Joshua found her intense, dangerous eyes troubling – that look was a look of a special agent – capable of discerning fault.

"What?" Ben whispered.

"I need you to go home, DePaula," the chubby-headed police officer said calmly, scribbling a note, closing the file, and putting down the ballpoint pen. Two pale hands rested on the dark desk like pink slugs, one over the top of the other. Then, the officer brought his hands close together, made a steeple of his forefingers, and stared at Ben with watery brown eyes. "You have been given a second chance. You cause another offence hampering us, the Actionman will get arrested. What a shock that would be on worldwide news. You're lucky. Your leg injury looks bad, so you need to go home, do your job, or chat with your marine friends." His watery eyes roved upwards, glancing at Pounders, Joshua and the other marines. "As a matter of fact, the marines look desperate to talk to you."

Ben shook his head, his face a rictus. "What about what I just told you?

Why the hell are you letting this guy go? I know him. He's dangerous."

Joshua glared. *Know him? God, I'm missing out on so much context!*

"As a member of the Federal Bureau of Investigation, everything is under control," Brianna said.

Ben turned to Judd Pounders, and, pursing his lips, he snarled with a milder tone, "What's going on, Colonel? Long time no see."

Judd beheld Ben in such astonished silence, the room felt like it would spontaneously combust the way the poor air circulated in the humid room from a rickety old fan in the corner. It was May, and a police department could not even afford proper air cons? Joshua's clothes darkened with sweat, and he mopped his brow. What Ben had just shown everyone in the parking lot would have immense consequences; Joshua felt as if he had just been thrown into the deep end of a chaotic crisis.

"That was James Casbolt," Ben gushed suddenly, sounding out of breath. "You saw him? It was him! In the parking lot, I looked into his eyes. They were blue, like an Aes Sidhe! It was him! Damn the super soldier bullcrap! Thomas Jones . . . He's James Casbolt!" Ben chuckled, shaking his head and pointing accusingly at Pounders. "The hell is *happening* to this world!? My father is dead and – Pounders you know this because you enlisted Casbolt! And Ian Mastemah that *moron* you sent to supervise the marines, he killed my father when I got back here. And then, this . . . Oh, Ian Mastemah, you see, he *knew* about Casbolt. He *knew* about the Aes Sidhe. I'm telling you this because you freakin know that son of a bitch Ian scammed you! I knew Casbolt was mad! And yet, you enlisted him!" Tears brimmed Ben's eyes, pain and anguish frothed from his quivering voice. "I could have prevented this. Casbolt took my daughter. He took . . . He *took Veronica* from me!"

"How could that be James Casbolt?" Joshua rasped, perplexed. From what Joshua could remember, that peculiar man that did not talk much, was a resident alien, had an unfortunate dissociative identity disorder, joined the Baghdad raid, and wrote a book without any academic discipline. "What do you mean?"

"Ben," Judd Pounders took a deep breath. "You're crazy to think that Thomas Jones is James Casbolt. Take a chill pill. The man, like the rest of the Shinar Units, are still overseas. You sure you're alright, Ben?"

"Hahaha. You think I'm making this up?" Ben said harshly, sparking a stichomythia.

"I am not. I—"

"Why do you think I'm making this up?" Ben rose from his seat, gripping his crutch like a mace.

"Hey. Hey. Hey."

"Hang on! Why do you think I'm making this up?"

"We thought you were dead, Ben. I couldn't have known—"

"None of your business. You think I'm—"

"What on earth happened to you, damn it!?"

"No, I'm asking *why I would make this up?*"

"I'm not saying that. Just listen. Everyone—"

"So, you can wring out *every* little bit of information you can *squeeze* out of me, for your *little* superiors?!"

"*Listen to me,*" Pounders spat, getting into Ben's vitriolic face, fists balled. Joshua worried that with Ben's height and build would end the heated goading quickly if it got out of hand. Joshua could feel the grievous conflict stirring in his stomach.

Every once in a while, Pounders looked over his shoulder at his audience, face flushing due to Ben's infantile outburst.

"Where have you been, Ben," Pounders asked softly. "Just tell me."

"Stuck in my freakin' father's house, when he got murdered, that's what!" He turned desperately, pointing at the head officer. "Arrest Thomas Jones!"

The head officer stood up. "You're going to have to trust me, Ben. Keller and I have been trying to get as much out of him as possible, but he wouldn't budge, so we're wasting time on this guy."

Ben's eyes went wide. They were glazed, and Joshua saw a visible shiver racking through him, giving Joshua goosebumps in return. This was a man physiologically broken from the stress of war, murder and kidnaping. He leaned on his crutches, as if they would support him from his wobbling knees, leaning on them so doggedly he made them creak under his weight. "I promised Veronica that I would be there to protect her . . ."

Pounders went to speak, but Ben stormed out of the room, crutches banging on the door as he left.

Brianna sighed deeply, throwing back her head in annoyance. "Sir," she said, leaning to the head officer. "I must go to speak to him."

"You will, Ms DePaula," the head police officer said. "But first, I have a few questions. Do any of you have an explanation for Ben's misconduct of Thomas Jones?"

"Officer, Ben is struggling after what happened to his father," Brianna said defensively.

"I can see that."

Joshua saw her shift as a hint of understandable mortification lingered within her, yet she held her ground, clenching her fists. "I'm required to continue investigating Joseph DePaula's murder and hunting down Ian Mastemah."

"You are dismissed then, Agent DePaula," the officer said, sighing.

She nodded. As Brianna departed, Pounders stopped her and, looming over Brianna's shoulder, he said, "I want to know everything about Ben. What he has done. What you have seen. What he has told you, right now." Brianna looked on ahead at him, the tendons in her neck tightening and her disciplined eye fixed ahead, aloof. Sweat trickled down the side of her face.

Joshua shivered – very rarely had he seen Judd Pounders appear so paranoid and so stern as he was now.

—

Under the lurid sky, under the mangled tree bush overshadowing the nature strip, Ben tottered, each step a flare of pain. The struggle to reach his small truck made him hunch slightly from the taut ligaments and muscles in his hip; it had worsened after the struggle with the police. He instantly felt a clot of guilt cleaving to his chest.

I must find Thomas.

Why does he look so much like James Casbolt? I need to see what he knows. Casbolt knows very well who I am. Yes. Do it. Follow Keller. Yes. Find what the Navajo code means, find out who killed dad and who took my daughter. Done.

His objective had been set. He would restore his life.

Throwing himself into the front seat, fighting his crutches which got jammed between the door, hurting his hip once more, he endured a shock of blinding pain. In vexation, he yelped, placing them over the glove box, over on the back seat. Exhausted, he turned the key once so that the car remained off, but the radio came on.

It is in suffering that we often draw closer to the divine, the voice from the radio said. *Affliction shows that compared to God, you are wretched and pitiable and poor and blind and naked. This is what the true and faithful witness, the originator of creation, says. 'Buy gold refined by fire to become rich, white clothing, to be clothed from naked shame, and eye salve so that you can see'.*

So, this is what I'm going to do, Ben thought. *Thomas Jones – James Casbolt – is out there and I have to find him, I have to talk to him, do whatever it takes. But where shall I go? Where . . . No, don't follow Keller, he might know.*

He was drifting away. Drifting.

Ben slumped his forehead on the wheel, cringing. *Why did I have to do that in front of all those people? Why?*

He would make up for what he had missed out on. For everything was collapsing, and Ben knew he had to face it alone, trying hard to hold everything together as it crumbled at once.

"I will soldier through this," Ben muttered to himself, slumping in sinking humiliation. He closed his eyes and pressed his head against the wheel until the leather marked his forehead painfully. He sat like that for a long time, castigating himself.

The voice on the radio preached on. *Never expect blessing. Dead flies make the perfumer's ointment give off a stench,*

so a little folly outweighs wisdom and honour.
A wise man's heart inclines him to the right,
but a fool's heart to the left.
Even when the fool walks on the road, he lacks sense,
and he says to everyone that he is a fool.

Staring at nothing, Ben lifted his head from the wheel, turning on the engine.

"What was I doing?" Ben spat, as he pulled out of the driveway. What difference would it make, now that the rumours would spread out of control? He had lacked sense, just proven to the world that he was a fool.

Why are you focusing on your reputation, you fool! What if what I'm doing is all wrong? No, it is wrong *for me to do nothing!*

What was wrong was letting child kidnappers get away with their crime. Something in the heart of most human beings simply cannot tolerate pain inflicted on the innocent, especially children. Even compromised persons will often first take out their own rage on those who have caused suffering to children. Even in such a world of moral relativism, causing harm to a child was *objectively wrong.*

So, Ben must punish Thomas Jones.

Ben's bowels bubbled with desire of what he could do to make that piece of crap miserable. And yet, Ben also felt guilt. Never would he permit himself to betray to everyone of what he actually felt, not even with Brianna his wife - of all who could see so deeply into him.

First, go to the church where this James Casbolt is, kidnap him, take him to mother's old house. Tie him up or something so he doesn't escape, and then, go and look for a Navajo reservation . . . But where in the world . . . Navajo?

For some reason, the closest place in mind that he could think of regarding Native Americans, was the Grand Canyon National Park. Surely there would be a Navajo reservation there. He would need a map just to make sure. But stifling all doubts that it was all out of the way, Ben patted his pocket containing the CD.

The clue to where his daughter was.

"It makes perfect sense now," Ben said faintly to himself, voice dripping sarcasm. "James Casbolt is steeped in conspiracy theories, explaining why he has the CD. He's invested in Julian's stepchildren, explaining why he was in a van and took my daughter. He's a DID meaning he is a complete liar."

That rationality sounded right in Ben's ears, so pulling out of the parking lot, he went to track down Keller Butcher, to find that church, to gather and take all that he could.

42

MARPLOT

"I saw that under the sun the race is not to the swift, nor the battle to the strong, nor bread to the wise, nor riches to the intelligent, nor favour to those with knowledge, but time and chance happen to them all. For humanity does not know his time. Like fish that are taken in an evil net, and like birds that are caught in a snare, so the children of humanity are snared at an evil time, when it suddenly falls upon them."
—From the Wisdom of the Qoheleth, the Solomonic Dynasty, 970 – 586 BCE.

The rest of the day in Phoenix Arizona was sweltering. As night swallowed the land, it descended into a fierce winter cold, that the trees, the ground and cacti seemed to creak with stress from the riddling frost.

Hopping from house to venue, Keller Butcher ticked off his lists of all the local sex offenders in the city of Phoenix recorded in the police department's archives. He'd even approached one guy, the mayor of Glendale in Maricopa County who had hard Mexican teenage porn magazines in his closet.

But he'd only gone to those suspected places to see if they'd been involved. None of them owned up to or even had a clue about the disappearance of Veronica DePaula and Zoe O'Leary – they were local perverts who barely recognised the girls' images.

So, Keller would try one last place.

Circling around, down highways and streets and houses, the church of Youngtown rose in the evening bands of a wild pink sunset, the spire with its infinitesimal knobs and decorations of a medieval castle rising in powerful silence, a relic of a past reality that had been dismantled. The church was a city within a city.

He entered the dark church and immediately felt the floor reject any of his footfalls cast upon them. A small scruff bounced around sonorously, in a slow, fading echo. Every sound Keller made felt like a disturbance. A transgression.

The church was utterly empty, no signs of children anywhere. Turning around, Keller recalled the small presbytery just across a small nature strip, where stumped cacti, bloated and blighted, sagged in patches on the dry cracked dirt under the unforgiving sky. Stalked plants rose like spikes, shadows stretching pensively across the gloomy land – even the roots of trees made the earth undulate as they tried to writhe out of the cracks to breathe.

Arriving at the front door, he knocked, ringing the doorbell insistently. When no one replied, Keller waited, balling his hands in his coat pockets feeling the cold lather around him, hearing the bleak desolate wind slithering through the trees.

Nothing. *Is Father asleep? Is he even home?* Surely, Thomas Jones would be inside, somewhere.

He knocked once more. "Father, open up! This is the FBI! The police!" Without an answer, he sighed, walking down the steps, seeking a window.

Peering within, he saw the TV still on in the living room, but with no sign of anyone inside. Keller pried opened the window; it slid open, and slithering himself in between the sill and the open beam, he then squatted, jumping inside, dusting off his hands.

He'd confirmed the priest was fast asleep on the couch, snoring heinously, near his dangling hand on a small wooden coffee table, which held a bottle of vodka.

Keller crept, slowly inspecting every nook and cranny, everything that would be of the least bit of interest to the investigation. "Father?" Keller said. "Father?" The old man snoozed, utterly knocked out. What had he been doing drinking such strong vodka? Were priests allowed alcohol? "You mind if I take a look around?" He spoke to the sleeping man, who hardly stirred. *Well, I'm not going to nudge him awake, he's in a deep sleep.*

Keller proceeded down the hall – plain and drab, floorboards creaking, so he tiptoed – seeking Thomas' room. The young man was fast asleep. Searching for signs of anything to do with little girls – clothing, or even for drugs – Keller walked back into the kitchen, until an oddity caught the corner of his eyes.

The fridge was placed against the corner where the cable, attached to its back and plugged into the wall socket, was taut.

Keller took two steps, scrutinising, thinking. "The hell?" he whispered. Who in their right mind would leave a taut fridge cable out like that near a walkway? And . . . telltale signs of a pair of scuff marks on the floor tiles paralleling the wall meant . . .

Keller moved the fridge, sliding it away from the wall to the left where it should have been, in front of the wall socket. As he suspected, behind the fridge, a door was revealed.

Suspicious, Keller opened it and hissed a curse, almost tumbling off a ledge, straight down eight feet into the basement. He gripped the wooden beam of the door frame, pulling out a flashlight. "The heck!? No stairs?"

The basement was stuffy and dusty, the darkness concealing much. *A dungeon perfect for stashing away little children,* Keller thought, and he wondered how to descend without smashing something, without breaking a leg, or perhaps startling someone innocent that could most certainly be dwelling down there, hungry and thirsty, tired and frightened.

Keller's heart palpitated with passion as he got on his bottom and scooted on the ledge. Not too sure how far down the ground was, he took the risk.

The ground was hot earth, so dusty that it powdered his boots. He meticulously searched the dungeon, brick fountains, pipes, very low ceiling, and oppressively silent. No signs of life but cobwebs.

A ghastly form. Cowled. Pale and statuesque.

Keller cursed, flinching. His light beam revealed a glazed statue of the Virgin Mary, pretty head inclined with a whimsical smile, her hands in prayer. Cobwebs weaved around her azure and white garments, and the rosary dangling down her elbows. Another statue, next to her, was a marble figure of a bearded prophet with a bound book in his hands and goat horns on his head. Moses?

Sweat bursting from his skin, Keller pointed the flashlight in the other direction, finding more religious statues, covered in spider webs, dust covering them in thick silk. There were winged cherubs and holy saints, petrified statues like Medusa's garden of petrified gnomes. Keller, heart throbbing in his chest, kept low, skulking towards a section of the dungeon behind the statues, where the power for electricity would be running. The walls were brick, covered in mud and more cobwebs so thick they could have passed for draping veils. *Who would store so many statues down here?*

Keller crept on his boots hardly making a noise; everything outside of the spotlight seemed mysterious until he cast it into his view.

And into his view came a toppled chair. A single chair, wooden, on its side. With the body of a human being, inert, still sitting on it.

Keller squatted by the body's side. It smelled decayed. The man had duct tape over his mouth and strapped to his body, binding him to the chair. His neck was bent at a distorted angle, suggesting that he'd died in a middle of a struggle to free himself from captivity. His skin – charred and black with soot – looked crinkled, mummified almost. On his neck was a tattoo of an elongated diamond with geometric lines running through it, connected by ten circles. Gleaming in the flashlight, on his chest, was a pendant attached to a necklace.

A pendant with an oblate cymatic pattern.

—

Outside the presbytery, parked next to the church on the other side of the road, Ben watched from his small truck, Keller barging out of the house. He hauled an old man out into his car, and then drove away.

Now with the priest gone, Ben felt a strange sensation of freedom – refreshing ecstasy of anticipation – a swelling thrill of finally having a chance to find answers. He could find his daughter now without hinderances and have everything in his own hands.

That asshole is sleeping in there. Or, I hope Keller has James Casbolt arrested. But if not, Casbolt's got the answers. He's got them and I've got him. There is simply no other way possible out of this.

Once Keller had pulled away, Ben crept into the open door, and saw Thomas Jones/James Casbolt standing in the hallway, dazed and confused. Alone and free.

"Hey! Hey bastard!" Ben hollered, bounding towards the whimpering boy. God, he hated the crutches, it made him so loud and slow! Like a box, Casbolt tossed against the walls, trying to run away. He whined muffled squeals, falling on his knees, crawling back into his room doggedly. So-called super soldier! What had the DID done to him to make him this insane? For a staggering moment – a tiny second – Ben considered if what he was doing was correct. That this man, who looked exactly like Casbolt, was perhaps not it – his behaviour resembled the Aes Sidhe to naught. No. Casbolt or not, the deranged lunatic was the *only one* that could have taken Veronica. "Get back here! You're not running away from me! Come here you asshole! Come here!"

The young man's blue eyes bulged, and he screamed like a woman. Ben, grabbing his crutch, began to beat Casbolt.

"Tell me!" Ben growled, hammering him with a flurry of vicious punches with his hand. After the bout of violence, he bellowed. "Tell me! Tell me! Tell me! Where is my daughter!?"

Casbolt squealed. He put up a good fight, so Ben had no choice but to bash him some more, smother him some more with the pillow, until he wormed out of his grasp, biting his hand. Grunting, Ben staved Casbolt with his crutches, driving the asshole to the ground. The brawl felt like an eternity, but Ben got the upper hand, bashing the crutch on Thomas' head against the floor to cease his thrashing. Ben was sweating after the ordeal, his hip on fire, spurring on his angry agony. He felt exhausted, bitter bile forming in his throat. He loathed to consider what he had to do next: to drag the unconscious body out of the house across the road hoping that no one would drive past and see him, then get him in the car to take him to his mother's old house.

"F you, Keller, you good for nothing! I shall do this myself!"

Lugging this asshole made his hip hurt even more, tearing at the sinew. He gritted his teeth and roared at the constellations above him. He could have hauled Casbolt on his shoulder, but considering that would put his hip in too much peril, Ben, spitting and swearing, dragged and kicked the moron, tossing him onto the trailer of his truck.

The drive to his mother's old house at West Jomax Road took half an hour. The house was a demeaning thing. It resembled a large modest mansion, like a doll's house. Strange brickwork glowered over Ben, the front lawn overgrown with cacti and shrubbery, pocked marks strewn like grim bones. Silent darkness played tricks on his mind, but it wasn't the shadows Ben was afraid of. He was glad for it, to conduct his secret interrogation. He'd known times when inanimate objects seemed to have facial expressions, and Ben thought his pareidolia confirmed he was seeing things that were not there: ghoulish imps swinging in the tangled bramble, demonic faces and heads popping in dark gloom and at the fragmented fence where the cacti to the left rose like towers, snagged over, sprawling chaotically into the driveway.

"I am not mad," Ben muttered to himself. "For people who go mad think everyone else is going mad." Did real insanity curse this place of his childhood, did it create hallucinations? Those drooping trees and gunky cacti black with enmity were pareidolia.

Discreetly, Ben hobbled, dragging the unconscious body of the asshole. Dumping the body on the door mat, Ben unlocked the door, pulled the body inside, and relocked it. Then came the stair climb – the drudgery that disjointed Ben's mind insipidly. After a good hour struggling with crutch and body, he'd lugged the asshole up the stairs, across the landing, past winding corridors strewn with wooden beams, peeled plaster, and unfinished maintenance work, and threw the moron into the bathroom.

Ben groaned in weary pain, resting his hip and his sweaty body. Switching on the lights, he got back up again, tying Thomas' hand around the pipe underneath the bathroom sink.

Only then did Ben collapse against the wall moaning, panting, yearning for a bed to sleep in. But the beds in this house had been taken out long ago. His hip throbbed like a heart; it kept him from having a deep nap. The persistent pain never alleviated, irking him to banal madness.

"Why, God?" Ben moaned dozing off. "Why? Why?"

What did Ben do to deserve this? He was simply trying to do the right thing by trying to spend time with his family; to reconcile with his father who he'd neglected for eleven years and with his daughter. And one thing after another, it all fell apart.

Commotion in the house jolted Ben awake. He grabbed his crutches, shuffling into the bathroom. Thomas Jones had awoken, sobbing, tugging desperately at his hand ties, trying to free himself.

"Oh no you don't. You have to talk to me first." Ben searched for his work bag that he'd left behind on the woodcutting table. He searched for some cloth, wrapping it around his fist. "Your gonna talk? Talk!"

Casbolt shuffled frantically against his bonds – boorishly tugging so hard, until Ben heard the sink pipe dislodge with a terrible grinding sound.

Stuff this! Binding the cloth tightly around his right fist, hopping on his crutches, Ben loomed over the squealing asshole, stabbing the crutch into the man's chest. The back of his head hit the basin from the force, winding his sobs. His crystalline blue eyes widened in fear.

The police did *crap nothing*, but Ben would knock some truth out of him for sure. The sore hip did not help as Ben got into the most comfortable position that he could in his condition, mounting the asshole. His injury pain galvanised the red rage, lodging in his bosom.

"This is your last chance," Ben snarled, hovering his fist before Thomas' wide eyes – the blue eyes belonging to James Casbolt. "I know you want to go home. I know you're scared. I know. I know, I hate what I am doing, but you got me into this. I don't want to hurt you, but you need to tell me where Veronica and Zoe are."

———

Early next morning, Keller come back from tracking down the owners of the North Mountain National Park. Getting word of the autopsy report on the corpse found in the man's basement reminded him that he needed to speak to the priest.

Duplicitous and corpulent – with hair white as snow – his name was Neil, and he stubbornly refused to be called Father.

"How are yah doing, Father?" Keller said, entering the solitary interrogation room – windowless, small, with only a desk and two chairs facing one another.

"Call no man Father," Neil insisted, his voice peevish.

Keller sat down, slithering into his seat, lacing his fingers together. Picking up a laminated copy of the images taken of the corpse in the basement from inspectors, he held it up for Neil. "Who's your buddy here? Do you know his name?"

"The Little Ladykiller, Detective Butcher," Neil whispered. He sat all poised and tranquil, hands in his lap. "He was shaven and wore red and black like a ladybug. His fingernails were polished pink and was covered in Satanic tattoos. He came to me to confess his sins. He wanted deliverance."

"From what?"

"He said that he kidnapped eighteen children, and had sex with teenagers – both boys and girls. He *bragged* about it."

A sign that Keller was coming closer to the truth. "Bragged, huh?"

"Yes. He abducted them from families. He was deranged in the head, if you ask me. When he came begging on his knees at my doorstep, I knew, by God's grace, that he had delivered this wicked man into my hands. So, I arrested him myself, held him prisoner, and locked him up in my basement."

"Why? Why didn't you call the police?"

"Sir, I didn't want to cause trouble. I prevented the evil by letting him die. I did nothing wrong, Detective Butcher. Trust me. The Bible says that when a criminal comes into the city of refuge, the avenger of blood cannot touch him. As a priest, I am a Levite, and I own a city of refuge – a church. I am divinely obliged to not hand this wretch over to the avenger." His milky blue eyes glanced up at Keller. "I personally don't trust government authorities staying at my retirement house doing tests and taking my stuff. It's not right, you know."

Keller licked his lips. "So, you're telling me you found the offender and . . . you killed him? You know by killing the offender, it will forever hamper police investigation?"

"I am sorry. I didn't kill him. God did. I don't trust the government as having my best interests in mind. I have a holy responsibility for the Kingdom of God."

"But I am the law, Father. Surely, your Kingdom of God has law."

Neil's face contorted in derision. "Yeeaah no. Let's not get into that. I told you; I didn't kill him."

"You could have really saved me a lot of hassle turning the man in," Keller said, grinning, letting out a little chuckle. Surprisingly, Neil grunted out a laugh. "Tell me," Keller hardened his voice. "Why didn't you call the police?"

"Oh, Detective, I'm sorry. You don't understand."

"No, no. Don't give me that. You know that the evidence as it is looks very suspicious. It looks too much like you have killed the man by refusing to turn him in. I don't want excuses. Not turning in crimes to 911 is just as much as an offence to the law as holding a civilian hostage, Father—"

"Call no man . . . I was just scared."

"Scared of what?"

"The demons sir. Ugh, sir, that is why I bury the statues and the satanic symbol on the man's pendant. Demonic entities are everywhere."

Keller raised his eyebrow. *Oh, this guy is one of those medieval maniacs!* "What else did Little Ladykiller say to you when he confessed? Did he say anything else?"

"Oh . . . He said, he was . . . waging war against God. And that he was losing."

Nuts. Keller smirked, hand stroking at his chin. Waging war against God by having sex with and killing little children? "Great," he tried hard to stifle his cynical snickering.

Neil eyed Keller gravely. To him, this matter was not funny.

"You scared the statues will kill God?"

"No. I'm worried about the Powers behind all things. All occult symbols, statues of anything in the likeness of holy beings is idolatry. Breaks the second commandment."

Keller, farrowing his brow, leaned forward. "So . . . you're not Catholic? What are you then?"

"Methodist, Detective."

"Why is Thomas in your house?"

"Oh . . ." Neil slumped, looking tired, and unwell. "Oh, you know, sir. Thomas Jones is without any family. He has no father nor mother. I'm his family. I look after him. He's a nice boy. I give him my van to drive – he doesn't go far. You know, he has successful schizophrenia? Yes, Detective, successful schizophrenia – the prognosis is very grave. Thomas has to minimise all stimulation or else he'll go insane. He can't live independently, hold a job, find a loving partner, get married, so, my house acts as a boarding school for him. I take him to the church with the other people of the community and the congregation, where he learns. I have full faith in that boy. Thomas says he hears voices – yes, he tells me he's heard these voices speak to him – he has a cognitive way to suppress them very, very well."

Successful schizophrenia? Boarding school in a Methodist cult? Keller wrote all that down. "Did you see Thomas come home in his van with two girls?" Keller said.

"No," Neil grumbled. "As I said, his diagnosis prevents him from even conceiving kidnapping children. No way, Detective."

Interesting. The condition, Neil implies, makes him innocent. Unless he had a medical certificate to prove this . . . That later. "Back to the man in the basement. How did he kidnap children? Did he say?"

"Oh . . . Oh yes. The Little Ladykiller claimed . . . that he took children in daylight. More than one at a time. Thomas . . ." Neil smirked smugly, as if an idea entered his mind. "He was one of those children. I protect him from those predators."

Keller slumped, scribbling the information down. *Ahhh, crap. So, he's claiming Thomas is a victim and not the instigator?*

"Okay . . ." Keller ran a hand through his hair, feeling a tremor of frustration for wasting a whole twenty-four hours with Thomas in ward. "How long was the man in the basement dead for?"

"Very recent. Three weeks ago."

Keller rubbed his face, but, before he could discuss the corpse, Neil continued to ramble. "Who are the girls you are looking for? What are their names?"

"Veronica DePaula and Zoe O'Leary," Keller said.

"As of this moment, Veronica and Zoe could be down the road, or they could be on a plane to LA, Columbia, Honduras. Child trafficking, sex trade and satanic ritual abuse is the fastest growing international crime that world has ever seen. More people are enslaved than ever before in the history of the world. It has past the Transatlantic Slave Trade, and it will soon pass the drug trade, because why sell one drug a day, when you can sell precious children, five to ten times a day? People don't want to hear it. I understand. It's too evil for polite conversation. But meanwhile, over six million children a year are being sucked into the deepest Hell. Trust me Detective. Because if you do *nothing,* this is going to spread and spread until the world is going to live in a nightmare it can never wake up from.

"So, here's the truth. You know why I bury these idols? Those dung gods are thirsty for the youth. They say that the olden gods needed statues and evil humans so they could inhabit their bodies as surrogate temples. These are the gods of darkness that want child sacrifice. The Canaanite deities in ancient times all demanded blood sacrifices of little babies. Oh yes, Detective, the old gods of the myths, they *demand children blood.* They need temples and statues – control centres where they can maintain order, make decrees, exercise sovereignty. It is because children are so innocent. So pure. Without sin. Perhaps that reveals the condition of these dung gods that they are full of vices and evil, that they need children to sedate themselves. Paedophilia – it's the Devil and the gods. This man, he was possessed by the gods for sure. So that's why I buried those statues and the man."

Keller considered the bottle of vodka from Neil's house and concluded, *Yeah, this guy is* definitely *having a hangover!*

"I hate immigrants," Neil muttered. "You know what happens when immigrants come to America, Detective?"

Keller frowned, fidgeting with his notebook page, with a strong distaste for this cult leader's bias for foreigners, reeking of supernatural superstition.

"They are untrustworthy, and they are scams. They take our children and bring their gods with them," Neil went on. "They bring their demons to oppress us. The Powers are not nice to human children."

"So, tell me, Neil," Keller sighed, swallowing, trying to get back to the subject from such a bleak digression. "When we searched Thomas' van, we found a Department of Defence CD containing files in there. Do you have an explanation what Thomas might be doing possessing such files?"

"I have none," Neil added. "As I said, Thomas is successfully schizophrenic."

"That doesn't make sense, Neil. Someone put the CD there. And you need to show me a medical certificate."

"You want me to drive back to my house?"

"Don't worry. How does Thomas own the CD?"

"It's beyond me. I'm sorry. I'm . . . just as confused as you are."

Crap! "Alright. Thank you for your very *informative* cooperation."

"Can I leave now?" the old man Neil said feebly, pushing himself up to rise, but Keller was already closing the door.

"No. You don't leave until the head officer says so."

—

Ben's shouts echoed across his mother's home, long into the gnarly night, bouncing off the walls of the forlorn house.

"Tell me where they are!" he snarled. "Tell me!"

Thomas let out a sharp cry, like a cloth tearing. He was whimpering, begging desperately.

"Talk! Come on, Casbolt! Talk! We've talked together before. You know me!"

"Crying . . ."

"What did you say?

"They were crying . . ."

"What?"

"They cried when I left them. I tried . . . Help them."

"Who!? *Who cried!?*" Ben waved his fist, a high hand trembling with exhilaration bending over the beaten body, ready to land a deadly blow. "You said *they* cried?!"

Casbolt blinked deliriously. His mouth and lips bled with dark crimson, blood dripping down his chin thickly like a beard.

Time and place seemed to distort as Ben persisted with some addictive impetus that kept him, hours on end, cajoled to break Casbolt to get what he knew was right in Ben's own eyes: answers.

"You said you heard them cry when you left them!" Ben punched. The boy grunted, flopping on the pillows Ben had propped up by the shower, so he could not suffer concussion. Casbolt moved weakly, his face buried, smearing the pillow with his lifeblood. He had been untied. He wouldn't be going anywhere.

With a trembling breath, Ben, yanking Thomas up to his face by the collar, raised his fist again. Blood squirted from between Thomas' teeth, gums and lips. Ben's hip writhed in surging waves of heat, and for support he leaned his underside on the wall. Sweat dripped down his face and his knuckles burned with blisters from hitting flesh and muscle, dislodging teeth and bone.

"Why will you not talk to me?! Come on, Casbolt, I remember you. You said you wrote a book. You wrote a freakin' book! Talk, you son of a—"

"Stop . . . Help them."

Ben could have imagined the rasping voice; it was so weak, so uncharacteristic of James Casbolt.

"Speak," Ben begged. He whimpered from his injury, squatting and bending over. He leaned on one leg. "*Come on! Come on!* Speak to me! *Tell me where they are!*"

Punch.

Crumpling into the pillow, Casbolt let out a guttural inhale, discharging blood and mucus out of his mouth and nose. Ben held him up again, hip scalding his body.

"Just tell me," Ben quaked, baring his teeth. Casbolt's eyes were closed, as Ben's mad breaths – hot and oily – engulfed his face. "Just tell me, and I'll stop hurting you."

Casbolt stared at him mutely and Ben, raising his bloodied fist, threw a punch.

Gagging, struggling to breathe, Casbolt fell flaccid into the pillow. Ben hauled him up again, fist raised.

His hip screamed! But he needed to find where his daughter was.

"Just," Ben moaned, jerking from his hip, letting go of Casbolt, sitting down on his bottom, wincing from the surging waves of pain. Iron, pungent and fresh, proliferated his nose. "Just . . . Tell me . . . where . . . they are."

Raising a limp hand, Casbolt lay in a heap. Ben grasped his arm, feeling the shock in Casbolt's body as he flinched and coiled into a ball.

Panting, Ben watched this man who he thought he knew, so vulnerable, so wounded, curl up to protect his vital organs from more beatings. But why, if he could just say something, if he could no longer take the torture? "Why . . ." Ben moaned, exhausted, resting his head against the wall. "Why won't you tell me? Why?"

Casbolt's eyes were shut, laying there still, in terrible agony. He opened his eyes which gleamed, knowingly. *He's playing games with me, is he?*

Catching his breath, Ben slumped, his vision blurred, gazing at a wheezing groaning wretch, his mouth black with gore, head arching back, screaming in silent agony, blood splattered everywhere, and arms twisted in unusual angles. He was groaning so feebly, as if moving a tad hurt him greatly.

Sympathy swelled up in Ben, and he raised his clenched hand to his head, feeling awful, filthy, unfulfilled by the ordeal.

"He knows," Ben whispered to himself, sniffing in the bloody iron. He lifted his head and glared at the despicable man. "He knows. I need to break his shell. I see it in his eyes."

Desperation then became the engine that fuelled his creativity for torture. That conserved Ben's functioning, keeping him awake all night.

Screwing his eyes shut, Casbolt groaned, as if dreading what next would be done unto him. He tried working his bloody lower jaw. Ben had broken it.

"I know you know!" Ben yelled. "Why aren't you *telling me!* WHY?!"

What should he do next? Get the hammer? No, what would be the good of that if he'd kill him in hot blood? Ben searched, grabbing his crutches, seeking for a way to . . .

Just behind the bathroom wall, outside, was a tap rigging. Two knobs. Hot water. Cold water. The plumbing linked to the shower just inside the bathroom. Thomas had to remain captured. Boxed in.

Ben gazed into the landing. The woodcutter table. A plank of wood. A new door.

Ideas wove in Ben's head, liquidating in his hardened mind. Pulling himself up, he found a place to plug in the electric saw, drew up the measurements that aligned with the shower, and cut out a frame from the large board of wood. Whirling metal buzzed as it sliced through the wood, along the measurements of the frame Ben drew.

The structure was simple. It took time, almost the whole night. He constructed a wooden wall frame, built into the bathroom shower, eclipsing all light from getting inside. It was cramped and squashy, barely enough room for another to sit down inside. All except for a small peephole to speak through, and for Ben to gaze into. Darkness and isolation would psychologically do its job to press the truth out from him. *Sealing him in there will do the trick,* Ben thought. *Then I will have the truth and I will set him free.*

The shower had knobs and a rig outside the bathroom wall, so he could control the temperature – it either came out scalding hot or freezing cold.

And, in case Ben started feeling sorry for Casbolt, he inserted a picture in between the door and the wooden wall. A photograph of the little girls trying out their go-cart. Sitting in the seat, Veronica in pink, displayed her muscles to the camera impishly, and Zoe, who had been pushing the cart from behind, hugged Veronica tenderly. Both were smiling sweetly, playfully.

After about four hours, opening the wall to his newly made torture shower, Ben limped towards Casbolt. "Alright," Ben growled, straining from the pain, kicking him into the small space. Casbolt whimpered, worming inside, trying to sob, but his bloody jaw caked with fresh blood prohibiting him from forming a wail. Ben grimaced at the gaping gory mouth. He poked the demonic thing with his crutch into a bunched heap in the corner of the shower, concealing him.

"Now." Ben heaved, tying Casbolt's hands back up again; he closed the door, casting Casbolt into darkness. Ben placed his own hands on the tap.

"It's going to burn you, or it's going to freeze you. Come on. Tell me. You're doing this to yourself."

With his good leg, Ben closed the door, and selected boiling hot water. Casbolt would not know which temperature would strike him, but better to psychologically torment him, than use the fist or the hammer on him. The latter was too bloody and messy, but he'd come this far into the night, and nothing could subdue his feverish insomnia.

Ben hovered his hand on the tap, considering what he was about to do. It daunted him, made his heart thunder, yet at the same time, it filled him with an intoxicating ecstasy. All was silence, except for the sound of Ben's heart pounding in his chest and ears. His arm grasping the tap almost quivered.

"Tell me."

Ben eyed Veronica and Zoe in the go-cart.

He twisted the knob. Water gushed in spurts.

Casbolt convulsed, mewling at the top of his lungs. The entire wooden frame of the shower trembled violently, shaking the wooden door.

"Tell me!"

Screams and wails cudgelled Ben's ears, turning his blood into ice, and at the zenith of strain, they dwindled into whines.

"Tell me!" Ben threw his palm into the door. Steam slithered out from the peephole, spewing into strands of smoke, becoming thicker as the water poured. "Where is Veronica!" Ben slammed the door, turning off the tap. Casbolt let out a ghastly wail, an inhuman screeching roar.

Ben slumped against the wall – defeated and exhausted. *It's been five days now since Veronica was taken. I'm running out of time. Hurry up!* Images of blood, Casbolt, his daughter, his father, the paladin and the child in the trash haunted his mind like scarlet cadaverous phantoms. Ben did not realise how tedious torture would be – it was a skill to torture someone to glean information via compulsion – one had to know what would be effective – the slow pain – the gradual isolation and time and dark confinements that would wear on the person's mind. It was more humane than killing them outright. In this way, Ben had confidence that the truth would crack out of Casbolt. Eventually.

But Ben resolved that he could give this asshole a period of respite, so he could rest. Later, he'd continue to gain some answers.

Vertigo seized Ben and he hit the wall, collapsing on the floor. Overwhelming exhaustion made him physically incapable of moving. He lay on his back, groaning, and deep sleep hurled upon him.

43

THE PEARL

"Therefore I strike you with a grievous blow,
*   making you desolate because of your sins.*
You shall eat, but not be satisfied,
*   and there shall be hunger within you;*
you shall put away, but not preserve,
*   and what you preserve I will give to the sword.*
You shall sow, but not reap;
*   you shall tread olives, but not anoint yourselves with oil;*
you shall tread grapes, but not drink wine."
—From the Scroll of Micha, Judgments against Israel and Judah, c. 735 – 700 BCE.

Brianna stalked into her house to have some breakfast after a melancholy night of tracking the Manicheans of Light. She went to open the door, finding it unlocked.

Ben's home.

In the gloom of the living room, an indistinct shape lay down on the sofa. Carefully, stealthily, Brianna took a step, making the floor creak weakly. She held her breath. In the deep silence she went on to the side to take another creeping step, but to her dismay, the sensitive floorboard only croaked louder.

Suddenly Ben yelped, rising from with a start, making Brianna yelp back.

"I thought you were Veronica," Ben said, hand on his heart.

Even in the dimness, Brianna could see her husband's haggard eyes.

"Where the hell were you last night?" Brianna questioned, bewildered.

Ben heaved out a sigh and said, "Looking for my daughter."

As a detective, Brianna never doubted potential truths, but she put them aside, hoping for the best of him.

"I spoke with him," Brianna said. "Judd Pounders, about—"

"What did you tell him?" His voice was dry.

"I told him you're distraught. He gave me some information about Ian Mastemah and the secret government agency, where this man known as Alfred Bonner who has been in charge of your deployment of Iraq and Ian Mastemah's affiliates since the very beginning. They both have information about your details."

"But that doesn't help us. Brianna, this is what I found out. Thomas Jones *is not* Thomas Jones." Ben was frantic, evading her inquiry, stumbling over his words. "He is James Casbolt! He looks exactly like him! I have no idea why this is the case, but whatever my father got himself into, I swear to God, I should have been more cynical towards that guy. Brianna, I knew about Casbolt! He is a soldier in the Marine Corps! He told me with his very words the night we were deployed that he wanted to find special children." Ben clicked his fingers. "I . . . I . . ."

"You need to wait for one minute!" Brianna shouted. "Because I have *no idea* what you are trying to say to me! I think you're conflating things, because Judd Pounders said James Casbolt is still in Iraq."

Ben threw back his head, hobbling for his crutches. "I have no time for this."

"Tell me the truth!"

"You can't *handle the truth!*"

"I'm an FBI agent. I can listen. Now, how did you come back from Iraq first off, and how and why did Ian Mastemah track you down? Ben, the missing piece of this puzzle is how you disappeared and came back to America. So, tell me what happened?"

"It's a long story," Ben grumbled. "Don't say I didn't warn you. It all began with James Casbolt and Julian's daughters. His conspiracy theories and his talk about secret societies and top-secret programs with alien genetics and crap. He joined us, and I swear to God he can control people's minds. Then at Haditha Dam in war, there was a burning building. I fell from it. I busted my *goddamn* hip and finding a baby in a *goddamn* trash can, and then when I thought all hope was lost, I meet a *goddamn* hooded alien that somehow knew about my family, then teleported me across the world with missing time, and then . . ." He took a deep breath. "And then I made my way back from Mt

Graham, my hip dying with a baby *pissing* on my face, and then by a miracle Daniel from South Africa takes the baby, not long before a stupid *Indian* tried to tell me that the giants are returning, and I have to reunite *stupid* whatever First Fruits!" Ben snickered with madness. "And *then,* I went to Dad's place. He got me fixed up and then all this *crap* hit the fan when Ian Mastemah barraged into the house killing Dad!" Ben spread out his arms. "And then Thomas Jones stole my daughter days after! Why!? Why me!? Tell me! Why is all this crap happening to me so suddenly? *Tell me* if I have *any* idea what is going on! There!" Ben threw the CD, tossing it so it slid on the ground, not shattering. "I told you now! But *no,* you're not going *to believe a single freakin'* word I said, because you think that I'm crazy!"

Brianna's mouth went dry, her eyes crossing. *My husband . . . he's insane.*

"Annnd there is more!" Ben slumped on the verge of tears. "This is Thomas Jones, Brianna! He had the CD! This stupid CD needs to be cracked! It is the *only way* for this to be possible – Casbolt's lookalike called Thomas Jones or whatever, has been programmed by some secret agents like Mastemah to track me down, to ruin me. Only Alfred Bonner and Ian Mastemah would have access to these files."

Brianna had to back off, now afraid of what Ben was going to do.

No . . . I will never leave him, she thought. *The cult of the Alliance and the Manicheans of Light are suspicious of him for a reason. But why is he so fed up with a worthless CD?*

"So," Ben poised himself, thrusting out his chin stubbornly. "There you go. The truth."

"Ben . . ." Brianna was stunned. What should she do? No one in their sane mind would believe Ben's story. Teleported by an alien? Indians? "I had to tell the truth to Judd," Brianna pressed firmly. "Those files are not going to bring your Dad or Veronica back, Ben. If anyone finds out—"

"How?!" Ben snapped. "How can you even say that?"

Brianna bristled. "But my point is . . . is it worth it? Is this CD and Thomas Jones worth risking everything? Keller last night has proven that Thomas is innocent! His guardian says that he was protecting Thomas Jones *from* predators! Thomas was a *victim* of child trafficking! The corpse of Little Ladykiller was found in Thomas' basement to confirm this. Thomas is innocent! The CD is out of left field."

Ben froze, his Adam's apple bulging. "Really?"

"Really."

"But how could a bum have gotten it?"

"That's not priority right now. Ben, it wasn't Thomas," Brianna said, watching stubbornness consume him.

"How dare you give up hope!" Ben trashed the coffee table, sweeping his hand across it, toppling everything on the floor. His body trembled violently. "No! No, they're *still* out there! You haven't given me our daughter's body, so she is still out there. Screw Keller! I'm going to find out what's on this CD myself!"

"But Ben! No! Forget the CD! Focus on the Manicheans of the Light! Judd said they are terrorists and what terrorists want is to spread a message. They inflict psychological trauma to do it. They want you to overreact, you understand? You will fall right into their hands or worse, you could become their decoy, their only way to escape being caught." Brianna took a brisk step forward. "You understand what I am saying? Do not go on with this. It is for your own good. Stop getting in the FBI's way, because you have no idea what you are doing! Thomas and the CD are *unrelated* to Veronica's disappearance!"

It was clear Brianna's retort did not cross Ben's arrogant mind, for the reply came viciously. "Stop doing this to me, Brianna! It's *you* that's getting in *my* way! If I find out you've got some insider agenda—"

Agenda? I'm trying to be objective here! "Excuse me!?" Brianna gasped. "Are you listening to yourself?"

Ben swerved his head back with distant eyes, blocking her out. "I need to find a Navajo reservation." He said those words dryly, but she noticed a hint of zeal in his voice, determination to fulfil a paramount duty. She could not think of what to do now that Ben, resolved and impetuous, had made up his mind. Denying the truth.

"I just . . ." she stammered. "I just need some kind of assurance if they are going to arrest you because of what you did to Thomas Jones in the parking lot." Ben smothered his face, as Brianna persisted. "Pounders now has to bite his tongue with whatever this Alfred Bonner figure is going to do now. If Bonner has the authority over the Manicheans . . ."

"Then Bonner should go to Hell." Her eyes dared him to say another word, but Ben sighed, grudgingly gazing at the floor. Brianna sighed deeply, so she approached his crisis tenderly, containing her calm. She needed to calm Ben down too, though it often felt like she was speaking to a brick wall, or rather to a baby having a tantrum. *Oh Ben . . . This is hurting you just as much as it is hurting me.*

Brianna needed to bring control, to impose order to this chaos.

"Ben, you're not doing this wisely," Brianna said, hoping her council would change his mind. "You're creating too many problems! The CD is worthless!"

"Agrh, I expected better from you, worthless woman," Ben exclaimed coldly. *But . . .* If words were knives, that would have left her bleeding on the floor with a nauseating laceration. Brianna set her jaw, debilitated as Ben stalked over to grab his red-flannel shirt.

"Have you ever thought that there might be something that you don't know? A perspective that you are missing? You *always* claim to be right!"

"Okay then, Detective! Tell me something I don't know?"

"We're still gathering facts and info—"

"Nah! You're wasting time that way! You can only say that if you deny Thomas Jones is guilty! The van shows he's guilty!"

"This is not about the van!" snarled Brianna. "It's about *you*, Ben! You're a morale pit!"

Ben harrumphed.

"I'm on your side, as I have always been. I'm your wife!" She emphasised the last words as Ben thrashed, frustrated, trying to put his jacket on. He picked up his handgun, slipped it into his holster on his back pocket, using his crutches to walk with a gimpy leg. "I lost my daughter too last week," Brianna said. "The world doesn't revolve around you!"

"It's been six days and we've found crap nothin'!" Ben snapped.

"Ben . . ." Brianna sighed, exhausted.

"It's complicated, Brianna."

"What?"

"Being me. These terrorists, this Alliance who killed my father and took my daughter are systematically trying to turn everyone I trust against me. It's clear these jealous lowlifes are bent on destroying my successful life. I shall *destroy* their lives for them doing so."

The *preposterousness* of that vendetta . . . She ground her teeth. "You really believe that, do you?" she rasped.

But he continued to run after his delusion recklessly. Picking up the CD on the floor, cleaning it with his shirt, he grabbed his crutches under his arms and hobbled out the door. Brianna stared. If this man, even inhibited by crutches, would be so stubborn to exert himself to get to the truth . . . Stress creased Ben's forehead, and his eyes were brimmed with tears. "I have to find her," he was mumbling. "Wastin' time."

"Why?" Brianna pleaded.

"I am doing this to save our family." Then, perfunctorily, he threw back an "I love you," and disappeared out the front door.

"Ben! Let the CD go!"

Shouting in vain, Brianna watched as Ben crashed into the car seat, tossing his battered crutches in the back, slamming the door. Brianna idly clawed the car bonnet as it pulled out with a screech.

"Did your dad want this, Ben?!" Brianna shouted marching down to the kerb. "This is not honouring him! Ben! Let the CD go! No!"

She watched Ben speed away hopelessly. Disgusted at herself and her spouse, she groaned in shame, weighing the outcomes and her options: the investigation, which was well under FBI jurisdiction, or ensuring her husband's safety. Following her own personal logic, Brianna had to commit to the most direct situation close at hand that needed to be resolved sooner before the other. It was triage time.

Her husband – lost and depraved – needed saving. He *needed* her above all else.

—

The solitary journey up north to the Grand Canyon felt spiritual.

It liberated Ben's clogged mind, releasing him from the bondage that had been Phoenix. He sped down the forlorn desert highway, the sun glazing the red burnt wilderness, the horizon blue and ochre. Sunburned eroded spires, jutting off plateaus covered with brush, thrusted up from a broken blistered land like ships sailing in oceans of blood. He kept his eyes on the highway and his foot hard on the accelerator, racing past Mazatzal Peak, cut through Oak Creek, Flagstaff, Cameron, and paralleling the Colorado River, towards Navajo Nation LeChee Chapter.

Ben wanted to tell Brianna that he was sorry, but saying sorry did not seem entirely adequate, and in any case, what he was sorry about seemed too deep and too evanescent for any words that he knew, it seemed so vastly more complicated – the immediate fact was that it was better for it to remain unravelled.

Ben flew down the snaking highway, eroded buttes to the right and the Colorado River valley to the left.

Once he found the Navajo Nation LeChee Chapter, Ben sat restlessly inside, not able to keep his good foot from jiggling up and down, holding his crutches up, waiting longingly for the decoding of the CD. The Navajo medicine man, Albert Tobadzistsini, had been generous to help him, and taking the CD, he had retreated into the office to translate the files. He told

Ben to remain in the waiting room, for the knowledge on the disc was sacred and guarded by the Navajo and the Department of Defence. Besides the rows of chairs set in a line against the wall, the cabin living room was particularly welcoming – it had a rug of an exotic sandpainting depicting animals and nature, feathers and figures clad in layered white, red, brown and light-blue garments and a garment of quality deer skin, all hanging on the wall. A small coffee table with a few books and a pot plant stood on top, and the wall was sparsely decorated with modest items like feathers, liturgical tools and the stuffed head of an elk.

"My friend, come here please," a masculine elderly voice spoke. Docile Albert emerged from the office room veiled by dappled light. His leathery skin glowed a glistening gold brown, auralike around his strands of long silvery hair draping over his shoulders. Clad in a crimson shirt, baggy pants, wearing leather moccasins, the medicine man wore a polished turquoise and silver bracelet and a necklace with a string of turquoise gems.

"Something hidden in the desert will be disclosed," Albert Tobadzistsini said as he eased towards Ben. "The truth will come from the sands of deception."

"Is that what the CD says?" Ben said.

Albert nodded slightly. "I'm entrusted to keep the knowledge burned on the disc safe. A time is coming when people will become blind and deaf – at war with themselves, and at war with others. They will forget that the mother is the centre of the family. They will forget that a baby is the same as an old person." Ben's body clenched with guilt. "Then, the truth about the Pearls of Power of the Anaye will be revealed. The truth about Alfred Bonner."

"You know about Alfred Bonner?" Ben asked, titillated.

"Before I became Chief and medicine man, I was a historian. The organisation of the Alliance began as a renegade activist movement that tried to expose ruthless child traffickers and Neo-Nazis by funding operations to hunt down paedophiles. Alfred Bonner had embarked on numerous rescue missions throughout his career. Driven by his passion for justice and his personal encounters with the horrors of child trafficking, Alfred through private donations and partnerships, played a vital role in disrupting trafficking networks and providing survivors with the chance to reclaim their lives.

"Over a thousand paedophiles have been captured by the Alliance. While Alfred's efforts have been widely applauded, he has faced many legal roadblocks. These evil people Alfred Bonner has tried to capture, try very hard to hide smuggled children for good. They take them into isolated territory, uninhabited places around the globe so they can disappear. Alfred Bonner is only one man, who's been through a lot. I mean a lot because he lost his daughter to these same traffickers."

Ben smirked. *What am I even hearing!?*

"But Alfred's job, has torn him to pieces," Albert said. "His cold-blooded hardness comes with his desire to rise up and defeat evil and now, he's become the very thing he wanted to destroy. He will be willing to take your daughter into the Underworld if you do not find him. He is an enemy that is bent on destruction. I have the information that will display the power that only Chief Cornerstone can wield."

"You saying Bonner has my daughter?"

Albert frowned. "I don't know. But what I do know is that your family is under the control of evil spirits. It is time for what I have kept hidden to be revealed." He led him towards the door and outside to the carpark, Ben hobbling after him on crutches. He yearned to learn more. They drove on the beaten track towards the canyon wilderness, the road rough and bumpy. Red swirls of dust rose from off the dry ground.

"What is hidden?" Ben asked.

"You will see for yourself." Albert left Ben seething in trepidation, his faraway expression forming on his face, looking into the hazy distance of barren wilderness strewn with thickets and red, pink boulders. They passed clustered campsites with a small shack or hut under a corpse of trees alongside a well. "Beware of the *Yee Naaldlooshii.*"

"Who?"

As they drove, Albert briefly spoke to Ben of the Skin Walkers: shapeshifters conjured by witchcraft, sedition and deceit. Skin Walkers could take on any form indefinitely, anything from animate to inanimate. Alive and extinct. Albert feared Ben's life was cursed as a result of the presence of Skin Walkers.

Albert spoke of the lore of the wars between the Navajo and the Utes who at that time were united with the Jicarilla Apache. For in that time, the Utes learnt of the ways of the Spanish and betrayed the Navajo, enacting various evils on them, abducting their loved ones. But this evil wasn't forgotten, some said that the Navajo in their suffering cursed the San Luis Valley between them and the Utes, while others said as punishment, Creator cursed the land with Skin Walkers to cover for the violence and bloodshed that racked the land mightily. And it was these demonic creatures that still lurked in the land to this day.

Of the Gateways into the Underworld at Sedona and Dulce Albert spoke, and of the First World - a primordial time when Creator communed and ruled with the humans and the Holy People, before Skin Walkers haunted the land.

"We will stop here." They had parked in front of a worn wired gate yellowed by dust. Once the engine stopped, everything was silent, so far from civilisation. Opening the door into the scorching heat, Ben hobbled to the creaking gate. Albert stretched out his right hand pointing to the wasteland ahead.

"This trail is very ancient. If we step forth on this trail, they will be watching you."

"Who? Skin Walkers?" Ben already had people on his tail though he expected that the stakes could get higher if he persisted onwards.

Then he heard the Chief whisper, "Shhh. Snake sorcerers. Shhh. We don't talk about this to outsiders."

"Why is that?"

"I don't like to talk about it," Albert said gruffly, face stern. His eyes thinned. "I don't like to give credit to the darkness. The Adversary's goal is to distract us and to deceive us from what is right and good. Taking things meant for good and perverting them for an evil end." Albert smacked his lips, in deep thought. "You now have a choice, Ben. This is a test. You will either follow the Adversary, or you will follow the Holy People."

Ben stared down at the rocky trail laying before him and said, "I just want to find my daughter. I just want to know why I was sent back to Arizona to find my father."

"You can learn the truth of these either by way of the Enemy or by the Creator," Albert said. "Choose."

What? Ben thought. *His riddles…*

As the two made their way cross the plateau, it was not long until Ben began to glimpse the vast Southern Rim of the Grand Canyon itself – a mere corner of the vast chasms. Shocked by how high he was, or rather, how deep those canyons were, for miles and miles in every direction they spread. Blotched shadows of fluffy clouds soared over the green plateaus, and in the bands of red and pink rock faces like the tendons and muscles of torn meat, majestic cliffs plummeted into a deep rugged gorge. The canyon looked rough, rockfalls precipitous with rifting inclines five hundred feet high. Wind swirled with a trill. Down below on the canyon floor, the Colorado River like a single metallic thread, eroded the earth.

Forcing his eyes from the walls of the canyon, Ben glanced at Albert who rested his foot on a stump of an old tree, squinting and pointing at something down the hilly slope ahead. "What you are looking for is down there," the

Chief said.

My daughter . . . Craning his neck, Ben followed the Chief's finger and looking closer to the right, at the foot of the flushed wall of rock, he saw it.

In the tangled brambles, nestled to the right inside a rocky cleft, was a slot canyon. A giant fissure cleaved right through the ochre wall that continued to form a precipitous rock face and a cliff.

Seeing the slot canyon made Ben curl his lips in a wry smile. The canyon's rosy sandstone seemed to gleam in the sun. His daughter could be down there – Thomas Jones had kept this sacred information secret.

Under the blazing sun, now slanting off to the west, navy shadows began to shroud the right spine of rock where the cave was, forming dense patches over the green thickets like the hide of a terraforming beast. With cautious steps, holding his crutches to stabilise him – not ideal using crutches on bush terrain – Ben followed Albert through the small wood, hiking across the slope. Rocks clanked and insects from within the trees and shrubs chirped by the disturbed rocks, the sound carried in the torrid air.

Once under the shade of twisted pines, the scent of their bark farinaceous, Ben and Albert stood on the sandy, tawny platform before the slot canyon.

The Chief did not say a word, and Ben, seeing that as a gesture to enter, embarked. He had been led here and, confident that answers undiscovered could at last be found, wondered if it really was worth it as Brianna had said.

Of course this is worth it, Ben thought, irked. *It is too late to turn back now.*

Ben proceeded into the narrow red scar cleaved through rock. It veered to the right downwards, and then all ambient noise – insects chirping, the wind – ceased. Everything went silent at once, as if nature were holding her breath. The only sound was his crutches rocking back and forth.

He entered a vast chamber, smoothed hard red edges with undulating flowing shapes and bands of swirling orange, brown, yellow and pink strata. Along the walls were strange petroglyphs, some thunderbirds and spiral tree motifs among many others: stick figures, zigzags, starbursts and animals. It had an emphasis on straight rather than curved lines, coloured in warm pigments made from the rich mineral deposits. The red walls ran in ridged runnels, eroded sandstone alcoves cut by flash flooding honeycombing the walls from ground to roof, overlooking a large rocky plinth at the centre of the chamber. In that centre was a round basin and inside that, were tattered blankets strewn across the ground and all manner of shining things.

But not Veronica.

In the middle of the central round enclosure basin was a small hole or indentation in the floor. In that nest was an alluring Pearl. Vaguely spheroid, diameter no bigger than two thumbnails, the Pearl shone with a faint radiance. Even with an iridescent nimbus, that pinprick marble of the purest of pale silver shone with a mother-of-pearl.

Ben stepped into the red-sandstone basin; his eyes hooked on the tiny pure-white star. In his tunnel vision was the Pearl and only the Pearl. Ben crept in a little closer; he wanted to take hold of it. Like his daughter – Ben itched to have . . . that . . . one . . . Pearl.

The ability to do whatever he wanted to find the truth. The power to destroy all those that came in his way, the power to restore his family. To gain all the knowledge of what happened to his father and to himself instantaneously. The power and strength to torture Thoams Jones, the might to take the truth from him.

Benjimin. Whispers, so faint. Still-small. *Benjimin.*

The Pearl, the wind, called to him. Desiring that the magic Pearl of Power was good, hand hovering over it, Ben shut his mouth. He had drooled. He blinked and felt lightheaded, requiring his voluntary effort to stand upright, grasping his crutches with both hands. His arms were quivering.

The good, beautiful Pearl *captivated* him. Feeling as if he had stumbled upon something – a prize that none but he had been most fortunate to find – Ben looked here and there, then went to grab the Pearl.

The Pearl cooed for him. It *needed* him. All his problems could be solved. *Yes.* Indistinct guttural murmurings.

A strange musky scent struck Ben out of his daze. Fear. Paralysis. The smell was chemically harsh, the odour of decay making his eyes burn faintly.

A ringing zipped in his ears.

At the corner of Ben's eye, a child covered in hair that had hit the gym one too many times lumbered into the rosy slot canyon on all fours, its massive back feet and hands, with pointed nails, lunged back and forth.

With coal eyes, the gorilla stopped at the rim of the basin, gazing at Ben.

Ben hissed, his crutches trembling in his hands, but he couldn't move. It wanted the Pearl! *I found the Pearl! It's mine, monkey!* Ben reached for his gun and aimed.

The ape did not charge. It simply stood up, standing on its two hind legs like a man. The spiky-headed gorilla, fearlessly mimicked Ben, hissing back at him. It hissed many times, then emitted a half roar, half snarl, protruding square-like molars as the primate opened its mouth.

But something strange happened as it hissed. The chimp's face *bubbled.*

Skin tremoring and melting like a fried egg on a frypan.

Ben's arm holding his gun suddenly felt heavy. His hearing buzzed, enhancing. He felt invisible probes vibrating his body and he was certain this demonic gorilla could hear and feel his heartbeat, feel and taste his fear, his blood and guilt coagulating his nerves. Shockwaves attacked him. Pain racked his bones.

The Pearl…

The ape screamed. The extreme sound drew up and let loose. The ape's whole face – eyes, nose, mouth and teeth protruded and contorted. It raised its arms and beat its chest, drumming it doggedly as it roared – a deep monstrous roar that the rocks themselves quivered. It cut Ben's ears, bludgeoning his brain. Ben slowly began to swoon.

Howls behind him erupted in the canyon. Ben heard keenly, the chanting songs – sonorous wails – cascading like an unseen flood. Unseen powerful forces channelled into him, crumpling him so that he could not fight back. Ben watched with teary eyes and heard with bleeding ears, as the ape dropped to all fours, and shot in a black blur like a lumbering Great Dane, in a flying gallop, disappearing.

Ben writhed in agony, vaguely aware of his body being lifted towards the sandstone ceiling, by clawed hands, carrying him away into the oblivion of darkness.

—

Brianna threw her car into the carpark of Navajo Nation LeChee Chapter, scrambling outside in haste towards the entrance of the reservation.

She needed directions. She needed to find Ben now, or risk wasting her time. For almost half the day she had been chasing her pathetic husband through the red arid desert and was not prepared to lose him now.

After knocking franticly on the front door with no reply, the phone in her pocket rang.

"DePaula," she answered curtly, out of breath. Sweat itched her skin as she paced, angry fists blanched at her side.

"You are a hard woman to reach." The stranger's voice on the other side sounded shrewd.

"Not hard enough apparently." Brianna felt her stomach twisting in knots from the menace in that voice.

"Where are you!?" The reply came with a stab of exasperation.

"Who are *you*, first off."

"I need to talk to you," the masculine voice said after a pause. "I'm the director of your husband's mission to Iraq and I have been aware of your current misfortunes. I have some news to break to you, to supplement your investigations."

Brianna marched to her car, sweating. She feared this was Director Alfred Bonner himself. "And what is that?"

"There are rumours about Ben, the mission, his father's death and his daughter's disappearance. There are all interconnected. Nothing could save your husband now unless he ceases from trespassing national government security. I'm trusting that you have come to stop him, FBI agent?"

"What do you mean?" Brianna said, matching the firmness of the caller's utterances. "I'm trying to protect him."

"Arrest him," the deep voice said. "That is what I'm calling you to do. Arrest him. He's deluded victim of post-traumatic stress. Unless you follow the helicopter down to the canyon, it will be too late."

Brianna gazed up at the azure sky, and lo behold, there she heard the faint sounds of spinning rotor blades.

"Tell me you're up there," she hissed. "If you kill my husband, I swear to God I will have the whole bureau hunt your Alliance!"

The man sniffed with derision. "I suggest you be quick, Brianna DePaula. I'm giving you a head start." The call finished.

Dazed, shoving the phone in her pocket, Brianna craned her head, shading her eyes. Fixating on the black helicopter soaring, she leapt into her car, starting the engine and pulling back on the road. She could see the ravenous vessel heading at full speed northwest.

Towards the Canyon.

God. She never thought the stakes were *this* high. And already she had a feeling she was going to lose.

She sped towards the Grand Canyon. The race for Ben's life had begun.

———

Chief Albert Tobadzistsini traced the rock and heard the scream.

The crying howl of the Big Fear sounded like a lion and an elephant and a blaring train rattling the body. It echoed from within the place where water runs through rocks, bringing Albert to his awareness.

The Big Fears were different for everyone. Darkness, enemies, heights, giants; these fears destroyed people and societies. These were the real giants, the violence, the destructive behaviours and the path of fear.

Perched on a single rock, with his back to the pinyon pine tree shading him from the scorching sun, Albert skimmed his hand fondly over the ringed lines of strata. He followed the journey of greys and blues sliding down into twirling yellow and reds, melting into saffron clay and granite pink – patterns that weaved time and history. The rock in which he traced was a familiar one. It was shaped almost like a seat.

A screech, a cracking whip, blared from the cave. Albert's heart beat faster.

For years Albert had known and protected this secret kiva of the Anasazi as a young man. The Great Spirit Nihitaa' told him too. The One Who Sees by the Sun, Moon and Star Light. The One Who Has No Name. Nihitaa' told him to protect and guard the secret slot canyon as a mountain lion protected her cubs. Knowledge – Albert protected it from the Hairy People.

Until now. The apocalypse was at hand. The essence of evil needed to be dealt with.

The Hairy People were wild. They could either act virtuously, ambivalently or with malcontent. They were from the Anaye – alien gods born as a result of a grand sexual experiment. Such beings influenced the Anasazi a thousand years ago. The Anasazi were a lost people who practised human trafficking, eerily echoing the actions of the secret societies. The Anasazi and the Anaye had a master, the Evil One who followed the bad way. And when he didn't gain the Pearls of Nihitaa', he went contrary to the Holy People, going astray with greed. He threw a temper tantrum, setting fire to the Second World.

The Power of the White Pearl destroyed the greedy Anasazi – violent people whose economy was based on slavery. A people who worshiped the darkness and participated in human sacrifice. It was the Holy People's way of punishment, giving these human traffickers the fruit of their actions. One file on the CD revealed a translation of an ancient inscription on a pottery sherd – now lost – which told the story when the Anasazi were here. It spoke of all the oppressed human slaves of the Anasazi escaping the walled settlements of Chaco Canyon, and of the Holy People bringing the walls down by a great and mighty storm. This was all thanks to the Pearl's evil.

The Pearls of Power was deceptive power over the five senses. But that power was self-destructive, for there could only be one Master of the Pearls. And true Power, could never be shared.

What worthlessness. Albert was called by the Great Spirit to protect this evil in the hands of evil, for the Pearls were dangerous in anyone's hands – as it had been when the Anasazi were here. And now, Nihitaa' said that his time protecting it was up. He had to let it go. For a wise Shepherd bonded with a Hearld will come.

Albert took a deep breath. Who could embody such wisdom? Many people of different tribes had different callings, although some people embraced knowledge eagerly and committed it to memory in exhaustive detail. Others were less successful; and while some were able to apply it productively to their minds, many experienced difficulties. Consequently, Albert could see wisdom in varying degrees, and only a few persons were ever completely wise. By virtue of their unusual mental powers, wise men and women were able to foresee disaster, fend off misfortune, and avoid explosive conflicts with other people. The wise were water because of its life-sustaining properties in the desert, wisdom was viewed first and foremost as an instrument of survival. People like Albert were mature spirit beings, emotional beings, rational beings and physical beings. Artisans of ethics, relationships and discerning between good and bad.

Wisdom consistently linked places, events and stories, but it was a body of knowledge. Wisdom was kinship, it was having a smooth, sound mind, that could see connections between place, knowledge and proper order.

Ben had none of this.

He will fail the test of the Pearl.

Albert would make a final stand to protect his people from the Anaye. From the stories, the Anaye monsters came after a battle in the sky world. They were always here, there was no return.

Only a resurgence.

Ben, unbeknownst to him, had brought the Anaye with him.

These shapeshifting earth dwellers – the *Yee Naaldlooshii* – the Skin Walker sorcerers, came at a time when Creator judged the earth. They existed in three worlds – the under, the above and the heavens.

"The time of the end is here," Albert intoned. "The restoration. Just as the Hopi people have said. Of the white people from the East bearing their sign of the cross, bringing their 'talking leaves'. They spoke of their rocky roads with their concrete forests, their iron ropes suspended in the air and the 'cobwebs' crisscrossing the skies.

"The sacred fire burns for eternity. The purifying fire shall burn. The Kingdom of Heaven will conquer Earth. The Holy People will arise."

Albert stood up to face the raging artificial winds stirring the pinyon pine trees. Albert took his stand – alone – against the monster coming from the skies.

The ominous beats of the helicopter vibrated, carrying the wind above the valley. Laying his hands down on the rock gently for the last time, Albert stood up as a gush of wind cascaded. The blaring roars rumbled and irritated the slot canyon, tossing sand into his eyes. Grunting, Albert buried his face in his arm, blinking hot tears.

Swooping in like a Tsenahale, the helicopter hovered slowly downwards, disgorging a hit squad, which poured into the slot canyon.

"Hey, you get away from there! Over here!" A voice bellowed over the gale. Obeying the authorities was right, despite how bent they were, so Albert meandered into the hovering helicopter.

"Albert – my dear friend." A voice trumpeted over the cutting beats of the rotor blades. He turned to meet the smug and spiteful owner of that boastful voice. A brawny man with ghoul-like skin and short white gelled blond hair. He sat poised on a seat in front of Albert, left leg crossing his right, his broad eye ridges shrouding his eyes in shade. That was Mr Forever Young. Alfred Bonner came from Operation Paperclip. A man of the Evilway.

Alfred Bonner rose and walked out of the helicopter into the kiva and soon he returned, striding out of the cave with soldiers bracketing him, holding the Pearl of Power of *Dokóóslit* in his hands. The White Pearl gleamed in the setting sun – a light emitting the divine.

"Why are you doing this!?" Albert yelled in woe. *Could I have done more? Could I have done more to prevent the Dragon from easily moving me aside? I let this happen! The Dragon could swallow my people!*

Alfred Bonner – the image of the Anaye – roared, saying, "I'm heeding Gilgamesh's call! It's time to cancel the Galactic Tyrant's invasion and it would be unwise to stand in my way!"

Albert gravely shook his head. *So unwise. Nihitaa' – the Great Spirit and the Creator - never loses to fallen star beings who rejected him. It shall not end like this. The Dragon is no threat to Nihitaa'. He controls the Dragon, using it to hand people their desires to rule with violence and conceit.*

Albert went to jump out the helicopter – he couldn't stand being in the presence of evil men – but the helicopter lurched upwards, forcing Albert to stagnantly grasp the handhold. Closing his eyes, he tried to ease his mind.

From generation to generation, history has determined to be in servitude to those that seek to control it. The Servants of God will always suffer. As Chief Albert Tobadzistsini buckled his seatbelt he didn't meet the gaze of the dragons but back down at the land – his life – peppered in green and orange. Unique yet familiar. He soared above his land – departing, taken into the sky, up into the space between the heavens. *Men will stamp over our oral memory, to quench the fire of truth. Such beasts who do such things, are Anaye. They will be burned by that same fire kindled by Creator, killed by the fire they wish to extinguish.*

Beware of their schemes for they are dangerous. Their narratives are written in blood. Yet their stories are grand displays on palaces, writings on a wall.

Sweltering in heat, Albert squinted; he saw his car parked down below at the gate, a contour along the scattered groves of junipers and thickets.

There were two cars parked there. A dark ant ran from the second car across the trail recklessly, desperately. Towards the kiva.

Ben had made a promise. His daughter had been taken by the Anaye. And Albert knew about promises. They crushed one's life and pride, preventing one from holding back mistakes.

If Ben is the Chief as the Great Spirit says, then he must fall, and rise a better man.

Albert kept on looking at the space whence land and sky met far away, tracing the line of mountain and horizon.

AFTERWORD

Thank you for reading Volume 1 of *Omega Plan*.

As you can tell, I've ended the story abruptly on a cliffhanger. This is because the novel isn't finished, it continues in *Omega Plan* Volume 2 which is a direct continuation of the story.

Because of the content, themes, characters and the foreshadowing that I wish to present in this book is on an epic scale, a short book would fail to convey what I want for this series. It needed to be this long, and in fact, I mean future instalments to be longer. Publishing *Omega Plan* in one massive thousand-page volume would not only be extremely expensive (to print and for customers to buy), but it would also be quite intimidating and, therefore, lose potential for success. Especially for a debut author in a very competitive publishing industry, this wouldn't be wise.

I hope you get what I mean.

Due to this, I selected the breaking point myself, where I saw fit. It could have been easier to break at the end of each of the three parts (or acts) and create a trilogy. However, this didn't feel right. Firstly, the three parts in this book are like three acts, the end of one sequence and the beginning of a new one. They couldn't serve as satisfying ends in themselves. Secondly, splitting *Omega Plan* into three Volumes would create the impression to readers that it is a complete series, not a single book.

So, I've broken the book in the middle after chapter 43, for this scene is extremely pivotal for not just the book, but for the entire series. It fulfills several plot cycles as well as anticipating future conflicts and answers. I want you to understand however, that *Omega Plan* Volumes 1 and 2 are a *single* novel. They are *not* two separate novels. I encourage you to read them as a cohesive whole, as it was intended to be.

I felt this would be necessary when I began my publishing journey and the team at Alkira Publishing also encouraged me to split it. Thank you so much to everyone that has supported me on this writing journey. It's only the beginning.

Find out what happens next in *Omega Plan* Volume 2!

Find me on Facebook - Jono Karagiannis
Instagram - @jonowarrior777
YouTube – Jonathon Karagiannis
Email – Antaresunit1@gmail.com

ACKNOWLEDGEMENTS

My literary journey began in 2018 with an idea to write an epic sci-fi fantasy mythopoetic saga based on the Book of Revelation and conspiracy theories. James Casbolt was the first character I envisioned, who would serve as the main protagonist in a TV show script I wrote. By 2020, I finished the script and realised I had created a nightmarish monstrosity.

During the 2020 festive season, I began converting the *Omega Plan* script into a fiction novel. By the start of 2022, I had the first draft of the novel done, but it was peppered with plot holes, info dumps, awful tangents, filled with on-the-nose preaching and cringeworthy episodes that made no sense. *Omega Plan* draft 1 was my greatest failure and at the same time, my greatest success.

But I couldn't stop there. From 2022 to 2023, I rewrote and edited the story so many times, weaving in new ideas and plots, tightening the story, refining the narrative into the form that you have before you today. I cannot explain how it all came together; I honestly believe the whole process was providential for the people in my life that helped the book come into its final form.

All this would not have been possible if not for the people who supported me. Firstly, I want to thank my family and extended family for believing in me from the start. I express my deepest love and gratitude to my father and mother who have spent countless hours and money to help guide and fund me through the five years of writing, editing and publishing this work. Thanking them here will not do justice. My parents are utterly remarkable. I want to thank my amazing friends excited for the story and for all those who prayed for the story. I want to thank my lecturers and teachers from high school, Monash and ACU for instilling within me the passion for academia in history, theology, literature and philosophy—the wisdom that reinforces this series. You know who you are if you're reading this. I want you to know that I would have never produced this labour of love without you. May God bless you all abundantly.

I also want to express my sincerest thanks to Kathy Betts (Element Eds) for her wonderful editing, proofreading and patience, Ludmila for the character POV artwork, my beta readers Ayebai-preye Iwowari, Harry Stone, Ifeoluwa Olorunniyi and Chizitere Godwin and Damonza for the Volume I cover design. I also wish to give a special thanks to Tahlia Newland (managing editor), Rose Newland (book designer) and the rest of the team from Alkira and Escarpment Publishing for helping me publish this big book.

I give thanks to all the people that inspired me and influenced me over these five years. I will also like to acknowledge the scholars and research I consulted for this book and the creators who helped shape the story: Brandon Sanderson, Jeremy Duncan (Upside-Down Apocalypse: Grounding Revelation in the Gospel of Peace), Tim Mackie (The Bible Project), Richard Bauckham (The Theology of the Book of Revelation), Greg L. Bahnsen (Victory in Jesus: The Bright Hope of Postmillennialism), Matthew Bogdanos (Thieves of Baghdad), Lawrence Rothfield (The Rape of Mesopotamia: Behind the Looting of the Iraq Museum), Nicola Crusemann (Uruk: First City of the Ancient World), Holly Baglio, Carmen Imes, John Walton, Tremper Longman (The Lost World of the Flood: Mythology, Theology, and the Deluge Debate), Michael Jones (Inspiring Philosophy), Michael Morales (Who Shall Ascend the Mountain of the Lord?: A Biblical Theology of the Book of Leviticus), William Paul Young (The Shack), René Girard, C.S Lewis, Brian Godawa, Denis Villeneuve, Ian Shaw (The Oxford History of Ancient Egypt), Jeremy Black, Andrew George, Amanda H. Podany (Weavers, Scribes and Kings), Wally Brown (Navajo Traditional Teachings), Chief Joseph RiverWind, Dr. Laralyn RiverWind, David Duchovny, Chris Carter, Joseph Blenkinsopp (Creation, Un-creation, Re-creation: A discursive commentary on Genesis 1-11), Michael LeFebvre (The Liturgy of Creation: Understanding Calendars in Old Testament Context), Michael Heiser, JP McMahon (the Way Biblical Fellowship), Dalton Thomas (Days of Noah), Gabriel Said Reynolds (Exploring the Quran and the Bible), Peter Berresford (Celtic Myths and Legends), Alejandro Gómez Monteverde (Sound of Freedom), Tim Ballard, Amar Annus (On the Origin of Watchers: A Comparative Study of the Antediluvian Wisdom in Mesopotamian and Jewish Traditions), Martti Nissinen and Risto Uro (Sacred Marriages: The Divine-Human Sexual Metaphor from Sumer to Early Christianity), Gregory Mobley (Samson and the Liminal Hero in the Ancient Near East), Fr. Stephen De Young, and Jonathan Pageau (The Symbolic World).

LITERATURE CITED DIRECTLY WITHIN OMEGA PLAN:

- *Holy Bible*, (quotations from the ESV and NIV with changes by the author. Tim Mackie's Literal Literary translation for Bible Project used with permission.)
- *The Birth of Civilization in the Near East,* Henri Frankfort, Project Gutenberg, Doubleday Anchor Books, 1956, (public domain).
- *Paradise Lost,* John Milton, 1667, Global Language Resources, Inc, (public domain).
- *The Book of the Dead or 'Book of Coming Forth by Day',* Translated by E. A. Wallis Budge, 1895, Sacred Texts, (public domain).
- *Desiring Divinity: Self-deification in Early Jewish and Christian Mythmaking,* M. David Litwa, New York, 2016, (used with Litwa's permission).
- *The Sumerians: Their History, Culture and Character,* Samuel Noah Kramer, University of Chicago Press, 1963, (used with permission).
- *The Deir Alla Inscription, Jordan, 8th Century BCE.* Translation by Baruch A. Levine, from *The Context of Scripture Volume Two: Monumental Inscriptions from the Biblical World,* William W. Halo, Leiden: Brill, 2001 (used with permission).
- *The Treasures of Darkness: A History of Mesopotamian Religion,* Thorkild Jacobsen, Yale University, 1978, (used with permission).
- *The Babylonian Gilgamesh Epic: Introduction, Critical Edition and Cuneiform Texts,* Andrew George, Oxford, 2003, (used with permission).
- *The Oxford History of Ancient Egypt,* Ian Shaw, Oxford, 2002, (used with permission).
- *The Treasures of Darkness: A History of Mesopotamian Religion,* Thorkild Jacobsen, Yale University, 1978, (used with permission).
- *Death of Gilgamesh,* translated by Jeremy Black, The Electronic Text Corpus of Sumerian Literature, Oxford, 1997, (public domain).

www.ingramcontent.com/pod-product-compliance
Lightning Source LLC
Chambersburg PA
CBHW050600170726
48283CB00001B/50